P

CW00537082

# THEIR BLOOD-SOAKED LIBERTY

UK Book Publishing.com

Editing, design, typesetting and publishing by UK Book Publishing

www.ukbookpublishing.com

ISBN: 978-1-916572-26-3

# THEIR BLOOD-SOAKED LIBERTY

## PREVIOUS PETE KALDER NOVELS

*Comrades Come Rally*

*Gone Underground*

*Dedicated to Alan and Audrey. For their love and support.*

# ACKNOWLEDGEMENTS

Although this is in no way a pandemic novel, a part of it was written during COVID. I like, the rest of the population, owe everything to the workers who kept the supermarkets full, the power on and the NHS going. Thank you to all. Clapping is not enough. Love to Mum and Dad for always being there. Thank you also to Ruth for your advice and Jay for your cover design, from UK Book Publishing. And of course, to Jane for all her love, support and putting up with all my doubts and dramas.

# CHAPTER 1: START OF THE HUNT

The semi-automatic rifle hung casually by the comrade's side, the barrel pointing directly at my chest, his stubby fingers hovering worryingly close to the trigger. I slowly moved my hand to my ID badge. From the faint orange glow on the top rim of his glasses, I knew he was scanning me. I didn't greatly fear for my safety; after all, I was who I said I was, I had a reason to be here, and I was on his side. He was being thorough. No doubt checking the state's watch-list of anti-revolutionary terrorists to see if my handsome mug was on it. Obviously, it wasn't, but then we weren't that efficient in its upkeep. The ongoing cyber-warfare meant it was taking the National Workers' Council a little time to rebuild the country's digital infrastructure.

Not for the first time, my intellectual vanity hadn't done me any favours. I had decided against the standard issue ID badge and had chosen, instead, a miniature of a Mondrian painting –a 1930 masterpiece – Composition with Red, Blue and Yellow. Not that this rather fierce militia guard looked too much as if he'd be interested in either what it was called or who it was by. My idea had been to turn a functional tool into a cool accessory, but that meant that it wasn't the standard issue badge, so this comrade didn't recognise it. That made him nervous. Which made me nervous. Not one of my best sartorial ideas.

Touching the red square, my ID flashed up: *Pete Kalder. C.R.I.B. Political Support. The President's Office.* Above the rather unimaginative Calibri font was a 3D image of yours truly – taken back in Spring, looking rather smooth in a dark blue pin-striped three-piece. The multi-media package was completed by a video confirmation from Jackie Payne – the very president of the workers' state, who we were attached to.

It had the desired effect and his hand moved away from the gun, and his facial muscles relaxed a touch. Not that he grew friendlier. He didn't even crack a smile at our name – C.R.I.B – *Counter-Revolution Intelligence Bureau.* Very quickly, we had lost the initials and had become a word –

Crib. This was our wonderful, shiny, brand new name. Or more accurately, our latest, because names for our unit were like buses: several could come along all at once. Mostly the ones you weren't waiting for. Certainly, Crib had attracted a fair amount of ridicule. It seemed that whilst the National Workers' Council had been elected to run the proletarian revolution, it appeared to have difficulties in naming departments.

He nodded, and with a voice so perfunctory that was above a mutter, 'Okay, comrade, sorry for the inconvenience'. Standing to one side, he resumed his gazing into the distance.

Although only a matter of fifty metres away, I re-started the scooter and turned into Mary Driscoll Avenue, past the newly-erected statue of the woman herself. I could see ahead, a group of people in the act of dispersing, heading off in obviously well-thought-out directions. In their dazzling bright colours and an admirable array of mini-skirts and shorts, they could have easily been mistaken for a neighbourhood committee preparing to set up a summer fete. Not that there was that excited and happy murmur you'd expect in such a situation. Here in the sweaty stillness, there was more determined talk. Obviously, they weren't about to set up the lucky dip or coconut-shy.

After ensuring that I didn't run over any comrade, I parked in front of number 14, behind a very familiar dark, very flashy – and very unrevolutionary – car. I smiled to myself at the thought of all the team crammed in it. It was Victoria Cole's pride and joy. Its red fists and party insignia incongruous with its conspicuous consumption. She was allowed to keep it post-revolution because it had been classified as a party vehicle. Its promotion hadn't stopped there, because now amongst the collection of badges along its chassis, there was an Everyday Drive Licence Plate. Thus, freeing her from the national eco-driving restrictions. Others in our team weren't cleared for Tuesdays, so either they had taken public transport, or had hitched a ride with her. I could just imagine them all wedged inside – in this heat!

Placing the helmet on the bike's seat, my smile broadened – *the team*. The thought still amused me that the four of us could be considered being a team. However, the fact was that we had the honour of being the first – the original – Crib. We had been in existence for a short time and still had only a vague idea of what our role was and how we were to perform it. Or indeed, what we were called that week. Teething troubles, I guess.

Behind Cole's car, was another, also boasting tinted windows and party insignia. It wasn't one of ours, but was definitely party transport. Quite obviously, the transport committee had seen too many gangster movies. Or we had nationalised funeral parlours. It was a black 4 x4 – less sporty and flash than Vic's – but bigger and more threatening.

The house was a four-storey Victorian house, which would have once housed hedge-fund manager types. In the front, was a bike rack, with space for six, but occupied only by two. I had never been a fan of that mode of transport – too sweaty, too uncomfortable, too much crotch-strain on suit trousers.

Past it, were concrete steps, once grey, now painted bright red and black, which led to the entrance of the main part of the house. The front door was slightly ajar. Pinned to it was a large poster with the simple, but a well-known slogan *YES TO NON* defiantly shouting its politics in green block letters. Next to it, stood a tall, young, barefoot white guy with dazzling orange nails, which matched his eyeshadow. He was wearing – just – an extremely short and intimately revealing pair of cut-off jeans and an equally skin-tight t-shirt, and was looking at me through large round green sunglasses. He didn't utter a syllable, but just moved out of my way. I sincerely hoped he wasn't tasked to keep the house secure. If he was, then his skill-set lay in other directions.

On entering the house, I immediately saw Roijin Kemal, standing in the hall. It had been a few days since we had last worked together, and in that time, she had, it seemed, treated herself to a trip to the hairdresser. Usually, when she tied her long, black, silky hair up in a forensic hairnet, it was a battle to get it all in, making the whole thing stand up like some Coldstream Guards' bearskin, but not so here. The hairnet was neatly down, with all strands comfortably contained. I dimly remembered her telling the office that because of the heat, she was going to get it cut into a high bob. Dressed from neck to feet in a white forensic suit, it contrasted starkly with her dark Turkish skin. Now, courtesy of the summer sun, an even deeper shade. She had been looking well recently. Regular visits to the 24-hour gym had toned her body. She may be in her mid-forties, but unlike most of us, appeared to be getting younger as she grew older. I, for one, would love to know her secret. Obviously, the current heatwave was doing her a world of good.

She was talking to Victoria Cole, defiantly pale as always. She was someone who loathed the sun. Her white skin and short, bleached, slicked-back hair seemingly designed to reflect all light. She was also wearing a forensic suit, but with her, it merged into her body. Their talking stopped and both turned to face me. Victoria looked as she usually did, without make-up, with smooth young skin and an almost boyish face.

'My God,' Kemal said with a mocking grin, showing perfect teeth and red lipstick, 'it's bloody Graham Greene. Our man in Havana!' Quite obviously, she thought this to be an utterly hilarious comment. 'Wearing a suit in this weather? You must be baking!'

Considering that they were dressed like a pair of heads poking out of toilet rolls, she had some nerve. But we had been instructed by the Central Committee to play nice with each other. I specifically had been told to remember that Roijin Kemal, Victoria Cole and Asher Joseph may have once been officers in the Metropolitan Police Service, but they had crossed over and joined the revolution. They had proved their loyalty and their commitment, and I should behave as a comrade to them. So, I bit down a witty – or more probably just plain nasty – reply and merely gave a polite smile.

She hadn't finished, though. 'Always thought you were more linen than Lenin, but I'm afraid you'll have to suit-up in a different way, if you go in any further.'

My smile stayed fixed. Being forced to serve the revolution with three ex-police officers was grim enough, but to have to suffer their "humour" was just plain cruel. Thankfully, she had exhausted both her stocks of puns and literary references, and finished her stand-up routine.

She leant down and took out from a transparent plastic suitcase, a forensic suit and a pair of over-boots and handed them to me with some Primary School forensic science: 'Don't touch anything.' Those plans of grasping misplaced knives, would have to be shelved then. She then announced that she was going to the kitchen, not troubling herself to explain why.

Victoria didn't try any humour. 'Was it a successful visit?' she asked, whilst I struggled to get into the ridiculous outfit that was necessitated by visiting a murder scene.

'Yeah, certainly was,' I replied between strains and gulping for air. 'The tip-off was...correct. Hidden in the storage unit was a whole gallery of concealed art... mainly late twentieth, with some early twenty... first century stuff. Amongst other things, we uncovered a few Damien Hirsts, several Tracy Emins... and even a Michael Craig-Martin. The owner has... already scarpered off to the States and was hoping to smuggle his art collection, to join him and his credit rating. Not now though... we'll have them in a public gallery in a matter of weeks.'

'Good. Obviously, you enjoyed doing it. Not bad – two big art recoveries this week, and it's only Tuesday. I know you'd much rather be doing your art historian thing than being here, but sorry, Jackie rang us personally.'

'And when Jackie Payne calls, we answer,' I muttered.

'Indeed,' she replied, pretending not to notice that I had almost lost my balance, whilst getting one leg in and had to grab hold onto the wall to stop myself from going arse over tit. I wasn't wearing my gloves yet, so grabbing at the wall had meant that I had instantly ignored Roijin's instruction.

Balancing myself against a wall, this time with gloves on, I pulled them over my shoes. What a waste. These were top-quality brogues. Finally, I had some energy to spare: 'So what's happened? What demands us being here – apart from Comrade Payne? You were rather vague on the phone.'

Cole replied with a look, which I couldn't decipher, 'One of the residents rang 147 to report a death of one of her flatmates.'

With my second boot on, I was dressed. I looked a prat; I was hot and I was none-the-wiser of what the hell had happened here. 'A death – and we think it's a murder?'

She pulled a face. 'Well, Asher and a team of forensic scientists from the Locard Laboratory are here. One of them, a Doctor Lopez, reckons it is as a result of a severe case of anaphylactic shock.'

So, I'd been dragged away from nationalising art to be sweating in clothing resembling a white tent – all so I could witness the demise of some poor bloke who had a medical condition. Tragic, but sod-all to do with us.

Cole was getting to know me and my facial expressions. She often knew what I was thinking before I did. 'It's best if you have a look yourself.'

I followed Victoria through the hallway, and into a large open-plan kitchen boasting of several ovens and top of the range cupboards, which no doubt opened as smoothly as exhaled breath on a winter's day. In the middle was a huge centre island. The type which had been oh-so fashionable back in the twenty-twenties. One half of the room was the kitchen, which shouted cooking virility and "look-at-the-size-of-the-utensils"! The other was a reception area that looked geared for breakfasts and snacking. In the corner, were what looked like folded banners. Neatly piled by their side, were seven portable virtual projectors. Essential kit for any activist. To their right, and in front of the large glass windows, were what I guessed were two hover-speakers. The kind used on political demos.

The cooking area was home to a round plastic table, surrounded by four chairs, all of different styles, colours and materials. None of them matched the work surfaces. The sofa in the far corner was blue but the armchair a faded orange. It was an odd juxtaposition of a room in an obviously wealthy home, but furnished with items taken from less-so-ones.

Again, Cole had read my thoughts. She had been detective once; now she was mind-reader. 'This used to be the London home of a PR consultant, until it was redistributed.'

I nodded; that explained it then. I didn't wonder where this PR consultant now lived. To be honest, I wasn't that bothered. Instead, I turned my attention to a slim woman in her thirties, who was sitting on one of the mismatched chairs. She was also in a forensic suit. She briefly looked up at us, but said nothing, and returned to look at her palm computer. I couldn't see what was so interesting: it could have been data about the death, or she had just received an amusing gif. I'd never know, because my attention was suddenly grabbed by the sight of the body of a young man lying at her feet. In my short time being involved in crime detection, I did find that dead bodies often did that. Even though I was beginning to see a few of them, they still had a novelty aspect to them. So, the dead fella was why Roijin had gone into the kitchen.

The body in question was lying on the floor in that classic dead person pose, you know the one which often had a chalk outline around it. Face down, one arm higher than the other, and the legs likewise. It was as if he was climbing the floor, practising his moves for scaling a local peak. This chap, though, wasn't going anywhere.

He was wearing black knee-length baggy shorts but nothing else. From his bare feet to his closely shaven head, he was covered in small to large angry red sores, which were bursting out of an inflamed skin. Once, he might have been considered fit and lean, and possessing slightly tanned white skin. Once. But now he looked like he'd been dumped at sea and had been nibbled by a shoal of fish. If one was simply to judge by appearances, then his final moments had been very painful indeed. His hands were like claws, almost embedded into the stripped pine floor. I peered over and saw that his head was tilted to one side, his tongue almost unnaturally sticking out. Twice its normal size. His lips were enlarged too – two giant red squashed cylinders clamped either side of it. The rest of his face was massively swollen too, almost swamping his nose. His eyes had become a boxer's after a particularly brutal match against a superior opponent. Swollen and closed. Not, then, a pretty sight. Not one for his dating app.

Looking at his legs and arms, they too were swollen and covered in spots. I jettisoned the fish simile – nibbling was too nice, too sweet – not nearly nasty enough. No, this was more like he had been engulfed by a swarm of angry bees, suicidally attacking every square centimetre of his body; or that he had been given a serious beating from a heavyweight champ. Or both.

Looking away from her computer, the woman finally noticed me. 'Hi comrade. You must be Pete Kalder. I'm Dr Jada Lopez, from the Locard Lab. The council sent me.' She spoke in that controlled professional voice, which medical and science type people have, which often has a hint of condescension. We humanities types often have the latter, but coupled it with vague amateurishness.

I nodded 'Hello' and waited for her to say more. But if I had been expecting a cosy chat and a slice of lemon cake, then I was disappointed. She got straight to the point. Which was fine by me – she might even explain why I was here.

'From my initial tests, I'd put this young man's age at 26 years old or thereabouts, died from anaphylaxis, a severe allergic reaction from traces of nuts contained in the milk he was drinking. My estimate is that he died within the last three hours. If I was forced to, I'd say it was around about,' she looked at her watch, '10am – but I repeat, *about*.' She switched to looking at her palm computer. 'From the number of mediators and the level of white cells, I would say that death was in a matter of minutes. There is a small amount of vomit by his lips.'

She let me look. I did, just to please the good doctor. Yep, puke. Yep, by his lips. She then reeled off all the tests which she had performed since her arrival. The words 'initial' and 'preliminary' seemed to prefix every result. Assuming she hadn't been sponsored by a charity to say them as often as she could in a minute, they all pointed to one thing.

'So, you're saying you think it was anaphylaxis?' I asked, reluctantly looking at the body.

'Certainly looks like that.'

My eyes met Victoria's. She replied to my silent question. 'Have a closer look at him.'

I knelt down and looked at his face, having no idea what I was looking for. Or who he was. His face looked like mashed potato to me. I got closer, and thought I recognised some of the features. Or rather of how they might have been before the reaction. His top lip resembled a Cumberland sausage. Which it had to be said, went nicely with his face, with some of the spots resembling small tomatoes. A sort of dinner combo. In amongst it all, I could just detect a brown birthmark on his right cheek. That rang a bell. It got louder. Then it got very loud. 'Mike Stewart!'

She nodded.

Dr Lopez looked up, interested. 'Mike Stewart? I wondered if it was him. Isn't he one of the leaders of the Now or Never movement? Hence,' she pondered her new discovery, 'the poster on the front door.' She looked down at him. 'Poor man,' she sighed. 'So young. So gifted.'

Victoria wasn't one for sentimentality, and cut her short. 'Dr Lopez, is there anything else?'

The good doctor looked rather taken aback, but did not argue. 'I can say that there appears to be no other violence inflicted on his body. There's no bruising that cannot be explained by his fall, and subsequent life-struggle. Initial observations indicate that there's no bruising around his neck or arms, which would have suggested that he was held down and forced to drink the mixture. But these are all prelim findings. That's as much medically and scientifically I can tell you at this stage. I'll be able to tell you more later.' With that she turned her attention to the body and to her palm computer.

'Let's talk to Ash and Roijin,' Victoria suggested, no doubt realising that for the time being at least, Dr Lopez had said everything she wanted to say.

She pointed to her two soulmates: the pair who had left the Met Police with her and joined the United Revolutionary Socialist Party before the revolution, and who were now half our team. They were standing with their backs to the large glass doors, looking into the room, listening to us. Roijin Kemal smiled, my second from her within five minutes. We'd be dating at this rate. Asher Joseph though, wasn't in any courting mood. He just grunted a greeting. He, like me, was doing his best to be nice, but also like me, was finding it a long process. A few months ago, he would have snarled and growled, so it was progress, but we were not yet having a bromance. We got on okay in the office, and whilst we never saw each other outside of work, it was polite and civil. Comradely, you might even say.

His speciality was forensics and in the past few weeks, he'd become a very happy forensic chappy, with the union representing the forensic scientists finally agreeing that they would work with the National Workers' Council. Asher now had some playmates to hang out with. No doubt, they had some on-line forum where they excitedly conversed about insect larvae and show saucy photos of bullet casings. In actual fact, I had no idea what he was interested in, other than the state of the revolution, and forensics. My history of dialogue with comrade Joseph, outside of those two areas, centred almost solely on how many sugars he was having in his tea that week.

Still, hopefully he could explain what was suspicious about Mike Stewart's death and why we were sweating calories in these suits. Judging from the shine on his black skin, beads of sweat forming necklaces – great chunky ones – Asher was also on a similar imposed weight-loss regime to the one which I was presently going through. He looked as if someone had had to lever him into his forensic suit. To be honest though, he could do with losing a few kilos. But I thought it best not to mention that. I could play nice, too.

'I've tested the milk he was drinking and there are definite traces of almond in there,' he said, answering a question which I hadn't asked. But would have.

He paused to wipe sweat off his face.

Roijin added, 'His NHS medical records are intact and they do show that he did have a certified chronic nut allergy. It's a possibility then, that he missed the warning on the packaging that there may be traces of nuts in the liquid. These warnings are so ubiquitous that they've become like wallpaper and people don't always notice them.'

I hoped so. Then I could get back to relieving rich folk of their art treasures. That was my idea of having a good time. Spotty corpses didn't do it for me. Still, I should at least look prepared to see a reason for our presence. 'Could it have been put in by a third party?' I asked. I mean, we were talking milk here, so why not grasp at straws?

'Possibly,' he replied, 'but we can't say for sure. I dusted the glass the milk was in and only found his prints. It could have been put in the carton but I would have thought it is a somewhat hit or miss way of killing someone. So why do it? Surely there are more effective ways of killing someone.'

'Could it have been forced down him? Dr Lopez hasn't found anything to indicate that, but what's your opinion?' Vic asked.

'Follow the science, and the science will give you the evidence, which will give you the direction to look. And like Jada said, we haven't found anything to suggest that. It looks like a severe allergic reaction.'

'So probably, a tragic accident.' I sighed. All attempts at being interested were rapidly disappearing. This was getting boring and very repetitive. Could someone please say why we were here? Alright, it had been decided that we would primarily be concerned with combating the former ruling class's attempts at undermining and destabilising the workers' state, and Mike Stewart could be regarded as a target, but murder by almond? I had seen my spy movies so knew anything was possible, but putting a nut in a carton of milk? Really?

Noting that there was a silence – but not being trained in graduating silences – I couldn't say whether it was an awkward one or not. But it was deffo a silence. I pointed out that okay, so it was sad, and he was famous – politically famous – but that didn't mean we had to get involved.

Roijin agreed, then turned to face the window and pointed to the back garden. Asher and Victoria turned to do likewise. No-one had told me why we were doing this, but in the spirit of synchronisation, if not solidarity, I did so too. Perhaps there was a rare bird nesting, or a lovely refreshing water sprinkler. No, it wouldn't be that – there was a water shortage and a ban was in operation and these eco-warriors wouldn't waste such a precious resource. What there was, was a stunning wild garden. To an untrained eye it would seem neglected, but I could see that great care and skill had gone into its planting.

'Not the mess of a garden,' Roijin chortled. Ah, there was the untutored vision. 'But sitting in the middle of the weeds, is...'

'Switchgrass,' Joseph corrected her. 'Prairie Sky Switchgrass, I think.'

She shrugged, not impressed with his knowledge, although for once, I was. Gardening, I thought to myself. If the sugar conversation ever runs out, try gardening. 'In the Switchgrass, is his flatmate, the woman who found him. Her name is Fiona Bailey.'

Interesting. If the Anarchist Federation believed in, or even admitted, such things, it could be argued that if Mike Stewart was in the premier league of green activists, then she was pretty much up there with him. She was at least in the promotion play-offs.

Roijin added, 'It was comrade Bailey who rang 147. I've only had the briefest of introductions, and it would be useful to talk to her in greater depth. Although, all things considered, I think it best that we don't crowd her. I think...'

She was interrupted by a voice at the door of the kitchen. Although the speaker was attempting lightness and politeness, her voice was undercut by annoyance. 'Okay! Okay! Don't panic! I know I'm not allowed in because of contamination, I wanted you to know that I'll be in my car. Anyway, you've got all my clothes, you've done your body forensic scan, and I'm in these bloody forensic overalls you gave me, so I assume it'll be okay. Thom's staying in the front room, but I thought I'd do some work, whilst I wait for Comrade Cole to find time to talk to me. So...'

Her familiar voice came to halt when she finally saw me. She was more used to seeing me in sharp suits, rather than in this garb, so hadn't recognised me at first. But I had her – Marie Williams. She had formerly been a medical professional, but was now a party full-time Central Committee member. She had also once been one of my closest friends, but now was someone who probably would wish I was lying dead next to Mike Stewart. Or more likely – that I was suffering severe and agonising pain – as I lie dying by his side. It had been the Alan Wiltshire case which had first brought me into the orbit of Victoria Cole and friends, and which had turned Marie from close friend to what wouldn't be too much to describe as an enemy. I knew for a fact that she had called, on more than one occasion, for my expulsion from the party, and even that I should be arrested and thrown into prison. She hadn't specified what should happen to the key but it was a fair assumption that she hadn't wanted it kept safe. She wasn't a fan.

Her green eyes focussed on me and I could have sworn that they turned red. 'Hello Pete, should have guessed that you'd be here.' Both her words and tone couldn't have been more civil, and yet. And yet, beneath the polite, political and professional voice was violent repugnance.

To my surprise, I felt a little intimidated. 'Hi, Marie. Good to see you.'

*Good to see you?* Could I have come out with a crasser reply? No, it wasn't! It wouldn't have been good at any time, let alone with a dead young man on the floor and the quite obvious fact that it looked like that we would need to interview her, which was bound to be a hellish experience.

Victoria covered my stupidity, by sounding effortlessly efficient. 'Thanks, Marie, sorry to keep you. We'll be with you in a minute. But it would be easier if you stay with Thom in the lounge – cheers.'

For a second, it looked as if there was going to be a confrontation, and a refusal to do as asked. The two women looked at each other with that cool calmness which women seem to have, which can be bloody intimidating and yet appear so reasonable. If there was to be a battle, then it would be a close call as to who might win. Marie was one tough nut. The sort you would definitely get a reaction to if you came into contact with.

'I think it's obviously an allergic response, and I really don't see why...' She stopped herself from going further. 'Of course, comrade. I'll do as you ask.' Evidently deciding not to have a big bust-up, she gave a regal nod of acknowledgment and agreement, a shake of her mop of auburn hair, and then turned and left us.

'Shit,' I muttered to myself. I sensed that my three colleagues agreed.

# CHAPTER 2: OPHELIA

'We'll need to talk to her,' Victoria said, gazing at the space Marie Williams had just vacated. I wondered if she could sense the hostile aura that Williams had left, or whether it was just me. 'We also need to have a chat with...er...the other guy, er,' she thought for a second, 'Thom Simons. Both of them arrived at around about the same time as Fiona Bailey.' She paused, getting her mental filing in order. 'But they can wait; we should talk to Fiona first. Roj and Ash, why don't you stay here and finish with the prelims.'

Asher nodded. 'I'll make sure that we get Stewart taken away as soon as possible. I don't want him staying too long in these temperatures. Never mind the loss of any forensic evidence, the smell will start getting rather ripe soon. We don't want to be the cause of a migration of neighbours, do we?'

Cole put her hand on the sliding door handle, but momentarily stopped, and lowered her voice. 'Bailey agreed to being body-scanned, but I've only had a chance to have a brief word with her. I thought as things stood, it would be better if you spoke to her.'

Before I had a chance to ask what exactly these 'things' were, she pushed the door open. The heat hit me like an American football quarterback running directly into my chest.

'Fiona?' Victoria shouted. (Though, I had no idea why – it was a London back garden not the Serengeti.)

'Yeah, here,' she replied. She'd not been eaten by the lions, then. Within seconds and not requiring Satnav nor safari park rangers, we found her. She was a tall, slim, white woman in her mid-twenties, whose long legs were crossed beneath her. She sat, surrounded by the Switchgrass, and was playing with her long waist-length red hair. Brighter and far more vivid than Marie William's, which was probably true of their respective personalities too. She was also dressed in a white forensic suit. The scientific wing of the team certainly had been busy in the short while they'd been here; folks had lost their clothes quicker than a Roman orgy.

Bailey's longish, pale face was the type that suggested that she had attended a private school, with interests playing hockey and spending her inheritance. The type who sometimes wander into acting and are always being cast as minor members of a royal family. But looks can be deceptive. Both her parents worked on the buses and had been members of the Labour Party. She and her many supporters were fond of splashing both her face and life story across social media. I had never met her before, but I had seen her everywhere. She'd even featured in one of those late-night bio-docs of people considered to be the leading movers of the moment. It appeared that young folks seemed to like them. I was yet to have any take an interest in making one of me.

Standing over her, Victoria introduced me. In reply, she looked up, forced a smile, and mumbled a perfunctory hello. Neither were convincing. Then to my horror, it looked as if Victoria was going to join her on the ground. No chance! Not at my age. Before we started to impersonate a scout camp, I asked Fiona if she would be kind enough to stand because I wasn't sure I'd get back up. Despite her reputation of having a love-hate relationship with party comrades, she looked straight at me, nodded and in one swift, but graceful movement, joined us on two legs. She possessed, if I'd been keen to rehash a cliché, the elegance of a gazelle. Slightly taller than me, she tilted her head a fraction to look at me. A serenity emanated from her, but one that had something else within it. I looked at her eyes and her mouth, and saw sadness, and the first signs of grief.

Vic quickly got down to business. 'I'm sorry to bother you again, Fiona. We're all really appalled at this tragedy, and we all understand how painful for you this must be, but we need to ask you some more questions. This is Pete Kalder, he's also with Crib. Could I ask you to repeat, for Pete's benefit, how you found Mike Stewart? And could you please go through it in as much detail as you can. Nothing is too mundane.'

Fiona folded her arms and snapped, 'I don't think anything about Mike's death is mundane.'

Through tight lips, Vic replied, 'You know I didn't mean to imply that. I mean, any events surrounding the time of his discovery.'

No more resistance was given and after thinking for a second, she concluded that she would cooperate. Her voice was quiet, quiet from the obvious pain which she was feeling. It was almost one long anguished sigh. 'Sure, of course. I'll do anything to help – if you think it will help catch whoever did this – I...er...have been staying around at a friend's.

I'd been working a long shift. I work on the trains, you see. As a guard. Transport runs in our blood.' She smiled to herself. The smile got a little wider. We said nothing to hurry or interrupt her. 'Anyways, I thought rather than travel all the way back here, I could go and visit Janine, she lives in Hammersmith, that's where my shift finished. We went out for a bite to eat and I stayed the night, then came back here in the morning. I've got no work today so I thought I'd make a leisurely return, then have a shower and some breakfast, and do some voluntary stuff at the local canteen.' She stopped and looked into the middle-distance.

'What time did you get here?' I asked, trying to move her along. I mean, no-one wanted to rush her, and I sympathised with her loss, but I was bloody melting in the plastic suit.

'Oh, I suppose it was about half ten. I can't say exactly, because I didn't have reason to check the time, but it was about then. Marie Williams could tell you. I met her on the doorstep, she was already here. She'd rung the bell, but no-one had answered. Which was odd, because she was due to meet Mike, so he should have been in. I called out his name when we came in, but didn't get an answer. Well, obviously I didn't, but I didn't know that then. We both went into the kitchen and it was then that we saw...Mike. He was on the floor. Marie went straight over to him, but, well, he was...' Her answer drifted off into the vapours of grief. Judging from how many facts she had fitted into a minute, these were answers to questions, which had already been asked of her.

'What was this meeting about?' I gently asked.

She shrugged. 'Don't know for sure, but I'd assume that it had something to do with his plan to give power to the localities. Williams would know.'

Now, we live in highly political times. If you said, "Good Morning", someone would reply that *yes, it was, because the old ruling class had been overthrown.* But here, I deliberately avoided an obvious question as to what that exactly meant. Now wasn't the time. Instead, I asked her if she had known that Marie Williams was going to be here or was it unexpected to find someone like her at her front door? She nodded, and said that Mike had mentioned it a few days ago. 'And you let Marie in?' I asked.

'No, not really. I mean, I opened the door, but it was unlocked. It always is. Marie felt that she couldn't just go straight in – bourgeois concepts of property are hard to get rid of, I suppose. I didn't think anything about it, I just thought he was lost reading a book or something. Or designing his cities of the future – reimagining London or Bristol or somewhere.' For a moment the memory of her housemate took her away from us. 'Anyway, as I said, we went in, and I shouted out for him and looked around, and went into the kitchen and that's where we found him.' She paused and looked towards the house. Again, we let her have her space. 'We went into the kitchen and found him,' she repeated in a trance. 'I kinda went crazy and tried to revive him. I think I even tried to give him mouth to mouth.'

'But you didn't get his EpiPen?' Victoria said. Her question surprised me – I thought I was supposed to be the one doing the questioning.

The comment flicked something in Bailey's brain. It had sounded too much like a copper coming down on an uppity teenager. Coolly, but with every word dripping with disdain, she replied, 'Your comrade Marie Williams told me that there was no point. He was obviously dead.' Her eyes pierced Victoria's. It wasn't love. 'And as I understand it, your comrade is a medical professional.'

'I've been told that somebody called Thom Simons was here too. Is that right?' I asked, perhaps quicker than I should have, but I was keen to pick up this lead of the interview I was supposed to have, and take it for a walk, at least up to the first lamppost.

'Not then, no. We were already in the kitchen when he arrived.'

'So, he wasn't on the doorstep with Marie Williams, then?'

'No, he came in later. About two minutes later. We probably left the front door open and he just came in. I know that I was shouting and yelling, Williams had to calm me down, so he probably heard me.'

'Can I check something? You said that both you and Marie came straight into the kitchen. Is that right?'

'Er, yes, well, I poked my head around the lounge door and looked in to see if he was there, and then we went into the kitchen. I thought he might be having his late breakfast in the garden.'

'And you didn't go anywhere else? Not upstairs?'

She told me no, and repeated once more that she had gone straight to the kitchen. I stroked my chin both in thought and also, so I could swipe away a very annoying bee which had been attracted to my cologne. I know that they are essential to life and all that, and Stewart and Bailey probably had spent hours encouraging them into the garden, but I hated the furry little bastards. I simply wasn't a fan of anything which could hurt me. Cole gave me a knowing look. She had guessed what I was thinking. Not about the bees, she probably could sting them back a lot harder, but the fact that no-one had gone upstairs.

'So how long were the three of you in the kitchen?'

From Bailey's puzzled look, it was as if my question was either amazingly original or just dumb. 'Oh, I er, would say that we were there until the ambulance arrived.'

'Which was how long?'

'Not long. Probably about five minutes. Actually, less. Say three.'

I again swiped away the bee from my face. 'Who is this Thom Simons? Is he one of ours or is he AF? I've not come across his name before.'

'Don't think he's either, not everyone is, you know, but to be honest, I've never spoken to him before this morning. Not a great way to get introduced,' she said dryly.

I decided to move the timeline along a bit and maybe even find out what these "things" I was supposed to be *negotiating around* were.

But before I had a chance, Victoria interrupted. 'Then what did you do?'

'I rang 147.'

'And asked for?' If this was taking a backseat, I hate to think what she looked like sitting on the bloody bonnet, pretending to be a hood ornament.

Pretty sharpish it became obvious that one of these "things" was that these two women weren't on what could be called friendly terms. Whether it was personal or political, or both, I couldn't at this early stage, say, but there was definite tension between them. Victoria had asked the question in the manner of an accusation and the look she had received in reply, had poison written all over it. My guess was that Fiona wasn't relishing having to answer questions from an ex-cop. Anarchists didn't have a great track record with the forces of law and order. Although Bailey had the reputation of being one of the more fraternal AF members, she was still wary of us. So, Cole was hardly high up on her birthday party invite list. Not that I was sure that her type of anarchist celebrated birthdays.

Because of recent successes, our Crib had received a fair amount of publicity, so Bailey would have been well-aware of who we were and where we had come from. The general consensus was that we were a small group of oddballs, but who were fair and honest. Even if she had a fondness for eccentrics, we were a Crib, and the AF were far from keen on Cribs. Actually, the AF hated Cribs. Plus, it had to be admitted that Vic's manner could easily be described as being, well, police-like. The AF hated the police, even more than Cribs. It seemed, however, that Fiona Bailey had taken a decision to avoid confrontation. Maybe, having a flatmate dead indoors brought out the pacifist in her. 'I asked for the Crib, well to be precise, I first asked for the NWC Investigations, before I remembered that you've had a name change.'

Victoria didn't this time jump in. She didn't need to. Instead, she just let the fact sink in, and it did, like a penny in a melting marshmallow.

I kept my voice level and reasonable, keeping the surprise down to a minimum. 'Sorry, Fiona, I do need to get things as clear as possible in my mind, I apologise if I seem intrusive. You say you asked for us?'

She looked straight at me. 'Yes.'

That was surprising. Unusual even. No, make it, odd; odd like a sheep knitting a fur coat to be worn on a day like this. Or wearing goggles in a shower. *That odd.* 'But aren't you against units like ours? I've seen you on TV denouncing Cribs as a dangerous development – anti-democratic, anti-revolutionary and anti-a-whole lot more. You and allies have been airing concerns about us for weeks. Wasn't it you who called us Payne's secret army? Actually, didn't you nickname us "Payne's Pains"? So, it's strange that you asked for us. Not to mention, that 147 gives a range of options, one of them includes a direct line to the nearest worker's council Good Social Behaviour Unit, who deal with basic law and order issues. I think I'm right in saying that Cribs are not even mentioned.' I glanced at Vic, who nodded.

For a moment I thought I'd been rather too brusque. Maybe my loveliness was being worn away by the company I was keeping. Or that bloody bee. It was still buzzing around, and even with a green-anarcho here, I felt like drowning it with insecticide. Something though, other than the insects, was stressing her, I could see her arms tightening.

'No, but I have the power of independent thought, so I asked for you. We're supposedly building a world for individuals, not routines.' She'd spoken perfectly calmly, but it had been intended as slap around my face. 'I also understand that in certain circumstances you've no choice but to seek the aid of people you might rather not do so.'

I didn't flinch. If I could stand in this heat, wearing this absurd white forensic suit without feeling any shame, with a sodding buzzing bee, I could take anything. 'And you got through to...'

'She spoke to me,' Victoria said.

I was now really confused. Hadn't Victoria told me as soon as I had arrived here that Jackie Payne, our esteemed president of our newly created workers' republic, had been the one to contact us?

Not speaking allowed Fiona to turn the tables, and ask a question herself. I would guess that Fiona was trying to avoid becoming antagonistic but whether it was from the difficulty of the situation or political dislike, I couldn't say, but her tone was edging towards a growl: 'And what, Cole, did you say to me?'

If Victoria was surprised by herself being questioned, she didn't show it. 'I explained to you that even suspicious deaths are investigated locally, under the auspices of the local workers' council. Probably by calling a Community Information Meeting. You told me that I was a bureaucratic chancer, who wants to turn back the gains of the revolution, and corrupt its creativity into a technocratic round of meetings.'

Not exactly a cry for help, then. But I let it go. 'So, what happened next?' I asked, still being in the dark as to how I came to be here.

It was Cole who answered, 'She contacted a comrade, sorry, 'brother', from the Now or Never movement who paid Jackie Payne a visit and repeated the demand. Jackie agreed, rang me, and told me to get the team here.'

Funny thing was, we were smack-bang in the middle of a tropical heatwave but it suddenly felt as cold as the Arctic out here.

'Sibling,' Fiona replied, 'we prefer calling like-minded activists sibling, rather than sister or brother, it's less gender specific.'

'Okay,' I said, really not wanting to get into some political bun-fight here. Especially not over forms of address. I was already feeling like I was being consumed by a giant blancmange. The more I struggled to understand why we'd been called, the less I did so. 'So, Jackie just says yes to this "sibling" and contacts us? Why? Jackie's a very busy woman. She's not easily bullied either. Numerous jailers can testify to that. Right now, I'm struggling to see why she would instruct us to get involved.'

Victoria made a rather showy look of focussing her attention on the younger woman, as if to say, 'well?' like a mother might to a petulant daughter.

Fiona though, wasn't one to be intimidated. 'Is his death not important enough to interest you? Is that what you are saying?'

I stumbled, stuttering a nonsensical reply. This was getting ever more uncomfortable by the minute. It was becoming quite apparent that this was especially so when Victoria spoke. I silently wished for her to get the hint and do as we had arranged, and for me to do the talking. But then, it was Victoria Cole.

She looked at her intently and, with a slight shake of her head, said, 'Maybe the fact that Fiona directly asked for you, Pete, might have something to with it. She appears to be less hostile to you personally than she is with the rest of us. This "sibling" repeated the demand, quite passionately, according to Jackie. It's you – Pete Kalder – or no-one.'

I hadn't expected that. Was this another of the "things"? My mind though, wasn't up to processing it. Feeling like you might if you had been struck by a large comedy mallet, I merely asked, 'Why?'

'I think Mike's been murdered. I wanted – I want – you to look into this."

'Why?' I asked again, summoning up my enormous mental dictionary.

Fiona replied – to whom I wasn't sure, because she appeared to be looking at something in the grass. At what I couldn't tell, maybe there were more bees. I guessed it was to me because it was said in a friendly tone, 'I think Mike's been murdered, and I think the counter-revolution are behind it. It's well known that you have had dealings with them, you know what they can do, and how to deal with them.'

I didn't say why again. Nor did I dwell on the reason why I had a new fan here. My charm could turn a frosty morning into a summer's day, but we could discuss exactly why she wanted my autograph later. Instead, I asked her what was it that made her think it was murder. As far as we could see he had been killed by a catastrophic reaction to a nut contamination of the milk he was drinking.

She looked directly at me; her jaws set. 'Mike was a strict vegan. He'd never drink milk. He saw milk as the stolen produce of an exploited animal. I mean, as far as he could, he didn't even touch plants. He preferred FermFoods – fermentation foods made in science labs. He just wouldn't have touched milk. He would have seen that as exploitative, and oppressing the captivity of a cognitive being. He would have no more drunk that milk than you would have murdered a child. Isabella is the only one in the house who isn't a vegan. That's why there's a small fridge on the kitchen work surface. It's where she keeps her stuff. Mike used to joke that it was her stash of stolen booty. I know that she has tried giving them up but, well, basically she can't. Not yet. Mike, nor anyone else here, gives her any grief for it, although we do insist that there is a complete separation of her food from ours. Everyone in the house knows that.'

'Isabella?' I asked, having no idea who she was.

It was Victoria who replied, 'Isabella Torres, another house-mate.'

'And she's where?'

Again, it was Victoria who answered my question, 'Apparently, she returned to Portugal, where she's from, a few days ago.'

'She and her partner went back there. With the invasion of the counter-revolutionaries in the north, she felt that she could do more good there than here.'

For a moment, there was silence. I couldn't say why these two young women were quiet, but I knew why I was and that was because I was still somewhat confused.

Finally, Vic spoke, not about the troubles which our sister revolution was experiencing, but about dairy matters. 'There's a separate fridge,' she confirmed. Adding, 'With only Isabella's fingerprints on it. No others.'

'Okay,' I said, deciding to hitch a ride on the milk float, 'is it possible that he was a secret milk drinker? We aren't perfect, we all have our weaknesses.'

She laughed. It was a rather harsh, mocking laugh. Not one you'd get at a comedy store. 'No chance. Mike was the most committed and principled person I've ever met.'

Which at your age wasn't that long, I thought. You might just yet find another one.

But she wanted to make sure that I understood that Mike was a non-dairy kind of guy. Or would that be, non-dairy kind of sibling?

She continued, 'If he thought it was okay to drink milk, he'd have said so. No need to hide it. It was a personal choice, he wasn't strident vegan, let alone Ferma Foodie. He advocated veganism, and even the use of fermentation foods, but he was never evangelical about it; it isn't the most important thing right now. But if there's one thing I know, it's that he didn't drink that milk. It's a set-up. Set up by someone who may have known of his allergy, but not his personal politics. Someone knew that he didn't eat murdered animals, but not that he was a vegan. No way is this an accident.' She paused, before looking me straight in the eyes. 'He didn't drink that milk.'

So that was why we were here – milk.

'You said Marie was with you when you found him – did you tell her that you thought it was murder?'

'I *know* it's murder, and yes, I did.'

'And what did she say?'

Fiona flicked her hand, dismissing the idea, just as I do to members of the Apidae family – or sodding bees, as they are known to most people. One of which had just been joined by a mate and were now buzzing around my ear. 'She thought pretty much as you appear to – that I was being a silly little girl. Making up horror stories. She made a big deal of telling me in no uncertain terms that she was trained in medicine and knew exactly what had happened. I was, she reckoned, just being ridiculous. Actually, she got quite irritable, told me that I was wasting Jackie Payne's time. She rang the local hospital. It was then that Thom Simons arrived. Apparently, he was supposed to be at the same meeting that Williams was having, but had got waylaid.'

Victoria stroked the back of her neck, and thought for a second, before speaking in her cool professional voice, 'Okay, Fiona, we'll have to take down all the details. Roijin will get all this recorded. We're also going to have to ask you about who lives here and their movements.' What she said was all pretty normal, but there was an unusual tone to it. If I hadn't known better, I'd swear that she sounded compassionate. Perhaps the talk of milk had made Cole retract her claws. She then added, 'But that can come later. Would it be okay if you and Pete talk a bit more about Mike, and perhaps look in his room?'

'Yeah, no prob.'

Victoria nodded. 'Thanks. Sorry, Fiona, but Mike will still be in there. We haven't had a chance to have him taken away yet, and we're still doing a forensic sweep. Because, you may not believe this, we are taking this seriously. Are you okay with that?'

'Sure.' She passed Vic and into the house; jaws firmly set together.

I noticed nobody had asked if it was okay with me. Hanging back slightly, Victoria turned to me and whispered, 'We need to talk to Marie next.' I sighed heavily as if the world's problems were on my weary, but well-tailored shoulders. Victoria looked at me and gave a faint smile. 'Okay, I'll do her, and Thom, you stay with Fiona.'

# CHAPTER 3:
# RIVER WITH POPULARS

---

S tripping off in in front of someone is usually stressful. There may be self-image concerns; maybe performance issues; maybe you wish you'd put some clean boxers on. Real life isn't like the movies. Usually, disrobing is just plain embarrassing. Certainly, I've never heard that it was a prescribed way to release tension. Well, except for naturists. But I've never been a member of that particular group – I love my clothes too much. However, peeling off the forensic suit in Mike Stewart's bedroom, whilst a traumatised Fiona Bailey looked on, seemed to be a previously unknown method of calming down a witness. She was sitting on his bed, making no attempt to hide her amusement at my ungainly attempts to take the blasted thing off. I sucked in the humiliation – grateful that I wasn't adding to her trauma.

Before we'd gone upstairs, Roijin had informed both of us that the forensic sweep had been completed and we could change back into civvies. Bailey hadn't been wearing anything underneath hers, so she'd gone straight to her room and changed. Although hers was directly opposite Stewart's, and I merely had to take the forensic layer off, she had changed and reappeared before I'd even managed to take both the over-boots off. No doubt, she didn't want to miss any of the fun.

Bailey was sitting barefoot, in tight fitting three-quarter length blue jeans and a t-shirt emblazoned with a green campaign from before she had even been born. She was talking ten to the dozen about what a wonderful man Mike had been, whilst all the time, barely even pretending to stifle giggles at my expense.

Taking it off was proving to be more time-consuming than putting the damn thing on. My arms were flailing around his room, attempting to keep my balance and not crash into anything. Her smile was becoming more pronounced by the minute. My self-respect and any thoughts of coolness evaporating quicker than the sweat beneath the plastic. Her fear that I was the heavy hand of state oppression was doing likewise.

Finally, human again, I put it into the sealed plastic bag which the ever-efficient Roijin had provided me with. I smoothed down my linen jacket and trousers, straightened my shirt and ensured that all was well with my collar.

Now that all was good, I asked Fiona to tell me a bit more about the deceased. She didn't demure: Mike Stewart, she said, had been a charming and friendly guy, with a gentle sense of humour. Everyone liked and, indeed, loved him. I refrained from commenting that if he had been murdered, then there was at least one person, who didn't. He had a gift, she said, of being able to mix in any circle. It didn't matter the class, the age or the interests of the people he was socialising with, he would charm them. He also had that knack of introducing politics into the most unlikely occasion, and win people over. Sometimes without them even knowing that they had been in a political discussion.

'He was the most gifted orator I've ever known,' she said. 'He could speak to an individual or a meeting of thousands.'

I nodded. 'So how long have you known him? Personally, I mean.'

She looked into a space, where no doubt memories were appearing. 'About five years I suppose. Yeah, five – give or take. I moved in here about two years ago.'

Suddenly, I was struck with what to do with my hands. On TV, the cops always have a palm computer or a notebook to fiddle with, but since I had finished my comedy strip, I was somewhat at a loss as to what to do with them. Thinking of nothing else, I shoved them both in my trouser pockets.

'Anything more than a flatmate?' I asked, hoping my charisma would make a very personal question seem less intrusive than it actually was.

A gentle chuckle proved that I'd managed it – she hadn't taken offence. 'Oh no, Mike may have been totally open to relationships with any gender, but that's not me. Women only.'

'*Was* he in any sort of relationship?'

She shook her head. 'Only with the movement. Anything with people was purely to meet sexual needs, or just a way of him being sociable. He was totally committed to saving the world. It was him who came up with the slogan – Now or Never. If we don't do something drastic in this country and spread it across the globe right now, then we'll face the environmental catastrophe that we've been warning about for decades. *It literally is – now or never.*'

For a fleeting moment, I considered how having sex could merely be sociable. I usually just said hello and talked about the weather (when being sociable, that is, I couldn't remember what sex was). Visions of anarchists passing around plates of vegan crisps and offers of oral sex flashed into my head. Trying to lose them, I looked around the mid-size room. On the walls, framed posters had been carefully positioned, which demanded environmental justice and green power. Smaller historic leaflets circled them, framed in twos – all barking support. The only non-explicitly ecological print was two of architectural icons – the Weissenhof Estate and Chilehaus Building. Icons both.

The only photograph I could see was of a middle-aged woman decked out in hiking clobber up some foggy mountain.

'His mum – Pauline. Nice woman.'

I didn't say anything and continued looking around. Everything was neat and tidy, polite and ordered. It looked like a showroom to me, the type you'd find in a newly-built housing estate, and, pictures aside, with all the charm of an estate agent in a coma. For someone so brilliantly intelligent and beguiling, this was one boring room.

'Did he have any other family?' It was for background information but also there was the small matter of informing next of kin.

She took a deep breath before answering, 'I don't know about his family details too much, but he is – was – close to his mum, Pauline. I've met her a few times. I don't know what she does, or what's her politics. She'd come around after shopping and have a cup of tea. I don't know of any other family. I got the impression that he was an only child.' She paused and looked intently at the photograph. 'Would you like me to tell her...' Her control was beginning to crack. She gulped down a silent sob. 'Do you want me to tell her about Mike?'

I gave a sympathetic smile. 'That would be helpful. Thank you. But, Fiona, could you leave the cause of death open. Say it as it is – that it looks very much like anaphylactic shock, a tragic medical accident. However, we are looking into it, *just in case*. Would you agree to that? To keep your belief down to a suspicion.'

For a moment she looked doubtful.

I poured out my reassuring voice, 'Fiona, not for my sake, or Crib's, but his mum's. She doesn't need that stress on top of her grief. Would Mike have wanted his mum to go through that? We shall inform her of anything we find – I promise.'

A look of agreement crossed her face. 'Okay, understood. I think you're right. Pauline doesn't need that. She doted on Mike. I won't even mention my concerns. You can trust me on that. I'll just say that you are checking for confirmation of the cause of death.'

After a few minutes of rummaging through his clothes, I re-entered the world of discourse. 'Fiona – you really believe that Mike was murdered?'

She tried to look defiant, but instead looked more vulnerable. I would have to tread carefully. After all, we were talking about the passing of a dear friend. I didn't want to upset her more than was required. In my new line of work, a certain amount of toe-stepping often couldn't be avoided, but that was not to say that I enjoyed it. Science might be saying that it was an accident, but she had lost someone. Plus, I had to admit that she had sparked my interest.

'And you think that he was murdered because of his beliefs?' I asked, as I picked my way through his socks. Which were all black – anarchist socks had to be, I guess.

There was not a doubt in her mind – he had been murdered because he was a threat. I didn't ask a threat to who. Things were sensitive between the AF and the party at the moment, but we weren't at the stage of open warfare, just yet. It was true that some of my fellow party members did view people such as Stewart as a threat to both the party and the revolution itself, but none surely thought of murdering them. Surely, even the most conspiracy-minded of anarchists seriously believed that? No, the obvious answer was the forces of reaction, but then they rarely used subtle means, or took much time in hiding what they were doing. Bombs, shootings and drone strikes were more their style.

But Fiona Bailey had made the accusation of murder with the firm conviction of a priest announcing that the bread was the body of Christ. Like them, she appeared to have only faith to support it.

'Have there been any direct threats to his life?' I asked.

If I had expected a sudden flash in enlightenment, or an Old Testament style revelation, then I was disappointed. Her reply was as evasive as a tail-end batsman avoiding a bouncer. 'Vague stuff, nonsense really,' she muttered. She'd dodged the question, but it was ungainly and unconvincing. That rather threw me. She demands we act, but won't give me a direct answer to what seemed to me an obvious and important question.

I tried again, 'Could you be more precise, Fiona. What was the nature of these threats? How vague were they and why were they nonsense? Fiona, if we're to help, then we need to know everything. This could be important.'

She looked uncomfortable and I began to wonder if she regretted mentioning them, or indeed involving us in the first place. Her answer was a shrug and, 'Just the usual crap, the usual stuff.'

An experienced interrogator would have pushed harder and tried to pin her down. But I'm not one. In actual fact, it was actually my political experience which stopped me. We had an uneasy alliance with the AF, and she and Mike Stewart were important voices for the continuation of their relationship with us. They were critical, but still believed that the revolution was best served by at least temporarily supporting the workers' state. If any AF member could be described as being supporters, they were. For me to go barging in and pissing her off, would be politically foolish. Instead, I decided that I would return to it later.

Around the room, I couldn't see a computer of any description. Her response had made me want to check his media footprint. If we could see any abusive or threatening communications, then that might give credence to the belief that this was something other than a severe medical reaction. I asked her where he had them. She replied that he had several and they were usually kept in his workroom. A workroom? That conjured up images of lathes and milling machines, which made me somewhat interested in seeing it. What little I knew of Mike Stewart, hadn't made me think of him as a craftsman, with calluses on his hands, slaving over hot metal.

But that too could wait. I went back to the drawers. Only his tee-shirts appeared to be anything other than perfunctory. Many had environmental slogans, but rather surprisingly there were several with iconic buildings on them. I turned and held up one with the Dancing House in Prague, and raised an eyebrow.

She shrugged her shoulders, in a "What can I say?" way. 'He loved his architecture.'

'So, who else lives here?'

'There's me and of course Mike. Upstairs, there's Eduardo and Isabella, they have two rooms. They're a couple, they've a bedroom and a living room, and...'

'Tell me about Eduardo and Isabella. AF members?'

She jutted her jaw forward and thought for a second. I hadn't noticed before, but she had quite a pronounced jaw, acute you might say. Not that it was unattractive; indeed, it went rather well with her hair.

Oblivious to my thoughts, she gave a pair of brief character sketches, 'Isabella is, but Ed isn't. I think, last time I talked to him, he was nominally a member of yours. But to be honest, he changes organisations more often than I change knickers. Both are a little older than me – late twenties, early thirties. She's an optician and he's a chef. They're a nice if a little quiet couple. You won't see them; they went back home to Porto. They felt that with the difficulties they're facing there, they would be more use back in their home country. I don't know whether they will be returning or not. Depends on what happens, I suppose. They do need to let us know soon though, it's socially irresponsible having two rooms unused. If they're not coming back, we should be offering their room out.'

After we had sorted out the death of one of their house-mates, I thought to myself. I know that usually outdoor space and kitchen rotas were the main topics of debate in shared households, rather than sudden deaths in the kitchen, but I would have thought it was of some importance to have a house meeting about.

'What is – was – their relationship with Mike?' I asked.

'Friendly. But then Mike was pretty friendly with everyone. Well, except Fascists and,' she grinned, 'coppers.'

I ignored the implication. 'How long had they known him?'

She didn't know. Indeed, she didn't seem to know much of anything about them, despite the fact that she had shared a house with the couple for over eighteen months.

I made a mental note to check them out. 'Anyone else?' I asked. In my experience, anarchist households were usually busy places, with dozens of people per square metre. This was a largish house, and I figured that there would probably be more than five living here.

'There's DD – Dave Donaldson – do you know him?'

I did. He was also what you might describe as a leading member of the NONs. What I didn't tell her was that I found him to be a very strident and angry young man. Compromise was not in his vocabulary. What words were, always had to be delivered at a high volume. He was articulate and well-respected, but personally, from what I had seen and heard of him, he was a self-obsessed berk. He would regard himself as one of the leaders of the revolutionary period; I, thought, more a revolutionary of the lunch period.

'And where's Donaldson's room?'

'Top floor, Ed and Isabella have a bedroom and they share the lounge with him.'

'How do you all get on?'

'Fine.' If she wondered at the implication of my question, she chose not to say anything. They seemed a fairly self-contained couple who didn't really mix. From her tone, she thought that this was an unusual, if not a reactionary, way of living. She'd be appalled at what an anti-social git I was. As for Dave Donaldson, he hadn't lived in the house for long. Less than a year, possibly a fraction more. She didn't have much dealings with him either.

'And where is "DD" right now?' I asked.

She shrugged, and gave me a blank look. 'No idea. Probably at work. He works part-time at a street cleaning centre – maintenance section. He wasn't in last night, I'm pretty sure of that, he left a verbal note on the HomeChat, saying he was out for the night.'

Another one to have a little talk with, then.

'So, Mike was on his own last night?' I asked.

'As far as I know. But then he could have easily had someone around for the evening or even stay the night. Or have people – plural – around. What I can tell you is that earlier in the evening he was at the rally just up the road in the Unity Stadium. I saw him on the telly speaking. He was his usual brilliance – clear, passionate but human...' Her eyebrows crossed. 'Why are you so interested in the night before? I thought Mike died this morning?'

'He did, but it might help us know what he was doing in the hours preceding his passing.'

She didn't argue, but did think for a second, narrowing her eyes as if to get a better view of something. 'I did mention it on NONChat. I figured that having this house empty with so many rooms not in use was criminal, so I put on that if anyone needed a place to doss for a night in London then they should contact Mike and they could have a place to stay.'

'And did anyone?'

She paused, and a wetness appeared around her eyes. 'I don't know, I really don't know.'

I smiled and quietly said, 'Okay, Fiona, don't worry, we will, but it would be helpful if you could yourself ask around to see if any one did. It might be more diplomatic if such enquiries came from you rather than us.'

She agreed.

'Thank you,' I said in one of my schmooziest voices. Then, it went up a level. 'Now, Fiona, you mentioned some recent threats.'

She didn't answer for a second or two. Focussing on something invisible, somewhere in the near distance. 'He'd received death threats. I don't know how seriously he took them. That's why I'm not sure it's worth you knowing. They might just be trolls. But...' She sighed heavily. 'You should know, I guess. Just recently, he started to think that these were not just the usual run-of-the-mill type, which we all get.'

I sensed that she was going to tell me more, the more which might give us an indication of where to start the investigation, or indeed, whether there was any need for one in the first place. 'How did he receive them? Email? Messaging? InstantReply? BlackCloud?'

'No, he said that was what made them so sinister – they were whispered to him in crowds and hand-delivered on paper.'

'Sorry?'

She repeated what she had said.

'He received whispered and hand-written death threats?' I asked in disbelief.

My response hadn't been what she had hoped for. 'I know it sounds far-fetched, but that's what Mike told me,' she growled.

'Whispered? How can that be done? Wouldn't he have seen the person doing it? How do you whisper in a crowd?'

'You wanted to know, and I'm telling you. He said that he would hear snatches of threats, from behind him. Mike might have been a gentle soul but he wasn't soft. If he said he heard them – he had. If they worried him, there was a reason for that.'

Frankly, I was nonplussed at what she had just said. It all sounded Victorian cloak and dagger to me – men in long black capes, swirling moustaches and floppy black hats, whispering dire warnings. 'When did he hear them?' I asked, hoping that my voice didn't betray my scepticism. I didn't ask if there had been a cackling laugh accompanying them.

'The most recent was a few days ago, at Paddington Station.'

It had been blisteringly hot for several weeks, so there'd have been no black robes. I thought it best not to make the joke. Keep it serious. 'Did anyone see or hear these whispers?'

'No.'

'Did he see who made them?'

'No.'

Must have been the bloody Scarlet Pimpernel then. 'Okay. You mentioned that some were written – did *you* see them?'

'I saw three of them. They were handwritten in blue biro. Neat like a child's. The lettering was small and well-formed.'

Moving away from marking his handwriting, I asked if I could see them. She replied that she didn't know where he had hidden them, though they must be still in the house somewhere. We were free to look around.

We will. 'What exactly did they say?'

She pouted, elongating her face. 'They were all pretty similar. I can remember the last one I read, word for word.' In a careful, solemn voice, as if she was reciting an oath, she recited them: '"If you continue to undermine the revolution then you will be seen as an obstacle to the progression of civilisation, and thus will require elimination".'

I laughed. It wasn't the time or the place, but I couldn't help myself. She looked at me with more than a touch of annoyance. In my defence, this was all just a little bit comical – whispering at railway stations, and then a note sounding like that? 'It doesn't sound convincing to me at all, Fiona. Are you sure they weren't a joke? It sounds like something Eliza Doolittle might say after being taught to 'talk posh' by Professor Henry Higgins – type of language is that for a death threat?'

That had been a misstep. Clearly angered, she snapped, 'And that's your only comment? You don't like the pomposity of the language.' A sneer curled her lip. 'Although, I'd say, referencing George Bernard Shaw is rather pompous in itself.'

She had a point. 'Touché,' I replied, before smiling. 'And I guess answering in French could be considered so, too.'

'Oui en effet,' she replied, before allowing herself a grin.

'Okay, I hear what you're saying,' I said. 'But you must agree that the syntax of the letter is odd. But let's put that to one side. However, it's written, it sounds like it's from someone who supports the revolution, but not his political outlook. They support the workers' state but not the AF. Indeed, it sounds like a party member of mine.' Which might then not make the wording absurd – I'd known a few pompous party twits in my time.

'That's exactly what we both thought, and, like you, we both thought it was crap. It's meant to sound like that. Neither of us particularly trust you lot, but sending death threats isn't your style. No, the wording is deliberate. It's meant to appear that it's from you, and written in such a way as to draw attention to itself. Its artificiality made it sound genuine. The usual threats are online from the far-right, with a liberal amount of abuse. From the left, he got lengthy lectures. He reckoned you were more likely to bore him to death.'

I wasn't too sure about her logic. Nor was I appreciative of her opinion of the party, but there was no doubting that she sincerely believed that it had been genuine. That she had swallowed both her pride and even principles, and had contacted us, proved that if nothing else, she believed that they had been real. The death of her friend so soon after he had received them, would appear to support her in that.

I asked, 'How many did he get?'

'Oh, he said about a dozen. What really freaked him out was where he found them. They'd appear at places he was visiting. Sometimes he had only decided to go there at the last minute or he hadn't told anyone that he was going.'

'Such as?'

'Oh, well, a few weeks ago, he had decided to visit the new Colne Valley solar farm and was in the toilet when he found the envelope addressed to him.'

'Did he tell anyone there, or ask who might have left it?'

'No, he said that it was too much of a shock. As soon as he got it, he came back home.'

'Did you see it?'

'Yes. But he wanted to keep it secret. He felt that we're living with enough paranoia as it is, publicising it would only undermine what he was trying to do.'

'How seriously did he take them?'

'Let's just say that he, like most of us, have a healthy respect for the depths which they will go to in order to destroy the revolution.'

'And I want to be clear – *you* believed them to be real – to be genuine?'

She looked at me as if I was a complete and utter idiot. 'I had my doubts, for pretty much the same reasons as you obviously do, but then he's now dead. A bit of a coincidence, isn't it? That's why I contacted you, didn't I?'

'And why us?'

She breathed out heavily. 'The workers' councils are still in the early stages, and, shall we say, are not as effective as they might be. That's especially true about how our law and order is working. The anti-social behaviour stewards might be able to cope with everyday misdemeanours, but not this level of stuff. I don't think they're yet capable of taking on the forces of the former state.' She stopped and almost looked abashed.

That was it, then. Basically, she was arguing against everything that the Anarchist Federation stood for. Bailey was known to be more equivocal, less strident, in her criticisms of the party's initiatives than many of her siblings, but this was somewhat more than that.

She regrouped and pulled up her defences a notch. 'That doesn't mean that I don't believe that they won't, but right now… You and your colleagues have proved that you do. The others in your Crib might be hacks, but not you. From what I've heard, you've even managed to get the backs up of quite a few of your party's top dogs. You don't care who you piss off to get the job done. Word is, that the fact that you're still a member is solely down to the support of Jackie Payne.'

Bailey was closer to the truth than she probably realised; Marie Williams was downstairs and was probably half-way through making a voodoo doll of me, as we spoke.

'An enemy of my enemy, is my friend,' I said.

'Yeah. Something like that, or if you want another cliché – needs must.'

I nodded. That made sense. I looked at her and kept her stare. She was a dedicated and serious woman. She hadn't done this lightly. That was good enough for me. 'I think it's time I see this workroom of his,' I said.

Her shoulders seemed to relax a little. She almost seemed to bounce out of the room. She'd made her political confession and I hadn't mocked her. Her penance was going to be having to rely on us.

The workroom was across the landing. She opened its door in a manner you might for a bride entering a room. The first thing I noticed were the city plans which lined the walls. But what was the most impressive was what occupied the space between the walls. The room itself was huge, three times the size of his bedroom. Fantastic models of urban centres were everywhere. On tables and shelves, tiny scenes dominated. In each, there were sublime, delicately made buildings, crafted out of wood, with detailed figures of people living their daily lives. Green trees and shrubs surrounded, stood by and intermingled with them. Fiona didn't say a word, but remained silent, like a proud family member.

Walking around, I could see areas I recognised: there was central London, around the Buckingham Palace Museum and there were the southern areas of the city. One of the streets around here was featured

– I recognised the historic neo-castle like architecture of the Bryant and May factory and the circular vehicle charging point. But all had been dramatically changed, looking less like cityscapes and more nature reserves which happened to include buildings. Sky pavements, tramways and cycle lanes linked the different parts of the dioramas. On a table by the window, there was a neatly racked set of tools.

I found myself talking in a hushed tone, 'Is this Mike's work?'

She beamed delight, her nose moving up her face. 'Sure is; when he wasn't working or protesting, he'd be in here, building these. Though it would be fairer to say that all three were different aspects of the same thing. Mike was a trained architect; he was very much concerned with how cities could be adapted or built to harmonise humans with the wider environment; stopping further damage and even slowly repairing it. He called it City Nature Synthesis. He felt that capitalism had shaved functionality in our living spaces to the bare minimum – of eating, sleeping and watching TV. So, we were rested for the next day's work. But now we have the means of production, the function should include love and happiness, space to grow individually, which has to incorporate the wider, natural, world. It was his life's work.' She pointed to three laptops on the side-bench. 'There's far more in them. He called these hard-models, his thinking exercises, his real work was in the virtual field.'

'We'll have to take these virtual fields away with us.'

She nodded. 'Some can be accessed now. Move your hand.'

I did as she had suggested over large walls lining a building which looked as if it had square plates strapped to its side. An enlarged image of the wall appeared in front of me. Then a 3D image of Mike Stewart appeared. He looked younger, his birthmark more visible against milky skin. His hair was longer than I'd seen downstairs in the kitchen; it was blonde and floppy. His eyes sparkled as he spoke, 'The concept of bamboo absorbing Carbon Dioxide is decades old. But we could do more in western countries – use the hotter weather to more actively grow bamboo forests and to integrate them in our cities. They've been a staple of middle-class gardens for a long time, now we should use them for more than ornamental purposes.' I waved my hand again and it stopped.

Moving along to a park. I gave my hand another bout of exercise. Again, Stewart appeared. 'Islamic societies have long seen public spaces as being important, where individual rights and ownership are not the important factors but the space itself. We can build the future by actually building it...'

I couldn't help but admire it all. 'This is truly Impressive – the craft and skill on show is amazing. The ideas and application are quite awe-inspiring,' I said. It was indeed.

'Mike firmly believed that this was the future we should be building. He called it *communityism* – it was his little joke. If we concentrated on building a future, it would keep the revolutionary forces together in positivity.'

I could have listened for hours but there were more pressing matters. 'Fine thoughts. Now, can I see the other rooms?' I asked.

She looked surprised. 'But both your militia, and that Cole comrade of yours, have already searched them. Did it when they first arrived.'

Actually, it was *our* militia, and Vic was *our* comrade, but I let it pass. Instead, I put on a cheeky grin, aiming to charm. 'I know, Fiona, and I realise that it's an awful invasion of privacy, but the more eyes are used then the more likely we will find something.'

'Like what?' she exclaimed. 'He was poisoned, how's looking in my bedroom going to help?'

I told her honestly, 'I don't know. Probably nothing. But it would be procedure in any type of investigation, by any type of state. There might be a chance that we find something that gives us a clue as to who might behind this. We might even find those threatening notes.'

She looked unconvinced.

I changed tack. 'There's also the chance that if someone did kill him, they might have gone upstairs.'

'Why? Do you think they dragged Mike downstairs?'

That was highly unlikely. 'No, but you said yourself, when you and Maria arrived, you both stayed in the kitchen, leaving the front door open.'

Realisation dawned. She looked horrified. 'Are you suggesting that someone was upstairs when we were in the kitchen?'

I shrugged. 'It's possible. It's certainly worth a look. Fiona, you've called us in and if you want us to investigate then you have to let us do our jobs. You can't have it both ways – demand that we get involved and then obstruct us when we do.'

She didn't put up any more opposition and relented, asking me where I would like to start. I pointed upstairs. We started with the Portuguese love-couple's bedroom, which appeared to be rather small for them. Furniture was rammed in there, side by side, with no space for the walls to breathe.

Behind me, on the bed, Bailey's eyes followed my every move. She didn't say a word, but I could sense her growing dissatisfaction. She had a point – if he had been assassinated, then the answer was highly unlikely to be in these rooms. However, on one of our interminably-long training days, Vic had been at pains to point out the importance of a fresh crime scene. There could be all kinds of details hidden, which at a later date we might use. We had no idea why Mike Stewart had been killed. Or indeed, if he actually had been. However, we needed to gather as much evidence as possible. What Bailey didn't realise was that it was far more invasive than she thought it was, because within my snazzy ID badge was a microscopic camera, which was filming everything I saw and did, and what she said and did.

After half an hour of rooting about, I pronounced myself satisfied and we moved into the small room which had been designated as their upstairs lounge. I would have called it an office, full of activists' detritus but nothing more of interest.

Donaldson's bedroom was slightly neater than their living room but not by much. It was smaller, and appeared to be used simply as somewhere to sleep, and store clothes, primarily on the floor, it seemed.

Then there was one more bedroom to go. The one which I was dreading. Hovering outside her room door, I turned and exchanged a look with Bailey. I received a horrified stare, before it opened up into a huge grin and she gestured with her hand, the world-known one of saying *be my guest*.

On the walls were prints of Franz Marc and Ernst Ludwig Kirchner. 'A fan of German Expressionism, I see.'

Sheepishly, she smiled.

I was tempted to engage her in a discussion on early twentieth century art because what I was going to have to do next wasn't something I was looking forward to. I leant forward and studied some photographs.

'Mum, Dad, friends at uni and my younger sister, Viola.'

'You know what I've got to do, Fiona, sorry...'

'Enjoy,' she replied simply, with more than little sarcasm in her voice.

I opened the wardrobe and flicked through her clothes. Her taste could best be described as relaxed fashion. Then I turned my attention to a large blue wood-stained chest of drawers. Taking a deep breath, I opened it up. Feeling like a perv, I rummaged through each one, attempting to apply the lightest of touches, as if that made this any better. Out of the corner of my eye, I could see a sly smile on her lips. I had a distinct feeling that she was enjoying my discomfort. This didn't faze her one bit. She had suffered for her politics in her life, so me going through her clothes was pretty small fry.

Ten minutes later and my agony was over.

'Done?' she asked, now not even hiding her obvious joy at seeing me cringe.

I closed the last drawer and stood to face her. 'Yes, er, thank you.'

Folding my arms, I tried to regain a modicum of authority and returned to the main issue here. 'I assure you, Fiona, that we will investigate Mike Stewart's death to the best of our abilities. If it's murder, then it's also an attack on the revolution and we'll treat it as such. We will utilize the forces of the class to avenge it. But I think it's important to be honest. We will keep an open-mind, but in all honesty, my first impression is that there isn't anything to suggest that this isn't simply what it seems – a sad death of a young person from anaphylaxis. You've said he received threats, but as you alluded to, so have I, so have many people in the public eye. That they were so bizarrely delivered is unusual, I grant you.

'Then you say, he didn't drink milk. Again, that's an odd fact and one we'll look into, but you must admit, it's not much. It could of course be an assassination, dressed up to be an allergic reaction. Subterfuge like that has happened before. If it is, we shall find out. Can you think of anything else which might help us?'

Her reply consisted of repeating what she had already said alongside some idle flattery. My ego was a big fluffy thing which had a big tongue to lap up the idlest of flattery, but even so, I wasn't finding much here in the way of nourishment. All was watery and thin, and unfulfilling.

Just then, a message came through my hidden earpiece. *We need to meet. See you and Vic in my office in an hour. Jackie Payne.*

# CHAPTER 4:
# THE GRAVENOR FAMILY

E go and stubbornness are often close allies; certainly, they could claim an inglorious victory over eco-socialism and discipline with Vic and I driving separately. So much for the state's strictures protecting the climate.

On my two and her four wheels, we had made good time, encountering only a modest amount of traffic, on our way to Marylebone. The early morning food queues were now just down to a few late-risers and we had missed the rush-hour.

I was a little surprised that Jackie Payne was there, seeing that the National Workers' Council was presently based in Manchester, and would be until its year was up, when it moved on to Durham.

I snuck in behind Cole's car, parking in front of the square three-storey Georgian building, which housed her offices. Such was my role in life – to tuck in behind. A faded sign spoke of the past owners – Gravenor Family Solicitors, which peeked out between the two large red drapes that hung down its cream brickwork, either side of bomb blast-proof windows. The decor was completed with iron bars, CCT and surveillance drones. Divorces could get messy, but assassination was a popular hobby of the reactionaries, so it was safe to assume that these were here because comrade Payne was. Gone were the days when you could just amble in for a chat. It was getting to the point that if you were foolish enough to try that, you'd instantly find yourself spread-eagled on the floor, pinned down by militia-comrades. Not being in the slightest chatty.

Four of them swiftly came to meet us, toting guns, square sunglasses, plastic earpieces, revolutionary zeal and shorts baggy enough to hide an entire battalion of the workers' army. Dismounting before Victoria got out of her car, it fell to me to explain the reason for our visit. I took off my helmet to reveal my boyish smile, and friendly eyes. Hopefully that would be enough, I didn't fancy being pistol-whipped by the leg of one of those shorts. They were flapping like sails.

I pressed my Mondrian badge. After scrutinising it, a complete change of attitude overcame her. The big gun dropped, and a big grin appeared. 'It's okay,' she muttered to the others. 'They're sound.' They backed off and moved to where they had previously stood, to concentrate on looking mean and controlling those shorts. She didn't. Instead, she introduced herself as Adina. Adina was clearly excited by the news of today's art reclamation and my role in it. She'd seen me on one of the party's news channels, she babbled. If you ignored the sub-machine gun, she could easily have been mistaken for a teenage fan at a pop concert.

Vic rolled her eyes. 'Is the nation's cultural warrior going to come in, or do you want to stay out here, signing autographs?'

Yeah, funny.

My new-found art-loving pal threw her a look. Luckily for Vic that was all she threw. Instead, taking the subtlest of unsubtle hints, she touched her earpiece and spoke. I didn't catch what she'd said; I presumed she was letting Jackie know that we were here. Either that, or she was making a complaint about the shorts. Surely, there were limits to what a worker's state could demand of people. Then again, maybe, she simply had an itchy ear. Whatever it was, the front door opened. We were let into the building by two track-suited comrades, who ushered us through an X-Ray machine.

No sooner had we passed through what I guessed had been nicked from Heathrow, when Jackie's voice filled the hall, 'I'm up here!'

The first thing which hit me was air conditioning, which it had to be said was hugely welcome in this heat. The further up the stairs we went, the cooler it got. The room temperature, though, wasn't the only thing on my mind. Ever since I had received a text, I'd been wondering why she had been in such a hurry to get involved.

Still, whatever the reason, it was good to be finally here and not just for the aircon. I'd never been before, and it was certainly nice to have at least an acquaintance with the offices of power. I'd been to the others. One, in particular, I remembered had been a claustrophobic cubby-hole above a warehouse. I had gone to pick up some placards with a young woman who I had recently started talking to, and who that day had decided to join. Her name had been Jackie. It still was, and now she was president of a workers' republic.

The floor was one large open-plan office with the overriding design philosophy of a scatter-gun. Chairs, sofas, tables, books, computers, hovering 3D and 2D images were everywhere. None were in any apparent order and sometimes were colliding with each other. Interacting with all this were a dozen people in differing states of concentration. A hum of activity filled the air.

Jackie Payne was sitting in the middle, on a battered brown leather armchair, sunglasses resting on the top of her closely cropped head; she looked all ready for a summer vacation. Her long black legs stretched out from red shorts, which were matched by a three-quarter arm loose-fitting blouse, whose red was interrupted by large white spots. A white necklace hung low off her neck.

Seeing us, she pushed aside a 3D visual and beckoned us over. In front of her, sitting on armchairs and surrounded by objects which resembled twentieth-century phone directories, were two men who turned and rose on hearing our arrival.

The youngest was very tall, just under two metres. He was in his early thirties and looked of Indian descent. I vaguely recognised him as being one of our comrade soldiers. Not that you'd guess that from his appearance, not with him barefoot, in a plain white tee-shirt and blue shorts. He looked as if he was joining Jackie on her hols. His shorts, I was gratified to see, were much better tailored than our friends' outside. Hopefully, there was no rivalry over the matter. He had a slim good-looking face, almost boyish in features, which was highlighted by his short black hair. Only his muscles looked military.

The other guy was almost as tall, but older, in his fifties. with barely any flesh on him he didn't look military, more emaciated. Mixed race, Sudanese and Maltese, with a shiny shaved dome of a head, he possessed a face that oozed a condescending attitude. Everyone knows that looks can be deceptive, but they weren't here in this case. This comrade I did know – this was Noah Walker. He was a man who rated himself highly and who never knowingly indulged in what he would consider as the sin of modesty.

We'd met a few times, mainly because he had been one of the most vociferous supporters of the creation of the Cribs. Not that he was celebrating his victory, because comrade Walker considered us to be too weak. He was now demanding that we should be beefed up with extra powers and the scope of our operations widened. The state shouldn't be too liberal – it should defend itself by whatever means, was his oft-repeated mantra. Or one of them. Liberalism merely played into the hands of the reactionaries was another. I was never quite sure which he hated more – liberals or reactionaries. He was an Old Testament type of comrade – all fire and brimstone. But then, with a name like Noah, he couldn't be anything else.

Not that the Noah here looked remotely like God's wrath, not with him wearing the most ludicrous and hideous luminous yellow baggy trousers I had ever seen. Bearing in mind that I regarded, as every sane person did, that all baggy luminous yellow trousers were inherently ludicrous and hideous, that was really saying something. They were less trousers and more pantaloons. Then again, if fire and brimstone was all about the torments of hell, then his attire could certainly achieve that. Christ, what did comrades wear in the summer? The party really did need to get a grip on the issue.

He gave me a playful slap on the arm. 'Pete! How are you?'

'Yeah, fine, Noah. Good, yeah.' I forced a smile. It had stung a bit.

He smiled at Victoria. She didn't get the honour of being struck, and had to just make do with a nod of his head.

Our arrival marked their exit. Jackie got to her feet. 'Cheers, Reyansh. I'll call you in a few days. I think we're at least agreed that we need to carefully consider our response. I appreciate you trekking over here.' She switched attention. 'Noah, we'll arrange something for tomorrow, but I think it would be useful if you were in on the call with Reyansh. Believe me, I do hear what you're both saying.'

Reyansh, yes of course, this was Reyansh Anand. He was indeed one of our star comrades in the military. He'd made his name organising the defence of Leicester in the civil war. Nowadays, things were a little less exciting and he could often be seen at meetings by the side of his louder friend here, also arguing for the state to have a bigger stick. I suppose being confined to barracks, cleaning your rifle and watching re-runs of old TV movies was a bit boring for such an action man. I also seemed to remember him recently having several spats with Mike Stewart. Stewart had felt keenly aggrieved at the continuing involvement of the military in the day-to-day politics of the country. Anand in turn, had felt that Stewart was a delusional fantasist, who didn't appreciate that one of the reasons for the republic not being attacked by a foreign power, and an invading army marching up Pall Mall, was because of the position of the armed forces' rank and file. It would be true to say that they didn't see eye to eye.

I didn't catch Anand's reply, because at that precise moment, Noah Walker moved closer to me, clearly wanting to have a quiet word. Not that I could imagine Walker's words ever being anything but booming. A remarkable feat, considering his slender frame. He spoke, as he usually did, when speaking to me, as if I was a child who required firm guidance from an older and wiser head. That he was younger, and definitely not wiser, always had a remarkable effect of making me want to disagree with him, whatever he said.

'Just wanted to say, Pete, I think you're doing great work, important work. I don't think I'm being boastful here, if I say that I believe that I've been proved right about the importance of Cribs. And if you need more help, give me a ring.' He looked deep into my eyes. Romantic it wasn't. This was Noah Walker emoting sincerity. My breakfast moved closer to my mouth.

Obviously deciding against putting his tongue down my throat to meet my toast halfway, he instead turned his attention to Victoria and nodded. 'As always, Vic, good to see you.'

The pair of us replied with a small array of bland platitudes, whilst I avoided looking at his pantaloons. I was also trying to think what a "supporter" of mine actually did. Did they make up chants? Wear rosettes with my face on?

Jackie and Reyansh Anand had finished whatever they were talking about. He gave Walker a knowing look and then he marched out of the room. Did all squaddies move like that? Marching everywhere? To the pub, to the bathroom? Taking it as cue for him to go as well, Walker again said goodbye and followed him. Less of a march, more of an awkward lope.

Jackie Payne turned her full attention to us. She smiled. 'Pete, Vic, thanks for coming. Sit down.' She indicated the two newly-vacated chairs. Something caught her attention. 'Pete, I've always loved that suit. Takes years off you.'

I smiled a thank you. There was no fashion critique for Vic. Which was a shame, because she looked effortlessly cool today. Wearing tight white jeans with an equally tight-fitting black tee-shirt, topping off her look with small round sunglasses, made her resemble some aspiring actress about to jet off to the south of France. Not that Vic wouldn't be too bothered by her exclusion. When Vic was working, all she thought about was the work. And all Vic seemed to do, was work.

The same was true of Jackie. She was called many names; what they were, depended on which side you were on. As for me, she was president, leader, comrade, but most importantly, friend. But despite the attempt at a warm welcome, it had felt just that, an attempt. She was meeting us as president. Something was seriously worrying her.

We all sat down. This signalled the end of the ever-so small talk. It was time for us all to get down to the business of why we were here. Settling herself, Jackie smiled. 'So, tell me, what have you found?'

I let Vic answer. She liked that sort of thing. She did so, quickly and with preciseness of a pro, finishing by reiterating that it looked like it was the case of an allergic reaction.

Jackie looked at her closely. 'But you will treat his death as highly suspicious and act accordingly?'

'We will keep an open mind, and if...'

'Vic, I want Crib to proceed on the assumption that he was murdered.' It wasn't a suggestion; it was an instruction. Our investigation had barely started and she had just told us that Mike Stewart had been bumped off.

Her tone might have surprised Vic, but she remained calm. 'Jacks, it does really look like it was a severe allergic reaction. So, we will not proceed with such an assumption because that could skew our investigation.' She almost sighed, wanting to relay what we were doing, even if our president appeared to be not that interested. 'But we'll keep an open mind. We've started to set up the required investigation structure. The Hackney Bow Workers' Council will be the organisational backbone of it. They'll decide if a Community Information Meeting needs to be organised and a judge and prosecutor elected. People are already taking statements from neighbours. Crib is there purely as support at the moment, because as we said, it looks like an accident...'

'If it walks like a duck, sounds like a duck, and looks like a duck, it probably is a duck,' I said.

They just looked at me, and didn't say a word.

I put it another way. 'It just looks like an allergic reaction, Jacks. It really does.'

I got the look. The look which Jackie could unleash when she wanted to. Calling it withering did not do it justice. Annihilating would be a better way of describing it. 'Why, have you something better to do?' It might have been said with a half-smile, but there was an edge to her voice. Her eyes had flashed. 'You know full well the situation we face. Our position isn't easing as we had hoped it would. We'd hoped that with the Portuguese revolution, our isolation would lessen, but it's proved to be quite the opposite. Events in Portugal have terrified other nations, who fear that they could be next. Reports are coming in on a weekly basis of sabotage and terrorism. We have heard for some time that they have been preparing for what they call 'an event'.

Vic looked her squarely in the eye. Not even the leader of the revolution could pressurise Vic into rushing things. 'We know, but that doesn't mean that this is murder. We cannot let paranoia corrupt our judgement.'

Vic didn't speak, but the power of Cole's glacial facial expression meant she didn't need to. These two really had some good looks. It was like an Olympic final of glaring. There was a thundering aura of suspicion emanating from Vic – one which could no-doubt be seen from space. Green Martians sitting on their green Martian chairs, could see that the female human-being, known by the name of Victoria Cole, did not for an Earth-second, believe the reason being given by the female human, by the name of Jackie Payne, for her thinking that there was something suspicious about Mike Stewart's death.

The Martians weren't the only beings who could see it, Jackie could as well. Her arms stretched upwards and she clapped her hands together. I have to admit that I slightly jumped; I hadn't expected that. Was she about to start singing? In a loud and commanding voice, she instructed her fellow office worker to give her some time.

I couldn't speak for Vic, but I for one, was utterly amazed. Those on the floor looked up and I could see from some of the faces that I wasn't the only one surprised. But after a few brief conversations, the projections closed and people started to file out. Jackie didn't watch them go, but somehow could sense when they all had.

Then she spoke. 'There's also the Fool's List.'

I laughed, thinking that she was joking. Had she cleared the office floor for this – a new one-liner? The piercing stare she gave me, informed me that she wasn't, and that she had.

Cole didn't find the comment amusing, but neither did she think it something worth taking seriously. 'I thought we'd pretty much dismissed it as being just a sick prank,' Cole said. 'Released on April Fool's Day simply to scare people. No-one takes the notion seriously that you'd publish a list of people whom you intend to murder. Not outside of thrillers, that is.'

'Maybe, maybe not,' Jackie replied. 'But on the list, there's thirty of the leading AF members and Mike Stewart is the fourth to die since it was released. That alone should make us want to investigate it closely.'

From memory, I could recall that one in Scotland had been as a result of a traffic accident. The second, which had been in Newcastle, had either jumped or been pushed from a window. The third had been shot by a sniper, whilst taking a dip in the sea at Hastings. So that one couldn't be explained away, but then shootings were sadly not that unusual. They weren't as common as getting run-over, not yet anyway, but the way things were going, they might well soon be. The list had largely been ignored when it had first appeared on social media. All but a few conspiracy addicts, in dire need of human contact, saw it as a hoax. After the deaths, all manner of wild conspiracy theories started to gain traction. Some were even saying that it was actually the party who had published it in order to cower our allies. They were becoming rivals for power and so needed to be eliminated, or at the very least, intimidated. True, there were also party members on the Fool's List, including Jackie herself, but the conspiracy enthusiasts dismissed that as being mere camouflage. As far as I knew though, the majority still thought that the Fool's List was simply a hoax.

Cole certainly did. 'But it's bogus! A stunt! Jacks – you, yourself, denounced it, denounced it publicly as fake news.' Disbelief and a touch of exasperation were evident in her voice.

Jackie's was level, but determined. 'All I'm saying, is that we keep an open mind. The news of Mike Stewart's death has only just been released and already the Fool's List is trending. More people are starting to take it seriously, even if you don't. Four of the thirty anarchists on the list are dead. That's just over thirteen per-cent of them. Whilst, no party members have died.'

That was zero percent. Even my maths could work that out. I could also work out pronouns, and noted that she had said "you", not *us* in not taking the list seriously. She hadn't included herself.

When she next spoke, there was an incremental heightening in the tone of her voice. Seasoned Jackie Payne watchers would know that it tended to happen when she was making a key point, and one which she felt needed to be defended vigorously. 'Which means we should keep an open mind about it.'

Neither of us argued.

Jackie nodded, accepting our acquiescence. She became, if not softer, then a touch less strident. 'And I admit that this is slightly personal. I've had quite a lot of dealings with Mike and always found him an amiable and fraternal guy. Always enjoyable and pleasant company. He had a lot of interesting ideas on redesigning our cities. I won't pretend that we didn't disagree on a lot of things, because we did. He was, for me, far too idealistic and pre-emptive about dismantling the state, but our relationship was always friendly and professional. He's a sad loss to the cause. I'll miss him.'

Silence resumed. I didn't know what we were supposed to do with this knowledge. In all honesty I wasn't quite sure what was happening here. We'd plainly said that we were going to look into his death further – what more did she want?

'If it wasn't an accident, we'll find out,' Vic said, with no fear of repeating herself.

'Thank you.' Jackie sat forward in her chair, coming closer, as if she was going to whisper something. There was nobody else here, I didn't understand why she was becoming even more secretive. She'd be tapping out Morse Code at this rate. If I wasn't imagining it, her voice was indeed quieter. 'The footwork will be conducted by the Hackney Bow Workers' Council. Roijin and Ash will give support. But I want you two to act more independently. Report regularly and personally back to me. Especially if there's anything which suggests that there is MI5 involvement.'

That didn't sound like our society's acclaimed transparency and accountability principles. I waited for Victoria to raise an objection. Surprisingly, she didn't. Nor did I.

'And if we find nothing to suggest that it is anything other than what it looks like?' Victoria asked.

Jackie's reply was short, to the point and to be regarded as the final word on the subject, 'Then keep looking.'

She stood. Obviously, the president had ended this cosy chat. She smiled, and added, 'Thanks.'

We also got to our feet and I promised that we'd keep her informed. Vic did not say a word but just nodded goodbye. Not wanting to leave on a sour note, I smiled at Jackie. 'We appreciate the pressure you must be under. You must be at your wits' end.'

She grinned at the mention of our familiar mantra which we had been saying for years, and gave the standard reply, 'Oh, I'm way past that.'

The instant we had left the building, and had passed some quizzical looks from the displaced office workers, Victoria reached inside her trouser pocket and pulled out a packet of cigarettes. Standing by my bike, she lit up, and asked, 'When did you two start that little call and response thing you have? The wits' end thing?'

Looking at her drawing down the nicotine, I sensed an element of hostility in the question. I told her that I couldn't remember, 'It's just a silly thing which reminds us that we've known each other for a long time.'

She flicked some ash onto the pavement and pulled a face. 'And in all that time, how often has she lied to you?'

I was taken aback by the question. Not least, because I thought Victoria rather idolised Jackie. I told her that I thought Jackie had never lied to me.

'Well, that's the first time then – you've lost your virginity.'

I was totally confused. What was she on about? What was in that fag?

'Jackie *knows* it was murder.'

'And how do *you* know that?' I asked.

'Because,' she sighed, 'as every fucking person on the planet keeps telling me – I used to be a copper.'

# CHAPTER 5: RIVER FRONT OF NEW SOMERSET HOUSE

B y the time we had arrived at Somerset House, news of Mike Stewart's death was spreading as quick as a flash flood in Cumbria. The location of our base had originally been chosen, purely because we hadn't been able to think of anywhere else. But it had gone from a stop-gap measure to more permanent one. At present, we could boast of occupying two small rooms and a share of a toilet. Langley, CIA headquarters, it certainly wasn't. Still, our neo-classical building was better than theirs. We did have a receptionist though – Odette Lecomte, whom we shared with other misfit departments of the state.

One of which, I'd been working for this morning – the Art Repossession and Transfer, otherwise known as ART. They themselves were next to the new Lissitzky Exhibition Space for Revolutionary Art, which had opened three weeks ago, joining the more established Courtauld Galley. Knowing the Courtauld so well, had been the reason for my proposal in the first place. Little did I know that it was to become my place of work. That we were still here, was, in part, due to the aesthetics of the building, because Jackie Payne thought that if we moved to a more modern glass and steel, virile and thrusting type office block, it would give off the wrong image, making us look far too Orwellian. The fact that Somerset House was a former palace, which had once included the Royal Navy as occupants, had seemingly not been a concern for her.

Odette was at her desk, fanning herself with a sheet of paper. Her long-tanned legs were crossed on top of her desk. She was as tall as Fiona Bailey. Both were just under two metres, but whilst you could imagine Bailey in an athletics competition, Odette would more likely be on the grass, having a picnic and reading a book of poetry. On my first meeting with her, she had, with all the enthusiasm of youth, informed me of her life story. Such as it was, her being all of seventeen years of age. Her parents were French, but she was from West London; she'd dropped out of school when the crisis had come to a head, immersing herself in political activity. She'd even been in prison for it for a short while. She now boasted of being a party member for all of fourteen months. Thus, making Victoria seem positively an old timer. As for me, she treated me with a mixture of awe and respect for my longevity, seeing me as a museum piece from a bygone age. Which was pretty much the case.

With her usual machine-gun delivery, she had in a single breath: welcomed us; asked if we'd heard of Mike Stewart's death; informed us of all the theories already developing around it; apologised that she was finishing work at five pm today because she had a meeting to go to, but we were not to worry, because house security would still be here; admired my suit but fretted that I'd be too hot in it – she had gone for shorts and a baggy cotton shirt herself; and finally, that there had been another cyber-attack, thus disrupting our power supplies.

That explained why the air-con was so crap at the moment. Relying on back-up, things were working at only ten percent. Such attacks were now common. We did have enough power to run the country but it could still be disrupted through cyber-terrorism. We blamed China and the USA; they blamed our incompetence. It was a sign of the times that it was so old hat, that in conversational terms, Odette had ranked it last on her list.

Thanking her, we had opened our office door. There was no impressive visual announcement that we were defenders of the socialist revolution. We didn't even have a sign – it was just a plain white door. I placed my helmet on my desk, hung my jacket on the back of my chair, took a swig of water, and proposed that today was an ideal one for the 'team' to go to an outside lido. Ignoring my flippancy, Victoria instead suggested, in that way she had of making it sound more like an instruction, that we start setting up an information display, with visuals, both 3D and 2D. Her mood began to lighten with the thought of setting up an incident room. She had been rather spiky with Jackie Payne; I was pleased to see her relax into work. There's nothing like an information board to raise the spirits.

Luckily, it was standard practice to charge our array of tech, so the low power situation didn't affect us too much. Even our trusted office AI was operating. Vic instructed it, in much the same voice she used with me, to sort the data into the areas on the board.

In its centre was a large hard-copy photograph of Mike Stewart. Smiling and looking happy, it could have been of any twenty-something on holiday. The pic of his corpse next to it rather spoilt that vibe. Around both, were virtual images and the data which the AI had found in the initial searches. Above them, in a line, were smaller, equally as real, photos of his house-mates – Fiona Bailey, Dave Donaldson, Isabella Torres and Eduardo Almeida, alongside Marie Williams and Thom Simons. Information began to appear below each in a variety of forms. Under Isabella and Eduardo, a lovely scenic postcard appeared of where they were thought to be. There was also the footage of my house-search, surely destined to be a block-buster, and the statements we had taken.

Victoria had further 'suggested' that I see if I could find Mike Stewart's speeches, film clips, and as much personal data as I could find. She did likewise for Fiona Bailey. On the left was the list of her initial thoughts and questions raised. Not to leave him out, there was a virtual column for Thom Simons appeared. He might have arrived after Marie and Fiona, but he was still to be treated as someone of interest. Looking at Marie Williams was rather disturbing. I would never have imagined when I had first met her when she had been a twenty-year old medical student, that I'd be investigating a murder, in which she was a key witness. But then, it wasn't the first time. We had so much history. I had even held her new-born kids in my arms.

When Roijin Kemal finally arrived, she had paused for some refreshments, before joining the game of pinning the data on a virtual donkey. We had been transformed into a Year One class on a sharing afternoon. The slight difference being, that it wouldn't be favourite teddies and books, but suspects and evidence.

Two hours of focussed activity passed, and the room's central space had quickly become an impressive array of images and text floating in front of us, with sections joined by colour-coded CGI ribbons. The restoration of full power had given the images a far clearer quality.

'Right,' Roijin announced, indicating that the review meeting was about to start. She had left a space for a full-size 3D visual link to be used, so as not to get tangled up with all the other projections. "Keeping our view clean" was how she had put it.

The link had opened and hovering in front of us, was Joseph in a pristine white overcoat, with Dr Lopez behind him. Both were looking busy with what looked to be medieval torture instruments, but were no doubt tools of the trade. Two young men could also be seen in the background, but we weren't given introductions as to who they might be. They were either scientists at the lab, or tourists with very particular interests.

Asher spoke first, 'Hi. I know it's my turn to chair, but as I'm in the lab would it be okay if Roijin does the honours? I can then concentrate on what we find here.' No-one had any objections, including Roijin, who asked me to start.

Why not? Choosing not to stand from fear that I might collide with one of the images, I strutted my political stuff: 'Michael Dean Stewart, known as Mike Stewart – twenty-six years of age. A leading member of the Anarchist Federation – although they deny having such things. But we all know that they do. Certainly, he was one of the AF members with the highest profile, which is at least partly due to his clear articulate manner and being very media-friendly. He had possessed an uncanny ability to make even the most extreme position, sound sensible and mainstream.

'He became politically conscious when he was at school, during the children strikes of fourteen years ago. Unaligned, but involved in various campaigns, until ten years ago, he joined the then fledging AF. An architect by trade, he had a deep interest in how the division between urban and country could be made less divisive and more harmonious. He founded the Now or Never movement, otherwise known as the NON, which is a group focussed on the environment and is within the AF umbrella. I won't go into details of the amorphous mass, which is the AF. Not that I can claim to be an expert on how they work.' I wasn't actually sure that most AF members could explain it either. 'Basically, it's a loose alliance of groups and organisations, of which the NON is a part of. Whether technically there is a membership or not, your guess is as good as mine, but if no-one minds, because it gives me a headache to even attempt to work out their structure – or even if they have one – I'll use the terms we use in the party. Even if they don't. As you'd expect from an AF 'member', Stewart favoured loose alliances, and opposed formally structured organisations. I'm sure he hated labels, but basically, he was a syndicalist, with your typical anarchist suspicion of parties. Pro-community self-help and against state control, including the NWC. That said, he supports the workers' state, but sees it as transitional. Whilst critical of us, he wasn't overly hostile, and was seen as one of the most fraternal of the AF cadre. This has led to accusations by some of his 'siblings' of being too close to us.'

I paused for questions and to take a drink. Receiving none, and taking a sip, I continued: 'As for his personal life, he was an only child. His mum's still alive; his dad died several years ago of natural causes. Mike was a well-liked man. Even allowing for the traditional hypocrisy of post-death amnesia of antagonisms, the initial response to his passing has been uniformly one of grief. And that's from across the revolutionary spectrum, from the softest Democratic Lefts to the nuttiest of AF members. He also seems to have had a wide range of friends, although no-one appears to be anyone special. Basically, he was a nice bloke.'

Short and sweet, I had said all I had to say. It was now Vic's turn.

She decided to stand, moving to a picture of Fiona Bailey who was dressed head to toe in leather – boots to tight trousers to jacket. I presumed that it was fake; her animal friends would have a meltdown if it wasn't. Pointing at the picture, she spoke, 'A train technician, twenty-three years. A leading member of the NON-eco-socialist movement.' She smiled and gave me a look. 'I agree with Pete, it'll be easier if we use those terms. She returned home in the morning after staying with a friend in Hammersmith and found Mike Stewart. That was approximately at 10.30am. This is confirmed by Marie Williams, who met her on the doorstep.' She pointed to an image of Stewart in denims, scaling a wire fence on an anti-military demo. Just in case we'd forgotten who we were talking about. 'On entering the building, both Bailey and Williams went into the kitchen, where they found Stewart lying on the floor. We're all pretty familiar with Marie Williams, she's 66, a former medical professional but is now a full-time Central Committee member of the United Revolutionary Socialist Party. It was she that made the original diagnosis of death from a massive anaphylactic reaction. At 10.37, Bailey rang the 147-emergency number and directly asked for us. Despite not being a choice on offer. She was insistent, and specifically named Pete as someone she wanted to speak to. Sadly, for her, she only got me.'

The room chuckled.

After the shock that Vic Cole had a sense of humour, she resumed her talk in an effortlessly professional manner. 'Two minutes later, Williams called the Hackney Hospital and reported a death. After talking to me for ten minutes, Bailey hung up and called a Christopher Jameson, a NON-member and friend of hers, who went to see Jackie Payne and convinced her to instruct Crib to be formally involved.'

'Who is this Jameson?' I asked.

'Someone Jackie works with at the NWC London offices. He's part of the skeleton staff there, whilst the rest are up north. He spoke to her at 11am. Three minutes later, she rang me, and I, in turn, called you.'

I had another question. 'Why were you originally so hesitant for us to get involved?'

She pulled a face. 'I thought it was rather premature. We're a specialist unit, which deals with anti-revolutionary terrorism. This could well be nothing of the sort.'

This prompted Roijin to speak, 'But Jackie thought otherwise.'

A curt 'Evidently' was Vic's reply.

Sensing that she probably wouldn't at this juncture get anything more from her, Roijin invited Asher to speak, 'And I think, Ash, this is where you need to come in.'

He nodded. 'Myself and Dr Lopez arrived at 11.47am. We conducted preliminary tests on the body and blood, temperature, Th2 cells and the levels of costimulatory molecules and B cells...'

Charts, graphs, and enough data to keep a stats junkie stoned for years, appeared in front of us.

'All these were consistent with what you would expect from a massive allergic reaction. Interleukins activate eosinophils, a type of white blood cell, was way up. This all unleashed histamines, which in turn made blood vessel walls extremely permeable. Basically, it caused a chain reaction. Since coming here and doing more tests we can confirm this. More detail has been sent to you.'

He pulled the virtual sheet back to show Stewart's neck. 'This caused internal swelling, severe bronchial swelling, and externally swelling across his body, including his throat which started to suffocate him. We found fluid in the lungs. Neither of which were cause of death. Here in the lab, they have a DBCS,' he paused, and smiled to himself. 'Sorry, a Debakey Cardiac Scanner, which we used to monitor the sinus nodes and the electrical activity of the heart at the time. Basically, the allergic reaction caused a heart attack. It was that which killed Mike Stewart.'

Still standing, with her arms crossed, Vic nodded. 'So, put simply – he drank some milk which had almonds in, which triggered a reaction?'

'That's correct, Vic.'

'Okay, next question, can you match the milk and almonds in his system, to what is in the milk carton?'

'It's a total match. The milk/almond compound came from that container.'

'Okay, so – sorry, Ash to interrupt your flow – but we need to know how the almonds got in the milk. Is there anything to show that it was artificially put in especially for this purpose?'

He blew his cheeks out. 'Too early to say. Certainly, there're no puncture marks on the container, and the compound of nut and milk seems to be of a level which suggests a long-term mix. There is a warning on the cartoon that it may contain traces of nut and we know because of the US led embargo, our usual supply routes have been disrupted, so we are getting food, where we can.'

Roijin nodded thoughtfully, and decided to change tack. 'Anything which might suggest force?'

Joseph shook his head. 'We'll do the more invasive tests later, but the surface scanner can find no entrance or exit wounds to suggest either a knife or gun had been used. No bullets or foreign objects have been found in his body. There are also no signs of blunt-force trauma or from any physical attack. There appears to be no bruising or abrasions on his body, which cannot be accounted for stemming from the reaction. There are bruises on his knees and under his arms, which can be linked by our Trauma Gauge to him hitting the floor. There's also one on his forehead. Its shape and depth do not suggest a blow having been delivered, rather the edge of the table. The TG supports this theory. There are cuts under his fingernails, but with traces of wood and varnish, they suggest that he clawed the floor.

'Any sign of poisoning?'

He replied that the first toxicology tests had come back as negative, but they'd look further, before adding, 'Although you could logically say that the almond in itself was poison to his system.'

'So, unless the butler did it, using an iron in the library,' I muttered, 'it looks like accidental death?'

'Oh, if he had been hit by an iron, I'd know.' His serious face, only moving into a hint of a grin after he had delivered his line. Then allowing himself a smirk. So, did I. We had shared a joke. A first. A plaque should be put up.

After a brief moment of bonding, and before there was any high-fiving, he told us that he would continue examining the body.

'Okay, thanks,' Roijin said. 'Anything of forensic note around the building?'

'Well, that's still continuing but we've found no evidence of forced entry. Which maybe isn't surprising because the front door is always unlocked. We've completed a full body scan and hope soon to have any indication of foreign fibres on his body. There was also a ground scan, which, again, we should have the results for pretty soon.'

He stopped and waited for questions. None of us had any. Let's face it, the main question was whether or not his death was as a result of a murder. Seeing that there were none, Roijin again thanked him and then volunteered herself to speak: proceeding to tell us about the activities of the workers' committee and their neighbourhood information gathering.

As she did, I stared at the framed Goya print which hung in the office to remind us of a previous high-profile case. Images and statements appeared from neighbours. As did a timeline. All, she explained, would have to be followed up. I translated it all in my head – no-one dodgy-looking had been seen near the house. So far, no-one had seen anyone entering or leaving Mike Stewart's home, aside from Fiona Bailey, Marie Williams and Thom Simons.

'Which brings us onto the other residents of the house,' she continued. 'We can list them as these individuals.' She pointed to the photographs of Bailey, Donaldson, Torres and Almeida. After a bit of confusion, as to how many have actually been staying there recently, we're certain that it's primarily these four. There's been the odd person crashing, but we're pretty sure, not in the last few days. Although, even Fiona Bailey was unsure about that.'

'She probably sees numbers as hierarchical,' Vic snarled.

'Which they are,' chuckled Roijin.

Vic ignored the comment. 'Find out everyone who's been there and get them talked to.'

'Sure thing, Vic. Anyway, there's Dave Donaldson, who as yet, we haven't been able to contact. I've left messages on his phone that we want to talk to him. He should be back tonight. I'm afraid, I haven't been able to find anything about him or his movements, yet.'

I gave a brief thumbnail sketch of the man, keeping it as neutral as I could. I wanted to sound professional rather than bitchy.

Roijin thanked me. 'The other two of the house are a Portuguese couple Eduardo Almeida and Isabella Torres...'

'The milk drinker,' Asher muttered.

This time it was Victoria who spoke. 'Indeed, the milk carton belonged to Torres, who does drink dairy products. Anyway, both have returned home to help with their own revolution. We've tried to contact Border Supervision and from Almeida's family, who've been told they are staying with to verify this, but so far, we haven't had any luck, but we'll keep trying.'

Roijin nodded. 'That should be a priority. Do we know anything about them – especially, Isabella?'

I shook my head. The others did too.

'Okay, we need to fill in some background on them, we could ask Odette to do that.'

After picking up a small hand-held fan, Victoria nodded approval. 'I'll ask her. Okay, so what about Bailey – what of her movements?'

Roijin answered – cool, fluent and without notes: 'She says she returned from a friend's house at just after 10.30am. I phoned this 'friend' and after listening to her views on Cribs for ten minutes, she confirmed that Bailey stayed there and graphically went into detail how they spent their time. I'm assuming that was intended to embarrass me. I guess she thinks I've time-travelled from the 1950s. A neighbour, Jon Conway – a party member – who lives two doors away, who was on his way to college, also saw her. Five minutes later, she met Marie Williams on the doorstep, who'd arrived for a meeting with Stewart. Together, they found him in the kitchen.'

'What else do we know about Bailey, that might be useful to share?'

Roijin turned to me. 'Pete?'

I was popular today, wasn't I? I'd need a publicity agent soon. Still remaining seated, I started by repeating what Roijin had already told us, 'She's been involved in direct action since she was eighteen. Studied at Farnham Ashley Wickes College. There, she studied politics and got involved in the green movement. She served two months for trespass, when she broke into a car factory. Soon after her release, she met Stewart. They became friends, sharing similar politics and then moved into the house. Like him, she's wary of us, but not fantastically sectarian. Like Stewart, I'd call her a syndicalist and like him, she'd hate being labelled. She believes in keeping an eye on the party, but isn't opposed to cooperation. She's popular and well-respected.' I paused. 'I don't know what else to say?'

Roijin pulled a face, a frustrated face. 'So, we know about Fiona Bailey and Dave Donaldson, but not the other two housemates, but does that actually matter? As far as I can see, there's nothing in the slightest, to suggest that this was anything other than a fatal allergic reaction.'

I pointed out the obvious, which had already been, er, milked. 'There's still the question of why he would drink milk.'

Roijin sighed. 'True, there is the milk, which is something which cannot easily be explained away. Any ideas why he might do so voluntarily?'

'He was thirsty?' suggested Asher.

Usually, it was my role to come up with the unhelpful quips, but I was happy to share the load. With a slot vacant for someone answering sensibly, I decided to take it (at least temporarily). 'According to Fiona, he could have been dying of thirst in the Gobi Desert and he still wouldn't have touched it. He was committed to what he saw as a life which did not exploit animals.'

'And if by magic, we return to the beginning – again!'

I think it was true that we all shared her frustration.

'Have we anything to suggest that it was anything other than an allergic reaction?'

Victoria didn't take the questioning badly, but nodded agreement, pulling a face which can be only described as one of bafflement.

Still occupying the mature seat, I piped up. 'We may not have any forensic proof of murder, but Fiona did tell me that he'd received death threats in the previous few weeks. Ones that the pair of them took seriously.'

That got the attention of the room – both physically and virtually present.

'They were delivered as hand-written notes and comments made in public.'

Bafflement entered the room and waved a flag. 'What does "comments made in public" mean?' asked Roijin, on behalf of everyone.

I told her, and was met by even more astonished faces. Even Dr Lopez, who had only been half-listening and had been busy in her lab, turned and looked at me. Feeling, maybe, that his new white-coated chum needed clarification, Asher repeated what I had said, and then in a slow deliberate voice, said, 'So Fiona Bailey is telling you that somehow, strangers would pass him in crowds and whisper in his ear that he was going to die and then they would disappear into the ether?'

What could I say? Don't ridicule the messenger. They had good reason to think it was nonsense. Not least, because I did. I tried to give it some credibility, 'Well, Fiona believes it. That's partly why she was so insistent that we be called in. Considering how much she hates the concept of Cribs; it must have been pretty persuasive whispering.'

'Okay,' Victoria said, sounding about as convinced as you might after hearing that Puss in Boots had traded in his boots for a pair of eco-friendly moccasins. 'What about these *notes*? Does she have any of them?'

'She said that he had received several. They were handwritten and in blue biro, and explicit threats to his life. I didn't see any of them and she didn't know where he'd kept them, or if indeed he had...'

Vic interrupted me and looked at Roijin, 'Did we find any of them in the house?'

'No.'

'Well, although I have to say that it sounds rather odd to me, I do think we need to get forensics to conduct a full search for them.'

I replied, 'She did quote from one: "If you continue to undermine the revolution then you will be seen as an obstacle to the progression of civilisation and thus will require elimination".' I got the reaction which I had expected – a mixture of disbelief and amusement. 'Yeah, I know, it all sounds Miss Marple, but that's what she claimed they said. She was quite certain.' I shrugged. 'Whatever. We have to look into it, and see if there's anything to them.'

'But she didn't actually show you any of these notes?' Roijin asked.

I repeated that she hadn't. We were in danger of becoming dizzy going around in all these circles. Valiantly, Roijin had been trying to keep the obvious feeling of incredulity out of her voice. But she was failing. 'The trouble is, comrades, that we found no trace whatsoever of these letters. Nor did we find any direct or credible threats on any of his private messaging services. There are a multitude of them on social media, which will take some looking at, but on first glance they look pretty much like just the bog-standard anonymous types made by bots and bored Tories. Frankly, we get just as many. Especially you – Vic!'

We all laughed. Though Vic didn't.

That did raise a question in my mind. 'Assuming they're genuine, and I can't see why Fiona would lie, and if she was to, surely she'd come up with something more believable, why would the secret service publicise a threat? They would surely know that Stewart wasn't a man to be intimidated. And why use such archaic methods, which frankly sound almost twee?'

All three nodded. Lopez was too busy looking busy to make any type of head movement.

Then Asher spoke, 'Are we suffering from tunnel vision here though, comrades? Does it have to be either a natural occurrence or state security, couldn't it be more personal? The causes of death are non-binary.'

Cole shook her head. 'I can't see a lover going to such lengths. If, and I say – if – this is a murder, then it was well thought-out and well-actioned. That doesn't sound, to me, like a jilted lover. But then again, we're back where we started – that, as of yet, there's no actual proof that it *is* murder.'

I agreed. 'It's also not going to be a business rival, is it?' I laughed at my joke. No-one else did. 'Nor is it going to be theft related. He had sod all to nick.'

'Political rival?' Asher asked.

'Maybe,' I conceded, but I wasn't convinced.

Roijin filled the void. 'Bailey is certain that it's state-sanctioned murder, from the former state that is. Which means that we should carry on for at least a while.'

'Agreed,' Cole said, with even less feeling. Indeed, a half-asleep sloth, after a night out in sloth nightclubs, drinking too many sloth alcoholic beverages, probably had more conviction about it. 'Although it's an odd way to proceed, on just the opinion of a grieving friend, we're brought in to investigate. But then, Bailey isn't the only one who has doubts...'

I translated – 'Jackie Payne.'

'What makes Jackie think it's murder?' Roijin asked, plainly interested.

'The Fool's list.'

Roijin looked at me as if I'd dropped my trousers. They should know that I'd never have done that – not to leave this quality of cloth on this floor. 'I thought "the Fool's List" had been pretty much dismissed as a joke in bad taste,' she said.

'Except as Jacks pointed out to us, this is the fourth name on it who's died in the past few weeks and they all happen to be AF.'

That appeared to appease her. 'True. Certainly, social media is full of it. Pretty much half of it believes it to be genuine.'

'Yeah, I saw that,' Joseph said, whilst fiddling with something in front of him. I truly hoped it wasn't a part of Mike Stewart. 'And a good number of those who think it's real, think we're behind it.'

Victoria frowned. 'They probably also believe that there's a tiny human being with wings who slip coins under pillows if they leave a tooth.'

'Does give Jackie a very good reason to want us to act on it though, doesn't it?' I said. 'I mean, to dismiss such conspiracy rumours, not the existence of tooth fairies.'

Roijin spoke with authority. 'Yes, it would, although to be honest, I think we mustn't get distracted by it. Essentially, it's peripheral to the task at hand. Like it or not, comrades, we've been called in to investigate and that's what we should do.' I could tell that instructions were on their way. Victoria used the same tone of voice when she was giving out orders. They must have taught them it at cop school. 'Vic, I think you need to look into

Stewart's personal history to see if there's anything there. Ash, could you continue to examine the body. Pete...'

I was right, here was the to-do-list.

I spoke before I had been given my chores. 'Well,' I said in the superior way that I saved for special occasions, 'I'm going to leave you all to ponder the whats and whys. I fancy talking to some real people and am going on a trip to the Shard. If I know my activists, there'll be a remembrance meeting organised, where the phrase, "Let us not mourn, let us organise" will be uttered by every other speaker. When I'm there I might learn something about Mike Stewart RIP. My betting is that Dave Donaldson will be there, and I'll have a chance – amongst all this not mourning and organising – to have a chat with him. And my bet is that Fiona Bailey will be there too, and I think another chin-wag with her would also be rather useful.'

Dearest Asher was surprised. 'They'll know you're a party member straight away!'

'Good,' I said, opening the desk drawer and pinning my party badge next to the Mondrian ID on my lapel. 'I'm not going undercover – they're our allies you know.'

Victoria went to get up too. 'I'll come with you...'

I laughed. 'Please don't. If you come, we'll both be thrown out the fifteenth-floor window. No, I can do this.'

I left the room, to shoulders being shrugged, heads shaken and eyes rolling. It was like a new zombie dance craze.

# CHAPTER 6:
# THE GRAHAM CHILDREN

B y the time we arrived at the Shard, the afternoon was mutating into early evening. Not that there was any noticeable change in temperature. Before I'd left, I had dropped in to speak to Al Handley, chairperson of the committee overseeing the Courtauld and Lissitzky Galleries. Although always good to chat with him, it wasn't social. I wanted to know if he knew anything about Mike Stewart's Nature City Synthesis plans. The fact that they were designs for redeveloping cities into more green and habitable places, might fall under his general remit. The Courtauld often hosted such design proposals. Genius that I am, I was right. Handley had enthusiastically talked about them. Interestingly, he had added as an aside, that Jackie Payne shared the same view.

The Shard was very possibly the total opposite of what Stewart had believed was progressive architecture. He liked low density, low height buildings, with nature being a key feature of the design. Being a giant phallus, there wasn't much in the way of areas for roof-top foliage. In all its years of standing tall, the skyscraper had enjoyed a variety of occupants and uses, but I doubted very much whether the original architects had ever in their wildest dreams have imagined who would presently be occupying it. More the stuff of their nightmares. All the rich folk who had once lived – or at least housed their tax returns – there, had been evicted. Companies using it for office space had suffered the same fate. A few months after the revolution, and without waiting for the NWC to come to a decision for its use, the Anarchist Federation had seized it and, with impressive speed, moved homeless people into the posh apartments and gutted the rest, converting them into communal spaces. This now included, what they called, "Democracy Floors". These were essentially, used for debate and decision making. Effectively, the Shard was the AF headquarters, although that was a word which would rarely be uttered there – far too hierarchical. Which was ironic, considering all this building seemed to do was to go upwards. You would have thought a bungalow would have been more architecturally correct.

I walked towards the glass idol of capitalism, which now had huge banners of black, red and orange, hanging down its sides as if rubbing the fact in that whatever pretensions it may have had, it was now firmly under the control of those who would have once been lucky to get a table in the restaurant. With so little breeze, the banners were barely moving.

On entering the ground floor, the sweat on my back turned to a sheet of ice as the air-con hit me. Second to welcome me was a huddle of children and a cat; followed quickly by several armed guards. The AF, like us, had been forced by the violence of the previous state, to curb their beliefs and trim their principles. Many despised violence, but finding that flowers and gentle words weren't that great a deterrent, they had been required to protect themselves in more traditional ways. Three gun-toting volunteers of ages between the teens and ancient, stood in front of me, preventing any further incursion to the building. The youngest who looked to me as if he had only recently stopped drinking hot milk and cookies, asked firmly, but politely, for my details and why I was there. They studied my ID but did not say anything. Then again, they did not move either. I explained what I was doing there, which seemed to do the trick; they nodded and then scanned me for any bombs, knives or guns. My mind being the only sharp thing on me, they let me through. I stepped over the cat, and did some scanning of my own – with my eyes – at the floor-guide and thought where I should go.

An AI infobot hovered towards me. I assumed it was a hangover from the previous building management, although as soon as it spoke, it became obvious that someone had reprogrammed it: 'Welcome, sibling, to our freedom space, how can I help you?' it said in a techno Essex accent.

'I need to find Fiona Bailey.'

Its metal dome head shook. 'I must apologise, friend, but we don't like to invade anyone's personal space, it compromises their right to freedom of privacy.'

I sighed. A right-on robot, just what humanity needed. 'No chance of any gossip then?'

With a metaphorical shake of the head, it told me: 'I'm sorry, friend, but we do not like to invade anyone's personal space and compromise their right to freedom of privacy.'

'Socio-political lectures from a robot – bonkers!' I said to myself.

'My friend, I must question your flippant and reactionary reference to mental illness.'

Feeling that a career in either stand-up comedy or computer programming, or indeed, comic computer programming, wasn't for me, I thanked it and headed to where every self-respecting detective would go – the bar.

The lift rocketed past the residential floors and stopped in seconds. The bar wasn't what one might expect if you said "anarchist bar". There wasn't a dog to be seen, let alone one on a piece of string, and I could only see a few young white men with dreads. And, if I wasn't mistaken, they ironically, happened to be party members, like me – just not so smartly dressed. Or so damned old. There *were* bean bags on the floor. Quite possibly the worst creation of capitalism, and that included tanks and warplanes. They were designed to make you look absurd and cause back pain. Thankfully, as the bar inhabited the whole floor, they had found space for chairs and tables as well. I could just imagine them having a three-hour debate on what seating was required.

The bar itself was circular (it would be, wouldn't it?) and was in the middle of the floor. I decided to have a look to see what drinks they had. As I'd come on my scooter, I couldn't have too many, but one wouldn't do any harm. The drink that immediately caught my eye was the USURP Slurp. Usurp was the nickname, not entirely a friendly one, for the United Revolutionary Socialist Party, of which I was a member. So, it was a drink which I couldn't resist. The barperson, whose minimal dress-sense extended to her shaved haircut, was quickly with me. She had that disconcerting look that some people have of seemingly being able to know everything about you. Her smile met me at about the same time as she clocked my party badge. 'Now I can see the USURP Slurp is the just the drink for you.' Without asking, she explained why it was called that: 'The ingredients vary, but they're always correct. Whatever has got past the embargo, or is home produced, mixed with any citrus fruit we can find, and a secret ingredient.'

Being one who could appreciate friendly sectarian banter, I was sold. It took her several minutes to make. I looked around. There were about forty people, of varying ages, races and genders here. Some were negotiating the bean bags, but many appeared to have wisely chosen the more ergonomically sensible seats which ringed the floor and which gave them glorious panoramic views of London. After getting my drink and agreeing to an acceptable price, I headed for one.

I sat down and gave it a taste. It wasn't that great, but it was bearable. A bit too much orange and she'd been over-generous with the gin for my taste, but it was quite acceptable. I sat admiring the stunning view of the Thames. My contemplation was interrupted by a woman's voice in my ear. 'Of all the squatted bars in the world, you choose this one.' Looking around, to see who was paraphrasing the great line from the movie Casablanca, I saw that it was Fiona Bailey. She was chewing gun and holding a pint and an affectionate smile. She was now in a pale orange vest, which boasted the word NON in huge green block letters, black shorts and a black cap to match.

'I'm guessing that it's no coincidence that you're here,' she said, before taking a large swig of her drink.

I shrugged. 'You wanted me to investigate Mike's death. And that's what I'm doing.' I tried a smile. It was meant to indicate friendliness, but probably merely looked like I had just been hit by the after-taste of my drink.

She hadn't taken offence. Indeed, she looked relieved, and leant forward. Momentarily, the chewing stopped. 'So, you believe me now, that Mike's death wasn't an accident?' The words were a far more potent cocktail than my drink. Hers were of hope, desperation and a search for succour, and also maybe a touch of anger.

'That's why I'm here.'

'Not tempted for a more progressive path than your dated ideology?'

Seeing as she was attempting humour, I smiled. 'No, I don't think so. I'm pretty dated myself.'

She quietly chuckled. 'So, tell me, seriously, why exactly are you here?'

Her tone was still affable but there was an undercurrent of hardness. She was being fraternal and welcoming, but there was a slight suspicion of my motives. I had nothing to hide because basically we didn't have much in the first place to keep out of sight, so I told her that as Mike spent so much of his time here, it made sense to come and see if I could find anything out. My explanation sounded as weak as watered-down lager.

But she didn't argue and just breathed out heavily, and took a swig of her drink. I hadn't a clue as to what that signified. Possibly, she was feeling hot. Nothing was said, which was understandable, as I hadn't asked anything. So, I tried a question: 'Please think – was there anyone you've seen hanging around the house, or who kept appearing when Mike was present, someone who looked out of place?'

She shook her head. 'Like I said before, it looked like any other morning. Then again, I don't know exactly what "looked out of place" means. There's people coming and going all the time. As for anyone following him. He never mentioned it. It's not like I followed Mike. But then, if as he said, people were threatening him, they must have been.'

These enigmatic folks again, the ones who whispered threats in his ear before departing. Aside from sounding hammy in the extreme, I did wonder at the staffing levels MI5 must have, if they could have them scattered across the nation, all at the ready to whisper sour nothings in his ear. It sounded like a spook job creation scheme.

Bailey, though, certainly took it seriously. 'All I can say, and I've been thinking about this since I found him. Believe me, I'd tell you if I had.'

Fair point.

She seemed to drift off. Remembering the wise words of the drone downstairs, I gave her some space, before, in my best compassionate voice – the one I keep for special occasions – I apologised for keeping asking, but could she think of anyone else.

Cradling her sculptured chin in the palm of her left hand, whilst her right did likewise with her drink, she didn't answer straight away. After a moment or two, she told me that she couldn't. 'I didn't see any black cloaked assassin or a smoking gun.'

Funny. That was my type of wit. I could see why no-one ever laughed. I ignored it. If we were going to play the battle of sarcastic quips, I'd win. I am a finely-tuned expert. The black belt master of banter; the champion of causticness and the high-priest of put-downs. But searching through my holdall of skills, I uncovered a dusty and cobwebbed file marked – maturity. I opened it, vaguely remembering it. 'Understood,' I replied neutrally. 'If you do think of something, let us know.'

Emboldened by my passivity, she decided that it was her turn to ask a question. 'Are you here just to repeat the questions I've already been asked?'

The nicey, nicey mask had slipped a bit, and she was showing some fangs. Again, I didn't respond, but then again, I was in no mood to bare my neck. 'We heard that your "sibling" housemate Donaldson would be here.' Once more using my best Switzerland voice: 'It would be good to ask him a few questions.'

Her mouth straightened and I thought I could detect a hard glint in her eyes. Seems sister Bailey here, wanted us to investigate in theory, but if that in practice meant investigating here, questioning siblings, she wasn't so keen. Maybe I was being over-sensitive, but she wasn't thrilled to see me at anarchist headquarters. (Or should that be anarchist-non-specific-body-part-quarters?) A flash of red appeared under her freckles. 'Why do you want to talk to DD? He wasn't even there!'

'True. But, Fiona, according to you, everything was normal and no-one was there, not even someone with a cloak and a recently fired gun.' My maturity file had been put away for another decade. 'We've only just started, and apart from what you've told us, or rather *alleged*, we don't have much to go on, so a good way to start is by talking to anyone who knew Mike Stewart.'

It wasn't an answer which heralded a return of her good humour – she all but spat out, 'He won't be any help to you. Start looking for the real killers? It's quite obvious who they are!'

'Is it?' I replied, looking at the young woman and wanting her to again verbalise what she thought was going on here. '*Who* do you think did it?'

She sighed heavily, and I could see that she was getting irritated. 'Them. The fuckers we thought we'd got rid of – MI5 and the like.' She took what could only be described as an aggressive gulp of her drink. Then she moved closer to me. It wasn't for a kiss. This woman was angry – 'I really hope you're taking this seriously!'

'I'm here, aren't I?'

It wasn't an answer she found acceptable. 'As to exactly why you're here, you still haven't really explained to me. I do hope this won't turn into an excuse to harass us. I trust you, Pete.' It was touching, but the way she had snarled "trust" had slightly undermined her stated belief in me. I also worried she might have accidently swallowed her gum. The last thing we needed was her choking to death in front of me.

My patience is always a rather timid beast; right now, it was fast asleep at home, in bed, with ear plugs in both ears, hiding under the duvet and with a sleeping eye-mask on. Through gritted teeth I said, 'Fiona, you insisted that we get involved. *You* wanted us involved, and that's what we're doing – getting involved. So, I'm going to ask you some questions. You're going to give some answers. Then you're going to introduce me to 'sibling' Dave Donaldson, who I'm also going to question. It's that, or I leave this shower, go home and take a shower, and forget about Michael Stewart and his nuts. I'm sure that the rest of the team would be perfectly happy to knock it on the head. Understand?'

If I had expected her to recoil, or to get angry, I was disappointed. She burst out laughing. '"Leave this shower and take a shower!" What cheap novel did you get that from?' She giggled so much that some of her beer splashed onto the floor. 'Yeah, fair enough, Inspector Clouseau, ask away.'

I didn't need any more prompting. Glancing at my mental maturity file, I didn't defend the – rather amusing – shower comment or tackle her calling me Clouseau. Instead, I went professional. 'Let's start again. You spent the night at a friend's. Martina Cowell-Brown confirms that you stayed the night; she said that you had been on late shifts. You finished your shift near her, and went to her place. She estimates the time at being just past nine pm. You had a meal and then went to bed early. The next day, the day of his death, you arrived home, 14 Mary Driscoll Avenue, at just past ten in the morning. A neighbour, Janice Brompton, who lives two doors away, who was on her way to college, confirms this. You exchanged comradely greetings. You arrived at the front door at the same time as Marie Williams, who was arriving for a meeting with Mike Stewart. You both go in and find him dead. Our problem, Fiona, is that so far, we haven't found anything at all, to suggest that it wasn't anything other than a tragic accident.'

She matched my irritation with her own. 'I told you. He didn't drink milk and he'd been verbally abused and received threatening notes, so...'

'We'll look into those "verbal threats", although as you yourself cannot expand on them any further, as to who may have made them and where, I'm not sure how we can do that. As for the notes – we've not seen a single one of them. We've searched the house, but found nothing. If he considered them serious, why didn't he keep them? Why not tell more people? I mean did he, Fiona? Did he confide in anyone other than you about them?'

'I don't know. I really don't.'

'I would have expected he would have told someone in the NON-movement, or the AF, even if he didn't trust the NWC.'

She shrugged.

'We also haven't found any direct and credible threats on any of his electronic media.'

'Well, that isn't surprising!' she protested. 'They might not want to leave concrete proof of what they're up to.'

'And instead, they write notes? Presumably using a quill!'

When attempting to illicit help, it was probably best not to scoff and deride them. This was especially the case if they were grieving the untimely death of a close friend. That was no doubt written in a sleuth's textbook somewhere, or if it wasn't, maybe I should write one. Her glare indicated the truth of this. I needed to soften my tone.

I moved into my best cuddly teddy bear voice, 'Fiona, I'm personally committed to looking into this, but I need help, I really do.' It was a voice so silky, it could have charmed birds off their branches.

Not anarchists though. The glare remained.

My reserves of powers to captivate and bewitch were legendary in my own mind, but presently they were being rationed. Still, I was here to do a job. 'Just to make an old renegade happy, tell me again about his mood in recent weeks.'

After a brief complaint that she had already gone through all this and it was getting boring, she gave in, with a theatrical sigh. 'Mike was devoting his energies into the NCSS. He had great hopes for it. Throughout history, cities have been ill-planned with areas created either by groups' own self-determinism, or more usually, by class. His vision was to change that, and make them a cohesive whole. It excited him, but a few weeks back his mood substantially changed, he seemed pensive. I mean he didn't go around moping, that was never his style, but he seemed worried.'

I took a slurp of my USURP Slurp and considered that we now had a slightly worried vegan as evidence of a dastardly deed. Call out the red army! 'When exactly was this?'

'He first told me four weeks ago. Then a fortnight ago, he was upstairs fiddling with some of his model skywalks.' She smiled at the memory. 'He said the threats had become more direct. He believed that he didn't have long and even made me promise that if he was killed, I'd take the lead in pushing the scheme. He was afraid, very afraid. He didn't want to die, but his principles wouldn't let him give up. But, Pete, he was scared, I mean, *very* scared.'

'Have you any idea why he would be a target? Okay, he was a figure in the movement, but there's plenty of others of an equal standing, I presume you're ruling out disgruntled property developers.'

She didn't appreciate my comment. Her look suggested that it wasn't appropriate.

'The Fool's List,' she mumbled.

'Ah yes, that.' This thing was steadily moving from a joke to something more believable, or at least more people appeared to be believing in it. 'Is that the view of your AF siblings?'

It was her turn to adopt a dismissive tone: 'There's all sorts of rumours flying about in the social media. You must have seen them. Most seem to share your view that Mike's death was just an unfortunate tragedy. There's already lengthy obituaries to his genius and bemoaning what an appalling way to die in such a freak accident!'

She was right, the theories were stacking up. We'd yet to have him alive and well and secretly living on a desert island with a cryogenic Elvis Presley, but give it time. I wanted to hear what her siblings were saying. 'And what are the theories? I presume you haven't shared your thoughts with anyone else?'

'Of course not!' she snapped, obviously outraged at my suggestion. 'It doesn't need me to stir up the gossip-mongers. There's a whole array of rumours circulating. And I have to say, a lot of them agree with me, that it's MI5, CIA or some other bunch of toe-rags in the employ of the former Prime Minister. Or if not him directly, then some cabal of the disenfranchised ruling class.' There was a momentary pause. 'There's even a few, shall we say, of our younger, more eager siblings, that are talking about the possibility that it could be the work of USURPs.'

'Us? My, we are held in high regard, aren't we? They don't have your view on things then?'

She shrugged her slight shoulders. 'Whoever said the internet was a haven of sensible thought? But like I said, I don't buy that. If, or when, you need to shut down opposition, you'll do it using bureaucratic means.'

I wasn't sure whether that counted as support or not. But before I could question her any further, she downed the drink, and announced that she had to go. 'On Democracy Floor 1, I'm going to talk about Mike. You should come. I expect DD is going to speak as well.'

# CHAPTER 7: THE CONDUIT PIECE

**A**rriving at the meeting, I saw an elderly guy, probably even older than me, standing in the middle of the expanse of the floor, explaining, or at least trying to – above the general pre-meeting hubbub – what the main focus of tonight's discussion would be. For those who were new to these gatherings, he also outlined the rules of debate. Politeness and fraternity appeared to be the basis of it all. I smiled to myself and thought – "We'll see about that".

In the vast single room, like the bar downstairs, which took up the entire floor, the chairs were arranged in ever decreasing circles around the central area. I sincerely hoped that if any walls had been removed, consideration had been made to whether they had been load-supporting ones or not. I feared that it had been some over-enthusiastic AF member wielding a sledgehammer, and yelling that the walls were tumbling down. I had no wish to be crushed to death. Especially not with this lot.

We both found somewhere to sit. Any further chat was prevented when the chairperson spotted the woman next to me. A solid silence spread around the room. Obviously, I'd missed something. Were they about to lynch me?

'Fiona, if you wouldn't mind saying something.'

She got to her feet and a floating microphone hovered above her. 'Thank you, everyone. I just want to say a few words about the loss of Mike, Mike Stewart – something which I know we all feel. He was a towering figure in our wonderful movement...'

She continued with her tribute for several minutes, rarely consulting her notes, which she tightly clutched in her hands. As she progressed, occasionally she stumbled and sometimes stammered, as the emotion of the moment began hitting her, but generally she was thoughtful and clear. Being so close to her, I could see her hands were shaking and a sheen of perspiration was appearing around her temple. She interspersed the personal with the political, some anecdotes, with the recounting of moments in the struggle, in which he had participated. She had been speaking for almost ten minutes when she stopped. Her voice lowered, 'I know online there's been a lot of debate concerning the manner of Mike's death. I don't want to go into that here. What I will say is that Jackie Payne has personally assured me that his death will be closely looked into.'

Murmurs, shuffling of feet and tapping of electronic devices, circled the room. She paused for it to pass. 'Friends, whatever we might think of Payne, and you all know that I'm not a fan, we have to accept that she does wield power and if, in the name of the revolution, she's using that power to investigate his death, then we should welcome it.' Again, though not met by anything resembling opposition, one didn't have to possess a doctorate in meetings to judge the mood being one of uneasiness. Jackie was thought by many present, to be at best a necessary evil. The feeling of distrust was palpable and seemed to be oppressing Fiona. Her speech slowed and the confidence began to wane. 'Payne has assured...er... me that...uhm... this will be done properly. Next to me, is Pete Kalder. Many of you will have heard how he unearthed the MI5 agent just a few months back. He's one of those who have been asked to investigate it.' If I had expected a thunderous round of singing and backslapping, I was disappointed. There wasn't even a clap. Instead, I received a few smiles but also several concerned looks. Obviously, I was seen as Payne's boy and therefore also to be viewed with at least some level of mistrust. Fiona must have sensed this too, as she gathered her words, upped her passion, and spoke of how we must work together and remember who the real enemy was.

She looked around to see as many people as possible, and reminded the audience of Mike Stewart's belief that we were entering a new phase of the revolution and that we should view the United Socialist Revolutionary Party as having played an important role. It would start to decline, to be replaced by a new, less rigid, movement. That received a few pockets of applause. 'However, he passionately believed that we should work together, whatever our differences. We are confronted by murderous thugs who will stop at nothing to overturn the revolutionary gains. You all know that I, too, share this belief. We mustn't be divided because that makes us weaker. Unity is strength isn't just a phrase!'

She received loud applause. I wondered though, if people were applauding her political points or the memory of Mike Stewart.

When silence had returned, the chairperson thanked her and announced there was another who knew him personally and who wanted to speak.

A needle-like white man, probably in his mid-to late twenties, got to his feet. He had a dark purple beard which was in desperate need of a trim, but which perfectly matched his hair, which also needed being introduced to some care and attention. With what passed for a stomach was on show between his low waist and very tight jeans, and high t-shirt, he might have passed for a rock star. If, that is, you ignored what looked suspiciously like breadcrumbs on both shirt and beard. He stood scratching his wayward beard, picking out the bits, whilst he marshalled his thoughts. If they were like his clothes, this might take a while.

Fiona leant across and whispered, 'That's Dave. Dave Donaldson.'

This would be interesting. So, this was the fabled DD. When he spoke, he did so with a London accent and one full of confidence that he knew what he was talking about. You could immediately tell that he was one of those blokes who did so, even if he didn't have a clue about a subject. I'd met a few in my time – kings of bluster and bullshit. If it was possible to quietly bellow, then his voice could be described as that. That wasn't surprising, his type always did. He thanked Fiona, and then went on to repeat much of what she had said, including some of her anecdotes. Which, considering that some of them had happened years ago, was rather cheeky. He hadn't known Stewart that long and wouldn't have been around when they had occurred. Yet, he made it sound like he had. But then, it had to be said that he made them sound a lot funnier than she had, receiving more laughter. He made it sound as if they had been life-long buddies. Ones, though, in which he was the dominant alpha-bud, who had taught Mike everything he knew.

It was after almost five minutes into his speech, that he deviated from what Fiona had already said. I began to really listen. He acknowledged that questions were being asked about Mike's death but we had to remember that it looked very much like an accident. 'We shouldn't fall for conspiracy theories. As it happens, all the medical experts are saying that it was a severe allergic reaction. The doubts are mainly coming from President Payne's office!' That received applause, and I, a few looks. Fiona did not move, either to indicate agreement or otherwise. He continued, 'I agree with my very good friend Fiona, that we face severe challenges, but let's not forget that threats to the revolution actually strengthen Payne's regime. Their argument is – "Don't criticise us, don't oppose us, because that only strengthens the reactionaries". They make it "our way or fascism – socialism or barbarism". As it happens, Payne has a vested interest in making this look like a state murder. It's not that I think that the former reactionary regime isn't capable of such acts – of course they are! But, siblings, don't take everything at face value! Questioning those who would lead us becomes *more* important when there's danger and it makes it even more important that we have allies who we can rely on and not ones who will dispose of us if we become too threatening. We can all remember the things Payne and her acolytes have said about us. The scorn and ridicule they have heaped upon us – the cheap jokes and the dismissive way they treat us, just because we don't believe in an old fashioned and discredited structure of organisation.' More clapping met this last point. Sitting between nodding heads, I pondered the possibility that I was being bugged, taking the mention of cheap jokes and dismissive air to be a direct personal reference.

On he went, countering any praise for the party's achievements with far longer sections attacking us. All were interspersed with the phrase, "as it happens", which he appeared to use as one might a comma. But even accounting for the regular appearance of "as it happens", he was an articulate speaker; indeed, on this showing at least, far more so than Fiona. Unlike her speech, though, there were times when I seriously wondered what the hell this had to do with Mike Stewart. When he was mentioned, it was done so to argue the direct opposite to Fiona. Finally, he sat down. The room had liked what they had heard and gave him rapturous applause. I hadn't, and didn't clap. Fiona did, but in a very polite non-committal kind of way.

One person who was slapping their hands together as if their life depended on it was a woman sporting a black bob and incredibly long eyelashes. When she blinked a tornado swept through Europe. Although difficult to tell, I would guess that she was just over one and half metres tall and fifty kilos in weight. But then, with those eyelashes, who could tell? She was wearing denim knee-length shorts and a blue t-shirt. She lowered her hoverchair and manoeuvred the microphone so she could speak.

Fiona leant across and whispered, 'Sophia Brownswood. She's a sibling in the AF. This might be a little awkward for you; she's not what you call a friend of your party.'

She spoke, with a strong, yet calm voice: 'Friends, I want to whole-heartedly agree with the previous speaker. Yes, there've been changes and improvements since the revolution, but they've been too little, and too reluctantly made. Payne and her USURPS are great at making grand gestures and epic speeches, but as for action, they're sadly lacking. Look how long it has taken to close the eco-violent power supplies. How hard have we had to push for climate catastrophe policies? De-carbonisation should be the priority, nothing less. The world is like a balloon and it is rapidly losing air. It's deflating by the day.'

She paused to wait for the applause to subside. I tried to work out what her metaphor had meant.

'The USURPS are keener on strengthening their own powerbase than saving the revolution. They talk of it being in danger and,' she paused and made air quotes with her fingers, '"of consolidating the gains" but they're purely excuses, reasons to drag their feet. Why haven't we built upon Portugal? The workers seized power months ago, yet, far from spurring us on to greater radicalisation, we seem to be becoming ever more isolated. How come we still have diplomatic ties with the capitalist countries? The sight of 'comrade' Payne cuddling up to the leaders of Germany and Singapore made me feel sick. We should be shunning them and talking only to the radical movements in other countries.'

For a few minutes she continued bemoaning the fact that Jackie didn't beat the shit out of any prime minister or president she met. This, it seems, indicated that we had sold out.

'Then there's the justice system in this country. We had fought for a whole new way of doing things, not just a red version of the old ways, with ex-coppers and lawyers parroting the odd Marxist quote.'

I was sincerely glad that Victoria hadn't come. I really did dislike having to defend her; it was bad for my image. She spoke at length of the dystopian world we had created. As her oratory increased, so did the applause. She was a gifted speaker, articulate and thoughtful, but in my esteemed opinion, she was plain wrong. Obviously, I was in the minority here. Most were lapping up what she said, like some thirsty Labrador at their bowl. Although, I could see that there were a few who didn't entirely embrace the attacks on us. Fiona next to me, for one, seemed to have doubts, even occasionally grunting disapproval.

Brownswood's voice increased in urgency, which I presumed meant that she was coming to her conclusion. I was right, for she was now demanding that the revolution had entered a new phase. 'Payne is more tin-pot than Pol Pot. But we must not let the freedoms which we have fought for be lost, or perhaps to be more accurate – taken from us. I don't want any dictatorship – be it the proletariat or of Jackie Payne!"

Hearty claps echoed everywhere. There were even a few cheers as people stood. Weaving in between the adulation, Brownswood manoeuvred her way back to her original position in the audience. Fiona gently clapped and remained seated; it was polite rather than political. I didn't move.

The next speaker was waiting for the room to quieten. A small, slender, elegant woman of South-East Asian descent stood, looking the epitome of serenity: long black hair, white linen trousers with faint stripes, a white shirt and despite being indoors, round sunglasses. But it was the badge she was wearing which was more interesting – that of the United Revolutionary Socialist Party.

Fiona turned to me. 'Do you know her?'

I didn't. Adding that being a mass party meant we didn't all know each other. We had long gone past that. It wasn't as if we wrote out May Day greeting cards to each other.

'Her name is Phan Bien, she's often here, arguing your line. I'd guess that she has been sent here to do just that. I think she's a student at the LSE.'

Eventually the room went quiet. Despite there being several hundred in here and probably only a handful were comrades, she looked totally at ease. She smiled and with both hands in her pockets thanked the chair for letting her speak. She spoke with a level voice, but after the initial courtesy, showed her teeth.

'As always, comrade Brownswood spoke with a great deal of feeling. Sadly, and I mean no disrespect, for I do hold her in the highest regard, there wasn't much sense accompanying it. Speaking personally, as someone whose great-grandfather emigrated from Vietnam to Cambodia, only to end up being tortured and murdered by the Khmer Rouge, I really don't appreciate the snide reference to Pol Pot. It may get an easy laugh, but it doesn't really get us anywhere, other than providing the sister with a soundbite and proving she has no understanding of history.'

Ouch. That was sharp. It was met by a few heckles, but also, surprisingly, a few people clapped. Most though, just sat and listened. That included Sofia Brownswood, who did so with a wry smile.

'I will, if you don't mind, miss out the more ultra-left elements of her speech and those which indicated that she wanted an all-out war with every other nation on this planet. Never mind the carnage and loss of life, what about the carbon footprint that would entail?'

It seemed that whilst attacking another woman for un-fraternal digs, she was quite happy to do some of her own. That prompted more heckles and no clapping. Although I was truly tempted to put my hands together. I did appreciate a barb when I heard one – if it was from my side. However, I was here to investigate, not to antagonise. More's the pity.

'No, I want to counter what the comrade said about what we had done since taking power and overthrowing the former capitalist regime.' She took her hands out of her pockets and counted them off: 'We've built a number of large-scale carbon scrubbing and carbon capturing plants, and which are now in operation, taking considerable amounts of carbon out of the atmosphere. We're now self-sufficient in energy which is non-fossil, and that's because we embarked on the biggest building programme of green power sources anywhere on the planet. There's been a radical refurbishment and renovation of buildings – insulating them and making them energy efficient. Finally, all petrol and diesel cars are banned, with even electric and solar being limited in use. I'm sorry that the fact that flights are allowed upsets sister Brownswood, but the sanctions are stopping most, so she no doubt is happy with that. Her and the American president appear to be on the same side on that issue.'

There were more heckles. And a bigger grin on my face. I could feel Fiona next to me, shaking her head at my reaction. However, whatever the audience did, or didn't do, Phan Bien didn't stop. Neither did she even pause, nor quicken her pace, but with almost deadly calm, laid out the party's position.

'We've severely dented the carbon curve. We've gone from tenth in the world league table for green policies to top, with our sister nation – Portugal – second. Of course, we cannot do it alone. That's why we have been reaching out to all progressive movements across the world, and yes, sometimes to capitalist leaders. However, the basis of our politics remains in spreading the revolution. Not to do so, not only would endanger the revolution, but also the project to save the planet. Unlike what some believe, it's not down to personal consumption but the system; it's the system which we have to change.'

She paused. 'I want you to sincerely remember Mike Stewart. He was a friend of mine and, although we had our political differences, he was sincere in his belief that the majority party, and all radical, anarchist, liberal and green parties should work together. Now's not the time to attack each other. He wanted cooperation. A true remembrance of him, a proper way of honouring him, would be for all of us to instigate the radical reshaping of the cities, which he was suggesting. Let us not mourn but organise...'

Ah, I had been wondering when that would be said.

'Thank you, sisters and brothers. Onwards and upwards for the green-red revolution!'

She gave a slight bow with her head, and returned to her seat. A number of the audience gave her what could be described as polite applause. Most didn't, and in fact, didn't respond in any way, other than by not responding. Brownswood sat and talked to someone next to her, quite obviously making a point of ignoring Phan, and giving the air of someone who was on home-turf and had no worries about being criticised. A number of what I guessed to be people who wanted to disagree with Phan, were lining up to speak, but I wasn't going to stay and listen to what they had to say, because I had just seen Dave Donaldson leave the meeting and he was one little anarcho-bunny that I was keen to have a word with.

I could see his coat-hanger shoulders disappear into the lift. Which posed a problem: I had no idea where he had gone and this building was bloody big. But then if I was inexperienced in detection, I was an old pro at meetings, and I knew that following a lively discussion, there'd be only one place where most people would go – the bar.

As the doors opened at the bar level, I was pleased to see that I had been right and could see his loose-limbed lope by the window seats, with a pint in his hand, and actually managing to keep some of it in the glass. Deciding that looking casual would be a good look, I got myself a drink. To show our anarchist friends that we party members could drink any old shit, I ordered another Slurp.

Armed with it, and a cool vibe, I idled over to him and took a seat by his side. 'Mind if I do?' I asked, already sliding onto a stall and not giving a worker's token if he did or not. Judging by the effort it took him to tug himself away from his phone screen, and then his look of utter indifference when he saw me, I guessed that he felt pretty much the same. But he didn't speak, and just shrugged his what he had of shoulders.

I introduced myself. 'Pete Kalder, Crib – I'm looking into the death of Mike Stewart.'

Not surprisingly, it wasn't met with whoops of joy. 'Yeah, I heard Fiona say in the meeting. Guess the revolution takes all sorts, to do all sorts. So, you think it was murder, do you?'

Straight to the point; no shilly-shallying about; no small talk. 'No idea. But we owe it to him and the movement to find out.'

'Do you?' he sighed, in an impressive display of sarcasm, whilst using not the slightest bit of effort.

'Don't you?' I said, trying to match him.

'I heard it was a severe allergic reaction, anaphylactic shock.'

This wasn't turning out to be one of the most exhilarating conversations I'd ever had.

'So, it seems, but it's odd that he would drink milk when he was a vegan.'

We were now competing for who could be the most laconic and laid back. At this rate, we'd be getting out the fold-up beds, and having a snooze. He stroked his beard, picked at it and then turned his attention to his head. He was in his late twenties, but up close, looked over double that. And acted even older. He had very pale skin, which was rather wrinkled for someone his age. But then, maybe old was the new young.

'An accident?' he finally mumbled. This was not one of the great discourses of our time; hardly Shakespearian rhetoric. We'd be grunting next.

I didn't give up, although every cell in my body was willing me to do so. His lethargy was catching. But it was all just an act; he'd been a lot livelier in the meeting. This was him letting me know that I wasn't worth making an effort for. I'd had done my research on him. Once my enquiries had been on great works of art, and great artists; now it was scruffy and surly anarchists. Somewhat of a difference, but the skills were pretty much the same. And if young DD here had been a piece of art, he was now doing a rather lame impression of a still life. But what I'd seen of his background, this was deceptive; he was far more like an action painting. He had been politicised when he was very young. Brought up solely by his mother, it had been catastrophic for him when she had been killed in severe flooding in Yorkshire. He himself had only survived because he had been visiting friends. He had moved to his grandparents in London, when he was fourteen. The traumatic experience had encouraged him to join the more radical elements of the green movement, and, I assumed, lose his Yorkshire accent, because I hadn't detected even a hint of it when he was speaking. Judging from I had learnt, he was far from being a quiet reluctant activist, but was one who believed that what got things done was direct action. The more direct, the better.

I didn't react to his attitude. After all, I was in his world, and as far as I knew, he had done nothing wrong. 'You seem keen to see it as an accident,' I said. 'Yet I don't see how accidently he could have gone to the wrong fridge, accidently got non-Vegan and hypo-allergic food out of the wrong fridge, and then eat it accidently. In my experience, vegans are very careful about what they eat, for obvious and deep-rooted reasons, as are, of course, people who have severe allergies.'

That got a reaction. Not like Stewart's, but he looked surprised. Maybe it was because more than four words had just been spoken by one of us. But no, it was astonishment at kitchen appliances. 'Separate fridge? What separate fridge?'

It was now my turn to look surprised. 'You're not aware that Isabella has her own small fridge, on the side, because unlike the rest of the house, she isn't vegan?'

He gave me a blank look; this time it wasn't a deliberate wind-the-old-guy-in-the-suit-up, blank look, which he had been sporting for the last few minutes, but looked like a genuine one. 'No,' he simply said.

I laughed. 'Really? I'm right that you're a vegan?'

'Yes, as it happens, been one, since I was fourteen...'

'And you live in the same house, yet you don't know that she eats dairy products? You share the same kitchen and you haven't noticed the small fridge? You didn't notice the fridge-like thing, separate to the bigger fridge-like thing? Only with stuff like milk and eggs in? You never knew it was for Isabella Torres? Are you joking? How could you not?'

He was defensive when he replied: 'As it happens, I've only been there for a matter of months and to be honest, with my shifts, I don't really see much of the household. It's not like we go on picnics and have away days. It's somewhere to crash. That's it. Anyway, on the very rare occasions that Mike and me were both at home, he was usually in his room, playing with his city models, dreaming of being Christopher Wren.'

'And Isabella? Her bedroom is on the same floor as yours!' I asked. 'Surely, you've noticed her!'

He shrugged. 'But she's usually either working, doing political stuff or hanging out with her partner, er, um, Eduardo. I wouldn't say we're close. There's kinda more important stuff going on in the world, than making friends. Anyway, I always eat at the Shacklewell Kitchens. I'm not really into privatised dining.'

We sat there for a few seconds in contemplation. I was pondering whether knowledge of the existence of a separate fridge or not was a detail of great importance, or whether it was truly ludicrous in its triviality. I took a large sip of my drink, in part to cover my thinking time, and for another, to see what the taste of this one would be. It turned out that this Slurp was a lime-gin combo.

Donaldson had swiftly returned to his phone, which I took to mean that it was interesting and that I wasn't. Tough, I wasn't stopping. 'So, let me get this straight. You're saying that you personally had very little to do with Stewart?'

Pulling himself away from his device, he sighed, as if he had been forced to separate from his one true love; nonetheless, he deigned to answer me: 'Yeah, I guess you could say that.'

'He wouldn't have confided in you?'

'Confided? About what? His love life?' He laughed, his small round eyes glistened, his chin nodded up and down. Crumbs scattered all over the place.

He was deliberately being obtuse. I didn't react, he wouldn't have liked it if I had. He didn't know me well enough to know what I could be like. If he wanted to play angles then, boy, I could be one sharp, acute one. Instead, I smiled. 'Fiona has told me that he confided to her that he had received threats. Did he ever say anything to you?'

'No, nothing. Nor did Fi. It's news to me. He never mentioned anything like that.' He paused before adding, 'Not that we talked much.'

'And Fiona never said anything?'

He shrugged, and attempted to adopt a bored look. 'Like I said, I didn't have much to do with anyone in the house. It's a place we share to kip, it's not like we're in some club. I'm not surprised if Mike confided in Fiona, they were close, those two.'

'Yet, you're comr...siblings...in the same organisation.'

'So? Are you best friends with everyone in your party?' he asked rather pointedly.

The truth was probably exactly the opposite. 'Can you remember when you last saw him?' I asked, keenly aware how that question might be received.

Judging from the look he gave me, I had been right. He wasn't pleased. In his view, I was behaving too much like the old repressive state apparatus and oppressing him. Poor him. The thing was that he might be too dense to notice the difference, but I wasn't a cop, I was working for a different society, for a different reason. He'd have to live with it. Fiona Bailey wanted me on this case, so he could swallow his tender feelings and start cooperating.

To my surprise, I didn't get a lecture, or even a snarl, I simply received an answer. 'I'd guess that would have been a few days ago. I was coming in and he was going out, and if you're about to ask how did he seem – I'd say that he appeared to be appreciative that I held the door open for him. He was off to the NWC London offices, to discuss what, I have no idea.'

'He didn't seem worried at all?' I asked.

'No, the offices are quite friendly. Even your lot have been known to sometimes behave like humans. No, he seemed happy and relaxed.' If I had hoped that his straightforward answers would herald a thaw in our communications, I was to be disappointed. 'He seemed oblivious to the fact that someone was going to murder him in a few days...*officer.*'

I let it go. It had been a pretty weak dig; surely, he could do better than that.

Phan Bien was now circulating the room. From her inquisitive eye movements towards several other people, I presumed that they were party comrades who were doing likewise. I caught her attention, as she attached herself to a small group. We exchanged a knowing look, one which seemed to pass comment on where we found ourselves.

'When did you hear of his death?'

'That morning, Fi rang me. After, that is, contacting you lot.'

It was obvious that he approved of the former but most definitely not the latter. I nodded, and thought about the next question. It wasn't going to go down well, and I was thinking how I could sugar-coat it. Trouble was, I didn't think there was any way of doing that, and he probably didn't eat sugar anyway, so I just asked straight out: 'So where were you that morning?'

He raised an eyebrow and then shook his head, but did nothing else. Disbelief that I was doing this, here of all places, was anaesthetising outrage, and he answered coldly: 'I was on a late shift. I work on the clean – at the central cleaning department – Euston. Monitoring the automated street cleaners. When I finished, I went for a drink.'

'With anyone?' I asked.

His skin reddened, clashing terribly with his purple beard. But still no explosion came. 'As it happens, it was just me. And before you ask, no I don't know if anyone can verify that. It was the Railway Arms just up the road from the station. I needed a drink after a tough day. You can check.'

'We will. Do you think Stewart was murdered?'

'Possibly, but what's the point? We're a non-hierarchal movement. What would killing Mike achieve? It's very sad, but that's about it. Surely, they'd use their time better. Killing individuals won't get them very far. And anyway, why kill like that?'

I nodded. There wasn't much there that I could disagree with. I think we'd all said that since we'd heard about his death. 'Okay, what possible reasons can you think of *for* killing him?'

He didn't answer for a second or two. Finally, though, he did speak. 'To demoralise us? Maybe even terrorise us into submission? Or at least that's what our enemies might think; it would be wrong, we're too strong for that to happen, but that doesn't stop them thinking that.'

'And who might "our enemies" be?'

For the first time since I had joined him, I saw him look me straight in the eye. The bland lacklustre couldn't-give-a-damn attitude had gone. Instead, one of strong conviction and defiance had taken its place. 'Well, the obvious is the one you're pushing – the former state. But then,' his voice became steely, 'it could equally be the present ruling class – the working class – or at least the self-appointed vanguard of it. We're your rivals, after all. We may need to be eliminated. Maybe revolutionary democracy's time is up.' He started to move and get out of his seat. 'Which I think is also true of our little chat. It's been a blast; however, sadly, I must reluctantly go. I've got some people I need to talk to, about more positive and concrete matters. So please excuse me, 'comrade', but I will bid you farewell.'

When he had left I turned my attention to the view. Despite the directives limiting light pollution, there were still enough building lights to give London that vibrant buzz, which it always had. The Tower of London was lit up. The red militia guarding both it and the treasures which it contained. When the Royal Family had fled the country, there had been an attempt to take the crown jewels, but the Tower's staff had stopped that. We had paid for the jewels; they were ours to keep. Now the castle was ringed with armoured cars and armed workers' guards. I had no idea what the ravens were doing. The Tower had seen many murders and crimes in its day. Dave Donaldson was of the firm and sincere opinion that we were equally capable of such.

My thoughts were interrupted by the arrival of Phan Bien, who from seemingly nowhere was sitting beside me.

She smiled. 'Comrade…'

I returned her smile. 'That's the first time tonight someone has called me that and it hasn't been a term of abuse.'

Her head went back as she laughed. 'Oh, don't take it to heart. They're pretty friendly here, just passionate in their beliefs. Just as we are.' She slid a drink towards me. 'I believe you're drinking this muck. Wasn't sure whether to respect your individual right to poison yourself, and get you another, or think of my collective responsibility to step in for the good of the class and get something less toxic. In the end, I thought, a leading comrade would have their reasons, so I should follow the line, so here's another one.'

'Cheers, I mean for both calling me a leading comrade, and the drink.'

She laughed again. 'Well, Jacks rates you highly.'

I noted that she had referred to Jackie as only friends and close associates would. Was that something she naturally did, or was she signalling that she was in the know?

'You spoke very well,' I said.

'Thanks. They're understandably feeling concerned at the lack of progress.'

I took a sip of the new Slurp, to discover this appeared to be an odd mix of what tasted like lager and whisky, and possibly chocolate. Somehow, it tasted even worse than it sounded. My head would most probably be going swimming around, with too many of these. Or maybe worse. Christ, Bien wasn't wrong, I was going to die here.

Seeing the collapse of my entire face, she howled with laughter. 'Told you!'

A smile didn't even get within nodding distance of my face. I stayed serious. The taste having obliterated any humour which I might have had. 'You never had any inclination that Mike Stewart had been threatened?'

She shook her head, but added that he would have hardly have told her if he had.

'Can you think of anyone who would want to kill him?'

Her mood dramatically changed. 'Only the obvious. Let's face it, we're uneasy allies here.'

As if perfectly choreographed, Sofia Brownswood came past on her chair. Her grin and a raised right hand clenched in a closed fist were symbols of friendship and solidarity, and yet, and yet, she managed with both to say fuck off.

# CHAPTER 8:
# INTERIOR WITH A TABLE

---

S treet fighting in Lisbon dominated the morning news. A thumping, skull-cracking headache dominated me. It was throbbing – *really* throbbing. Throbbing as in a ferry boat engine on a conveyer belt. The pain was all down to last night's Slurps. I'd like to believe that the anarchists had used it as an obvious revenge tactic to destabilise party members, but regrettably, reality was that it was all my own fault. Phan Bien had warned me. But being one whose middle name was contrary, I had just carried on drinking them. Now I had acquired several more middle names – dry throat, nausea and rumbling stomach amongst them. My surname was guilt, as it was becoming a habit riding the scooter whilst drunk; I could I have killed myself, or worse, someone else. It was irresponsible, reactionary and stupid, and needless, considering the fact that public transport was now the best it had ever been.

Lack of sleep hadn't helped. That was partly down to the booze, but it was also down to a big black dog running across the road. I had tried to swerve and avoid it, but the car had crashed off the road. It was a familiar nightmare. The dog had made that run hundreds of times and I had never managed to avoid it. There had always been broken glass and death – the death of my wife and daughter. Maybe that was the reason for my reckless riding, the guilt from my anti-social activity was nothing compared to guilt I felt from the road accident of a few years ago. That the accident had just been that – an accident – and I had been stone-cold sober, didn't matter; it felt like it was yesterday and it felt like it was my fault.

Pushing such thoughts back into the dark recess I had created for them, I tried on my best swagger and strolled into the building. The first person I saw was Odette, who was nominally sitting at the front desk. In fact, she was in the middle of a conference call, with whom and what about, I had no idea, but it was painfully loud and the phrase 'picket line' was being repeated on a regular basis.

It had just gone eight and all were already here. Roijin and Victoria were busy at the virtual incident board, or the VIB as we started called them. The new socialist society which we were creating may have shortages of many things, but initials and acronyms were something which we had an abundance of.

Roijin was in blue jeans and a nondescript green tee shirt. Victoria was in a tight-fitting white tee and what looked like black leather trousers. They wouldn't be. Not in this heat. Not unless she was wearing them to deliberately antagonise Bailey, Donaldson et al. Which was entirely possible, but more likely it was the fact that they were made out of some material which had become the vogue recently, which had the look and texture of leather but was deemed to be able to keep one's skin cool. I couldn't remember its name; with this head, I could barely remember my own. Asher, meanwhile, was in white canvas shorts and a Hawaiian shirt. He was writing something on a notepad. Obviously, they had taken the same happy pills as Odette and all loudly said hello. This included Vic who had her back to me but had sensed my arrival. I hoped it wasn't from the smell of cheap booze. I again grunted, and got myself a large glass of water. Then I sat by my desk and hoped I didn't look too green.

Vic turned around, saw me and let out what could only be described as a guffaw. 'Too much socialising last night with our black flag comrades?'

The others looked at me, and fell about laughing. I looked green, then.

'Yeah, funny. Very amusing. Yes, actually, but I am willing to suffer for the cause.'

More merriment followed; whether it was still at the way I looked, or for my witty repartee, I couldn't say.

When, finally, they had finished their morning laugh-in, Roijin suggested that we should make a start and share any progress we had made since yesterday. She looked at Asher and asked him to update us on the forensic side of things. Speaking without notes and promising not to use jargon, he confirmed the cause of death. 'Basically, the headline is that it still looks like anaphylactic shock. Nothing we've found points to anything suspicious. All our tests show a massive allergic reaction to the consumption of an allergen, in this case, traces of prunus dulcis – almond, in other words. Personally, I love them, but not our friend here.'

A three-dimensional picture of a naked and very swollen corpse appeared on the VIB.

'As you can see, he is covered in hives and the swellings, especially around the throat, lips, ankles and hands. My estimate is 70% coverage. The partially chewed allergen was found in his lower throat. The lower section of the Laryngopharynx was especially swollen and enflamed as you'd expect it to be. From there, the reaction spread to the rest of his body. It affected different parts in varying levels of intensity. Some like his right arm, both hands and his kidneys were worse than others, but there's nothing unusual in that. We didn't find anything which shouldn't have been there – no poison or anything suspicious.' He stopped to let us ask questions.

Roijin eagerly did so. 'So the nut didn't reach his stomach? Is that unusual?'

Asher corrected her, 'Nut traces. There wasn't an actual nut. If there was, I don't think he would have put it anywhere near his mouth.' He shook his head. 'No. Severe reactions can start before the object has reached there. It started almost immediately; the throat closed due to the swelling and he suffocated. It would have been quite quick.'

'Can you say how quick?'

He shrugged again. His large shoulders making the remarkably loud shirt he was wearing flash upwards and downwards. I feared having a reaction myself. 'Five minutes at most.'

'Still no evidence of poison or other stimulants?' Roijin asked.

Asher shook his head. 'Toxicology, so far, has come up with zero.'

'Any sign of struggle? Physical trauma?'

'Only what I told you yesterday – nothing which seems extraordinary. I had a chance to create a virtual recon.'

A three-dimensional image of Mike Stewart appeared. Drinking milk, he clutched his throat, then his chest, then, bouncing off the table he hit the floor. There he appeared to be digging his fingernails into the floor as he attempted to crawl, presumably to the sink. He then grabbed his arm, then his heart and collapsed. It hadn't been pleasant. I'd seen better movies. I wondered why we had to see it, because it hadn't exactly furthered our understanding of his final seconds. Maybe, it was just Asher's new toy and he wanted to play with it.

Roijin spoke again. 'Are there any results that we should note?'

He shook his head. 'I did the SV double R test and it corresponded with an 89% probability of what he might have done. Grabbing his neck, falling to the floor, hence the knee wounds and then crawling using his hands, hence markings there.' Right on cue, high-res photos of his hands and knees appeared.

Victoria had yet to say a word. Maybe she was mesmerised by Asher's shirt. It really was one of the loudest I'd ever seen, red parrots seemed to compete with yellow canaries and fruit of many types. Looking at it, I wished there was a bloody volume control. It was making my head thump even harder. Finally, she spoke. Probably to detract attention from his shirt, which would not have looked out of place on a student from last century. 'So, to be quite clear, you have found no evidence of anything which could suggest anything suspicious?'

'None.'

Roijin asked Cole if she had anything to add.

She shook her head. 'All seemed as you'd expect. Everything looked perfectly normal. Nothing out of the ordinary at all. An upturned chair was all we found.'

The visual confirmed everything she was saying.

'Most of the neighbours have been interviewed. No-one saw anyone go into the house, though one – a Janice Brompton – a fourteen-year-old who lives with her mum a few doors down, confirmed that she saw Fiona Bailey arrive at the time she said she did. She was quite clear on that, Fiona stopped to ask her how she was enjoying the summer holidays. Janice looked at her watch because she was due to meet a friend and was running late. We also have witnesses who saw both Marie Williams and Thom Simons arrive at pretty much the times they said they did. Neither Williams nor Simons spoke to anyone. So far, no-one has said they saw anything of note in the area or anyone who was acting suspiciously. Nothing which might be worth looking into. Both the council and the neighbours are working well together, we're already getting a clear picture of people who were in the area at the time. We'll continue today. All in all, we haven't found a great deal.'

Roijin turned to me. 'Pete, you spoke to Dave Donaldson yesterday, did he say anything of note?'

Typical. It wasn't that long ago that she'd have ignored me even if I was rolling barrels of dynamite down a hill, stark naked and singing a collection of jazz classics, but now, when I could have done with some anonymous time, she wants me to speak. Not seeing that I had a choice, I recounted my evening.

With nothing to get excited about, Vic summed the mood up, 'So, I guess we've no choice but to continue with the routine stuff. To be honest, it looks to me very much like there's nothing at all to investigate, but we'll give it a little longer.'

Asher concurred, with the same lack of enthusiasm. 'I'll do few more tests. There's a specialist in anaphylaxis, who has agreed to look at Mike. I'm hoping that she'll be here tonight.' He almost spoke in a sigh.

'Routine stuff' it was, then.

We all got to our feet. I did so, slower than the rest, due to wanting to avoid any sudden movements to my swollen brain.

Victoria gave me a look, which I wasn't used to – sympathy. 'Pete, you need to get home and get some kip. You look wrecked.'

I went to protest. She held up her hand. 'I'm not being funny in the least. You need to sleep. Might as well. Don't think you'll be missing much.'

Asher leant over, and in his large black hand, two small white tablets rested in his palm. 'Take these. They're not your common or garden painkillers – prescription only. They'll get rid of it within an hour. These babies could kill the pain of having your head decapitated.'

Could you actually suffer pain when your head had been cut off – wouldn't you be dead and so there would be no electrical impulses which conducted the sensation of pain? I then wondered if I could arrange someone to lop my head off.

Before they had a change of mind, I headed off to the loo. With great age comes great many visits to the toilet. Then after mouthing goodbye to Odette, who was still on the phone, I clambered onto the scooter. In all probability, I shouldn't have got on the bike, but one downside of the people taking power was that the traditional reserve on public transport had waned and everyone was friendly and chatty. My head couldn't take that.

Twenty minutes later and I was home. I was surprised Red hadn't meowed and run to meet me. Probably chasing a mouse somewhere; there was little in the way of species solidarity with my cat. Once again, the toilet called. With me, hard-boiled detective referred to my bladder.

Washing my hands, I thought I heard the cat – there was a noise coming from the stairs. I paused. Something seemed odd; he was getting fat in his old age, but he didn't make that kind of noise. It was too heavy and sounded more like two, rather than four, legs. I turned the tap off. There it was again. Someone – a someone who I was now certain was human – was coming down the stairs, coming down *my* stairs. The stairs, which were right beside my downstairs toilet. The one I was presently in. Suddenly, the hangover disappeared. No headache, dry mouth or stomach pain. I had found the fabled cure – terror at the fact that someone had broken into my house and was heading towards me. I looked around for a weapon. The militia-allocated pistol was locked safely away upstairs; the upstairs where this person was coming from. Which meant that at that present moment, my armoury consisted of two loo rolls, a soap and a variety of hair products. Trouble was, staying put wasn't an attractive option. The lock was long-ago broken. I'd always meant to get it fixed but had never got around to it. I lived alone except for Red and he couldn't reach. I hadn't really banked on uninvited visitors. I stood behind the door, fists clenched. If I charged out, I'd have the element of surprise but then even in my youth, I'd been more cerebral than sinewy. So, I stayed, frozen with fear.

For a moment, I sensed them hovering directly outside. I could almost feel them placing a hand to the door. I held my breath. If the door opened a fraction, I would pull it, and launch myself at them. What I lacked in strength, I might compensate with surprise. True, the toilet paper had a greater robustness than my plan, but I had little choice. Shouting 'occupied' wasn't really a viable option. But something made them move on. Whether it was from the desire of avoiding being seen, or what they themselves might see if they opened the lav door, I didn't know, but I said a silent prayer to the god of bathrooms, when I heard the front door open and then close.

Gingerly, I left my sanctuary and looked both ways. Seeing that it was all clear, I ran full pelt up the stairs and went straight into my bedroom. Standing by the front window, looking out, I saw a figure quickly departing through my gate. I couldn't see any features, because they had their back to me and were wearing a large blue hoodie and baggy black jeans, which managed to conceal what gender they might be.

Hastily, I knelt down and opened my bedside cabinet. Taking out the false back, I showed my right eye to the eye-recognition lens and laid my right palm on the scanner. It opened and I grabbed the pistol. The horse may have bolted, but it made me feel safe. Holding it with one hand, I ran downstairs and out into my road. I saw my hooded visitor get into a mustard-coloured car and drive off. As they did, I could have sworn that through the back window I saw them waving goodbye. Or were they signalling to someone else? Had I just run out, and left an accomplice of theirs in my home? I turned, and held my gun firmly in my hand.

# CHAPTER 9: SOUTHWARK FAIR

I t had taken Roijin and Victoria half an hour to reach me, which had been time enough for me to conduct a nervous, but armed, search to see if there was anyone else lurking in the shadows. Or the cupboards. There hadn't been. All I had discovered was that I possessed an incredible ability to sweat profusely.

Despite my assurances that I had already checked the house, they'd insisted on doing their own. Immediately, they had whipped out their guns and had gone room to room. I had remained in the kitchen, hoping that they didn't look closely in the laundry basket. It had been a while since I had emptied it. Red sat on the dining room table looking at me, purring and wondering why they couldn't just have taken my word for it. But whilst they played knights in shining armour, I played the damsel in distress, and poured out some beverages.

Victoria returned, first, holstering her gun, but without any of my dirty shirts, or indeed Roijin. The latter, she explained, was looking at my home security system. This was the same system which Roijin herself had installed, and which she had boasted was impregnable, but today it had spectacularly shown that, actually, it *was* very pregnable.

For a second or two, I drifted off, wondering why the negation of pregnable was used but the word itself wasn't so much.

'Pete! Hello! You okay? Did you hear me? As I said, there's nobody here now.' Victoria touched my arm, her voice dripping with concern, fearing that I was suffering from post-traumatic stress, not realising that I was pondering semantics at a time like this.

'Er, yes, sorry, just thinking. Er – here.' I handed her a cup of coffee. Deciding that my rarely used machismo should be given some exercise, I assured that I was fine. 'Like I told you, Vic – I'm okay. Just need a coffee, although–' I did a truly awful fake laugh– 'ha, I'm not sure that what I really need at the moment are more stimulants.' I smiled, hoping that my nonchalance would hide the fact that every bodily function I possessed had liquidised. I nodded towards one of my genuine 1950s dinner table chairs, and suggested she use one.

She shushed Red away, referring to him not by name but simply as 'Cat'. Then she sat. 'So, what happened? Tell me again – tell me *precisely* what happened.'

I joined her at the table, and once more told her of my adventures.

'Did you get a look at them?'

'Sort of, they were walking away. Walking quickly, but they weren't panicking. I'd say quite the opposite. I didn't see their face, they always had their back to me. They were wearing a grey hoodie, blue jeans, and...' A solitary detail pierced my head full of shock. 'They were wearing bright green trainers – the new Karnazes, I think. But, sorry, Vic, that's about all I can remember. Their hood was up and the clothes were so large and shapeless, that they could have been any gender. They looked medium height, but to be honest I'm not even sure about that.'

'Weight – skinny, fat, medium?'

I grimaced again. This was proving to be embarrassingly difficult. Could I be any vaguer? I was supposed to be an investigator and I couldn't remember anything about the person who had just scared me shitless. 'Er, maybe overweight, 75-odd kilos? Possibly heavier, but then, the clothes they were wearing made it hard to see their figure. I don't know if that was because they themselves were, or it was just baggy.'

She didn't mock but sympathetically smiled. 'Don't worry, that's natural. Did you see the car?'

'Er, yes, it was mustard, looked electric, not brand new, not old. I think it was a Tokyo FT5, reg ended in 67GY.'

She nodded. 'Okay, it's unlikely there's a record of it, but Odette can check. Can't see them using their own in any case. We'll go house to house, see if anyone saw anything, and we'll see if there any traffic cameras still up. You never know, the odd one might be.'

'Maybe,' I said unconvinced. We'd been pretty hot on dismantling the old state round here. 'What I should tell you, Vic, and I know this will sound ludicrous, but when I saw them drive away, I am sure that they waved at me!'

'Waved?'

'Yes, really! They waved! It was as if they really didn't care that I'd interrupted them.'

'I've never before heard of burglars waving. Do you think it was some kind of taunt?'

'That's a good way of putting it. It was as if they were ridiculing me; showing me that they couldn't give a toss what I might see or do.'

Roijin entered the room, grabbed a cup and joined us at the table. Her face clearly indicated puzzlement. 'I looked at the locks and it's pretty obvious that a pro opened them. From the timer, it took the intruder 5.3 seconds to disarm the alarm and open the front door. That's amazing. I think, even if I knew the combination and how to bypass the eye-recog, it would take me longer. I presume, Pete, you haven't told anyone the code.' I shook my head. 'No run of the mill burglar could do that.'

'Have you checked to see if anything's been disturbed?' Victoria asked me, clearly treating the question as one that she should ask, if only so she could tick a box.

'No. I only had time to see if there was anyone else here before you turned up.'

With the cup to her lips, Roijin, nodded. 'Understandable.'

'But this isn't,' Victoria said. 'Our intruder waved at Pete as they left.'

Roijin looked astonished. 'Waved?'

I confirmed that she had heard correctly. I fully understood that it sounded absurd. But perhaps indicating what a surreal period we were in, Roijin didn't feel the need to query it further. Instead, she suggested that Victoria and I should see if anything had been taken. We all agreed that it was unlikely, but we had to check. Roijin, on the other hand, would do the opposite and see if they had left anything behind – surveillance equipment or microscopically forensic.

After scanning Vic and I for DNA and fibres for use in elimination, Roijin took the downstairs, holding something which resembled a showerhead in her hand. Vic and I took the upstairs. I suggested we go into my bedroom first because I had something to show her that I had noticed when I was searching for a possible second intruder. She followed and stood behind me as I pointed to an expensive vintage watch, which sat proudly in its case, on my chest of drawers.

'This was my father-in-law's. He left it to me when he died. It means a lot to me, mainly because Caroline always said it reminded her of her him. Which in turn reminds me of her. It has a lot of sentimental value to me.' Especially today, I silently said to myself. 'But it also has a great deal of monetary worth. We know that there is a thriving black market in antiques and retro products, which are being smuggled out of the country. But look – it wasn't taken.'

She looked. 'You're right. Even if they don't have the contacts to get it abroad, there's still plenty of chances to sell it here. They wouldn't get the full value, but it would still get them a tidy sum. At many of these pop-up retail events, you'll see stuff like this for sale, because there's still a market for them. Any thief would know that, yet they left it here. There's not much else in the house worth nicking. I mean you've got your compact disc and book collection, but unless they have a specialist antique dealer lined up, there's not much call for such dated tech.'

Victoria was right. If rude. 'Yeah, most break-ins at the moment are professional and are stealing from the state to send overseas to rich collectors. Stuff like ceramics, fine art and furniture, and I'm guessing you haven't anything like that here.'

'I keep the Monets in the shed,' I quipped.

She smiled. 'Okay, we'll leave the hidden masters 'til last. Let's see if we can find anything which gives us some idea of what they were really doing here.'

'You take the spare room, I'll take mine?' I suggested.

I received a look which was quite obviously one which was calling me a prize twit. 'I'd suggest that we stay together as, to put it bluntly, if we're looking to see if anything is taken, how on earth would I know?'

Good point. The prize twit neon sign above my head was on and glowing.

In the event, everything was in order and nothing was missing from my bedroom. All was also correct in the bathroom, not a razor out of place.

I could hear Roijin coming upstairs scanning with her showerhead thingy. She shouted to us that she had conducted a tech-sweep downstairs and could find no bugs either in my communications equipment nor in the rooms. She was now sweeping the upstairs rooms. As far as she could tell, though, nothing had been tampered with, and she hadn't found any evidence of listening or viewing devices having been planted. The house anti-surveillance screen was still operational and had not been breached, so no satellite could peek in.

Both Vic and I were now in what used to be my daughter's bedroom. For a long time, it had remained exactly as she had left it, with every piece of clothing being in the same place she had dumped it. The very clichéd shrine to a loss. The same had been true of my wife's clothes. But one frosty morning, I had decided that I should move on. They lived on in my memory and I had no need of their stuff to remind me of what I had lost. Interestingly, it had happened after the first time I had worked with Vic, Roijin and Ash. I had tidied up Lisa's, which had been quite a formidable challenge and given most of hers and Caroline's clothes away. A few still remained stored away, ready for when I had a free moment to make the final emotional journey and pack them up as well. We looked around the room. As we did, I felt Vic keeping an eye on me as well as what was in the room. Whether this was to see any reaction to something being amiss or from any possible emotional effect of searching my dead daughter's room, I couldn't say, but she was certainly searching for something in me.

In the event, she found nothing in either, so we went into the last room. Once it had been our spare room but it was now my library, and boasted floor to ceiling bookshelves. I looked, as I always did, first at the large photograph of my daughter and then at the books, and felt a huge sense of tranquillity. They weren't just a collection but were a physical history of my life.

'Your bedroom is clear!' shouted Roijin, continuing her tech-search, which was sounding more Hollywood than anything rooted in a realistic possibility.

They wouldn't see much if they had a camera in there. Maybe, me sipping a cocoa and reading a book, but that was about it.

Then Roijin came in, and scanned my personal library. It really did look as if she was going to give the books a good hose down. A blue light shone on its white plastic casing. 'Here's clear as well. I'd say with 99.9% certainty that in the e-dimension at least, the house retained its integrity. I cannot find any evidence that any of your devices were hacked. Nor is there any electronic surveillance in your house. It looks like an old fashioned, hands-on, break-in.'

Victoria turned away from looking at something on my desk and asked her if that was what she had expected.

'Frankly, no. With the skill they showed getting in and past the alarms, it wouldn't have taken them very long to set something up, or even take something away. From the timing on the door alarm, they were in the house for just over fifteen minutes before you got here. Easily time enough. What's even odder is that discounting us three and your cat, I can find no fibres which have been left in the last twenty-four hours.'

Vic looked at her. 'Nothing?'

'Nothing at all.'

Judging by the fact that their eyes had widened, and presuming that neither had recently taken any stimulant stronger than my coffee, they were showing surprise.

Roijin explained, 'You'd expect something off clothing and even if they were wearing gloves, then that would have left something, even something microscopically small, but there's absolutely nothing. It's as if nobody has been here except for you and the cat.'

'Red,' I said, trying to give the poor animal some semblance of a personality.

'Yes, of course, Red.'

Vic stood thoughtfully stroking her nose, and returned to what had been previously interesting her. Roijin stood there looking at the books. I had no idea what was going on in her head. It wasn't the most dynamic of moments.

The lull was finally broken. 'What a fantastic atlas!' Vic explained, sounding almost lustful.

Glancing down, I remembered that I had been looking at it last night. Why, I couldn't remember, but in my drunken condition, I no doubt had a good reason. It wasn't that unusual, my night-time ritual usually included some pictorial fix – art, photography, or in this case, maps. Then I would get into bed with a novel or some nonfiction.

Victoria continued cooing, 'The Aladdin Historical Atlas. 2024 edition. Nice book.'

One of the few things I had found out about Victoria was that she was greatly interested in maps and the history of cartography. Something which I wouldn't have guessed. But then, whatever turns you on, and it was rare I'd heard Victoria get excited about anything.

She then made a tut-tutting sound. 'Shouldn't fold down corners, though. I'm surprised you'd treat such a lovely book like that.'

'That's because I don't!' I muttered. Did this woman not know me at all? I was outraged. Suddenly, thoughts of revolution, counter-revolution and murder disappeared; I wasn't going to be dissed on alleged mistreatment of books. I stared at this alleged crime.

She pointed, and shook her head, in a schoolteacher kind of way.

To my total and utter horror, she was right. The top right-hand corner had been turned over.

'Not by me!' I stammered. I felt like some kid at school who had been accused by an adult of defacing a toilet wall with graffiti. I could also feel Roijin's disbelieving eyes boring into my back. Likely, not from any similar horror at a lack of care of books, but more from a thought of *What the hell are Pete and Victoria going on about?* A suspicious death and a break-in were slightly higher up our list of priorities than mishandled books.

'That wasn't me. Look at any book here—' I swung my arm expansively around the library. 'You won't find a single page turned back in here. Caroline didn't either. Even Lisa – who had a life's mission to do everything the opposite of her parents – never did.'

I looked closer – it was the Middle East in the early thirteenth century. It hadn't been that page I had been looking at last night. I turned the pages over to show her what I had been looking at. I explained, 'I'm reading Livy's Rise of Rome, I was looking at Rome.' I swear, I could hear Roijin's eyes rolling. Yeah, it sounded pretentious, but this felt somehow important.

Victoria was getting used to me and what she perceived to be my funny ways. She got the importance. 'And you're certain, that you didn't do this?'

I again swore my innocence. Roijin joined us. I would have expected that she would have simply discarded what I had said. What the hell has a turned-over page got to do with anything? But she too had been observing my little eccentricities. Getting out her fingerprint scan she went over it. Looking at a small monitor, she then looked at me. 'Well, it was turned over recently, possibly last night, although, quite equally, it could have been this morning. But what I can say for certain is that it was touched by someone wearing gloves.'

Cole thought out loud. 'Definitely not you, then. Let's say it was our intruder. That means that they take the trouble to break in and in their limited time, they don't take anything, they don't plant any surveillance equipment or anything, but what they do spend time doing is have a look at your atlas.' Not action movie material, it had to be said. 'Furthermore, they go to the trouble of not leaving a speck of forensic evidence that they'd been here, but they do turn over a page corner.'

'Which you'd notice,' Roijin said, continuing the train of thought. 'In fact, maybe, *only* you would. It may seem petty to everyone else, but not to you. They know how anal you are. In itself, it's slight, but it's enough for you to notice it. It lets you know that someone has been here. They weren't counting on you being here yourself, so this little thing was designed to freak you out – to threaten you. To mess with your head.'

It had worked, then.

Victoria agreed, and then asked, 'Is there any significance to the page?'

I couldn't think of any. Not to me personally, certainly. I hadn't even visited the area. The closest I had been was the southern coast of Turkey. I mean, I know a few people from the region, but they're not anyone close.

'Politically?' Roijin asked, looking up and down at the map.

'Nothing jumps out,' I said. 'You could argue, that ironically, the Middle East is quieter now than it's been for decades. The troubles are elsewhere in the world.'

'What about the historical period?'

I looked again. 'Well, about the time was the Fourth Crusade. Round about 1202, organised by Pope Innocent two or three, I can't remember. Anyway, it set off to retake Jerusalem from the Muslims, but got diverted to do some robbing, murdering and raping in Constantinople – a Christian city, in actual fact. Could it be a comment on treachery? A betrayal of supposed civilisation?'

Both women were pulling faces. Had I gone over the top? Shown off a tad too much? Did they have indigestion? No, it seemed that neither thought that could be the reason – too arcane.

'I really don't think they'd break in on the off-chance of finding a book which could act as a metaphor for treachery. I can't see a hard-nosed right-wing fanatic riffling through your book collection for literary or historical references that they might use.'

Victoria's imagery made me laugh. 'The secret librarian.'

She didn't see the humour. 'We should talk to the neighbours, see if anyone saw anything. Who's the road rep?'

'Er, Bill, number 76. Party member, I'll give him a ring. He's cool.'

Just then Roijin's phone went. It was on 2D voice. 'Hi Ash, we were going to ring you. Yeah, he's fine, just a bit shaken. It looks like...' Her expression changed. 'What?' She turned and spoke to us. 'Seems we've a pack of reporters outside the office. The rumour mill is in full swing and we've become celebrities. Listen, Ash, I'm putting you on 3D full.'

He appeared, and before telling us why we were now famous, adopted an *oh you poor lad* expression and asked how I was. After assuring him that I was okay, he quickly went on to the real reason why he had rung which was that stories were now going viral concerning the death of Mike Stewart. We had moved to centre stage of the news world. All three of us rapidly took out our phones to see what he meant.

As we did, he précised: 'So you don't have to wade through them all, I can tell you they can be sorted into two groups: Firstly, there's those arguing that we're about to declare it a murder, and use it to bring in emergency powers. The other, is that it was the party itself who murdered him, and we've been brought in to cover it up. Hence the pretence that it was a severe allergic reaction. Either way, we're up to no good.

'By the way, Pete, there's a lot on you. Indeed, you seem to be the main focus. They've found records from the Anchorage about your stay there for mental illness. There's also, what they call, and I stress Pete, I'm using their terminology – *the suspicious death of your wife and child*.' He stopped and looked at me. Even to a professional cynic such as myself, I knew that it was a look of compassion. I smiled and blinked to indicate that I was okay, and he should carry on. 'Also, they mention the death of a suspect, which you were involved in.' Here, he hurried his words, not wanting to dwell on the matter, for the obvious reason that it was a shared history that none of us were proud of.

He turned to look at Victoria. 'You're in there too, Vic. Including police personnel files, which we all thought had been destroyed in the civil war; seems like someone found them, or had them tucked away. They talk of the time you were accused of framing a suspect. The fact that you were cleared and it was later found to be itself a frame-up in an attempt to discredit a leading party police comrade, isn't mentioned.'

'Oh Lord,' Roijin muttered.

He could see the news report which she was looking at, describing her as "Cole's loyal faithful Turkish assistant" and painting a highly unflattering picture of her. The crux of which, was that she was corrupt and willing to work for the highest bidder. I wondered how she could be both faithful to Victoria and willing to work for anyone – surely that meant she'd be *un*faithful and *dis*loyal?

'Yeah, not nice,' he said. 'Note the "Turkish" references. Some of these have been written to appeal to two diametrically opposite audiences – one audience is the shaky left, those who fear that power is corrupting the party and we're readying ourselves to grab monolithic power. But simultaneously, they're appealing to the right – to racism and base prejudices, and I should say, misogyny and homophobia – there are less than subtle hints that Vic, you're, both Jackie and Pete's, lover.'

He couldn't help himself smirk at the thought. Vic though, looked positively nauseous.

'Oh, and they haven't forgotten about me. I'm pretty much like you, Roijin – an amoral, corrupt accomplice. You'll find that they make a great play that I served time. Which of course, I did – for being a party member. But there's also frequent references to me being black and Jewish. All the usual racist memes that you'd expect are there and a few new ones. Not so much dog whistles for racists, as bugle horns.'

'We're the story,' I said.

He nodded, before adding, 'And that story is making a lot of people very angry – angry at the four of us.'

# CHAPTER 10: BEER STREET

I t had been after midday when Victoria and Roijin had finally left. I had intended to collapse into my bed and sleep off the rest of day. But I hadn't been able to rest. The cocktail of Asher's pills and the litres of water had dulled the physical pain, and my unknown visitor had so powered up my adrenalin that it made sleep impossible. Today was always going to be a rough day, but I hadn't envisaged it was going to be quite this bad. This had been a 60 grit, course sandpaper-type of rough day. I buried myself in my work.

For most of the afternoon, I had further researched the life of Michael Dean Stewart, taking several hours, and numerous cups of coffee. Then, after I had exhausted a number of meandering avenues of enquiry, I moved onto his flatmates Fiona Bailey and Dave Donaldson. That had taken another hour or so and had been as fruitless as an empty Victorian china fruit bowl. Probably wanting to forget my unknown and unwanted morning visitor, I moved onto Stewart's invited ones – Thom Simons and Marie Williams.

Not unusually, there were large holes in what information was available. Despite our best efforts, the cyber-blockade, not to mention the cyber-blitzes, it resembled a threadbare woollen jumper from your youth. But total genius that I am, I had managed to get a fair bit.

I had also dived into the history of the Middle East to see if I could find anything which might link what we were doing with the page of the atlas which my uninvited guest had chosen. I pretty much agreed with the consensus of my comrades' opinion that the choice had been arbitrary; the point was simply to freak me out, but – and call me Comrade Committed – I looked anyway. I did manage to find a motley crew of Nazis who had set up various grouplets, who looked to the Crusades to dress up their far-right fantasies. This included actual dressing up. They seemed at the moment to be just small sects – more sad than sinister. The real right-wing action was happening at international government level, not with a few lardy blokes with St George crosses and swastikas tattooed on their arses. That had been my afternoon – comprehensively failing to find anything useful. I had needed a drink and there was one place to go.

Soul Shack was heaving as I arrived just after nine pm. Squeezing past a huddle of people, who didn't appear to want to move, I edged along the entrance wall, which was covered with film posters that heralded the fact that this was a nineteen-sixties/seventies theme bar. I could see that the place was full of people dancing, chatting and drinking. I was welcomed by hearing the classic "I Spy (For the FBI)" by Jamo Thomas on the sound system. Considering the world, which I now appeared to inhabit, it seemed quite appropriate. But then, shouldn't that be the CIA rather than the FBI? I negotiated myself around two guys snogging and reached the bar. Maurice, the owner, had just finished serving a group of thirty-somethings and turned – 'Friend, what can...' before recognising me. 'Pete! How are you? It's been a few weeks. How's things going in the land of law and order?'

I lied, and told him that everything was just fine. He had probably seen the day's news. Despite being publicly non-political, he was always well appraised of national and international events. I wouldn't be surprised that he knew full-well that one of his long-standing customers was being described variously as insane, an arch-reactionary, a rabid revolutionary, a lone-wolf, a ruthless murderer and part of a sinister conspiracy. I had developed quite a CV, but I had no wish to discuss it. He didn't say anything. I knew that if I wanted to talk about it, he'd listen. But I didn't. He didn't push it.

As he always did, he looked the height of sophistication and cool. Today, he was dressed in a green two-button suit, obviously with only the top one done-up, over a pure-white small button-down collared shirt, which had a nice detail of emerald green buttons. There was no tie. He was the only person I knew that was more clothes conscious than I was. We'd first bonded over it, though I strained to overlook that he always looked so effortlessly cool and so much better than I. Plus, despite him being my age, there wasn't a line on his smooth handsome black face. His powerful genes, he'd told me. Whatever it was, I was jealous; my face became more like a tube map every day.

We leant across the bar, he with his height advantage, finding that far easier than I did, and kissed each other on the cheek.

'In for the northern soul night?' he asked. 'You used to be a regular, if I remember correctly.'

Of course, he did; where his clientele was concerned, Maurice forgot very little. I smiled, and told him that it was a pure coincidence. But it was a happy one, and was about the first thing which had been positive all day. He didn't disagree, but there was a disbelief in his eyes. I decided to tell him the truth. Not, that is, on how my day had passed, but my reason for being here. Well, why not? After all, he'd always been present for them. On hearing it, he nodded and muttered a heartfelt, 'Oh yes. Sorry. Of course. I should have remembered that.' He closed the subject, realising that I had no wish to explore it anymore, and instead repeated that it was great to see me. Then, as usual, we shared compliments over our clothing.

I decided on a lager. It was a hot evening and I required quantity in my liquid. Also, after last night's bizarre anarchist cocktails, I needed a proper non-lethal drink. After handing it to me and scanning my phone for the worker's token, he looked across the bar. For a second, I thought he might be checking out the moves of the dancers. Certainly, the three teenagers nearest to me were going at far too fast a pace. They seemed totally oblivious to the tempo. Still, they were young and had the energy. And anyway, maybe dancing in time was a bourgeois concept? But no, he was looking past them towards the large framed photo of Charlie George scoring for Arsenal in the 1971 FA Cup Final. Not being as tall as Maurice, I couldn't see what exactly he was looking at.

'Come on, Pete,' he said. He flicked the bar top up and walked out, with the elegance of a ballet dancer. This was his stage, and he was the premier *danseur noble*. Trying not to spill my beer over my jacket, I meekly followed. I was obviously the bloke who had wandered into the *corps de ballet* by mistake, after taking a wrong turn at the stalls. People parted to let him through, greeting him, and commenting favourably on the evening. To each, he bowed his head and thanked them, always finding something different, something personal, to say to each. I followed in his well-tailored wake. Approaching the poster, I could see that beneath the picture of an exultant Mr George, sat a couple tapping their feet and watching the dancing. On seeing them, it dawned on me, what was going on.

'It's not necessary, Maurice, I can sit anywhere,' I said, trying to make myself heard above the music, but I merely spoke to the elegant back of his neck.

He approached them and bent down, with one hand on the back of the man, and with a friendly smile, started talking to the couple. By the time I got there, they were looking at me and nodding seriously. I caught the woman telling him that it was no problem and there was no need for a free drink because they totally understood. Moving off, they passed on their sympathies. I sat down on one of the vacant seats. He gave me a knowing look and told me that he'd sort the music.

Before he had gone a few steps, Henry Mancini's "Peter Gunn Theme" started to play. This prompted the crowd to adopt what they felt were the coolest poses. This appeared to consist of nodding one's head and miming putting shades on. Those who were already wearing sunglasses, adjusted them. I sat, imagining myself as the American 1950s TV private eye, from which the theme tune was taken. At least I had the suit. A million years ago, when I was a somebody in the party, or at least a something, I'd written a book on the history of fictional detection, and I vaguely remembered that Peter Gunn used to hang out in a club too. I had Soul Shack, he had a jazz place – Fathers, Mothers, Mother-in-law – something like that. Not a huge amount in common, then. He had it easy. He could rely on an army of informers, and didn't have the dubious joys of a devastated internet and an over-active social media to mislead him.

The first half of the lager went down quickly, then I slowed to gentle sips, looking out over the dance floor. I remembered the many times I had sat in this seat, watching Caroline on the floor, imploring me to join her and not to be a boring old fart. Today would have been one of the few times I would have, it being her birthday. That, and our wedding anniversaries, had been the only occasions when I would have been found on the dance floor. Caroline was dead but it made no difference. I came to celebrate her memory, and to grieve. But I drew the line at dancing. For the past few weeks, this day had been hanging over me. It always meant that the loss got that little bit sharper. That was the reason for the dream about the black dog. We had been on holiday, driving along the Italian coast. That dog had run out in front of us. I had swerved to avoid it. I had missed it, but had killed my wife and daughter. Sitting here somehow helped. The three of us had always come here.

Lisa had gone from childish joy at being with Mum and Dad, to extreme embarrassment. At the time of her death, she'd reached the pinnacle of that, finding anything and everything I said or did to be just ridiculous. That provoked a memory. She had – as usual – cringed at my dad dancing. I had hit back that it was my Dada dancing. That had just made it worse. 'Oh, let's remind ourselves that Dad is an art historian. Pretentious, moi?' I laughed at the memory. Taking another sip of the lager,

I wondered if she would have grown out of that by now. I'd never know, because for eternity she would be embarrassed by me.

Just then, the music changed to a very familiar song. "Too Hot to Hold" by Betty Everett. Causing the movement on the floor to go to Go Go. I caught Maurice's eye and nodded. He smiled, acknowledging the thanks. He knew that this had been Caroline's favourite.

A slight disturbance appeared to be affecting the movers and shakers, very quickly I realised that it wasn't due to change of dance style. Parting like the Red Sea, people moved aside to let a Moses through. This one though, was an attractive middle-aged woman, striding through the throng with a glass in one hand and a delicate and well-crafted handbag in the other. Her hair was swept back to a smooth shine, and to reveal a slight tan and an expression of bemused tolerance. Wearing a tight-fitting black dress with large red flowers spread across it, like some ten-year old's art project. The lipstick on her pursed lips matched the roses. The whole effect was one of cool sophistication, giving off the aura of someone at a summer party. And she was going to be very choosy about who she spoke to.

Reaching me, she smiled, raised her glass and said, 'Of all the dingy bars, in all of London, you have to choose this one.' This was the second time in as many evenings that someone had paraphrased the line from Casablanca. Either it was on rotation on a movie channel or I had a striking resemblance to Humphrey Bogart. I hoped for the latter, but guessed it was the former.

'Sophie! What brings you here?' I asked. I was shocked to see my younger sister in a place like this, knowing that she considered popular culture to start and finish with Chopin's Preludes.

Pulling a chair back, she carefully placed her drink on the table as one might place a foot in a minefield and in one graceful movement sat down. She lowered her voice, as much as she could in this place, into what I knew full well was her practised sympathetic tone. 'I thought you might want company today, as it's Caroline's birthday.'

That was the second surprise – how did she know? She had never bothered on the previous ones. 'Your PA remind you, did she?' I asked, rather ungraciously.

A very familiar smile appeared on her lips, one that conveyed the utmost belief that she was tolerating her wayward, and rather simple, brother. 'Actually, Peter, I don't have one anymore. Not now that your glorious *comrades* have closed all the fracking sites. I have been redeployed.

I've lost my office as well.'

'What a tragedy. We must do something. I wonder if I could arrange a sponsored run or something, to raise funds.'

She took a sip of her drink and predictably pulled a face to register the fact that it wasn't the quality of alcohol that she had been accustomed to before the revolution. 'You may mock, but you and your Reds are endangering our power supply. Especially now the nuclear plants have also been closed. I have no idea why, I thought they were carbon neutral. But that's by the by, it's hardly a surprise that we are having so many power cuts!'

'Nothing to do with cyber-attacks from foreign powers then?'

'You and your conspiracy theories, Peter. You'll be telling me next that the world is flat and that it's world capitalism's fault.'

There was no point in arguing with her. For Sophie, any action taken by our former prime minister was justified in restoring democracy. Anything we did, was a small step away from totalitarianism. Her position was further complicated by the fact that she wanted a return to parliamentary democracy but did not want bloodshed to achieve it. Any attempts to use it, she opposed, but none of it in her view could be placed at the door of our ex-PM or his new best pal, the President of the USA.

She took a sip, pulled another face, then shrugged, as if to indicate that whilst it wasn't up to her usual standard, she would be a trooper and plough on. 'And anyway, seeing the utter rubbish they've been saying about you, I thought you might need a shoulder to lean on.'

The thought that I had a new-improved empathetic sister who offered shoulders for support was easily the most bizarre thing that had happened in one of the most bizarre of days, in one of the most bizarre years. But I didn't say anything, and softened my tone. 'It's good to see you, Sophie. Thank you for coming, I appreciate it.'

She leant forward in a hammy impersonation of someone about to share gossip. 'So according to certain online sites, which obviously I don't visit,' she stopped and mimed inverted commas, '"someone in the office" told me, that your Victoria Cole and she-who-must-be-obeyed-Payne, are having an affair! Did you know?'

I shook my head, indicating that I wasn't going to play her game. She might think it was funny, but after this hellish day I was in no mood to get my cards out. I knew full well that she felt gossip was what the secretarial class indulged in when they were drinking cheap non-fair-trade tea. I didn't answer.

That didn't stop her. 'I also noted that some of your "comrades" aren't too happy about the fact that some former members of the police service are now working for the revolution.'

She suddenly turned serious. 'Though to be honest, Pete, some of the shit they've been saying about you, isn't quite so funny. There are all sorts of theories popping up about your involvement in the investigation of the death of that poor boy. I've seen some saying that you're involved in a cover up and even that your "baby cot" were the ones who actually did the killing. Good heavens, there's even some saying you and that Victoria Cole are lovers. Now that is disgusting. I hope to God that isn't true. I could handle you being an assassin, but not for goodness' sake, you sleeping with *that* woman!'

'Sophie, you know full well, that we're called a Crib, not baby cot. Actually, to be more precise – *the* Crib.'

She was right though about it not being that funny. The lovers' angle was just tabloid nonsense, but some of the other stuff had the potential to be dangerous. Online media speculation had the habit of becoming regarded as the bone-fide truth. Even the most ludicrous of stories if repeated enough could convince people to move from fantasy to fact. From there's no smoke signals without fire to there's no trending without the truth.

Unlike the others in our Crib, I had a whole number of titles – "former psychiatric patient", "alleged killer" and "uncontrollable maverick" being just three of them. I had tried to laugh them off. I had tried. But then, I had tried to get interested in cricket once. I had failed at both. Some things were just impossible.

Obviously, my face betrayed what I was thinking, because, as if this day couldn't get any weirder, it then did. Sophie put out her hand and held mine. 'You, okay?'

I looked at her and saw concern, love even. For a split-second I wondered if someone had slipped something into my drink. Hopefully they had, because Sophie being loving and caring was just too freaky to comprehend. I reacted as she knew I would do: 'Who are you and where's the real Sophie Kalder? You're an imposter! My sister would never be like this!'

She pulled her hand back slowly and grinned, giving out an exasperated sigh as she did. 'You do know, Peter, that I've always only had your best interests at heart. And anyway, *you know* I don't use Kalder, I use my married name – Humes, I am Sophie Humes.'

'And how is hubby? Still hiding in New York until the nasty lefties go away?'

She smiled. But I knew my sister very well. I knew her colour chart of smiles. This one was fake – she had a number of them to cover all manner of real emotions. This was number 17, and was her way of deflecting serious pain.

Guilt pricked my throat and my brain registered a rebuke to myself. That was petty and spiteful. Grief didn't have to be always about death; you could lose your partner in other ways too. Ways such as crossing the Atlantic and leaving you here, just so they could protect their assets. Sophie may be his wife, but obviously he didn't consider her an asset.

'Sorry. That was below the belt. How is Michael? Hear from him much?' I sounded about as sincere as a train announcer apologising for a major delay. That was strange, because actually I was being sincere. Then again, so probably were the announcers.

'And who are you? And where is my brother? You've apologised, showing the self-awareness to know when you've said something wrong. And the clinching piece of argument – asking after Michael! Indeed, actually bloody calling him by his proper name, and not by the "hilarious nickname" which my brother thought of all by himself. Well, unless this brother in question had organised a "humour" caucus and came to it by committee, you cannot be my darling bro!'

I lifted up my glass to acknowledge her comeback. Sophie didn't stay down for long. 'Well, how are you?'

She took another sip, with yet another grimace, and then another shrug of her bare shoulders. 'Oh, I'm okay. I've been moved to a department coordinating energy supply. My role now is to help manage the final national change to complete reliance on more eco-friendly renewable energy. Most of the people are fine. Well meaning, but naive. Most are party members of yours, but they're friendly enough. Don't think any of them know we're related, which after today, is probably a blessing.' She gave me a grin. This was number 35 on the chart – a cheeky affectionate one. It was rarely used. 'I have to share an office now. I even have to get my own coffee!' She spoke in a mock tone of an aggrieved victim.

'Good God,' I said in playful sympathy. 'Where will it all end?'

Shouting above the noise, we tried small talk. Both of us were crap at it, but as politics was a no-no and there was still no footie, and neither of us had any contact with our extended family, it was pretty much all we could do. Awkwardness buffered us like people in a crowd. Occasionally, we lapsed into reminiscing. Nothing could be too contemporary because frankly we knew little of each other's lives now. Things did relax a little, the more we drank. My words became ever more slurred; hers, of course, remained perfectly articulated. Sophie could consume a whole vineyard, alongside a vat of spirits, without showing any noticeable effect. What was annoying was that with every word I mangled, a look of saintly but amused tolerance sparkled in her eyes. I had last seen her drunk when she was sixteen, before she had decided to be a Tory, pronounce her Ts, and pretend to have been raised in some nice middle-class home.

Looking at her watch, she announced that it was 11.15. I wasn't sure whether the time indicated something, but it was followed by a strange look, as if she had seen something unusual in the distance and for a brief moment, I wondered if there was something she wanted to say. It was an odd look. One that, for once, I couldn't decode. But then her being here was odd. It only lasted a second before she announced that she was going to the "Ladies". Maybe, the look was just that she needed a piss -—or pee as she would delicately call it – and was horrified that she could hold it no longer, and would be forced to use a public one.

Leaving me, without asking me or anyone else where they were, she headed off to them. Typical of my sister, she would instinctively know where to go. I wouldn't have put it past her to have examined plans of the building before getting here. Sophie never left anything to chance.

Looking around, I noticed that it had become even fuller. Two women were dancing dangerously close to our table, and what was left of my fifth beer looked in peril. Vernon Garrett's "Running Out" was now playing and the dancers were trying some strident moves. The cacophony of sound had increased and now snippets of conversation, like torn bits of newspaper, were being blown about by the thumping of the music. Clinking of glasses and raucous laughter accompanied them.

The women moved aside, not as I expected to let my sister return, but to my surprise, to allow Victoria to reach me. My Lord, was everyone here? You come to a bar to lose yourself in a crowd and enjoy some good old solitary self-pity and the whole bloody world turns up.

'Hi!' she yelled after giving the dancing pair a glare that told them to back away. 'You need another one?' she asked, indicating my nearly empty glass.

I thought for a second, before thinking hell, why not? Wasn't that what revolutions were for? To be able to go to work with a hangover two days running? I didn't say that though, because Vic was still in her earnest newly-joined mode and no doubt would give me a long lecture on alcohol and alienation and how both will decrease as the new society is built. Instead, I just said yes. 'Oh, by the way, Sophie, my sister, is here.'

She hesitated. This, I knew, would not be welcomed with open arms. 'Yeah, I saw her in the loo. I popped in as soon as I got here. So, er, why is she here?'

'Oh, we've been having some sibling bonding.'

Cole looked at me if I was mad. Which according to a multitude of blogs, I apparently was. Which in turn, had sparked a debate online of what constituted mental ill-health.

'Get her a glass of red. You don't need to worry about remembering the type, there's only one.'

She nodded and headed towards the bar. The dancing bodies closed in around her, only to part again, as my sister appeared. It had been so magnificently timed, a choreography of avoidance, that I wondered if it had been planned. I knew that they didn't like each other very much. I didn't have a chance to ask her, or indeed, sit back and watch the fun of two alpha females in combat, because, she immediately said, 'Well, Peter, I must go. I've stayed late enough. Now I have joined the heroic proletariat, I mustn't be late tomorrow and must always do my best for the brightly coloured future.'

'Oh, okay, but Vic's getting you a drink.'

'Victoria Cole is here?'

'Yes, Sophie – according to online gossip – my erstwhile lover, and of course, according to these same experts, also the lover of Jackie Payne. She has found time not only from rampant sex with the pair of us and from being an ex-cop, the betrayer of revolution and basically being responsible for all the world's ills, to be here at Soul Shack.'

She grimaced. 'Please don't put that picture in my head of you and her. That makes me feel even more ill than the liquid they serve here and call alcohol.'

'Didn't the pair of you just meet in the toilets? She said she saw you.'

My sister looked defensive. 'Did she? Why – what did she say?'

God, these two women did not like each other one bit. 'Nothing, only that she saw you and she's getting you a drink.'

'Even more of a reason to make my apologies. Much as I would love to sit and discuss Miss Cole's love life with her, I haven't yet given up the will to live. And to be honest, any more of the sweet-berried tasting drainage cleaner and I will lose the coating of my throat.'

She leant forward and kissed my cheek. 'Take care, Peter. You have your faults but you're still my brother. It will all blow over. Hopefully, one day, we shall come to our senses in this country.'

With that, she left. I watched and wondered when was the last time we had had a drink together. Probably, a lifetime ago. Vic returned, balancing the drinks and preventing any further thoughts. Surely, she was in some theatrical farce with Sophie: one enters through stage door left, whilst the other exits on the right.

'She's not back then?'

'Astute of you, Vic. Learn those observational skills at police training?' I said, as I unloaded my drink from her hands. 'She had to go. She sends her apologies.'

I was met with a strange questioning look. 'I'm sure she did.' With one swift movement Sophie's wine was consumed and Vic took a sip of her own lager. She looked like she wanted to say something, but was reluctant to do so. I had seen such a look before, but not often. Rarely was she reluctant to speak. Finally, she spoke: 'Was she upset about something?'

I was surprised. 'Well, apart from the death of her glorious Rule Britannia, the fall of the monarchy, the creation of the workers' state, and also that horror of horrors, she has to share an office, she seemed okay. Why?'

Clearly, Vic was reluctant to explain her question. 'Er, I saw her crying in the toilet. She didn't see me because I was around the corner, but I heard her, then saw her.'

'Sophie? You must be mistaken. Sophie never cries. Cut both her legs off and she'd only say in that affected voice of hers, "Oh dear, that's an inconvenience". She didn't even shed a tear at either of our parents' funerals. I was bawling like a baby, but she was stony-faced and dry-eyed.'

'It was her, Pete. She was crying.'

That was strange. I didn't say anything; for some reason I didn't want to explore what had possibly so upset Sophie. I'd give her a ring tomorrow. But for now, I sat and people watched. Sensing that it was a topic which I did not want to broach, Vic did likewise, absorbing her surroundings. Her nose turned up. 'You really do love this music, don't you? I mean, it's classic, but most of it is at least eighty years old. My grandfather listened to this stuff.'

I shrugged. 'It's a 1960s and 1970s theme bar – what do you expect?'

'Don't get me wrong. It's fine, but, Pete, there's so much good stuff being made now. It's a golden age of music. Do you even to listen to bands like Irresponsible Gardening or Affecting the Blinds?'

I used my 'of-course-I-know-them-who-doesn't?' face and then the fail-safe reply for such occasions, 'Yeah they're good, although I think they need to develop their sound a bit'.

Actually, I'd never heard of them, and hoped she wouldn't enquire any further about the two bands. I was tired and my blagging batteries were almost empty. Luckily, she wasn't greatly interested in my opinion of contemporary music. Instead, she moved her chair closer. 'You okay, Pete?'

That threw me. I was only just recovering from my sister's unexpected discovery of human emotion, and now Victoria does likewise. I mumbled a non-committal reply, then changed the subject, I asked her how come she was here. Her reply wasn't what I had expected. 'It being Caroline's birthday, I thought you would be.' Good grief, she knew as well! This was even more of a shock than Sophie doing so. After all, my sister had actually met my wife.

Seeing that I was need of an explanation, she told me that when we had first met, she had done a full background check on me. 'I learnt a lot about you, Pete, including about Caroline...' She paused and added, 'Sorry. Back then, I had to see if you could be trusted.'

'Glad I passed,' I mumbled, feeling rather aggrieved. 'So how did you know I would be here, and not at home?'

'You are a creature of habit. I bet you come here every year.'

'I don't actually'. My lie was said with all the conviction of a twelve-year-old.

She shrugged, obviously not believing it. 'Anyway, after today, I think we both could do with a drink.'

She wasn't wrong. It had started with a hangover and got worse. But then, Vic hadn't had the greatest of days either – being in the spotlight had hardly been a barrel of laughs. Seeing and hearing your name and reputation being trashed was more painful than I had imagined, and I was old, cynical and not that bothered. I didn't think I had a name or a reputation, and if I had, they had been pretty much kicked to hell and back in the past couple of years.

'Pity I can't use my truncheon on them anymore,' she joked. I half-wished that she could.

Trying to forget our brush with the sticky pot called fame, I changed the subject. 'What are Roijin and Asher doing tonight? They coming here?' I wouldn't have been surprised if they were. Seems like my dead wife was now public property. Grief had been nationalised.

After pouring her drink down her throat in one go, she answered, 'Roij is at home with her family. They've taken the media circus quite badly. Ash is still working. And me? I intend to have several of these and you're going to join me. We are going to try to forget that today ever happened.'

Seemed like a plan to me.

# CHAPTER 11: AN EXPERIMENT ON A BIRD IN THE AIR PUMP

It was an unearthly hour. Such hours shouldn't exist – or at least, I shouldn't be awake to experience them. My rather inebriated, dry-mouthed stop-start sleep had been rudely interrupted by a very excitable Asher Joseph, phoning. Semi-awake, I had mistakenly used the housecom to answer, which had meant that I had his voice ricocheting off my bedroom walls. He had insisted that it was vitally important that I get to the office immediately. After two excitable minutes, he had hung up.

I wasn't as young as I used to be. (Which was quite possibly the silliest phrase ever thought of, I mean, unless you could go back in time, who *isn't* as young as they used to be?) But that was too much for my frazzled thought-processes to untangle. Thankfully, the hangover wasn't as savage as yesterday's, but even so, my head still resembled a soggy jelly. Soul Shack could boast that its booze was better than the Shard's, but it was still booze. Which wasn't the greatest advertising slogan that there's ever been.

I passed the building's security, then Odette's empty desk (the lucky sod was probably still in bed) and headed into the office. Asher and his huge smile were the only ones in. Obviously, he had big news, because not only did it warrant the call, but he had made an effort getting dressed today. This news warranted sartorial effort. He was wearing quality jeans and a stylish linen jacket. He even had a shirt on, which looked as if it had once said hello to an iron. This, for Asher, passed for formal wear, especially in this weather, which although still early, was warming up to be one steaming day. My delicate state seemed less important right now because I was intrigued to know what the news was: Had the blockade been lifted? Had revolution spread to other countries? Or was he dressed like that because he was going for an interview? Seeing me, his smile got even bigger, threatening to submerge his face into his mouth. He really was in a good mood.

'Pete, hi, mate. Sorry to get you in so early but this is important.'

It must be. He had just called me "mate".

'No problem, Ash,' I said, refusing to return the "mate", but still keeping it light and friendly. I returned the smile. I could do matey, if not mate, even at this hour.

Just then, before we started hugging each other, the female members of the team arrived. Obviously, neither of them had got the 'dress smart casual' memo and had turned up in shorts and t-shirts, looking all set to go camping.

After the standard morning greetings, they grabbed a coffee each and sat down. Roijin smiled. 'Going for faded grandeur today, Pete?'

Vic grinned. 'Isn't that his usual look?'

I forced a smile but didn't reply.

Their witty repartee exhausted, it was time to get down to business.

'I think, Asher, you'd best start,' Roijin suggested. 'You were rather vague last night, but it's plain to all of us that you've found something.' She gave an affectionate and knowing smirk.

It was a good idea. If he didn't tell us soon then I feared that he was going to explode.

'Well, first things first. I've been puzzling over the TOD – sorry, time of death – because certain indicators confirm Dr Lopez's initial estimate that it was 10am, but when you analyse the rigor mortis, body temp and lividity they seem to contradict each other.' He paused, before adding, with an obvious implication, 'I'll come back to that in a minute.'

He turned to a 3D image of which, he informed us, was a blood cell from a body which had suffered a severe anaphylactic shock. After pointing out some of its characteristics, he showed another photograph. 'Now look at this one.'

Another cell, looking to me like some alien being on a cheap Sci-Fi movie, flashed up on its right. We looked at the two, and I couldn't see anything remarkable. Judging from their polite but blank looks, Roijin and Victoria seemingly didn't either. If we had been rung up at a ridiculous time to admire pics of his favourite cells, then I would find it somewhat difficult to keep our new-found friendship going. My patience was feeling severely dehydrated.

This seemed to excite him. Our ignorance of what he was showing us, that is. I sincerely hoped that he hadn't clocked that me turning up to work with a hangover was becoming a bit of a habit. No, his happiness was definitely supported by two large baroque pillars of his knowledge and our ignorance. He told us to look closer. 'Look at the slight pimples on the right.'

We peered; he enlarged the image, and yes, we could see them.

'I told you that I was getting an expert in. Well, actually I got three in, and they noticed what I'd missed, and that was these cells around the stomach. We weren't sure what they were at first, only that it was an anomaly. But,' he paused. 'What we did notice was that they had similar profiles of cells which have come into contact with accelerants, accelerants which pharmaceuticals use to propel medicines around the body. As the name suggests, accelerants are used so that the medication in question is pumped to the area which it is required for, in as quick a time as possible. Such accelerants have a pimpling effect on certain cells. We did further checks and found that our suspicions were right. It's not one that is used in the health service, certainly not one used in this country or indeed any that they are aware of. But we're certain that it is a type of accelerant. That would explain something which had also puzzled both Lopez and me – anaphylaxis can be quick, but our tests showed that it had been rapid, and I mean unusually rapid.'

He took a sip of water, before continuing. He knew that he had our attention. Even I was beginning to twig what he was talking about.

He continued, 'Now, there are key differences between this accelerant, and ones used in mainstream medicine. The health-care compound ones aren't as strong as the traces we found. Think of it as the difference between 5% and 100% alcohol.'

To be honest, I didn't want to think about any type of alcohol right this second, but I caught his drift.

'Also, despite being less powerful, they tend to linger in the body. This one appears to disappear from the body extremely rapidly, leaving no trace. Convenient for a poisoner, don't you think? The evidence destroying itself.' He put up what he informed us was film of a collection of cells in Stewart's bloodstream. 'I took this at the house, as soon as I got there. If I magnify it, then you can see those pimples. But if we look at these.' Another film appeared. 'Taken from the same spot in the body. If you excuse the pun. No pimples. The second was taken only an hour later.'

Okay, it wasn't Saturday night at the movies, but the films were effective. It showed to all of us that there was an artificially inserted accelerant, which covered its tracks by disappearing. We all could see it; nobody needed to say it. But I did. It was rare that I understood anything scientific so I might as well take my chance.

'Absolutely!' Asher said, after I had stated the obvious, that this could only be there if someone had somehow got an almond mixture into his blood, with the specific intention of killing him. 'So, we investigated further, and by looking at the chemical reaction the cells make, when losing the accelerant, which from our small sample, we could see, we traced the process of disappearance.' Yet another diagram appeared in front of us. 'Watch the red!'

Victoria, who was keenly looking, felt the need to commentate, 'It starts from the A section of the intestine and the extremities, with the exception of the left arm, then moves along until it reaches the throat and the left hand.'

'Exactly, this is if you like, the process in slow motion reverse. Where the red starts, is where the accelerant was the last to dissolve, therefore the furthest from the point of origin. You could say that where the red finishes, is where it began.'

'At the throat, where he swallowed the milk,' Victoria said.

'Yes. But look! Look, at the same time as the throat is reacting, so is the left hand.'

'And why would that be?' she muttered.

'Indeed. Why? There's no link between the throat and the hand. This can only mean that there were two points of entry. That was our theory, so we thought we better have a closer look, and this is what we found.'

Stewart's hand appeared, slowly rotating. As it did, the image zoomed in to the fingers, to the forefinger, then towards the skin. Then to what looked like bits of wood. 'These are splinters from the floor, where he clawed the floorboards. Nothing unusual in that, the floor was fairly worn around the table, with the varnish gone in some places. But then we get closer. Look at it now. The puncture wound is not the same shape as the splinter. Nor the depth. The wood has an irregular hexagonal shape to it, but the wound is cylindrical, and the splinter is half the length of the wound. Which is exactly the puncture hole a micro-syringe might make.'

Victoria had caught my bug of repeating what he had said, just to make sure that I had understood. I was glad that I wasn't the only one in the room who had skived off Chemistry lessons at school. 'So, you're saying that he was injected with the almond mixture, alongside this accelerant?'

'Yes, Vic – in a solution. I still can't be sure of the sequence of events, he certainly did drink the milk, but that could well have been soon after the initial injection, which basically incapacitated any clear-thinking. He may have grabbed the glass, or somehow it was poured down his throat by the same person who had injected him. That would make sense, as it would camouflage the injection into his finger. I think if I hadn't been lucky enough to take the Bloodcam then we may have never noticed. I will, of course, have to do further tests.'

Roijin looked puzzled. 'But you can't find any sign of bruising or anything which suggests that it was forced on him? Nothing around his arms or wrists, suggesting that he was physically restrained?'

'No. Not yet. But the key thing is that this accelerant is not naturally found anywhere. It's totally synthetic. Indeed, I can't find any mention of it in any database. As far as I can judge, this is a new formula, and one, which suggests somebody has quite extensive facilities to come up with such a sophisticated compound.'

We all knew what "extensive facilities" meant.

He straightened up. 'I think Fiona Bailey's been right all along. In my opinion, Mike Stewart was murdered. And this is the proof.'

For a moment or two there was silence, as we digested the fact. Then Vic spoke. 'We need to talk to Fiona again. And for that matter – Marie Williams and Thom Simons, seeing as they were either there when the body was found, or at the very least, arrived soon after. Dave Donaldson also needs to be interviewed again. Like it or not, there needs to be some close questioning. Pete, could you arrange that?'

I nodded. Although the thought of having to have face to face contact with Marie Williams again was not one to make my delicate heart go all aflutter. Especially when it entailed "close questioning".

'Good. Thanks. Asher, get your team to go over Stewart's body again. I know you're probably sick of doing that, but I want every test known to humanity performed – and a few that aren't. There's still a few things we don't understand. Like, for example, as you yourself said, how did it get down his throat? The media's been taking an interest in this, and will get a lot more so when they hear of this. We need as much in the way of facts as possible because the political sandstorm is going to make finding them very difficult. Roij, send over a team to go through that house again.'

'No prob.'

'Okay, Pete, you and me need to do the interviews.' Vic paused for a second. Immediately, I realised what she was going to say and why she was desperately thinking how to phrase it. My therapist, Dr Brakus, would call it "overcompensating previous emotional friction". Or in Kalder speak, "trying not to open old wounds with the touchy thin-skinned fella sitting opposite her". She wanted to say that as she was the ex-cop, and I was the new kid in police town, she would have better questioning skills than me. It wasn't easy being PC, and a PC.

I put her out of her misery. 'Good idea.'

She smiled, grateful for the save. 'We now have solid grounds for thinking this is a crime. Ash, could you also organise a Community Information Meeting to be set up in the locality, with reps from the area, local councils and the militia. I think I need to ring Jackie Payne as well. She needs to know, as this is going to make the headlines. She can talk to their leaders – or whatever they're called.'

'And,' she paused, starting to become more hesitant, a little less confident, 'I think we also need to trace exactly the route that Williams, Bailey and Simons took to get to the house. We have a vague idea, but we need to double-down on this.'

We all looked at her. 'Are we now formally considering them suspects?' I asked.

'If nothing else, we need to do it to eliminate them from our enquiries.'

I wish I had a workers' token for every time I'd heard that said in a detective show, I'd be a rich man. But then, we're against personal wealth.

She stared into space, before adding, 'Oh and the NWC public relations section need to be in on this. Like it or not, we need them to be kept informed, because the last thing we need is even more journalists getting under our feet. I thought Odette could cover that.'

With that, we got active, and started to organise what was to be done.

Fiona Bailey was the first person I contacted. She answered after a few seconds. 'Hi, Pete. What's up? Is there any news?' Her voice sounded urgent and needy.

I could see that she was on a tram, surrounded by people off to work. I asked how she was doing.

'No, I'm off to a meeting at the Shard. I really should take a few days off. I can't seem to concentrate on anything. I keep bawling my eyes out. I just can't get Mike's swollen face out of my mind.' A look of anguish shot across her face. I commiserated. I knew what locked images could do to one's mental health. I had several in my life and none were fun. They were never positive.

I softly administered my best Florence Nightingale advice on how to deal with grief, which boiled down to sympathetic noises, and muttering that time healed. Then after seemingly curing her sense of loss of a dear friend and sibling, I quickly got to the reason of my call. 'Look, sorry, Fiona, but we need to talk to you again.'

'Sure, yeah of course. Why don't you come to the Shard? I'm guessing that you need to talk to DD, cos he'll be there too.'

That would be convenient, I thought to myself, and asked if she could arrange that then it would be great.

She looked at me, her watery eyes questioning me. Why, she was wondering, did I need to talk to her. What was new?

I thought for a second, debating with myself whether I should tell her over the phone or not. Telling someone that their friend had been murdered whilst on public transport, wasn't ideal, but shouldn't she be told?

'Fiona, there's no easy way to say this, but you were right – Mike was murdered.'

# CHAPTER 12: THE VILLAGE FETE

T he Shard isn't that far away from our office and on a sunny day like today, it's a pleasant 40-minute stroll. We could have walked it easily. We *should* have walked it, but Victoria had insisted that we drive. It would be useful to have transport, because it allowed us freedom of movement, she said. Probably true, but I suspected that the real reason was from a desire to make a statement to our erstwhile anarchist allies. What that statement was, I could only guess, but it probably had something to do with power and prestige. Back in the day, we called it showing off. Truth was, me and her were more alike than either of us cared to admit.

For our short journey, she'd put the car on auto, and watched television. It was the news. That was no surprise – whilst chemical addictions in the country were on the decrease, news junkies were on the increase. Still, just occasionally, Victoria, I thought, could lighten up a little. The news today remained the growing tensions within the NWC. On the one side was "a growing and significant minority" in the AF who were arguing that they should withdraw from the alliance. There was to be a debate at the Shard on the matter, which was why Donaldson and Bailey were going to be there.

In turn, the party ultras were denouncing the AF as lightweights. Predictably, Reyansh Anand had been on, pointing fingers and accusations. Seemed that he and Noah Walker was going to be partaking in similar debates today.

It was just before 11am when we entered the Shard. But it already felt as if most of the day had already passed. Two AF guards, each the size of a heavyweight boxer, strode over. Both were wearing matching orange and brown camouflage trousers and jackets. I wasn't too sure why you would require camouflage in a skyscraper, perhaps that was the colour scheme here, so they could merge in with the soft furnishings. I didn't have time to ask, because, after a brief welcome, they scanned us. By doing so, they noticed that we were both armed. Neither panicked, but their own guns did noticeably rise up to waist level – ours. Politely, but firmly, they requested that we hand them in. They would, they said, give us a ticket, and we could collect them as we left. Just like you might a brolly at a gallery. It was a reasonable request, so I started to do so.

My partner didn't. 'Sorry, comrade, I'm afraid we can't agree to that. We have authorisation from the NWC to carry arms and to do so when we deem it necessary to do so. And we deem it so now. With that in mind, they'll have to remain with us.'

Victoria's officious tone had slightly irked me, and I was on her side, so I expected a severe reaction from the guards. Impressively though, their politeness remained: 'I'm sure that's so, sibling. But there's no need for weapons, here. We're all friends. I'm afraid that we've strict rules against firearms being in the building – this is a place of peace and support.'

'Really? Why have you got one then?' she snapped.

They remained smiling. 'True, but we're here to defend the building.'

'So are we!' she replied.

This went on for a couple of minutes. Throughout the verbal arm-wrestling, I had been holding my gun rather pathetically in mid-air, as if raising a glass to toast a marriage. Not wanting to see a painful divorce here, and one which as far as I could see, would entail us being the losers in any settlement, I made an exaggerated gesture of putting it on the table and flashing the little fireball standing next to me an angry look.

She didn't move, and didn't say anything.

Somebody had to break this impasse, so I turned to her and in a voice, which attempted to balance comradeship with authority, said, 'I think you should hand it over, Vic. You're of course absolutely correct, but here, the importance of our relationship with our allies overrules that. I'm the political support in the Crib, and in matters concerning areas not directly involving detection, I take precedent. Vic, please.'

She looked at me. Several possibilities flashed through my mind as what her reaction was going to be – none of them pleasant.

She breathed in, as if in the middle of some yoga exercise, surrounded by scented candles and water features. But she was feeling far from serene. In a controlled voice she replied, 'Okay. You're right. Sorry, comrades.' She even attempted a smile but that was about as genuine as a second-hand car dealer's. Nonetheless, she took out her gun and laid it down.

That done, they thanked us and waved us towards the lift. She said nothing. Nor did she look at me. Not even when I informed her that 'I told

Bailey that we'd meet her in the bar'.

I looked at my watch, although I knew full well what the time was. I just needed to think. You could have cut the atmosphere with a knife, if such weapons had been allowed. 'Their meeting starts at 11.30, so we've got half an hour. Marie Williams and Thom Simons will also be there.' She knew all this, because I'd arranged it back at Somerset House, but I didn't have anything else to say. 'They're both due to be here for the debate. Showing cooperation and love, I guess.'

Her reply was crisp: 'You lead. I'll chip in.' Then, just for a second, the facade slipped. 'You are, after all, the *political support.*'

I didn't have time to reply, because the lift doors opened. Despite the comparatively early hour, the bar was about a quarter full. A hubbub of conversation greeted our arrival.

I immediately saw Sofia Brownswood, by the far window, in her hoverchair, which for the moment was on the ground. She was in a deep conversation with Phan Bien. Although, perhaps a better description would be a hostile rant. She appeared to be about to lose her temper at any moment. If she hadn't already. There was a lot of gesticulating and spittle flying out of her mouth. Her face was distorted by anger. Not a good look. Not that anyone would be foolish enough to say that to her face. Comrade Phan, in stark contrast, looked pretty much relaxed, nodding occasionally, palms up, as she attempted to make her point against what appeared to be a cascade of words. Her whole demeanour whispered cool, as did her attire – three quarter length cream linen trousers and small collar-less linen shirt.

Victoria elbowed me in the ribs. Thankfully, it was a gentle one; not one stemming from her unhappiness with me. That could come later. Nodding towards a white guy in his early thirties, with long hair, tied in a ponytail, she muttered, 'That's Thom Simons.'

Walking towards him, I saw out of the corner of my eye, Fiona Bailey. She was on the far side, by the large curved windows which ringed the room. She was walking around the perimeter. Briefly, she nodded hello, but didn't deviate her direction. It looked like she was heading towards Brownswood and Phan. I wondered what the dynamic would be when she reached them. Things appeared to be getting even more hostile between the two women. Bailey and Brownswood were allies, but equally, she was opposed to needless hostility between the two organisations.

Alas, I was to never find out because just as Bailey joined them, and before she could try her peace-making skills, Phan walked off, shaking her head and waving her right hand in a dismissive gesture. Her face, whilst still far from angry, had lost its calmness, and was instead starting to show annoyance. It seemed that even she had limits to her patience. Brownswood had activated her chair and was hovering behind her, her dark eyes and black bobbed hair making her look for all the world, like some early twenty-twenties comic book super-villain. I – indeed, all the floor, and probably half the city – could hear her accusing Phan of undermining the gains of the revolution. We needed some calming influence here, and it appeared that Bailey was volunteering to be the one to do it. She had increased her pace to try and to catch up with them. Phan, though, had seen me, and no doubt wanting to seek some solidarity from party comrades – moved sharply to her right. Joining us by an empty table, she grinned and rolled her eyes. 'Is it too early for a drink?'

I was about to offer some words of comfort, something witty and succinct, when suddenly one of the large windows shattered. A loud crash burst in our ears. Instinctively, both Vic and I crouched down, looking at where the noise had come from. Glass was showering downwards and inwards – everywhere. Someone screamed. Then others did.

A strange grinding and clanking noise started, like someone riding a bike with the chain off. It was coming from Sofia Brownswood's chair. Losing height, it smashed into the carpet. Her face registered shock and she almost looked insulted. My mind sent a message that she needed help, but there was no time to act. A moment later, a second crack rang out. This time, no glass broke because there was now none to break. This time, everyone knew what it was – it was gunfire. A piece of the table flew up by my wrist, as a bullet ricocheted off its corner

'Get Down! Drone attack!' someone shouted.

The second shot had missed Phan by millimetres. But she hadn't moved, standing stock-still, like a statue. She was in total shock. I grabbed her and pulled the pair of us under the table as further shots rang out. Clinging onto each other tightly, I could see Brownswood was alive, but from the blood appearing on her side, obviously she had been hit.

Victoria sprinted forward, lunged and rugby-tackled Fiona Bailey, who only had time to look startled as Vic collided with her. The pair's momentum took them rolling onto a large empty sofa. They'd hit it with force at its base, then in one rapid but graceful movement, Vic used their legs as a fulcrum, pulling the sofa down with her free arm over and on top of them.

Meanwhile, Brownswood was frantically attempting to get her chair moving again, and to head away from the window, hoping to get to somewhere safe.

'Sofia!' Phan Bien called, holding out her hands, in a desperate attempt to help.

Brownswood rose again to about a metre above the carpet. Looking at us, she moved forward. Fear and desperation streaming out of her eyes.

Phan called out to her, 'Quick, Sofia!'

But Brownswood's progress was halted by being hit by another shot. She screamed, it screeched. It juddered. Lurching forwards, it ploughed into our table, pushing it back several centimetres. Desperately clutching onto her, we recoiled. Thankfully, we remained under cover. Another shot rang out. Again, jolting our table. Then another. Brownswood was still in her chair, but was at a right angle to us, wedged against the table's edge. I could see her stomach was now a mass of red, but could see no breathing. Thoughts of hauling her under the table disappeared, when the firing intensified. Now it was long, repetitious and continuous. Bullets were ricocheting everywhere. Carpet, wood and metal were flying up in all directions. Bottles from the bar were exploding at the impact of the bullets.

Screams and shouts were everywhere, contesting with the gunfire to create a cacophony of horror. From my obscured vantage point, I could see that people were finding whatever cover they could as the room was raked with bullets. Phan was shaking and muttering, 'Oh my God! Oh my God' over and over again. If this lasted much longer, I would be offering some sort of prayer myself.

I looked across at the upturned sofa, where Vic and Bailey had found refuge, and was relieved to see that for now at least, they seemed to have been left unscathed except for a covering of debris. They'd been lucky that it was big enough to house Bailey's tall frame.

'Where's the fucking defence drones?' someone yelled above the screams.

I lay with Phan, the pair of us tightly holding onto each other as a series of mini-explosions went off around us. It must have been less than a minute but it seemed so much longer. God, I hoped the table was bulletproof. But then, Brownswood was, in effect, shielding us.

Before I had had a chance to experience guilt at feeling relieved at her being so used, I saw two pairs of legs pass us. Both sets were in hideous orange and brown camouflage. I guessed they were the building security. Their bravery wasn't, it seemed, solely confined to their dress sense, but more importantly, that under continuous machine-gun fire, they were running towards the window. I presumed – I hoped – that they were going to shoot the fucking thing down. May their aim be good and the sight of those outfits confuse the drone's targeting systems. I wasn't sure how long our table could survive this onslaught.

They were out of my line of vision, but I heard rapid bursts of automatic gun fire from inside the building.

One of the security guards yelled in triumph, 'Yes! You little piece of tin shit. Got you!'

The firing into the room stopped.

'It's hit!' someone shouted.

Another, obviously peering out from where glass used to be, announced that it had just crashed onto the pavement below.

Some people cheered; others sobbed.

Like animals emerging after a storm, people started to crawl out from their hiding places. Many were crying, whilst others stood like zombies, silently looking at the wreckage. The attack had only lasted a few minutes, but the room was trashed. Furniture was splintered and cut to ribbons. Glass was everywhere. I looked over towards the sofa, which thankfully still looked untouched, to see it pushed aside, the wreckage above it sliding to the floor, and Victoria and Fiona Bailey appearing, apparently unharmed.

Getting out from under our table to join them, I helped Phan out after me. Neither of us spoke. If she was feeling anything like me, then her body would be as if some giant dentist had injected a large dose of anaesthetic into her body. I was numb and unable to speak. Despite the weather, I felt very cold.

This apparently wasn't the case with Vic, because, instantly, she took charge. Looking at one of the security detail, she asked, 'It's definitely been deactivated?'

He nodded silently. His joy having swiftly been replaced by horror at the extent of what had just happened.

She congratulated him, 'Good work, comrade!'

He didn't look like he was in the mood for celebrating.

Nor was Fiona Bailey, who was kneeling down by Brownswood and soundlessly sobbing.

Vic addressed the other people in the room. 'Comrades, we need to act quickly. We need to see who's been hurt. Get the first-aid. There must be some in the building of this size.' An elderly man being helped to his feet, answered that there was indeed, medical rooms. 'Good, let's get some of the casualties in there.' She pointed to another guard, who was staring out the glass-less window. 'You.' Then after receiving no reply, she raised her voice – 'You – contact the emergency services and tell them to get both ambulances and the militia here now!'

It had the desired effect and jerked him out of his shock, but as he did, he must have remembered who the person barking orders at him was. For a second, he paused. Vic was, after all, an interloper here, with no standing whatsoever. She might want to play the general, but she wasn't even in the same army. Seeing his hesitation, Bailey stepped in and told him to do as Cole had said. But before he could do so, a familiar voice spoke. 'No need. I've already contacted health emergency, they're on their way'. Marie Williams was standing by the lift.

Phan was now kneeling as if in prayer. She was by Sophia Brownswood. I joined her. I could see why she might have been doing that. There was nothing an ambulance could do for Brownswood. Half her head was missing.

# CHAPTER 13: AFTER THE HUNT

N ot wishing to either contaminate the scene nor get in the way of the emergency health workers, we had adjourned to the floor below the bar, which was usually used as a place for residents and visitors to obtain supplies. Resembling an indoor market, it contained a couple of dozen or so stalls, boasting a whole array of domestic goods which any person desiring a world built on cooperation might require in their daily lives. It was painfully apparent that that included a selection of easily accessible puns, of the variety which can usually only be found on seafront shops of coastal provincial towns. There was a fruit and veg section with the sign – *Lettuce Help You* and the one nearest to us – *Paws for Thought*, which was for pets, or as it put it, "Our non-human co-inhabitants".

The groans weren't from the postcard humour, but from the injured. Tables had been cleared to act as temporary hospital beds. Marie Williams had quickly divided up the victims of the attack according to the level of care which they required. The seriously injured had been taken straight to hospital. Those requiring minor medical attention, but who she deemed as being non-emergency were in the medical rooms, where she and other medically trained residents were with them. Those needing only plasters, sympathy and cups of sweet tea were here. The dead remained in the bar.

I stared at one of the building's vision enhancers, which were showing what was going on the streets below. Although a long way down, the sense of shock, anger and pain were clearly visible. No different from up here. Ambulances and fire engines stood swamped by a gathering crowd. News of the attack had travelled fast. Little over ninety minutes later, and there was a sizeable number of people surrounding the building.

They were here in solidarity, but even from twenty-five floors up, it was obvious that it wasn't that straight-forward. Amongst the workers and students, I glimpsed uniforms of the militia. They had been called to protect the building, but from what, and where, was sure to be an issue.

Circling the Shard, they were intended to control the situation, but the crowd pressing against them might well see their presence as being both an antagonistic and an anachronistic one of control. Many of those "being controlled" would regard the building as their home, their sanctuary, their base. Yet now they were being kept from it. It didn't look violent; people generally regarded the militia as sisters and brothers. But there would be tension. Tempers could easily start to fray. The militia would overwhelmingly consist of the party. Were *we* keeping *them*, from *their* building. It wouldn't be helped by the snatches of green I could see. Not, as in the politics, but as in khaki. Worryingly, soldiers were here. And like some fashion show for uniform outfitters, they were standing by figures in much brighter ones, from the London Trams. They had a depot nearby and had instantly responded to an emergency call. Even their presence wasn't that simple; sure, they'd be AF supporters amongst their ranks – as they'd be within the militia and army – but again, we would be the majority.

I looked sideways at Jackie Payne, who had arrived ten minutes earlier. She was standing erect, her back perfectly straight, arms folded across her white t-shirt, also watching the dance of the revolutionaries, below. 'This is going to have to be handled with sensitivity. Things could easily turn nasty – very easily.'

Now was the time for me to speak. The little pill I had taken ten minutes earlier, was beginning to work; I couldn't just stare at her, glassy eyed; I had to say something.

'Yeah,' I muttered.

It wasn't my most articulate statement. She looked at me with concern. 'You sure you're okay, Pete?'

On her arrival, she had given me a hug and warm words, and it looked very much like as if she was going to do so again. I had felt tears welling up when she had done it the first time and I wasn't sure I could hold out again. Crying my eyes out wasn't a good look for a Cribber. I forced out a reply, 'Looks pretty friendly, at the moment.'

'For how long, though?' she mused.

I wasn't sure if she was referring directly to the events occurring below or in the wider scheme of things, but I didn't ask her to clarify. I wanted to speak as little as possible. Then, I heard my name being called. Turning around, I saw that Victoria had finished her conversation with the building security. Seemed peace had been at least declared between them. A good shoot-out was obviously a useful bonding exercise. They had even returned our guns. With two pistols and a big smile, she said goodbye and walked over to us, tossing me mine and holstering her own.

'Was this the event they've long been threatening, I wonder?' Jackie asked.

I didn't have a chance to reply when one of the lift doors slid opened and Asher stepped out in all his forensic glory. Suited and booted up in his forensics, he headed towards us. Simultaneously, Roijin emerged from another lift. She wasn't alone. To my utter surprise, and it was obvious from Jackie's expression – hers too – she was followed by Noah Walker and a fully uniformed Reyansh Anand.

'What the hell are they doing here?' I asked.

This had put the pill into gear.

'Don't know,' Jackie admitted. I could tell from her voice that she was none too pleased to see them. Judging from the looks they exchanged, Roijin and Asher weren't either.

Several AF siblings had clocked their arrival, but were too busy with the aftermath of the attack to challenge them.

'Comrades!' beamed a cocky Noah Walker. We were now one heroic magnificent socialist seven. From his whole demeanour, you'd never have guessed that four people had just lost their lives and at least another seventeen were seriously, perhaps critically, injured.

Jackie was clearly in no mood for a big love-in. 'Can I ask what you're doing here?'

Her somewhat negative reaction upon seeing him, prompted only a slight change. He was still brimming with confidence, but there had been a small spillage. That was no surprise, no matter the size of one's self-admiration, there were few people who wouldn't take a step back when opposed by Jackie. 'Rey and me were at the Britain Today TV studios, which as you know, Jacks, aren't that far away.' Despite her look of daggers, he continued, 'We saw the NWC call for aid, and came straight here, to offer solidarity and offer support.'

Jackie's face grew sterner and clenched. 'I know where you were, and know only too well why you were there, but...' Her emphasis on the t of the but almost shook the building as much as the machine gunfire had. 'Your contribution can be discussed at a later time. Do you honestly think for one minute, that you might be of help?'

I thought I could detect another slight drop in his cockiness level. But it was only a minute one – like evaporation off a puddle on a warmish day. He shrugged. 'As the late and much missed Mike Stewart once said, "When the forces of reaction strike, we must lay our differences aside and fight as one".'

Never had a quote, which had the perceived intention of support, sound so scathing and belittling. He believed that as much as I did in Santa. Less so, probably.

Jackie was still far from satisfied. Anger was now so close to the surface, it was about to emerge like a bull shark, baring its teeth. You didn't often see her lose her cool, but when she did, it was best to take cover. A nuclear bunker was usually what was required. An awful mixed metaphor, but in regard to Jackie's temper, you needed as much figurative language as you could marshal. Not that she shouted; she didn't need to. Speaking with barely concealed annoyance, she hissed, 'Your animosity to the AF is well-known. This is a delicate situation, which we need to handle with the utmost care. The party turning up mob-handed – *with unformed soldiers, for heaven's sake* – will only make matters worse!'

Hearing the reference to the army, prompted Anand to speak for the first time. 'Sorry, Jackie, but they were with me at the studio and I thought if they came here, they might be of help. I did what I thought was best. After all, it was a military attack.'

Young comrade Anand here, might think that putting on a soothing tone would mollify her, but I knew better. Walker might think standing legs apart and oozing bravado might be a useful counter, but again, I knew better. Jackie and I went way back. I knew that neither sweetness nor machismo won an argument with her. Only logic and politics did. Walker had poured the petrol on the floor and Anand had just lit a match.

Her eyes blazed. 'Why the hell you were in uniform at the debate I have no idea – wearing the uniform in a civilian environment is prohibited. It was the wrong move and politically naive at best – provocative at worse. As for bringing a delegation from your barracks – in full uniform – to the studio, that was dangerously stupid. Bringing them here was – *comrade* – verging on anti-revolutionary behaviour. Let me remind you, comrade, that it clearly states that "uniformed military will not be allowed on the streets and will not be under the command of officers – including elected officers – unless directly ordered to be so by the NWC Executive". Did you get that order, comrade?'

'No, Jackie...'

'Comrade President, please!' she snapped.

I swear his back straightened and he was almost standing at attention. 'Apologies, Comrade President. No, it's true that we didn't, but...'

'I thought not. In which case, I want you, and your soldier comrades, to get away from here immediately, and return to your barracks.'

It looked as if he was about to argue, but a shake of Walker's head indicated that it was unwise to do so; unwise, as in bloody suicidal. He was no doubt brave, but he wasn't stupid. He nodded and marched over to the lifts. We Crib had just been spectators so far, but if we thought it was time to speak, we were mistaken. Comrade President hadn't finished just yet.

'And I would have expected more from you, Noah. You have every right to express your views, but you also have responsibilities, which you need to honour. Discipline, comrade, is sometimes called for.'

He wasn't one to be easily cowed. His haughtiness might be slightly less than what it had been, when he had first arrived, but he wasn't a wilting flower just yet. 'Frankly, I think you're rather over-reacting, Jacks...comrade president. Reyansh came here to offer assistance. I mean, two of his squad are AF members. What were we supposed to do? Just sit on our hands?'

Her lips pursed. 'To be honest, that would have been preferable. Look, Noah, I know that you're worried about the situation. We've discussed that, but as I've told you before, we need to be careful with both our rhetoric, and our actions. If new laws are required, then we will patiently explain why, and win people over. Abusing them, denouncing them as liberals, counter-revolutionaries, won't do that. They are not our enemies. Start using your brain!'

He shook his head. 'But their ultra-leftism leaves us exposed. The right-wing cabal hanging out in America are growing in confidence. As I always say – "Those who make revolutions by halves do nothing but dig their own tombs".'

I rolled my eyes on hearing the much-used quote from the eighteenth century French revolutionary, Louis Antoine de Saint-Just, which Walker had just requisitioned.

On he went: 'Look around you, Jackie, they've organised a drone attack in broad daylight. Yet, this lot want us disarmed and hand out flowers. Well, we're not in utopia just yet. This is the dictatorship of the proletariat and dictate we might well have to. If the AF succeed in taking the revolution forward too quickly, it will leave us open to counter-revolution. In that case, de-facto, they're our enemies.'

This was all fascinating, and an important discussion, but these two having a political fisticuff wasn't appropriate here – now wasn't the time. Not in the middle of people who had just had their arses shot at. 'Comrades, should we be discussing this here?' I nodded to the security detail, who were taking a keen interest in their argument.

Jackie agreed. 'Pete is right. Crib have my full confidence to deal with this. Their presence is useful. Yours is not. Now please leave.'

He was about to argue, but before he could make another lofty bout of verbiage, Jackie turned to the security. 'Siblings, would you be kind enough to escort comrade Walker out of the building. Make sure he's safe, and doesn't get lost.'

His jaw dropped. Frankly, so did mine. The beefcakes didn't need asking twice, and led him to the lift before he had a chance to say another word. Each one wore an amused smirk.

As the lift closed, so did Jackie's eyes and she sighed heavily. After collecting her thoughts for a second or two, she asked for a quick resumé. 'Could one of you briefly tell me what is happening and what you are going to do about it. And I emphasise the word *briefly* because I need to travel up to Manchester, to speak at the NWC, as soon as possible. I don't need to tell you that this is turning into one hell of a nightmare.'

Victoria nodded. 'Okay. At 11.05am a drone opened fire on the main bar of the Shard. The drone had been one of the building's security, but its systems had been hacked. The attack lasted less than two minutes and resulted in four people being killed: Sofia Brownswood, Thom Simons, Mohammed Aydin and Bruce Jenkins. Brownswood was a leading...'

Jackie cut her short. 'I don't need the details, give me just the outline. When you report to the NWC, I'll see them, then.'

Vic didn't argue, and kept it concise: 'Our initial theory, and it's only a theory, is that a defence drone was hacked into, which took it out of the control of the Shard's defence technicians. The whole defence system had been accessed, with the other drones disabled. That meant that the attack drone was able to fire without opposition.'

Vic turned to Roijin to continue, who took a step forward, like a Year 4 child at an assembly. 'That, in itself, tells us something, Jackie. I've only had a chance to have the briefest of looks, but from what I can see, it would have to have been a very sophisticated operation, done by a pro. We've cordoned off what's left of the drone so I can have a good look at it.'

'Okay. So, Ash has been looking at the bodies. Jackie, do you need him to say anything?'

She again shook her head, muttering, 'I think we can assume that this isn't a supposed allergic reaction. So, no, I don't need to know.'

Poor Ash, his big moment lost. He did look a little crestfallen, but Vic didn't get a violin out. 'Me and Pete, with some of the militia, have been taking statements, and Roij has been feeding them into a simulation unit. They don't film their debates here because they believe it infringes on their freedom, but this'll be just as good. We're doing as much as we can, but we're having to tread carefully.'

She nodded understanding. 'So, with regard to "treading carefully", how's that going?'

Victoria frowned. 'Well, they're having a meeting right this minute, to discuss our presence here, and whether to chuck us out or not.'

For the first time in a while, I spoke, with the help of the pharmaceuticals. 'Ah, the new world of law and order – endless meetings and motions. Less arraignments and more amendments, politics not precedents.'

No-one fell about laughing or stood in awe of my profundity. It hadn't been one of my best. Instead, Jackie looked at me, and simply said, 'I think law enforcement has always had a political element to it and has always involved meetings. Usually behind closed doors. I should speak at it,' she said.

'Do you think that's wise?' I said, feeling chemically unabashed. 'You could stir up even more trouble. You may be more popular with the AF rank and file than Walker (but then I'm hard pressed to think of anyone who isn't), but you're still not the belle of the ball.'

'That's as maybe, but I think I should.'

She had a point – for the president to arrive at the scene of a terrorist outrage and not say anything to the victims would look appalling. Both heartless and uncaring. 'Let's do some groundwork, see if we can have you introduced.'

'Agreed. What do you suggest, Pete?'

'Fiona Bailey's still here. She's actually been a great help in coordinating things and easing cooperation between the AF and us. I think, if we asked her, she'd talk to the meeting, and ask its permission to allow myself and you to address it. Technically, of course, that's not required, but it would give off the right signal. I'd tell them what we have been doing and what we'd like to do. That would include our investigations into the death of Mike Stewart. I could take the opportunity to formally announce that it is a murder enquiry. Then you'd speak.'

Jackie theatrically sighed. 'Good Lord, what strange times we live in – Pete Kalder talks of diplomacy.' A slight smile appeared. She looked at the other three. 'What do you think?'

Asher answered first: 'I think it's a sound idea.'

Roijin and Victoria agreed. Then a strange expression crossed Victoria's face. She spoke in a serious voice. Not that she'd been cracking jokes before, but she sounded even more determined and resolute. 'If we're to be believed that we have no hidden agenda, then we shouldn't have one. Pete should be completely honest and open about our investigation. There needs to be total transparency. Pete, you answer to the best of your ability any question they ask.'

I concurred, although I wasn't sure about what the "best of your ability" meant. But Victoria had something more important to say: 'That includes you, Jackie. You need to be totally transparent. And *that* includes whatever you knew that made you so sure that Mike Stewart had been murdered. They've lost friends, so they deserve to be levelled with. In any case, they're not stupid. I may have serious disagreements with the AF, but I've always found them to be committed and astute people.'

Nothing was said for a moment or two. Jackie just held her chin in her right hand, proving if nothing else, that her purple lipstick was non-smudge and that her fingernails matched it nicely. We just waited for answer.

'I think you're right, Vic. Let's talk to Fiona and see if we can address this meeting.' Then with a chuckle, added, 'And watch Pete be "diplomatic".'

# CHAPTER 14:
# THE POLITICAL ARGUMENT

F iona had agreed and was addressing the meeting, whilst we lingered outside. She hadn't held out much hope that it would be of any use. The expression on her face was one you might expect to see from a woman stepping into a lion's cage – a lion that hadn't had a decent meal in weeks – with said woman attired in a piece of red meat. Not the most appropriate of comparisons, considering the veggie composition of the meeting.

After five minutes, Jackie indicated that we should go in. I went first, full of fake confidence. My heart resembled a hummingbird's wings. It was a full meeting, with not many spaces available. I went up one of the aisles, looking for a seat, attracting a few glances, whispers, and awkward looks. At the front stood a middle-aged woman, dressed in overalls. Presumably, she was chairing the meeting and not here to fix a pipe. In front of her, Fiona was talking. A friendly face caught my attention and Phan Bien beckoned me over, pointing to an empty seat next to her. I wondered if that said something about the party's popularity in this part of town. She smiled, sending tiny, but raw, shrapnel cuts sliding diagonally across her face. Cupping her hand to shield her mouth, she whispered, 'Fiona's just been paying tribute to those killed, giving obituaries are coming a bit of a habit.'

Like wind crossing a field of corn – not that being a city boy, I'd ever seen such a thing – a hush spread around the room. I turned to see the cause. Not that I needed to. Jackie was at the back, politely asking an elderly man if the seat next to him was taken. Finding that it was free, she sat down. Half the room were openly staring at her, and the other half were pretending that they weren't.

Phan looked at her, and then me, open-mouthed. Now it was my turn to use my hand as a sound muffler, and spoke as quietly as I could, telling her what we hoped was going to happen. She shook her head in disbelief, saying only – 'Good Luck.'

Then Fiona got to the crux of her speech, that Crib should have full access to the Shard. No-one heckled but there was a lot of moving from one buttock cheek to another. Their discomfort wasn't from the chairs, which were actually rather comfy. The majority of the AF were in favour of working with us. But there were limits. She emphasised that it would only be for a short time, but those arses on those seats weren't reassured, and we risked an epidemic of haemorrhoids. Then it got even more uncomfortable. 'That's why I'm requesting that we welcome Pete Kalder and...er...Jackie Payne.'

Jackie seemed to be unmoved as she received looks ranging from the frosty to the Siberian. In return, she tilted her head and smiled. Several of the audience even shouted out comments. None could be construed as chants of support. Fiona ignored them and continued with her proposal. After a few minutes, it was plainly obvious that whilst there were many in the room who agreed with her, there were also many who didn't. Some being very vocal in their opposition. It seemed that a quiet respect for the fallen didn't last too long, here. As we had feared, the arrival of the army had angered a lot of people, and both Anand and Walker were both name-checked. It wasn't from a place of love.

Phan leant across and whispered, 'If it goes to a vote, it'll be lost. Fiona's always been a superb speaker, but she's barely making sense here. Just recently, she's really lost it. Not surprising I suppose, considering what she's been through, but the fact is, there's no way the vote will be won. Do you want me to speak again?'

She was right, Fiona had been as effective as jelly scaffolding. I looked down at Phan's rucksack by my right foot. 'Open your bag,' I murmured. She frowned, but did as I asked. I slid my hand into my inside pocket, palmed the gun out and slipped it in. Phan looked astonished, which wasn't surprising – she was used to arguing politics, not hiding firearms.

I stood up and walked towards Fiona. She hadn't expected that. The idea had been for me to wait for the vote, but we couldn't risk it. She paused, but did not say anything. I gave her a warm hug and thanked her loudly. Then turned around and faced the meeting.

I didn't focus on a particular face or concern myself with what they might be feeling, I just moved my head, attempting to visually connect with as many people as possible. In my best humble but assertive voice, I spoke: 'It's an honour to be here, although obviously I would have preferred to be so in less dramatic and tragic circumstances. But I can honestly say that I'm pleased to be here. Just over two hours ago I thought I wouldn't be. Not breathing anyway. That I am, is down to Miguel and Dom, who you'll all know are two of the security here. They, under a shower of bullets, heroically ran towards the drone, and shot it down.'

'Whilst you hid under the table!' yelled a familiar voice. Dave Donaldson was standing, in full sneer. 'Typical of your lot. Hide and let others do the work, until it's safe to make the speeches.'

I smiled, and not just at the sight of the ridiculous skin-tight t-shirt he was wearing, which had last been washed in 1997. I wanted to avoid conflict but not so, Phan, who leapt to her feet, angrily replying, 'Yeah, he did, mate. It was Pete who had dragged me under the table and saved my life. Where were you there, DD?' He didn't answer. 'No. Probably home in bed, in your jim-jams, whilst we were being shot at. What else was Pete going to do? He was unarmed, for Christ's sake!'

With a bashful smile, I unbuttoned my jacket, to show the empty holster. Noticing that the jacket had red silk lining, I improvised – nodding towards it. 'As you can see, friends, we party hacks aren't allowed to hide our politics.' That received some chuckling. I'd hoped for more, but I guess that four deaths made for a tough crowd. 'And I should add, Dave, that my colleague and comrade Victoria Cole was also hiding. She likes a bit of luxury though, she was under a sofa.' Fiona had forgotten to mention her, probably thinking that a reference to an ex-cop wasn't wise. She was probably right, but you might as well be hung for a sheep as a lamb. 'I think you'd agree, Fiona, that you would have been killed if it hadn't been for her leaping at you and dragging you under it.'

Fiona nodded.

DD wasn't beaten just yet. 'Okay, so fair dues to you both. As it happens then, you did the right thing, but the fact remains, that you're now manipulating the situation for your own benefit. You've flooded the Shard with your comrades, ringed it with militia, keeping us all inside and preventing people from entering. It must be a dream come true for you. Taking over this building. As it happens, this 'unit' of Kalder's consists of only his party. The militia is 75% them. We've even had the army here. And now Payne arrives to lecture us, no doubt to lead us naughty boys and girls onto the right path. They do this in the name of our security, but it isn't. If we allow this, then what comes next? Big round-ups and arrests for "our security"? Maybe we should feel honoured that woman has left her limo and is slumming it with us poor folks!'

It had been quite a rant. Spittle was dribbling down his purple beard. He had received some applause, but he had made a mistake. Passion is a good thing, but there's a time and a place for it, and he had overdone it. Phan was about to explode, but I gave her a look to leave it to me. She played an important role here and shouldn't risk alienating anyone. As for me, I might never come here again. Certainly not to have a cup of tea with DD. She understood and forced herself to sit down. Out of the corner of my eye, I could see Jackie coolly watching the proceedings. Her attention was now focussed on me. It was my move.

Dave Donaldson was still on his feet and sweating profusely. He looked directly at me, and sneered 'Well?'.

Jackie's mouth twitched into what could possibly be an affectionate smile. She knew me well. She'd seen me at my best and at my worst. And she knew that very few people intimidated me. True, if they were holding a gun, then that often did the trick, but certainly not someone in a meeting. I never got brow-beaten. It only spurred me on. In my time, I'd had run-ins with most of the leaders of the party – certainly in the years with Jackie herself, and even with the 'Old Man', the founder of our organisation. Now retired, but in his day, was one of the most formidable of speakers. He would have had Donaldson for breakfast, and then asked for more toast.

I spoke in my softest, most gentle voice. What I was intending to say would create its own volume. I framed my opening sentence as a question: 'If I may answer your questions and concerns?' I stopped and looked at him. So, did the room. It was his choice now – harangue me or sit down. He chose the latter. I started slowly, once more agreeing that what had just happened had been a cowardly crime and a tragedy. The loss of life was appalling. I also agreed that it was far from ideal that there were so many party members here, but with a shrug, I explained that the situation was what it was. We would not have planned to be in the room during the attack. 'Surely, that shows that whatever our differences, we face the same enemy?' I did not wait for a reply because, it was time for a quick barb before I went on. I had shown that I was a kitten, but I also had sharp claws. 'It is a stressful time for all of us. And that's why you called Jackie Payne "that woman". I think in calmer situations you'd never have made such a sexist remark.' Nodding heads greeted that, but I did not pursue the matter. 'We find ourselves in a challenging period. I know that many of you have profound disagreements with the party, and with Jackie. But she doesn't come here as the president of the United Revolutionary Isles of Britain but as a life-long fighter, offering support and solidarity. You're wrong to think she avoids a fight. Let's not forget that she was imprisoned and tortured under the old regime. She's been arrested and personally attacked, probably more times than anyone in this room. How hard do you think it is to be a black woman at the front of the movement? You may say that is all limos now – though I don't actually think that's her style – but what do you think it was like when she was in a tiny organisation confronting arch-racists and fascists on the streets? Did she lack courage then?'

Donaldson gave me a scoffing look but it was noticeable now was how many of the audience were nodding. The people here were sincere revolutionaries who didn't go for simplistic sectarian abuse. 'And, siblings,' I smiled, as if sharing a joke. 'About our unit, yes, we're all party members. (And yes, by the way, Crib is a crass name.)' A few chuckled.

'However, other Cribs are not. I believe that Luton's Crib 19, is actually all AF.' I looked at Jackie, who nodded. 'But that's not by design. We didn't know this was going to happen. If we had, I would have made sure to find a better hiding place than a bloody table!' There were a few more chuckles. 'Yes, there's ex-police officers in our unit, but we're answerable to the NWC and to a Community Information Meeting for any case which we're investigating. And, siblings, do you think I've been a party member for over forty years, just so I could work with ex-cops? I can tell you, that was never my heroic dream. Storming the barricades maybe, but grubbing around after reactionary terrorists? Nah. If you want to know me and my personal history, well, it's splattered all over the internet. You'll see I'm no apparatchik. I don't blithely follow orders.' Despite telling them that they could find out all about me online, I proceeded to give them a personal potted history in any case. I wanted them to see me as a human, and not just as a functionary.

Now it was time to get to the point. 'We were asked by Fiona Bailey to look into the death of Mike Stewart. To be honest, it looked for a long time that it was simply an appalling accident. That is until this morning, when we found a chemical compound in his body. It's alien to the human body and it's used to accelerate a mixture which was injected into him. This mixture contains almond and was there to make it look like a severe allergic reaction. Fiona was right – Mike Stewart was murdered. Let me repeat, and I'm saying this officially – that Mike Stewart was killed. And we can prove it. Feel free to get any expert from any organisation you like, to verify that.'

Shock waves went through the room. It had been rumoured on the internet but now it was official. 'It's now a murder enquiry. Frankly, it doesn't matter who is running it, but it needs to be done. Then just an hour or two after such an enquiry is launched, this attack happens. Coincidence? I presume, Dave, you don't think we are to blame for both?'

He moved awkwardly in his seat, but didn't say anything.

'That said, something is odd about this attack. Your defence systems here were hacked. Someone managed to get through your security protocols, which Roijin, our ICT expert –' I rolled my eyes in a comic what-can-you-do expression. 'And yes, another ex-cop.' A few smiled. 'Assures me that it wouldn't have been easy. From what she's seen, and it's only been a cursory look, because we want your permission to continue, whoever did it, knew exactly what they were doing, suggesting a familiarity with it.'

That gave Donaldson something to say. 'So now you're accusing one of us for this? See what I mean, siblings! See their game?' A few heckled, agreeing with him.

Still in soft mode, I responded, 'It goes without saying that any such investigation would be under the strict supervision and observance of AF members. That could include you, Dave – if you're interested.'

That took him by surprise. But he didn't answer, which I had guessed would be the reaction. I drew to the close. 'So yes, we're asking for permission to investigate what has happened here. The NWC rules state that if deemed necessary by the local workers' council, a Community Information Meeting must be organised to help oversee the investigation and assist it – we're suggesting that this forum takes on that role.' After many years, arguably far too many, of being in meetings, you develop a radar for the mood of one. My radar was buzzing that the tide had turned.

I paused and looked at the woman, who'd been doing a rather flimsy job of chairing the meeting. She coughed and asked if there was anyone who wanted to speak again. To my surprise there wasn't. Even DD felt that he had said enough. The vote was taken. We won a narrow victory. We were in.

I thanked them and asked if a similar vote could be taken to allow Jackie to speak. I laughed. It was a false laugh, but I was still in self-facing mode, and said the intention as Fiona had indicated, was that I too was to ask permission to speak. 'That's obviously too late now. Sorry, friends. Maybe it's the company I'm keeping.'

Another vote. Another victory, but by a larger majority. Jackie was to address the meeting. She rose to her feet and walked down to the front. I returned to my seat and discreetly reclaimed my gun.

Jackie began by thanking the meeting and talking about those who had been murdered. She talked with respect and some affection as she recounted the numerous times she had crossed swords with Sofia Brownswood. She wasn't going to patronise people by pretending that they were friends. 'We were, though, two strong sisters fighting for a better world!' That received applause although DD kept his hands firmly in his lap. She then moved onto the political situation as she saw it and how the NWC was proposing to deal with it. It was then that she said something which got everyone sitting upright. Including yours truly.

'In this cyberwar we have had some successes, we have managed to hack into a phone we took off one of their agents and although we can only decode a small percentage of what's being sent, we did find an underlying electronic tag to their messages. It was explained to me, and I'm sorry but I lag well behind technological innovation, so things do need to be explained as simply as possible...' Some of the room laughed. 'That it's like a verification code, assuring the receiver, that it's legit. It's like an electronic ID. We picked up a lot of e-traffic on social media, with references to Mike Stewart. None of them were outwardly suspicious, some were just conversations. However, several of them had this tag imbedded in them. Two days later, Mike Stewart dies in a supposed "natural way".'

DD jumped to his feet. 'So, you're saying that you knew he was at risk but did nothing!'

Murmuring spread around the room, as all eyes stared at Jackie, waiting for her to say something. I myself was keen to hear the reply.

She remained unflustered. 'We had no idea what it meant. Superficially, all the messages were innocuous, and we haven't worked out what the tag is, or what it says – if indeed, it says anything. Let's be honest here, you yourself, Dave, have been highly critical of us, accusing us of exaggerating security threats for our own purposes. I remember that in a recent online debate, you used a rather clever, if insulting phrase, that I was, "using the deaths of revolutionaries to clothe myself as the gravedigger of the revolution". Indeed, you also accused Pete of being just that only a few minutes ago. Without solid evidence and an explanation of what we'd found, we risked being charged with scaremongering, of doing exactly what you accuse us of. I mean, siblings – what could we actually say? That attached to some messages about the rights of eating plants, there was some electronic bleeps? If we had, you'd have crucified us, and we'd have alerted our enemies that we had this fraction of a lead. We always intended to go public as soon as we could.'

'So why tell us now?' he snarled.

She met his aggression with a placid smile. 'I don't think we have a choice now, comrade. As Fiona said in her speech, we need to forget our differences and unite. Otherwise, the revolution will be buried. And we will all be in the coffins. The enemies of our movement won't give a toss of a coin whether we are Trotskyist, Anarchists, Anarcho-Greens, Trotskyist-Greens, Popular-liberalists, freedom warriors, Syndicalist or whatever. To them, we're all the same – we're all reds – who they will do their best, and that will be their most murderous best, to see dead.'

# CHAPTER 15:
# TWO BOYS BEFORE AN EASEL

S itting next to Asher Joseph on a two-person plaid sofa, which recently had enjoyed a radical redesign from a spray of bullets. Forensics had finished with the bar and we were waiting for Roijin to finish the final touches to her virtual rerun. A gentle and very pleasant breeze drifted through the shattered windows. Not so pleasing were the multiple pools of blood which were across the floor. Most had dried in the stifling heat but there was enough to satisfy a number of flies which had been drawn to them. The metal of spent bullets, half buried into the walls, the floor and the furniture, glistened in the sunlight. I wasn't aware of any smell, other than the stench of spilt alcohol. The room was like an alcoholic's sodden-dream, the carpet soaked and the walls splattered with the stuff. But whatever the reason, there was no death or pain filling my nostrils. Hot metal and torn flesh had been overwhelmed by the booze. If any of it combined to make a USURP Slurp, they'd have a terrible time removing it from the furnishings. It might even be combustible. It pretty much had that effect on me. Whether that held any deeper meaning, I couldn't say. Such things were for the poets, and I've never been one of those.

In front of me, Victoria was standing legs apart and offering encouragement and unasked-for suggestions. I had just arrived from the meeting and was still trying mentally to process what had so recently happened.

Asher looked at me and smiled. 'You seen one of these before?'

I shook my head.

'It's pretty surreal when you first see it. Avatars acting and moving, looking like the people involved, reliving their final moments. It's especially unnerving if you happen to be one of them. To go through it again by watching yourself must be an odd experience. It's never happened to me, but we'll see both you and Vic in all your glory here.'

'Nothing surprises me at the moment. I've just come from a public meeting, where a key bit of evidence was announced, before notifying the actual people investigating the crime.'

Asher shot me a quizzical look. Both Roijin and Victoria turned around and stared at me. 'What do you mean?' the latter demanded.

I told them what Jackie had said about the electronic tagging.

'Why didn't she tell us?' Vic demanded. Obviously angry that it had confirmed her suspicion that Jackie knew more than she had been telling us, which was why she had been so sure that Mike Stewart's death was not from natural causes.

I shrugged. I had no idea. It made no sense to me.

'And she announced this at the meeting? In front of *them*?' The second explosion in this room, in a matter of hours occurred. She erupted with profanities and rage ricocheting around the room. If they had been physical entities, there would have been even greater damage than what the drone had so recently managed. Nobody said a word. I'd never seen her like this. Usually, she was as refrigerator cool, but this was hot rage. Finally, with her face now a deep shade of pink, she all but hissed, 'Has *she* gone?'

Fearing that Victoria might search her out and lamp Jackie, I felt like lying. But I didn't. 'No,' I admitted. 'She's still here. I left her debating future environmental policies. I think she's rather enjoying herself. Nowadays, she spends less time out with people and more running the country, so this is like a return to the old days.'

'I'm glad to hear it,' Vic said between closed lips. 'Maybe she could later entertain herself by talking to us about what else she knows?'

It was a question that I didn't really have an answer for. 'Well, Vic, I agree that would be a good idea, but I doubt it. She's missed one train already. Whether she likes it or not, someone will go in there and drag her out. Otherwise, she'll be in there for days.' Or thumped by Vic, I silently said to myself.

She didn't respond. Her jaws were firmly set, and I could see that beneath her lips her tongue was going over her teeth. Pure rage was running through her like an electric current. Alternative energy was one of the key topics of the moment; if we could tap into what was convulsing Victoria, then that would be one issue solved.

Ostensibly addressing me, but in reality, allowing Victoria time to cool off, Roijin proceeded to explain that the data we had collected would be used to create the avatars. And, we were pretty much ready to run. We could stop, rerun, or even focus on a detail, at any time we wished. She paused, but nobody said a word. Asher and I were simply waiting for the show to begin. Victoria was still fighting a temptation to get herself a drone and murder a few people; quite possibly starting with a certain workers' president.

Asher gave an almost imperceptible nod of his head, to Roijin. She took the signal. A 3D image of a machine, looking like a toy aircraft, appeared in front of us. It was about the length of small car. 'This is the type of drone which was used in the attack. It's a Krac 987BX, Polish/American design. Used in several countries by their military. Including ours. During the Civil War, it was given to the AF by troops loyal to the movement.' She moved closer and pointed to its nose. 'It's loaded with two Ognia machine guns. Top of the range, heavy duty fire-power. It also has two Dart sniper guns, meant for more accurate assassination assignments. The military one also carries four Thor pocket missiles, but this one had had them removed. As for control, it can be programmed to act on its own, using either facial recognition, or by using its AI to evaluate what is the best course of action. Or it can be controlled old school – manually.'

'Any ideas which it was in this case?' I asked.

Roijin thought for a second. 'Not as of yet,' she replied. 'I hope to have in the near future. I think if we run through the sequence of events, it might. And also, to guess what its purpose was. I mean, was it simply to kill as many people as possible, or was someone – or some people – targeted?' She paused. 'Okay, it begins when you two arrive. The norm with these things is to have the first take to be in real time speed. So...'

The drone disappeared, taking its virtual position outside, ready for the performance. Then it got all weird. Suddenly, the room was reconstructed, tidied up and populated by people positioned at the moment when the lift doors opened, and Vic and I walked out. It looked spookily realistic. Like I was watching a film of myself, but the film was real and I, the viewer, was the replica. As it began, I felt a melange of feelings: intrigued to see what it would be like; a touch of excitement because of it; vanity, to see myself in the centre of things but also, I had to admit – a great deal of trepidation.

In the recon we walk towards the man I had been told was Thom Simons. Slightly behind him, Sofia Brownswood and Phan Bien are having a blazing row. It was happening as I remembered. Phan breaks away and heads for us, Brownswood follows her, shouting. It is then, I notice something which I hadn't at the time, Simons turns and goes to join them. As he does, he's stroking his ponytail.

The windows shatter when the first shot is heard. In real-time, no-one had appeared to be hurt, but now you can see that Brownswood has been hit. Her chair hovers for a second, then wisps of smoke appear from its rear, before it drops like a stone to the floor. A second shot hits the table, worryingly close to both Phan and myself. Being the nearest to Phan. I grab her and pull her under the table.

Victoria runs past at the same time, tackling Fiona Bailey around the waist, and in one movement pulls her to the sofa and onto the floor She pulls the sofa down over them. Being slightly larger than the one we are presently sitting on, it completely hides them. Watching it again, I'm rather impressed with Vic's agility.

In obvious pain, and with her chair unstable, Brownswood shakily moves off the ground. Simultaneously, another shot rings out, it hits her in the top of her back. Exiting at an angle, it hits Thom Simons on his right side. This I hadn't seen before. She crashes into our table. He falls, arms outstretched, behind her.

More single shots ring out. More than I remembered. She is hit twice more. He, once more in his neck. One further shot hits a tall, slim Asian guy, who appears to have also been running towards our table, presumably in a bid for cover.

The two guards could now be seen running out of one of the lifts. Their guns aimed towards the smashed windows. They run forwards. It was then that the rate of firing increases. Holes pepper around us. Without any apparent concern for their safety, the guards manage to reach the edge of the room, and fire back. The drone continues firing for several seconds until eventually it explodes.

Then the recon stopped.

I had the distinct feeling that if I hadn't popped one of my blue pills straight after experiencing this for the first time, then doing so for the second, would have played all kind of havoc with my bodily functions. Dr Brakus would have a fit if she found out, but hey, if you couldn't self-medicate after a deadly drone attack, when could you?

'Comments?' Roijin asked.

My mouth opened and I spoke before I had activated my brain. 'Judging from that, I've lost weight.'

Roijin and Asher laughed, which seemed to break Vic from her anger mismanagement trance, and after a brief look of disapproval, joined in with a reluctant chuckle. For the first time in quite a while, she spoke. 'Good work, Roij. Could you play it again? Only at half speed. And I think we should walk around to see if anything looks strange.'

'Strange? Strange, apart from being raked by bullets in a bar high above the Thames?' I said. How strange did she want?

'Yeah, apart from that.' She smiled.

So once more we took a stroll down murder lane. In slow-mo on it went, the first shot, we could now see entered Brownswood on the top of her spine, and judging from the bits of her chair splintering outwards, imbeds itself into her chair. Then almost at the same time comes Phan and my dive under the table, and Vic's lunge at Fiona. Sofia Brownswood attempts to get mobile again, but gets hit by a bullet. Impressively, or disturbingly – choose the adjective – the reconstruction included the bullet entering her body and blood spraying outwards. Then, after hitting what I guessed was her ribcage, it exits at an acute angle. It is this freak event, which makes it change direction and hit Simons. She collides with the table, and stops with arms spread in an almost crucifixion pose. She is hit twice more, once in her right and then once in her left shoulder.

At that point, Victoria asked for it to be frozen. Looking closely at Brownswood's avatar, and the direction of the shots, she spoke in a tone, which I had learnt was her professional voice. 'Pete, what do we know about her?'

The question took me by surprise. The attack had been barely three hours ago, and I had been in a meeting for much of it. I did my best. 'Er, well, Sofia Brownswood was twenty-six years old. She was high profile and well known, and I should say, a highly respected revolutionary. She lost the use of her legs when she was sixteen, demonstrating against building on the Green Belt when a bulldozer ran her over, crushing them. She received a living allowance from the AF, which allowed her to be full-time. She was known as someone who wasn't afraid to put herself at risk for her principles. As was the case with the loss of her legs.

'She was imprisoned in the Big Crack Down and by all accounts, was harshly treated.' I paused. The three looked at me with questioning eyes. Perhaps they were waiting for a sarcastic comment about what they were doing eight years ago, and who they'd been beating up. After all, they had been serving police officers then. But whether from a growing maturity, or the meds, or simply that I was really just one big puppy dog, I didn't. I wasn't thinking about them; I was thinking about a far more important subject – me. I had been caught up in the sweep. I had been lucky when they'd banged me up, being one of the last to do so, and the movement had been of such a size that it had soon forced Parliament to release all detainees. Also, they had been pretty okay with me. The odd punch and push, but not much more. Not like the treatment Jackie had endured. Or indeed Sofia. 'They took her chair and forced her to crawl – and a lot more. It wasn't pretty.'

Asher gave a look which I assumed was one of sympathy, but equally it could have been from indigestion.

I continued, 'Not that that got anywhere close to breaking her will. She was a revolutionary to her core. No fan of ours, mind. She felt that we're too statist, and as such, are holding the revolution back, preventing it from reaching its full potential. If she had been in the meeting earlier, she would have vigorously backed Dave Donaldson in opposing our involvement. She would have hated it. In her time, she had repeatedly clashed with Mike Stewart over their relationship with us, considering him far too soft.'

Vic nodded and quietly thanked me. 'Ash – anything to add?'

It turned out that he had as little as me to say. 'I've only had time to perform the briefest of examinations. I mean, there are four bodies, so I haven't been able to open them up. Also, I have not had time to have them removed to the lab for more extensive tests. All I had on me was my carry-kit, although luckily it does have two mobile scanners.'

"Open them up" – what a charming and delightful phrase. He had a way with words did Asher. And many of them were being utilised to explain away why he had found out very little. 'Sofia Brownswood was the first person hit by the attack. She was struck by a Dart XV3 bullet, averaging a speed of 3000 kph. It entered through her left shoulder, smashing her shoulder blade – then miraculously missing all her vital organs – exited through the left armpit. In itself, it was not fatal. Or as insensitive as it might sound, that serious. If that's all it had been, then she might even have been able to make her own way to hospital. It was the following bullet, also a Dart XV3, which proved fatal. By the time she was hit in her shoulders, she was already dead.'

Victoria had heard enough for the moment. 'Okay, thanks, Ash. Roijin, could you run the last few seconds again.'

Even in slow motion, in that short amount of time, we witnessed Thom Simons being hit in the back, followed shortly afterwards, by Mohammed Aydin. Roijin stopped it.

I was getting the hang of this game. We watched the grisly movie, then I gave a short political profile. I duly obliged. 'Thom Simons. Twenty-three years old. Been a member of the unaligned movement for two years, came fairly late to the cause. I don't know what attracted him to them. He's a social worker in Brent – *was* a social worker – something to do with family support. Politically, he involved himself in local health and community initiatives. I didn't know him at all. He wasn't that high profile. From what I can gather, he pretty much agreed with Mike Stewart's outlook, being relaxed about working with us.' I stopped. The sad thing was that those few sentences were the sum total of what I had to say about him. I looked at Asher. Your turn, mate.

'One shot, another Dart XV3 bullet, enters through his back, smashing the T4 vertebra, then ricocheting around, and exits via his heart, exiting through the vena pulmonar, bursting it apart like an arrow through a watermelon. Death was instant. One more bullet hit him, through his skull, as he lay on the floor. Aydin is hit two seconds later, again through the back, the C7 vertebra to be precise, again the direction of the bullet is deflected, and it exits through his left lung. He survives this, but it's the head hit, which kills him instantly. It enters through the occipital bone and exits out through his mouth. Again, they were Dart XV3 calibre bullets.'

No-one said anything as we gazed at the macabre scene in front of us. It was like the worst slasher movie you could imagine. Finally, Victoria spoke: 'And Mohammed Aydin. What do we know about his life?'

I sighed. I knew even less about him than I did for Simons. These people deserved more than what I could give them. 'Thirty years old. Journalist. He had flown in from Chicago, via Cuba, because of the American blockade. Been in the country for less than 48 hours. He was here to report on the progress of the revolution for an online news site. This was his first meeting. And his last,' I muttered.

We watched what happened next without comment. Seeing the guards run in, getting involved in a fire fight with a drone, made me wonder if we'd ever get to a place of safety in this country. We were all living in a bloody computer game. The rate of firing increased dramatically, with the whole scene exploding. Glass shattering. Chairs being torn to pieces. People writhing in agony. Then I saw something which I hadn't seen before – crawling on his hands and knees, away from the window, was a large man in a white coat. His back exploded as dozens of bullets tore into him, turning him into pulp. Flesh nor muscle nor bones were a match for them.

This was Bruce Jenkins; I had been given his name but not seen his demise. Now I had.

I whispered, rather than spoke. 'Local butcher.' What a cruel sick joke that was. The butcher, butchered. 'As far as I can find out, he was pretty unknown here. He'd been to a few meetings and talked to some people. First impressions were that he was a nice bloke. Most saw him as being intrigued by what went on here, rather than a possible recruit.'

I stopped. This was so flimsy. Good grief, this was turning into some sick murder thrills flick; we didn't even know his age or address.

It was obvious that I wasn't the only one who was being weighed down by it all. When Asher spoke, he sounded weary: 'Jenkins was hit by multiple bullets - fourteen in total; Type Ognia 7LT machine gun calibre. Basically, they obliterated his spine and heart, lungs and kidney. Death would have been instant.'

Victoria appeared to have no self-doubts. 'Comments?' she asked briskly.

'That it's a fucking massacre!' I growled.

Asher nodded, and agreed. I had come to regard him as a faithful, dependable and highly capable professional, who only displayed emotion when getting angry with me. True, that had been more than once, but even then, if I was being honest, he wasn't alone in that. Not everyone found me charming. But now, he looked almost crushed by what we were witnessing. Nobody answered Vic. Roijin busied herself with some gadgetry in an obvious way to avoid having to do so. I didn't have any one-liners to liven up the proceedings.

'Anyone notice the pattern of the firing?' Vic asked, hoping to prompt some sort of reaction.

I looked up, and bit down a desire to simply repeat that this was a massacre. I didn't get what she was talking about. The room had simply been blasted to smithereens. Bodies were everywhere. We knew what had caused this – it was a drone. We knew it had been used by the enemies of the revolution. What pattern was she banging on about? Did it all make some herring bone design? We were dealing with amoral assassins, not a fabric obsessed super-villain.

Her question, however, prompted Asher into losing his lethargy. He circled the room and started to nod. The nods grew in frequency. He pointed to where I had been taking shelter with Phan. 'Initially, it's single shots, using the Dart sniper rifle. They're all clustered here. Around the table. Look – Brownswood, Aydin and Simons – all killed within metres of you. So close indeed, that they created a human shield, protecting you both. Otherwise, I think you might have ended up being one of the fatalities.'

I looked at him to see if I could detect any wishful thinking, but happily couldn't see any.

'Then the machine guns are turned on.'

Victoria was now nodding furiously as well. So much so, I feared she'd get whiplash if she wasn't careful. I had no idea what was exciting them so much. So, drones had different types of guns. Whoopee!! Break out the balaclavas and let's play war games!

Roijin understood. 'So why didn't they start with the machine guns?'

'Indeed,' nodded Victoria. 'If their intention was simply mass slaughter, then why start with the sniper rifle? By doing that, it gave people a chance to seek shelter.'

'Because they were after a specific target.'

Even I could see the logic in that. The only problem being, that if you followed where it led, it ended in a place which I didn't care for.

'And when they do use the machine guns, can you see where they fire?' Victoria asked.

Roijin was now also doing this strange circler nodding head dance. Was this something you caught like a virus? If so, I was obviously immune. She had also twiddled with some switch or button, because we now could see a plan of the room, with each location of an impact of a bullet shown in red. This hovered above the repeat of recon scene at the point when the firing went from Dart to Ognia. It was an arc which went around the sofa hiding Victoria, like a waning crescent of the Moon.

'They were aiming all their fire power on one section of the room. That's why the guards avoided being hit. They ran into the area which wasn't under fire. The question is, why was that? Maybe it was because of the position of the drone.' The image of the drone came up. 'You can see that its positioning is ideal if you want to reach the part of the room where Aydin, Brownswood and Simons were. If they were interested in the largest number of casualties, then all they had to do was move it. But they didn't.'

'You seem to be implying,' said Asher, as he moved closer to the plan, 'that this was a targeted killing and the use of the machine gun was just to cover that.'

'That's exactly what I'm saying,' Victoria replied.

He thoughtfully stroked his chin. 'Okay, if we dismiss Jenkins, because he was killed by the Ognia machine gun, then, in all probability, the individual who they were after, was maybe one of that group – Aydin, Brownswood and Simons. But we should perhaps include Phan Bien and,' he paused and turned to face me, 'Pete.'

'A hammer to break a nut,' I muttered half in humour, half to make a point.

'It does seem an over-the-top way to kill someone,' he agreed, missing the joke, or at least, not regarding it as being worthy of note.

Victoria agreed, but made the point that the change of approach happened almost immediately after the death of Sofia Brownswood. 'She's the person who was hit most by the sniper bullets so it's a logical assumption to make that she was the target. But whilst I acknowledge the fact that it could be a presumption too far, I think we can also discount Aydin, he's just a journo. Which means it certainly is a workable premise that one of the people you mentioned, and yes that includes Pete, was the focus of the target. And in particular, Sofia Brownswood.'

'Still seems OTT,' he replied.

'Unless they were in a hurry.'

'You mean, straight after the discovery that Mike Stewart was murdered?'

'Yes, Ash, I think it's at least worth a consideration,' Vic replied.

'Quite a difference between the two,' I said. 'One was a cunning and sophisticated way of killing someone, and then there's this. This is hardly cunning, and certainly it's not sophisticated. From a scalpel to a bludgeon.'

Victoria walked towards me. 'That's true, Pete. But let's look at this again, from the perspective of the personnel involved. Not only were Pete and I here, but so were Thom Simons and Marie Williams. Okay, Williams only arrived at the end, when it was all but over. But the fact is, that both Mike Stewart's visitors on the morning of his murder were present. Then there was his returning flatmate, Fiona Bailey. She was also here and only barely escaped with her life.'

'And Dave Donaldson,' I added. 'He was downstairs in the foyer, after arriving from the TV debate.'

'So that's both visitors, both flatmates and the both of us here. And the attack comes immediately after we find evidence suggesting that Stewart's death was murder. In fact, it happens exactly when we arrive, wanting talk to them.'

'So, it was to shut one of them up? Or to shut us up?' I asked.

'Good question, and one which I don't have the answer for. But look, okay, the methodology of killing Stewart and the four people here, is totally different, but the overlap of people involved is telling, surely?'

I was still rather unclear on what was being said here. 'But if we think they're somehow linked, the question is raised that, apart from us, the only person who knew that Mike Stewart had been murdered was Fiona Bailey, so does that implicate her?'

Roijin grimaced. 'Well, no, not quite Pete. Following protocol, I informed Jackie Payne. Who told me that she would contact the NWC Security Committee. Who in turn would have probably immediately contacted someone in the AF leadership.'

I groaned. 'So basically, the world and their gender non-specific partner knew.'

The grimace grew grimmer. 'Yeah, I'd say so.'

'Okay, what do we do now?' I asked.

Usually Vic would answer that, but she looked deep in thought. Perhaps she was considering the joys of transparency in detection. Instead, it was Asher. 'Odette can see if she can trace who had been told about our findings on Stewart's murder.'

Roijin nodded. 'The murder weapon here was the drone, and in a sense, it was also the accomplice, so I'll stay and concentrate on finding out as much as I can from it. Or to be more precise, what's left of it.'

# CHAPTER 16:
# THE ARTIST'S SON AND NURSE

Feeling desperate to have some control; having some sort of say in what I did, no matter how little, I told Victoria that I should take the lead when we questioned Marie Williams. She didn't argue, which was perhaps a shame, because, to be frank, I wasn't too sure that I was the person to do it. Marie's view of me was not one to warrant flowers and chocolates. Unless it was Deadly Nightshade and a Hershey Bar. No doubt, there were people in the world she despised more, but not many.

We'd been told that she was in the Pastoral Room on the seventh floor, which had been converted by the new(ish) residents for on-site medical matters. Previously it would have been used for more minor ailments, such as headaches or strains; not airborne assaults. On entering the room, I was immediately hit by the familiar nasal attack of antiseptic. But the walls weren't the traditional white, which one would usually associate with such a smell, but were a pale green with framed prints of countryside from around the world circling the room. I recognised a few of them – there was a lovely one of Powys, South Wales – but I wasn't here to be a stationary tourist. The actual reason was disrobing from a green plastic gown and gloves. She was talking to someone similarly attired, but who looked about half her age and was sporting a bald head with AF tattooed on the back.

'Have you a disposal unit here?' she asked, in her best medical professional voice. She hadn't been in the NHS for over thirty years without mastering that voice they have – calm, professional, reassuring and to the point.

He nodded towards a white and steel bin in the corner. 'And how's little un' here going to be then?' he asked, not referring to Victoria, who had entered the room behind me, but to a young boy, who was probably ten or eleven years old, and had been partially obscured by Marie.

Peeling off her gloves and studiously ignoring our arrival, she replied, 'Just a few cuts from the glass. He'll be fine. Won't you, Adam?' She smiled and playfully patted his shoulder. 'Although I doubt you'll be wanting to come to many more political meetings after that one.' The smile remained fixed; as did any acknowledgement of us. We were two metres from her, in a room a mere twenty metres square, so unless we had slipped an invisibility potion into our morning coffee, she was making a point.

'But remember, keep those cuts clean, and get your parents, or, er, another responsible adult, to take you to a GP if they look like they're getting worse. Yes? Promise?'

He nodded, which I took to be a promise in his world.

Addressing the adult, and still ignoring us, she asked him if we knew where Adam's parents were right at this moment. 'They've been taken to hospital because...' He paused, obviously not wanting to go into details in front of the lad.

She nodded, understanding the unspoken diagnosis. Turning her attention to the boy, she assured him that his parents were in safe hands and would be okay. To be honest, he didn't look that bothered. Kids today – your parents get mashed by machine gun fire and it worries you less than losing at a computer game. Wasn't like that in my day. Fewer machine guns, I guess. 'Is there anyone you can be with?' she asked him.

He replied in a voice dripping in unconcern, that it wouldn't be a problem as his family actually lived in the Shard and they had neighbours he could stay with. In fact, he called them 'neighbouring siblings'. They started young, here. Sibling no-hair said that he knew the family well and would arrange for the lad to be looked after. That seemed to satisfy Marie, before she added, 'Now, Adam, remember what I told you about shock. You say you're alright now, but shock is like a monster hiding behind the corner. You don't think it's there and then it jumps out! You will talk about this to your friends, or family, won't you?'

He nodded and so did her hairless assistant. With that, both passed us. Neither said hello or goodbye. I began to wonder if we had drunk that potion.

But we hadn't. 'Pete...' she said finally, in a voice you use for tiresome teenagers. 'How can I help you?' It was a question that was designed not to be answered, because she had as much desire to help us as you might a very hungry, angry cobra. Me and her had once been close. Her family and mine had even been on holidays together. But that was gone. All because on a previous case I had accused her of being a hired killer for the reactionary forces of the world capitalist class. She hadn't liked that. People could be a tad touchy about that sort of thing.

'And *will* his parents be okay?' I asked, trying to be as cool as the atmosphere.

She breathed out heavily, taking the plastic skullcap off and putting it in the bin, 'I don't honestly know. It's been awhile since I've worked in A&E. If they're the couple who I think they are, then both looked pretty bad. But I've just been concentrating on the minor cuts and bruises; the serious injuries were dealt with by the ambulance crews. They were here pretty quick so let's hope that we'll have no more fatalities.' She sighed, and then turned and faced us. 'I see you two are unscathed. That's good.'

A loose translation being: 'how come you two bastards are unhurt – I was hoping to see your bloodied corpses piled on the street below'.

I smiled, and simply said, 'Luckily, yes.'

A loose translation being: 'Luckily, yes.'

With the bedside manner formalities done with, her tone altered a touch. 'So is that why you're here? To see what the final body count is?'

I decided it was best to get to the point and take no bullshit. Young Adam might take being shot at in his young stride but not old me. Regrettably, it wasn't the first time, but I wasn't quite yet accustomed to it.

I spoke with what I hoped was assertive officiousness. 'Of course not, comrade. You know that we're charged with looking into the death of Mike Stewart, who *you* found. As soon as we arrived, the attack was launched. With you here *again*. It would suggest that they're linked and we were wondering if you might be able to help us find out how they may be.'

She gave a slight nod of her head in acknowledgement. It wasn't going to be 'a bunch of flowers', but equally it wasn't going to be a fist fight.

I seized the moment. 'Why exactly, were you at Stewart's house?' I held my hand up, before she had a chance to protest. 'Yes, I know you've already told Vic, but if you wouldn't mind, I myself would like to hear.'

She didn't complain, but instead, in a very controlled voice, explained, 'The party and the AF want to set up neighbourhood health and wellbeing centres. They'll act as super-powered health centres, but will be far more than GP drop-ins, acting as cohesive units of social support and organisation, operated by the local community. The anti-social stewards would also be based there. Both organisations see this as an important way to empower localities. I was there in my role as both medical workers rep and CC member.'

'And Mike Stewart?'

'He was a leading advocate for it. He also wanted to synthesise them into a whole new way of structuring housing, which was part of his vision for a new way of urban living.'

Impressive jargon. I wasn't too sure what it meant, but as we were agreed that he wasn't murdered because someone opposed giving power to the localities, I didn't ask for clarity. Instead, I gave my best knowing look. Then asked, 'So what role did Thom Simons play?'

'He was the national rep for the social workers; it seemed logical to have that aspect included. Plus, the fact that he wasn't in either organisation made it look more like a broad-based approach. We were to come up with proposals and then present them to the workers' councils across the British countries. The hope is that we can launch it next year.'

'Was there anyone else in this, er, organising group?'

'No, just us three.'

Which was now one. One could almost believe that someone had a serious grievance against street well-being centres. Maybe they thought it would spoil the neighbourhood? Drone attacks and secret poisonings, though, seemed a bit extreme. At the very least, it suggested that it was one committee you wouldn't want to be on. With two-thirds of the present one now dead, volunteer replacements might prove to be hard to find.

'How long's it been going?' I asked.

'This would have been our second meeting in a fortnight. The three of us worked well together, I think we would have had something concrete to put to the councils in a month or two.'

Concrete again. She did like that word. Was it one of the party buzz words of the month? They were always popular, and whatever it was, it would be used endlessly by the hacks for its duration. Then again, Marie was no hack.

I thought for a moment, I needed to get away from these neighbourhood centres, and also any question which might provoke Marie into answering with the word "concrete". 'Why did you come here?' I sincerely hoped that the answer wasn't to borrow a cement mixer.

'Partly, I wanted to pay tribute to Mike. He was a good man, a good revolutionary, a good class fighter. But also, to keep the initiative going.'

'Who knew both you and Simons would be here?'

She shrugged. 'Everyone. It was on both the Red and Black Clouds.'

So that was no help. I did have one more question and it was one which was at ninety degrees to the previous ones. 'So, what do you know about the discovery of this electronic tag? Jackie mentioned it in the meeting, but didn't have time to elaborate.'

She looked blankly at me, before answering in a voice which contained what could only be described as a scoff, 'Tag? Nothing whatsoever. I have no idea of what you're talking about. Playing at secret agents is more your scene.'

It was a good try, but I'd known Marie for decades. She was a great medical professional and a great socialist. But a really crap liar.

'Marie, it really isn't the time for secrets. Be political and tell us what you know.'

She continued playing dumb. 'Why would I know? I'm NHS not MI5.'

'Hardly, Marie. You're close to Jackie. Let's not forget that several times the party has had to set up important committees and you've been involved in all of them. Not least on the eve of the civil war. You'd be involved in the discussion of the finding of this tag, or at the very least know about it. We need to know, Marie. We're on the same side, after all.'

She considered what to say. On the one hand, she knew full well that Jackie in particular and the party in general, supported Cribs and our work. Jackie trusted us. Trusted me. Even if she didn't. On the other, there had obviously been a good reason to be so hush-hush on this electronic tag thing. Behind me, the so-far patient Vic could be heard shuffling from one foot to the other. Either she was desperate for a pee or she was eager to join in.

Finally, Marie came to a decision: 'I'm being totally honest, Pete, I don't know the details. But I do know that our tech people noticed that in messages we'd identified as originating from various foreign security services there was a tag hidden within the message. Different codes, different languages, but the same tag. It's a way of guaranteeing it. So even for those we can decode, we can't hack them, not without this tag, a tag we can't replicate. We did find it attached to The Fool's List. I assume, you know what that is?'

I nodded.

'Also, we noticed that in social media it could be found. We think, and again, this is only guesswork, that it's a way of communicating messages without it seeming to be anything but social media chatter. Hidden in plain sight you might say. For example, we found that amongst the usual right-wing abuse of Mike Stewart some comments which had the tag. One of which simply said, 'That dick needs to go!'

It sounded innocuous, if not destined for the bumper book of quotes, but with an accompanying tag of authority it goes from juvenile abuse to a death threat.

At this point, Vic decided to speak. 'And the party wanted to keep this secret because we don't want to alert our enemies that we knew of it? That's why Jackie was keen to get us to investigate Mike Stewart's death, but not willing to spell out why?'

'Yes,' Marie answered, simply.

'So, when did you find out about the threat to Stewart?'

She looked a little embarrassed. 'Sunday afternoon,' she muttered. 'But we weren't really in a position to warn him.'

Now that *was* dynamite – the party knew two days before his death that there was a credible threat to Mike Stewart's life, but had not acted upon it. If our friends in the AF heard this, there'd be uproar. What position did we have to be in to warn allies that their life was in danger? Seemed to me, that the position we had been in was prone, semi-comatose. I turned to look at Victoria, who was standing arms crossed and was intently looking at Marie.

'Anyone else been threatened with the tag attached, apart from Stewart and everyone on the Fool's List?' I asked, turning back to face Marie. I was reeling from what I had just heard.

'Anything else?' I asked. 'Like an event?'

'Yeah, there was some chatter about that, but many of us felt it was rather vague.'

'You don't think that this is the event that they were referring to?'

A pained look crossed her face, but she didn't say anything.

# CHAPTER 17:
# A CONVERSATION PIECE

**W**alking towards the lift, and being gifted with the ability to simultaneously walk and talk, Vic was on the phone to Roijin, telling her what we'd just learnt.

For a moment or two, Vic didn't speak, but listened to Roijin. Then, finishing the call, she turned to face me and informed me that in her opinion, which she immediately made mine too, we should have a word with Dave Donaldson. Roijin had had just found out that dear Donaldson, house-mate of the sadly deceased Mike Stewart, also happened to be on the team who operated the defence drones.

'Communal Rooms. Floor 3,' she told the lift panel.

I downloaded the fabled Fool's List. It only took a moment's glance to notice a few things. For starters, neither Victoria nor I were on it. We weren't that important. My ego flinched, but the upside was probably that with all things considered, not being on a kill list was a good thing. I looked to see who was on it. As you'd expect, there was Jackie Payne. Marie was also there, as were the rest of the party's Central Committee. I could see both Mike Stewart and Sofia Brownswood. It wasn't in any order, certainly not alphabetically, or by organisation. I presumed that was too much of an intellectual push for the types who had written it. Other names included Reyansh Anand and Noah Walker, who no doubt saw it as a badge of honour. I then noticed Fiona Bailey's name and just below hers, was her flatmate, Eduardo Almeida. His partner, Isabella Torres, wasn't on the list. Hopefully, that hadn't caused any domestic friction. Was there a right of appeal, I wondered, where they could request inclusion? Would she feel that it was a sexist oversight that the male in the relationship gets noticed, but the female is ignored? But then, Thom Simons wasn't there either, so it wasn't just me and Isabella, then, being out of the in-crowd.

The lift arrived, the doors opened and we went in. I kept looking at the list. Near the bottom, I saw Dave Donaldson's name. Such a sententious man wouldn't like that, he'd want to be top – in big bright bold letters. I slipped it in my pocket, and busied myself picking bits of glass and unidentifiable materials off my jacket. We arrived at the floor and found where these "communal" rooms were located.

DD wasn't lying down, having a nap, or thankfully doing anything else horizontally. Instead, in a small – no, make that claustrophobic – room, he was gazing out the window. The room had all the charm and decor of a budget travellers' hotel. He swung around as if he'd been raided by the police. Which, in a sense, he had.

Without any formalities or niceties, Victoria barked, 'Comrade!' It wasn't the politest of greetings I'd ever heard.

'What do you want?' he demanded. 'How dare you barge in without permission!'

Vic snapped back, 'I thought these were "communal rooms", well, we are the community!' Obviously, she had forgotten the 'tread carefully' strategy.

Talking in a volume a little below hollering might be useful here. I leant around her and in a quiet, but less confrontational tone, answered his question, 'Sorry to come in so abruptly, but we do need to talk to you, Dave. If that's okay?'

'No, it isn't,' he snapped. 'Who gave you permission to kick your way in?'

You couldn't keep Vic down. 'The meeting upstairs did, the one you were in less than an hour ago. We had a vote – you lost – remember?' She really didn't have much patience with this scrawny, aggressive hobbit.

But when she next spoke, she did lower her voice a fraction. 'Now we've settled that, and you know our credentials for being here, perhaps you can tell us why you didn't immediately go to the meeting when you first arrived at the Shard? We know you were at a TV debate. It isn't far from here, but even so, to get here in such a short space of time, you must have rushed. Witnesses say that you arrived sweaty and out of breath.' No shilly-shallying around, she had got straight to the point. 'And yet, when you arrived, you didn't go directly upstairs, which would have been what was expected.' Just in case he was getting confused with all the meetings they had around this place, she reminded him. 'This was the meeting which became somewhat bloody, when it was fired upon. You must have all but run to get here, yet, the building security informed us that you spent ten minutes in the foyer.

Which coincidently was the length of the attack.'

'What the hell are you inferring?' he demanded, shouting even louder. Although, this time, I figured he might have some justification in raising his voice a little. 'Who the hell do you think you are? You…' He took a few steps towards us. If the desire was to intimidate us, then he had no chance with Vic. He was hardly a boxing champ – his body resembled a sixth-form classroom skeleton, used in biology lessons. His ribs visibly poking out of a badly ironed shirt. Not that I blamed him. We had just barged in and aggressively fired off a barrage of questions at him. Our approach was very similar to a male from the Bos Taurus species scampering about in a shop selling ceramics.

'Stay there, tiger,' she replied coolly, unknowingly swapping species.

*Tiger*? She had called him – "Tiger"? Really? Oh, I would bring that up at a later date.

'As it happens, it hadn't started, they were in the bar. So, I didn't need to rush.'

'And you knew that, did you?'

He stumbled and muttered something unintelligible.

'Sorry?' Vic said, not being at all sorry.

'I had some calls to make,' he repeated. 'Personal calls, in my *personal space*. Or aren't we allowed a personal life? Have *the party* banned them?'

'Yeah, we're going to ban friends and families,' she replied. 'Who were these calls to?'

His answer was more barely inaudible noises.

She sighed. Previously, I would never have thought that a sigh could sound threatening, but now I was enlightened as to how it might be. I knew a threat was coming.

'You'll be aware that the NWC has recently reorganised its anti-social detention centres. Or what used to be called prisons. They've a different name, and there's different ways of being sent to them, but because of the decriminalisation of a raft of offences and the release of a large number of inmates, they do have plenty of room. You'll also be aware that four months ago, the NWC passed *Amendment 1V2. Emergency Threat Powers* which give Cribs temporary powers of detainment.'

He stubbornly kept his jaws clenched.

'We need to find who was responsible because more lives might be at risk.'

'Donaldson, for goodness' sake, grow up and cut the crap! Who were you talking to?'

'You don't frighten me. I'm not interfering with your work. I just don't see that it has anything to do with the attack. I think you're just behaving as if nothing has changed and the revolution never happened. You think your sort can still bully working people around.'

Vic just stared at him. Then he gave in. 'But, if you must know, I was on the phone to my mum, she's not been well.'

If it was possible to have explosive anti-climaxes, then here was one.

Disbelief dripped from her voice. 'Oooookaaaaaaay, can we have *Mum's* number?'

Her request surprised him. Perhaps he didn't know his mother's number. Perhaps he dreaded her talking to Victoria, and his mother telling her all his childhood misdemeanours. Or probably worse for an anarchist, what a nice polite, well-behaved boy he had been. But then it was my turn to be surprised, because he told her. Relying on her memory, Victoria didn't write it down. Impressive. I was getting to the time in my life when I had to write my own name down in case I forgot it.

'And the others?' she asked. 'You said you made personal *calls*.'

His response was almost a sulk: 'Why are you being so aggressive? Playing Gestapo and KGB, intimidating people. You'll do more damage to the revolution than any bloody drone attack.'

I was tempted to question whether we could be both Gestapo and KGB at the same time, but thought better of it. Now wasn't the time to split authoritarian hairs.

'The problem is, Dave, that you've been very keen for us not to be involved in investigating these deaths. And I'm beginning to start to wonder why that might be. You can hurl abuse at us all you want, and hide behind libertarian principles, but the problem is that you happen to be a flatmate of Mike Stewart. No big deal, that. But we're unable to find any witnesses to corroborate where you were at the time of his death. Still, not such a big deal. But you were unhelpful when we approached you. Then, when we've proof that he was murdered, we come here and within seconds a drone fires upon a room full of people. Not you, because you've been delayed downstairs, making "personal calls". You refuse to tell us who these calls were with. The deal is getting bigger. The drone is for building defensive one and you're on the team which operates it. *I would call that a big deal.*'

'To Penny, my girlfriend. We're having issues.'

He left the word "issues" hanging. If it had been up to me, I wouldn't have asked what they might be. I did have sympathy for the girl having to get her hands on that bony body of his. It wasn't up to me though, and Vic did ask.

'No, I won't tell you my personal life – it's not relevant. However, you can have both Penny's and Mum's numbers so you can check. You're right, you've been tasked to investigate this atrocity, so if it helps, and eliminates me from your snooping, then I'll give them to you. Anything, so I don't have to go through this police shit again. Surely, you must have electronic surveillance to confirm when and where I made the calls, so I'm not really sure why you're asking. For your own amusement, I guess.'

Vic ignored the petulance and thanked him.

His shoulders relaxed a bit, but he was worried. 'Surely you don't seriously believe that I have anything to do with either Mike's death or this attack? My friends were in there, for heaven's sake! Check with Penny and Mum, how could I be on the phone to them and operate the drone at the same time? I realise that it looks dodgy that I'm involved in both, but it's coincidence – that's all it is – a coincidence. Yes, I'm on the aerial security team, but there's another ten siblings who are too. It could be one of them. Or more likely, it's none of us, and it's just you trying to fit us up. I mean, wouldn't it be pretty simple for the security forces to hack into the system remotely? It doesn't have to be an insider. You don't have to be physically standing in the control unit to control the drones. Check it out for yourselves!'

'Thank you, Dave. I appreciate that we're being intrusive but we're doing what we need to.'

Leaving the room, I grinned at her. 'Well that was fun! For a second, you had me believing that we were actually going to cart him away and bang him up as a terrorist!'

'It was a real possibility,' she muttered. 'We need to talk, Pete.'

Seemed that *we* had "issues" now.

She had decided that any further interviews could be conducted by the militia and announced that we had to go. As we did, she swung around and walked towards where the much-mentioned drone lay smashed to the ground. Roijin and Asher were already there, surrounded by people in those funny white coats that are the in-thing to wear at crime scenes. Militia guards ringed them, separating the team from the crowd. At a rough estimate I would say that between two and three hundred were now there.

If the pair of them had expected a friendly chat, then they would be sorely disappointed, because immediately Victoria reeled off a whole list of jobs for the pair of them to either do themselves or delegate to others. Pausing for breath, she added, 'We'll meet at the office.'

I had expected her to jump into her car, command drive, and speed off. All in a dramatic, tyres screeching, rubber burning, action, with the car being thrown side to side. But it wasn't quite like that. Instead, we got in, she switched the windows to deep tint, and pushed her chair right back. Taking off her shoes, she put her feet onto the steering wheel. Was she about to have a snooze? She had a small heart tattooed on her left ankle. I wondered if it held any significance. A past lover maybe? Our friend DD would have said that it was there to remind her what a heart was.

'I'm flattered, Vic,' I said keeping a straight face, 'but romps in the car with a woman are in the past for me. The gear stick tends to get stuck in my back.'

She forced a small smile, and then feigned a grimace. 'That really is an appalling thought, Pete.'

'So,' I said, 'having established that this isn't a romantic liaison – I can see that you want to talk about something – what is it?'

She didn't answer straightaway but when she did, it was a Victoria Cole whom I had only partially glimpsed before. She spoke in a heavy voice: 'I just don't know whether we're capable of dealing with this. This isn't the type of policing I was trained for. It's a totally different world. Aerial attacks weren't the usual stuff you learnt about at police college. On the rare times it was murder, then nine times out of ten it was someone the victim knew. Usually, a lover or partner. Serial killers were even more of a rarity, but even then, they had a tell-tale signature to their killings. A particular method of murder. Or way of operating. But what is there that links a fake anaphylactic shock and a fucking drone?'

'We can but try.' How could she not be motivated by that? 'I think we're right, there's too many coincidences.'

'But then, why kill Stewart first?' She gave a heavy sigh. 'Oh, I don't know.'

The world appeared to be weighing down on her. 'What would you do have done when you were a copper?' I asked. Catching her wary look, I explained that – for once – I wasn't having a go. 'What would have been the procedure?'

She folded her arms, dug her hands into her armpits, and recited almost as a mantra: 'Collect evidence. Check it. Evaluate it. Then follow it.'

'Isn't that what we're doing?' I asked, thinking of all the people who were taking statements around Mike Stewart's home; the ongoing forensic study of his body; the statement-taking at The Shard; Roijin examining the drone – to name just a few. She knew what actions were being taken because she had organised most of them, but she was having a confidence-wobble. Personally, I thought everything we had set in place was impressive. 'If I remember my true-life crime stories, wasn't police work mainly painstaking evidence gathering?' I resisted adding, "or fabricating it". Once more, I had resisted an obvious chance to diss the police – I must be going soft.

She agreed, she understood full-well that we were all working hard. 'But this is spy work, and Pete, neither of us are spies.' She rubbed her face, then forcefully ran her hands through her short hair. 'I mean, Christ Almighty, Stewart and the Shard attack are completely different in style. Not even remotely similar. What are our lines of enquiry or anything resembling a working hypothesis? We could be collecting data for decades and all of it would be pointless.'

Something had been rattling around my head for the last half hour, so I thought I would take it out for a walk. 'Thing is, Vic, let's look at all of this politically. They've tried assassinations before and it got them nowhere. In fact, most agree that it backfired. So why start it up again? Sure, they're getting desperate so it simply could be that. But let's go with this Fool's List. What strikes me is that there are some pretty heavy-duty names on it. None of whom were in that room. Arguably, Mike Stewart could be regarded as one of the B List, but the others, those killed in the Shard, wouldn't be classified that highly. I know that sounds harsh, but the top people are elsewhere. Most of them are up north in Manchester at the NWC. So why attack the Shard? In the cold logic of what would destabilise a movement, it wasn't the most effective target. Wouldn't you agree?'

Vic leant forward, her knees going further upwards, as if she was about to rock herself. 'Go on,' she said.

'It just doesn't make sense. If they were going to hack into a drone defence system, then attack the NWC itself. Most of the bigwigs from all the parties are there right now. That's why Jackie had to rush off. But guess what the effect of the attack on the Shard has had up there? You can bet your last worker's token that security has now been tripled, that they've checked and double checked their drones. Why did they choose to use their best move against Division Two opponents, when they could have gone for the Premier? Like I said, I can't see the sense in it.'

Vic nodded. 'Good point. So, you discount the Fool's List theory?'

'Well, it's very nice of them to let us know who they intend to have a pop at, isn't it? And this handy little tag to let them – and us – know which are the legit messages is a wonderful example of transparent planning. They've clearly learnt a thing or two from us about the importance of accountability.' I stopped to let the weight of my irony have an effect. 'But is that really how they operate? It isn't, is it? Something about all this doesn't make sense.'

She gave me a faint smile. 'From what I understand the tag isn't some kind of large flag but a minute piece of coding. It's probably taken the tech-team a lot of hard work to uncover it.'

I didn't say a word, but I wasn't convinced.

'So why the drone attack, then? Do you think it could have been aimed at you?'

That took me by surprise. 'Me?' True, many people weren't aware of all my positive attributes, but I had never imagined that I would warrant a drone attack all to myself. 'That's just wishful thinking on your part.'

She didn't laugh, but looked at me earnestly. 'I'm sorry to have to suggest this, but we can't forget your mystery visit, can we?'

That stopped my heart for a moment or two. My unhealthy self-belief did feel that there could be some logic to her suggestion. Maybe, the few successes which the Crib had enjoyed was making us a target. The trouble was, my renowned intellect wasn't buying it. 'If they wanted me dead, my personal burglar would have just done it then and there. One bullet would have been a lot less effort than hacking into a drone. And with far less mess.'

She nodded acceptance, but didn't say anything. She was now almost in the foetal position on her chair.

We spent the next few minutes just sitting there, listening to our breathing and the chants from the crowd around the Shard. The latter were now growing in numbers. We were a few streets away, but the periphery of the demo was beginning to reach us. Finally, she moved the chair forwards and instructed the windows to a lighter tint. 'We need to get back to Driscoll Avenue.' Turning the ignition on, she leant out the window and in her best polite, but authorative voice, asked people to move out the way. Luckily, they did. Then, as soon as there was a space, she drove off at speed.

# CHAPTER 18:
# THE DRAWING ROOM

N ews that the party knew of the electronic tag followed us back. By the time we were parking, there had been the further revelation that we had good intelligence that Mike Stewart had been at risk. It wasn't just the weather which was hot and sticky.

Outside the office was Odette, but she wasn't at her desk. She wasn't even on her phone. Nor was she eating a piece of fruit. This was a first – I don't think I'd seen her not doing at least one of those things. Instead, she was sitting on the sofa which occupied our foyer. We had inherited it from the previous occupiers, who presumably had visitors who used it. We certainly never did. Well, not until today. Odette was leaning forward, with her arm around the shoulders of a woman who looked in her fifties. I couldn't see any family resemblance with Odette, but that didn't mean that they weren't related.

Both looked up at us when we entered. The unknown woman had short hair and large gleaming earrings. Something about her nudged my memory. I knew her from somewhere. Her red eyes and blotchy cheeks showed that she had been crying, and crying a hell of a lot. It was that which reminded me who she was.

Odette gave a faint smile. 'Pete, Vic, this is Pauline Stewart, Mike's mother.'

I smiled back at the woman, nodded and said a gentle hello.

Odette explained why she was here, although she didn't really need to. 'She'd to talk to you about the investigation...'

Pauline Stewart meekly interrupted, 'If you have the time, Mr Kalder, that is.' It was almost apologetic. Noticeably, she had addressed only me and not the pair of us. That could quite possibly be a hangover of gender prejudice, but then in this day and age, that was unlikely. More likely, it was because Vic was hanging well back, almost to the extent of being in hiding.

In the course of looking into Mike Stewart's life, I had learnt that his mother was a mechanic, and so without wanting to stereotype, was hardly likely to be a wilting flower, but here, every petal had been knocked off. Any colour or vibrancy had been swept aside in the strong winds of grief.

'It's Pete, and of course I have, Pauline.' I suggested that Vic and Odette prepare for the meeting.

Victoria didn't argue and indeed, even looked grateful. She did, though, dare to take a few steps forward and address the grieving mother. Gently, she said, 'Ms Stewart. I am truly sorry for your loss. Please rest assured that we're doing everything we can to track the killer of your son. We shall not rest until we have. Please ask Pete anything you need to, and if you need anything else, the team are just through that door.'

Her thank you was almost inaudible.

Odette rubbed Pauline Stewart's shoulders and unfurled her long legs to follow Vic. When they had left, I sat in the armchair opposite her and leant forward. I knew painfully only too well what she was going through, and I knew that there was nothing I could say, or indeed do, to lessen her grief. The only thing I could do was to attempt to reassure her that we were doing our best. That, after all, was the truth. The worry is that our best might not be good enough. That she didn't need to hear. As far as she was concerned, we had everything under control. I repeated the condolences and although, just like Vic's, they were sincere and heartfelt, they sounded tame and fake. 'How can I help you?' I asked.

Her reply consisted of informing me that Mike had been her only son and how wonderful he had been. His father had left when he was six and she had never seen him again. Again, and again, she told me how proud she was of "her Mikey". Finding a passion from some space where anguish hadn't taken up residence, she went into great depth on how he had wanted to make a better world. She explained what his City Natural Synthesis idea was and how it would be his legacy. I sat there, nodding and making agreeable noises. She needed to say this, even although she had probably been saying nothing but this since it had happened. If this helped her deal with her agony, then I wasn't one to stop her.

'So,' she said, 'you'll understand why I so need you to get the person who—' she gulped, almost choking on the thought. Summoning every ounce of strength she had, she forced the words out— 'who took Mikey away from me. I can't believe anyone would want to hurt Mike, I really don't. Everyone loved Mike. He was so loved.' She gulped down a sob.

It had been a while since I had said anything, but I judged that now was the time. 'That's what we've heard, Pauline. He was a lovely man, everyone who ever met him, found him to be an extremely warm and friendly person. I wish I had had the honour of knowing him. You're right, Pauline, he was also a very intelligent young man, one who had fantastic ideas. But I don't know if this makes what you're going through better or even worse.' I paused. Fact was, I didn't. A part of me thought it might make the pain deeper. 'But it wasn't personal. This was a political assassination. They wanted to get rid of those fantastic ideas, but you're absolutely correct, Pauline, they'll live on. Mike was too much of a visionary to be simply removed from our history. Jackie Payne has personally told me that she will push the City Natural Synthesis through. It will be going to the NWC next week, and will be proposed by Jackie herself. She is going to call it Mike Stewart's Vision.'

For the first time, a smile fleetingly appeared on her face. 'Yes, the president rang me yesterday. She was very sweet. She's invited me to the NWC, as her guest, to see it. I wasn't sure at first, but I think I'll go.'

That was typical of Jackie. It was a nice gesture and one that obviously meant a lot to Pauline.

'Then you'll know that whatever has been said on social media, we've taken this seriously right from the start. That's true, Pauline. Even when it looked like it was an accident, we kept looking, which is why we found out that Mike had been murdered. We will not give up. I give you my word. We will continue until we've arrested whoever took Mike from you.'

Wiping her eyes, she nodded. A glimmer of hope sat by the misery. 'President Payne said that too. She said that I could trust you, Mr Kald... Pete. She said that you'd stop at nothing to get him. You don't care whose toes you stepped on; you'd track them down.'

I wasn't too sure about the reference Jackie had given me; I'd talk to her about that at a later date. It did, though, explain why Pauline had seemed to only want to talk to me. It hadn't been my warm and cuddly demeanour, then.

'I just needed to see you and tell you about Mike, from someone who knew him best, his mum.' She paused and looked at me, as if weighing me up. 'Have you a son or daughter, Pete?'

'I did have,' I quietly replied. 'But she was killed in a car crash, a few years ago.'

She nodded and didn't pursue the matter. She understood that it was best not to. Instead, she returned to the investigation. 'I wanted to see for myself the person who's now looking after my Mike.' Her look grew in intensity. 'Are you close to finding out who it was?'

Looking deep into those eyes of raw agonising pain, I wished I had some secret piece of information to tell her. I wished that we had a prime suspect who was looking likely to be in handcuffs very soon.

'We've a few ideas, Pauline. Obviously, I can't say too much at this moment, as we don't want to prejudice any trial.'

She looked at me. I felt my heart thump hard as I inwardly cringed at just how naff that sounded.

'You have someone in mind, though?'

Despite my best intentions, I lied. 'Yes.'

Now wasn't the time to consider whether giving her false hope was the correct thing to do or not. The brutal truth was that the truth was brutal. She had been hurt enough; she didn't need any more pain right now.

'I'm just worried that with the attack on the Shard, which I know was awful, and I feel so sorry for the friends and families who lost loved ones, I really do; but I'm worried that Mike will be forgotten about.'

'He won't, Pauline, I promise you – he won't. Every person in this country is valued. Every person has the right to live in freedom and without fear. They have the right to achieve their potential. In return, they will do nothing to infringe on anyone else's. Taking their life, breaks that contract.'

She didn't reply and just got to her feet. I did likewise. Immediately, she wrapped her arms around me. Still, she didn't say anything. She just held me. I could feel her chest breathing hard against mine, and her hands pressed on my back, pushing me harder onto her desperation.

It was only for a few seconds but it felt like a lifetime. After a moment of being held onto as one might to a life buoy, she pulled back. 'I trust you, Pete. I pay internet gossip no mind. That's just electronic waffle. I know you will do it. Get them, get them for Mike.'

'I will.'

She mouthed a thank you and left.

I exhaled heavily, and tried to return to some semblance of control. Blinking rapidly, I tried to get rid of the wetness in my eyes. Having been slowly developing a self-image of being the hard man of fighting counter-revolution, I liked to think that it was a touch of hay-fever. The realist in me knew that I wasn't allergic to pollen. Rather overcompensating, I shoved the door open. Everyone looked up at the entrance which you might expect from a gunslinger in a Western.

Victoria was sat by the window, looking out. I sincerely hoped that she hadn't spotted an angry anarchist mob on its way here, armed with grievances and pitchforks. The latter was highly unlikely in this day and age, but you never knew with anarchists, what with their being at one with nature, and all.

'She okay?' Vic asked, and in doing so, won the coveted communist medal for asking this month's stupidest question possible.

'Not really,' I replied in a masterful understatement.

'We can show that we're not a part of some kind of cosmetic exercise, by getting down to work. Ash, update us on what you've found at the Shard.'

He cleared his throat and spoke: 'Well, our investigations came to an abrupt halt when it was announced that we had foreknowledge about an attempt on Mike Stewart's life became public.'

'Yeah, we heard that on the way.'

Roijin facepalmed. 'It's pretty widespread. We started to hear it by the drone. Most dismissed the accusations as being ridiculous and libellous. But then news of the ComMessage came out and that really stirred things up. I spoke to the militia-lead and advised him to leave as well. He's an old comrade, so he agreed immediately. I have to say that a lot of the younger members were confused. There were a sizable minority who were angry.' She looked at Asher for confirmation, who nodded.

'ComMessage?' I asked.

'Between Glen Bale and Jackie. It confirms his belief that it is an electronic tag and is nine units long. They register as if it was an electrical inference. He couldn't say whether they're letters, numbers, shapes or just noise. But this message proves that the party knew.'

'Jackie told the meeting at the Shard that we knew of this tag. All the ComMessage does is to add some detail to it.'

Roijin answered, 'But seeing it written down makes it worse. Especially when accompanied by the second one.'

That surprised me. 'Second?'

'There's one timed at an hour and a half later, again from Bale to Payne. In this, Glen says that they are fairly sure: the exact quote is that "We are seventy-five percent certain" that there will be an assassination attempt made on Stewart, which will be made to look like an accident. It even gives a four-day window of when this will happen. And guess what? Mike

Stewart dies smack in the middle of it.'

'What?' This was a total nightmare. The type which you awoke from kicking and screaming. 'We knew that much detail?'

She shook her head, making her bob, well, bobble. 'Bale immediately went online, and whilst admitting the first communication was his, denied the second. He said that it was fake. Then someone pointed out that the cyber-coding was his, so, therefore, the communication must have come from him. He responded to that by saying that he'd been hacked.' She all but flinched, adding, although she really didn't need to, 'But the general consensus is one of disbelief. He is, after all, the much-heralded IT expert and hero, who's been defending us against capitalist cyber-attacks. Jackie, you'll remember, described him at the most recent International Socialist Revolutionary Conference, as our 'Cyber-Shield'.

Victoria was now all but holding her head in her hands. If those pitchfork anarchists arrived, our look-out wasn't concentrating. She spoke as if she was weary from a long-distance train journey: 'One who's now claiming his shield's been dented.'

For a moment or two, no-one said a word. There wasn't much to say. I didn't believe that we would have deliberately withheld such important information, but I wasn't sure many others would. If we were talking general consensus, then the one in the room could be best summed up in one word – four letters, beginning with S, ending in T, and rhyming with bit.

'This is politically very sensitive.' Once more showing that my skills at masterly under-statements was unmatched. I'd be saying the Titanic had a sticky maiden voyage at this rate. Nonetheless, I ploughed on, 'I'd imagine that the debate in the NWC is going to be angry and bitter. I'd bet, too, that the councils, be they workplace or geographical, will soon be meeting to consider their response, and if they disapprove of what their delegates are saying, they will instruct them to change their line. Or replace them.'

Asher looked concerned and stared at me intently. 'Where does all this leave us?'

Us meaning whom? I wondered. There were many types of us. I took an educated guess at the pronoun he was referring to. 'I think this Crib simply carries on doing what we've been doing, until instructed otherwise. Whatever the mistakes the leadership have made, real or otherwise, we ourselves have treated this totally seriously from the minute we were called in.' A thought raised an arm and waved a placard. 'Which is a point – have our leadership said anything?' I asked.

Roijin answered, 'A statement is expected within the hour.'

'Probably trying to find a shovel big enough to dig themselves out of the hole they've got themselves into,' I said, with a level of resentment that was surprising. ' I mean, let's be honest here, it's not exactly been well-handled, has it? Even if we take Glen Bale's word, and I do, that the second message is fake, this has been one huge cock-up.'

Vic had pulled her head out of her hands. 'The fact remains that Jackie was reluctant to say anything, even to us!'

I myself had plenty to say on the subject and most of it wasn't good. The party had screwed up big time, and as far as I could see had very little defence. Okay, there had been a couple of times recently where important information had been leaked. The AF wasn't as tight organisationally as we were; telling them something and asking for confidentiality would ensure that everyone would know about it within the hour. The joke was that if you wanted an event well-publicised, then tell the AF that it was a secret. But that was no excuse. The party, and Jackie in particular, had made a whopper of a mistake. Relationships are built on trust, and this was on par with if your partner had come home early and found you in bed with half the neighbourhood. With the other half at the door waiting to come in. This was an epic error in judgment.

Emotions were running high everywhere, including in the office. With the notable exception of Odette, who looked the picture of composure cross-legged on her stall, chewing on an apple. I could almost feel the agitation. I was also beginning to feel a delayed reaction of what I had just gone through at the Shard. Raked by machine gun fire, I had recently learnt, wasn't good for the nerves. I tried to keep it level. I didn't want them to see me weakening. 'Obviously, we need to keep an eye on national developments, but let's not get side-tracked. We now have five murders to solve. That's our job.'

Vic agreed. 'You're right, Pete – five murders and…' She looked at me with a wry smile. 'Something *in my gut* tells me they're linked.'

The fabled copper's gut instinct. Once, I thought they only existed in whodunits; in real life, a copper's gut instinct referred to knowing where the nearest kebab shop was. Not now.

She continued, but didn't mention donors or shish kebabs. 'I know this sounds strange, considering what me and Pete's just been through, but I think we need to go back to Mike Stewart, I think that it starts in his kitchen. Agreed?'

We did. Pauline Stewart was nodding in my head.

Vic brought up a map, showing the surrounding area of Mike Stewart's house in a 3km radius. Avatars appeared, ready for instructions. 'Let's look at this. The militia and the Bow Workers' Council have been very thorough interviewing people who either live in the area, or were seen going through it. There're still some people we have yet to trace, but we're slowly getting a picture of the timeline of events. So far, we can pretty much trace the movements of Marie Williams, Thom Simons, and Fiona Bailey. Marie came by her NWC carpool car, via the A12. Traffic Control Stewards saw her drive along there and an elderly pensioner saw her arrive at 10.20am. He knows the time exactly, because he's housebound and was waiting for his day's shopping. Seems, it should have been delivered at 10.15, but there was a delay at the food distribution centre. Marie stayed in the car for just over five minutes. She told me that she rang the party offices. I checked, and they confirm that she did. She got out the car and met Fiona Bailey on the doorstep, who had just arrived. They both entered the building together and found Stewart dead on the kitchen floor. She says she saw no-one other than Fiona in the vicinity.'

She stopped and looked around, waiting for any questions. None were forthcoming. I couldn't think of any, either. 'And Thom Simons?' I said.

'Thom Simons, who of course is also sadly one of the victims of the Shard attack, travelled from his home in Walthamstow on the No 9 Water Bus, along the River Lea. He got off the boat at the B & M Stop. From there, he walked to the house. We've witnesses confirming that he was on the boat, but not for his movements between the river stop and the house. From his disembarkation, and walking at an average speed, and for that distance, you would have expected him to arrive at 14 Driscoll Avenue twenty minutes early. However, he arrived ten minutes late, at 10.40.'

'Do we know why?' Asher asked.

'He said he got lost on the way there. We need to look further into that.'

'And Bailey?' asked Roijin.

'Fiona Bailey travelled that morning from Hammersmith, after staying at a friend's place. She took the tube, and then the A33 bus, which terminated at the Bow Garage. Staff there logged the bus in at 9.45am. She walked to the local neighbourhood organising centre, where she used the copying and computer facilities. Roijin, you looked into that.'

'There wasn't anyone in the centre, but both a computer terminal and 3D copier register being used during the time when she arrived there at

9.50am and the house at 10.30am. She used the centre's database to check on the results of a travel survey which the train workers union have been conducting. She also sent several ComMessages, to the union and train operators, making suggestions on changes to the timetables. I accessed them, and it confirmed that they had been sent from a terminal at the centre, at 10am, ten- and fifteen-minutes past.'

She had accessed them? Hacked, she meant. She was investigating a murder on behalf of the NWC but it was still a border-line illegal thing she'd done. Not so long ago, Roijin would have been up in arms against such abuse of our power. Those were the days. No-one now uttered a word of protest.

'I also checked the 3D copier. Bailey spent ten minutes creating a new black rucksack. The old one was full of holes, apparently.'

Victoria took over again. 'Which, Marie says, she was carrying when she arrived. We have a Janice Brompton, a fourteen-year-old, who was off out to visit friends. She confirms that she stopped to talk to her a few hundred metres from the house. They talked about the weather. It's hot, apparently.'

We all laughed. It was a better reception than I ever received. Probably not because she was more amusing, but that people were trying to lessen the tension.

After the rather synthetic amusement had stopped, she returned to what needed to be done: 'We haven't had time to look at Dave Donaldson's alibi, which is something we urgently need to do. He was on a nightshift at the street cleaning centre. We need to find out when he finished, and where he went afterwards.'

She paused and took a sip of water. Perhaps I was imagining it, but a change of mood appeared to come over her. I sensed that whilst previously she had been professional and working through a set-out procedure, she now appeared, if not excited, then keen to tell us something. 'I think we're all clear that we need to further look into the movements of Williams, Simons, Bailey and Donaldson. We also haven't nailed down exactly where Torres and Almeida were. We've reports that they left for Portugal, but I'd be happier if it was more concrete. There's also this person here.' She pointed to an avatar of someone of an indistinguishable gender, wearing a blue hoodie, loose trousers and bright green trainers. 'There appears to be gaps in where they first appear and then disappear, but please note that three people saw this person, near Stewart's house, at approximately 10am.

Nobody has any idea as to who this could be. All three witnesses say the person seemed keen to hide their face. None of the other people who were seen, are wearing anything resembling this. This is a person we really do need to talk to.'

I stared in astonishment. I had seen that person before. Or at least those clothes. 'The person who broke into my home, was wearing those.'

They all looked at me. Vic nodded. 'Indeed.'

'Do you think it's the same person, Pete?' Asher asked.

'I can't tell. Vic, was there any description of them at all? The avatar's face is blank, which I presume means that we haven't received any.'

'Correct. But it obviously becomes a priority. I think it would be an enormous coincidence if there were two people wearing the same clothes. The hoodie obscured their face and the baggy clothes hide any physical features. Which in this heat, wearing such clothing might hide their identity, but it also makes them stick in the memory of anyone who saw him, or her, whatever pronoun they prefer to use.'

Roijin looked closely at it. 'And we've no idea which direction they came from or where they went?'

'Not so far. Tonight's Community Information Meeting will be organising the follow-up investigation. One of us obviously needs to address it.'

Blue hoodie was someone we really did need to talk to, and do so very quickly. Because unless blue hoodies and green trainers had become the fashionable thing to wear, the same person who had broken into my home had also been seen around Stewart's.

Victoria turned to Odette, to ask if she had anything to add. A smile almost cracked her face open. 'Thanks, comrade. I looked into the personal history of Dave Donaldson. He's been very busy over the previous weeks, mainly attacking our conduct and policies, in virtual and physical meetings. He's ever-present at demonstrations. They're all accessible there.' She pointed to the file floating to her left. 'From his speeches, it's quite plain that he's hoping to be elected to the organising assembly of the AF and standing on a platform of hostility towards us. He began this political positioning...'

What followed, was a tsunami of information. Odette was a very thorough, if indiscriminate researcher, who had a rather loose grasp on the concept of editing information. It had been several minutes and we had only covered the last ten years. I feared that when she reached his puberty years, we would have a run-down of his acne. Luckily, she stopped before then. 'Putting it simply, I haven't seen anything which might interest us. He doesn't like the party, and is an ultra-leftist, but I can't see much more. Neither from his personal history, nor his communications. They...'

I interrupted her, 'Communications? What do you mean?'

She looked as if I was a complete idiot. 'His phone, laptop, use of the AF com systems, ComMessages, social media, stuff like that.'

Roijin's black pencil-thin eyebrows went up. This meant it was serious. In my experience, Turkish women could say a lot with those eyebrows, and Roijin was shouting with them. 'Are you saying that you hacked into Dave Donaldson's private communications?'

'Yep, it was no problem.'

Roijin was spluttering with shock. 'N-n-no, problem? How easy it was, or wasn't, isn't really the point! Our licence at present, only covers matters that directly touch upon the time of Mike Stewart's death. To widen that, we need to obtain permission from the NWC.'

Odette looked sincerely puzzled. Like a child might when they've discovered Father Christmas isn't real. 'But you asked me to look into his life? Let's face it. Post-rev, online records are a mess; what there is, is of little use. I mean, they're hardly going to leave incriminating evidence on there, are they?' She was smiling with pure innocent contentment. 'I thought it was more beneficial to see what he said in private. Though it looked all uncontroversial to me. I've loaded it all on the office server for you all to look at.'

Roijin again tried to explain why it was wrong. We were allowed to use intrusive methods but the state had to sanction it. We couldn't just do it on a whim.

Noticeably, Vic hadn't said anything. I wondered if she had condoned Odette's actions, or had even instructed her to do it.

Odette couldn't see what the problem was. 'But you lot frequently do the like. I thought it was the thing we did here. Didn't Roijin just say that she had done the same at the neighbourhood centre? Surely, it's just bureaucratic niceties we're talking about here?'

She had a point. We'd been bending rules so much that they now resembled coils. Perhaps the real reason why there was unhappiness at her actions was more to do with our own guilt, than condemnation of hers. Not so long ago, we had stood tall on principles of justice and human rights; now we were breaking them ever more frequently. But we consoled ourselves that we did so knowingly and reluctantly, and with an email saying that we could. But what we had actually done, was to start to create an atmosphere, where such anti-revolutionary methods were beginning to be seen as a norm and someone completely new, just came in and adopted them. She had modelled her behaviour on ours. That was why she was getting the reaction. She was correct: we had little basis on which to judge, and so, we judged ourselves, and didn't like the verdict.

At that precise moment, I shivered. It wasn't from the situation we found ourselves in, but my phone vibrating. I looked down and saw that it was my sister Sophie. Now wasn't really the time for family reunions, so I stopped it and turned my attention back to the meeting. No-one, I noted, had said anything more. There was a little shuffling, but not much else. Well, there couldn't be really.

Roijin changed tack. 'But what if he traces your hack? We're in enough trouble as it is. Actually,' she paused, as her face registered a thought, 'how did you get past the security protocols?'

Odette leant across the desk and took an apple, which I think had been Asher's early evening snack. It became Odette's. Taking a large bite, she grinned. 'Piss easy to get in and out. They won't know I've been. I mean, their defences are pitiful. Someone should have a word with the AF. I thought ours were bad, but theirs were even worse.'

'Ours?' Roijin almost choked. Something had just dawned on her.

Odette happily clarified that what Roijin had just thought. 'Yep, I thought I'd have a close look at Marie Williams' too. Again, there wasn't much to see; what there was, I've saved it to the server, so you might spot something I didn't.'

She had hacked a Central Committee member of ours. Without anything even resembling permission or a request for one. Not even from us. She had just gone and broken into Marie Williams' systems. She was right to say that we were hardly virgins in the invading privacy world, but this was a shameless orgy.

'And before you start worrying, I got in and out with ease. No-one will ever know I've been. Roijin, you do need to find a subtle way of telling comrade Glen Bale that he needs to up his game and improve our security. It really is poor.' She smiled an innocent smile.

Rojin looked stunned. It was, after all, Glen Bale *and* Roijin herself who had created the security systems. And Odette here had breezed right through them.

Roijin attempted an oblique defence of it. 'I can't believe that you weren't detected. It can't have been that easy, surely.'

'It really was.' She took another bite of the apple, then laughed. 'Although to be fair, I'm bloody good at this – if I say so myself. I was the one after all, who, a few years back, got into the world's four major arms dealers and published all their sordid dealings. Got me a prison sentence and expelled from uni, but it was worth it.'

She was certainly throwing surprise bombs in the room. We looked at her in total disbelief. Even Vic. We all knew the revelations about the armaments industry, which she was referring to, because they had made world-wide news, but we had no idea that it had been Odette. It had been *our* Odette – the fast-talking Odette, who sat at, and sometimes on, the desk outside, and did the odd bit of office work, between phone calls – who had blown the whistle on the arms industry. Odette had once been the heroine of the hacking world.

I had to admit to having a touch of admiration. Not so Roijin, who was still attempting a last-ditch defence of her own computer capabilities. Stuff rules and civil liberties – her skills were being called into question. 'Well, comrade, you may not be as good as you think you are. You got caught, after all. So, maybe we should be worried about you leaving an e-footprint.'

Odette brushed the comment aside. 'Nah, they never caught me. You could say that my love life did. This prick I was going out with got the hump when I dumped him and grassed me up. They never knew they'd been hacked, until he put it online. And they never knew who it was. Not till dickwad informed on me. I'm too good for that.'

There was silence.

I asked a question which I really didn't want to know the answer. 'Odette, was it just Williams and Donaldson, or is there anyone else you've hacked?' I had feared the worst. Actually, no, what I had feared was merely the very bad; the answer was far, far worse.

Tossing with an expert aim, she threw the apple core into the bin on the far side of the office. She beamed with pride. Which was ominous. My bet was that it wasn't from her throwing skills.

'I thought that I might as well look into Mike Stewart himself, and Fiona Bailey and Thom Simons. Then when I heard that they'd been killed in the drone attack, I had a peek at Sofia Brownswood, Mohammed Aydin and Bruce Jenkins. Oh, and I picked up on who were responsible for the drone defence, so I did them too.'

Good God. We were into double figures of those we had cyber-hacked into. And it was only seven hours after the attack. She didn't hang about, did she? At this rate, by the time the day was over, she'd probably have hacked into half the country. I didn't need to ask Roijin whether we had NWC permission to take such action because we hadn't had the time to make the request. Obviously, there was no moral conscience or anything even resembling doubt, which slowed her down. Whilst I might admire her speed and sense of action, if this got out, we'd be finished. But something she said had worried me even more. 'You "picked up" on the names. How?' I had visions of her hacking into our personal phones.

'Roijin rang and told me.'

A clearly dumbfounded Roijin dumbly nodded that was true.

Oh, thank you, sweet heavens for small mercies. She hadn't hacked us.

My phone went again. This time it was a message. It was from Sophie again, and it said simply, "Ring me when you can." Despite what Odette had said, I had an uneasy feeling that Odette would know exactly what the message had said, who had sent it, who Sophie was, and what she was wearing. To keep what there was of my shaky sanity, I put that thought, and my sister, to one side.

Vic broke the silence, looking at me; she sounded cautious. 'Well, the deed is done, so we might as well have a look to see if there is anything of interest in what Odette has found. Ash, anything else?'

'I can confirm that Stewart had been injected with a mixture containing almonds and an accelerant which would have heightened his allergy. It was injected under his fingers, and from the direction of the puncture wound he must have had his fingers either outstretched, flat or at ninety degrees.' He demonstrated with his hand.

'What, no 3D visuals?' I muttered. This was a bit old fashioned, I thought nowadays they went with everything, like French Fries at a burger bar. He looked at me, not catching what I said. 'Nothing,' I mumbled.

An alert appeared in front of us. Victoria explained, 'I set my com scanners to pick up anything of relevance to the attack and it looks like something is coming up. Looks like from Network 56 News.'

'The party statement?' I asked. Hoping that we had something to say about this mess we were in. Jackie was a brilliant speaker, and she'd have to be, to salvage something from this.

'Er, no. It's an interview with Fiona Bailey.'

A murmur of apprehension sounded in the room. Except that is, from Odette, who had found another apple and had taken a large bite out of it. Before our collective groans and darting looks had time to finish, the visual of Bailey appeared in front of us. She was being interviewed by Art Parker, the Network 56 News' lead news anchor. Vic's alerts were seemingly on a go-slow because it looked like the interview had already been going for several minutes. Like so much else, we appeared to be behind the game.

In his hushed mid-Atlantic voice, he asked her, 'So, Fiona. You found him – Mike Stewart –who you have just described as being a close personal friend, and a fantastic sibling, dead in your kitchen. You say that you immediately suspected foul play, because of the milk. What did you do?'

'I rang the emergency number and asked for a Crib, well, *the* Crib. Specifically, for the one with Pete Kalder in. But...'

I shared a look with Vic. This wasn't going to be good.

And it wasn't. Fiona Bailey, the most fraternal of the AF, and a close friend of Mike Stewart, quietly and reluctantly, but brutally eviscerated the party's conduct over his murder. I could feel Pauline Stewart's hands still on my back.

'And you haven't any ideas why they didn't warn him, or indeed inform the AF?'

'No idea. But I think questions need to be asked.'

He didn't pursue the matter and just flashed his eyes. 'Then, there was the attack on the Shard...'

# CHAPTER 19: THE VIOLINIST

A public dressing-down from someone claiming to be on our left wasn't a particularly pleasant experience. Negativity wrapped around us like a damp blanket on a rainy day. Even Odette could only manage a smile, barely above the thin. She had, to be fair, attempted to chat with Roijin, but after receiving a series of monosyllabic replies, had given that up. Instead, she quietly hummed to herself.

The programme had been a deeply unsettling and uncomfortable one to watch. This was no crazy anarchist blindly ranting at us; she had sounded calm, logical and reasonable. Halfway through, Vic, sounding decidedly not calm, or reasonable, had declared that she had seen enough and turned it off. With that, our little dispirited gang had attempted to put the interview to one side, forget about its wider implications, and get down to work.

Odette, our Little Ms Commissar for Sunshine had gone next door with Roijin, to attempt to discover if there were any secrets hidden in the drone, specifically, whether the drone had been manually controlled or not. And if it had been, whether we would be able to find the location. Roijin might even heal her bloodied ego. Roijin had accepted Odette's offer of help with impressive grace. Despite the feeling that it was the case of *the Queen is dead, God save the Queen*. Obviously, Roijin was more of a grown-up than I was.

For some reason, Vic had thought it a good idea to have us all linked by video. A sulk shared, is a sulk halved, I supposed. Odette herself, had remained subdued for as long as ten minutes, before a smile had returned. Followed by her voice, was the one which could be heard the most, as she shared ideas and theories.

We were much quieter. Vic was clenching her jaw ever more tightly. The interview had really irritated her. I was in a slightly less stressed frame of mind, and amused myself, if that was the correct phrase, in adding to our files of each person of interest. Vic and I were, in the main, silent. I had started with Marie Williams.

Asher, meanwhile, was speaking at the Mike Stewart Community Information Meeting via a 3D link up. He, too, had adjourned to next door; wanting to have the felled drone as a backdrop. Making us look as if we were in the thick of the action, as opposed to being thick, or the marginally corrupt and majorly incompetent lackeys of the power-crazed Jackie Payne.

Usually, I had only seen him in action peering at, over or inside, dead bodies, so it was instructive to see him socially interact with the living. He was impressive, it had to be admitted. Cool, professional and lacking any the waffle, which we all could be sometimes accused of. He seemed to be enjoying it too. No doubt it made a nice change from cadavers. After the CIM had been given an update, Asher had informed them that the mystery green-shoed and blue-hoodie person, was someone we really would like to identify. It seemed friendly enough to me. Nobody appeared unduly hostile, and all were quite willing to help. Social media bitching about us hadn't yet appeared to have turned them against us. Nor had Bailey's interview. Or they hadn't seen it yet. The CIM moved onto allocating the tasks to those assembled and I lost interest. Time to get back to what I was supposed to be doing. In all honesty, I was finding snooping into Marie's personal communications rather awkward. Not because of guilt or embarrassment, but for the more straightforward and prosaic reason that with some of them, the lack of context meant that I had no idea what they meant. Who, or what, the hell was TLS, for example? Looking at the dates when TLS came up, it was noticeable that they coincided with Stewart's death. There was a direct relation between its appearances and incidents in the case. Its usage definitely had increased in frequency in recent days, and as it did, it became obvious that it was a person and most probably a male.

Then, something interesting occurred, listening to a phone conversation between her and Bale, TLS again cropped up. Williams used the term and Bale laughed, though advising her that she should stop using it because she risked Jackie Payne hearing about it. 'And you wouldn't want that, because...' I pressed the headphone deeper into my ear. 'She's fond of the little shit.' So, TLS meant *The Little Shit*. With that, it started to become obvious that this was no secret code, but a term of snidy abuse. And then came the punchline. Williams replied, 'Yes, well, so was I once, 'till he betrayed me and accused me of being a spy. Kalder can piss off as far as I am concerned. Little shit describes him to a tee.'

The mystery had been solved. I had spent the last twenty minutes hearing myself ridiculed. I pulled the plugs out and closed my eyes. Victoria looked across. 'You okay, Pete?'

'Yeah, fine,' I lied.

For a moment it looked as if she was going to enquire further, but my face quite obviously deterred her, because instead she just looked doubtful and returned to her work.

I hadn't really finished mine, quite possibly there may be more to find about Williams, apart that is, from her clever wit. But frankly I wasn't feeling exactly motivated to do so. Ear-wigging was always a dangerous game because you never knew what you were going to hear. Then again, what choice did I have? So, TLS got back to work. Thankfully, I didn't find any more insults, but then, I didn't find much of anything. So, I moved on, for quite a while, finding sod all. But then, I saw a file marked meetings. Opening it, I saw the magical letters CC. This would be interesting. Metaphorically rubbing my hands and thinking that this little boy had just found Santa's grotto, I opened it and excitedly prepared to watch our Central Committee at work.

Then two hours passed, and I was still watching the first CC meeting, and had come to the realisation that the inner workings of the revolutionary leadership weren't all flashing lights and prancing reindeer. It was business-like and repetitive.

My self-flagellation in the cause of the investigation was interrupted when Asher's voice came through the intercom. The CIM had finished. They had ComMessaged all the residents and two had replied that they had indeed seen blue hoodie man in Mike Stewart's road. It was progress, but not much. He was now back off to the lab to see if anything could be discovered from the bodies in the Shard. Daddy was going home. It said a lot for our company that the cutting open of five bodies was preferable than being here. Exhausting all his energies on the living, he needed some quality time with the deceased.

Vic returned to whatever she was doing, and I moved onto Dave Donaldson and Fiona Bailey. I might as well trample over the AF rights, as I had done with the party's. Well, to be accurate, it was Odette who had, but then I was an accomplice. I quickly discovered that finding a coherent and cohesive life story for each was somewhat challenging. I had the basics from my previous search, but Odette had managed to find far more. The trouble was that fundamentally, it was still a hotchpotch of data.

Nothing shouted MI5 at me. Actually, nothing said much of anything. Certainly, nothing which helped us. What school they went to wasn't that useful. Nor did the fact that Odette had got hold of recordings of their many, many, many meetings. Of those, it was all pretty predictable, their prime concern being what they called, the 'Second Revolution'. Nor was the tedious amount of analysis on their relationship with us. But being a good boy, I watched. And, I watched. And watched some more.

Getting myself a coffee and a sandwich, I sat down and summoned all my willpower to see what wonderful things Thom Simons had for me. Having been a researcher in my pre-revolution life, I thought I was inoculated against boredom, but this was beginning to take its toll. I could feel the tedium infecting my soul.

Chewing a cream cracker, Vic turned to me. 'I've just found two witnesses who say they saw Dave Donaldson on his phone, near the Shard entrance. They're pretty sure that he was having a 2D visual call. I called both his mother and partner, and they, after much coaxing, agreed to speak to me and both corroborated his version of events. Of course, they might be lying. I'll get Roijin to see if she can trace the calls. What about you, Pete? Find anything of use?'

'Nothing.' I didn't mention TLS – she didn't need to know that.

'Where you at now?'

'Just started with Thom Simons.'

'Okay, I'm looking at Mohammed Aydin and Bruce Jenkins. Nothing so far.'

I was glad it wasn't just me being a kennel without a dog. Maybe artificial intelligence would do a better job, so I requested the office computer make a search on any links between Mike Stewart and any of the five who had lost their lives in the drone attack. But it didn't. I tried again, but again, I got no response.

I spoke to Roijin. 'The AI's not responding, I'm not getting anything – just blankness. Have we been hacked? Are you in?'

Before she had a chance to answer, Odette poked her head in a view, gave an enthusiastic wave, then grinning, replied, 'Hi-ya, Pete. Sorry to butt in but you need to ask Yelena for help.'

'Yelena?' I asked, confused.

'Yeah, I've named the AI – Yelena. She'll respond if you ask her by name. I thought as she is an important part of our team, she should have a name.'

She had humanised a computer program! I was sure that I saw Roijin's eyes roll.

I swallowed a sarcastic comment. 'Er, thanks, Odette.'

'No probs. Have fun.'

I looked over at Vic, who merely shrugged.

'Er, Yelena, er, could you find anything which links Mike Stewart with the five who were killed in the drone attack on the Shard. Er, thanks.'

Good grief, I had thanked it. I truly hoped Vic hadn't heard me. It took the AI – Yelena – less than three seconds before it came back with over four hundred possibilities. Maybe politeness worked, even with computers. Looking down the list, I noticed that both Stewart and Jenkins had in their time possessed a loyalty card for a well-known health food shop. MI6 hadn't wiped that, then. Which now meant that I knew that they liked eating organic noodles. My God, this was going to take a long time.

My self-pity didn't have time to marinate because a high-pitched scream bounced off the walls. Was our AI rebelling against her name? Did it object to being assigned a gender? Startled, I looked up at the screen, and saw a triumphant Odette. 'We've cracked it. We're in.' For a moment or two, they could only be seen punching the air. As television drama went, it was fairly lacklustre.

'And?' Victoria finally asked, getting tired of just watching them.

It was Roijin who spoke: 'Well. I was right – the drone wasn't on automation – someone was controlling it. Its cameras were on and were being used to direct the fire. The commands are coded from manual control.'

'You're sure?' Vic asked.

This time, it was the younger of the IT sisters who answered. And she did so in a voice you might use if you'd just received the bike for your birthday – one which you had always wanted. 'Def. Someone was operating and directing it, which means...'

Roijin finished her sentence: 'They were making a concerted effort to ensure the correct person was killed. This wasn't a splatter-gun attack. This confirms what we thought – they were after a specific person. They had a target. Which makes it even more likely that one of those killed was the intended victim. I think we might discount Jenkins, he was just unlucky, wrong place, wrong time. He was just collateral. He was killed by the machine gun, which I think was intended purely to act as cover for the more accurate sniper fire.'

I could forget about the health food shop loyalty card link, then.

Odette was exploding with glee. 'The drone's control line has been traced, so we'll be able to find out where it was controlled from. We're guessing that the reason for the memory of the link still being there is due to the damage which the drone sustained, either by the security gun fire or the crash, which created a malfunction, so preventing the automatic wipe being activated.'

'In English, please,' I asked, not understanding what had been just said.

'We've located the phone used to operate the drone,' Roijin replied, getting to her feet, pointing at a map projected in front of her. Beaming with pride, like mother about her new-born baby, she yelled: 'Look and there it is! It's in a storage building!'

We joined her in the silent standing ovation, holstering our guns. Odette looked at all of us with almost innocent surprise. Victoria noticed, and told her to stay here – she could continue the background checks on the drone defence team. I could see that Odette was relieved that she wasn't being called on for anything more than her usual invasion of people's privacy. Trampling on workers' rights was no problem for this girl. 'I'll ring the MComs,' she announced.

'The what?' I asked, having no idea who she was on about. Was it a fast-food chain? Was she hungry?

Vic shook her head as you might when your dad hasn't heard of a new band. 'Militia Comrades, MComs. The militia!' She laughed. 'MComs is what the young people call them. Odette is what you call a young person. Anyway, come on, Granddad! Let's see if we can find the person on the end of the phone!' Still laughing, she had left the office, before the 'a' in ha-ha was out of her mouth.

It took us just over twenty minutes to drive into deepest Lambeth. For once, eco-conscious, we had all piled into Victoria's car. It was also a lot quicker. The women were in the front, whilst I was at the back being hurled around as she took corners far too quickly. On the way, Roijin informed us that the phone was stationary. Predictably, it wasn't registered to anyone. She could identify the building as being a storage facility. Our friend with the phone might be hiding something away.

We arrived at an anonymous building, which could have easily passed for the headquarters of a bank, all darkened glass and pastel concretes. Considering the fact that Roijin had reeled off a dozen or so organisations which were using it, I had expected something much bigger. But from the look of it, I would have put it as being no more than six storeys.

Reading my mind, Roijin explained that it was an iceberg building.
'Cold, is it?' I quipped.

'It means that the majority of the floors are below ground. That is
where this phone is. On Floor -7, a storage facility owned by Katarina
Safety Company.'

There's nothing worse when you pretend to be stupid to get a cheap
laugh, and someone takes you at face value. Joke fails. You now know
that the person thinks that it is quite possible that you are that stupid to
genuinely think that.

'So how do we get in?' Vic asked, looking both at her dashboard
monitors, and through the windows. She pointed at the reception. 'In
there, I presume.'

Roijin shook her head. 'No, Vic, if you take a left, you should see a
vehicle entrance at the back. I'm guessing that's how they get the bigger
items into storage. They're not going to be ferrying sofas through the front.'

The car swung to the left, followed along the building's side, and then
just as it looked as if we were going to pass it, we saw to our right, what
she had been referring to. It was like a small concrete bum-bag on the
main body. Probably only three storeys high, it was about 30 metres long.
It looked impregnable. There appeared to be no windows or doors. It was
just a smooth blank sheet of blue. We turned into an equally bare forecourt
and stopped.

'Okay,' said Vic, 'I'll ask again – how do we get in?'

There should have been cheers and bells ringing, because I knew the
answer to that. I had been to one, very similar in style, only a few days back,
to recover some art thefts. I leant forward. 'Either side, will be cameras.' I
saw one. 'Look. That will be reading our number plate and matching it to
their files. There won't be a match, so it all stays shut. What you need to
do, Roijin, is hack into it, insert our registration number. Then the doors
will open.'

Roijin made a sound which I took to indicate that she was impressed,
but alas, there wasn't a firework display. Instead, she pointed her phone at
the camera and punched in some codes. A minute later, and the sheet of
blue in front of us started moving. A large swing-door appeared and opened.

The two women exchanged a look. Victoria turned to face me, with a
smirk. 'Well, Odette will be dazzled by your skills.' There was a pause before
we all burst out laughing. Turning back to the front, she drove forward.
'Okay, let's get serious. We don't know what we'll find in there. I'm putting

this on auto and I think we should get ready.'

"Get ready" meant one thing – get the guns out. The three of us did just that. 'We could wait for the militia,' she said. 'But I don't want to be waiting here, whilst whoever is in there, escapes.'

'Agreed,' we replied.

We drove into a large, spotlessly white room, with no windows nor any other door than the one we'd just come through. And that was closing. We stopped, and got out of the car. Guns in hand. Both women looked at me. I pointed at the cameras ringing the room. 'Vic, look into one of those. Roijin, hack into it and insert her image.' Both did as I had suggested and a door once again appeared and opened. 'He's just showing off now,' she cracked.

Victoria looked through it, first with the barrel of her gun, and then her eyes, as she poked her head through. She turned around and informed us that beyond were the doors to what looked to be a lift. 'Where to?'

Roijin replied, 'It's not moved. Still on the seventh basement floor. Shall we go?' It was a rhetorical question; Victoria was already pressing the lift button.

Seconds later, the door opened and the lift, big enough to take a large van, opened before us. We left the car and went in, instructing it to go to -7. After just a few more seconds, we were there and the door opened. Leaving it, we headed towards the storage unit where the phone was signalling from. We could now be more specific. It was Unit 19 on floor -7.

Victoria and Roijin took the lead; I the rear. The corridor was totally silent and featureless. The only noise I could hear was the sound of my nerves jangling like cats on dustbin lids. Like everything we had so far encountered, there appeared to be no doors or windows in the corridor. They were concealed until activated. It was light, but I couldn't see any light source. Nothing was visible, not even a pipe. This was one upmarket storage building. Built when the rich wanted places to store their stuff in as minimalist buildings as their designer homes. All that could be seen were a few red spots, which I presumed were cameras. We walked along the corridor, whilst Roijin scanned the wall with her trusty phone.

Something moved to our left. The edges of a door started to appear. 'Let me see if anyone is in...' she said.

But before Roijin had a chance to find out, or indeed decide on what we were going to do, the door swiftly swung open. We were now already on the system and it knew we wanted to be in there. The three of us stood facing a fast-appearing room. I was now drenched in sweat; my heart was doing a fair impression of a bebop drummer. We could be about to face an armed MI5 assassin; and call me a big yellow-hearted cowardly custard, but being shot at had a limited appeal. Quite frankly, the drone attack had satisfied all my death-defying needs for the month.

What we saw surprised us. What confronted us wasn't a crouching class killer, with us in their sights, but a wall of jumbled furniture. My first thought was that this looked very much like a make-shift barricade and that there could be a dozen British secret agents behind it ready to blow our brains out. The second, lurking by its side, was that if MI5 had been forced to retrain and become interior decorators, then they had appalling taste. With all the stripes and loud checks, it was like the festival of the chintz. But nothing moved, except maybe my stomach. Roijin was skilfully manipulating her phone with the same hand she was using to hold her gun. I did hope that she wasn't making a call at this fraught moment. Dinner arrangements could surely be made at another time.

'All clear,' she said. 'Picking up nothing in there, nothing living. That is, except us.' She holstered her gun. We followed suit. 'The phone *is* definitely in here, though. It's behind this junk.' She walked around the boxes of memories. Out of one, I could see a bald teddy bear, a pair of grotesque vases and a broken violin sticking out. Behind the pile of auctioneer's rejects, was a room about the size of a small bedsit. Towers of crates were everywhere. Uniformly, they were all two-metre-long grey cuboids, reaching from the floor to the ceiling, taking up almost every centimetre. The whole of the back wall consisted of them, possibly four-deep. In front of the wall of crates were three more, sitting alone, acting almost as benches.

'Tell me it's not in one of these,' I said. Envisaging spending the rest of the year going through them, tossing out piles of knick-knacks, as we did. There were dozens of them.

Roijin kept looking at her phone and went to the far corner. 'Well, it's somewhere near here.' She started to look around one of the towers. We joined her, and Vic turned her phone to the torch setting. There was a gap of thirty centimetres between the end of the crates and the wall. Roijin pressed her back against the wall, and whilst squeezing herself in, tried to crouch down and search the floor. This failed, with her muttering about her knees. She came back out and then re-entered by sliding headfirst along the floor.

'There's a bag!' she yelled as all but her feet were now wedged between the grey tower and the wall. She started to shuffle back, cursing as she did.

'Give us a hand!' she demanded.

Getting one leg each, we pulled her out. Coughing and sneezing as she came. Her right side was dirty from the dust and cobwebs from the floor. In her hand, she triumphantly held what looked like a bright green overnight bath bag. I held out a hand to help her up, but she just smiled and sprung to her feet.

Roijin unzipped the bag. 'Well, there's toiletries in here. But...' She lifted out, using the tips of her fingers, the phone. There wasn't a round of applause, but there should have been. She placed it on the floor and then scanned it with hers.

'Locked, and the security level is *Potentia*.'

'Power?' I said, trying to remember the basic Latin that I had been forced to learn in the role I had held in my previous life.

'Yeah,' she replied. 'In this context, it basically means that the security is bloody good. It's so good, in fact, that I'm going to have to take it back to have a look at it. I'll have no chance here. But give me an hour or two and I'll get in.' She scanned it. 'No prints. Wiped completely clean.'

Behind her, Victoria had slipped on some gloves and was looking into the bag. She pulled out a small gun and some ammunition. 'This looks interesting. Roij?'

Roijin joined her and asked her to hold them up. She did and after a few seconds, again announced that these too had been wiped completely clean of fingerprints. The two women shared a look which I couldn't decipher. They did this often. It was probably a cop thing. Thankfully, for one who didn't fit that category, they said their thoughts out loud.

'So careful about that then,' Roijin mused.

'But not in regard to the signal being kept on, which led us here,' replied Victoria.

'Yes. Strange that. But...' she got up and walked to a red light in the corner of the room. 'This is, I'm guessing, a part of the internal security set-up here. They won't have internal cameras in here, because of the concern of the privacy of the users. Before the revolution, who knows what loot was kept here. They only come on if the system doesn't recognise the faces, when the tenants of the room get alerted, with a video of the uninvited persons being in here. Like a burglar alarm.' She caught my startled look. 'It's okay, when we opened the door, I neutralised any such set up. I figured they'd be. It's pretty standard. All they're seeing is a loop of what the room looked like before we came in. We might be able to find out more from it though. We got in by placing our faces into their database. So logically, we can do the reverse and see what other facial images have been used to gain entrance.'

Victoria was rustling about behind us. I had no idea what she was doing. I doubted that she was looking for something nice for her flat; I presumed she was looking for evidence.

Roijin was half talking to me and half to herself, 'Okay, so we're in FRecog, we just have to get past the protocols, and yes, there we are…' Two faces appeared in front of us. Below each was their name and their log in times and dates. Both had been regular visitors here. 'Christ!'

I think I said something similarly New Testament.

The faces of Dave Donaldson and Sofia Brownswood were staring at us.

'Good God!' Victoria yelped, behind us.

A right old Bible reading group, we had here.

In a stunned tone, Victoria though, was ignoring her, 'Pete, Roij – look!'

We both turned to face her. By Victoria's feet, was one of the crates on the floor, which I had just assumed was used as a bench. She had taken its lid off, and I could see that it was made of a type of plastic. Guessing that wasn't the cause of her surprise, the pair of us joined her to see what was so amazing. I had presumed it was just more house clearance crap. But looking into it, I discovered that if it was, then it was one very strange house. There weren't any pots and pans but instead, it was packed full of rifles. At a guess, then I'd say there were twenty of them. Roijin opened the crate next to it. In this, were machine guns. But before we could discuss what this meant, we heard voices outside. 'Comrades? Pete Kalder? Victoria Cole? You down here?'

'MCom! Brilliant timing!' Roijin exclaimed in jubilation. 'They can help us open up all this lot and move it.'

I wasn't so sure. My mind raced, possibilities popped up like toast. Looking at the crates, I came to a decision. 'No. You two stay in here, get behind the furniture. Don't make any noise. I'll go out and talk to them – and send them away.'

Both looked puzzled, but I didn't have time to explain. I wanted the militia in here as much as I wanted curry powder in my underwear. 'Trust me – just do it!'

I marched out of the room, quickly but hopefully not showing that I was in a rush, and into the corridor. I had my hands up, but it would have been a lot safer if I hadn't had my phone in my hand; however, speed was of the essence here. I was confronted by five armed militia of varying ages coming out the lift. They looked surprised and raised their rifles. I gave my best boyish smile, and quickly identified myself, 'Comrades. I'm Pete Kalder. May I?' I nodded towards my ID badge, then slowly touched it. Up came my ID and authorisation. Noticeably, though, they had been lowering their weapons even before they had seen it.

The oldest, a man in his sixties and impressively still with a full head of hair, returned my smile. 'It's okay, we know who you are, comrade. Couldn't fail to, your lot are all over the news.'

It was a fame that didn't quicken my heart or make my chest swell with pride. Frankly, I could do without media attention and speculation, but it might work to my advantage here. 'Comrades, you've been called on a false alarm, I'm afraid. Sorry. There's nothing here, just a pile of furniture from some ruling class traitor who wanted to hide their stolen wealth.' I pointed to furniture behind me and hoped that they weren't expert designers, because this was no horde of treasures which had been gained by the exploitation of the working class. It was junk. I shook my head and made an expression which I hoped conveyed one of embarrassment. 'Just what we need! If this gets out that Crib called you out for a collection of soft furnishings, I'm going to be crucified. I'm getting a bad enough press as it is, without this.' I rolled my eyes.

They all laughed. Maybe, too heartedly. Judging from the speed at which they accepted that we had made a huge mistake, they were ascribing to the social media portrait of us being incompetent, as opposed to cunning and evil. I wasn't insulted, just relieved. I was in no danger, so they headed off to a workers' cafe to get themselves a brew. I waited to ensure that they had left, before returning to Roijin and Victoria.

No other crate had been opened, but both had their phones in their hands. Roijin was scanning a tower of them, whilst Vic was being traditional and actually using hers to quietly make a call.

'Well?' I asked Roijin, who I assumed was using her X-ray app to see what was in these crates.

Her reply was one of shock and surprise, 'All of them are full of weapons. I've scanned a couple of dozen and they're crammed with them. Of all shapes and sizes. Rifles, pistols, sub-machine guns. Even hand grenades. We've found a bloody arsenal in here. Perhaps not enough to equip an army, but certainly a battalion.'

I nodded. I had guessed as much. Vic got off her phone and told us that Jackie Payne wasn't answering. I had assumed that she'd ring Jackie.

It was, after all, of some importance to find an arms stash belonging to a supposed ally. Strangely, it might work in our favour that she had been unable to contact her – it gave us time to think.

'Why did you turn the militia away?' Vic asked.

The two women looked at me, intently.

'Think about it,' I replied. 'We've just discovered a storage room filled to the ceiling with what Roijin has eloquently described as containing enough weaponry to arm a battalion. And we've discovered that on multiple occasions, two leading members of the Anarchist Federation have had access to this room – to this arsenal. On top of that, there's the fact that we've found what we believe to be the device used to orchestrate an attack on the London home of the AF. Think – what effect do you think the news of this will have when it comes to light? And it will. That's why I sent our friends in the,' I did quote marks, '"MComs" away. I'm sure they're all good, disciplined revolutionaries, but how long do you think it would take for this little find to get leaked, if they'd seen it? Now, I'm all for accountability and transparency, but at this precise – very tense – time with the party and the AF trusting each other about as much as one of Casanova's lovers might of the man's fidelity, this could be explosive. And no, no pun intended. It would be a gift to party hardliners such as Noah Walker and Reyansh Anand. The likes of which, would use it as ammunition – again, no pun intended – for their argument that the NWC needs to severely clamp down on opposition. And as for the AF, a sizeable number of them won't believe it; they'll see it as a Crib set-up to act as an excuse to turn on them.'

Victoria might not have believed that the puns had been accidental, but she at least agreed with my reasoning. 'Yeah, you're right, Pete, we need to think very carefully how we handle this. This is a room which could easily enflame passions.'

'Or start another civil war,' I added.

Victoria closed the door and turned to me. 'Okay, so what are you proposing?'

I looked at her, and considered for a second that the proposal in my head might well seem logical, but I wasn't sure that it would do so when spoken out loud. Deciding that whether it would or not, wasn't really an issue, because it was the best that I could come up with, I told her. 'We can't do anything until we talk to Jackie. This is too big, with too much at stake, for us alone to decide on. We need to take a moment to think what our strategy will be. But surely, we need to know a little more about what we have in here before we start to advertise its existence.' My brain formulated one of the oddest to-do-lists I'd ever compiled: 'Roijin, is there a chance that you could by-pass the phone's security and get in?'

She nodded. 'Easily.'

'Good. Vic, take a closer look at the guns in here – see if you can find anything more about them? For example, if we can trace the history of them, how they got here and such like.'

'Okay.'

Noticeably, neither had seriously questioned what I had in mind, or had offered any alternatives. My guess was that their heads were goldfish bowls of doubt and uncertainty, just like mine. I tried to sound confident of what I was doing. 'Cool. I'll take a peak again at the security systems. Now Roijin has got us in, it should be easy for me to see if there's anything of interest in the dates and times this room was visited.'

Then, just before everyone set off to work, I added, 'Take photos of where everything was before you move anything, because we'll want to put everything back in its exact position. And also,' I said, thinking of something else, 'we need to tell Asher and Odette, that if anyone asks, this was a false alarm. I'll have a look to see what's in the neighbouring rooms and choose the most harmless. Ash and Odette will also give out the wrong storage unit number. That way, people can mark it down to one more Crib cock-up. And they stick to that line. No deviation. Not even to friends, loved ones, or comrades – no matter how high the cadre. Right at this moment, the only people who need to know the truth, are the three of us in here, Ash and Odette. And of course, our new friend, Yelena.' I grinned. 'The line will be that we came; we saw naff all; we went home with our tails between our legs.'

I stopped to let them disagree if they so wished. Let's face it, I was suggesting that we conceal the fact that we had just found an illegal arms dump, which it didn't take a military historian to work out, was probably intended to be used against us – the party. They were being kept here just in case they felt the need to attempt an overthrow of the workers' state, with more than slogans. In other words, this was really heavy shit. Neither said a word, but just looked very serious. I guessed it was their *this-is-heavy-shit* look.

Seeing agreement, I said, 'Okay. Roijin, you ring Ash, and I'll ring Odette?'

'Sure,' she replied, still with that look.

Chores designated, I made the call. Odette didn't even blink, let alone give me 'the look', when I told her that she was to lie, and what's more, I wouldn't tell her the reason why. I had a whole spiel ready, about the importance of the revolution and how unusual our work was. But it wasn't required. She just gave a smiley 'Sure, no probs', and then, a quick, 'See ya!' and she was off. I wasn't actually sure whether her reaction had been a good thing or not.

Pulling out an old wicker chair – after photographing its exact position – I sat on it and downloaded the log of who had been coming to this little arms store. The room had been rented under the name of Jamille Cronin. Jamille Cronin, hey? It had been rented just over twelve months ago. I checked the file containing the lease contracts. Looking down to find the one for this room, I made myself a little bet that the birth date for the hirer would be the 17th February. Now, I was still a system's beginner, certainly I couldn't claim to have the expertise of Roijin or Odette, but once in, I was good at searching. I smiled. There he was. And look, on the 17th of Feb, he'd be getting out the balloons and candles. It was indeed the Jamille Cronin I knew. There was even a photograph of him. That was interesting because sibling J Cronin had been dead for over four years before the day he apparently had taken this contract out. I knew that for a fact. Actually, most people did. His murder had become notorious, with both the day of his death and his birthday becoming international anarchist remembrance days. The photograph itself was a familiar one, which had been copied many times. He was sitting on a high wall, simultaneously smiling and shouting, with one hand stroking his closely cropped hair and the other outstretched in a fist. Dressed in tight fitting jeans and a bomber jacket, it had become an iconic image. It was one that captured what had made Cronin such a pin-up, even before his martyr status.

He had been shot dead by armed police during the long years of dual power, when both the NWC and parliament had been in existence, playing a game of existential chess. He was remembered for the wanton murder by the former state, as a symbol of their barbarism, and the anarchists' bravery. But more recently, his memory had also become a symbol of their distrust of us. Before the fatal demo, there had been a huge debate between the party and the AF as to whether the demonstrators should be armed or not. The party had argued for them not to be, as it would be seen as provocative; the AF had said we'd be walking into a trap. As it turned out, they had been correct.

Now, years later, he comes back to life and gets himself a storage unit. An odd thing to do with your resurrection. Either the people who ran this place didn't know of him, which I doubted – his face was regularly plastered all the media – or they didn't care that it was fake because they had been induced in some way. Or that they were AF supporters who were happy to go with the ruse.

My thoughts were running around my brain like kids in a playground. I leant forward and brought up another screen, and looked closely at the dates of Brownswood and Donaldson's visits here. According to this, no-one had been here for several days. The last person logged in had been Donaldson himself, and that had been the day before Mike Stewart's death. Brownswood hadn't been here for over a week. Which made finding the phone interesting. How did it get here then? I went to the files again and it was confirmed that no-one had been here for days. I tried again, going to its hard drive to see if the file imprint was still there. Quickly, I found that it was. Even to my untutored eyes, the record of entry had been deleted, but I was unable to find anything other than that. The time, name, let alone facial or number plate recognition memory, had been erased. I called Roijin over to see if she could do her magic. But after twenty minutes, she admitted failure – this had been professionally done, according to her, we couldn't even get a slither of data from it.

I asked the question before I had thought of the implications: 'Do you think Odette would have more luck?'

I received a withering look from Roijin, who muttered, 'Possibly. But I doubt it. The phone's the same, a top job.' She grabbed a chair and sat by me. From her face, I guessed that she was feeling as frustrated as I was. We had been in here now for just over an hour and a half, and I was feeling rather claustrophobic, thirsty, and in need of the loo.

Soon, Vic joined us. She had just made another attempt to reach Jackie. Yet again, failing to do so. 'And?'

I told her and Roijin that I had basically found out that the most vocal critics of ours appeared to be making regular trips here. Judging from how often, I'd say that our first impression had been correct and if you discounted the possibility that they were storing their old chairs and tables, this was their preparation for the "Second Revolution".

Roijin, asked, 'Is that legal?'

Predictably, Victoria quoted the regulations: 'The NWC passed Workers' Rights to Defence Order #143, which was, shall we say, a compromise between the party and the AF. Workers are allowed to have access to arms, but only if the local council is notified, and then, they must be kept under its supervision. There's quite an extensive list of regulations. Although nobody wants a society with such things on the street, we have to recognise that our enemies are constantly trying to undermine us, including by force. Weapons though, must be expressively only for the defence of the NWC, and not the restoring of the old order, or,' she again summoned up a quote: '"Be used in detriment or opposition to the aims, principles and rules of the National Worker's Council".'

Some people recited poetry, I was prone to do so with old song lyrics, and some even said prayers. Victoria quoted the rule book.

'And what does all this fall under?' Roijin asked pointedly.

'Good question,' I hastily replied, not wanting to hear another rule. 'And one that quite possibly has a far-reaching answer. But I think we can take a guess that whatever its use, it's not under the control of the Lambeth Workers' Council. No, this is a little hideaway for a rainy day. Whose umbrella it's acting as, is something we need to find out about.'

Victoria added, 'From what I can make out, the guns here are a mixture of ex-Brit Army and smuggled imports from Croatia and Greece. I have been able to the identify the fingerprints of both Donaldson and Brownswood on several of the crates and on some of the weapons themselves. There's a few I can't identify, because we haven't got them on file.'

Roijin frowned. 'Mixed results, I'm afraid. I got in – eventually – and I can say that this is definitely the device used to control the drone.'

'Definitely?'

'One hundred per cent, Vic. The operator must have assumed that the crash had cut the link. But it hadn't, hence us being here. I can also say that whoever it was controlling the drone, they were doing so manually. The 3D Virtual screen was turned on, and was being used at the time of the attack, so they would have had a visual of what the drone could see right in front of them. They used that projection to guide it by eye – like a virtual TV screen. Its AI was switched off. It was operated in or around the Shard of a maximum to a 5km radius of it. Further bad news is that it is totally wiped clean of prints or any identifying traces on the software. A real pro job.'

'Which is interesting,' I said.

Victoria agreed, 'Yes, isn't it? They are incredibly thorough in removing any traces of themselves with regard to the Shard attack, but then leave facial recog and fingerprints all over the guns. A strange mutually exclusive dichotomy; on the one hand, a thoroughly efficient operation, which doesn't leave a trace and on the other, they might as well have scrawled on the wall, "I woz ere!".'

'And why leave the phone here?' Roijin asked. 'Why keep it at all? It's a throwaway, so why not throw it away? Like you said, Vic – they went to a lot of trouble to clean it of anything personally incriminating but then they leave it in a room, which has nothing but that.'

We had a lot to think about. Not least, Victoria Cole coming out with the phrase "a mutually exclusive dichotomy" and what exactly that meant. Had it been used in an NWC mandate?

'I think it's time to leave,' I said.

Vic looked thoughtful. 'You sure this will work?'

'I hope so.'

'Totally. They won't know we've been here.'

'There is though, the slight problem of the arrival of the militia. They saw we were in here. No-one's going to believe that we came in, guns out, militia on call, and we just came in and not open a single crate.'

I grinned. 'Actually, I had thought of that.' I waved my phone in the air. 'I synchronised my phone with yours as you were hacking into their systems. I thought it would be useful if we all have access to the system here. I reached the militia before they could see where I'd emerged from, and I opened another unit. They had their eyes on me and not a door opening. The fact that the doors here are silent and very quick, helped. They were wondering who I was, and what I had in my hands, rather than looking around. By the time, they did, it was open and I was pointing at the wrong one. What they saw was another room with just a few armchairs and sofas in. That was ideal, they thought it hilarious and only added to the picture I was painting of it being one big cock-up. The story they'll be no doubt telling everyone is what a chump I've been.'

Despite themselves, Roijin and Victoria were impressed.

'It's not full-proof, but it'll have to do until we've a chance to talk to Jackie.'

# CHAPTER 20:
# ELECTION PROPAGANDA

T idied, closed and cameras reset, we left the storage unit. I had volunteered myself to look a bit closer at what Donaldson was doing at the time of Mike Stewart's murder. DD had suddenly become very interesting to me.

Getting off the bus, I headed to the Railway Arms. Predictably, it was near the railway station. There would probably be scores of them called that round here. It was that sort of workplace that pubs were called after. Market Tavern was another one. But you never got The Crap Plastic Arms next to a recycling plant, or the Make it Last next to a benefits office.

It was a lovely, balmy, orange summer evening and people were out and about. The Railway Arms wasn't far and could easily be spotted by a dozen or so people standing outside with glasses in their hands. Whoever had designed the pub had the imagination of an ailing amoeba. Pictures and 3D visuals of trains were everywhere. I made my way to the bar, which appeared to have the only non-railway themed picture in the place, and that was only because it was a large 2D TV screen. The sound was down, but it was obviously the news. I could see a number of delegates being interviewed in front of the Manchester NWC building.

I got a lager from a skinny kid with bad skin and very long hair. I paid and pressed my ID. He knew immediately why I was here, and it wasn't to admire the trains. He didn't even wait for me to say another word, before informing me that he had already told the militia everything he knew. Remembering the interview notes, I said, 'Then, you must be Ray Christensen.' And "everything he knew" amounted to very little.

'I know you did, Ray, but just to make sure we've everything, could you tell me.'

He shrugged. Basically, taking out the multiples of 'maybes' and 'possibles', he simply repeated what he'd said before – it had been busy and he hadn't taken too much notice of who was in. Looking at the vacant look in his eyes I could believe that. If his mental focus had been an apartment, then it had been a long time since a tenant had lived there. I projected a picture of Donaldson for him to look at. That achieved nothing.

'You say that there were a lot of people in?' I asked, thinking that even in these days of a workers' paradise, 9am was a tad early to be drinking, for most. Turned out though, as well as the stations, there were several 24-hour nurseries and assorted other workplaces who all kept to non-traditional hours.

I tried again. 'He works at the cleaning control depot, just around the corner. He might have worn a lanyard or a high-vis.' Or eulogised the cleanliness of the road to socialism.

'Yeah, I know the place. Still don't know if he was in, though. Sorry.' Then something disturbed his mental lethargy. He turned to the woman on the stool who had been pretending to be watching the TV and sip her drink, but had been ear-wigging our conversation. 'Gem, you were in here that morning, weren't you?'

'Last Tuesday morning,' I added, helpfully.

'Yeah. You know, the same morning we saw those horses.' Both started laughing. 'Never did find out where they came from.' For a few moments they shared the memory.

She began to wipe tears away, especially the thought of the piles the horses had left behind. 'I remember. I was in here with Nat and Franz, colleagues of mine. Good craic it was.' She explained. 'We were sitting here and suddenly a group of horses just wandered past. No riders, no saddles, nothing. No-one was with them. They were all alone. Just them, in the middle of London! Where the hell they came from we never found out. It was like a scene from a cowboy film.'

I showed the photographs of Donaldson. 'You don't remember this guy being in here at the same time, do you?'

'Sorry, comrade. It was quite busy in here. We were just happy to have finished work. For a few pints and a laugh. Certainly got that with them horses!'

'He doesn't ring any bells at all?'

She took a sip and thought. A light went on in her head. 'Only that obnoxious bitch, sorry, for my sexism there, but, well, she was. Good God, she was full of herself. Telling me to pull myself together and not to be so childish. We were laughing too loudly apparently. Laughing too loud? Calls herself an anarchist and she hates people laughing.'

The bartender tilted his head at an angle. 'Well to be fair, Gem, it wasn't quite that. You did spill her drink all over her. I think that's what she objected to.'

'Anarchist?' There were quite a few around nowadays, but still, my interest was piqued.

'Yeah. She had an AF badge. Alright, we were being childish, and a bit lively, and I'm sorry about spilling her drink, but I did apologise. She was just being moody. I mean, I get being in a wheelchair is crap, even if it is one of those hover things, but lighten up, girl.'

She now had my full attention. Even the blasted virtual-reality Flying Scotsman, which was hurtling past my ear, was ignored. I showed her projected Sofia Brownswood. 'It couldn't have been her, could it?'

She looked closely. 'Yeah, that's her. Bloody big gob.'

What a small world we live in. 'Do you remember who she was with?'

She shrugged. 'Some bloke, I think, but I had a few words with her, bought her a new drink, then moved well away from her, so couldn't say for sure.'

That made me think of something which was blindingly obvious, but for some reason, hadn't occurred to me before, and my betting was that neither had the other good comrades. 'Most people use tokens to pay, could you check to see if Donaldson had done so?'

Raymond looked at Gem, who looked at Raymond. It wasn't love, he was wondering if this infringed on his citizen's rights and in particular, this Dave Donaldson's, and so was she. They didn't need to, because I could have told them both, that yes, it did. But here, the few might have to have their rights infringed, to protect the many, in the name of the many. I didn't need to try out my 'this is our law and order' speech, because with a shrug, he went to the till and tapped two buttons. Up came an itemised bill for Dave Donaldson, registered at 09.13. He had purchased one orange juice and a pint of Cornish Bitter.

'If he was with her, then the bitter was for him; she was having the OJ. That's what went all over her,' she smirked.

Nothing else afterwards came up for either of them. It didn't prove anything one way or another, but it did suggest that they had left afterwards. Assuming that it took them ten minutes to drink it, it would give him enough time to get home and kill Stewart off. It would be a rush. And was that really the behaviour of a killer – sup a pint, then dash home and fatally inject the target?

Still, it was worth following up. I phoned Roijin and told her what time he'd left. 'We need to find where he went after leaving here. We'll have to talk to him. Also, is there any chance you could get into the personnel records of the Euston Cleaning Control Depot and see which party members work there?'

'No problem. Get back to you ASAP.'

Raymond and Gem were now deep in conversation about what the collective name for horses were.

Always happy to help the proletariat, I told them, 'There's a few – herd, stable, harras.'

We didn't have time to explore why there were so many before Roijin had sent the list of comrades who worked at Donaldson's workplace. One stood out. One who might even be classified as a friend – Cathy Smith. I gave her a call. My Cribber's luck was in.

'Pete! Long-time no hear! I figured that you were too busy battling reactionary drones!'

Looking behind her, I saw what looked like an office. 'Hi Cathy. How are you?' I continued with a few minutes of pleasantries, asking after various mutual friends and family members of hers, but then after I felt that the social etiquette had been followed enough, I got to the point. 'You at work?' I asked with fingers crossed.

'Here until eleven. Why? Ringing up to complain about your road?' She laughed.

'No, that's just fine. Good work! No, I was wondering if I could come in and talk to you?'

She looked surprised. 'Er. Yeah, sure, that would be fine, but why...?'

'Good. I'll be there in ten minutes.'

Cathy Smith had joined the party the same time as Jackie Payne had. I must have been on fire back then, because, it had also pretty much been me who had recruited her. I'd met her on a demo and we had got talking. Two top recruits in the space of a month – that happened rarely back then to anyone, let alone me. There had been periods when she had drifted in and out of the party, but the ins were longer than the outs. She had been extremely supportive over the death of Caroline and Lisa, and my subsequent breakdown. Or she had tried to be, but she was one of many that I had just pushed away. Doing that had been a far more effective way of hurting myself than my clumsy attempt at cutting myself.

She was waiting for me in reception. Her whole face turned into an affectionate smile, and she ran over and wrapped her arms around me. For someone so short, she had quite a hug. I could only see the top of her short grey hair as she buried herself into my jacket.

'It's been too long, Pete. It's great to see you!'

'I'd say the same, but I can't actually see you with your face down there in my jacket. Mind you don't crease it, this is quality linen. And if you're not careful, Cathy, you'll drown in my armpit sweat.'

She pulled away sharply, and gave me a gentle slap on my arm. 'That's disgusting, Pete!'

She hadn't changed that much since the first time I'd met her. She was a bit wider in the waist, which with her short hair, and side parting, gave her the resemblance of a tennis ball.

After straightening her glasses, she asked why I was here.

'Is there somewhere we can go?'

She led me up to the third floor. It was open plan, all new looking, spic and span, tubular steel and plastic compounds. There were approximately half a dozen people in the room either at physical screens or fiddling about with virtual ones.

'What do you do here?'

'Maintenance and control,' she explained. 'The cleaning vehicles are AI, we're here just to oversee and monitor them. We can talk over there.' The corner, she explained, was both her work station and also the mini-kitchen for the floor. 'Rep's perks.' She grinned. It would mean that we would be well away from the others and could enjoy some privacy. Like the perfect hostess, she offered me a chair and a coffee. I accepted both.

Putting the kettle on, she passed me a plate of biscuits, which I swooped on, realising that I hadn't really eaten a great deal today. She laughed. 'Hungry, are we? I can make you a sandwich, if you want?' With a mouthful of digestive, I nodded. 'Cheese okay?' I nodded again, and mumbled a thank you. She apologised that she couldn't vouch that the bread was the freshest. 'It should be okay, but when I went shopping, they hadn't much in. It's a few days old, but it's been in the fridge. Anyway, it's that or nothing.'

'It'll be fine. Cheers.' I looked at the five screens above her desk. They were feeds from cams on the different cleaning vehicles. 'These on every bot?' I asked.

She turned around, bread in hand. 'Yeah, most of the time, we barely notice them. They're just on in the background. You forget about them after a while. We only take notice if there's a problem. It's a live feed, so it's like a mobile wallpaper.'

'Do you keep copies of them?' I asked, thinking that if they did, then that might be useful.

She shook her head. 'Nah. We'd have endless hours of rather boring footage, which would serve no discernible purpose.' That was a shame, because I could think of at least one. Especially if they happened to be operating around 14 Driscoll Avenue at 10 am on Tuesday morning. 'Unless there's a problem,' she added. 'We do save it then.'

'Problem?'

'Yeah. Mainly anti-social littering or rubbish. Anything which is deemed to be against the ethos of healthy and community living.'

'And how could I find out if there's been a problem at a particular place, at a particular date and time, and whether it had been saved?'

If Cathy was surprised by the request, she didn't show it, and indeed, didn't even break her buttering. Instead, she just told me to simply request the file for a particular place, being as specific as possible, giving the time and date.

I did. It was an outside chance, but maybe we could get a glimpse of our mysterious hoodie. The local council had been trawling vehicle sensors, such as on buses, and cars, to see if anything could be seen, but I hadn't heard of anyone checking street cleaning. Nothing, though, was referenced. Must be a trouble-free neighbourhood. All litter bins emptied and roads cleaned. Drawing a blank, I did the same for the area surrounding the Shard at the time of the attack. Here, there was something: a cleaning vehicle had hit a van. There was five minutes of footage. All high-res and with sound. The problem was that it was eight months ago.

Cathy joined me, passing me a mug of coffee and plate full of delicious looking sandwiches. I pounced on the food. The bread was fine and the cheese tasted even better. 'I assume, you're not here to see old – and neglected – friends, but for the case you're on. Get anything useful?' she asked, nodding towards the screen. I shook my head. 'So, you're working with Vic, then?'

'You know her?' I asked, through mouthfuls.

'Not well. She's not the type to be known well, is she? I was in the same branch as her for a few months. She's dedicated and hard working. Always focussed, rather spookily so. I never found her unfriendly, but she's very careful about telling you anything personal. It's politics first, last and only.

It must have been about six months that we were in the branch together; I know her name but not much else. I don't even know where she lives.'

'Well, that makes me a bosom buddy, then,' I said, before inserting another one of the orgasmically good sandwiches into my mouth. 'I've been to her flat, even had dinner there.'

Cathy's eyes widened in mock surprise, and a salacious smile crossed her lips. 'Wooo, is there some luuurve to be told here? Romance in defence of the revolution?'

'Hardly. I don't know much more about her than you, but she's okay.'

Cathy's face was still straight out of a Christmas Panto. I half expected her to yell, "Behind you!". 'I'm only pulling your leg, Pete. I didn't mind her, actually. In fact, considering that the reaction of most comrades when she joined was somewhere between suspicion and downright hostility, it was commendable that she changed sides at all. Anyway, enough of that. I'm guessing you're here about DD? He said you've been asking about him.'

'What did dear Dave think about that?' I asked.

'Let's say, he wasn't best pleased.'

'Shame. Tell me, what he's like to work with?'

'He's okay, actually, despite our political differences, I'd even go as far as saying that we're friends. Or at the very least, we're friendly colleagues. His persona of the hard-man of the revolution isn't quite the whole story. Don't get me wrong, it's not an act – he passionately believes in his politics. He has profound disagreements with us, but he's always been willing to support anyone he feels is on the wrong side of oppression or exploitation, and he's very good at it. I have got to say, Pete, I like him. He's committed, and yes, even charming, in his own way.'

I almost choked. 'Charming? Well, that's a side I haven't seen of him. Charmlessly, full of his own self-importance, yes – but not charming!'

'Pete, you find an awful lot of people arrogant and over-confident. A psychologist might have a field-day discovering why that might be.'

I ignored the implication. 'They try, but haven't managed to yet. But let's return to our charming Dave – has he been acting oddly recently?'

'Can't say as he has.'

'What about the day of Mike Stewart's murder?' I reminded her of the date.

'Can't say I remember anything out of the ordinary.'

I told her what time he had given us for when he had left work.

'Sounds about right. But let me see.' She looked at her screen and it confirmed it.

'Do you remember where he said he was going?'

She looked at me blankly. 'How'd I remember that? I don't keep tags on people!'

'Try, please Cathy. It's important. Maybe mentioned Sofia?'

She looked truly puzzled. 'Sofia? Your sister? Does she know him?'

It was my turn to be confused, until I realised what the misunderstanding was. 'No that's Sophie. As far as I know, she's fine. No, Sofia Brownswood. AF leading light, killed in the Shard attack.' I described what she looked like. Or at least used to, until a drone had drilled her with bullets.

'Sorry, I don't remember.'

'He didn't mention that he was going to meet Brownswood at the Railway Arms?'

'Don't know how long it's been since you've been in a normal workplace, Pete, but here, we don't feel the need to inform each other of where we're going, or who we're meeting...' She stopped. A thought had occurred to her. She stroked her neck. 'But...now you mention it, he did say he was meeting her. Yeah, that's right. Said he was going for a swift half.'

'Did he say what he was going to do after it?' Like maybe to murder a flat mate? I thought to myself.

'No, sorry. No idea.'

That was something I would have to chase. 'Okay, could I have a look at his desk please?'

She wasn't too happy about allowing me to do so, but she didn't say anything, and led me to it. A picture of Jamille Cronin sat prominently on top. I nodded towards it. 'His hero?'

An affectionate smile met my comment. 'More like his inspiration.'

A look of horror crossed her face, as I went through his drawers. I wasn't sure why – what did she think I'd be doing, giving it a light dusting? She looked around to see if any of her colleagues had noticed. Whatever she had intended, she was now my look-out. But I found nothing but the usual desk crap.

'Is this his personal computer, or are they all linked?' I said, pointing to the two hard screens on top. She replied that they were networked, all data was shared. Which, if that was the case, then no MI5 agent would leave anything incriminating on it. 'Do staff have their own personal space on them?'

'No, he'll have his own – this is purely for operational purposes.'

'Is it here?'

She looked around. 'Not that I can see. He usually leaves it on top.'

I stood thinking; it made me look impressive. 'Does he ever get visitors?' I asked.

'No. Not that I remember. He leaves his political activity outside, we all do, helps keep the peace in the building. Not that we hide our politics, but it's controlled. And before you ask, I don't tend to listen to colleagues' phone calls, so I've no idea who he's been in contact with.'

'Okay, I won't ask. I will ask, though, if he ever talked about Fiona Bailey?'

'Only in passing. She's an AF sibling and a housemate, after all. Dave considers her to be too soft, too trusting of us. Pretty much like he saw Mike Stewart. Not that he openly criticizes her, he wouldn't do that, especially not in front of me, but some of the comments he makes have an undercurrent to them. But, like I said, it wasn't anything major.'

Nothing major; but it was worth noting. 'What about Isabella Torres or Eduardo Almeida?'

She looked at me blankly.

'They're also housemates of his.'

For a few more moments, she thought. 'He may have; Spanish, aren't they?'

'Portuguese.'

'Uh, okay, Portuguese. Certainly, the name Isabella rings a bell. Sorry, Pete. Can't think what it was, something mundane and domestic, I'm sure. Nothing important, I'm certain of it.'

And with that, the big interview petered out.

# CHAPTER 21: MEDEA

O n leaving her, I phoned the office. As I did, I noticed that I
had two missed calls from my sister. I couldn't actually recall
a previous time when she'd made this much effort to get in
touch. A worry wormed itself into my brain. Then, there was the fact that
Vic had seen her crying in the Soul Shack toilets. This wasn't the sister
I knew. It had prompted me to make a bold and almost unprecedented
decision: I'd go and see if she was okay. I phoned the office and let Roijin
know what I was doing.

Sophie had phoned from her home com system, but that didn't mean
that she'd be home. When she had been once the queen of all she surveyed,
you could have almost set your watch by her movements, but nowadays,
who knew? When the mighty fell, their time schedules took a battering. But
something made me want to see her face to face, so I would risk a wasted
journey. I had decided not to do the obvious and check first to see if she
was home because in all probability she would just palm me off with an
excuse and tell me not to come. In any case, paying her a visit also gave me
some time away from our investigations, and I had often found that a break
meant I could return to a problem with fresh ideas. Or at least attempt to
have an idea in the first place.

Anyway, for better or worse, I was here, outside her two-storey terrace
Georgian house. She answered the door and smiled. 'Peter, what a pleasant
surprise.' If she was surprised then she was too cool to show it, and if it
wasn't in actual fact, a pleasant one, she was far too concerned with social
niceties to say otherwise. 'What brings you here? On the run from feral
anarchists and looking for a safe house?'

I smiled back and wondered how my younger sister could always
manage to make me feel like a naughty ten-year old. 'No, I've come to
requisition your house for the state.'

'Well, in that case, you better come in.' She turned. 'I'm slobbing in
the garden watching the news.' Seeing her well-tailored red summer dress,

I considered that her idea of slobbing was very different to most people's. Perhaps we did have some things in common, then. 'By the way, your friend Cole has just been on, skulking around in the background of some of the reports. I think I even saw you at one point – although, it may have been a homeless person.' I saw the back of her head shake. 'You do look rather crumpled, Peter. Usually you're at least well-turned out. All part of the Philip Marlowe vibe, is it?'

'No, it just comes with hot weather, and having your arse shot at by drones.'

'Sympathies. Still, you survived – that's the main thing. The country really has gone to rack and ruin – still, if you will abolish the judges and the police, then I guess that's what happens.' She didn't give me time to reply, not that I had any intention of doing so – it was too hot for political ping-pong – especially with my dearest sis. She pointed at the French windows. 'Go into the garden and I'll get you a drink. Wine? Beer? Coffee?'

I went for beer. The garden was as you'd expect it to be – immaculate, carefully planted and oozing politeness. It was fairly small, and there wasn't a leaf or petal out of place. Hovering above the lawn, was a 2D image, roughly a metre square, of a reporter from one of the more right-wing broadcasters. A retro deckchair and matching table were positioned in front of it. A wine bottle sat in a small, equally retro, last century, ice-cooler. A half-drunk glass of wine kept it company. I walked up to the rectangular mosaic covered underground shed. Her husband had – ostentatiously – shown me it on one of my rare visits here. I pressed the small discreet control panel to open it and then engage its small lifting gear. What rose from the depths wasn't Hades – he'd never afford the rent in this neighbourhood – but a deckchair.

I positioned the chair on the other side of the table and sat down. And there, hovering in front of me was Noah Walker. Christ, I couldn't get away from any of them. I turned the sound down. He was on his familiar hobby horse of the state being too weak, but I was saddle sore. Just then, Sophie came back out and handed me a bottle. It was an American import beer. 'How did you get this past the embargo?'

Her bare shoulders shrugged, and gave me a cheeky grin. 'Where's there's a will, there's a way.' Then she let out a squeal, which was as genuine as a fish on a skateboard. 'Oh, look, Miss Bailey! How wonderful! Our very own, anarcho wet-weekend! Turn it up please!' She slid a pair of red sunglasses onto her nose, and sat down, theatrically striking a pose of the utmost interest in what Fiona was going to say.

'Actually, Sophie, do you mind if we turn this off? I've had enough.' I stroked my brow, and closed my eyes for a few seconds. When I opened them, the screen was off and I could see her looking at me. 'Are you okay, Pete?'

To my surprise, I decided to tell her about the Shard attack – second by second. I went into such detail that if she had been planning on making a movie, then she had the scriptwriter right there in her painfully manicured garden. It was like one of Roijin's virtual recreations. I didn't need my ever-faithful counsellor – Dr Brakus – to tell me why I was doing this. She would describe it in some painfully elongated swimming metaphor, but I called it just getting a shit day off my chest. Whilst I spoke, Sophie delicately drank from her glass and listened. I had come here to see what was troubling her and yet here I was, unburdening my problems onto her.

When I had finally finished, her face showed concern. I liked to paint her as a heartless Tory git, but that wasn't quite true; she did have a heart – somewhere. I apologised again, and tried to pass it off as just the result of a hard day.

She leant across. 'Peter, should you really be involved in all this?'

I went to protest, but she held up her hand, her fingernails matching both her sunglasses and the rose bush behind her. 'No, I don't mean politically, I'm not picking a fight here – honestly – I'm not. No, I mean, your investigating job. You have to admit that it puts you in a lot of danger.'

I took a swig from the bottle and reflected that it was a shame that these beers were so hard to come by, because the taste was smooth and thirst quenching. 'I'm okay,' I said, not wanting to spend too much time on the subject of my mental health because a sympathetic sister was far more disconcerting than any drone attack. I changed the subject with the subtlety of a terrorist outrage: 'I'm fine, really. Actually, I am more worried about you, Sophie.'

'Me?' She pushed her sunglasses slightly up her nose. It was her way of showing cool control, but in actual fact, it was something which she did when she felt far from that. She was weighing up what to say to me.

'Yeah, I'm worried about you. Something isn't right. You rang me – three times.'

'Can't I ring my brother? Or is there an NWC directive on that?'

'There isn't, but there *is* a Sophie directive. In the past, we've gone years without communicating and yet you turn up on Caroline's birthday, then ring three times.' I left out the fact that Victoria had seen her crying in the toilets, because the only purpose that would serve would be to embarrass her. An admission that I knew something, which she would perceive as weakness, would prompt such a cold reaction that would make the ice-age seem like a temporary chill. However, by not doing so, I had given her an easy reply.

'I'm worried, that's all.'

And that, my friends, was her reply. But it was nonsense. Obviously, she had changed her mind and now didn't want to talk about what was worrying her. However, I knew my sister. You could tell when Sophie wasn't going to back down, when she was breathing and conscious. I also knew that even the tiniest sub-atomic times when she would, it was, never, ever, when she fractionally pulled the glasses forward, and then back. Her high-end sunnies were her drawbridge. I decided to retreat and observe. I muttered something about being mistaken and tried out some small-talk moves. So, we sat relaxing in her urban retreat, whilst I consumed three more bottles, before I said I should go. She smiled, said that she understood, managed to get a few digs against both Vic and Jackie Payne, then led me to the front door, presumably to ensure that I didn't seize her precious pottery collection on my way out. Opening the door, she clumsily kissed my cheek. Clumsy, not from the wine, but the utter novelty of it.

I was on the street and the evening traffic was humming past.

'And you *are* okay, Pete?' she asked. 'You don't think that drone attack was personally meant for you? I mean, you are beginning to make a name for yourself.'

I reassured her that I sincerely didn't think it had been. Half-turning to go, I added, 'Let's face it, Sophie, if they'd wanted to bump me off, they'd a much better chance to do so, and they didn't take it.'

Her eyes narrowed. 'Why?'

Turning around, I explained, 'Oh, I didn't tell you, did I? They broke into my home, and I interrupted them. I was a sitting target – in the downstairs loo, armed with some super-soft bog paper, whilst they had a gun. Hardly an equal match, but they just left me alone. If they had wanted to get rid of me then that was their chance. To be honest, Sophie, I don't think the Crib is that much of a threat. It was probably just to scare me. All they did was to leave a page of an atlas open.' I laughed.

She didn't join in the humour; instead, she went pale, paler than usual. 'An atlas?'

Quickly glancing at my watch, I noticed the time, and thought I needed to get back to the others as soon as possible. They might not think they needed me, but they did. 'Yeah!' I shouted, hurrying off. 'It was a historical atlas, of all things. They left it open at the Middle East. My guess is that if it means anything, probably something to do with crusades and such like. That's what they think they're on, isn't it? Don't worry about me, Sophie. It was just to spook me. Anyway, got to go! Keep safe!'

As she closed the door, I could see a look on her face, a look which I had only seen once before. It was of fright. It was one of terror.

That look haunted me on the tortuous journey back to Somerset House. Several times, I thought I should turn back and see what was really the matter. But I didn't. Instead, two buses later, both crawling at the speed of the continental shift, I arrived there at a time when evening preferred to be known as night. Darkness was all but in control.

Entering the office, the smell of Chinese food hit my nostrils, enticing me to partake. Small silver foil boxes covered the desks. I had arrived at what was obviously buffet time. Roijin and Asher were seated, each tucking into a plate of delicious looking takeaway. Vic was standing, helping herself to a chicken wing. She looked at me and smiled.

'Ah, he's back. All these damned murders do tend to interrupt your life. Class war can be hell on family life.'

'Sorry, I had to see my sister.'

Her reply was flippant: 'In that case, with a sister like yours, hell is family!'

The other two laughed. But I saw what they hadn't – the more truthful response in her eyes, one which was asking me if all was okay.

I surreptitiously nodded, but continued the act. 'Ha, ha, very funny!'

I eyed up the dishes and in particular the one containing Kung Pao Chicken. I hadn't realised that I had been quite so hungry. But then, doesn't the smell of Chinese food always make you hungry?

'So how is the delectable Sophie?' Vic asked.

'Fine,' I said, helping myself to a plate and scooping food onto it. 'Where's Odette?'

'Gone home,' Asher replied, then after swallowing a noodle, he added, 'It's good you're here, Pete, we've some news which might be of some use.'

That was a shame. I could have used her technical skills and her ambiguous morality. I had decided that I needed to act, and act in a decidedly questionable way. Finding a chair, I shovelled down some more of the rather fine food and nodded. 'Good,' I mumbled through it. 'But mind if I say something first?'

Vic waved her hand, indicating the stage was mine.

I recounted my visit and that I had got the distinct impression that Sophie was hiding something. They all sat politely listening, but with the possible exception of Vic, they were more focussed on forking food into their mouths than what might be troubling my sister. It didn't seem much more that tittle-tattle to them. I went on, regardless, 'Then when I was leaving, she again asked if I was safe, and so in passing, I mentioned the break-in. Her attitude changed. She seemed worried. And then when I mentioned the atlas and the Middle East, her face fell. She had a look, one which I have seen before, but only the once.' I paused, remembering it. 'We were out in a dinghy, in the Med, when we were kids, and Mum fell into the water – she wasn't a good swimmer, and for a minute, it looked like she might go under. In the end, Dad jumped in and got her, and she was safe. But Sophie was terrified. She thought Mum was going to die. Sophie had that same look, when I told her about the atlas.'

Roijin wasn't impressed. Swallowing down some rice, she brushed it aside. My comment that is, not the rice. That either went down her throat or stuck to her lips. 'She's just worried about you. Okay, you two have your issues, but she still loves you. Hell, me and my brother fight like cats and dogs, but I love the little bastard to bits.'

Asher nodded. 'Yeah, what's the big deal? What you've been through recently, wouldn't it have been a bit weird if she wasn't a bit bothered?'

'Not necessarily; I know my sister. She didn't have that look when I was telling her about the drone attack and not even when she heard about the break-in. No, it was when I said which page it was that shook her. I think my sister knows what the significance of it is. We might have just dismissed it as a prank, but somehow I think it's more, and I think she knows that.'

'How the hell could she?' Asher scoffed.

'I don't know,' I admitted. 'I didn't ask, I came here.'

'Did she know of the attack or your visit when she rang? I mean, it would be natural to contact you to see if you're alright – surely?'

Time to get to the point. 'No, not my sister. It's most definitely not natural. Which is why,' I turned to Roijin and took a deep breath, 'I want you to tap all her comms systems.'

'What?' Her mouth opened and thankfully the rice fell off her lip.

I repeated myself.

'On what grounds?' Roijin demanded.

'On the grounds that MI5 have tried in the past to recruit her and used threats to my safety to do so. I think that they're doing it again. I think that's why she's been behaving like that. Sophie is caught between a cause she believes in, against a regime she detests, but a reluctance to act which will lead to violence. And like you said, whatever the stuff that lies between us, she's equally reluctant to do anything against me. I honestly think that break-in was to both freak me out, but also – somehow, and I don't know how or why – to send a message to her.'

Asher pooh-poohed my logic, 'Sounds a bit far-fetched.'

'Ash, *I know* it sounds far-fetched – but I saw the look. It resonated with her – she understood it.'

I could see Roijin was about to say something; I answered her before a word had left her lips. 'Yes, I should have pressed Sophie more. I should have tried harder to find out what was troubling her. But I didn't. Maybe that's because I'm a crap Crib detective, or maybe I'm a crap brother. But I *know* something is up and I've a feeling that it's because they're trying again to contact her. They wouldn't for a second expect us to do something like tapping her communications. So, if we do just that, then we might find something out.'

Roijin was far from happy. 'But, Pete, it would be illegal!'

'Roijin's right,' Asher added, licking his fork. 'Your sister might not consider herself a worker, but she is covered by the same rights. We can't just trample all over them. That would make us exactly what Dave Donaldson says we are. No, Pete – no way.'

'That's the Dave Donaldson who collects crates full of guns?' I snapped. 'Some of us have books stored, or old photographs bagged up in the attic, but DD has an arsenal. This is a vicious class war, comrade. One which will shape the future of humanity. We really don't have the luxury for liberalism.'

He shook his head, almost in sorrow. 'Pete, mate, you sound like Noah Walker – the ends justify the means, and the end is socialism, shtick.'

I wanted to slap the pair of them down, but the problem was that they were quite right. That pissed me off. Ex-coppers lecturing me on democracy and freedom in the workers' state, really was the pits. And that they were right to do so, made it even worse. For a few minutes no-one said a word as political, moral and philosophical mental wrestling matches took place in our heads.

Predictably, it was Vic who first returned to the land of the vocal. 'You sincerely believe this, Pete, that your sister is being threatened by the security services?'

'Yes, I wouldn't suggest it otherwise.'

'To bug your own sister?'

'Yes.'

She gave Roijin a meaningful look, who looked back surprised. 'You can't be serious? I know I've been willing to bend a few rules recently, but that's been for concrete reasons, and involving particular targeted people, who we've genuine concerns about, but this?'

'Family members always bug each other. That's what families do.' No-one laughed. It hadn't been one of my best. I decided being grown-up was a better strategy. 'I know it's morally and legally dubious, Roijin, and I wouldn't suggest such a thing lightly, for anyone, let alone my sister, if I didn't think it was necessary.' Good grief, I was turning into Odette.

What would she decide – would principle win? But pragmatism was more brutal. 'Okay. I'll do it before we go.' Her reply was little more than a resigned whisper.

'Good. Thanks, Roijin.' Vic's body language indicated that she was keen to get down to business. 'Okay, that's sorted. Let's start with Mike Stewart's murder. We know how he was killed. He was injected, under his fingernail, with a substance which faked anaphylactic shock. Ash, do we know anything more about this?'

He slid his plate to one side. 'I did a few more tests and managed to find minute traces of Fododrozine in the compound. Fododrozine is a fast-acting drug used to tranquilise wild animals. It's been around for a few years. Usually, it's easy to trace. I mean, there's no need to keep it hidden. But some of the chemicals in this compound acted on it, intending to remove all traces of it – the Fododrozine – as well as the other active ingredients. Like I said, the Fododrozine is well-known, but despite contacting every lab in the country, and some in Portugal, the compound as a whole, remains a mystery. A friend in Lisbon did say that they had heard that the CIA have developed something like it.'

He paused. If he was waiting for gasps and wows, he was disappointed. It was hardly news that the CIA was taking a keen interest in chemical terrorism. Receiving no standing ovation, he continued, 'It's known that shock can be induced, leading to paralysis, to anything which seriously disturbs the area, between the fingernail and skin. It's a natural reaction.

That's why tearing fingernails has been a torture of choice for centuries. So that, and the Fododrozine, explains why there was no struggle. If you could manoeuvre the hand and swiftly insert the syringe, then it would have been pretty quick and simple.'

Victoria thought for a second. 'Ash, you previously you told us that the hand would have been horizontal when the syringe went in.'

'Yes. From the small hole it suggests that. I'd guess that he had his hands on the table flat.'

'Hmm. Anything else?'

'We did another low-count DNA sweep of his body but only found Marie Williams' and Fiona Bailey's, but that can be accounted for by the murderer wearing gloves. However, we had more luck in your hallway! We found fibres from Stewart's kitchen, there, and microscopic particles of Stewart's wooden flooring on your carpet. Also, using geolocation technology we can make a direct link between the pavement outside his house and yours. In other words, we can be sure that the same person was at both. I'll do further tests to see if we can find other places they might have visited.'

'Good. That gets us a little further.'

'Yes, it does,' he replied with more than a touch of deflation in his voice. To be honest, I didn't blame him. Because of him, we could now place our mystery man *inside* the house, which surely could be classified as a breakthrough. But Vic thought it just got us a "little further".

"Ash, you've been liaising with Stewart CIM, you need to inform them of these findings and treat locating this mystery hoodie person as a priority.'

'Will do.'

'Great, so okay.' She looked directly at me. 'Pete, you've located Donaldson before Stewart's death.'

Now it was my turn. Lucky me. I told them about the Railway Arms. Then about the visit to his workplace.

I expected some dismissive comments at that, but to my surprise Roijin actually looked impressed. 'Good work, Pete. The road cleaning department wasn't allowing me access. I did get access, though, to the tram, bus and car sensors in the vicinity. There are clips of Bailey and Marie Williams, but nothing of the mysterious hoodie. Got nothing around Pete's at the time of his break-in either.'

'And Thom Simms?' Vic asked.

'Nothing so far.'

No-one spoke. Vic was deep in thought. Or she was dizzy from the circles we were going around in.

'What about Torres and Almeida – the Portuguese love birds? Have we confirmed that they're both on Lisbon?'

Roijin answered, 'We're still waiting for confirmation. Things are a bit tense there at the moment and they have bigger things to worry about than a Brit murder enquiry, but we're hopeful we'll hear something soon.'

Not having anything resembling a reply, I just humphed, hoping it sounded profound and astute.

Whether Vic considered it such I would never know, because when she finally alighted from her train of thought, it was at a completely different station. 'Okay, maybe we should put aside the Stewart murder for a while. Ash and the council can continue with that. Let's see what we have about the Shard – Roijin?'

Impressively, the change of focus didn't faze the woman one jot. 'It's difficult to know what to look for, Vic. The drone was controlled by a phone and there's plenty of footage from car sensors and the like, within the possible radius, of people using them. It's hardly a unique sight. Even by discounting those of different models to the one we found in the storage unit, it still leaves half a dozen people who it could possibly be, including our friends Donaldson, Walker and Anand. It's difficult at this stage, to even attempt a match with ours because it's completely clean inside and out.' Then her regretful intonation became slightly less regretful, and a note of optimism could be heard. 'But I think Ash has something.'

A detail of the 3D recreation of the Shard shooting appeared. It was of Sofia Brownswood slumped in her chair and over the table. Hiding underneath were rather disconcertingly lifelike images of Phan Bien and my good self.

He drew up another screen. This one was an even more disturbing image, of the real Sofia Brownswood, lying flat on a mortuary slab. I really hoped that Roijin's new-found positivity was warranted. Certainly, when Asher spoke he sounded a little upbeat. 'I looked closely at the entry and exit wounds, and it looks to me like the firing was deliberate, not just random. Look...' He pointed to the virtual recreation. Red streams of light helpfully showed the trajectory of the bullets. 'The drone could have continued firing straight into her, but it looks to me, like it's trying to get around her. If that's the case, then we could presume, or at least entertain the notion, that she wasn't the target, but was simply in the way. Look, the other bullets are either side of her.'

Roijin got to her feet, when a visual of the drone appeared. 'Look at how the drone slightly changes its position; I think that supports this theory. As I said, I haven't had much luck with the phone, but I did manage to find a transmission from it at this time, which our AI has identified as being used to change direction of its aim. This was deliberate targeting.'

Bless Yelena, she was a great AI. She should get a reward, maybe a vocal upgrade?

Asher added, 'Look at the projection lines...'

I got their drift, which frankly was more of a shove. 'So then if she wasn't the target, it was either me or Phan.' They nodded. 'And if that's true, then that offers two more possibilities. If it's me, then we, or I, have found something of importance about Stewart's murder, which requires my elimination. That's possible, but then we've the same question as we've always had, and that is, why would they kill me in such a crude and dramatic manner? Why not kill me when they had the chance in my house? Or knock me off my scooter? And surely, if I know something, then so do we all. They'd have to eliminate us all.'

I sipped some water. 'But it makes more sense if it's the second – it was Phan Bien, who was the intended victim. If so, then the link to Stewart is quite obvious. Both wanted closer cooperation between the two organisations and have long been campaigners for such. Get rid of those two, and not only do you remove two high-profile advocates of unity, but you actually ramp up the tension. As we've seen today, it's a fraught time, and it doesn't take much to increase the temperature. But then, why do it in such a public manner? Why not do it in an underhand way, like how they eliminated Stewart?'

Vic nodded. 'But if this is to create friction, then the Shard attack makes sense because it's such a news-worthy event. Small isolated murders don't have the wow factor that a full-on airborne attack does.'

'Okay, I follow all that, so why not do something dramatic for Mike Stewart's murder? Why make it look like an accident?' I was speaking to myself as much as to the others.

Victoria pondered the point. 'Perhaps the fact that we originally thought it was an accident made it possible to give the impression that we're both incompetent and corrupt in covering it up.'

That made sense. 'And by extension, so was Jackie. When you add the outrage of the news that Jackie had been forewarned of a threat to

Stewart, it was like lighting a fuse. It created an explosion of mistrust and a crisis, which is growing by the day. I mean, even someone like Bailey, who's committed to unity and cooperation, is doubting us. If she is, then there's a whole layer of AF and NON-supporters out there having more than doubts. That's why the murders are so different, because they were to be used in different ways. But with the same goal...'

Victoria finished my sentence, 'To further mistrust. Sounds plausible to me.'

'Then it becomes obvious that the probable intention is to create a fracture in the NWC, which would weaken the revolution, indeed, might even destroy it.'

Asher wiped his mouth with a tissue. 'Agreed, Pete. The question is then who's behind it? I don't mean, which organisation, I don't see that we have the resources to find that out, and anyway, that's almost an irrelevance. I mean the individual – who had their hand on the trigger, so to speak. Or to be more accurate, their hand on both the syringe and the drone. Our problem is that it could easily be someone who we've not heard of. In which case, we stand little chance of getting them.'

'True, but I think this is up close and personal. It's someone we have come across. This is a carefully choreographed plan, it isn't just carnage for the sake of it. They know exactly what they're doing and have carefully set it all out. Their next move is either about to be enacted, or it already has. I think, organising from afar wouldn't have that kind of control. I get this feeling, this sense, that we've spoken to this person.'

We were being guided by a sense and a feeling, not exactly science, but then I didn't have a better idea.

Our forensic expert also had a feeling. 'Doesn't Dave Donaldson, then, fit the bill? He's, after all, the arch proponent of the AF breaking with us. He's been cropping up on a regular basis throughout this investigation. We can't seem to turn around without him coming into view.'

'Possibly, Ash,' Roijin agreed. 'But we've not the slightest slip of proof against him.'

'Well, apart from a storage unit full of guns,' I said, thinking that in my day, that would have been enough to get you into serious trouble.

'But it doesn't prove that he killed Mike Stewart,' Vic replied. 'It proves that he distrusts us – in the extreme – but not that he killed him.'

I told them what I'd learnt from the visit to his workplace. 'We can concretely place him at the Railway Arms. And whilst it would mean getting a move on, he could have made it to his house in time. We need to check where he went after the pub.'

Asher nodded, and threw another metaphorical dart at DD's face. 'It's also a bit iffy about where he was at the time of the drone attack.'

'Though, if the criteria for being a suspect is that they're promoting distrust, then there's quite a few who should also be considered; more than quite a few. Certainly, we could factor in Mr Comrade Conflict himself – Noah Walker. And let's not forget Reyansh Anand. He's military, so operating a drone would be a piece of cake, for him.'

'I wouldn't let that influence you, with AI and navigational support, anyone could have controlled it. Even you, Pete.'

# CHAPTER 22: SUMMER EVENING

I t had been a long day setting our surveillance into motion. 'Long' being a euphemism for dull and repetitive. The heat was still oppressive and all-consuming. Every pore on my skin seemed to be weeping. Even on my scooter, there had been little relief in the way of a breeze. Simply, there wasn't any. My mood had lightened on the way home. The traffic was light, so I could just motor along. I was knackered and just wanted to get back.

Getting closer to my personal nirvana, my mind was racing was faster than my scooter. I wasn't concentrating on what it should be, keeping safe on two wheels, but on the morality of what we were doing. Whether we liked it or not, and on this the Crib was unanimous – we didn't – we had found ourselves caught up in a national debate as to how the revolution should handle the crisis and the growing instability, which the violence against us was creating. The controversy was dominating the news; Mike Stewart had almost been forgotten about, with the Shard attack the lead item across every format you could think of. A leading party cadre in Swindon and two more AF members from the Fools' List in Coventry had also been murdered today, but were mentioned more to add context to the debate, than to mourn their loss. The crux of it all was that the revolution's principles and values were making us vulnerable. Some supporters were even questioning our open borders policy, which, they said, was allowing foreign reactionaries to come into the country.

Whatever pretty revolutionary socialist principles I could mouth, the fear was that our unit was behaving just like the old regime, and for the most part, I was either actively agreeing to it, or worse, suggesting it. I wasn't even talking about those principles anymore. Or at least not doing so very often. Our defence was based on the context, on who our actions were for and who they were against. Ironically, Walker and Anand would agree with that one hundred per cent. Funnily enough, both Donaldson and my sister would be pretty chuffed too, because it confirmed everything which they were accusing us of.

I pulled over to the side of the road. A thought had just occurred to me; relaxing at home would have to wait. I made a call and received a very surprised answer. It was late and phone conversations between us had been somewhat limited just recently. Her shock increased, when I told her that I wanted to meet her at the Soul Shack. To my surprise, she had said yes. I started up again, and took the next right and headed to the bar.

Entering it, I saw Marie Williams immediately, sitting at the far side, in a small snug. Behind her was a large still from the 1970s TV series *Bewitched*. Considering that it was midnight, it wasn't too busy, with just a scattering of groups, standing or sitting. There appeared to be little dancing because tonight, the music appeared to be soundtracks from the nineteen sixties and seventies. If I wasn't mistaken, and I was rarely was when talking about music from the period, the tune was from Roman Polanski's Chinatown.

Marie was in a casual dark blue short-sleeved blouse, which probably had last been fashionable when the film had premiered. Her hair was tied up into a denim cap. She wasn't looking around, which was what one usually did when they're waiting for someone. She was watching TV clips from various American shows. Directly in front of her, on the fake Formica table, was a tumbler full of, I presumed, a double gin, with a touch of tonic and three cubes of ice. That had always been her evening drink.

I walked over to her with a beer, regretting that it was sadly not of the standard of my sister's black-market stock. Marie looked up with an expressionless face. She had been here several times before with Caroline and myself. That had been back in happy times of friendship, of love and cheer. Not now; she'd cheerfully tear my head off.

Being a friendly chap, my natural reaction on seeing someone I had known for decades was usually to give them a hug, or at least a smile, but instead, I tried to match her blank face. She reacted by crossing her arms.

'Thank you for agreeing to meet me,' I said formally.

She didn't reply straight away, but just gave a slight tilt of her head. It was preferable to the reply I had expected. So, I took it. She stared directly at me and got straight to the point. 'I can only give you half an hour. To be honest, it's been a while since I've been out at such a time. Normally, I'd be tucked up in bed. So, what do you want from me? Is this an official meeting?' She looked around. 'It's an odd place to hold it, I must say.'

'I thought we could twist the night away.'

As ice-breakers went, it wasn't a great success – the muscles on her face didn't move a millimetre.

'It isn't an official meeting. Marie, I need your help.'

'Really?' She tilted her head. 'All not well in the vanguard of fighting bourgeois insurrection?'

'Less vanguard, more guarding the van,' I replied.

It was an old joke, one which had never been funny, and still wasn't. She pursed her lips. 'Okay, well, I'm always happy to help you with *your enquiries.*'

Leaving the intended snarky undercurrent to sink under its own weight, I explained. 'I want to ask you about some of the people we've been looking into. You know everybody and have pretty much worked alongside everybody, so I thought you might be able to add some depth to what we have found out.'

Her tone moved along the hostility colour chart from pale crepe sneer to fuchsia antagonism. 'You want me to snitch on comrades?' I could also detect just a hint of chartreuse bemusement. She now had such a low opinion of me that it couldn't sink any further and so, couldn't take offence at anything I might suggest. She just thought it mildly amusing that I would think that she would do such a thing.

'No,' I assured her. 'I just want...' I paused, trying to grapple with the best description of what exactly I wanted her to do. An idea strolled past, I lassoed and corralled it. 'All I would like you to do is to give me your opinion of them, of their politics, and what positions they took at important key moments.'

'How on earth will that help you?'

I had been thinking about that. 'Most murders are all about ownership. Some occur in the course of taking one thing from someone else. Deaths through domestic violence, also have their roots in ownership. When one human believes that they either own, or part-owns someone else. In both cases, these are privatised killings, involving private motives. In war, it is slightly different, the basis is ownership, of land, assets, markets, etc, but it's nationalised. We're in a class war, where it's about who owns the world we live in. The motive here will be political, so having a better picture of the politics involved is essential. Just as important as forensics or eye-witnesses.'

My opinion didn't receive ridicule, nor applause; she didn't indicate whether she thought it profound or pretentious. 'But I would presume that I'm a suspect. Let's not forget, that very recently in a previous investigation, you bestowed such an honour on me, so I couldn't imagine not having it again. After all, I was one of the people who found the body. If I remember my Dorothy L. Sayers, correctly, those who found the body are often the guilty ones. In which case, surely I'm not a reliable source of information.'

I took a sip. 'Good point, except that actually, it's rarely the case, except in certain sub-genres. And anyway, you're not a suspect, Marie.'

'No? That's a surprise. I must put that on my CV.'

*Not now*, I should say. We've checked your movements at both the time of Mike Stewart's death and the Shard attack, and both check out. You have a timeline, where we can trace where you were for virtually every minute up and till then. You didn't have a chance to kill him, and then reappear in time to be met by Bailey. In any case, the murder was by injection and medical in nature – so it's hardly likely that you would have chosen to kill in that way, and with you there. You've worked in hospitals all your life, so it would have been an act of supreme bravado to do something which would focus attention on yourself. And to be honest, Marie, you're worse at tech matters than I am, so I seriously doubt if you could control a drone.'

I waited for an explosion of outrage, coupled with a lengthy lecture on ethics and comradeship! But none came. She sat their arms crossed, staring.

Receiving no verbal opposition, I tried to soften her body-language. 'Marie, I know you're still furious with me for falsely accusing you in a previous case. You feel personally betrayed and insulted. I get it. It isn't just the hurt of being a long-time comrade and being suspected of being a counter-revolutionary, it's being so accused by a friend. As was. But please remember, that it was political, and so is this. We need your help.'

She picked up her glass and after a swirl of the ice, took a large sip and then nodded. 'Okay, Peter, I'll cooperate. So, who are we talking about?'

'Thom Simons. You were with him at Mike Stewart's house and he was also at the Shard. What do you know about him?'

'Hmm, not a lot. He's a member of the undecideds. Been one for a couple of years, I believe. Although, why the so-called Unaligned Movement don't just disband, I don't know. I mean what do they believe in? How can you not be aligned in this period? He was a social worker. Nice enough chap, if bland, like the majority of the undecideds. He was involved in the community health care initiative with me and Stewart.'

'I specifically want to know about the civil war. As you'll remember, I was enjoying prison hospitality during it, so I'm a little hazy on the details. Was Simons involved?'

She laughed. 'Well, as much as any of the Unaligned Movement were. They're not known as the undecideds for nothing. I think they still haven't decided if they were for it or against it. I really can't imagine MI5 wasting a good agent on them. And let's face it, if he was one, then they sure did screw that up in the Shard, didn't they?'

The amusement stopped, and a cloud crossed her face. 'No, that was wrong. That was a tragedy and I shouldn't be so dismissive of him. He was a good decent socialist, who in the limited amount of time I had with him, came across as a nice bloke. He didn't deserve that.'

I nodded. It was pretty much what I thought too. Okay, so onto someone whom many might struggle to describe as a nice bloke. 'Tell me what position Dave Donaldson took on the seizure of power.'

'Donaldson?' She quietly laughed to herself. 'He's pretty straight-forward, he thought we should seize power and had held that position for at least two years prior to when we actually did. As no doubt you have found out, he's a blow-hard. As soon as the National Workers Council was formed he was arguing for revolution. Then, as now, he considers us to be conservative and lagging behind the class. You may remember several half-cocked and premature attempts at uprisings a few years back. They were flops. Donaldson was linked with several of them. His denials were never that strenuous. He's always the ultra-left.'

'These risings – could they have endangered the movement?'

After a moment's thought, she pulled a face. Maybe it was to give it some exercise, or to check that her muscles still worked, but more probably, it was to indicate that whilst my suggestion was a possibility, it was unlikely. 'Well, insurrection is both a science and an art form, and timing is important, but we never feared that it would lead to a precipitous rising. They were fruitless adventures, which tragically led to some pointless deaths. I'm not sure that Donaldson himself actually believed they would be the push to set the revolution in motion. We trod a fine line over them – understanding the impatience and supporting the ideals of those involved, but criticising the timing and the lack of accountability. There was also the fear that it would give Parliament the excuse to reintroduce draconian laws and herald another clampdown.'

'So, you would describe Dave Donaldson as an adventurer, but is a sincere revolutionary?'

She gave me a look. 'I guess so, yes. He's bombastic and arrogant, but he's highly effective. What dealings I've had with him, have been business-like, if I can use such a term, but not what I called friendly. To be honest, I find him boring in the extreme. But I have to admit that he's effective – people listen to him. He can win arguments, that's for sure. And whatever some of us think of him, he's capable of inspiring people.'

'Has the party ever had doubts about his commitment to the revolutionary cause?'

'Not his commitment, no. His politics are a different matter! Putting it plainly, the Central Committee think that he's a gung-ho ultra-left whose passions overrule any common sense. His approach often resembles a First World War general whose only strategy is to go over the top and charge. Give him credit though, unlike them, he himself would be running into no-man's land. But I guess what you're not so subtly asking, is whether we ever thought he was a spy. In which case – no. Not that I'm aware of. But then, we never spend much time thinking about that sort of thing. I can say that I've never heard any rumours or suggestions that he wasn't anything other than what you see, *and hear.*' A grin almost appeared, before being shooed back into its place.

She recounted various moments in his life, when their paths had crossed. She did so, in a cold professional manner. One could almost call it robotic. She was willing to help but that didn't mean that she had forgiven me. That would be a long time in coming, if it came at all.

'Did he ever take any decisions or political positions, which seemed out of character?'

I had asked this for the simple reason that if the counter-revolution had people in positions of power, then it would make sense for them to be more than just conveyers of information from the movement to their handlers. Surely, if they had a profile to help shape events, they would do so. She, though, couldn't think of any, although, she did say that one never knew with the AF.

'Does the Central Committee think that he represents a threat to us?'

'No. Donaldson's just hot air. His hatred is of the capitalist order. He merely dislikes us.'

If only she knew. I thought for a second and took another large glug of the average lager. I wasn't about to inform her that we had found a large quantity of guns, which appeared to belong to him, and were not intended for a clay pigeon shooting competition. That was something Jackie needed to know first.

'Does the friction between the party and the AF concern the CC?'

'Of course. We're the two major organisations of the revolution and if we're fighting amongst ourselves, that can only but weaken us. However, we've no choice, we have to tackle the more extreme elements of the AF and their political misconceptions. That's why the NWC and the workers' councils across all the home countries, have been holding such debates. They're heated and passionate, but they are crucial. It's our belief that we're not in the position for the state to instantly wither away. If we do that, then the US Marines will just parachute in and create their own.'

'Which is pretty much the argument Noah Walker and Reyansh Anand use.'

'True, but they go too far in the other direction. Why? Are you interested in them as well?' she asked. Her voice sounded incredulous, half-meaning it as a joke.

'We'll get to them later. Tell me about Fiona Bailey.'

She finished her drink and held the glass up. I took the hint, and got up and went to the bar and got her another one. She savoured the new drink, before passing on her thoughts concerning sister Bailey.

'Fiona's okay. Friendly and someone we can always work with. She has important differences with us, no doubt, but she's fraternal. You don't get the sectarian hostility from her that you do from Donaldson. Not that she's push-over though, she's well-thought out and very articulate. I'd say that she's a far superior speaker than him. I've seen her myself win over an audience, no matter how hostile. She's written much on cooperation of the left. There was even talk of her and her faction leaving the AF and joining us.'

'The AF splitting? When was this?'

'Last year. There were secret talks between her and the CC. We thought we were close to coming to an agreement, but it wasn't to be.'

'Why didn't it happen?'

'We were never sure, but I think it was the news that Portugal could be entering into a revolutionary phase. And of course, it was. That seemed to change her mind; Jackie thought that she and her group believed that it would be best to stay in the more flexible, less disciplined AF. But whatever the reason, it wasn't to be.'

'Did Donaldson or Sofia Brownswood know of this?' I asked, thinking that it was the first I'd heard of it.

'Not that I'm aware of. It would have made news if they had. I don't think I'm exaggerating, when I say that there would quite possibly have been violence, if it had been publicly known, with Donaldson's wing and Bailey's fighting in the streets. Something which would not have done us, or the revolution, any good whatsoever. The party would have been in the middle of it all. It might have been worth taking the risk if everything had been agreed, but not over exploratory talks. That's why we kept it so quiet. Why we still do.'

'Was Mike Stewart involved?'

'Oh yes, he and Bailey were the prime movers of the talks. We always had the impression that he was perfectly happy to have continued with them, but was outvoted by the rest of the faction.'

'I'm surprised,' I said. 'After all, when all is said and done, we are a centralised party, which both Bailey and Stewart dislike. There must have been concessions offered.'

She sighed. 'Well, we were proposing that they would be confederated with us. We were working out the detail of what issues a party line would be binding, when Portugal started to kick off, and their faction pulled out. We were willing to make further, quite major, concessions to have them on board.'

'But that would have involved a national consultation in the party, and then there would have to have been a member's vote on it.'

'Yes, but we were confident that the numbers involved and the security it would have given us would have won the rank and file over.'

'Who knew about this in the party?'

'Just the CC.'

I thought for a second and looked across the bar.

Three-dimensional imaging had begun to our left. It had been created out of the early nineteen sixties British TV series *The Human Jungle*. I knew of it, because it centred on Herbert Lom starring as Dr Roger Corder, a psychiatrist who could treat any mental disorder. My own personal brain doctor – Sarah Brakus – had sometimes referred to it as an example of sowing misconceptions on mental health. I had no wish to watch it, let alone interact with it. The last thing I was interested in was joining the cast in its fictional dissection of neural diversity. I had enough of my own to deal with. At the best of times, I couldn't see what the teenagers found so amusing playing in 3D interactive showings. Let alone this one. I looked away and returned to the scene of my creating: 'What was Bailey's and Stewart's position on our seizure of power?'

'Both supported it, although they did have certain misgivings, if I remember correctly. But then, the actual organisation for the defence against the coup was kept pretty much in-party for obvious security reasons, so the AF really only knew about it after it had already started. That irked them. Basically, they weren't happy about being kept out of the loop. Not that I blame them.'

'You were one of the central figures in organising it. Did you ever have concerns about whether there was a traitor in the movement?'

She looked at me with an expression of disbelief. 'You'd know more about that than I would. That's how you made your name, after all! It was your first case, I mean...' She stopped, I could tell that she felt that if she continued with her train of thought, then this could very quickly become antagonistic. Remaining disciplined, she steered it into the sidings. 'But that's another matter. No, no-one in particular, not even the one you, er, uncovered. We have always known that they would have people involved in the movement, but the seizure of power was organised by a small group. The political groundwork was of course open and public, but the detailed organisation was only shared with a select few in the party. Bailey and Stewart didn't know until after it had happened. They did air concerns that we might have gone too soon and be vulnerable to a counter-revolution.'

Obviously, my face showed what I was thinking. 'You shouldn't read anything into that; it was a nervous time. And in some cases, this nervousness led to opposition, but Bailey and Stewart never went that far, but many did, even in the party. That's to be expected, a revolution is something you don't go into lightly. Sometimes even the most hardcore can get the wobbles; I mean, even Noah Walker did.'

'Walker opposed the revolution?' I was stunned.

Marie seemed not to share my surprise. 'He was worried, yes. There's no shame in that. Let's not forget what the situation was. There was dual power, with both the NWC and Parliament claiming to be the legitimate government, meaning that there was a daily power struggle. The Prime Minister dramatically changed all that when he attempted a coup. His desperate attempt to topple the NWC and to purge Parliament forced our hand. It wasn't the situation which we wanted. We had no choice but to defend ourselves, and to do so effectively, we had to seize power. But many people had doubts and worries. Jesus, I did, and I was tasked with helping to organise it! So yeah, Noah had concerns. Very few people didn't.'

'Was he one of the chosen few who knew what we were planning?'

She shook her head. 'No, he knew at pretty much the same time as everyone else did.' She laughed. 'Maybe that's why he had worries, because he wasn't involved.'

'Have you ever doubted Walker's honesty?'

'Pete, if he's an agent of world capitalism then he's a very odd one indeed, considering that if he had his way, they'd all be against the wall, in front of a firing squad. He hates the ruling class with a deep passion. He really does hate them both as a class and individually.'

That was true. He spat venom whenever they were mentioned. 'How long have you known him?' I asked her.

'Oh, I guess it must be about nine years now. I met him soon after he came up from Southampton. He was one of the leaders of the Small Firms Strike down there. On strike for almost three months. After its defeat, he was sacked, so he came to the Capital. Very committed and hard working. I would also say, very reliable. I don't agree with everything he says, but he's honest and straight-forward. I don't have any personal problem with him.'

'What about Reyansh Anand?'

'Eh? Reyansh? Why you asking about him and Noah?' She scoffed, when it dawned on her why. 'Surely, you can't suspect them?' Before I had a chance to say anything, she raised her hand. 'Okay, don't say anything. I know. I know. Your job is to look at everyone in the name of defending the revolution – I've read the brochure and seen the movie.'

She shook her head with the absurdity of it all. 'Okay, let's talk about Reyansh, well, he's a good comrade, an excellent comrade. Been in the party for about six years and has done great work within the military army rank and file. His work is largely why we've such a large membership there. As far as I can remember, Reyansh was in favour of the seizure. Because he sat on the army council, he was one of the members who knew in advance what was going to be required. He's always believed that the workers' movement has to have armed support from the military. To believe otherwise, is just naive and...' She abruptly stopped and stroked her chin. 'Actually, come to think of it, he did have a connection with Mike Stewart.'

'Which was?' I asked. Pretty much instantly, I guessed what she was going to say, but I wanted to be sure and hear her take on it.

'He had a number of rather heated debates with Stewart over the role of the army and what should happen now. Sometimes it almost felt as if it was just man versus man. Stewart felt that the party was not demilitarising the streets and disagreed totally about the formation of the army council, whereas Anand thought the exact opposite.'

'Was it ever anything other than "heated debates"?'

'No, just good old passionate democracy.'

'You've no doubts about him, then?'

'Well, if I was being honest, I do think he has lost his way recently. That's the influence of Noah Walker; but that said, even some on the CC are being won over by Noah. Personally, I think he's travelling in a very dangerous direction. I'm no pacifist and I know full well that sometimes we must do certain things, which we'd rather not do, but I think there are lines which shouldn't be crossed. If democracy is too compromised, then it ceases to be democracy, and we lose the state we're supposed to be defending. I think the partnership of those two comrades is unhealthy for both of them. And, I'd say, the party as a whole. What worries me is that he has quite a following in the army councils.'

'You think he might use that influence against the party?'

'No, not really. He's a disciplined comrade.'

'Okay, one last question – if you pick one issue which is worrying the Central Committee the most, what would that be?'

She finished her drink and gave what I had asked some thought. 'That's an interesting question; well, we've been spending a lot of time discussing food distribution and protecting supply routes, because both China and the States have been bullying others to join the embargo. We've been both talking to friendly nations and developing domestic production. The fact that after Portugal, our influence not only hasn't spread, but in some ways has shrunk. The fear from the international ruling class has increased their hostility, and has increased domestic oppression abroad. Their working classes have fought back, but many aren't in the position to adequately defend themselves. That's been a concern for several weeks.' She paused. 'But I doubt if you'll be surprised to hear that right now what's been top of the agenda has been the dropping in support for the party. We've had several NWC reps replaced and we fear that more will follow. Bound up with all this, is the growing tension between us and the AF.'

She was right, I wasn't surprised.

Realising that my time was up, I thanked her for her help. Marie stood and nodded. As she was leaving, she turned. 'I should have asked earlier, how are you, Pete? What you went through in the attack, must have been terrifying.'

I gave a small smile. 'Yes it was, but I was lucky. I'm okay.'

For a split-second, I thought she was going to say something else. A look, which I couldn't decipher, flashed across her face. But whatever she was going to say, she decided against doing so. Instead, she just nodded again, and walked out. I drank down the dregs of the beer and followed her out into the street and to my scooter.

The journey home was uneventful. Arriving at my house, I first saw Victoria's car, with the roof off, confidently glowing with style and cool. The woman herself matched it. Sunglasses on, feet up on the retracted steering wheel, she was talking into her phone. Pulling in behind her, I saw the second addition to my road – a man and a woman, in their thirties, whom I vaguely remembered, sitting on temporary chairs in my front garden, chatting to each other, and enjoying the warm evening.

Turning the bike off, I went up to Vic. With perfect timing, she finished her call and turned to greet me. 'Evening, or should I say, morning.' She grinned.

'Sorry, if I've kept you waiting.'

'How was Soul Shack?' she asked, in an unconcerned voice.

That took me back. 'How, how did you know that?' I asked, before answering myself: 'you put a tracker on my phone?'

She shrugged and smirked, as she got out the car. The roof started to come down.

'I presume the reason for the presence of the tracker, and for you being outside my home at this time, and for our two friends there, is that whilst we've pretty much agreed that it was unlikely that I was the target for the drone attack, you're taking precautions just in case. The office talk was just to reassure me. Meanwhile, you arranged this.'

'You're far too valuable to lose, Pete. That and the thought of spending more time with you was too good an offer to decline.' Said with all the sincerity of a plastic duck in a zoological park. 'But the emphasis is still on Phan Bien. We still think it was her who they were after. You just happened to be there, but we don't want to take any chances. Ash and Roijin are with her, with rather more militia.'

'I'm touched. How long do you intend to stay?' I asked. A worry was starting to gain momentum in my brain.

'All night. Killers don't tend to work office hours. If there's a problem I can stay in the car.'

It was an idea. Just recently, the only living thing which had slept under my roof with me, had been the cat. Now it seemed, Victoria would be. The two red warriors presently sipping water and resting rifles on their laps, by my front door, would presumably also be demanding a bed to crash in. The thing was, although the new society was creating all sorts of original and exciting social conventions, I wasn't sure there was one concerning bodyguards and sleeping arrangements. However, getting her to stay in the car was rather ungracious, so I asked her to follow me, and I'd do us a drink and something to eat.

Passing my personal protection, I invited them too. We were attempting to create an equal society, so I couldn't just leave them outside. However, they assured me that they were fine and thought it best if they stayed out front to act as a visible presence.

'That'll get the neighbours talking.' I smiled.

'Oh, they know,' replied the woman. 'The street committee has been informed.'

'Oh good. Now I'm the postcode's celebrity assassin's target.'

Whilst contemplating my new-found fame, Victoria announced that whilst she had scanned the house, she wanted to make doubly sure by conducting a physical search. The priority for me was getting fed; an assassin would just have to wait their turn. By the time she had returned, I had made a start cobbling together a meal of sorts from what food I happened to have in the house. I hadn't been shopping for ages. Not the best policy when the blockade-hit shelves could often be patchy. Detective work and saving the revolution was hell on domestic chores. I hadn't been swimming for I don't know how long, either. Not good. Not healthy.

'Salad okay?' I asked. 'I'm afraid that I haven't got much in, so it's going to be what I can find and throw together.'

'That sounds great. What I could do with, though, is a shower and to wash these clothes.'

'Yeah, that's fine. Although, the dryer operation of the washing machine is buggered, so you'll have to let them dry naturally. Apparently, the part which is needed is in short supply in the country and we are waiting for them to arrive. But in this weather, it shouldn't take too long for them to dry. In the meantime, I suppose you could borrow...' I looked at her; she was far too petite to fit into my clothes. 'Er, I think Caroline's will be too large because, she was far taller and her...er...'

'Tits were much bigger?' She smirked, enjoying my evident embarrassment.

'Er, well, yes, I guess so. You could try Lisa's. She was more, um, your size.'

She nodded, then looked at me seriously. 'And you're okay with that?'

It was my turn to smile. 'Well, if it's the choice between that, you wandering around semi-dressed, or ruining a pair of my trousers, then yes, I can cope with that.' I took out half a lettuce from the fridge. 'The bathroom is upstairs on the landing and Lisa's...'

She was already turning before I had a chance to complete my sentence. 'I know. I've searched this house twice now, I know my way around here, pretty well.'

I put on some 2020s neo-soul and continued attempting to create something edible. Seeing the state of the cucumber, mushy and wet, I decided that it wouldn't include cucumber. I poured out some water into a jug. Opening the French windows, I laid out the garden table, making it as welcoming as I could. My activities did not go unnoticed. Red meowed and emerged from under the holly bush and came to check me out. Despite it being ridiculously late, I also got a wave from my neighbour and via ad-hoc sign language, made an enquiry as to whether all was okay. I nodded and pointed to the two glasses. Comforted that I wasn't about to be slaughtered, he disappeared.

I sat down, closed my eyes, and tried thinking of absolutely nothing. My self-imposed semi-coma was interrupted when I heard the washing machine's door being closed. Victoria appeared soon after. Her hair was wet, and she was wearing one of Lisa's black and white V-neck short sleeve shirts and cream cotton shorts. She saw me looking at her.

'You're sure that this is okay?'

I grinned. 'Yeah. I'll be honest, it does bring back memories, but Lisa would never have been barefoot – she hated her skin touching the ground.' The thought of her warmed my heart. 'And,' I nodded to her waist, 'she didn't usually tend to carry a gun.'

Victoria returned the smile, but didn't say anything. Instead, she made some polite noises about the food. That lasted seconds, before she was forking the quiche into her mouth. She was hungry, I cleverly deduced. For a little while, we sat in silence, eating. Red looked quizzically at her, wondering what this person was doing in his chair. The only sound we could hear were a few birds, some early morning insects, and music wafting from a few houses down. When she did finally speak, it was to suggest that she'd wash up, whilst I showered and changed. It was a good idea, but I worried at what had prompted the suggestion. I was truly tempted to sniff my armpits and check out in the mirror to see if I was looking that bedraggled.

The shower was more than good. I spent ten minutes letting the water cascade over my face, cleaning off the shit of the day. I took out some fresh, well-ironed clothes and slipped them on. I felt human again. Or as near as I could.

I arrived back downstairs to find Victoria sipping a beer and smoking in the garden. She had taken a bottle out for me but hadn't asked if I minded her having a fag. To be honest, even with the so-called healthy varieties of cigarettes, she was in a miniscule minority. I guessed that was half the attraction. She must have read my mind, because she immediately put it out and placed it on the small dish, which she had been using as an ash tray. Both went onto the wooden decking.

'Thanks for that. Just what I needed. Hope you don't mind but I got these out.' She pointed to the bottles. I didn't have time to answer her. 'Nice garden, by the way.'

I thanked her. We then played a gentle game of polite chit-chat ping-pong, before we got back to work and I told her of my conversation with Marie Williams. She listened, and Red jumped onto my lap.

She made a few comments before returning once more to silence, looking out onto my garden. Silences are funny things; they can have so many meanings. I grew up being told that the Inuit have lots of words for snow. I don't know if that is true, but it would make sense. We should have for silences. You can have so many types. There are shocked ones, embarrassed ones, those for remembrance, astonishment, uncertainty, thoughtful – the list is endless. Ours, there in the garden, cradling beers in our hands, was one of quiet reflection, and judging from the smile resting on her face, relaxation after a stressful day.

For no apparent reason, I finally broke it by managing to say something so mundane that in the mundane super-league knock-out final of the mundane, it would have mundanely won by three mundane points. 'You're the first person I've had here for years.'

She looked at me, processing what I had just said: surprise greeting the break of the silence, then a puzzled frown flashed across her forehead, before she started to laugh. 'Well, I guess I should feel honoured.'

I caught her laughter, and started myself. Which, in turn, made her laugh greater. Her head went back and I saw a level of amusement, which

I hadn't often seen in her. Red sat there looking at both me and her. I wondered if cats have multiple words for "humans behaving oddly", or does "human" simply cover that?

As it began to subside, I apologised for my banality. 'Yeah sorry for that. Sophie has always said that for all my self-belief that I'm as articulate as a knife, and that I consider myself supremely witty, I say an awful lot of dumb things.'

'Can a knife be articulate?' she asked, before laughing again.

Once more, I joined her and through repetitive giggling, managed to say, 'Which Sophie would use as a prime example of proving her point.'

Victoria started laughing again. I hadn't seen her so relaxed, nor seen her laugh so much.

'Well,' she said, 'let's be honest, Pete, there's not been much to laugh about recently, has there?' She started to pull herself together. 'So would you say, you and your sister are close?'

'Sort of,' I replied. 'When we were kids we were. We drifted during her time at uni. Politics got in the way. As for now? I don't wish her ill and she doesn't me, but I doubt if we're going to spend holidays together any time soon. You close with any of your family?'

She took an almighty slug of her beer and shook her head. 'All my close family are dead. I suppose the one I was closest to was my dad. Daddy's girl and all that. He was very proud of me getting a degree – the first in the family – and then me entering the force. He died six months after I finished my training. Mum died the year before.'

'Was it a surprise, you joining the police?'

'Ah, if you mean did I spend my childhood playing with plastic guns and handcuffs then no, I didn't, and so I guess it was. I was a fairly ordinary girl. I liked dolls, but I also liked football. I'd climb the odd tree, but I'd also spend hours on my phone playing computer games. They hadn't pushed me to be a copper, nor did they oppose it – they were fairly neutral over the service. They just wanted me to be happy. It's not a big story, very ordinary, really. How did your parents react to your politics?'

'Oh, they were classic Labour Party members, sincere, well-meaning, but ultimately naive people. They were very active in the area. Well-respected, and I'd even say, loved. But they thought I was the sincere, well-meaning but naive one.' I smiled.

'And what did they think about Sophie's Toryism?'

I remembered the blazing rows that she and they had had. For them, she was the one who they didn't understand, and she was the one who felt the need to change their parents' views. 'Let's say that they loved her, and were happy that she had own beliefs, but didn't share them.'

'An understatement?'

'Oh yes.'

A silence returned. One which would be more difficult to categorise, but it was still one which had a warm relaxed feel about it. I was interested in finding out more about Victoria Cole. Being enigmatic was all very good but I was intrigued about this woman I was now spending so much time with. Closed books were more interesting when opened.

'What about your friends? First joining the force, then joining us, one or the other, or both, must have ruffled a few feathers either side.'

Her answer was reflective: 'Yeah, you could say that.'

'An understatement?'

She smiled. 'Oh yes. Being brought up in Tottenham meant that I lost a few friends when I joined the service. Though, to be fair, some were okay about it. Then I lost a further few when I joined the party.'

'What about in the police? You keep in touch with any? I mean those who didn't follow you over to the party?'

'Well, we don't have reunion drink-ups if that's what you mean. Most cut off all communications with me. They did the same with Ash and Roij. As you know, only a tiny minority joined the party. There's a few more, who whilst not being actively pro the NWC, are willing to work with it. Most, though, are downright hostile to the revolution. Some have turned to direct action, although I'd reckon most are sulking at home, hoping that things will change. I do keep in touch with some ex-colleagues. Obviously, not those actively engaged in counter-revolution, but there's a few who will talk to me. Does that shock you?'

She had asked in an unusually soft voice. I'd expect such a question from her to have sounded more like a challenge. But this sounded more like a genuine enquiry.

My answer was a chortle. 'We can't solely have politically-pure friends; I mean, you've met my sister.'

'She'd get on a like a house on fire with some of those I used to knock about with. So, maybe a reunion drink-up would be a great idea. She might even find someone.'

'Nah, she's never been unfaithful in her life. Hubby may have left here, but she feels that ring on finger is binding in more ways than one. Anyway, she may love to publicly praise the police, usually to wind up any liberal within half a kilometre of her, but she wouldn't want to socialise with them, certainly not the lower ranks. Useful idiots, is how she views coppers.'

'Then, you do have some things in common with her.'

'I never said they're useful.' I grinned.

'Oh, but they can be. It's a good way to gauge what's happening by what they're saying.'

She was being enigmatic again, but she had piqued my interest. 'Which is?'

'Put it this way, Pete, straight after the revolution most didn't say a word; too scared of what was going to happen. They had visions of the streets running red with the blood of executed police officers...'

So had I.

'But now, more and more are becoming vocal. They are beginning to sniff weakness.'

'Especially now, I bet.'

'Yeah, especially now.'

Silence crept back and any chance to delve deeper into the private life of comrade Cole was lost. Politics had flexed its muscles and swept it aside. After a few minutes, she yawned and said she was going to hit the sack. I thought it a good idea and suggested she sleep in Lisa's room.

# CHAPTER 23: THEY SCRAMBLED UP THE PARAPET

S
lim and dressed from head to toe in black, except for a pair of designer green trainers, he slowly drew up the blinds. I lay asleep on top of the duvet. He had gained entry because the window had been left open in a fruitless attempt to get some air into the stifling bedroom. Once in, he had given me one quick sly look, waved and then opened the blinds. Outside, now with a clear view, the drone manoeuvred into place and fired. Bullets tore through the window, into the bed and into me. Blood splattered against the wall. My body exploded.

I awoke, burying my head into my pillow, drenched in sweat and shaking. Then, after a split second wondering how I was still alive, I realized that it had been merely a bad dream. Nightmares, I was fairly used to. Although they usually featured my Caroline and Lisa. There'd never been a drone before. I let out a long sigh of relief. Sitting up, I tried to get my breathing back to a regular speed. Slowly, it did, as my body and brain returned to normality. Or what passed for it, in my life. Terror of death was now replaced with that of possible embarrassment – had I screamed out? If so, had my house-guest heard me? I sincerely hoped not.

The more pressing issue, however, was what to wear today. The forecast was that it was going to be in the high forties, so common sense and the need for practicality over presentation, demanded shorts and t-shirt. Problem was that common sense was something which I had only an occasional acquaintance with. And the concept of presentation being anything other than in premier position was something unheard of in the Pete Kalder universe. With the day we had in front of us, I needed to feel confident, and shorts didn't exactly radiate authority. Not unless it was who was going to get the ice-creams. Thus, common sense had been summarily dumped for a higher judgement. I'd gone for a lightweight pale blue two-piece suit, skinny trousers and a one-button narrow lapel jacket, which was baggy enough for the accessories of phone and gun. Acknowledging the heatwave, I had chosen a pure white, crisply ironed t-shirt underneath. All finished off with white trainers and for that final funky detail – no socks.

Downstairs, I found Victoria lounging on an armchair, her bare feet slowly swinging over the leg of the chair, whilst she intently looked at one of my vintage compact discs, with an expression that an archaeologist might have when discovering a new tomb. Looking up from her deliberations, she quickly appraised my attire, but decided not to compliment the fine balance of style, formality and practicality. Instead, I got an ironic smile. I hoped that her nonchalance meant that she hadn't heard anything of my nightmares.

'Morning.' I smiled.

'Hi.'

She was back in her own clothes. She thanked me for their use and for letting her stay.

'No problem, you were playing bodyguard for the night, so I could hardly let you camp out in your car, could I?'

She grinned, looking younger than her years. 'Not so long ago you would have!'

I affected a *what-can-you-do?* shrug and replied, 'Sometimes you have to work with the devil himself, or with his grandmother, so tactics change.'

'Nice allusion. Not sure whether I'm the devil, or his elderly relative,' she tilted her head, 'and the quote you're paraphrasing, is I think, not *that* appropriate. Not yet, anyway. Leon Trotsky was talking about temporary alliances against the growing threat of Nazism in Germany.' She was letting me know that she knew her history too.

I didn't respond. I mean, what did she want me to do – give her a diploma? Instead, I did a fair impression of a B&B owner on uppers, asking her if she required anything to eat or drink, and so on. I discovered in the ensuing conversation that the pair of us shared a whole heap of morning rituals in common: we were early risers; we both almost medically required two cups of strong coffee for breakfast; and there was the pathological need for early exercise. In her case, a 5K run; mine – a swim. We both experienced an almost over-powering feeling of lethargy if we went without any of these. Rather impressively, she had already completed her morning routine.

I downed my coffee and said nothing. She put the CD back and told me that we were to be at the office for eight. We were to have another meeting. What the need for this one was, I had no idea. I didn't have time to find out, because she instructed me to be quick, as 'we didn't want to be late'. Like a good doggy, I obeyed, ran into the kitchen and washed my cup. Then after holstering my gun, I returned to the lounge and moved the CD into its correct place. She had put an Ornette Coleman Quartet album back in the Qs; I moved it back to the Cs. Basic mistake. She, though, had gone. Already out the door, she was saying goodbye to the relief militia, who had taken over from the nightshift outside my house.

It was already warm outside – *very* warm. The summer sun was already carpet-bombing the city with heat. The traffic wasn't too bad, but noticeably, the morning commute did have a worrying addition, with a number of militia vehicles on the roads. There had also been a couple of military ones. Soldiers could be stood outside NWC buildings, soldiers. They weren't in the numbers which they had been in the civil war, when they, and even tanks, had been a common feature, but their presence was troubling.

A bomb had gone off in the party offices in Solihull during the night, which, whilst there had thankfully been no fatalities, had hospitalised six. Reports were coming in that all workplace and geographical councils were meeting to discuss the situation. Some of the reps had already been replaced with those who believed the revolution should be more pro-active. A harder line all around was taking place.

Arriving at Somerset House, we were immediately met by a group of motorcycle militia, incongruously leaning against posters for the Courtauld Gallery for their upcoming exhibition of contemporary sculpture, entitled *Peace and Art*.

Everyone was already there. In the far corner, Odette sat in front of four projections, sipping orange juice and munching on a croissant. I guessed that she was watching the footage from the hacked-into phones. I wasn't certain that we had ever made a definite decision on the matter. It had seemed more that we had just stumbled into doing it. In any case, whilst the intention was to allow us to peer into their lives, all we were actually seeing were ceilings. One of which was painted cream, the other pale blue. True, there was the excitement of seeing an elderly woman in conversation with Reyansh Anand. Hovering beside it was a transcript of the conversation and information of the woman. It was his mum. She was telling him about her backache. The last one was pitch darkness. All in all, hardly blockbuster Oscar movie material. Asher was by his desk looking at his laptop, doing what, I couldn't see. Maybe, it was to look at another ceiling. Roijin was nearest to me and didn't look too happy with life. So perhaps she had indeed found something out last night that warranted this meeting. Or maybe she was tired after staying awake all night, guarding Phan Bien.

Victoria had seized the middle of the floor. But if we were expecting to start, we were disappointed. Excitedly, pointing at a far table with a plate of pastries, Odette announced, 'Look what I managed to find! Apologies, comrades, I have to admit that they're black-market, but still, they were only five Fists for the lot! I mean, five Fists! And they are fresh and very tasty – help yourself!'

I looked at her. 'Fists?'

She in turn, looked confused, 'Yeah, Fists, Fists – Workers' Tokens!'

Roijin came to my rescue. 'Fists are what young people have started calling Workers' Tokens. It's because of the large fist on them.'

'Oh,' I replied, duly educated.

I could see that my ignorance had amused Victoria and Asher. Odette looked sincerely puzzled that I didn't know what a Fist was. Maybe that was why Victoria started with an attempt at humour. 'As you can see, Pete survived the night with me. With everything intact, except possibly his handle on youth trends.' I politely smiled. The other three chuckled. A career in comedy though, would have to wait. Not receiving a standing ovation, she continued, 'And I understand, Ash, Roij, that Phan Bien is also safe and sound?'

Asher nodded. 'Yes, she's fine, in a secure location and heavily guarded. Not that she's happy about that. She had to be practically dragged there. She's especially narked she's had to leave behind all her electronic devices because they could be traced.'

Odette looked genuinely concerned. No doubt considering it to be a torture not worth enduring, not even if your life may depend on it. The rest of us gently laughed. Seemed, I missed the memo on adding humour to these briefings, I'd also missed the one on what was top of the agenda.

Vic looked intently at Roijin. 'Okay. Let's start with this, any news on Pete's sister?'

Roijin's large eyes got even larger, as she stared in surprise, before shooting me a look. She wasn't the only one who had been taken aback.

Victoria read her thoughts. 'Odette knows what we are doing. We're all comrades here!'

With as much decorum as she could muster, Roijin muttered, 'Okay.' Then, still looking at me, forced a smile, and quietly, in what I took to be Roijin being understated, told us that she hadn't found anything incriminating in my sister's communications. Sophie was unhappy with the workers' regime, which I knew – we knew, *everybody knew* – unless they'd been holidaying on one of the moons of Jupiter. 'Your sister doesn't believe in keeping her opinions to herself, that's for sure.' Roijin paused. Concern filled her voice. 'There does seems to be something worrying her at work, though. I'm not sure yet what that might be. I get the impression that it could be that there's bullying going on. Perhaps because of her political views.'

I thought about what she had just said. The idea that Sophie could be bullied was one that stretched the imagination, but then, in the right context, couldn't we all?

'What makes you think that she's having trouble?' I asked, feeling concern beginning to grow in my head.

'Things she's said. Nothing specific, hints she's dropped. But, I'll keep with it, Pete. I promise.'

I nodded. I knew that Roijin was thorough and dedicated. I didn't need to say anything; if Roijin said she would keep an eye on Sophie, then that was exactly what she would do.

'Nothing else to report?'

'That's it, Vic.'

'Okay, Roijin – you've also been keeping yourself busy 'round at Phan's.'

She seemed to relax at the change of subject. 'I tried out a few computer simulations, and it confirms what we've been thinking – Phan Bien was the target. She and Bailey are the top conciliators in the country, but they couldn't get to Bailey because she was hidden under the sofa. Basically, Vic, you saved her life.'

I felt like pointing out that I had done likewise for Phan Bien, but didn't. I could play modest. Certainly, no-one else made a reference to it. Instead, Roijin told us that she was planning on having another look at the drone operating systems, and was hoping to pinpoint exactly where the drone had been operated from.

Vic didn't take a bow, but continued, 'We need to look closer at the movements of Reyansh Anand and Noah Walker at the time of the attack. Conduct phone traces and look at footage of the TV broadcast that they say that they were at.' It was, she loftily announced, 'time to ask some serious questions'. Presumably, they'd only been giggly, half-arsed ones so far. 'Odette, have you anything to tell the group?'

With joyous abandon, our young comrade gave a brief but breathless account, of what our quartet of suspects had been doing since we had further trampled on their rights. Nothing sprung out as being unusual. Aside from contact with friends and family, all were busy contacting people to build support for their political positions. 'The people who they are contacting, are in turn, doing likewise.'

'Classic faction fighting,' I muttered. 'Shore up their support and build on it.'

Asher agreed. 'Yeah, Pete, and they are well within their rights to do so.'

Odette shrugged. 'So far, it's just democratic debate.'

'And Fiona Bailey?' Vic asked.

'She's been pretty quiet. I haven't heard her directly get involved in these discussions. I mean, she's been in contact with some political siblings, but in the main, she's pretty much been consoling herself and others, over the death of Mike Stewart. Mainly crying and reminiscing. Pretty sad really.'

'She's not been involved in any way with the political manoeuvring?' I asked.

'Naah, not really. I mean, she's commented on it, but she's been pretty much the spectator in it all.'

Victoria thanked her. 'Keep watching.' Then, she turned her attention to Asher. It was his turn in the spotlight. 'Have we anything new from the Stewart murder?' she asked.

'Sorry, Vic.' Asher moved forward in his chair, looking as if he was about to stand, but at the last minute decided against it, so he sort of hovered above the chair as if he was going to fart loudly. 'Nothing more than I said yesterday. An injection, with a compound that included a tranquilizer, injected under the fingernail. I think we have reached about as far as we can on that.'

After giving us a regretful look, he tried to look more hopeful. Announcing that he and the Bow Workers Council would continue to look into the mysterious hoodie who had been seen both around Mike Stewart's, and mine. 'We still don't even know their gender,' he muttered. But our mountain Ash knew full well that in our Crib, if you weren't doing at least four jobs at the same time, such as eating lunch, running 10K, playing Mozart's Symphony No 40 in G Minor K on the piano, and discovering a new species of insect in the Amazon Rainforest, then you obviously were a counter-revolutionary scab. So, as well as everything else he was doing, he would continue with it.

The bored teenager in my head again mumbled a moan – hadn't we already been through all this? Weren't we just going around in circles? What exactly was the point of this meeting? I was developing a strong feeling that we were lost and Vic had called us here with the vague hope that something would emerge out of it. With the exception of the ever-jolly Odette, who reminded me of Tigger from Winnie the Pooh, there did seem to be an atmosphere in the room. An atmosphere which was heavy, despondent, and even a touch oppressive.

Then the thunder broke. Victoria stuck her chin forward and announced, 'I've taken the liberty of requesting a *Protocol #5*.'

We all looked at her. We all knew what *Protocol #5* was. It was an emergency procedure – a BIG TIME emergency procedure. A few months back, under pressure from Noah Walker's faction, the NWC had reluctantly passed a provision which allowed for extraordinary powers to be granted in the event of the state being under "a direct and serious counter-revolutionary threat". Things were a bit spicy at the moment and tensions were rising, but we had experienced a lot worse. They were hardly in the tongue-exploding league? Amongst other things, it, if sanctioned by the security committee of the NWC, Cribs were granted a licence to do a range of things, which I for one, wouldn't exactly be comfortable doing. I wasn't the only one with misgivings.

Roijin's eyes widened. 'What? I know things are serious, but is it really that bad?'

Coolly, Victoria replied that she thought it was. Then just to stir things up even more, she told us that *obviously* she had done so in my name, because I was the political support in the unit, so *technically* I was in charge here. Well, *obviously,* and *obviously* it was only *technically*. Great, thanks Vic. Another thing I'd been volunteered for. I, though, was too gob-smacked to speak. That wasn't the case with Roijin; her anger was visibly rising. She demanded to know what Jackie's response had been. We were informed that our president was preoccupied by wider matters, and hadn't actually given one.

'So, it's not been activated?' replied a clearly relieved Roijin.

But Roijin didn't know her sub-clauses. 'According to *Sub-Section 4d,* if the governing panel of a Crib – and as we're attached directly to the president, for us that means Jackie – is indisposed then, we can, in an emergency, assume it has been agreed. I believe that this is an emergency, so we can.'

Roijin's shoulders tightened up again, so much so, that you could have easily used them for a spot of drumming. She responded with strident opposition. An intense row erupted between the three of them. Asher and Roijin were clearly unhappy at what we were doing. Actually, make that furious. No, wait, make that exploding with apoplexy. This, on top of tapping important revolutionaries without the proper democratic control, was too much. Odette just sat there, listening intently. She was enjoying the debate and didn't seem over-concerned by it. From her brief track record with us, that didn't surprise me. I didn't say a word, either. I was concerned but not as much as I would have once been.

Every so often, Ash and Roij had called on me for support, but all they received was inarticulate indecision. After five minutes, both came to a halt and stared clenched-jaw ahead of them. Arguing them into submission, Vic had, indeed, got her way. With that came silence. If I had expected a leisurely coffee and morning chat with my colleagues and tasting these "Five Fist croissants", I was mistaken. Victoria moved, not to get the pastries, but instead she walked past Odette, to the end of the room, to the cupboard.

'Roijin, if you could...'

Roijin's face fell. It made a change from her eyes. It was obvious that Roijin hadn't expected whatever Victoria was asking her to do. However, Roijin didn't refuse, but instead followed her. Simultaneously, they both leant forward and looked into retina scans, and placed their hands on the palm pad.

The door opened and was met with audible gasps from Asher, and, I had to admit, from me as well. The small room held at least ten full racks of guns. I could see several rifles and small machine guns in there. And who knew what else? Although Victoria Cole no doubt did. It wasn't of the scale of the Dave Donaldson's arms store, but it was still one to be taken seriously. Did everyone have their own arsenal, nowadays? Was it the new household accessory, like greenhouses once were?

'Christ!' I said. 'I thought that was the stationery cupboard!'

Victoria turned and gave me a dismissive look. 'What – with this level of security?'

I shrugged my shoulders. 'Paper's in short supply.' Looking at Asher, I asked if he had known what was in there.

'Nope. But then I never gave it much thought.'

'I did,' replied Odette, whose smile seemed to almost go around her whole face.

'How?' demanded Roijin.

'It was obvious that something important was in there, so I couldn't help myself. I overrode the security systems, and took a peak.'

Roijin's nicely tanned Turkish face instantly changed from angry red to pure white. 'H-h-how? How did you...' She stopped herself, and held up her hand. 'Never mind. We'll talk later.'

'Okay,' Odette replied, oblivious to the fact that the rest of us were all pretty much stunned, either by what was in that cupboard, or that Odette had easily broken into it. Or both.

Victoria didn't dwell on the issue. She was keen to talk about her toys. She hadn't opened it, to hand out pencils, or even to show the great carpentry skills, which the party's direct labour Corps boasted. *Protocol #5* granted Crib's authorisation to carry heavy-duty weapons. We had, she reminded us – again – been attacked by a drone and there were still people whose lives might be at risk. I hadn't forgotten that. As the years went by, my memory did get worse, but being shot at by aerial automatic weapons was better than tying knots in a handkerchief as a memory aid. Just a bit messier. Victoria went on to once more list the latest terrorist outrages which had recently taken place across the country. These all required us being better prepared.

When she had finished, I commented, 'You sound just like Noah Walker.' It wasn't a compliment. I had enough political, moral and sartorial issues carrying a revolver, but now she wanted me to lug a machine gun around with me! 'No chance, Vic. Not in a million years am I carrying one of those things. It ain't going to happen!'

Ash and Roij looked almost relieved that I had got off the fence; the creosote metaphorically staining my arse. Vic took a second to think about what I had said. She knew me well enough to know that whilst I could be convinced of many things, I did have a particular tone, which although used very rarely, was one which signalled that I was not going to change my position. She nodded acceptance, before turning to Roijin and Asher.

Asher spoke, 'Sorry, Vic. I understand your reasoning, but we're not at that stage yet. I'm with Pete. No.'

Roijin nodded. She too was with me. It was almost a Spartacus moment!

Piping up, Odette slightly spoiled the moment of solidarity, by saying, 'It wouldn't have bothered me, but then, I'm not sure I have a vote. I'm not sure that, technically, I'm even a part of this Crib. I'm supposed to be purely admin-support.' She laughed.

'I think you're well-past being just that,' I said.

That brought a small ripple of laughter in the room, momentarily lessening the tension. It also allowed Vic time to think. She had found herself in the unusual situation of facing losing a vote. I couldn't remember the last time such a situation had occurred, and it was going to be interesting to see how she reacted. But there was no outrage or temper tantrum; there wasn't even any further argument or impassioned pleas. Instead, she simply said, 'Okay. Let's close it, Roij.' But behind her eyes was disappointment.

As they did, I wondered to myself if it would be useful to have a look behind some of the other doors round here. What I had assumed was a fire exit might, for all I knew, turn out to be the way to a tank park.

# CHAPTER 24:
# THE WESTERN BROTHERS

Victoria marched out of the meeting like she might if she was invading a small country. Annexing the general foyer, she announced that we needed to find decent projectors. I refrained from pointing out the obvious, that the best ones in the building were back in the office. She knew that. But for some reason, she had wanted to leave as soon as possible. I had no wish to be taken prisoner, so I kept my mouth shut, and simply followed in her wake.

The answer to the problem appeared as if by magic. Al Handley, the gallery's director, strolled up to us. Handley is the gentlest of souls. He never raises his voice, or gets angry, always keeping his whole aura on an even keel, and he is the type who would have an aura. You could measure his emotional state with a spirit level. I genuinely envied that. His voice always has a smooth relaxed tone to it, which perfectly matches the serenity of his face, which is always underlined in a soft smile. Handley is more Monet than Francis Bacon, tranquil rather than turbulent. But as he approached, I could see that something was irritating him. Well, as much as he could get irritated. Great! I was with two unhappy kittens, now.

He nodded a hello. There was no smile. This was bad then. For him, this was an explosion of anger. His voice though, was as pleasant as it always was. 'Hi Pete, Vic.' I moved by Victoria's side, who I presumed had also noted that comrade gallery director's brushes were missing a bristle or two. She answered his greeting, but by our secret non-verbal communication, indicated that I should handle whatever the problem was.

'Hi, Al. Everything okay?' I said in my breezy voice, which I saved for special occasions when trouble was looming.

He looked pained. 'Look, I'm really sorry, but I think there's an issue with you being here.' He furrowed his brow, to further indicate just how much he didn't want to be saying this. Not wanting me to think that he meant me personally, he clarified, 'Your Counter Revolutionary Intelligence Bureau, that is.' He hadn't really needed to elucidate; I was pretty secure in my own loveliness to believe that there could ever be anyone who wouldn't want me near them. He'd used our full title, so it was obviously serious. It's like when your mum calls you by your full name, you know you're going to bed early. 'The thing is,' he continued in his gallery-level quietness, 'that with the situation as it is now in the country, I totally understand that your, er, department, unit, erm, your "Crib", is of great importance. You know, Pete, my politics, and you know how supportive I am of the revolution, but I think that we might need to iron-out some problems with your residency here.'

I smiled, and tried to frame my face into an expression which conveyed that I understood how hard he had found saying that. Avoiding confrontation was central to his being, and he had pretty much succeeded in doing that with what he had said. The problem was, that in doing so, I had no idea of what particular thing could be the cause of a disagreement. Could it be the cupboard? Was that the problem with our "residency" here? 'In what particular way, Al?' I asked so gently that a lamb would have felt secure.

'That,' he replied simply, nodding towards a heavily armed guard by the door. 'I'm sorry, but whilst I totally understand, and I really do, believe me, the need for your unit, and the protection it requires, it's just that having this level of security, isn't really, er, conducive to an area dedicated to creativity, emotional and intellectual enquiry.'

I looked at the guard. She was a tall, strong woman who had more muscles in her arms than I had in the whole of my body. He did have a point. One shouldn't stereotype, because whilst she looked as if she could crush a coconut between her biceps, she might also be a connoisseur of Spenserian sonnets. But then, that didn't really matter, did it? People would be noticing the muscles, the fixed jawline, the machine gun slung across her chest and taser on her belt, not pondering her literary tastes or what her inner-soul was like. Fact was, she didn't look like she was someone who had an aura.

I conceded, it wasn't what you really wanted to see when you were entering an art gallery. 'I sympathise,' I said, wondering how I might allay his fears, 'but to be fair, you did have security before we even got here. State-owned centres of art or culture are seen as legitimate targets by our enemies. We all remember the fire-bombing of the People's Gallery in Huddersfield.'

'True, Pete. Very true. But not at the level it is now. I've only just got off the phone to the Thames-side Workers' Council, when I had to firmly – but politely I hope – refuse to allow the stationing of an armoured car here.'

At this point I could have pointed out that it was only a few months ago he had actively commissioned the stationing of two such vehicles in the courtyard. True, they had been painted pink, had flowers growing out of them and had large fluffy teddy bears inside, but they had still been armoured cars. That had been an installation by the Welsh artist, Blue Silver. But I decided not to. Instead, I went for a three-pronged strategy of platitudes, waffle and delay. The first two were delivered in a voice and expression which tried to match his, although I doubt if I ever could be as laid back as him. Not whilst I continued to breathe, anyway. Then I adopted a look which was meant to mix the thoughtful and the concerned, and told him that we would see what we could do, and that we hoped that we could end the crisis as soon as possible. Whilst I was attempting to reassure him that we weren't a unit which invited violence, I tried my best to banish the memory that our stationery cabinet housed enough weaponry to give this kindly, passive man a fatal heart attack.

Luckily, he had no idea what we stocked instead of rubbers and sharpeners, and so, superficially at least, accepted what I said. He thanked me. Not that he believed me – he was serene, not stupid. It was just that he wasn't, at this precise moment in time, willing to push the point. How long that might last, I didn't know. People would be foolish, indeed, to mistake his demeanour as a sign of weakness; when he needed to be, he could be as assertive as anyone. It was just that he was choosing not to do so now.

Not wanting to hang around for when he did want to change his mind, I asked if the virtual sculpture room was free. He affirmed that it was. 'Mind if we use it for a while?' I asked. I was sure that I could see a pained expression flash behind his eyes. Chasing killers hadn't been the purpose which he had hoped his exhibition space would be used for. Visualising hope, life, the human condition maybe, but not crime detection.

But he didn't oppose us, and politely agreed, 'Of course, you know the way, Pete.'

After thanking him, I led Victoria to large empty room, which didn't possess a stick of furniture or indeed, a window. The only thing other than the white walls in the room was a one metre black square by the door we had come in by. This was the control panel, which I instructed to start the projection link up. Feeling her sullen silence to be as oppressive as any installation in the room could ever be, I decided to find out what was so pissing her off. I had my suspicions, but they turned out to be laughably incorrect.

'Are you upset about our reaction to the *Protocol#5* being requested?' I asked. 'I know you feel that we should be better equipped but none of us want to be a military unit. It's no disrespect to you, Vic, it's just that it's a step too far.'

She looked at me as if I was an idiot. Shaking her head, she replied, 'That doesn't bother me at all. Christ, Pete, do you think I'm some paramilitary nut? I'm not keen on the idea of being armed to the hilt, myself. But then I'm not keen on the idea of us being shot at whilst we hide under the furniture either. What do you take me for?'

'What's troubling you, then?'

She turned on her phone to link up with the projector and then went serious. 'It's just so fucking frustrating. We're trying our best. All four, well, five now I suppose – with Odette – are doing what we can, but Pete – is it enough? Is it enough against such a well-funded committed and coordinated enemy? Let's face it, we are up against a whole number of different nations' secret service agencies, who are trained in all this. We simply don't have resources. We're guessing. We *feel* that it could be Walker or Anand, but just how weak does that sound?'

'We're doing the best we can.' It was a reply so lame that even Jesus would have difficulty getting it to walk.

Handley's karma had rubbed off on her; she shook her head as if to cast away her doubts. 'Don't mind me, Pete. I'm just having a wobble. We don't have a choice. Come on, let's get down to work and see where we can place Noah Walker and Reyansh Anand at the time of the Shard attack. We can pinpoint where their mobile phones were at any given moment, and like most people their phones have a health-app, so we should be able to tell if they were further from it than a couple of metres. Roijin also informs me that the TV studios had CCTV coverage for most of the building, and we've also the television footage itself.'

A map of the surrounding area of the TV studio appeared in front of us, with two blank avatars heading towards it. Victoria explained that these were their phones – red was Walker and Anand was the blue. 'Unlike the phone used to control the drone, these have not had their SatID wiped so we can follow them.'

Both arrived separately, but within minutes of each other. As they entered the building, we linked into the building's CCTV, their features appeared. Victoria zoomed in. Anand arrived first, upright, with a uniform so well-ironed that its creases could cut through silk. Speaking as someone who was a slave to his iron, I gave him a silent salute. Anand was a handsome guy, smooth skin, with features that I knew many would consider, well… handsome. He walked several paces in, and then after surveying the area, made a call. Victoria informed me that we had traced it to a comrade in the army.

It was just over a minute later, when Walker appeared. He did not look either smooth or well-dressed. On entering the building, he too had looked around, then on seeing Anand, headed over to him. Anand had quickly finished his call, and firmly shook his hand. Then he said something.

'Is there sound?' I asked.

'No, 'fraid not. More's the pity.'

'Vic, I think I've got something which might be of use to us.'

I tapped a few keys on the control panel and engaged audio-lip synchronisation. 'This won't be perfect; artists use it for some of their installations. There was one who dubbed an old 1920s silent movie into Portuguese, relating it to the revolution.' She gave me a doubtful look, which I think indicated what her opinion might be as to the value of such a thing being classified as art. But that didn't matter; what did, was that we could use it to 'hear' what they were saying. 'It lip-reads what is being said, and then vocalises it. It isn't perfect. It relies on the CCTV, which might be missing moments. Such as people walking in front of them, or they themselves walking behind something which obscures the footage. However, if there is even a partial view of the lips, the system's AI can infer what's being said. Not fool proof but it should be enough.'

'Good idea. The police have used it for years. I should have thought about it before.'

'We're ready to go,' I said smugly. 'Let's rewind to when Anand enters the building.'

Once again, we saw him arrive. He looked around and then took a position where he could see all entrances. Considering there was going to be a major TV debate, there appeared to be very few people around. He looked at his watch and took out his phone. A generic male voice came into our room, as Anand started to speak into it. The voice sounded nothing like him. I spoke to the AI: 'Synchronise with known recordings of Noah

Walker and Reyansh Anand.'

A few seconds later, the voices now sounded like who we were looking at. 'James. Hi. Yeah, I'm at the studios now. Where are you? In bed? Fuck, man, it's easy for some. Yeah, yeah, I know...' The sync went silent for a moment, unable to read his lips, then followed with random words, which made no sense, before picking up his speech again. 'In full uniform, yes indeed. Yep, gonna get hell for it but that's nothing to what will hit the fan after this morning. Yeah...' More random words followed, until we heard, 'Look, Jim, mate. Gotta go, Noah's here. I'll let you know how it all goes.' He chuckled. 'Or you'll see it on the news. See ya!'

At that point Noah Walker ambled in, almost in complete contrast. Anand was smart and cool; Walker certainly wasn't. Wearing those hideously garish trousers which looked to me like pantaloons. He was also sporting a pink flat cap. He looked like he was off to the circus. Or had come from it. And this was for when he knew that he was going to be on TV! I shivered to think what he wore chilling out at home. The only thing being worn which didn't scorch the eyes, was his navy-blue rucksack.

They shook hands and Walker said something. He had his back to the camera, so we had no idea what.

'And you, my friend,' Anand replied. 'I totally agree.'

This was all very basic, very last century.

Anand was pointing at something towards the front desk. Walker moved to see what he was looking at and nodded agreement. As he did so, his mouth came into view. 'I think we need to sign in there. Then we'll go through and take our places. Have you seen one of these 'The World's a Stage' broadcasts?'

Anand had now moved, and with Walker's shoulder partially hiding his lips, the AI made a guess that he was asking about the broadcast.

Walker spoke: 'Okay, well it's pretty unlike most programmes. Its layout is loosely based on what the original Globe Theatre might have looked like, with the stage in the middle, and everyone else milling around it. On the stage is a randomly chosen panel who discuss what's been said and vote on it. The audience can move around as they wish, talk to each other, ignore the cameras, or speak at them. Stand or sit. They can also address the panel directly. As we agreed, I've managed to get a few of our supporters in there to put our case. You and I will of course speak, but not too much, we need to be intermingling with the audience. If we can get as many people as possible to make contributions, it'll look a lot more convincing.'

Anand replied, but we had no idea what it was. But whatever it was, after saying it, they both walked off and spoke to a woman who had an E-Clipboard. She checked it, and let them through. They disappeared. Their images had gone and we were back with the avatars, now in a plan of the building.

This was bloody frustrating. We were looking at something which resembled an early computer game, meanwhile, the CIA were probably right now, analysing my brainwaves and close up visuals of my cat, whilst following the movements of anyone who has so much as thought of signing a petition.

Vic could sense my frustration. 'Roijin informs me that there's no CCTV in the part of the building which they've just entered. The next time we'll see them, is when they enter the audience area, where the cameras are used for the show.'

She was right. They reappeared, entering the second ring and then split up. Victoria looked at me. I smiled. 'That's not unusual, split up so you don't look like a bloc, go in different entrances, so you seem to be a part of the broad sweep of the audience, not some pre-planned intervention. Standard stuff.'

At that moment, Dave Donaldson appeared in the corner, having been picked up by the reception area's CCTV. He didn't so much walk, as shamble in, all the time scratching his beard almost as quickly as he moved. He went up to the receptionist and asked in the computer's monotone, rather than his, if the debate had started. She informed him that it was about to and that she would escort him in. I instructed the AI to change the vocal to his.

Like an old Whitehall stage farce, he disappeared from our visual and Walker and Anand appeared in the audience area, at opposite sides of the stage. 'I've set Donaldson as a green avatar,' Victoria explained. The studio was full, which was in stark contrast to the reception area. There were people already on the stage and cameras were hovering all over the place.

'They've cut it fine,' Victoria said. 'It's about to start in one minute.'

And then in exactly sixty seconds it did. And as it did, Donaldson emerged a few metres from where Anand had previously entered the area. We stood, leaning against the gallery's walls and watched the debate. Victoria had set the screen to freeze whenever a camera picked up a facial recognition of any of the three, or if it picked them up speaking. For the first fifteen minutes, the panel members spoke and put their individual political positions to the audience. Once or twice the camera would pick up our trio, but for the most part, we simply were following the avatars moving around.

We got further glimpses when the audience started to make contributions. You could see all three circulating, talking, debating, arguing. Twenty minutes in, and Walker put his hand up and spoke to the audience. He did so calmly, logically and sensibly. Only his clothes spoilt the image of the reluctant idealist being forced into restricting our freedoms. It just made him look a berk.

It was then that Donaldson's dyed beard flashed onto our screens. What Walker had just said had clearly got his goat, or at least his goatee. His tone was angrier, more accusing. He fiercely pointed at Walker and denounced him as laying the foundations of tyranny. He received slightly more applause that Walker had. The camera moved onto another speaker and Donaldson disappeared into the crowd.

The debate continued. Generally, it was civil, but understandably, there were times when passions rose. All three disappeared from the visual, and we were back to our avatars. Ten minutes later, Donaldson's avatar left the studio. A minute after that, and he was once more in all his glory, walking through the reception area.

At the same moment, Anand's visual appeared as he spoke. There was a sharpness to his tone. Tempers were now increasing considerably. For the next twenty-three minutes the debate went back and forth.

In the far corner of our room, Donaldson's green avatar was heading ever closer towards the Shard. With no satellite surveillance and no CCTV in the streets, this was all we had. We believed that he hadn't made a phone call until he reached the Shard, when he would ring his mum and then his partner. Seemingly quite innocuous, it did mean that he wouldn't be in the bar for the attack. The question was, was that good luck or good judgement?

Victoria nudged me back to the TV footage and pointed to the clock hovering in front of us, which was showing the time the recording had been made. The drone attack was about to start in ten minutes. Victoria and I would be now entering the building and having our guns confiscated. Donaldson was almost there. We could see snatches of Anand's uniform and Walker's ridiculous cap, but not much more. As the panel on the stage started to sum up, the cameras were solely on them. So even the glimpses of Anand and Walker's clothes disappeared and the avatars representing their phones replaced them.

What in real time was minutes, in our recon it was seconds and became the time at the Shard, when I was diving under a table with Phan, and Victoria was pulling Bailey under a sofa. It sounded as if it could have so easily been a wild party or frantic orgy, but instead it was four terrified folks, grabbing whatever shelter they could.

Only a few minutes later, and obviously news of the attack had reached the TV studio and was announced from the stage. Shouts of outrage echoed around the studio. People reacted in different ways: some ran out; others restarted the debate, some just stood in shock. We searched for our two. We first saw Anand who was looking around, presumably for Walker. A minute or two later, we saw him. They headed for the nearest exit. Shock and anger flashed across their faces. Anand was calling soldier comrades. They were off to the Shard to give support; or to seize the limelight.

I stopped the footage. 'Doesn't really help us, does it?' I said.

'No,' she sighed. 'According to Roijin, the drone could have easily been operated from almost anywhere. She said it was a radius of 5 kilometres, but that still means it could be from Hackney or Dulwich, or points in-between. The stark fact is that we if can't see all three clearly for every minute of the duration, we can't rule any of them out of the reckoning. I think we need talk to Walker and Anand, again. Odette's told me where to find them, so let's go. My car or go separate? I'm afraid, Pete, I'm ruling out the option of hitching a ride on the back of your scooter.'

'Sharing yours would seem the most sensible. Assuming that you haven't filled it up with anti-aircraft guns, bazookas and rocket launchers, that is.'

Leaving the room, she turned and smiled. 'Oh I keep them in the cupboard under the stairs.' Then she headed out. I switched everything off and followed her. I had decided to treat what she had just said as a joke.

A question was nagging at me. 'What I want to know is, if it was either Walker or Anand who had operated the drone-phone, how did they manage to get it to Donaldson's arm's dump?'

She stopped by her car. 'Good point.' Touching her earpiece, she said, 'Odette, could you do us a favour and trace where Noah Walker's and Reyansh Anand's personal phones were between the Shard attack and when we discovered Dave Donaldson's storage unit. Specifically, if either have been anywhere near it. And could you do likewise for Donaldson himself as well. Cheers.'

The car door opened. 'Come on. Let's pay these alpha-comrades a visit,' she said, sliding herself in, and the steering wheel emerging from the dashboard.

Noah Walker was the nearest to us. Indeed, he was only fifteen minutes away in Jackie Payne's Marylebone office. It seemed that whilst she was ensconced in a frantic whirl of meetings up at the NWC, he was making use of her stapler.

Not that he was doing so when we arrived there. Instead, he was carefully monitoring the morning news. No-one else was present. He had the place to himself – just him and the lurid headlines of friction between the ruling NWC coalition. The stapler was nowhere to be seen. Hearing us enter, he switched the screens off and turned to face us. As he did so, he crossed his legs, clearly displaying today's leg-attire, which were bright lime green jeans. For a second, I feared that my retinas would burn out at the sight of them. He was wearing an orange and yellow t-shirt which just added to the glare. The whole neon ensemble was topped off by his face, which had become even redder than previously. He really should consider a stronger sun-block.

'Pete, Victoria – welcome. What can I do for you?' he asked, giving off the bonhomie which you might expect from a host at a barbecue party. The offer of drinks, veggie sausages and burgers usually followed, but he just smiled, and waited for our reply.

'We just need to clarify a few things,' Victoria replied, speaking with a distinctly unsociable voice.

Maybe she didn't do barbecues. I wasn't too keen on them myself.

Vic sat down without being invited to.

'Sure, happy to help. I must say, I was surprised to hear that you were outside. Actually, I'm surprised that you knew that I was here. I must be bloody predictable.'

'What exactly *are* you doing here?' I asked, grabbing a chair and placing it next to Victoria. This was an interview not a soiree.

He looked at me, somewhat startled by my attitude. He hadn't been party to our discussion on the way here of what our approach should be with both men. On the one hand, they were leading members; on the other, they might also be traitors and renegades. Then there was the small matter that more deaths could be on the way, so perhaps politeness and respectfulness weren't the main things to worry about. Now was the time to stop farting about. Or as Victoria had succinctly put it, 'They want the strong state, we'll give them the strong state.' This was my strong state look.

It had some effect. 'I, er, Jacks wants me to coordinate the London party branches, whilst she's up at the NWC.'

'And strengthening your position at the same time, which is convenient,' I said, looking directly at him, partly to add to the authoritarian vibe, and partly to avoid looking at his clothes.

I might have momentarily wrong-footed him, but he wasn't intimidated, and answered in a calm and relaxed way, 'I think, comrade, you'll find few complaints about me.' Then a puzzled look crossed his face. 'Can I ask why you're here? I've told you why I am, but what about you? What things need "clarifying"?'

'We're interested to know why you spoke so little at the TV debate,' Vic replied.

'What?' he spluttered, finding the question highly amusing.

It was my turn. 'Having seen you talk many times, it frankly surprises me that you kept your contribution to a minimum. I mean, with all due respect, comrade, usually no-one can get near the microphone when you're in a meeting. You usually speak so often that you start collecting loyalty points – so why be so shy at this one?'

By the time I had finished, I was pleased to see his humour had departed, and his expression, at least fleetingly, was one of serious displeasure. 'I think, comrade,' he said carefully choosing his words, 'that your tone is inappropriate. I don't think it has a place in conversations between comrades, and if I might say so, I find it confrontational and rude.'

I replied: '"One shouldn't hide behind dated petty bourgeois notions of politeness and decorum when the arguments are central to the defence of revolution and freedom. To do so, is not polite, but cowardly."'

He smiled slightly at me, recognising the direct quote from an article of his. 'At least you agree that the revolution is under threat.'

'Comrade, please remember that we were at the Shard,' Victoria crisply replied.

'Indeed. But you still haven't explained how I can help you with your investigations. You tell me how, and I will happily do so. I'm your greatest supporter.'

Before he started a terrace chant or waved a scarf about, I got straight to the point. 'So can you confirm that you didn't see Reyansh Anand leave the debate at any time?'

He looked at me incredulously. 'Surely you're not suggesting that Rey has anything to with the attack? We were nowhere near it!'

'Well, comrade, a short walk away, actually.'

'I don't know if you know, comrade, but as I understand it, drones can be operated anywhere. Let's face it, a drone isn't a kite, you don't have to be there with a piece of string. They're pretty old-tech. You must have had one when you were a kid.'

I gave him a humourless smile. 'Not with revolving machine guns, I didn't.'

He shrugged. 'Anyway, the capitalist military have been operating them across continents for years. How do you know it wasn't the case here?' His voice oozed patronising condescension.

A thin smile crossed Victoria's face, and she met his comment, with a barely concealed sneer. 'Because, Noah, we might not be as efficient or muscular as you'd like us to be, but we're getting there. For starters, the CIA disruptive cloak was operational, so nothing could be remotely operated at any great distance. We also know that it was operated within a 5-kilometre radius of the Shard.'

'And anyway, Noah, how do you know about the military drones?' I asked.

He shook his head at what he considered to be a daft question. 'I know they've got nuclear submarines, but I've never been in one. Furthest I've been underwater, is in the local swimming pool.' He wasn't in the slightest ruffled by our questions, adding in a voice with theatrical weariness, 'And knowing it's a 5-kilometre radius, is hardly pin-point accuracy, is it? That's basically central London. But to answer one of your other questions, there were quite a few people in the debate, but no, I didn't seen Anand leave at any time. As far as I know, he was in the hall the whole time. I can't imagine Rey just leaving.'

'Did he make a call or use his phone?' I asked.

His answer was similar to the first, that there were a lot of people in the audience and he had better things to do than constantly be on the look-out for Anand, 'He's not my lover nor my child. And before you ask, I didn't leave the debate myself or make a call. Feel free to check, though.'

Victoria leant forward. 'We will. Although, I must say, Noah, that you don't seem to be over-worried about what we're asking you. You're an intelligent person, you'll have guessed why. We won't bother giving you any guff about painting a picture of the events. The truth is, that with the assassination of Mike Stewart, a major opponent of yours was removed. If Phan Bien had been killed, that would have removed two leading advocates of detente.'

'So, strengthening your faction.'

He threw his head back and laughed. 'Good God, if only it was that simple. Kill a few key speakers and you get your way. In that case, why have we spent decades, centuries even, painfully building a movement, when all we needed was a bomb? I thought we were against individual acts of terrorism, comrade.'

'We are,' I snapped. 'But they're not.'

'And you honestly think Reyansh and me are "they", do you?'

I didn't answer. Victoria did: 'And are you?'

His laughter abruptly stopped, and his expression changed. 'No, comrade, I'm not. I've spent almost a decade building a revolutionary movement. Five years before that, I was a leading trade-unionist. I'm proud of what I've achieved. My record speaks for itself.'

Neither of us commented. Neither of us sang the Internationale or composed a folk song in his honour. Victoria changed the subject and abruptly asked him, 'Where were you Monday at 10am?'

He all but choked, though we didn't get a howl of innocence but instead he roared with laughter. 'You don't believe in subtlety, do you?'

'"Subtlety is just polite flim-flam",' I said, again quoting one of his phrases.

This just amused him more and he nodded in appreciation. 'Fair enough. Live by the sword etc, etc. So yes, go for it. Let's see...' he thought for a second, before remembering, 'I was at Rey's.'

'And would you mind saying why that was?' Victoria asked, sounding exactly what she used to be – a police officer. Staring at him, I noted, that that fact hadn't disturbed him. Or me.

He laughed again. I couldn't tell whether it was genuine or simply to hide his annoyance with us. 'We had a meeting. I'm sure you can guess what about.'

'When did you leave?'

'Oh, the meeting went on for a while. We had a nice breakfast together. Were these two men inseparable? Did they live together now? Was there a big ultras house, where they all swapped stories of paranoia?

The grin became something you might find lying on the top of an oil slick. 'Revolutions aren't 9 to 5, revolution is 24 hours a day.' Confidence radiated from him.

It was a good quote – it was Jackie's.

Victoria got to her feet. We had decided on keeping this short and sour, but the suddenness of movement startled even me. 'Good. Thank you, comrade, we need to get going. I must inform you that we will be checking on what you've told us. We'll be in touch.'

'That it?' he said.

'Yes, thank you. You've given us everything we need,' she replied. 'One last thing, though: have you used, or ever been to, a storage unit, recently?'

His eyebrows went up, and looked surprised. 'Storage unit? No, why? What would I need one of them for?'

'Nothing. Well, thanks, comrade. You've been a great help. We'll let you get back to your work,' and with that, Victoria started to leave the room.

I nodded and thanked him for his help. He hadn't been, but that's not what we wanted him to think. 'As the comrade said, we'll be in touch,' I said. That much was true.

Recovering his balance, he resumed his nonchalant air, before making a humourless quip, 'And I'm greatly heartened to hear how acquainted you are with my work.'

Victoria's response was to hold up a hand up, and without turning, replied, '"It pays to know who you're up against, their thoughts, their beliefs, even better than they do".'

It was another of his sayings. He had many of them.

'Ah, my ego swells...'

I seriously doubted that his ego needed any enlargement.

On our drive to Camden, Odette had rung back, and confirmed that Dave Donaldson had been to the storage facility several times since the Shard attack, but according to the phone locations, neither Walker nor Anand had. The nearest that either of them could be located was two kilometres away.

'Odette, could you look into Walker's whereabouts at the time of Stewart's death. Check up on his communications and get a local militia worker to interview Anand's neighbours. See if they support his story.'

Odette agreed, but before she hung up, she gave us the latest news: 'By the way, Walker is on the phone right now to Anand, telling him all about your visit, what you said and implied.'

'And what does he think we implied?' Vic enquired.

'He said that you were treating him and Anand as possible suspects for both the Shard and Stewart. He had no idea what you had to warrant this or what made you think that they could do such things, but that he should expect a visit from you two in the very near future.'

'And we only inferred that?' I said in pantomime shock. 'I thought we did a lot more than that. We're going soft.'

Vic smirked, but didn't reply. She did ask, 'Did he sound worried?'

'Vic, to be honest, more amused. It was Anand who sounded annoyed, and I mean – very annoyed, I'd say, angry. He felt personally insulted by the accusations. The pair of them even discussed the possibility of making a complaint to the NWC Standards Committee.'

'Did they now? Well, I hope their feelings get better soon. Okay, thanks Odette.'

During the drive, I thought about our brief tete-a-tete with comrade Walker. Well, for some of the time. For the rest, I wandered down memory lane, thinking of the times Caroline and I had gone to Camden for drinks, a meal, or to buy clothes. Things had changed since then; although the market remained, it was smaller, moving from teenage mock vintage fashion, which we had known, to today's families selling second-hand clothes and furniture as the economic blockade began to squeeze harder.

The meeting Anand was attending was being held in what had once been a supermarket but was now a distribution centre. From the sounds of it, over a thousand were there, either physically or digitally. It had been called to discuss the political situation and he had been invited to be one of the guest speakers. We arrived a few minutes after it had finished, with crowds of people streaming out to go back to work, or to home.

Anand was still in there, standing close to the main rear exit. Vic drove, rather too quickly for my comfort, up to the building and parked. We got out. Putting on my shades, I leant against her car, crossed my legs and folded my arms. Looking at me, she laughed. 'You're loving all this, aren't you?'

'What?' I asked innocently.

'You know. Look at you, posing by the car. All you need is a fag in the corner of your mouth, and you'd be all set.'

'Says the woman with machine guns in the stationery cupboard.'

She grinned but didn't say anything. Anand was leaving the building. Once again, he was in uniform. In itself, this was designed to be a statement. He was busy saying friendly goodbyes and shaking hands. From where we were standing, he looked to be a popular bloke. When the chairperson had thanked the guest speakers, he had singled out Anand, describing him as a 'leading revolutionary' and praising his 'articulate and thought-provoking speech'.

He didn't look thoughtful or articulate when he saw us. He looked what could be best described as being narked. So much so, there was probably a photo of him in an Anglo-American phrase dictionary, so across the Atlantic, they could know what the word narked meant. But he didn't miss a step and just carried on walking directly towards us.

Then again, where we had parked, he could only avoid us by heading back into the building. He was never going to do that. Whatever other faults he might have, cowardice and backing away from a confrontation were not amongst them. His stride was confident and purposeful. Victoria put on her sunglasses and stretched. Whether it was intentional or not, it meant that he had been treated to a flash of her holstered gun. Neither her shades nor gun, deterred him. I guessed in the army, he'd seen more frightening sights.

When he reached us, he changed his look to one attempting a friendly demeanour. There was even a hint of a smile. 'Hi, Victoria, Pete. Were you at the meeting?'

He knew we hadn't been; whether he was covering his tracks or having a dig at our expense, I didn't know. I would have guessed that it was the latter. But we didn't call him out on it. Instead, Victoria asked him how it had gone. He told us. But didn't need to. We had recorded every second. Including his *thoughtful and articulate* speech.

'So why are you here?' he asked, knowing full-well the answer.

'We want to talk to you about Thursday's TV debate,' I said, and then not bothering to wait for another one of his fake questions as to why that may be, I told him. 'We're looking into the movement of people connected, no matter how loosely, with the Shard attack.'

His response was calm – too calm, too accepting. It was as if he knew why we were there. Which of course, he did. 'Sure. No problem. What do you want to know?'

Victoria moved towards him ever-so slightly. 'We'd like to know whether you were in the debate for the whole of it, or did you leave at any time?'

His answer was too pat and too thought-out. He assured us that he hadn't left for a second, not even to go to the loo.

'So, you were there for every second of it?'

'Pretty much.'

'Does that mean all of it or for most of it?'

'It means, comrade, that from the time we arrived, until the time we left, I was in the studio.'

'And Noah Walker?'

'Well, there were a lot of people there, so I didn't see him all the time – but then, I wasn't trying to – but I didn't see him leave if that's what you mean.'

'Yes, it was,' I said simply.

Vic and I played relay with our questions but throughout he remained with his calm, cool vibe. I tried to match him, but I had to admit that I was being out-chilled. Maybe Vic was right, a ciggie would have aided my vogueish look; shame that I'd never indulged.

It was time to see if the man in green was as disciplined as he was pretending to be. 'I don't quite understand how the pair of you worked together at the debate. Surely, you'd be in contact with each other throughout? I mean, how did Noah get his instructions to you on what to say? Or did he brief you beforehand? How did you know when to speak?' It was cheap and insulting, which was exactly what I had intended.

He didn't answer straightaway, which was the give-away. If bodies had a language, then a slight tense of his shoulder muscles and the closing of his smile, was fairly easy to translate. I had succeeded in baiting him, but he didn't respond. Not in the way he wanted to; he wanted to tell me to take a hike and not be so condescending and rude. And not in the way that I had wanted – to lash out and say something which would give him away. When he spoke though, he was the epitome of reasonableness. 'I'm an experienced comrade, I don't need spoon feeding. I can think for myself.' Then with just the slightest hesitation. 'If I might say, comrade, there's been much written by the party on how we should respect all workers, even those in uniforms, so perhaps you may regret the tenor of your question.'

Neither of us responded. Instead, Vic asked, 'There was no contact between you two during the debate?'

'No. We both knew what the job was.'

'Which was?' Vic asked.

I wished she hadn't. We usually tried to be economical with our questioning, but this allowed him the luxury to speak, and speak at great length, about the state of the revolution.

As he paused for breath, Vic took her chance, interrupting his five-volume oral analysis. 'You didn't see him use his phone during the meeting?'

'Like I said, comrade. I didn't have eyes on him all the time. He's not a child!'

'Funny, he said the same. You haven't been in contact with him, have you, this morning?'

'No.'

Oh liar, liar, pants on fire.

'Was it his suggestion as well that you head to the Shard, when you heard of the attack?' Victoria asked.

'No, it was mine.'

'Why?'

For a moment he looked a little puzzled, as if it was a stupid question. 'To see if we could offer any assistance. I knew there were some soldier-comrades stationed nearby. I called on them. There might be an all-out assault on the building and we could help defend it.'

'It wasn't to take advantage of the situation, then?' I asked.

He wasn't provoked this time; he'd got the measure of me. 'Yeah, that's what Jackie thought, but it really wasn't. Anyway, comrade, I thought you were accusing me of conducting the attack? Are you now thinking that I'm just an opportunist who uses tragedy to further their cause?'

'Could be both! Organise the attack and then turn up and seize the limelight.'

He smiled, but didn't otherwise move a centimetre.

I tried another dig. 'So what *is* your cause?'

'The same as yours, comrade – the proletarian revolution.'

'Okay, good to hear. So, Reyansh, have you ever operated a drone in the army?'

'No, comrade Cole, never. Not my area of duty,' he replied. 'But from what I've heard, it's pretty much like playing a computer game. A few minutes' training and anyone can do it. Ten minutes' practice and you're an expert.'

'Assuming you'd be able to stomach the death toll,' I replied.

'From what I've heard, you're not that squeamish, Pete.'

Ouch. He should retract those claws of his, he'll snag them on my jacket. He looked pleased at his comment. Little things obviously impressed him. He had proved that he knew my personal history, good for him. All he needed to do for that, was go on the internet; it was hardly the discovery of the Rosetta Stone. I changed the subject. 'Could you tell us where you were when Mike Stewart was killed?'

He wasn't surprised by the question; after all, he had been briefed by Noah. 'So now it's time I provide an alibi for that? Okay, I'll play ball. I know you're doing what you have to do. I was with Noah Walker, we had a morning meeting at mine.'

'Anyone else there?'

'Zena, my partner, she was there for most of it.'

As he had finished, I knew what was coming. The second he'd finished, Vic had turned and opened her car door. 'Thanks, comrade. We'll leave you to get on with your day.' She got in and the car automatically started.

He looked astonished. 'That it?'

Taking my glasses off and putting them in my jacket top breast pocket, I smiled. 'That's it, comrade. Thanks.'

We pulled away even faster than we had arrived. Avoiding mass slaughter of the departing crowd, Vic kept her eyes straight ahead, but asked, 'Well, what do you make of those two?'

Good question. It was a pity that I didn't have a good reply.

She called Roijin, who answered immediately, but before she had time to say a word, Vic was distracted by the expression on Roijin's face. She looked worried. We could now see her hurriedly picking up her gun and bag. She looked worried. 'What's up? Vic asked.

'Look, I was just about to ring you. Pete, it's your sister. She's being attacked!'

# CHAPTER 25: PALLAS ATHENA

O ur dramatic exit was rather spoilt by the fact that before we could wheel-spin into the open road, three community transport buses had stopped directly in front of us, bringing us to a sudden halt. That never happened in the movies. They had stopped to allow a few more workers to get on. Worthy, but skull-crushingly annoying. Victoria had tried her best to get them to move, which had basically consisted of putting our emergency siren on the roof, and swearing a lot. Considering the crowd had all just come from a mass rally where they'd heard about encroaching state power, it probably wasn't the best of strategies.

But I wasn't really taking much notice of Victoria's efforts to antagonise the local population, because I was more interested in what Roijin was saying. 'Your sister went into a room, which I presume is the office copying room, and a guy followed her in. It was when he started talking, that I started to take note. It wasn't your usual office chatter either in tone or content. Basically, he was pressurising her about something...hold on...'

I saw Roijin on the dashboard screen, spin her steering wheel and leave Somerset House at speed. She didn't have any problems with a Hollywood exit. 'Sorry. Anyway, he was aggressive to say the least. I got the impression he'd been hassling her for some time, but she's been refusing to do whatever it was he wanted her to do. To be honest, he wasn't entirely convincing at playing the hard man, but there's no doubt that his intention was to be threatening.'

'What was he asking her to do?'

'That wasn't clear, but whatever it was, she just told him to piss off. Your sister didn't sound too concerned at first; seems to me, she's a woman who isn't easily intimidated. She sounded annoyed, angry even, but not frightened. She was definitely giving as much as she got.'

I could see Roijin's face – she, though, *did* look worried. That made me worry.

'But that changed. It was when he told her how sweet her house was. Described the wallpaper, the pictures on the wall. Then, he went on about her pottery, china, or something like that, I didn't understand...'

'Her husband collects Clarice Cliff pottery,' I explained. 'It shows he's been inside her home.'

'Yeah, but Pete, there's more. He mentioned *your* house. Talked about your cat, your CD collection, and listen, and I quote - "a lovely little atlas in his library. I've always been interested in the history of the Middle East".'

Could he be the one who had paid me the visit?

I took out my phone and rang Sophie. It went straight to voicemail. 'Fuck!' I yelled.

'Can you remotely change that?'

'Sorry, Pete, no, I've tried but haven't been able to.'

'Christ sake, move!' Victoria screamed out the window. Somebody answered back, but I couldn't make out what. I could, though, very easily hear Victoria's reply, 'I can see they're in a wheelchair, but it doesn't make the lift work any faster. I need to get through – there's a woman in danger, for fuck's sake!'

Roijin, unlike us, was at full speed, and with sirens blaring.

'What's happening now?' I asked, fear beginning to multiply and reproduce in my soul.

'Can't say. It's difficult to tell. Her phone's in her pocket, so's his. I can only hear muffled voices, but it sounds tense. and I'm sure I heard a cry. I've got the amplifier on full, but still, like I said, the sound isn't great.'

Finally, one of the transports moved, and Victoria thanked a deity which she didn't believe in, and hurtled around it. I lurched back as she accelerated.

'Wait,' Roijin shouted. I couldn't tell if it was to me or to a passing car. 'She's on the move. He's, I've got the sound translator on. It picks up background noise and estimates what it belongs to. The slight ping, and electronic noise is a sound of a lift.'

'We're on our way,' Victoria yelled at Roijin. 'Do we know who this person is?'

'She called him Albie. I looked at their HR files and there's an Albie Warrington-Bridges. Thirty-three years old, been employed at Sophie's office, since the different energy sectors were consolidated. He's from Bio-energy. Got a partner who's a journalist, and they've got two kids, both under two. He's a party member – a Rev Baby...'

Rev Baby was a description, a rather dismissive one, of someone who joined the party after we had taken power. It was usually used by comrades who we old-timers called in an equally dismissive way, 'newly-joins', as a way of pulling rank. No-one ever said that in a workers' state, backbiting would immediately wither away.

'Anything else?' Victoria asked, whilst driving straight through a red light.

'No. You know the score. The records are in disarray. Wait! She's leaving the building. Crap!'

'What?' I demanded.

'Traffic jam,' she replied. 'It's solid. I'll see if I can find another route. 'She's out the building. There's a bus stop and a staff car park nearby, she could be heading to either.'

'It'll be the car park. She hates public transport.'

'Yep, you're right. She's getting in her car. He's left the building. He's following her. Come on! Move! I'm stuck here, Pete. You'll be able to get to her quicker than I will! Come on!'

She spoke too soon because right at that moment, we came to a sudden halt. We too, it seemed, had hit a similar problem. Ahead were cars. Bloody dozens of them. Victoria slapped the steering wheel. The great gods of traffic control were against us. Our vexation wasn't helped by the commentary from Roijin. 'He's on the move now, in his car. From her computernav, she's heading home. Quite obviously, he's following her.'

If either car had had a swear box, we could have raised a fortune for charity, as frustration became physical and profane. Minutes seemed like eons. But then, finally, the traffic cleared. Thank Christ! Victoria saw a gap and seized the moment.

With her driving, it didn't take us long to reach Highgate. As we did, Roijin informed us that Sophie was now parking outside her house. Warrington-Bridges was fast approaching too. 'Pete, I'll be there soon after them,' she said, obviously trying to reassure me.

'I'm here!' she yelled. 'I see them! They're fighting! I'm getting out the car now!'

Victoria answered an unasked-for answer: 'We'll be there in a minute. It'll be okay, Pete. Come on, Sophie, keep him off. Just for a few minutes.'

It was then I heard Roijin scream and demand them to back off.

After what seemed to be an archaeological time-period, we arrived. As we did, we heard Roijin shout again to stop. This time, she was yelling,

'Stop, or I will be forced to shoot!'

The pair of us flew out of the car, before it had even stopped. Doors were left open and guns unholstered. We ran towards where we could see Roijin. She appeared to have her arms pointing downwards. From my training, I recognised it as the safety stance – holding a gun, downwards, ready to use it. Our view of Warrington-Bridges and Sophie was obscured by her car. My heart was beating fast, both from the exercise and from fear. Sprinting around the car, we stood next to Roijin and were confronted by a scene which I hadn't expected.

On the floor, whimpering, with blood pouring down from his nose, lips and cheek, was a tall skinny man, who I took to be Albie Warrington-Bridges. Backing away from him, was my sister. She looked totally unhurt, but had turned red with rage. Roijin was telling her to calm down and that we had it all under control.

Suddenly, Warrington-Bridges moved his hand towards his pocket. In that same second, Roijin and Victoria swung around and aimed at his head. Simultaneously, both screamed for him to freeze and not to move a muscle. He cried back, in a voice resembling a terrified boy wanting his mum, that he was merely getting his handkerchief. 'I'm bleeding. That bitch assaulted me.'

I was sure that I detected a slight self-satisfied smile on my sister's face. Roijin scanned him. 'He's unarmed. Okay, fella, get up.'

After ostentatiously getting out his hanky and mopping his nose, he carefully put his hands, palm down, onto the pavement. He then tried to gingerly push himself up. But he didn't get far, and screamed, holding his side. Between showing us that he was in pain and throwing accusatory looks and abuse at my sister, he looked straight out of an Edwardian melodrama.

It was at this point that a neighbour appeared. With their dress and accents, it was obvious that the notion that we had obliterated the middle class had been greatly over-stated. Despite that from behind their twitching Plantation Blinds, they'd have seen that we were armed, they weren't in the least intimidated. Guns were no match for their self-entitlement. Looking at Warrington-Bridges, who by now resembled Horatio Nelson dying on the deck of the HMS Victory, one of them demanded, 'What's the meaning of all this? What on earth is happening to warrant firearms?'

I pressed my Mondrian badge. The sight of the visual of Jackie Payne, almost visibly made their collective lips curl.

'So much for the president's promised to remove weapons from the streets!'

'And you are, friend?' Vic asked in her most amenable tone.

'Michael Graves. I'm a resident here. But more to the point, what are you doing here and what has happened to that poor chap! Have you attacked him? Because if you have, I will be making representations to our street representative.'

More people were emerging from their homes. All were sporting the latest in designer shorts and stern looks. The neighbourhood posse now numbered a dozen or so. All were in an unhappy, although faux-polite and well-spoken, mood. Any threats of shrieking outrage were pre-empted by my sister speaking: 'It's okay, Michael. That man there in the suit is my brother. I think you met him once at a party.'

He looked at me as if it had just stepped in something disgusting in the street. No recognition registered. Obviously, oiks like me didn't stay long in the memory. That was alright, mate – chinless wonders all looked the same to me.

She explained, 'The man on the floor, assaulted *me*. I defended myself, and well, that's why he's hurt. Pete, my brother, and his *friends* were actually trying to help me.'

That confused them. Sophie was bluer than all of them put together, and here she was, the duchess of the street, not only saved by the reds, but one of them was actually her brother. Oh, the shame of it all. This would provide the soirees with plenty of goss for a good while.

'I'll leave you two to sort this out,' I said to Vic and Roijin, as I walked over to Sophie. 'Come on, let's go inside.'

Sophie didn't demure, but then she didn't look eternally grateful either. Closing the front door, I left my two comrades to deal both with the local antagonised bourgeoisie and the poor wounded diddums on the ground.

Once inside, Sophie kicked her shoes off, after that is, a swift examination of the damage they had sustained in kicking Mr WB.

'Stay there,' I told her.

I'd seen Vic do this several times. It was my turn. I searched her house. It had taken five minutes, by which time Sophie had gone into the kitchen. She was standing by her huge, very expensive fridge and was pouring herself a chilled glass of Chardonnay. I guessed it wasn't her first. One hand rested on the workspace. She didn't speak. I told her that the house was empty. She didn't reply or indeed respond in any way. Recognising the mood she was in, and beginning to fear what might come next, I took my jacket off, then my holster, and laid both over the back of a chair, and tried to gain some time. Turning to face her, I saw that she was pouring herself another glass. Seemed that there wasn't to be any offered to me. Yes indeed, I recognised that mood.

When she spoke, her voice was heavy in sarcasm. 'Well, I'm safe and sound. That was exciting. And what a coincidence that you, Victoria Cole and that other woman...'

'Roijin. Her name is Roijin.'

'You, Cole and, *Roijin*, happened to be in the area. Visiting Karl Marx's grave, were you?'

'No,' I answered simply. I wasn't surprised that the first thing we were discussing wasn't a colleague trying to intimidate and threaten her. Not him chasing her home. Not the break-in to her home. Not the suspicion that he had broken into mine. No, topper most in her mind was the reason why we had been there. No surprise whatsoever. And I had no doubt that she knew full well the answer.

'So how did the three Musketeers happen to be in my street, hmm, Peter?' she asked.

It was pointless to lie, so I just came out and told her straight: 'I asked Roijin to hack into your communications systems, including your phone, so we could monitor you. That's how Roijin heard Warrington-Bridges threaten you.'

'Really?' she asked in fake surprise. 'And may I ask why?'

I took a deep breath. This was not going to be pleasant. 'Vic saw you crying in the toilets of Soul Shack, and well, er, I thought you seemed to be acting oddly. I thought something might be up.'

'Really? And this amounts to be enough reason to invade a person's privacy – *a citizen of the glorious workers' republic*, no less? Trampling over their rights and equality? Hmm, for years, your party have been telling us that such draconian and undemocratic methods are not the way of your, sorry, *our* state. It was slander to suggest otherwise. But I have a cry and apparently acting "oddly", and that was enough for you to infringe my rights.' For a split-second she paused, before shouting, 'For Christ sake, Pete – you spied on me!'

'I was worried about you, Sophie,' I said simply, and very weakly.

She finished her glass and poured herself another one. That was her third, in as many minutes. It was coming up to 4pm, so it was a little early for a drink. She also probably hadn't eaten for a while so, despite having a wine resistant stomach, it probably wasn't that wise. I decided against saying anything. Instead, I silently counted down. 5, 4, 3, 2, 1...

Then – boom!

'How fucking dare you!' she screamed. 'Who the fuck do you think you are?' Her eyes glared and I swear, she was baring her teeth. 'What gives you the right to do that to me? I haven't broken any laws. I have not taken arms against the state. Sure, I oppose it, but I do so peacefully and within the law. Pete – how could you?' She slammed her glass, spilling some over the surface. Not good for the glass, but probably good for her liver.

I attempted to mount a defence, although I knew full well that it was futile. 'I was frightened that you were in danger – because of me. If it's any consolation, the rest of the Crib were against it. It was my idea. I told them to do it. And yes, I'll probably get into trouble for this. But you're my sister. I was genuinely worried about you. And anyway,' I decided to try a different approach. It was risky, but otherwise, I was in for several hours of abuse. 'I was right. It was a good thing that we turned up when we did.'

She laughed, a rather harsh mocking laugh. It was a laugh that she was rather good at. 'Did I look in danger?' she demanded.

She had me there too. 'No. But you don't know what the repercussions were going to be from it. He did, after all, admit to breaking into both our homes!'

For a moment, she looked taken aback, as if she had forgotten that we had been listening to her. Then her eyes widened, as she remembered. It was going to be a toss-up between it reigniting her fury, or if not calming her down, then at least saving me from receiving the same treatment as Mr WB outside. She pressed her glass to her mouth but didn't drink. I took that for a good sign. Against the lips was better than pouring it down her throat. Or chucking it at me.

Thankfully, she decided that giving out one beating was enough for the day. 'That was to intimidate me into working for them. To make me feel vulnerable and to make me worry that you were too. When you told me about your break-in, I admit that it did freak me out, that is true. Before it happened, he told me that they were planning to pay you a visit and he said, that they were going to 'take you to Jerusalem'.

'Jerusalem?' I said, alarm bells going off in my head.

'Yeah. I think it was their way of sending a message to me.'

Another bell went clang, clang in my skull. 'You've said – they, them and their. They're all plurals, is that exactly what he said?'

Her eyebrows furrowed. She wasn't really getting the concentration of the plural pronouns here. I clarified that I wasn't giving a literacy lesson. 'He said – they, them, and their – and not I? Did he actually say it was him who broke in?'

'Does it matter? Surely, what matters is that they, he, them, she, whoever – did exactly what Albie said they, he, them, she, whoever – would!'

I nodded. I'd leave that for now. 'So, tell me about this Albie.'

She paused for a second, before picking up the bottle, and then paused again. Stretching up to one of the eye-level cupboards, she touched it and it smoothly opened, and she took out a glass. 'Join me?' she asked.

Feeling that saying no wasn't a possibility, I agreed.

'He seemed nice enough to begin with. A bit wet, and a bit dull, but okay. He joined the office at about the same time as I did.' She poured me a drink and passed it to me. I sipped it. It was cold, medium sweet, and hard to come by. Sophie took another sip of hers and continued, 'He was one of those office furniture types – he was there – you saw him – but you didn't take much notice of him. Then, a few weeks ago he started to talk to me. At first it was work related, then general stuff, but then politics. That was no big deal, it's what everyone is talking about, isn't it?'

Seeing her drift away for a second, I asked, 'Do they know your politics?'

Her head went back and laughed in a way that the middle classes do – loudly, assertively, wanting the world to know that they're amused. She must have learnt that somewhere because she didn't laugh like that when she was younger. Now, she had that neighing horse sound which they have. There's probably an online course you can take. Snorting to a close, she replied, 'Oh, they do. Yes, they do. I make sure of that.'

'And how does that go down?' I asked, not surprised in the least.

'Oh fine. I'm honest, civil and polite. I keep to the laws of the communist state, and cause no trouble, so I am not a threat.' She stopped and pulled a face, which I recognised. She was going to correct herself. 'That's not quite fair. They're all perfectly friendly. We do have discussions and debates, but it's all friendly. "Fraternal and comradely" is how the workplace rep calls them, No, they're okay. I think, I kind of amuse them, I'm the office blue. And to add to the amusement, I've a brother who is not only a party member, but is now becoming a semi-regular feature of the news, in his quest to hunt down conspiracies, both real and imagined. They find the irony very funny. Which, let's face it – it is. '

'And Albie?'

'Well that was what was weird, and made me suspicious of him. He was very keen to find out more of what I believed and what I thought should happen next. The others do a bit of that, but it's different, er, it's less intrusive, more a civil exchanging of views. He seemed to be snooping. Also, he claimed to be a member of yours, but he started to ask me a lot of questions about what he claimed was *his* party. Then he got onto asking me about you.'

'Such as?'

'Mainly, what you were doing and what's our relationship like, and how much influence I have over you.' That laugh came again. I feared that my eardrums would start to bleed, if she did it much more. 'I told him, very little, and as for influence – bugger all!' She stopped talking and suddenly, the humour ended. Instead, a steely look appeared. 'That changed. He got very nasty and spiteful. I would have simply told him to piss off. Well, I did. But he then started telling me details of my life and yours, stuff that I was surprised that he could know. Really personal stuff. Soon it became apparent that if he was a party member, then he was a very unusual one, certainly not a believer. Quite obviously, he was working for the old security services and basically, he tried to recruit me. As you know, they've tried before, and it didn't work that time. I sincerely want a return to parliamentary democracy and the England I love, but I'm not getting involved in violence and sabotage, and spying. That's not my way. And certainly, I'm not getting involved with a twit like him!'

I had finished my glass. Sophie opened up her fridge, which was large enough to house a family of penguins and took out another bottle. With a speed of a gunslinger from the old Wild West, she opened it, and poured both herself and me, another glass.

'And it was that which scared you?' I said.

She opened her mouth; she was going to disagree with my description. Instead, she thought about it, and just nodded.

'Especially the atlas. Tell me about that.'

'Albie sometimes seemed to be talking in riddles. One day, he kept talking about how they were going to lead you to Jerusalem. He kept mentioning Jerusalem. Jerusalem, Jerusalem, Jerusalem. I do have to say that if his way is their standard way of intimidating people, it's a rather boring method. But whatever, when you came around here and mentioned your atlas, and the fact that it had been opened at a page on the Middle East, that really did scare me. I suppose, when he brought it up again in the office today, I had had enough. Also, he was getting rather close, if you know what I mean. Whispering in one's ear is, to be honest, creepy as much as anything else.'

'And that's what he was doing?' I asked, noticing the similarities to the threats made to Stewart. Fury was rising up from my gut. I didn't blame Sophie from giving him a thump or two. I was considering doing so myself.

'Yeah, oh...' she laughed. 'Don't go all big macho brother on me. I know you, Peter. You're not that sort. No, he didn't harm me, or sexually harass me. He just kept whispering how close they were to you. How they could pull your strings.'

'Did he elaborate on how they were going to do that?'

'No. I stormed out at that point.'

We stood in silence for a moment or two.

'Sophie, you didn't think to tell me about this harassment? I could have done something about it – to him.'

She shrugged her bare shoulders. 'He warned me that if I did that, they would simply kill you. '"Liquidate" was his exact word. Rather Hollywood I thought, but then I don't move in your world, do I?'

'Didn't someone in the office see what was happening? Surely, they weren't all in on it? Couldn't you have talked to the workplace rep?'

She took a large sip and shook her head. 'No, he was too clever to be seen, I'll give him that. I think they thought him and me were getting romantically involved.' She grimly laughed. 'As if; as if with that snail! No, they didn't know. Maarav, he's the workplace rep, he definitely is one of your party, and he would, I know, have been horrified and reported him straightaway. He's a decent man, despite his politics. No, I didn't talk to him or the others for the same reason that I didn't go to you. They would have supported me, but that would have put you in danger.'

The silence returned. I couldn't tell what was going on in my sister's head, but I knew that in mine was a mixture of guilt and anger swirling about.

Finally, Sophie spoke. She looked straight at me, her eyes unblinking. 'So now I've told you everything. I've done so because you are my brother and I know you care for me. Also, in the absence of a national modern police force, the likes of you is all we've got. So, like it or not, if I must report this, then it has to be to you. But...' The word echoed around her kitchen. 'I have not forgotten that you infringed upon my personal space, my privacy. In doing so, you probably broke the law. And to add insult to injury, you got some stranger, this "Roijin" to listen into my life. That, Peter, is despicable and hurtful. No matter what the reason, you had no right to do that to me.' She took a glug of the wine and then stared at me. When she next spoke it was in a quiet voice, but it was one full of anger and fury. 'Pete, I want you to leave now.'

I opened my mouth to speak, but she held up her hand. 'Leave!' she repeated. Her voice was brimming with passion, and maybe even of hate.

I put down the glass, put on my holster and jacket, and left her, without saying a word. As I closed the door, I thought I heard the sound of a glass being smashed against a wall.

Outside, I felt as if I had left a part of me in there. In front of me, by her car, were Victoria and Roijin deep in conversation. As I approached them, I could see that in her car, a very tearful Albie Warrington-Bridges was sitting looking very sorry for himself. I shot him a look and he visibly flinched. Across the street we had two huddles of neighbours who were talking earnestly and shaking their heads. Their attention was shared between Vic and Roijin, the car, and now me.

'What's up?' I asked, nodding towards our audience.

'Ah, there, comrade, you have a microcosm of the contradictions of the state we find ourselves in.' Roijin grinned. 'Over there,' she pointed to the group who had first come out, 'are the long-term residents, they're appalled that what they perceive to be the Red Army, that's us, have assailed their peaceful and tranquil land. The other group are those newly arrived in the re-housing scheme. They obviously don't like the first group, seeing them as being privileged and snobby. The other group no doubt refutes that, but they do resent the presence of such lowlifes in their formerly high-mortgage London village. But the new residents aren't too happy about violence on their street either. Both have come to a temporary alliance and have decided to call an emergency neighbourhood meeting, and some neighbourhood reps are on their way.'

I mouthed a mock, 'Wow' and smiled. 'So apart from analysing the dynamics of the area, did you have time to talk to James Bond over there?'

Roijin spread both arms, as if to say, how could you doubt us? 'Yes, in between discussing law and order with the neighbourhood factions, we did manage to have a little chat with our friend Albie. But let's talk in my car, so we can get some privacy away from the spectators.'

Victoria agreed and used her phone to lock her car and tint the windows. 'He's not going anywhere.'

We got into Roijin's, who also tinted her windows. Then turned on her dashboard. 'Ash, you're on 2D image. Pete's here now so let's share what we know.' A small image of Asher appeared in front of us. He was still in the office. Behind him I could hear Odette humming some recent soul tune.

I told the three of them everything Sophie had told me. As I did, I found my stomach tighten. That would have been nice, if it had been the result of some gym toning up against the aging process; but the reality was that it was from the thought of her so upset, so angry.

They nodded. Victoria spoke first. 'Fits with what he told us. According to him, he was just relaying what he had been told to say. He claims that it wasn't him who killed Mike Stewart. He's given us an alibi for that, which we can check. He also denies that he had anything to do with the drone attack. And he says that it wasn't him who broke into your place, Pete. He was told about it. Basically, he's denying everything and claiming that he's just a nobody.'

'You believe him?' Asher asked.

Her brows furrowed. 'Well, unless he's a great actor, and I mean, truly great. He seems too petrified of what we're going to do him. Put it this way, judging from the smell, I fear that he wet himself, when he was taken to my car. I mean, I hope not. I really don't want the smell of piss in there.'

I chuckled. I couldn't help myself.

I received a stare of rebuke from her. I stopped. She continued, 'I really can't imagine him being cool enough to lethally inject someone or to fly a drone. Not when he can barely control himself. I mean, he hasn't stopped crying.'

I agreed. 'I think I believe him. I noticed that Sophie said he always used the plural, never the singular. That it was other people who were making the threats.'

'Lots of people refer to themselves in the plural. Hardly a new thing, Pete.'

I conceded that was a good point, but I got the impression that he wasn't doing that. 'And like you say, he doesn't come across as suitable for this kind of work. I mean, my sister managed to floor him, without him laying a finger on her. He may be a slimy toad, but that's about it. No, I see him as a messenger. Did he have any idea who was doing the asking?' I asked.

'Oh, in between sobs, you couldn't shut him up. According to him, he was contacted about eight months ago and told to get close to your sister. Then more recently, he was told to start trying to persuade her work for them. When that failed, he was to try to coerce her. He said that they told him exactly what to say. He never knew any identities. It was via disguised computer chat.'

'Why did he do it? Principles? Has he background of antagonism to the party? Or did he get disillusioned?'

Asher spoke: 'I think I can answer that, Pete, it was for money. Good old-fashioned cash. Whilst Vic and Roj were talking to him, I've been looking deeper into our friend. He was paid a hefty sum six months ago, and another even bigger one three weeks ago. Not in Fists either.' For a second, he grinned and shot a glance at Odette, who could be seen behind him. 'No, it was in US Dollars and from an anonymous account in Zurich.' He chuckled. 'Ain't that always the way. 'Anyway, he's already used a good chunk of it as a substantial deposit on a property in California. Family home, near the beach. Rather nice actually. Seems, he was planning to move into it soon, because recorded on his computer are searches for which flights are still in operation to Europe. There were also matching enquiries into onward flights to California. Now, as we know, there's a ban on emigration from Britain to the States, but I found a payment to the US Embassy which is tagged as being for a permanent visa. Seems our friend had friends in high places, and they managed to bypass all the bureaucracy for him and his family.'

'Which is exactly what he told us,' Vic replied.

Leaning towards the camera, Asher added, 'I should say, that there was no more security for his bank account or search engines, than is normal. Hardly what you would expect from an espionage professional.'

I thought for a second or two; was that all it was – the money? Or could it be just the cover for something deeper? I considered the possibility. 'My sister said that he whispered threats into her ear, which is rather bizarre and melodramatic, but it does coincide with how Fiona Bailey said the threats had been made against Mike Stewart.'

Vic nodded and thought about what I had said. 'Obviously, we need to question him further and see what we can find out about him, but something tells me he's not our man.' It was one of those hunches again, I bet. She started to pick her lip as she thought out loud. 'Alright, I know full well that spies come in all shapes and sizes, they are not all karate experts, but I have difficulty in accepting that Warrington-Bridges is one. His nerdiness and wetness could be an act, in which case, he should join a theatre group. I've only had a few minutes with him, but on face-value, what he says rings true. And if he's directly employed by some foreign power, then he's a lowly clerk, not someone who organises attacks.'

After what could have been described as pregnant pause – one quite possibly, in the first trimester – Victoria spoke again. Her voice had now lowered. It was the type of voice you might use when delivering bad news. 'Pete, he also told us that they had told him that they were planning to break into your home. He says it was to freak you out. The atlas was just a piece of luck because they had wanted to leave some kind of reference to Jerusalem.'

'Sophie said that he kept repeating Jerusalem!'

'It was just pure chance that there was an atlas there. One which they took advantage of.'

'Why?' My mind sieved through the multitude of possible reasons why they would want to draw attention to their involvement.

Asher spoke again. He had been reading my mind. 'Whatever the reason, it must mean something to them. I don't know why, but I remembered Roij saying that the computer tag they'd been using to validate their messages was nine characters long, so I raised some of the messages we had. Guess what? Jerusalem has nine characters long and when I inserted it into a message, up popped a confirmation. Simple as that. Jerusalem is the code. I did it with a few others, and got the same result.'

The three of us in the car just looked at each other. We were stunned. It was Victoria who said out loud what we were all thinking. In a voice laden with incredulity, she demanded, 'Why would someone, who is probably just a patsy, who crumbled after we asked him a couple of questions, be entrusted with a secret codeword? He didn't need to know, so why tell him?'

No-one had an answer.

Roijin posed another question about this hush-hush, highly secret codeword: 'And why go to the bother of breaking into Pete's house simply to leave a clue as to what it is. Why feel the need to be so melodramatic? Why be so, to be honest, I don't know how to describe it. it just seems all unprofessional, like someone playing pranks on us!'

The allusion to theatre struck a chord. 'Unless, it isn't important. They've either changed it, or it's like you say, Roij, it's a prank, one to fool us, to confuse us. It was never meant seriously, the tag was set up to be found, so they could mess with our heads. It was never important. It was just there to distract us, like dangling a string for a cat.'

Roijin agreed. 'Makes sense, I've always been puzzled at how crude and obvious it was.'

Vic thought about what had been said. 'We're saying that they were just trying to discombobulate us with misinformation?'

'I've read about similar things in the past, World War Two, the CIA in South America, that sort of thing. Misdirection. We look one way, and not notice what's really going on. Did he have anything more to say about it?' I asked.

'No,' replied Victoria. 'He certainly didn't know why the word was chosen.' Her expression grew serious and she looked at each of us in turn. 'But can we be so sure that it's fake? Do we take that risk? Are we aware of any particular counter-revolutionary activity from that part of the world?'

We weren't.

'Perhaps it was just chosen at random?' Roijin suggested. 'I mean, passwords don't have to mean something, do they?'

Victoria squashed her nose. 'No, not necessarily, but usually there's something relevant to the owners, even if it's their favourite holiday destination or the name of their dog. But let's not get too bogged down as to why it was chosen, what's important is that they were keen to shove it under Pete's nose. Roij, you heard him. They were determined to leave something. He said that they even had a copy of the Book of Revelation of St John Divine on them to leave if they had to.'

I was now totally confused. A pathetic 'What?' was all I could muster.

It was Asher who once again cleared the fog. 'Good grief.' He grinned. 'Does it take a Jewish lad to know the New Testament? Didn't you do Christianity at school, Pete?' He laughed. I remained none-the-wiser. 'In Revelation it refers to the "New Jerusalem". Maybe the allusion isn't to the modern geographical place, but to creating a new heaven on earth. A new England. Or in their case, the old proper England. The one they've lost.'

I caught on. 'As in William Blake's Jerusalem, more in the sense of the poem and the hymn, than the city in the Middle East?'

'Could be,' he said.

Victoria was sounding almost exasperated: 'What's the point of it all?'

The same question could be asked about the attempt to enlist my sister to spy on me? That was truly ridiculous. Even a cursory examination of our relationship would reveal that the limit to any confidences we might share would go no deeper than our favourite coffee blend. To me, it suggested just one thing. 'Obviously it's to confuse, deceive us, but it's also like someone's having fun at our expense. We're being fed red herrings, so many that I feel like popping out and getting a sprig of thyme and a few cloves of garlic...'

'You'll be lucky, with the embargo,' Asher quipped.

'Indeed, but the thing is, that the real story is unfolding in front of everyone's eyes. The ruling two organisations, the dominant ones in the NWC, are baring their teeth at each other. That's what they want, that's their goal. The snivelling wreck who's just got a kicking from my sister is just part of the game. As is this Jerusalem thing. They knew Crib would eventually identify it, but that's almost the point. They're saying that they know that we know our learning, but it doesn't bother them one little bit.'

Asher feigned mock surprise. 'Did comrade Kalder just suggest that we're more than simple coppers? That we "know our learning"?'

'I think he did!' Roijin replied, before all three grinned.

'Okay, okay,' I said, for once thinking such levity wasn't appropriate. However, I let it go. 'I admit that I've been corrupted.' Before steering them to a more important question – 'What do we do next?'

I, for one, thought we had just been led up the garden path, past the shrubbery and into a maze, to emerge at exactly where we had started. I hadn't a clue as to where that might be.

All eyes turned to Victoria. 'I think we just have to let everything we've set up run its course.'

Not a grand strategy, then – just wait and see. The masses weren't going to be dancing in the streets. Victoria frowned and shrugged her shoulders. 'I think it's imperative that we talk to Jackie. This has national implications and we need her advice. I'll give her another call.'

'No,' Asher replied, rather too quickly. 'I think it would be better if Pete did.' He stopped, and then looked at the two women. It was as if he was feeling rather abashed at what he was about to say. Taking a deep breath, he continued, 'Pete's a friend of hers. If you call, Vic, it'll be solely work-related, and she'll treat it as such. If Pete does, then it'll be personal as well as political. I think it will be far more effective, if he makes the call.'

Silence met his suggestion. I knew how proud Victoria was that she had a personal relationship with Jackie. For Asher to suggest that it was minor compared to mine would wound her pride. Not that she would ever admit to that; certainly not here.

But Victoria Cole might be a funny fish, in fact one of the oddest aquatic creatures you might find in a large pond of strange water creatures, but she was practical and committed to getting the job done. 'Okay,' she agreed. 'Pete, could you?'

I nodded.

'Good. Okay? Is there anything else?' When everyone said that there wasn't, she said, 'Well, I need to inspect the upholstery of my car. Cleaning it of piss, if necessary. I'll arrange a more thorough investigation into comrade Albie Warrington-Bridges. Pete, you make the call to Jackie Payne.'

# CHAPTER 26: TWO WOMEN READING IN AN INTERIOR

On the drive back, I watched the world go by, and thought about my sister. Sophie was angry at me. I understood why; let's face it, it didn't take a doctorate in psychoanalysis to do so. I knew I'd feel the same if the roles had been reversed, but that didn't make it any easier. She was *really* angry with me. So angry, in fact, that I wasn't sure that there was any way we'd recover from this. The irony was, we had been closer than we had been for years. Over the previous twelve months, I'd seen her more often than in the previous twelve years. I couldn't see us meeting any time soon in the next twelve decades, mind.

I was pulled away from family matters by Victoria's repetitious tapping on the steering wheel increasing in intensity. Either something was bugging her, or she was preparing for an audition as a drummer in a Goth band. Taking a wild guess that she wasn't preparing for a major career change, and I wasn't sure black spiky hair was really her, I guessed that something was troubling her. Ostensibly, we were returning to the office to continue our electronic surveillance, but I was beginning to sense that she wasn't looking forward to spending the rest of the day in front of a screen. Vic was an old school kind of detective who preferred being on the street. My Cole antennae picked up when she suggested that we should be proactive and I steeled myself for a suggestion.

The car turned into Holloway Road, and slowed to filtering speed. Vic herself moved up a gear. 'So, whoever we're after, I'm certain they're a major player. So, it's logical that in the course of their activities over the years, they might have aroused suspicions about their loyalty. Perhaps not directly, but there might be some comrades who they've worked with, and have had an uneasy feeling about them.'

I didn't speak, but I wasn't sure how much use comrades' feelings would be – most trusted each other unconditionally. The party functioned through good and bad times, by solidarity and trust. I mean, I had 'uneasy feelings' about a host of people, but it was never about whether or not they were a spy. Usually, it was simply that I didn't like them.

Vic couldn't read my mind because she was now assigning her logic to me. 'You've thought that yourself, Pete, that's why you talked to Marie Williams. I think we should continue along that line of enquiry. Talk to people who they were politically active with, in campaigns, workers' councils and so forth. See if anyone ever thought there was ever anything smelling dodgy about them.'

She had a point. I wasn't going to quibble about how much we should set in store with the 'uneasy feelings' or 'smelling dodgy' approach, even though it sounded like the actions of a flighty hippie herbalist to me, because I could see where she was coming from. As the stakes got higher, any saboteur would have had to take more decisive action, which inevitably would have risked drawing attention to them. She was right, I'd had much the same thought. Trouble was, that there were rather large implications to what she was suggesting. 'And we could see when exactly and how they joined. I presume that by "them", you mean Bailey, Donaldson, Anand and Walker?'

'I do.'

'That's going to be a lot of leg work.'

We stopped at some lights. Three mothers with buggies crossed in front of us. A little hand appeared from one of the buggies and waved at us. I returned the gesture. Vic didn't. She just looked at me as if I was a complete idiot. 'Okay, let's narrow this down. I think we can set aside Fiona Bailey because there's no way she was operating the drone. I was cheek to cheek with her under that sofa and I think I'd notice if she had been. So that leaves Anand, Donaldson and Walker. Want to choose who we start with?'

'Well, if I was to pick a lucky winner, then Dave Donaldson would be the one. He's the one with crates full of weapons. A falling out between us and the AF would suit him just fine. And let's not forget that he originally came to our attention because he just so happens to have lived with Mike Stewart. His alibi for the time of Stewart's death is flimsy to say the least. Add to that, just before the attack on the Shard, he arrives for the TV debate late and leaves early, despite the fact that the relationship between the party and the AF is one of the most pressing political issues of the moment. (And one which he's obsessed by.) At best it looks like a tick box exercise, which isn't Donaldson's style. Usually, he speaks and acts in exclamation marks. The only boxes he ticks have grenades in. But no, he stays for the barest minimum time, then rushes to the Shard. Whereas, I'd say that both Anand and Walker behaved as you'd expect in such a situation. They stayed the whole time, made contributions and circulated. They didn't rush off like Donaldson.'

Victoria agreed. 'But after rushing to the Shard, he *doesn't rush* upstairs to the debate; he hangs around on the ground floor, and rings mummy and his partner.'

'Indeed.'

The lights changed and we set off. With this quality of vehicle, it moved with the smoothness of silk and with the level of sound you'd get from a boy blowing air out through pursed lips. It was barely noticeable that we were moving at all. There was more noise coming from the cogs whirling in Cole's brain, than there was from her car. 'Okay, so we look at Donaldson first. Now, there's the small matter of how we do that. His anarchist friends aren't going to like that, not one little bit.'

She had a point. The fact that we were both party members and Crib investigators was going to make us as popular as the plague. Not to mention Vic's previous job. It was entirely conceivable that we might prompt Donaldson to unpack his crates.

We passed the newly refurbished Holloway Road Tube station in silence, its red tiles and six arches newly restored to their former glory, gleaming in the sun. 'We're going to have to be careful,' I said, once more giving the bleedin' obvious some airtime. 'But there's too much pointing at Donaldson not to take a closer look at him. We can talk to party comrades who've worked with him; that would be a little less risky than directly talking to AF members. That had been my approach at his workplace and I managed not to unduly antagonise anyone. We should do something similar… if we can.' There was a good tonnage of wishful thinking involved in this. Sooner or later, we'd have to have some awkward conversations about espionage and the loyalty of a popular and leading member of the AF – with sisters and brothers of that very same Federation.

She replied, with a voice laden with weariness, 'Any suggestions on how we're going to do that?'

An idea had occurred to me. 'Having people working for you in positions of power becomes crucial at critical points of events. We know what DD's public position is at the moment, and we know what he's preparing for in private. But what about at the other times, when history could have taken different paths?'

'The attempted coup d'etat?'

'Possibly,' I replied, 'but when I spoke to Marie Williams, she reminded me that the initial resistance to the prime minister's grab for power was primarily organised by the party. So, I don't think any leading member of the AF would have been of much use to them at that moment, for the simple reason that only a small group of party members were involved in the preparation. That doesn't stop there being agents embedded in the AF at the time, it just means that I don't think they'd have been able to do anything of noticeable importance. There would be nothing said or done which might help us identify them. But what about the days following – in the civil war?'

Recognition lit up her face. 'When it was touch and go, when we were shoring up support from other organisations, including the AF.'

'Exactly, so we need to find out what DD was doing, and how he was behaving, during the civil war, and whether there was anything suspicious. The rest of the office can continue the surveillance and the more direct investigations, but I think we should at least take a temporary step back in time.'

She was smiling, and noticeably changed the car to manual. Obviously, she was looking forward to a juicy dose of proactive detection. 'And you're going to suggest, just where we're going to travel back to, aren't you, Pete Kalder!'

It was my turn to smile. 'Well, Victoria Cole, although at the time in question, I was a spectator of events from inside a prison cell, I was a keen observer of them. If for nothing else, my life depended on the outcome. Which means that I do know that regional defence units were set up after the failed coup d'etat to protect the revolution. Knowing Donaldson's love of the spotlight, not to mention his penchant for firearms, it wouldn't be a street committee or workplace defence branch, it would be something with a higher profile – a DU. He works near three travel hubs – Euston, St Pancras and King's Cross – which were seen as vital to protect back in those days. There was a Central Zone Defence Committee based in what formerly had been the St Pancras Hotel. I bet, if we were to do a little nosing around, we'd find that he was heavily involved in it.' My grin broadened. 'And it just so happens that the CZDC, as it was known, still have staff there.'

Vic indicated to turn right, in the direction of St Pancras.

I made a phone call to Marie Williams. She had not only been central to the preparations to resist the prime minister's attempted seizure of power, but the aftermath too. Her links to the medical professionals had made her a vital component of it all. A bloodbath had been expected, but thankfully, although there had been loss of life, it had not been of the scale we had feared. She would either know who had been on the regional defence committees, or at the very least, would know where to point me to get the information. She answered almost straightaway, which was a good start, as it indicated that there had been no prevarication on taking a call from me.

Her make-up less face was perfectly neutral, neither showing pleasure, nor, as was more likely, wariness, at receiving yet another call. I had no illusion that whilst she hadn't broken off all diplomatic relations, she wasn't going to be inviting me to any family get-togethers just yet.

'Pete. How can I help you?' she said, keeping the Switzerland vibe going.

I explained. Unnervingly, she replied with a simple stare. For a moment, I worried that she was annoyed, but as her eyes looked to one side, slightly bit her lip, I recognised it as her thinking face. After a minute or two, of me having nothing to do other than study her pores, which it had to be said, were, for a person of her age, rather wrinkle-free, she answered.

'I think he was on the committee as one of the AF allocated positions on the CZDC.'

'What was his role?' I asked, keeping my smugness at being proved correct hidden.

With only her mouth moving, she replied that she couldn't remember.

'Were there any concerns or issues with the activities of the CZDC?'

She gave a humourless laugh. 'To be honest, Pete, at that time, there were concerns and issues everywhere! There were outbreaks of counter-revolutionary violence across the British countries and there was the very real concern that a section of the army would break away and join the counter-revolution. We already had the problem that the majority of the police weren't like Vic–' her eyes darted towards the former cop in question. Vic herself didn't respond, but concentrated – or pretended to – on driving. 'They opposed,' she continued, 'what we were doing. And added to all that, there was also the concern that we might get invaded by a foreign power. So...'

I interrupted her. I was quite knowledgeable of history, and not just the fine art variety, but of recent events, I could have written a doctorate thesis. I didn't need a refresher course on it. 'I mean, Marie, were there any concerns that the CZDC had made obvious errors? Or decisions which were inexplicable? Maybe, it was noticed that our enemies seemed to always be one step ahead of us there. Basically, Marie, was there anything which might be construed as looking dodgy?' I was sharper than I had intended, and I hoped that she wouldn't tell me where to get off, and hang up. It was just that Victoria wasn't the only one who was feeling that we were chasing our tails here.

But her face still not betraying any emotion, Marie replied simply that she hadn't been aware of any. 'But things were moving so fast, it was a crazy time, there could have been, but we just never got to hear about it. I'd suggest that you contact someone who was on the committee.' She rubbed her cheeks with her hand, and bit her lip. 'I'm trying to remember who was on it that you might contact.' A smile of satisfaction crossed her face. 'Cathy was on it, yes, Cathy Smith. She was, still is, I believe, a colleague of his at the cleaning...'

'Yes, I know. I've met her. Thanks, Marie.' I closed the connection.

Immediately, I checked to see where Donaldson was. I didn't want to phone Smith and talk about him if he was sitting next to her, sharing a coffee cream, and gossiping over a cuppa. But according to our tracking device he was at the Shard. So not at work – again. He seemed to barely be there. I was surprised that the streets weren't knee-deep in litter, considering how rarely he deigned to make an appearance at his office. I rang Cathy Smith, taking advantage of Donaldson's lax attendance levels.

She answered after a few rings. Unlike her anarchist co-worker, she was doing what the NWC paid her to do. 'Hi Cathy, sorry to disturb you again, but this is important. I understand that you are on the Central Zone Defence Committee. Is that correct?'

'Er, well, *I was,* but it's now really just a skeleton staff there...'

'They still based at the old hotel?'

'Er...yes. But, I'm at...'

'And Dave Donaldson was also on it?'

She looked at little disconcerted at my rather brusque questioning, but didn't complain. 'Yes, he was, but like me, he's come off and...'

'Okay, that's good. Could you please head for the hotel and we'll see you in ten minutes?'

'Er, why? Can't we talk over the phone, it's just that I have to...'

I didn't let her finish. 'Thanks, Cathy. Ten minutes it is then. Please don't tell anyone we're meeting. Just say that...' I thought for a second for a plausible excuse. 'That, we're checking on *present* security levels, in light of the Shard attack.'

Out of the corner of my eye, I saw Victoria smile and nod her head, approving at my little red lie. I didn't give Cathy a chance to object. 'We'll see you in the CZDC office. Don't worry, we'll find it.' I quickly thanked her again and rang off.

It didn't take us too long to get there. Even without a siren and flashing light, Vic was someone who didn't really do sedate driving. She barely slowed as we drove up the impressive arced driveway. Its mid-Victorian brown neo-Gothic frontage oozing the confidence of its age, when steam was king and so was the Empire. It always looked to me, as if it should be perched on some Austrian mountain, surrounded by forests and bears. Its fairy-tale look was somewhat lessened by huge rectangular strips of the rainbow colours of the various NWC supporting organisations hanging down in front of it.

Cathy had informed the reception to expect us. She was in room 12, on the second floor. We were pointed to the opposite side of the reception. Meaning that the NWC had kept a few of the better, older rooms, to work in. Naughty. All of a sudden, I felt youthful. This rare event was due to the fact that everyone enjoying tea and cake under the steel and glass roof, beside the palms, appeared to be at least two decades older than us.

I bounded over to the grand staircase. I had never been here before and wanted to enjoy its opulent design. I almost sank into the William Morris design of the carpet. I looked around and gawped. It was like somewhere you'd expect a Tsar to stay. The grandeur was almost laughable; glorious in its over-statement. Light steamed through the long windows, making it feel almost like a cathedral. I was perfectly happy to get lost in this former palace of early bourgeois travel. But it couldn't last. Within seconds, I remembered the tawdry reason why I was here. I guess that wasn't unusual – the meretricious could often be found in the luxury. I quickened my pace. Turning into the curved corridor, I saw Vic reach Room 12. Without bothering to knock, she opened the door and went in. I gave one more look of admiration for décor then dutifully followed her in.

What once had been a rather swish bedroom was now an office, with lush decor. There wasn't usually an oak fireplace and ceiling to floor curtains in the modern office. Along all the walls were virtual screens, although seventy five percent of them were presently turned blank. In the corners there were blue labels denoting that these had been once the property of the Metropolitan Police Service. Victoria didn't appear to be too choked up at being reunited with them, but was deep in conversation with Cathy. Both were standing behind a young black man, in his early twenties. He appeared to be totally oblivious to our presence, or at the very least, not that interested in it. His long thick black hair was held back by rather large headphones, and in front of his mouth was a retro-mouthpiece.

I joined them. Cathy was explaining that, until recently, many of the bedrooms had been converted into offices, used by the NWC during the civil war to serve as the CZDC HQ. This room housed the computers used for monitoring cyber-attacks to the central transport systems. Next door was used for similar purposes, but for the power and water supplies. Others were for controlling defence and surveillance drones. Approximately a third of them had been for surveillance and monitoring. The rest had been used to billet the CZDC militia.

She sighed, as if it had been heady days of wine and roses. 'All pretty much mothballed now.'

'What's the hotel used for now, then?' Vic asked.

'Therapeutic stays for the local elderly.'

That explained why we had appeared to be the arrival of the youth wing.

'There's only a few comrades still working here,' she explained. 'Like Jacob here. Just to keep an eye on things. Of course, with the privacy and citizen rights legislation, all the street drones have been grounded and all the CCTV has stopped.' She looked ahead, thoughtful. 'Although, with the situation as it is now, that might change. Talk in the office is that they might get reactivated.'

'Have you heard anything which specifically mentions that as a possibility?' Victoria asked.

Cathy shook her head. 'Oh no, just chatter over the sandwiches.' A cloud of sadness crossed her face. 'Of course, it would be very different this time. Back then, it was the united front of the pro-revolutionary forces against reaction. We had all sorts in here. There was a sense of solidarity, of camaraderie, fighting for a better future. But now, it won't be the AF and us sitting side by side. We'll be fighting each other, not together.'

Clearly not interested in guesswork of the future, Victoria asked about the past: 'How did it work? Did you have assigned duties, or was it all just free-flowing?'

'No, we had definite roles. Mine was based a few doors down. It's been converted back into a bedroom now, but then, it was pretty much like in here, except a bit smaller; it was to monitor the traffic. You'll remember that we had surveillance drones, which we had liberated from Special Branch. In that section there were nine of us, three teams of three.'

'And was one of them Donaldson?' I asked.

She shook her head. 'No. Dave was in charge of the provision of supplies.'

She saw similar looks of incomprehension on both our faces, so she explained: 'Armaments. Guns and stuff. For the militia.'

Once more, our faces mirrored each other. Both tried hard to be as placid and vanilla as possible, and not to register any kind of interest.

'Any idea, what became of them? The guns, I mean,' I asked, with fake nonchalance.

She replied that she didn't and had assumed that the Workers' State Defence Forces had absorbed them. She wasn't quite correct; they had been absorbed into Dave Donaldson's private savings for that rainy day, when you have an emergency, and need to fork out military armaments to various chums.

Victoria folded her arms, conveying the message that it was an area which we were not to pursue right here, right now. Reading her body language, I decided against jumping up and down, and screaming that he had them hidden – the naughty, anarcho beardy boy!

Nor did Victoria; instead, she asked what precisely his role had been.

'Well, like everyone delegated here, he sat on the defence committee and discussed how best to protect the area. He served on the surveillance rota, and if the militia were called out on an action, then he was in charge of distributing the necessary firearms.'

'Did that happen often?' I asked.

'A few times. But it had gone pretty well. We'd responded quickly, been well-supplied, and with as much force as had been required. Most here, think Dave was efficient and trustworthy. He did a great job.'

'Do you have a record of these "actions"?' I asked, before I got too emotional at how fantastic Dave was. Stirring stuff. We'd be renaming streets after him soon.

A frown appeared. She wasn't enjoying this. But she didn't protest, and began to start to list them. Victoria held up her hand. 'Is there a record?' She pointed at the computers. Cathy nodded, and rather sharply replied, 'Of course.'

'Good. Could you forward them all to Roijin Kemal?'

She nodded.

Then Vic changed direction. 'What area of London did this committee cover?'

'Does,' corrected Cathy. 'We still do.'

Unfazed, but with just a glimmer of amusement, Victoria repeated the question, but with the correct tense.

Seemingly happy that the grammar had been taken care of, Cathy turned to Jacob and tapped him on the shoulder. Smiling, he took off his headphones. She asked him to put up a map of operations. He nodded, but didn't say a word.

Seconds later, a map appeared in front of us. Jacob didn't break his apparent vow of silence, and just replaced his headphones.

Cathy explained, 'Those buildings and streets which the revolution has renamed, have both the new and old names.'

I looked at it with a combination of reverence and respect for the heroic actions of normal working people in defending their state, and rather less high-mindedly, to search those memories for anything which might finger Dave Donaldson. The area it covered reached Copenhagen Street at its furthest north and to the former Buckingham Palace in the south. To the east it stopped at the City Road Basin; to the west what had once been Kensington Palace. Basically, this was tourist London. The points of interest here though, weren't for that kind of guide; these were of murder and injury. This was an area of several flashpoints.

'So, you were at the centre of much of the heat.'

She nodded thoughtfully. 'Yeah, you could say that, Pete. It was pretty worrying for a while, that's for sure. But, well, we got through it didn't we?'

I didn't answer. It was too soon to do so. We weren't there yet. Headlines of successful attacks, attacks stopped and near misses, appeared in my memory. 'You don't have a list of all the "actions", do you?'

'I can do better than that.' She tapped Jacob's shoulder. 'Could you put the Action Log on visual?'

Colour flashed across the map. She now acted as tour guide. She didn't have an open top bus but she had the sights. 'The yellow flames which look like stubby fingers are bomb blasts. Those with a red cross, are ones which we manage to diffuse. The blue dots are drone strikes; the orange ones are missile. Any with a red cross, are those we neutralised. Green dots are sniper, or counter-revolutionary action by people actually on the ground.'

It was quite a picture. Central London had become a painful rash of irritation and sores.

Victoria asked if this too could be sent over. Adding, 'Actually could you send over all your files connected with the state of emergency? It would be useful if you also included the times Donaldson was on duty.'

Cathy blanched. 'Do you really need all that? It'll be quite a load!'

She received a focussed look, straight into her skull. 'If it's a problem, comrade,' Victoria replied, 'we can just access your entire system. We'd rather not, as that would appear to be somewhat impolite, but we can if we have to.'

'No. It's okay,' she muttered. 'I suppose it's important.'

'Thank you. Would you say that any of these attacks were preventable?'

She looked at me with confusion written all over her face. 'Is that in the philosophical sense, or in regard to the long-term strategy of the NWC?'

'Neither,' I replied. 'Was there anything which the CZDC could have picked up on? Specifically, were there any questions over his behaviour or decisions which he had made?'

Cathy shook her head. From her expression it was obvious that whilst the line of questioning wasn't a surprise, it was still rather distasteful. Rather like having to take a course of medical treatment. You do it; you know it has to be done, but it's still unpleasant. 'None. Dave's a hard working and honest revolutionary. I may disagree with some of what he says, but I trust him explicitly.'

'You can't think of anything, which rang alarm bells?'

'Not even a tinkle.'

Oh, she was attempting humour now. I smiled at the effort. Vic didn't. I asked again, 'So with all these attacks, there was never a time when people felt that something either could have been done, and wasn't? Or something which was done, which made it worse?'

It was obvious that Cathy considered that not to be the clearest question she'd ever been asked. But again, she answered that nothing of importance stood out.

'Really?' I asked. I found the answer to be a surprising one. I had been a revolutionary all my life and with the best of wills, we had made cock-ups left, right and centre. To be so efficient and error-free at this time, was gratifying, but didn't sound truthful.

Vic might not have the years that I had under my belt, but she knew enough to expect at least a percentage of mistakes to have been made. That had always been the charm of the British Left. Even when things appeared to be going well, we could always find a way of buggering it up. 'Think, Cathy. This is important. Was there anything, which didn't sit right with comrades here? Anything which raised eyebrows.'

We both stared at her as she thought. To say it was a meaningful pause, wouldn't have given it due justice. Finally, she replied: 'Well, I suppose there were a couple of times when questions were asked, three actually.' She took a deep breath. 'One was on the first day we'd been set up. A massive cyber-attack swept the system. Someone had launched a virus at us. We never found out who, or exactly from where. But it seemed unstoppable. It was lucky that Glen Bale was actually in the building – Comrade Bale is a Central Committee Member who is responsible for the IT security, he is now based...'

'Yes. We know him. What happened exactly?'

She looked at me, rather taken aback at my sharpness. 'Okay, well, ironically, he had just arrived to check on our security when it struck. As I said, it was a stroke of good fortune that he was here, because, it was moving at speed and bringing systems to a halt. I mean, transport, health, communications – the lot. If he hadn't been on the spot and able to block it, we could have been in deep trouble. Comrade Bale was furious. He couldn't understand how it had by-passed our security.'

Knowing that he had been the one who had set the security up, I guessed that his annoyance was at least in part from a slight dent to his enormous ego. 'And did he have any idea how that had been achieved?'

She shook her head.

'Could it have originated here?' I asked.

'No. He managed to establish that it was external to this building.'

Victoria led the elephant in the room over to say hello. 'Could Dave Donaldson have anything to do with it?'

She scoffed, 'I doubt it. Dear old Dave can barely use his phone, so setting up a virus is well out of his skill set.'

'Hmm, he knows enough to control the cleaning vehicles, though, doesn't he?'

'Well, he doesn't actually. They're run by artificial intelligence. He oversees any problems.'

Victoria interrupted, 'Was he here when it happened?'

She thought. 'Yes, I think he was. He'd had a bit of a barny with Bale.' She saw my look. 'Oh, it wasn't related to the cyber-attack. No, they've history. Can't stand each other.' I inwardly smiled. Donaldson wasn't all bad, then. I wasn't a Bale fan either. 'I think it was about the actions of the party, in particular, not consulting the AF about the early stages of the civil war. But, no, I don't think Dave can do much more with computers than turn them on.'

A look on Victoria's face indicated that she wasn't going to just accept that. She would be examining it further, but she said nothing except to ask, 'You said three occasions. What was the second?'

She frowned. 'Well, many people think that the missile strike at Workers' Hall should have been stopped. It's in our area, you see. We received quite a lot of criticism over it. As you know, the NWC had decamped from it, but we still lost some sisters and brothers.'

Workers' Hall had once been known as the Royal Albert Hall and had been the NWC's home. I remembered the attack well; although it had failed in its objective in destroying the revolution's leadership, it had still shaken the Brit nations. Thinking that it was such a tempting target, Jackie Payne had taken the decision to secretly have it evacuated. Sadly, however, that hadn't meant that there hadn't been any casualties, because a number of workers who had been brought in had been killed. Ironically, they had gone in as the delegates had left, and were there to ensure that the historic building would be well preserved. It was now a bombed-out ruin. The prime minister's much-repeated love and honouring of Britain's past, obviously hadn't extended to the Royal Albert Hall.

'We were criticized for not launching the defence drones to stop the attack. To be honest, comrades, I thought that was unfair. Okay, the Hall's in our area, but the attack came from the east. By the time the drones had entered our zone, it was too late.'

'Was Donaldson on duty then?' Vic asked.

Cathy shrugged. 'I don't know. I could check.'

Vic briskly brushed aside the offer, telling her that we would do it ourselves. 'And the third?'

Here, she looked a little guilty. 'Yeah,' she said slowly. 'That one is a question that needs answering.' She took a deep breath. 'There was a substantial quantity of weapons stored here for the militia. And I mean, a substantial amount. They took up nearly one floor. There were rifles, machine guns, mortars, all sorts of hardware. Well, after the civil war ended, and this place was demobilised, it was thought the safest option was to move them into a secure location. As we were doing this, it was noticed that some of the stock had gone missing. Because of all the upheaval, we never had proper records, so it was guess-work, but comrades who had been maintaining them were certain that quite a cache had gone missing. Like I said, we couldn't prove it, but that was the talk.'

I looked at Vic, before asking a question which I knew the answer to, because I had been told it only a few minutes ago, and although my memory wasn't what it was, due to the aging process, I could still recall it. 'And Dave Donaldson was in charge of armaments, yes?'

'Yes,' she muttered.

Rubbing her neck and closing her eyes, Vic clarified the situation. 'So, apart from a full-on cyber-attack, which we had previously assumed was impossible; a full-on missile attack on the NWC headquarters, and a substantial amount of weaponry going AWOL, there was nothing of any concern here? Everything was just perfect.'

That was alpha-sarcasm from my fellow comrade detective. I would have been proud of it, myself. Cathy didn't reply. There wasn't much she could say.

Vic didn't pursue it any further but stood thinking. I knew she was calculating what we should do next. I didn't see any point in giving my two pennies' worth because Vic was good at this, so why get embarrassed at being overruled with better ideas? This way, I could pretend that I had come to the same conclusion myself. Cathy looked at her, and then me. I returned her a look to say that this shouldn't take too long.

Finally, Vic spoke: 'We'll need everything you've got.' She tapped the young man on the shoulder and showed her ID. 'Jacob, isn't it? Sorry, but Crib needs your help.' He looked at her and then the ID, and then without seeming to be either concerned or annoyed, asked politely, 'Okay, comrade, what can I do for you?' Proving that he did speak.

'Thanks, comrade. I want the full log in times for Dave Donaldson for the duration that this place has been used as CZDC. When he worked here, what he was assigned to on each day, and how long he was here. Can that be done? I want any hostile reactionary activity which happened at those times to also be listed. Is that possible?'

His reply was slow and doubtful: 'It can... everything was automatically recorded, but...' He paused, not happy at what we were asking him to do and looked at Cathy. She nodded acquiescence. 'Okay then...sure, I guess I can do that now.'

'Good. I want you to send it all over to that terminal over there–' she pointed to the one nearest the window. Something to gaze out of, I guessed.

'I'll look over them. Cathy, you'll give us the security codes? I'll also want the precise dates and times of the three attacks you've told us about – the cyber, Workers' hall and the loss of the guns.'

She nodded.

'Excellent. Now, Cathy, I want you to search all of your records for any involvement of Fiona Bailey, Reyansh Anand and Noah Walker. Whilst you're at it, also have a look for Phan Bien, Sofia Brownswood and Thom Simons.' She saw an expression cross Cathy's face, and guessed what it signified. 'They are of course all leading revolutionaries. None are necessarily under suspicion, but we do need to find this information. I don't need to remind you that it is your revolutionary duty to cooperate with Crib investigations.'

If Cathy had been contemplating opposition, she quickly decided against it. The natural and inherent belief in freedom and opposition to control was beginning to be compromised by the situation we found ourselves in. That made our job easier, but it was also worrying. 'I'll do that now,' she replied and sat down at a computer next to Jacob.

I waited for my orders from Victoria. I had been expecting long hours poring over computer screens, but to my pleasant surprise, it wasn't to be the case.

'Pete, we've got this covered. I think you should try your well-renowned charm and see what people think about Donaldson. Ask around – party members, AF siblings, the lot. It will get back to him, but that can't be helped. We can't pussyfoot around for much longer. Try not to be too blunt though.'

'No asking if he is a murderous renegade, then?'

She grinned. 'Maybe not right at the start. But you've the political experience to sniff out anything which sounds dodgy. Also, you've a reputation of being far from being a party man, so the anarchists will take it a little better if you are the one asking the questions. It's better if you do so alone, than if I was with you.'

'Cheers. I *think*.'

I turned to leave, with Cathy and Jacob glued to the visuals. But before I did, I had something important to say. 'And Cathy, thanks for all your work back then in those crucial times after the seizure of power. It's appreciated. You helped defend the revolution.'

When the enemy seemed so much clearer then.

# CHAPTER 27:
# THE WATERING PLACE

O n the way out, I had an idea, which was the reason why my beloved scooter was huffing and puffing up the hill towards Alexandra Palace. With the stunning building on my right, and the fantastic panorama of London on my left, it was an effort to keep my eyes on the road. Unrivalled views of the city competed with the walls of white Huntington and yellow stock brick walls for my attention. I couldn't help myself and sneaked a look at its glorious Italianate style, rising up from the hill, imperiously looking down on the surrounding park, and the Capital beyond. London looked glorious in the fading sun. I passed the large blue and pale green circular feature window, framed with strips of red brick. Ally Pally couldn't decide whether it was cathedral or palace or coliseum – or a mix of all three. I turned right and headed up to the main entrance. I was making a habit of visiting Victorian architectural statements: the St Pancras Hotel, and now here. Both shared a design intended as a nod to past European empires, in an unsubtle attempt to give glory to the then British one. Both had been opened in 1873. Both had been commandeered by the revolution.

Alexandra Palace had been a host to many and varied events in its time, and used for a variety of uses. It had been known as the "People's Palace"; now it really could claim to be that, because the NWC had decided that the People's Museum of Revolution and Rebellion would have its home here. Many people – and from his computer files, it seems Mike Stewart had been one of them – had wanted a brand-new building to be built to house it. But the NWC had decided that the revolution had more pressing construction priorities, so it would be better to utilise an existing structure. And thus, the "People's Palace" had become the People's Museum. And elected to be its first curator was one Joni Feld.

I had known Joni since before I had joined the party. Basically, anyone who had been involved in the movement for even the briefest of time, knew her. She was an institution in the struggle. Now in her eighties, she had been involved in every movement, campaign, uprising or strike that you could think of in the last sixty-odd years. To my knowledge, she had never actually been a member of any party or formal organisation. However, many of her numerous children and grandchildren were. Because of her steadfast principle of not being directly affiliated, not to mention her extended family being scattered across the British Left, she was widely respected – and it would not be too much to say loved – by a wide range of socialists, anarchists, activists and trade unionists. She also had an encyclopaedic knowledge of the history of activism, which defied belief. This made her an ideal person to be in charge of the museum. And an ideal person for me to talk to. I wondered why I had never thought of doing so before.

I passed two guards, making a mental note to mention this to Al Handley that Somerset House wasn't the only cultural centre which had security. I walked into the entrance of Palm Court and immediately noticed a pair of British army jeeps on display. One had the insignia of the party, the other of Parliament. Judging from the bullet holes and burnt wheels, both had seen action. Large photographs of past violent crackdowns lined the walls. Cabinets full of artefacts stood, displaying repression and opposition spread across the room. Holograms of street battles filled the spaces between them and the vehicles. This was, after all, a celebration and remembrance of the struggles we had all gone through. Seeing a group of museum workers moving large boxes on a trolley, I stopped one and asked where I could find Joni Feld.

'Last time I saw Mother J was in the hall,' he answered.

'Cheers,' I replied and smiled at her nickname. It was one from affection and love, but she hated it. She said it made her feel old.

Along the wide corridor, William Hogarth paintings hung on the walls. I felt rather proud that I was at least partly responsible for them being here. They, like many of the artworks which could be found in the museum, had arrived through the nationalisation of private art collections. We'd also unlocked the vast storage-houses of the galleries and A.R.T had sent many here for display.

Arriving in the main hall, I found myself amongst a hive of activity. Noise and movement were everywhere. Museum staff appeared to be multiplying in numbers before my very eyes. Many of them were busy setting up avatars of mannequins of striking workers and demonstrators. It had to be said that they were disturbingly real, so the sight of them being carried on people's shoulders was somewhat surreal. I asked one who was holding the torso of a figure clenching a fist, where I might find her. He directed me to her office.

I went through some glass doors, along yet another corridor, and quickly found it. Stopping only briefly to politely knock, I went straight in. She was sitting at her desk, which barely had enough room for her to rest her elbows. Papers and books covered it in lopsided layers. A lone chipped Frida Kahlo mug stood in the middle of it all, half full of cold coffee. Behind her was a poster for the 1960 film, Spartacus, starring Kirk Douglas.

Today, Joni was sporting bleached blonde short hair, parted at the middle. It was always short and always parted in that way, but the colour changed at fairly regular intervals. Slightly tanned, she was wearing an orange and white shirt with large geometric flowers, and looked the epitome of summer.

Hearing me come in, she looked up and through her metal and gold glasses. A huge grin suddenly appeared. 'Pete! Great to see you!' She leapt out of her chair, and in one movement, came around and crushed the breath out of me with a hug. 'Come up here with a few repatriated paintings, have you?' Her north London accent cackled.

Not that I had a chance to reply, because at that very moment, her phone rang. 'Scuse me, Pete. Sit down, I have to get this.' She waved her hand in the vague direction of a chair, which was presently being used as a support for an assortment of items that I guessed were destined to be exhibits. I could see a 1980s megaphone sitting on several anti-Poll Tax t-shirts from the same era. She nodded towards them. Then with one hand on the phone, she closed the door with the other. I took up her offer, and put them carefully on the floor.

Hanging on the back of the door was the leopard-skin print coat which she was famed for wearing. That coat had been seen through decades of industrial and political struggles. I had no doubt that within the vast photographic archives that they had here, there'd be a whole volume of her in the past sixty years wearing it at demos, sit-ins, strikes, riots, festivals and uprisings. Che had his beret and Trotsky his glasses; Joni had her coat. She had always assured me that it was the same one, although I had my doubts, because it looked in good nick for something of that age. But then, the same could be said of her.

Cutting the call short, she apologised for the interruption and sat down heavily on her chair.

'A busy time?' I asked.

She chortled. 'Yeah, you could say that. We're supposed to open officially in four days' time! I've told the NWC that we are only half-ready, but they are insistent that it goes ahead; they see it as helping to give the revolution a sense of being established. Dunno how our humble efforts can do that, but who am I to argue with Jackie Payne? She can be a funny old sock when she wants to be.'

She chuckled to herself; I wondered if in all my time left on this planet, I would ever think of Jackie as being a sock, funny or otherwise.

'Course, she'll be there. But there'll be a host of other speakers as well. We've also a good number of international big cats as well – the president of the Portuguese People's Assembly is coming over, alongside leaders from the movement from across the world. We've also got music, art, a light display – the lot! It's gonna be the biggest event since the revolution! All we have to do, is to get it all ready.' She blew out her cheeks. 'Which ain't going to be easy. There's scores of volunteers alongside the full-time staff and they're all working their little shorts off, but it's going to be a close thing. I'm reckoning that we're all going to be here twenty-four hours a day 'til then. I'll be sleeping here. Just me and Kirk,' she giggled. 'It's bonkers – if you excuse my insensitive mental health vocabulary.' She laughed again. 'But then you ain't that good on such things yourself, are you?'

One thing she had said had interested me – she had said "event". Could this be the event that Jackie feared was going to happen? The "event" which had been in the communications we had intercepted? An attack on the leadership of two revolutions in the front of a world-wide audience would be a Godsend to our enemies. That really would be a world-wide event.

I played it cool. Having no wish to unduly worry her, I didn't suggest that I was entertaining a notion that that there might be a full-scale terrorist assault on her museum. 'Sounds like it. Have you, er, security sorted?'

She looked at me with a confused expression on her face. 'Well, we'll have stewards to help, but I don't think we'll have anything more, Pete. This is going to be a celebration of solidarity and love.'

Not everyone would be thinking that.

'You think there'll be trouble?' she asked, beginning to look a little concerned.

I tried a reassuring smile. 'Probably not, but, well, I suppose you've heard about the Shard?'

'Well, yeah, I get your point, like I said, we'll have some people here. But we don't want to spoil it by having dozens of armed militia running all about the place, waving guns about.'

I really didn't want to ruin her big day. Her only worries for the occasion should be what nibbles to provide, but my problem was that I would not be doing my duty if I didn't at least give some indication of a possible threat. I tried to find my reassuring smile. 'They'd hardly be doing that, Joni. They would be sisters and brothers from organisations committed to the NWC. I think you do need to face the unfortunate fact that the opening of this museum might make it a possible target.'

She shrugged. 'I'll talk to the stewards.'

'But...'

But what? I thought to myself, what could I say? Should I freak her out, based on what? Based on a guess? Based on the fact that she said the word event? If the word was a warning flag then that would make any sporting competition a target. Instead, I smiled and sympathised. Assuring her that I sincerely believed that the museum would be ready and not to mind me, it was the company I was keeping. Mentally, I was filing a to-do list to talk to Jackie and arrange some serious security.

She was right though, it would open in time. She may look rather so laidback that she could be a Pilates pose, and her office may resemble the aftermath of a drone attack, but she was an experienced and highly competent woman. It would not only open in time; it would be utterly fantastic. Joni was a woman who had an acute eye for style and design.

'That going in?' I asked, nodding at the poster.

She grinned. 'Nope. Kirk and his thighs stay in here. A perk of being commissar museum curator.' She looked around the room. It was a small room, barely big enough to fit the pair of us, and Mr Douglas, but she had lost something. 'Fancy a cuppa? The kettle is...er...' She scanned the room. It didn't boil, whistle or shout, 'Hi! I'm Mr Kettle, fancy pouring me?'

I decided to save her the effort of searching for it. 'No, it's okay, Joni, I'm fine.'

She shrugged. 'Fair enough. You here on ART or Crib business?'

Strangely, I had experienced a substantial drop in confidence in being here. I spoke almost in a whisper: 'Crib, I'm afraid. Do you have a problem with that?'

'You're a servant of the National Workers' Council, as am I, and the NWC is the servant of the people, so I can't see why I would. But then, I suppose it depends on what you are going to ask me.'

Good point.

Trying to regain my speech, I went for the direct approach. 'How well do you know Dave Donaldson?'

She looked at me closely, as if she was analysing me, judging my intentions – thinking how much she was willing to say. We both may be servants of the NWC, but I had the job of cleaning out the privy. She was wondering if she could handle the smell. Metaphorically holding her nose, she replied 'DD? Yeah, I know him. You know, I've probably known him for most of his adult life. Why do you want to know about him?' A thought struck her. 'Course, he shared a house with Mike Stewart, didn't he?'

I told her that was the case, and the reason for me being here was to fill in some background. That was partly true, but then we were doing so much of that we'd soon be able to paint forty Victorian paintings. The type with lush romantic countryside, the odd ancient Greek folly with a hunting dog in the middle.

I wasn't sure that she believed me.

'Okay,' she said. 'I'm afraid we might have to do it walking around the museum. Like I said, we're on a tight deadline.'

'Whatever you can give me, Joni. When did you first meet Donaldson?'

'Now there's a question. When did I first meet him?' She scratched her temple. 'Oh I know. I guess it was, yeah, it must have been during the Save the World occupations. What's that – seventeen, no eighteen years ago? He was with the group who'd taken over the London offices of a biotech company. He must have been barely in his twenties. I went over to interview some of them for an online magazine I was with at the time. And ever since, I've been bumping into him. Say what you like about DD, but he's always in the thick of it.'

'Such as?'

She sighed. 'Oh, you name it, he'll be there. I suppose the longest time I've personally worked with him was when he was in a group who sabotaged the Buckler Factories. Buckler made heavy weapons, you know tanks and stuff. The group was a hotchpotch of anarchist, radicals, feminists, peace campaigners; their intention had been to protest against the sales of military hardware to repressive regimes. Not that they managed to do much. I mean, I say sabotaged, but they barely broke the locks. Didn't stop the courts coming down heavy on them, though. The government wanted to make an example of them. Such actions were on the rise, and they wanted to stop any more. I was involved in the defence campaign. It went on for over a year. We managed to get quite a high public profile, actually.' For a moment, she drifted into a fond memory. Finally, she returned to me. 'They were known as the Buckler 12, you must remember them?'

I did. The courts had begun to dish out extremely long sentences, labelling the attack as an act of terrorism. A national campaign had been launched, led by MPs, trade-unionists, various actors and sports people and the left. I myself had been involved, but at a grass-roots level, giving out leaflets, mailing social media and such like. Because of the blatant over-hyping of the offences, the campaign had gained widespread support, eventually forcing the courts to change the charges to lesser offences. In the end, the defendants only faced minimal fines. They didn't pay, and no-one had the will to go and get them.

'He was one of the Buckler 12, was he?' I hadn't remembered that. Maybe even more worrying than the gaps in my memory was the fact that I hadn't found this out in my research. I had no concerns over my research skills, they were impeccable, what was the worry was just how depleted the internet was. I smiled at the irony of him being done for protesting against military hardware, when he had a room full of the stuff himself.

By all accounts, it had been hard for the twelve women and men. Some of them had suffered physical, mental and financial hardship. Three of them had never really recovered from the experience.

'Nah. He was lucky. He and another one of them were let off straight away. Cops said they didn't have enough evidence to charge him. Yeah, DD was lucky. Fair play, he used it to help the others. He threw himself totally into the campaign. He was at everything, doing everything. I always thought he felt guilty, not being one of them, but still.'

So, they didn't have enough evidence? Indeed, DD was a lucky boy.

For a few minutes she went through the many times when their paths had crossed. There were quite a number. Seems, if it moved, Donaldson would be there yelling through a megaphone. I listened with one ear, but my brain was more focussed on the thought that the police had been unable to find enough evidence. That didn't usually stop them. My attention was brought back to the present, when her phone went.

'Hello? Right, okay. Be out there in a jiff.' She looked at me and pulled a face. 'Sorry, Pete. I thought this might happen. I'm needed. Do you wanna come out with me? Join me, if you like.' She smirked. 'You'll be chuffed to see what I've got. There's a great photo of you...'

Now there was an offer too good to resist.

I followed her out of the office and into the main hall. She obviously had decided that my visit should include a guided tour because as we passed the exhibits, glass cabinets, video and 3D images, she gave me a personal commentary.

'We've got the history of agitation from the hand-written to the most recent. We've just been given a fabulous selection of Chartist pamphlets. "A donation" ...' She laughed. 'By a very rich collector who loved the idea of rebellion when it was two hundred years old and cost a fortune at the auction, but not in real life. He fled to Bermuda; we took them. That's happened a lot. You'd be surprised how many first editions of Marx, Lenin, Bakunin, and such like, we've got from nationalising ruling class collections.' She pointed at an old gestetner being unloaded. 'That's just arrived.'

'Let's go into the Windrush Hall. It's through here. As you've probably guessed, it's our room focussing on the struggle against racism in Britain and the immeasurable contribution that black and people of colour have made to the country.'

Like everywhere else, it was heaving with activity. Sitting on the floor two staff were holding consoles and were manoeuvring 3D virtual reality signs into place. Looking up I could see Notting Hill, Black Lives Matter, the Bristol Bus Boycott and SUS Laws appearing directly in front of me. A hologram of street clashes in Cable Street flickered above some more exhibits. Whilst there was much activity, it wasn't chaos. Even just standing here for a few seconds, I could see the kaleidoscope of history taking shape. Catching my look, Joni beamed with pleasure.

'Gonna be good, isn't it?'

'Yes,' I agreed. 'It will.'

I could easily find myself being lured into spending a good hour or two, looking around this place. A familiar image caught my eye. I wandered over to take a closer look. In an oval glass cabinet, I looked almost lovingly at the poster for the 1978 Rock Against Racism concert in Victoria Park. Below it were badges and paraphernalia from the era. I smiled, nestling in the warm comforting embrace of nostalgia. My grandmother had been on the march from Trafalgar Square to the park. She had that very poster, framed, in her hall, and I had seen it every time I had gone around for my Tuesday night dinner. It was from that delightfully loquacious and enthusiastic woman that I had not only begun my political education but my musical one too. Eighty percent of the music I listened to had been first heard when I had made one of my frequent visits to Nan and Grandad's.

'Pete, over here,' Joni called.

Turning, to see where she had wandered off to, I saw something that made me shudder. A large cabinet of uniforms seemed to snarl at me. This was one memory lane, which I didn't want to stroll down. The outfits might look like fancy dress outfits, but it had been no party when I'd seen them marching down various high streets. Worn by the country's most recent master race specimens, they had spread fear wherever they'd been seen. Which had been entirely the intention. The wearers had claimed not to be Nazis, and were merely patriots and concerned citizens. But they were Nazis. Their bid for power had been over a decade ago. We'd beaten them, but it had been bloody.

I joined Joni. She was pointing at an A3 photograph. I laughed. 'Oh my God! I haven't seen this in donkey's years.' There was I, a young me, with more hair and less wrinkles – standing proud and defiant. Next to me was someone equally as militant, with one fist in the air and the other holding onto a placard, like one might a baseball bat. It was a very young Jackie Payne. She had only just joined the party and must have been in her twenties. She sported tiny afro curls back then. Her face was a picture of defiant anger. A large gash above her eyebrow was oozing blood. That had been made from a policeman's truncheon. In actual fact, the same one which had caused the large red patch on the side of my face. That patch would soon turn into a huge bruise. I remembered it well. Beside her on the other side, was a young, beautiful Caroline. This was pre-Lisa. When we had a life.

'Oh my God, that's here?'

'Yeah. Great picture, innit? See the *i* with a fist in the dot. Press it.'

I did.

Up came a visual identifying the three of us and informing the observer what had become of each one of us. With mine, I was glad to see that ART had been given precedence. That said, it didn't quite have the power of Jackie's short bio.

'You'll be naming one of the halls after me soon!' I quipped.

She laughed back. 'Yeah, thought we'd have a mock-up dungeon for your Crib work for that.'

'Yeah, funny. I'd stick to museums if I was you, Joni.'

I noted that after being described as an activist and leading trade unionist, it said of Caroline that "with her daughter, Lisa, she had been tragically killed in a freak road accident whilst holidaying in Italy. In the car with them was Pete Kalder, who survived it".

Without a scratch, I muttered to myself.

'Why's our names in a different font?' I asked.

She positively grinned with pride. 'If you touch them, it links up with our entire knowledge store – hard copy and e-copy. You know we can boast a brilliant hard library here, well our online one ain't too shabby neither. Not just here, but with our sister museums in Glasgow, Manchester, Birmingham, Derry and Cardiff. From there you can access films, documentaries, anything they've written – everything and anything we can get our hands on. Try it, press Jackie's.'

I did and an extremely long index of subjects appeared in front of me. 'Looks a very useful tool for MI5 or the CIA!'

Her hand brushed the comment aside. 'Nah. You don't think they know all this stuff already? Anyway, all the confidential material they copied and wiped. You know that. I reckon we have ten-percent – at most – of what they've got on us.'

'So, I can search for anyone?'

'We've a good selection of the activists, socialists, anarchists and revolutionaries through history, who've been active or lived here. Not just the modern ones, you know, but Engels, Eleanor Marx, CLR James, Mary Wollstonecraft, Olaudah Equiano, Tony Cliff, Christine Pankhurst, the lot. I tell you, Pete, it's quite a resource. Just say a name.'

I did: 'Dave Donaldson. Anarchist Federation Member.'

Three names came up. Two lived in Scotland, so I touched the second – our one.

She looked at me with an expression, which I couldn't tell whether it was amused, upset or just resigned.

'Okay, well, Pete, if you don't mind, I have to get on and unpack a drone.'

For a fleeting moment I wondered if it was our one, the one which had tried its weaponry of Vic and I, before remembering it was back at the office. Still, yesterday's terrorist outrage, soon became ancient history. She left me. I thanked her and kissed her on her cheek. Both of us, for very different reasons, were going to be conducting historical research. Hers, the general sweep of its ebbs and flows; me, to the Buckler 12 Campaign.

# CHAPTER 28: BRITOMART

Hours later, and I was far too wired for bed. Outside the front and the back of my house, local militia were standing guard. Once more, they were there to prevent the possibility of my becoming the next target. Most of us thought the risk was remote. I certainly hoped it was. It was why Vic wasn't babysitting me for another night. But I was too tired to read or watch the news, so I stretched out on the sofa, feet resting on the end-arm, with a glass of wine in my hand, the cat on my legs and some jazz on the housecom system. Normally, I liked the physical aspect of putting music on, of feeling a direct connection to the choice, but my weary bones and brain frankly couldn't be bothered, so I simply requested Hank Mobley. Listening to his lush saxophone being accompanied by the sound of rain bouncing heavily off the window, I attempted to clear my mind of the job, and get myself into a mellower place. It worked to a certain extent, but every time I thought I had achieved a blank space, images and conversations from the investigation came flooding in, like the sea over a causeway. Too fast to stop, flooding everything before it. I decided that I required some mental coastal defence, so instructed the art file of great paintings to slowly be shown in front of me. Their familiarity didn't stretch my interest, acting instead, as a visual lullaby. With all the elements in place, it soon began to take effect – my breathing began to slow, and my eyelids to get heavier.

Another day had passed; another day achieving absolutely nothing. Dogs chasing their tails at least had fun when doing so. I couldn't honestly say the same. Vic had called earlier and said that she had found nothing suspicious about Donaldson's involvement in the Central Defence Zone. Well, aside from supervising movement of the weapons. She did say, that generally he seemed to have done a sound job. So, another wasted day. I began to feel sleep whispering that the day was ending.

My doorbell sounded. For a moment, I wondered if I had been dreaming. But then it went again. No, it wasn't a dream, but at five minutes past two in the morning, it was a nightmare time to call. Groggily, I asked the homecom, 'Who's at the door?'

Despite my speech being slurred through tiredness, the visual came up. 'Pete, there is a female ringing the front doorbell. She can be identified as being Jackie Payne. President of the United Workers' States of the British Isles. Since this system has been installed, this is the first time she has visited here. The probability, however, is that she has done so on numerous occasions before, because you have known her...'

'Okay, Okay. That's enough information.' I rolled my eyes – ask a simple question and you get a novelette. Roijin's security measures were all fine and dandy, but they did make me feel as if I was trapped in an online encyclopaedia. Shame it couldn't identify who had broken in.

I pulled myself up, launching Red into the air. After landing on all four paws on the floor, he flashed me a sullen look and moped off to the kitchen.

Opening the door, I was met with Jackie stood smiling in front of me. She was dressed in a figure-hugging knee-length sage coloured rubber raincoat, buttons done up as straight as soldiers, hood down. 'Pete,' she said.

'Jacks,' I replied. The rain was whipping into my face and being dressed solely in shorts and a t-shirt, I quickly concluded that anything more than identifying each other, would be better conducted inside. I muttered, 'Come in,' turned and went back to the lounge. 'Sporting the Little Green Riding Hood look today, Jacks?'

A smile appeared. 'And what's yours today? Thought you only ever wore a suit.'

Closing the door, she unbuttoned her coat and hung it up in the hall. Then followed me into the room. Her large brown eyes swept over the place, logging every book and compact disc I owned. A quick glance at the visuals prompted her to identify the picture presently been shown. 'That a Matisse?'

I looked at it. 'Yes, indeed. It's called The Moroccans. It's in the MOMA, New York.'

'Nice.'

'So, sister,' I said, underlining it for comic effect, 'what brings you to this humble home of mine at such an hour? I presume it wasn't to discuss twentieth century art.'

She smirked, raising an eyebrow. 'Sister? Are we being Marxist or Philip Marlowe here?'

'Nowadays, I try my best to be both.'

'You haven't got the lips to be Humphrey Bogart.'

'They're the Marxist bit, my walk's Bogie.'

She didn't reply, but caught sight of my wine glass, which was still in my hand. I didn't take the hint, but wondered about the significance of the fact that was the third reference to the iconic actor that I had heard in as many days. It would be nice to think that nowadays, I was looking noirishly cool. Perhaps though, not when dressed like this.

I tried again. 'Something up?' I hoped that my puzzlement wasn't seen as being rude. If I was going to have a house caller at this time, it might as well be Jackie. But still.

'Do I have to have a reason to visit my favourite Cribber in his Crib?'

'Oh please, don't you start.' As piss-takes on our name went, this was one of the weakest. 'Why the hell, do we have to have that poxy name? I know there's been a lot of discussion on what our units should be called, I mean this is our fourth title in a year. But Crib, really? It's by far the worst. I mean, we're named after a baby's bed, for God's sake!'

She was rather surprised by my opening topic of conversation for the middle of night. With this weather, from heatwave to rainstorm, the traditional one of the weather would have been more expected. She wasn't the only one. Often my mouth, being Humphrey B or not, talked before my brain had a chance to consider what was going to come out of it.

Shrugging, she couldn't see the problem. 'C.R.I. B, Counter-Revolution Intelligence Bureau. Sounds okay to me.'

She, though, didn't have to introduce herself as being from Crib. 'Yes, thanks, Jacks, I know what it stands for but, well, for starters, it can be misread to sound like that we're the intelligence bureau *for* the counter-revolution. We get it in the neck for being named after a bloody baby's bloody bed *and* for having an ambiguous name. Shouldn't an acronym be dynamic, or at least have some reference to what it's concerned with? Crib would just be great, if we worked for the state's childcare provision! What hack came up with that?'

A wicked grin appeared. 'Actually, it was Vic.'

'Really?' She hadn't told me. But then, that made sense. Vic had many gifts, but I didn't ascribe creative thought as being one of them.

'That's why every other Crib has a number attached to it – Crib 1, Crib 2 and so on. I think we're up to 34 now. Yours, however, is simply Crib. Not only denoting that you are directly attached to the president's office, but that you are the original unit.'

'How touching. I feel a tear welling up.' I shook my head in disbelief. 'I can't believe Vic has so little imagination. Then again...'

The grin remained. 'Says the man who came up with ART?' She laughed.

No, that was different, that's clever. A.R.T. – it had reference to the subject, and the words were unambiguous. Art, Repossession and Transfer, was exactly what we were about. However, I didn't pursue the point because at such an ungodly hour, bickering over names wasn't that smart. That said, ART *was* a good name.

'Fancy a glass?' I asked, finally responding to her darting looks in the direction of my wine.

She sounded relieved. 'That would be great. Thanks.'

As I headed into the kitchen to get the bottle and another glass, I thought about the pair of us. It felt like we were a middle-aged couple in a long-term relationship, with things not said. Simply, because there was no need. There was definitely something not being said right now. She hadn't popped around to discuss titles of organisations. If she had, we'd be here all night. Nowadays, there was a myriad of the things, all with an ever-lengthening set of letters. It was as if there'd been an explosion in a Scrabble factory.

I opened up the cupboard where I kept the surviving few glasses from my mental melt down a few years back. When, for reasons only known to the inner me, I had trashed the place. Four had escaped the carnage. Which meant wild parties were out of the question, but it did mean that I had enough to pour Jackie a drink.

If Jacks and I were acting like a middle-aged pair in a relationship, that was because we pretty much were. She was the friend I'd known the longest. Perhaps, in our own way, we could be considered as being close. Maybe, she was the closest friend I had. Because of that, I understood certain things that Vic and the others didn't. One such, was the reason why Jackie hadn't got in touch; it was mystifying Vic, but not me. It wasn't because she had been busy; Jackie was an Olympic champion at multi-tasking. If she had felt the need to contact us, then she would have. No, the lack of contact was because she had evaluated the situation, and had decided that leaving us to operate by ourselves was the safest option. Safe not for her personally, she didn't often think about herself. Her sense of safety, and her ego, were inextricably bound to political service. Ruling class politicians routinely uttered such sentiments, but unlike them, hers was sincere and not just for a soundbite. Not that she had a hero-martyr complex, it was just that Jackie Payne had total dedication to the cause. The revolution was what made her body work and her brain think.

Walking back into the lounge, I saw her sitting on the armchair nearest the window, gazing out, deep in thought. This was probably the first time today she had enjoyed some solitary moments. Certainly, her face looked relaxed, if tired. But then, I'd seen her looking far wearier than this. She was aging well, and only by looking closely could you see fine lines in her black skin. Some of her previously tight skin was sagging somewhat, but she still looked great. She smiled slightly, before her lips broadened into a huge grin. I wasn't sure whether her happiness was down to me or the thought of a glass of wine. But then, Red strutted past me and jumped onto her lap. Seems, it wasn't me or the alcohol, but our feline friend, who had brought cheer to her. She stroked him, and he nestled against her long fingernails. I passed her the glass. Nodding towards the window, she referred to the rain: 'We need this. You can almost hear the plants sighing with relief, drinking it up. Grateful for the refreshment.'

'Thought you were in Manchester,' I said, ignoring the frankly odd comment, fearing that she was turning into Dylan Thomas.

'I'm down for twenty-four hours. Got a few things to attend to. I'm catching the 09.14 train back.'

'And you found time to pop round. Sweet.' I wearily smiled, raising my glass as a salute. Then instructed the music and visuals to stop.

She took a sip and returned a tired smile. 'Spreading the love, Pete, spreading the love. Anyway, how's your sister – your biological one? You said she'd been attacked.'

I returned to the sofa, but this time sat up. Laying out full stretch, like some Cleopatra, wouldn't be quite appropriate. There was already one queen in the room. 'She's okay,' I replied. 'To be honest, the bloke who attacked her, got the worst of it, as his many bruises will attest. Sophie's fine physically, just very pissed off with me, I think she'll get over it.'

'Pleased to hear it,' she said simply.

Jackie hadn't taken my call as a cry for help too seriously, then. If she had, then she would be spitting fire and fury right now at being emotionally manipulated into seeing me, away from all that was going on, and all under false pretences. But she seemed perfectly relaxed. Nor did she enquire as to why Sophie would be angry with me. Either she already knew, or it wasn't important to her. Now was not the time to make house calls for old times' sake, especially at this time of day. Jackie was here for a purpose.

Not that she had asked anything more about Sophie's attacker, but I told her anyway. 'We've pretty much eliminated him from our enquiries. He has solid alibis for both attacks. We think he's just some stooge, paid off to mess with Sophie, and by extension me. None of us think they seriously considered there to be a chance of me passing on state secrets to her, and so onto him. Let's face it, I don't know any. We were told to investigate Mike Stewart's death but that's about all...'

She nodded agreement at our assessment of him, but remained passive at my final comment. It had been intended as a barb to prick a reaction. But instead, she just sipped her wine. I tried again to get to the reason for her visit. It wasn't concern over my sister that was now certain. Nor was it about how I was feeling. This time, I boldly tried to take subtlety for a walk. It rarely did do with me, so it would make a pleasant change. 'So, is the political situation as tense as the media are saying? Are we really so near to the coalition collapsing? Or is it just hyperbole to occupy the time?'

As political small-talk went, it was pretty weak. After all this was over, maybe I would check out to see whether amongst all the adult education sessions being provided, there was one on polite conversation, which I could attend. Or maybe one for probing questions. You never know, there might be a combined course of both.

She savoured the wine and nodded appreciation. This time I was graced with a reply. It was a reply that was placid and serene, like one you might expect from a yoga teacher. Jackie's legs though, weren't behind her neck, but were stretched out in front of her. 'Somewhere in between the two extremes. There's no doubt that the situation is worrying, and it's true that our sister organisations have concerns, but I feel confident that they can be addressed.'

This was Jackie-speak for now wasn't the time to talk about it. Trouble was, I was monolingual. 'You'd be surprised to hear that leading members of the Anarchist Federation are stockpiling weapons in readiness for an armed confrontation with us!' I replied tartly.

A thin smile appeared. 'I would question your terminology – and the premise stated – but in regard to a member of the AF having access to a store of weapons, no, it wouldn't surprise me. If for no other reason, that I do read my communications, and Vic is highly efficacious at sending them. I'm well aware of how your investigations have been progressing.'

'And you're happy there are piles of guns ready to be used, most possibly against us?'

Not a single feather was ruffled. 'Not particularly, but the CC is aware of the situation, and we have stationed comrades to keep an eye on them. There are, incidentally, a number of similar arms dumps in other parts of the country. So, with both the militias and you – the Cribs – I think they're pretty safe. Or rather, *we* are safe.'

'And that's the only action you're going to take?'

'For the moment, yes. The last thing we need is for the party's militia to go storming in and starting a civil war. We have to be very careful here, Pete. We don't want to do anything provocative. I am pleased that your unit thinks so too and has not gone barging in. I am relying on you to keep Vic's enthusiasms under control.'

'Which, I assume, is why you've not agreed her request for a *Protocol #5*?'

She took a sip, and I swear I could see her eyes sparkle with amusement. 'Yes. I really don't think issuing such an order is quite the thing right now.'

'Even though the party has picked up a communication mentioning that the opposition forces are planning an "event"?'

'Yes? And? How does that link with your investigation? From Vic's extremely extensive notes, I've gleaned that Crib's theory is that the primary reason for these murders is not to liquidate the individuals *per se*, but to help destabilise the political situation.'

'That's *one* theory,' I said so dryly that the Gobi Desert appeared to be rain-sodden.

'Well, if it is the reason, don't you think using the protocol to arm up the Crib, not to mention giving it extraordinary powers to curtail civil liberties, will do exactly just that?'

'Maybe, but calling something an event makes it sound extremely grand, and grand in this context, means a lot of deaths, and public ones at that.'

'Then, it's worth considering that the Shard is the event in question.'

'That could be true, but two things cast doubt on it. First is the remarkable coincidence on how many people connected to Mike Stewart's death were at the Shard. Plus, Roijin talked to NWC Tech Support and they said that within the communications there was a lot of talk of organising an event. It looks very much like it is intended to be something which is headline news across the world. They even used the word "major". Does shooting up an Anarchist bar constitute that? I 've witnessed for myself what they consider to be events.'

Her voice was equal measure ironic and disbelieving. 'You don't think a drone attack on a London landmark could be construed as being major?'

Despite the hour, she was playing games.

'Of course, it could be, Jacks. It *could* be. But it also *could* be that the event is still to happen. Add that to the small matter of our supposed allies storing weapons and that's why Vic thinks that issuing the protocol is important. '

'And what do *you* think, Pete?'

I paused. I had the distinct impression that she already knew the answer to that question. Whether it had been included in Vic's fabled notes or simply that she knew me well, I couldn't say. But I was sure that she knew.

Maybe I was a contrarian or maybe I didn't like having all my cards on show, but her attitude changed what might have otherwise been my answer. 'Let's just say that I have issues with the principle, but that's not to say that I don't see the logic.'

She didn't reply but looked intently at me. It seemed that I didn't have a good hand. I played my wild card: 'I spoke to Joni Feld earlier. She was telling me about the opening of the museum and how it was going to be an international celebration of revolution and resistance. Gathering from around the world, there will be leading figures from the movement. She described it, Jacks, as being – "*an event*".'

Jackie didn't, as far as I knew, play poker, which was just as well, because the passive face she'd been wearing for the last few minutes, suddenly didn't look quite so passive. Sure, there was no histrionics or expressions of horror, but I could see that I had made her think. After a moment or two, she spoke. 'And you think they might be planning an attack on the opening ceremony?'

'*Could* be.'

'What did Mother J say about your theory?'

'I didn't mention it; thought it best not to.'

She nodded, thoughtfully. 'I get what you're saying, Pete. I'll see what I can do.'

I put my glass to my lips to steady myself. Because I was tired, but I could feel frustration crawling up my throat. Frustration at how we could stop those bastards from winning; frustration at fighting an unprincipled enemy and frustration at being so uncertain what we should be doing. But then why was Jackie here? Was it just to kibosh *Protocol #5*? If so, then why not simply send a text? No, there was something more. Jackie knew such orders better than anyone else. Largely, because she helped write most of them. She knew full well that there was a provision allowing a Crib to assume that permission had been given if the situation was deemed critical enough to warrant it – even if a formal permission had not been granted. It had been incredibly controversial when it had been passed because it was suggested that it would give Cribs a blank cheque to take whatever powers it wanted. The rumour was that Jackie herself was unsure and had serious misgivings about it.

Was this about protecting the party? To avoid the difficult questions of how to defend the gains of the revolution, the party could step back and let us get our hands dirty. If events prompted us to use the powers, then she, and therefore, the party, had an escape clause. The action had not been officially sanctioned. I had noticed that of late, when Cribs, and in particular our very own, was discussed in the news, the party leadership spoke as if we were a separate entity to the NWC. It showed the independence of the investigation, but equally, it served as deniability if we cocked it up. I had always known that we served a purpose, which wasn't a pleasant one. Whilst that purpose wasn't hidden, neither was it advertised. But this was pushing it.

I could only hold my tongue for so long. 'The situation is growing graver. The counter-revolution is obviously stepping up a gear. In this case, we've already had six murders and there could, one way or another, be a whole lot more to come. Whether or not the Shard attack was the "event" mentioned, the fact is, we still have a killer on the loose, one who will strike again. But there's only five of us, camped out in two rooms in an art gallery. It's not really an equal match.'

She nodded, to indicate that she understood, and then said something which had much the same effect on me as one of Dave Donaldson's grenades might have – 'Jerusalem.'

'Er, yes, the, er.' I stuttered. My usual slick, precise, witty and erudite vocabulary was suddenly was reduced to primeval utterances. 'Er, yes, that's what the tag is. But we think that they're no longer using it, that it probably has always just been yet another red herring – to add confusion to an already confusing situation.'

She nodded in agreement. 'Otherwise, why use the atlas to give us a clue?' She flashed her eyes in the room's direction. Presumably, just in case I'd forgotten where my library was.

'Like some real-life crossword puzzle.'

'Not that it's got anything to do with geography. I'm sure you of all people have guessed that it's a reference to William Blake's poem – Jerusalem. Building a new glorious England, or perhaps resurrecting an imagined ancient one. They've co-opted it for their cause.'

'Yeah, I figured that.' Eventually.

I looked at her. 'Is that why you're here, Jacks? To be honest, at two-thirty in the morning, I'm not really interested in discussing how many angels can dance on a pinhead, you obviously know more about it than us, so what is it?'

'Slightly off with the angels' allusion, although I get the link, but there's at least hundred years or so between the origin of the phrase to indicate arcane discussion, and Blake.'

I rolled my eyes. People, it seemed, were lining up to point out errors or embroider semantic disagreements with me. Everyone was a know-it-all nowadays. Revolution liberated and educated the mind, but it also seemed to make us bloody smart-arses.

She held up the hand not presently holding the glass. Her fingernails pointing towards the heavens, indicating that I need not interrupt because she was getting to the point. 'There're some people who work for foreign states, who are also sympathetic to our cause.' She gave a knowing smirk. 'Don't look so surprised. We've our spies too. We've been in contact with them but they're unable to help you with your investigation. They know very little about it. So, you don't need to know about them. What they've told us though, is that there's a concerted attempt to unify and consolidate the actions against us by various hostile states. So far, they've all been doing their own thing, with only limited cooperation between them, but with Portugal's revolution following ours, they're worried about a domino effect and have created a management committee to organise themselves more efficiently. Rather than separate nation states acting alone, there's now an international task force which has been set up. Seems, they can be as internationalist as we can.'

'Jerusalem.'

'Correct.'

'Why the thing with the atlas, then?'

She shrugged. 'Perhaps they couldn't find your books on romantic poetry? Or couldn't decode your cataloguing system? It's not important though, is it? What is, is that future attacks are going to be far more efficient and targeted than previously.'

The news drained blood from my face. If I was right in guessing which powers were involved, then we were up against a formidable, well-resourced and powerful foe. David had it piss easy against Goliath, compared to what we faced.

I spoke to myself as much as to her. 'They're feeling so confident that it doesn't bother them that we know of its existence.'

*Protocol #5* was becoming ever more like a sensible option by the second. I was seeing Vic as less someone hooked on gunplay and more of someone who had a sensible grasp of the balance of class forces. 'Jacks, if that's the case, then we need to organise accordingly. Just the odd unit scattered across the country made up of radicals, a few ex-cops and a lab or two of scientists are no match for that!'

The smile stayed. 'Which is basically the argument that comrades Anand and Walker are making.'

'Not quite,' I snapped. 'They're asking for a whole lot more.'

'Which, incidentally, is – as far as I can see – the main reason for your suspicion of them. Many comrades, and I include myself as one of them, consider Noah and Reyansh to be two good comrades who've worked tirelessly for the party. They honestly feel that we're not responding appropriately to the threat we face. Basically, we're being too liberal. I may not agree with everything they say, but that doesn't mean that I consider them to be anything other than sincere revolutionaries. But you do, which is fair enough.' Her voice was smooth, but there was an undercurrent of toughness beneath it. I sensed that we were approaching the reason for her dawn visit. 'I haven't had the time to devote in studying the latest three volumes of Vic's notes. Tell me where you're at.'

I took a deep breath before answering. 'Basically, it's our belief that covert operations against us would be of little use on the ground, if the spies were in the rank and file. It needs to be more high-profile figures, who not only spy on and pass back information, but actively destabilise the revolution. Who...'

She did not say a word, but her expression indicated clearly that I too was being too wordy.

'We think the Shard attack was hastily arranged. If maximum casualties were wanted, then they would have attacked the meeting itself, not the pre-meeting drinks! Indeed, if they planned to use a drone, why not attack the NWC? There was a reason for it being the Shard, on that day and that time.'

'Which you don't know.'

'Which we don't know. But the timing of it, straight after confirmation that Mike Stewart's death was murder, makes us think the two are linked.'

'How?'

'We don't know that either,' I admitted. 'But the fact is that many of the same people are involved.'

'Nothing else?'

'Dave Donaldson has no solid alibi for Stewart's death either. He's been arguing for the AF to break its alliance with the party and incite what they think is the next phase – that gives him a motive. He also happens to have a store full of guns, providing him with the means. Then there's the fact that the phone used to control the device was found in his storage unit.'

'So why not make a citizen's arrest and question them closely?'

'Because we are acutely aware of the politically sensitive nature of doing so. It would be highly inflammatory. We'd be accused of victimising AF members.'

'It certainly would. And Noah Walker and Reyansh Anand?'

'They oppose cooperation with the AF and want to strengthen the state. They, like Donaldson, could easily be spies hoping to foment a civil war. They've also shaky alibis for both Stewart's murder and the Shard attack.'

'But as I understand it, against all three you haven't any eye-witnesses, and not a shred of forensic evidence?'

'Er, no.' Put like that, you'd be forgiven for wondering what we'd been doing. 'That's why we need help.'

'I can understand that,' she murmured.

She calmly finished her glass, put both it and Red onto the floor, and stood up. Feeling that I should too, I did so. When she spoke, it was to both enlighten me what the purpose of her visit was and to instruct me as to what was to happen next.

'I agree, Pete, with a lot of what you're saying. There's much to do and it's not going to be easy. I will not formally oppose the Protocol, so as to give you the leeway to activate it, if you feel that you have *no choice but to do so*. And if it is activated, it will be by your unit, not the president's office nor the NWC. Such an action would be distanced from the political apparatus. But as I said, Pete, I would strenuously suggest that you don't.'

She paused for a second and looked straight into my eyes. 'The fact is, I don't believe that there's a need. You're forgetting the power you already have. You don't need the trappings of a paramilitary grouping when you have a far more potent power – *the class*. The revolution survives not because of our armed forces – the USA alone could wipe us off the face of the planet in a matter of minutes. No, we're surviving because of the support of the working class both here and internationally. Use it in your investigations. Law and order is to be from within the class, not outside. It's not the case of them and you, it's collectively – us. Be open, honest and transparent about what you're doing. Contact officially both the AF and the party, and inform them that you're investigating members of theirs. Inform the individuals too, and remind them of their rights under the Republic's Constitution. That includes making representations to the relevant Community Information Meetings. You've set the CIMs up – so use them more directly. There's the help you need, right there. You have recourse to greater and more physical force if you require it, but the greater support you have, the less you'll need it. You and Vic are correct that we need to be more efficient with our security across the republic, but I'd also say, so do you.'

She stopped to allow me reply.

That was quite a speech. I almost felt like giving a standing ovation. I didn't have a reply of the same length, but what she had said was all very well, though she had neglected the continent's worth of elephants in the room. 'And what if the repercussions happen to create further friction between the AF and us?'

For a moment, she pressed her lips together and gently shook her head. When she did speak, it was in a quiet voice, one underpinned by a strength which few could match. 'You need to stop thinking like that. The us, is the class, consisting of all the organisations and individuals which support the revolution. That includes the AF. You'll be totally open in what you're doing. It demands sensitivity but you'll be dealing with serious, intelligent people; treat them so. Trust them. And let's not forget the crucial fact that you will be investigating your own senior party members as well.'

'Easier said than done. We could be roasted.'

'Pete, building a new world was never going to be easy. You know full well that you're accountable to both the workers' courts and the NWC. You clearly enjoy the public support and praise you received in your previous cases. It's true that this might be trickier, but that's the job, I'm afraid. You're accountable. Get the evidence, make the case and present it to the appropriate authorities. Then there will be an open and fair trial, where the case will be tested.'

She was right, though it may sound easy in my front room after a rather fine glass of wine, but in reality, it was going to be no such thing. We may be a Crib, but this was far from being child's play. But the truth was that she was right. I nodded agreement. There were no short cuts.

She put her hand on my arm. 'No-one admires Vic Cole more than I do. I trust and respect her, she's gone through a lot and made sacrifices, putting herself in severe danger. All for little thanks. That's all true, but it's still a fact that she still has a political education to go through. I know that could be said of all of us, but it's especially true for her. She's still thinking like a police officer. One that serves the revolution, but a police officer nonetheless. You've spent your entire adult life fighting for the revolution. Many times, it has been hard and dangerous, but you've carried on regardless... although,' she chuckled at the memory, 'usually the greatest threat was usually from lapsing into a coma from the boredom of routine work.' Her laugh grew, which in turn made me smile.

She walked to the door. 'When I arrived, you complained about the name of the unit; well, personally I think it's fine. But what I also think, and it's more important, is that your role is wrongly described. Your title is Political Support in the Crib; that's not quite correct – I think it should be Political Lead. That's your role, Pete – political lead, and that's what you need to do – *lead politically!*'

With that, she rubbed my arm and left.

# CHAPTER 29: BREAKING COVER

After Jackie had left, I had rung everyone and arranged a meeting. News of her visit, and its timing, not to mention my keenness for a meeting had surprised and intrigued them in equal measure. All agreed with no opposition. The next surprise was me volunteering to chair it, and be professional and to the point. I had kicked it off by informing them of Jackie's refusal to implement *Protocol#5*. The response had been minimal, and in the main accepting. Even from Vic. I'd skipped the verbal flannel and went straight into what was to be done. I thought it best to start with my well-dressed self, which incidentally was in all probability going to be the most controversial, that I was to formally approach the AF and inform them that we were investigating one of their members.

No-one disagreed, but Roijin did ask, 'Will you mention that we know about Donaldson's store room?'

'No, that'll be the limit of my openness. The security committees of the NWC are aware of it, so there's little need for me to do so. But whilst I won't go into operational details, I will make it clear that Dave Donaldson is a person of interest.'

Vic's right eyebrow raised a centimetre. Somehow it made a loud comment in doing so.

I went on. 'After that, I'll be straight off to the party's London HQ and likewise inform them that two leading comrades of the party are also of special interest to us. And I'll purposely use 'them' when referring to the party to emphasise our neutrality.'

I paused for any comments but there were none. The only sound which could be heard was Odette throwing a banana skin across the room, successfully finding the bin. The sound of Vic's eyebrow returning to its place was purely in my head. So, I continued. 'I think we need to put out a pan-media statement and arrange a press conference to announce how our investigation is proceeding. I'll do that, unless there are any objections?'

More agreement met my suggestion. Roijin smirked. 'Is that the reason for the tie today?'

I smiled and nodded in agreement. 'A nice pale pink, narrow one with a beige linen suit is a nice look. Politically neutral too.' Mentally, I reminded myself not to veer off into sartorial discussions because for this meeting, I was staying focussed. From the general approach to the specifics of the deaths: she should concentrate on the Shard attack. When she visited the building, it should be separately from me. 'I think it looks better if the sole purpose for my visit is to seek co-operation and share knowledge. Whilst you'll be there to investigate. Use their vote of cooperation to get help. Jackie has given me a couple of names of AF members who can help you analyse the data.'

'Will do, Pete.'

Victoria had been watching me with an odd expression on her face. I wasn't sure whether it was from being impressed or amused by my new-found focus, but in any case, it was her turn to get the all new efficient Kalder direction: 'Vic, I think you should go to the Britain Today Studios. Donaldson, Anand and Walker were all present for the debate, before travelling to the Shard. I think we need a face-to-face confirmation that Walker and Anand were in the debate for the whole duration. We still cannot rule them out. We also need to know what time Donaldson left, and indeed, what he was he doing whilst he was there.'

I paused. She simply replied, 'I agree.'

As I continued, I did begin to wonder, if I was allocating her tasks, which she had already decided to do, but I didn't stop. 'You should link up with the Thames Workers' Council, and there'll be a few trade union reps at the studios who might be able to help you.'

Once more, she simply agreed.

From drones to poison. Inspector Morse never had this variety. It was time to return to the death which had set it all off. 'Asher, I think you need to continue with the Bow Workers' Council investigating the events surrounding Mike Stewart's death. See what the latest is. Someone injected him with the almond compound and unless our foes have discovered a cloak of invisibility, someone must have seen them either enter the house or leave it. Issue another appeal for witnesses. It would be better if you went down and supervise it personally. We need to know every single person who was in the vicinity at the time of his murder, what they were doing, and what colour underwear they were wearing, if possible.' I paused to smile, just to indicate that the latter was not to be taken seriously. Vic could sometimes be over-literal. 'The mystery hoodie person is a priority. Surely, being so wrapped up on such a blazing hot day must have caught someone's attention!'

Asher nodded. 'Whilst I'm there, I'll do another forensic sweep. I might even extend the circumference of it. Any evidence will have been corrupted, but it's worth a go.'

'Thanks.' Now for the last person in our merry little gang. 'Odette, if you could stay here and act as link-up. I also think you need to keep a very close eye–' I stopped, noticing that she appeared to be distracted by the search for another piece of fruit to eat. 'And I mean, *a really close eye* on Donaldson's storage facility. Explicitly hearing that he's under investigation might push him to act and get them. Also, could you set up a programme, which lays out clearly all that we have so far done, including actions which we had no authorisation for? We will need that for the courts and for our report to the NWC.'

'No probs, Pete.'

'Good. Thanks.'

Victoria put her hand up. I wasn't sure if she did so from a sense of meeting etiquette or she was taking the piss. 'Odette, could you also look at the records for the Central London Defence Zone – for two particular times. I've bookmarked them. One's for the full-on cyber-attack they encountered in the early days of the civil war. The other is for the drone strike on what used to be the Royal Albert Hall – the Workers' Hall. You'll remember it, when they destroyed half the building and succeeded in killing a cleaning and renovation team.'

I looked at Vic, feeling puzzled. 'I thought you'd done that already and found nothing?'

'I did, but it won't harm to take another look. Something wasn't right about the Workers' Hall attack and I want to see if Odette can see anything, which I might have missed.'

Now with an apple in her mouth, Odette agreed.

'That's good then. Anyone think of anything else which demands our immediate attention?'

I looked around and saw Odette, Roijin and Asher shake their heads. Vic gave me a wry smile, and quietly replied, 'No, Pete. It all sounds a thoroughly sensible and logical plan of taking the investigation forward.'

Never had the words 'thoroughly sensible' and 'logical' sounded so full of ridicule. Quite obviously, Vic thought it was somewhat humorous to see me play the cop. She, however, kept the piss-taking to herself and instead, asked about Phan Bien.

'She's okay,' I replied. 'Before I got here, I took over a bag of books to her. She's not allowed anything electronic, in case it can be traced. Something which she moaned about at length. She looked at the books as if they were from another historical epoch.' I chuckled. 'But they'll give her something to do. She may be moved again, because we still can't rule out that the drone strike wasn't a targeted assassination attempt, and they may try again.'

With that, I looked around, but no-one had anything more to say. Even Vic had lost the smirk. The meeting then split up. I allowed myself a smile though; there hadn't been a wisecrack to be heard, well, not many. I could do serious when I had to.

My first job was to contact the Shard to request a meeting with a member of their Organising Committee. This was their top committee, if that is, they used terms such as 'top'. The receptionist asked why, and I simply replied that I was in Crib, empowered by the NWC, and was investigating the Shard attack. It was vital that I had to speak to someone from their OC. He then asked me to be more precise. I refused. After several minutes of going backwards and forwards over this point, he finally relented. The new no-nonsense Pete Kalder could be a persistent bugger and wasn't going to take no for an answer. Not even a maybe! Then he asked if there was anyone in particular I wanted to talk to. That sent me tripping headfirst over terminology. I wanted someone senior, but they don't believe in hierarchy. Senior is not in their vocabulary so how could I phrase that? Being unable to think of a translation, I decided to introduce the word. It was met with silence, before consulting a metaphorical dictionary, he pointed out that most of the OC siblings were in Manchester at the NWC.

My patience was beginning to look like old-person's rug – thread-bare. 'I understand that, friend, but I know that there's some still in London. Not everyone has decamped up north. I will be at the Shard at 9.30am, please arrange to have someone there to meet with me. Thank you. As I said, and as I know that you know, this is important.'

He didn't put up any more obstacles and agreed, saying that he would arrange it.

My next call was to the party's London offices, where went through virtually exactly the same conversation. Just that the committee's initials were different.

Next, I went on the official NWC news page, entered our password, and announced that there would be a Crib media conference concerning the investigations into the murder of Mike Stewart and the drone attack on the Shard. It was to be midday and would be held in the car park of Alexandra Palace. All news outlets were invited.

Grabbing a coffee and my helmet, I started for the door. Asher and Vic had already gone. Roijin was still there, waiting for me. She explained that it would be better if she arrived after me. Such was revolutionary diplomacy. At present, she was leaning over Odette, as they started to analyse the CLDZ data. Without turning, she gave a backwards wave and said goodbye as I left.

The first people I met when I arrived at the Shard were the orange camouflaged security guards, who instantly recognised me and sent me up to the Organising Committee offices where I was to have my meeting.

Arriving at the floor, I pondered whether there had been a fierce internal argument whether the OC should actually have their own offices – surely that showed preferential treatment. Putting aside such momentous philosophical debates, I knocked and went in. My immediate reaction was that in all probability there hadn't been too much of an argument on the matter, due to the simple fact that the office had the superiority and sense of power of a cupboard. It was the same size with the same décor. It contained three chairs and a flat-pack desk. Sitting behind it was a young woman tying up her long hair into a bun. I was surprised to see that the young woman was Fiona Bailey.

'Hi, Pete.' She smiled.

Clearly, my face showed what I was thinking.

'Is it going to be a problem, me being the OC member? I'm the only one in the building at the moment and we figured that this was only a courtesy call, so it didn't matter too much. But, Pete, if it is, then give me an hour, and I think I could find another sibling.'

I sat down so as to give me time to think, before answering. 'It probably shouldn't be you, Fiona, because you're involved in both the incidents we're investigating.'

And although we had pretty much ruled her out, she was still a possible suspect. It wasn't ideal. In the past, it wouldn't have been allowed. But I suppose back then, the cops wouldn't have been seeking the help of an anarchist organisation, either. I breathed heavily. Figuring that she was right, this was really only a courtesy visit, I couldn't see the harm. 'It's fine, Fiona. Actually, it probably makes what could be a rather difficult meeting, a little easier.'

She spread her long arms apart. 'So, what's up? I didn't quite understand the message.' Her mood changed for a second and with an ominous tone, asked me, 'Have you news?'

''Fraid not, Fiona. That's not why I'm here. You know, I'm from Crib, and that we've been tasked with investigating the poisoning of Mike Stewart, and also the drone strike against this building. That as you know only full well, led to the murder of Sofia Brownswood, Thom Simons, Bruce Jenkins and Mohammed Aydin. I'm here to formally represent the Crib, for two reasons. The first is to officially inform you that we're investigating a number of leads in regard to these atrocities. I'm not going to go into detail as to what we're investigating, but it's important that the Anarchist Federation are fully aware that some of its members are considered to be of interest. In particular, we are interested in Dave Donaldson.'

'Surely, you can't believe that DD is involved? Not DD! I mean, I know he's fiery, but he's an honest revolutionary. I mean, I've seen the online chatter, all the rumours, but...' There was real pain in her voice and disbelief in her eyes. I almost expected her to start to well up. But she kept control and said simply, 'I don't believe it.'

'Crib are keen to reassure the AF that we're completely impartial, whatever our personal political affiliations, we serve the revolution. We're accountable and answerable to elected officials of the NWC. Our only concern is to hunt down the reactionary renegade, or renegades, and to bring them to revolutionary justice. It doesn't matter what organisation these criminals are pretending to be members of. That is, if they're actually in one. The truth of the matter is that the organisation which they ultimately belong to is not the URSP or AF, but a counter-revolutionary terrorist one. You know from our record, and that of other Cribs, that we have unmasked conspiracies in different organisations, including the URSP and the AF.'

I tried to sound in equal measures sympathetic and authoritative. 'You'll understand that I cannot comment on the case. We do promise to keep you abreast of any developments and keep you informed as much as we can. I do realise, Fiona, that this is very difficult for you – not only is he a sibling of yours, but he's also your housemate. Which is why I wouldn't have chosen you to be the OC member to be here. But I think it would be impolite to ask for someone else. The important thing is that the AF understands that this isn't a sectarian attack on them... on you. It's not in any way subterfuge to undermine you. We honestly want to work with you over this. Everything is going to be above board. Everything will be democratic, and in line with the laws of the workers' state.'

I gave her time to reply, but she did not. She was more interested in what I had to say than imparting any points of view. After a few moments of polite silence, I continued. 'You should also know that after I leave here, I'll be visiting the headquarters of the United Revolutionary Socialist Party, to inform them that two members of theirs are being investigated.'

That really took her breath away. Her hands clasped together as if in prayer. Wishing that it would be a URSP member, maybe? 'Who?' she asked, moving away from hand shapes.

'Fiona, you'll realise that it's not for me to say. I'm sure if you look online, there's many names mentioned, and you'll get a pretty good idea, but it would be wrong of me to explicitly name them. Then again, so much social media, is digital gossip over the neighbour's fence; I have no doubt that Danton and Fidel Castro are also being touted as possible MI5 agents. What does matter, is that you fully understand that we will hunt down this person, whoever they are, wherever they are, whatever organisation they are cowardly hiding themselves in.'

'Okay,' she said uncertainly. 'But forgive me, Pete, I can't believe that you're really going to go after two of your own!'

I corrected her. 'They are not "my own", we are impartial, and certainly, if one of them is the renegade, they most definitely won't be.'

'Even if they are high profile leading members?'

'Even then. Let's not forget that there have been occasions recently when we have done exactly that.'

She seemed to accept that. 'Okay, 'nuff said.'

'Good.' I shuffled in my seat. There was still one rather uncomfortable thing I had to ask. 'Now, I have organised a media conference later today. I will be, at least to a certain extent, updating the progress of our investigations and countering at least some of the more ludicrous rumours.' Feeling oddly nervous at this juncture, I attempted humour. 'I can at least say that the absence of Cuban cigar ash means we can discount Fidel.'

It was a pitiful attempt, and was met with a blank look. She waited for what I was tentatively getting to. 'I'd like you to be there. Indeed, Fiona,

I'd like you to actually be a part of it.'

That particular idea had occurred to me on the way here. Having a senior (I couldn't think of a better word, so they'd have to lump it) sibling from the AF by my side would show that this was no sectarian escapade. I hadn't thought that it necessarily would be Bailey; my idea was that it should be whoever the AF had arranged to meet with me. But as it turned out, having lost a friend in Mike and nearly losing her own life in the drone attack, she was an ideal choice. Before she had a chance to say anything, I added, 'I'll be requesting that a CC member from the URSP be on the other side. This will clearly show that this is an investigation into counter-revolutionary activities and not in any way involved in the internal politics of the NWC. In one sense, it's true that Crib aren't neutral, we don't pretend to be non-political like the old police force used to fraudulently claim – we're political and we're biased – we exist to defend the revolution. However, we're not at any organisation's beck and call. With senior figures from the two largest parties, it will help diffuse any attempt to sew divisions between us.'

She rested her hands on her stomach. Not that here was much to rest on, it being as flat as a spirit-level. She was clearly taken aback at the suggestion. She hadn't expected that. But after only the slightest hesitation, she came to a decision. 'Yeah, why not. Okay, I will. Obviously, I'll have to speak to other siblings on the OC, but unless they object, I can't see any problem. Where and when will it be?'

'Twelve, midday. At Alexandra Palace, in the car park nearest the building at the rear. Thank you, Fiona. I think it will be beneficial.'

With that, we finished with a few seconds of social niceties and then I left her and the building.

Next stop was across the river. If the AF had taken over a major skyscraper which dominated the area, to send a message to all who saw it, then the present London offices of the URSP were sending a very different one. Not that I had the slightest idea what it might be.

Housed in the ugliest and blandest office block you could imagine, it only had two points of interest. One was simply the fact that it was still there. A low-level block still standing was unusual – in the past decades, most had been knocked down to make way for ever-higher ones. The other was just how bloody hideous it was. If you wanted a 1970s style cuboid office, to feature in a depressing social-realist film, then this was your building. It would be ideal to serve as a backdrop of a workplace, indicating how the main character, probably pale, spotty and with a crap haircut, worked in a monotonous, dead-end job. It was perfectly possible that some well-meaning hack had chosen it to reassure the population that we weren't going to set ourselves up as a new aristocracy, lording it up in stately homes. Not when we were based in this monotone monstrosity. But if it had been chosen to make a point then it was unfortunate that it looked suspiciously like something out of a Stalinist brutalist construction manual from 1950s East Germany. Which was exactly what some of our enemies were accusing us of wanting to copy. Inside was just as bad.

I was here to see Reeves Wilkinson. We'd met briefly before, although in all honestly, I didn't know that much about him. I'd been told that I could find him on the second floor. Most of it was open-plan but it seemed that my visit warranted some privacy so we were to meet in a smaller office, off the main area. The door was open and I could see him behind a desk, chatting to a couple of comrades. I quickly gathered that there was a problem with the air-transport unions. For a few moments, I stood in the doorway, not wanting to intrude.

Wilkinson was in his late forties but he didn't appear to have any of the attributes of a middle-aged man. His hair had only a smattering of grey and there was no sign of balding. His face was slightly tanned, with a few wrinkles but was firm in cheek and jaw. His body likewise had little in the way of flab, despite the fact that he had once been a manual engineer, but now worked at a desk. Muscles strained his tight t-shirt. It had been through the trade union movement that he had received his political education, which coupled with his strong physique, had led to comrades nicknaming him Wilkinson Steel. That was perhaps a touch misleading because in actual fact, he had the reputation of being one of the sweetest, mild-mannered of members. If the Central Committee wanted to charm and schmooze, then Reeves was sent out. He could work any room, even if it was full of giant carnivorous lizards; he'd have them eating off his hand in a few minutes. I wondered if it was purely chance that he was the CC member chosen to meet me.

Finally, he saw me. Giving me a broad smile, he said something to the two comrades who he had been talking to. Both turned and faced me, then as if by magic, they let me know that they'd let us have some time together and they would leave us. Obviously, news had got out that we had a date.

'Pete, I've been expecting you. Sit down, comrade, please. Tea?'

'No thanks, Reeves. This shouldn't take too long. You'll know that I work in Crib, and at present we are investigating two incidents which we regard as examples of counter-revolutionary violence, namely the murder of Mike Stewart and the drone attack on the Shard.' I then went through what I had previously done with Bailey, except I named Reyansh Anand and Noah Walker.

After I stopped, I looked at his face. No emotion registered at all. He sat passively, before replying in an even tone, 'Thank you. That's as it should be, and although without wanting to interfere, I am surprised that it could possibly be Reyansh or Noah. I've known both for several years – Noah actually hails from the same part of the world as me – and I've found both to be good solid comrades. I realise that you've an important job to do and I've no doubt that you'll conscientiously do it to the best of your abilities, but I do think you need to be careful when accusing comrades. Concrete proof will be required.'

'It will be,' I replied. Although it was not the reason for my visit, I thought I might as well take the opportunity to further our case. Reeves said he knew both, and so it would be interesting to find out what he knew about these two "solid" comrades. I asked him.

'I've worked with Reyansh during the civil war. We were both charged by the party to coordinate the military and civilian defence.' For five minutes, he articulated what he had seen Reyansh do and say. He sounded like a talking head contributor on a TV history documentary.

'Didn't like Mike Stewart, though, did he?'

The sharp question following the eulogy slightly took the wind out of Reeves' fluttering silk sails and it took a moment for him to collect his thoughts, before answering with a shrug, 'I wouldn't know. I'm presuming that you're referring to the arguments between them concerning the role of the military in political life. That's hardly a motive to bump someone off, is it? I would have thought that if someone was planning to assassinate someone, the last thing they'd do would be to have a very public spat? It was just a political disagreement, that's all.'

'I'm guessing that you're going to whisper sweet nothings about Noah as well?'

He chuckled and shook his head. 'I don't know about *sweet nothings*, Pete, but I've only ever seen comrade Walker put body and soul into the cause of revolutionary socialism.'

'Noah Walker has a soul?'

He ignored my comment, but whilst still beaming a butter-wouldn't-melt smile, shook his head, as if to say that everything he'd heard about me was obviously true. I wasn't surprised with his fondness of Walker. His comment of hailing from the same part of the world had reminded me that he had been a Southampton district organiser, so he would have come across Walker during the Small Firms Strike. I asked him about it, but he said that it was only when Walker had moved to London that he had met him.

'That surprises me.'

'No mystery, I didn't know everyone there. And as I said, I have only ever seen Noah give body, and...er...mind to the cause.'

I resisted the temptation to act shocked at the thought that Walker had a mind. Though I was happy to endlessly recycle jokes, I thought it probably best to keep to the subject. Instead, I asked if he could he tell me anything more about him. Once again, I received such a glowing reference that it was a wonder that we hadn't cast icons of the chap. For the last eight years Walker had been a superman, always leading from the front. After a few minutes, I indicated that I had heard enough. I invited him to today's media conference. As I did, I made a point of telling him that Fiona Bailey would be there as a representative of the AF. He, as she had been, was clearly surprised.

'I'll have to consult my diary,' he stuttered.

'Funny, Fiona had to consult her comrades to see if it would be politically appropriate. You, your diary. I sincerely hope that doesn't suggest the bureaucratisation of the revolution, comrade.'

He breathed out heavily and closed his eyes. He knew there was no way to beat me. 'Okay, Pete, I'll be there. When is it?'

When I told him, he looked even more taken aback. 'That's in an hour and a half!'

'It is, indeed, comrade. Should be enough time for you to put your glad rags on.' I stood up, thanked him and left.

On the way out of the building, I ducked into the loo and threw some water on my face. Thank goodness, I had got that over and done with. I checked myself in the mirror and ran my hand through my hair. I had grown it somewhat, so I can sweep it back and let it hang slightly off my ears. It was still off my collar but was a sufficient length to give me that carefully dishevelled look. I pulled the tie down a centimetre or two. Yeah, there was a reason for the references to Humphrey Bogart.

# CHAPTER 30: RETURN OF THE DOVE TO THE ARK

**M**y reception at Alexandra Palace was hardly a Hollywood star welcome. No red carpet, nor a flashbulb met my arrival. Joni Feld was definitely not a happy curator. She was exhibiting distinct irritation. She wasn't meeting me to ask for my autograph. Now, Joni was a woman who could speak her mind purely by the shape of her mouth. Those lips were not just unhappy, but somewhat angry. Quietly furious was a more accurate description. The mouth in question was stage 1 pursed, as if she was about to whistle. Immediately, I found out however, that it wasn't, in fact, intended for any kind of happy-chappy tune whilst sharing a pot of tea. More like it was a theme tune from an Ennio Morricone movie prior to a gunfight. She had marched up to me, and without even a cursory greeting, had snapped, 'I had the pleasure of having Jackie Payne on the phone this morning!'

I responded flippantly, 'Well, it's nice that the president is taking an interest in the museum and its grand opening.'

Her mouth got even tighter. It was actually a miracle that she was able to squeeze any words through it at all. 'She rang me to inform me that the NWC Defence Group would be providing extra security for our opening. They'd be helping the Anti-Social Behaviour Stewards. Seems she has received intelligence that we could be a target of an attack.' She stopped, her eyes matching her mouth for narrowness. My guess was that she was blaming me. Thinking that much more of this and her face would resemble a straight line, I didn't say anything. She continued, 'So we're to have the NWCDG hiding behind exhibits with whopping great machine guns – all whilst Payne cuts the fucking ribbon.'

'I would have thought that would be quite appropriate to have armed workers with some of the displays you've got here. You could say it's an interactive display. People might actually think they are permanently based here.'

I wasn't helping myself. Her lips grew tighter. We were at stage 3 now. If she whistled, only dogs would be able to hear.

She forced out the words: 'What I'd like to know is, who could have possibly whispered in her little earhole that we might be at risk? Who or what, might have prompted her to make that decision?'

Her finger wasn't physically pointing at me, but might as well have been. It was time to fess up but to do so unapologetically. 'In my experience, Jackie rarely requires prompting. But if you're suggesting that I spoke to her about it, then Joni, yes, that's true. I did voice my concerns, but to be fair, I only said to her what I had said to you.'

I had expected counter-fire over my reply, but none came. Comrade Feld had another issue to raise with me.

'And then we have your media conference!'

'Yes?' I said, genuinely not knowing how that might be upsetting her.

'Did you ask me if it was okay?'

'Ahh...'

Now. I genuinely knew.

'Yes, it's the 18th letter of the alphabet. Well? Did you ask anyone at the museum? Did you ask anyone on the management committee?'

'No, I'm sorry, I just thought you wouldn't mind...'

Her mouth was now transforming from a horizontal red line into a scalene triangle as a snarl began to appear. 'You say that you're worried that the museum is a target for terrorism, but surely any link with Crib magnifies that. What on earth were you thinking, Pete?'

'I just thought the building and the view of the city would make a nice setting to hold it in.'

Sometimes, something might well be true, but that doesn't stop it also being painfully naff. My reasoning could be categorised as such.

Joni almost choked. It wasn't from the shape of her lips. 'A nice setting? A nice – sodding – setting! Can you hear yourself? Do you hear how you sound?'

I did, as it happens, but didn't say anything. There wasn't much I could say, so instead I gave my best hangdog expression and hoped this would pass.

It didn't quite work.

'But don't you see how this will look, Pete?' She glared at me. 'This is a museum which is supposed to be about opposing the state apparatus. Like it or not, Cribs are controversial and whilst many see them as necessary evil, others see them as just being plain evil. Either way, they're evil, and it's not something I want people to think of when they think of this museum!'

My problem was I'd come by scooter, not a convoy of lorries carrying freshly baked humble pies. Luckily, time flew to my rescue, and noticed that the controversial media conference, the one with a nice setting, was due to start very soon. Using that as my escape hatch, I mumbled an apology and headed towards it.

I was relieved that the NWC publicity department had already set things up. Screens were in place for the 2D links and spaces allocated for the 3D. Camera drones were already hovering, and I could even see a few human operated types. A small stage had been built. On which, a technician, was doing technician-type of things. Behind him, was a large red screen. I was guessing that no-one could think of an appropriate image to come up with to be on it. I mean, what does go with a "necessary evil"? Three chairs and a table had been placed in front it, with the NWC flag draped over it. In front of them were far more chairs, set out in three rows for the visiting news-hacks. To my surprise, all were occupied. I had expected what interest there would be, would be via the net, but it seems our investigation warranted the old-school in-person touch. There were approximately fifty reporters there, chatting to each other and to colleagues back in the studio.

With one bound, and not bothering with the steps, Fiona Bailey got onto the stage and sat down. She crossed her legs and smiled at the people in front of her. Truth be told, she looked a little ill at ease, but then, that was to be expected; after all, I had pretty much ambushed her into being here.

Wilkinson followed her, deciding against jumping onto the stage, and instead took the steps. Carefully, taking each one. There was symbolism in there somewhere, but I didn't have time to think what that might be, because it was obvious that I was required to be up there as well. I decided on the Reeves approach, as jumping and falling flat on my arse wasn't the look I hoped I would be giving. I joined my guests, and made the introductions, although didn't need to.

'How are you going to do this?' Fiona asked, leaning across towards me.

Reeves looked at me, quite obviously also interested in the answer. Actually, so was I. Deciding that just replying that I was going to blag it, wouldn't be quite the thing to say to a CC member and a comrade from the AF OC, I took a breath and then blagged it with them.

Keeping my voice down low, I replied, 'Basically, it's vitally important that we reassure the class that the Crib investigation is totally impartial, not favouring one organisation of the NWC over another. We must show that the URSP and the AF are united and cannot be divided by the forces of reaction. We need to keep this bland, with the only thing solid, being the fact that whatever the political and strategical issues which lie between the two organisations, this investigation plays no part whatsoever in them.' I looked at them and took their nodding as agreement.

The technician bent down and said we had less than a minute to transmission. He passed me the earpiece and asked if I was ready to go. I was about to say yes, when I had an idea.

'Could you change the backdrop please. Red is associated with the USRP. Could we have a more unified image.' I searched my mental photo-library for something. Then it came to me. 'There's a photograph which was used widely of street celebrations in central Liverpool on the day that it was announced that the prime minister had failed in his coup attempt and the NWC was in charge. You must know it – it was everywhere. There's a gigantic balloon of the prime minister, looking like a toy soldier, floating above the crowds. Could you try to find it and use that?

The tech seemed to know what I was talking about and after a quick word into his microphone, the image appeared behind us. I smiled. Clearly visible were AF and party banners. It was a famous image of unity. Just the theme we were hoping to encourage.

'Thanks,' I said.

Sensing a change, Bailey looked behind her and smiled at me. Clearly, appreciating the choice.

'Ready?' asked the tech.

I nodded and he got off the stage.

In front of us, a small screen had appeared showing the three of us. I had one last chance to check how we looked. I was pleased with the new background and that despite my fears, it did look at least partially professional. But not too much so, an air of amateur but sincere revolutionaries doing what was necessary, was better than a cold efficient one.

It turned 12. We went live and I introduced Reeves Wilkinson and Fiona Bailey. They responded with the swiftest of hellos, which didn't give me time to prepare, so unless I was going to make a few human sculptural poses, I had to think on the hoof. 'This will be brief, and I'm afraid that there will be only a limited time for questions. We sincerely want to be as transparent as possible, but cannot go into too much depth concerning our investigations because we don't want to alert our renegade enemies, by giving out details, which they can use to evade justice.'

A murmur rippled around the journalists. They clearly wanted details – big juicy details. Details which could fuel the narrative that the revolution was going to drown in its own blood as the two parties ripped chunks out of each other. Details that would show that our Crib was planning to set up some poor sod of an anarchist as a way of discrediting them. It was pleasing that Fiona nodded in support.

Taking this as encouragement to continue, I did so, but just as I was about to, a leopard skin coat caught the corner of my eye. I decided to say something, before I got onto the case. 'I should have said first, that we're extremely grateful to People's Museum of Revolution and Rebellion for putting up with this.' I waved my hand in the direction of the media. 'Especially as I forgot to ask their permission beforehand.'

The journos laughed. Reeves and Fiona did likewise. I sincerely hoped that the occupant of the leopard skin appreciated it too. Having distanced us from the museum, I got back to the point and recounted our involvement from the very first call to investigate Mike Stewart's death.

I took a deep breath. Here was a sticky point to negotiate. 'We've all seen the widespread social media speculation concerning both attacks, and I won't be commenting on them either. Suffice to say, that none of it comes from official sources so none have any official standing. It is pure gossip. Unfortunately, included has been scattergun chatter on who could possibly be responsible. Frankly, this is not in keeping with what the republic sees as decent behaviour. Such accusations are hurtful and damaging, and serve no other purpose than to feed some alienated desire for tittle-tattle. Last time I looked, every leading member of every organisation has had a finger pointed at them. I think a few Disney characters have been named as well! The situation is ludicrous. We have freedom in this state, but we do ask that people don't get their source of information from these places. Having said that, I can confirm that Mickey Mouse is not wanted for questioning...' I paused to allow for some laughter. Thankfully, I received some. 'It's true that there are certain individuals who are fulfilling their revolutionary duty and are helping us in our enquiries. That doesn't mean that they're guilty of anything.' After a few more minutes of talking, I asked Fiona if she wanted to say a few words.

Speaking clearly and articulately she precisely outlined the position of the AF, emphasising their support for the NWC and for the role of Cribs. It was the best I had heard her speak. The AF were determined to capture the killer. Tellingly, she even alluded to the fact that this would be the case, even if they happened to be in AF: 'No matter how personally close this individual might be to me, or to the AF, we will support this investigation. As Pete said, if the killer does turn out to be associated with us, then we will remember that he or she is not a member of NON or AF, but of the fascist counter-revolutionaries. He or she will be no real sibling of ours.'

After she had finished, Reeves did his part and said much the same, only from the perspective of the URSP. He, though, wasn't quite as obvious.

I thanked him. 'Now, there will be a little time for questions. I'm limiting it to half a dozen.'

A hand shot up at the speed and direction of a rocket, from a woman sitting directly in front of me. 'With both representatives from the major parties of the NWC being present here, is this a signal that the talk of a fall-out between the two is greatly exaggerated? Is the marriage still sound?'

'Yes,' replied Wilkinson. 'Ignoring the allusion to a questionable concept, the revolution has nothing to fear from disagreements and a frank exchange of views. Which is simply what is happening between us and the AF.'

Fiona leant forward, as if she had an old-fashioned microphone in front of her, and said simply, 'I totally agree.'

The woman in the front still had her hand up, and before I had a chance to choose anyone else, she asked another one, 'Is it true, comrade Kalder, that Dave D...'

I jumped in, cutting her sound, 'No-one is to be named. This will not be trial by media. That isn't the democracy we believe in, so we will not comment on anyone who, as I stated a moment or two ago, is simply fulfilling their revolutionary duty. No guilt should be inferred.'

The next two were from virtual journos before we returned to the physical. The questions hovered around possible suspects and the effects on the alliance. Bland replies met both.

'Okay, I think that's enough. We'll end this here. Thank you all for coming.'

After some courtesy small talk with Bailey and Wilkinson, I headed back to the museum. Whatever the success of the media conference event had been, something in it had given me an idea and I wanted to follow it up. Walking briskly away, I received a text. It was from Jackie: 'Glad me and Mr Mouse are in the clear. Good work, Pete.'

Once inside, I quickly found a terminal and went online to their archives. It was half an hour of searching, before someone official got around to approaching me. It was Joni Feld herself. I had been right, I had seen her. Though the weather was cooler than it had been of late, it was still red hot, so she must really be feeling it in that coat. I bet she was wishing that her trademark piece of clothing was a straw hat. 'Thanks,' she said, with a smile. Referring to my reference to the museum.

'No probs. You were right, Joni. Sorry. I should have asked. Could you do me yet another favour, but am I right in remembering that you're archiving materials from industrial and political disputes?'

'That's right. Some as you've seen, are in the museum's archive cloud, but there's also quite a lot in hard copy, they're still in boxes, ready to be transferred.'

'Would it be possible for me to have a look?' I asked.

'Can't see why not, that's what they're for. They're in a bit of mess. I mean, they're boxed and parcelled and labelled, but that's about it. They're in the William Cuffay rooms.'

'Sorry?'

'The basement. At the moment, it's just being used for storage, but eventually, when we get it sorted it'll be open to the public to access the hard copy as well as the e-copy.'

# CHAPTER 31:
# A SHOOTING LANDSCAPE

T he William Cuffay rooms contained the archives much like a belt did on a middle-aged man's trousers, trousers which he had purchased in his youth, sweating and straining to keep them all in. They were crammed with the paraphernalia of struggle: pamphlets, newspapers, USBs, paper books, leaflets, newspapers, journals, banners, virtual projectors, placards, arm-bands, badges, blogs and Vlogs were all here. Only a fragment of the materials had been digitalised or been found homes for. I had personally found that out, when my search upstairs had ground to a halt, with several messages politely informing me that information might be found down here in four boxes of hard copy.

Luckily for me, Joni might be what she herself describes as a funny sock, but she was also extremely hard working, and in her own way, efficient. The boxes might be waiting to be unpacked, but she had labelled each and every one of them. All were in chronological order and within that, alphabetical, so it had only taken me a few minutes to locate the particular boxes that I was looking for. Again, I was in luck, because they had their own separate and small pile. It could have easily been the case that they had been on top of one of the ceiling high piles, or maybe even worse, at the bottom of one.

Then I got going. Joni had warned me that it wasn't going to be easy because what I was basically going through was the personal archive of someone called Booker Campbell. She had described him as, "One of those lovely dear-old real-ale types, all commitment and facial hair". (And who was proud to have a full set of minutes for the local committee he attended each month.) Whatever my frustration, she had been right when she had said that I was in luck, because brother Campbell was someone who was meticulous in his record keeping. Also, rather brave. Many people hadn't been, because holding onto such information could be dangerous. Over the years, when the struggle had turned against us, there had been several vicious clampdowns when any shred of evidence could be used against you. This sort of archive could very quickly turn from remembering our history, to making us history with a lethal injection. And there was more than a shred here.

It was all worthy and wonderful, but it wasn't helping me much. What I was looking for, I could not find. Week after week, month after month of meetings, and I found nothing. As the time passed, though, any frustration vanished as I began to realise that, in fact, I was finding out a lot. I think it was in King Lear that the phrase "nothing becomes of nothing" is said, or at least something similar. But in this case, nothing becomes most definitely something, something very substantial indeed. I had only just finished trying to think of what the exact quote was and who had said it, when my phone went.

'Vic, hi. I was just about to call you. Something I've found, or rather...'

She cut in, not letting me finish: 'Dave Donaldson and two siblings of his are heading to the storage unit – in a lorry. We think they're going to move the crates.'

My jacket was being slipped on, before she had even finished her sentence. 'I'm on my way.'

I had received a running commentary from Vic through my helmet speakers on the progress of Donaldson as I rode there. I wasn't too sure why she felt the need to inform me of every turn and stop he had made. We knew where he was going so unless we were about to publish a guidebook on anarchist routes, or she was monitoring his Highway Code skills, it was pretty irrelevant which direction he was taking.

I arrived soon after Mr D himself. I had been told by my very own personal human socialist satnav, that she was parked outside the block, feeling that being too near to him, in broad daylight, was being too obvious. She could have added, but hadn't, that it was especially a wise move because her car was a flash up-market sports number, which was incongruously covered with party insignia, and couldn't have been any more conspicuous.

Asher and Roijin were parked outside the other exit, in a somewhat more discreet vehicle.

Vic had given me strict instructions on what to do when I reached the storage buildings. She had even gone so far as advising me on my walk. I wasn't to, in her words: 'crouch down SAS style or to impersonate the Scarlet Pimpernel". Shunning the balaclava, and leaving aside the ruff and powdered wig, I casually strolled to her car. Her car, I noted, which now had all the windows tinted. And this was the woman who told me to play it subtle!

Getting in was like entering mission control. The inside of the front windscreen was now her computer screen. 'We're patched into the faculties' CCTV, and–' she pointed to a screen which was obviously from a camera hovering above the building– 'that's the NWC surveillance drone. We've notified them that we're here and that we're taking the lead. They'll not act unless we instruct them to.'

From the multiple screens, at multiple angles, I could see Donaldson locking the front door of a mid-size white lorry. It looked innocent in being so unremarkable. He was talking to two white men, who both looked in their thirties; all were wearing unremarkable clothes. Dressed to match the lorry. They hadn't gone for the SAS or Pimpernel look either.

'We've identified the taller one as Anthony Higgie and the other is Piers John. Both are two AF ultras – acolytes of his. He recruited the pair of them a few years back. They're forthright in their politics and make no secret of their belief that the revolution has stalled. But that said, they have never been known to be violently against either the party or the NWC.'

All three were heading to the entrance. Donaldson glanced up at the camera and looked as if he was staring right into our car. Despite knowing that wasn't the case, a shiver ran down my spine, only becoming a stroll when they he turned his attention elsewhere. They headed to the building. On approaching, a door appeared, and they went in.

The carcom automatically switched to a camera inside the building. We could now see them waiting for the lift. For people about to arm themselves for a resurrection, they looked very chilled; far more casual than I would have expected. But then, I wasn't too sure what wannabe renegades would actually look like. Not that they were without nerves. I could see Donaldson chewing gum as if his life depended on it. His beard was also getting a good scratching. But aside from that, from the speed of their jaws, they seemed to be relaxed.

'Is there any sound?' I asked, feeling that my lip-reading abilities were pretty amateurish.

Roijin replied, full of regret, 'No. I guess that they feel that there's no need.'

I could almost hear Vic's grin. 'Car AI, activate lip-reading translation.'

'Of course. Good thinking, Vic,' Roijin said in praise.

Vic flashed me a knowing look of recognition.

Instantly, three simulated voices began speaking. The one who was taking Donaldson's role sounded far too modest to be him. Strangely, the computerised voice sounded more human than his actual human one. We could now hear that he and his confederates were discussing the security arrangements in the depository. Donaldson was reassuring them that the fact that it was low-level was to their advantage because no-one would suspect that they would keep such an important store of armaments there.

Obviously, he was wrong about that. Presently, he was getting more attention than an A-list movie star at a world premiere. They reached the floor and Donaldson pointed at the camera, which meant, although he didn't know it, he was pointing directly at us, and asked the taller one, 'Higgs, access the vid-footage file, see if we've received any unwanted visitors'.

'But Dave, we're linked to the system – we see what it sees. That's why we're here. We know that Crib turned up but found nothing. If anything else had happened, we'd have seen it.'

He shook his head. 'That Usurp plod, Roijin Kemal, is a tech whizz, she could easily override that, and cut the link. But I'm betting that she won't know of the Hj shadow system Piers here, installed.' He patted Piers' back in tribute. 'It sits alongside the storage centre's own log. Let's see what that shows.' He chuckled.

Roijin grinned. 'They won't find any. This "tech-whizz plod" put a blanket over our visit, including the Hj shadow.'

'A blanket?' I said, none-the-wiser.

Vic shook her head in disbelief. 'Metaphorically speaking, Pete. Not literally. Roijin doesn't usually take bed-linen on her assignments.'

I heard Roijin and Asher laugh. I was tempted to point out that the AI lip-reading program had originally been my idea, but decided that right now, there were bigger things than my ego to worry about. After a few seconds of being amused by my presumed ignorance, Roijin continued, 'The story they'll see is one of us turning up and going to the wrong unit, finding nothing. The militia turns up and you turn them away. End result, their stash is safe, and we bungled. They're cunning and clever revolutionaries and we're dumb reactionary plods.'

True enough, Donaldson helpfully recounted just that story. 'A Kalder cock-up,' was his conclusion.

Roijin's satisfaction vibrated through our radio link. 'Actually, it's him who has only looked at the surface, he's missed what's just below the obvious. He knows that we're onto him and so left his personal phone at his workplace, guessing correctly that we're tracking him. But what he hadn't counted for, was that we're also linked into John's and Higgie's devices.'

Vic spoke: 'The fact that they've risked a visit here shows that he's spooked. There were some very heated conversations between them about whether they should move it or not. They'd been lucky once, with a seemingly failed raid, but they mightn't be a second time. But his arrogance is again his weakness, he reassured them that we'd been once and come away empty-handed, so we wouldn't come here again. "Hiding it in plain sight" was his highly unoriginal way of putting it.'

'Why is it that those with biggest heads have the smallest brains?' I asked no-one in particular.

No-one in particular didn't answer because we were now watching Donaldson slowly getting onto his knees. Was he going to pray? Then he lay on his chest. 'Now what's happening?' I asked, presuming he wasn't feeling tired and needed a quick nap.

'He's looking for the strip.'

'Okay, Roijin, what's that a metaphor for?'

'No, Pete. This time I'm being literal. He left a tiny sticky strip on the door. It was difficult to see with the naked eye, unless you looked carefully. It's an old, old trick, to see if someone has been in. If the strip is torn then the door has been open.'

'Jesus, so he'll know?'

I could hear Roijin's pride in her skills, when she answered, 'Oh no. I saw it. It's intact. Using such old-school methods is back in vogue with cyber-warfare so prevalent and skilled.'

'Which is probably why they used whispers and handwritten notes to intimidate Mike Stewart,' Vic muttered.

After a few grunts and groans, Donaldson got back on his feet and announced that it was still there. With that, they opened the door. But they did not go in. Instead, the man known as Higgie scanned the floor with his phone.

Until now Victoria had been so laidback that she should have reclined her seat and taken a snooze. There was, though, worry in her voice when she spoke. 'Shit! I didn't think of that. They're cleverer than I gave them credit! Shit! Shit!'

I looked at her. She was obviously agitated and more than annoyed with herself. 'What?'

Vic's explanation was delivered at double speed. 'Floor dust, it's another old trick. Put extremely fine dust on the floor. Any intruder will disturb it and his app will pick up any disturbance.' She slapped her knee. 'Damn! A simple bloody ploy – and we missed it – I missed it. He'll know that we've been. This will cause a shit-storm of all shit-storms. Your news conference panicked him enough; this is going to force him to act. We've no choice, we have to call the militia. Christ! We could end up in a bloody gun fight here. Just what we don't need. We need to be careful.' She pressed her hand to her temple, talking to herself; ordering herself: 'Quick, Vic, think!'

I had never seen her this het up. Our eyes met. It wasn't romantic.

Then, the calm smooth voice of Roijin once more floated over the radio link. 'Don't fret, Vic. *I saw it.* I re-spread the fake dust on entering the building, that image replaced the one he's got. It will be identical, because basically, it's the same photo. All is fine. He'll see nothing.'

A strange feeling came over me, and words came out of my mouth before I had a chance to think, 'Christ, Roijin, you're bloody good, aren't you! I feel like hugging you!'

'Me too,' sighed one relieved Victoria Cole.

Roijin laughed. 'So as to spare you any more heart attacks, I should tell you he put more strips on the crates, which he will no doubt inspect, and will again find that they've been untouched.'

She was right. He did.

Piers John didn't look relieved though. His nerves were fraying. 'We've been lucky so far, but how long can that last? Well? If this little lot is found then not only will we face the wrath of the Cribs and their Usurp backers, but most of the NWC too. We can't even rely on the sibs from the AF or NON. Too many are too naive and too trusting. Too many fucking pacifists. They'll be as angry as the Usurps. You know what I think, Dave – we need to move this now! We've got the lorry, let's just do it.'

There was tension too, inside the car. Probably more. If they did move this cache, then we would have to make the decision as to what to do. Vic's finger was stroking her phone. The call to the NWC Defence Corps was in the balance. If she made the call, then I had no doubt that no matter how much a fool Donaldson appeared to be, he would not easily give all this up. Donaldson was committed and ready to act. How and who for, was up for debate, but what wasn't, was that he would be willing to take any course of action which he felt to be necessary. And that included armed resistance. It would be a shoot-out that we would win, but it would be one which the counter-revolutionary forces would love. Not just a split within the NWC but a violent confrontation was a wet dream for the reactionaries.

Seconds passed and I began to find breathing difficult. Donaldson was looking at the crates and stroking his beard under his chin with the tops of his fingernails. Finally, he spoke: 'No, they stay. Moving them is too much of a risk. Now's not the time. We continue as before. Come on. We came here to see that everything was kosher and it is. Let's head back to the Shard. There's things we can do there.'

The sighs of relief from the four of us might have been audible kilometres away. Vic looked at me and smiled. She didn't speak but didn't need to. In the other car, Asher and Roijin didn't either; again there was no need. A very nasty and messy situation had been narrowly averted. Or at least postponed.

We watched Donaldson, Higgie and Johns leave everything as they had found it – the dust and the strips, and then head out to their lorry. Vic was staring at the screen, but I got the distinct impression that she wasn't actually looking at them. She was deep in thought.

'Something up?' I asked.

'Hmm. Very thorough, isn't he?'

I glanced at the screen to see Donaldson unlocking the lorry door. 'He's no fool, that's for sure. Underneath it all, he's got an intelligence, I guess.'

I couldn't see what the problem was. Surely, it was hardly a startling revelation that Dave Donaldson had a brain. I mean, he was quite obviously a somewhat sussed-out bloke. His track record clearly showed that.

'He checked everything,' she said so quietly that I almost didn't hear her.

Again, I agreed, not seeing what was odd about that. After all, what was in that storage room was highly controversial and valuable.

'Well, not everything.' She looked at me with meaningful eyes.

I looked back, trying to understand what the meaning was. Whether by telepathy or simply that I too had a brain, I eventually got it. 'The phone!' I mumbled. 'He didn't check to see if the phone was there. We took the phone which was used for the drone attack, yet, he didn't check to see if it was there!'

Roijin spoke, not understanding the significance: 'But I had replaced it. Even if he had, he would have seen nothing unusual.'

I knew what Vic was thinking. 'But the important thing is that he didn't check. The most natural thing in the world would have been for him to do so, but he didn't.'

The occupants of the other car clearly weren't tuned into us. Asher replied, 'Maybe, he didn't need to, because all his other little checks had come up as negative. The floor dust was settled, so he knew that no-one had got in.'

'Except, that he still checked the strips on the gun crates. He checked everything – except the phone, he didn't check to see if the phone was still there.'

Roijin understood. 'You're right. He *would* have checked, wouldn't he? Not least because of the threat that phone poses to him. If the guns are found, he has to answer for being an ultra-left. Many will, if not support him, then at least understand his motives. He will plead that they're only for self-defence. But the phone? If that's found it will prove that he was responsible for the attack killing AF members. No-one will support that! Certainly not, when it shows that he is a spy for the deposed ruling class. The most important thing in that room is the phone!'

I finished her sentence: 'The reason he didn't check for the phone, quite simply, is because he didn't know about it. *He did not know it was there in the first place.* Which means that he wasn't the person who hid it there. Which means that Donaldson wasn't responsible for the attack, and that someone else planted it there.'

'Bingo,' Vic quietly said.

'So, are we suggesting,' I said, not waiting for a diploma or awards ceremony for solving one of her riddles, 'that Donaldson may be hoarding illegal arms and advocating a second revolution, but he's not our killer, or at least not responsible for the Shard drone attack?'

'I think so,' Vic replied.

'Sounds right,' Roijin groaned. 'Which means we're back to square one. I suppose that at least he's one off the list. But let's face it, we haven't got much else to go on at the moment. We've come up with a pretty arbitrary list as it is. Where to now?'

I thought about my visit to the museum and what I had found. Or to be more precise, what I hadn't. 'I think I may have the answer to that.'

# CHAPTER 32: READER WITH A MAGNIFYING GLASS

After an impromptu conference, we had decided to concentrate on just the one line of enquiry. Initially, they had been rather sceptical of what I had to say, but whether by logic or persistence, I had ground them down. It warranted at least a follow up. Not that we were totally giving up on Dave Donaldson. However, we had come to an uneasy consensus of opinion that we should at least temporarily focus on one person in particular.

My job couldn't have been more straightforward. I adjourned to a cafe, ordered a coffee and settled down to making some phone calls. Straightforward, easy, but not very exciting. With each one, it was the telecommunications equivalent of knocking door to door. Each time asking the same questions.

After a while, I had another coffee. Then another.

Still, the cafe was a pleasant place to spend time in. I had found a corner which afforded me some privacy and settled into a work routine. The chairs were comfortable and the air-conditioning very pleasing, so there were worse ways to spend your time. That was just as well, because as the phone calls came and went, I uncovered very little in the way of information. Just as it had been back at the museum, there seemed so little to be found.

Needing inspiration from higher up, I rang Jackie Payne, who merely told me what I'd been told before. She did, however, suggest someone I could ring – Reeves Wilkinson, who was someone, frankly, I should have thought of in the first place. I didn't tell her that; I just lied, and said that I planned to do so next. This I did. Reeves Wilkinson answered my questions, but added absolutely nothing to my sum of knowledge. Except, that is, once more, suggested someone else I might ring. Seems I was in some sort of human pass the parcel. This one was called Booker Campbell, the very Booker Campbell who was the generous donator of all the boxes, which I had spent hours trawling through back at the museum. Reeves told me that if anyone could help me, then he could. I sincerely hoped that this would be the case, because even copious cups of coffee couldn't stop the yawns coming thick and fast.

Booker Campbell had been involved in the Small Firms' Strike right from the beginning and had been active throughout. There appeared to be barely a picket line, meeting or demo, physical or virtual, that Campbell hadn't been involved in. If he wasn't present, then in all probability, it wasn't a part of the dispute.

Without too much difficulty, I managed to hook up with mister mainstay of the strike –Booker Campbell. I applied to be allowed to go 2D visual and he accepted, his image appearing before me. He was a thirty-something dark-skinned black man. He was wearing a crisply ironed white shirt and his hair was cropped short. I received a polite smile when I told him who I was, who I worked for, and that I had got his number from Reeves Wilkinson. The smile remained, but the eyes showed puzzlement the moment when I told him that I wanted to talk about the Small Firms' Strike of eight years ago.

'Okaaay,' he said. He was understandably wondering why I wanted to talk about the strike – being from Crib, I wasn't about to be writing a history of pivotal moments in British labour history. 'Happy to help, but I'm afraid I can only give you five minutes though, as I've got to take an international call.'

'That's fine. It should be long enough. As I said, I've just spoken to Reeves Wilkinson, who you might remember was the URSP organiser in Southampton at the time, and he said that you were one of the leaders of the dispute, is that correct?'

He grimaced. 'Well, not exactly; Reeves is always too kind about that. I was one of many. My only claim to fame is that I was the first to suggest that we link up the small firms and the home workers to fight against the new tax the Government was proposing. So yeah, I played a part, but as I said, there were many others.'

He was being modest. The newscasts and the records showed that he had been far from that, but I wasn't contacting him to discuss the story of his life. The fact was, that everything I had seen had his face, name or signature on it. I was hoping that he would be able to discuss someone else.

'Why do you want to know? What could interest a Cribber from a dispute from another time?' he asked.

I used my old standby, 'Background.'

'For what?'

I told him what investigation I was involved in and that this might have some bearing on it, and then waited to see if he was still willing to help.

He looked a bit surprised. 'I've seen it on the news. Awful, just awful! Not sure how I can be of help and what something so long ago might have to do with it, but of course, I will help anyway I can.' After the slightest of shrugs, he asked what I wanted to know.

I said that he could start by refreshing my memory on the chronology of the dispute and the personalities involved. This he did, again modestly keeping his role to the minimum and maximising the praise for everyone else. He didn't realise it, but that was exactly what I wanted. In fact, I asked him to tell me more about the other people involved.

He spoke eloquently and with the precision of a history site. Even with my interruptions, he spoke in one flowing narrative. My guess was that he had often spoken of it. The dispute had been important to the class, but also to him personally. Maybe it had been the first one he'd been involved in. That would explain why he could recall so much detail of it. It would also explain the reason he had a large personal archive of it, which he had not only kept, but thought enough of, to donate it to Joni Feld. First disputes were like first loves, whatever the outcome and whatever you thought of them, you never forgot them. I remembered both. He finished, apologising once more, but he did not have much time because his "international call" would be in three minutes' time and he must take it.

'Thanks, Booker. You've been very helpful. Would you say that you have mentioned everyone who was involved in the dispute?'

'Er, yes. Everyone I can think of. A lot has happened since then. But, yes, I think I've about covered it. Certainly, all the leading activists – why?'

I believed him. So, we had finally arrived at the point of my call. I now had less than three minutes to get what I wanted. 'You were the chair of the disputes committee and by all accounts, knew virtually everyone involved in the strike, so I'm interested that you haven't once mentioned Noah Walker.'

He looked at me with face that had confusion written in bright red lipstick written across it. 'Noah Walker? Well, I don't remember him at all. I mean, I know who he is, anyone who watches the news would, and I know that he also hails from Southampton, but I don't remember him being involved in the dispute at all. Why – was he?' His voice sounded as non-comprehending as mine does when engaging in a conversation about the chess strategies.

His reply was interesting in itself, because Jackie Payne had told me that she had on more than one occasion, heard Walker say that he had been working for a firm called Strictly L Solutions, and it was whilst he was with them that he had got involved in the strike, and then onto the party. I asked him if he remembered the company.

Without pausing he answered, 'Yes, I do actually. They were one of the larger employers involved. About seventy, I think, with twenty home workers. If I remember correctly, the staff were mostly website designers. They were of the third wave of firms to come out – totally solid, with all except the owner out; stayed out for the duration. The owner was a total and utter bastard. I mean, many of the owners were keen to end the strike, which is what you would expect. Most were willing to consider concessions, but he wasn't someone who was keen to win *at any cost* and by doing *anything* to achieve that end. That's probably why his staff were so militant. A lot of the staff were actually pretty active during it.'

'And Noah Walker?'

He closed his eyes to dredge his memory, 'No, sorry. I have to say that I don't remember him; I suppose, he may have been involved at the final stages of it, by then, I was personally rather preoccupied, the police were beginning to go on the offensive and I was at the receiving end of a great deal of rather unpleasant harassment.'

That I could believe. The strike had become infamous for the violence which the police and private security had dished out.

'But you don't remember him?'

'No, sorry, comrade. Like I say, not at all.'

'Do you have any more information on this Strictly L Solutions?'

'Everything I had, I sent to Joni Feld.'

'Have you any idea, who might have? Employment records and such like?'

He thought for a moment or two. 'I can send you a few numbers of people who worked there, but...' he looked at his watch. 'But I really have to take this call. Sorry.'

I smiled. 'Okay, Booker, you've been a great help. I've transferred our contact details. if you could ring and give the phone numbers to someone called Odette, that would be really helpful. I'll leave you to your call. Bye.'

Consuming what was probably my millionth coffee, I thought about what I should do next. I really could do with looking at the personnel files of this company. Booker would be on his call now so he wouldn't be sending on the numbers of the Strictly L Solutions workers for at least a while. I checked online to see if their website was still up, but it wasn't. There wasn't any mention of Strictly L Solutions at all. Not even an address. No doubt another victim of the cyber-data wipes. So, what next? I ruled out heading to Southampton and roaming the streets to see if I could find some trace of them. Deciding on foregoing another coffee for fear of a caffeine overdose, I tried this thinking lark. That went on for a few minutes before my mental puzzle solving session was interrupted by Vic calling.

'Pete, how's it going?'

I sighed heavily. 'I think I've made some progress,' I replied, although I wasn't sure that was true. I told her that I had spoken to the leading activist of the Small Firms' Dispute, Booker Campbell. 'He'd no recollection whatsoever of Noah Walker during it and I'm sure that if Walker had been, he would have remembered him. That strike means a lot to him.'

She didn't react as I might have liked. Indeed, there was barely any reaction at all.

I persevered. 'Nor has Reeves Wilkinson.'

Vic could see where I was coming from, and could see the implication, but she wasn't just yet punching the air in triumph. 'All a little puzzling, I grant you, but it's hardly cast-iron evidence, is it? People don't always remember everyone who was involved in a dispute, a dispute which was eight years ago! There were lots of people in the strike. There were over three thousand strikers across the region who were eventually involved, and the nature of the dispute meant that they were dispersed across a large area. These were isolated people at home and small pockets of workers in small workspaces. That's why it was such big news; these were people who had previously been hard to organise.'

'True, but then there's the archives at the museum, there's not one mention of him. Not a single one.'

'A few boxes of memorabilia – hardly the British Library, is it?'

'All true, but I would have expected *some* memory of him. The Noah Walker we all know wouldn't take a backseat in a black cab, let alone in a strike. For all his faults, is no staffroom warrior, moaning and but doing nothing. He takes the lead.'

'It's a good point, but maybe this was the beginning of his politicisation?'

'According to Jackie, he's claimed to have been a Marxist for over a decade.'

She nodded. 'Well, I might have something which would add some support to your theory, even if it's no more circumstantial than yours. I'm at the TV studios and one of the cleaners thinks he saw Walker leave the debate. I should repeat, he *thinks* he saw him leave. He can't be certain, but he thinks it was him. Which if we can verify, shows that he at least lied to us. He said that he had been in the studio for the whole time, but if we can locate him outside, that will at least pose the question as to why he lied.'

'I thought we'd confirmed that he had been, by locating his phone in the studio for the duration?'

She laughed. 'The simple answer to that is that he could have left it in there while he went out. It's so bloody obvious that it's actually bloody embarrassing. Having said that, the cleaner was pretty vague, and was far from definite, but it's something to work on. I'm gonna chase that up. But let's not get too excited, we haven't found anything in the way of solid proof, and we cannot forget that it was only a few hours ago that we were convinced that Dave Donaldson was our man. But I admit that we may be seeing some daylight here.'

I thought that it was less a sign of daylight and more of a spotlight on our chum Noah, but she was the professional, I suppose. I was still new to this game and I was getting excited. 'If we manage to prove that he lied, then that will indicate some guilt.'

'Possibly, but in itself it doesn't prove anything. He can just say that he forgot that he had.'

'But it starts to paint a picture. Especially if we can find out more about his involvement – or otherwise – in the Small Firms' Strike.'

'Any ideas how you're going to do that?'

Now your average fictional detective might sink a whisky or ten, kick down a few doors, or thrill to car chases, but, I made phone calls. And what was worse, to the same people. I told her that I was going to ring Reeves Wilkinson again.

She hung up. I rang Wilkinson. When he answered it was obvious that my renowned coating of charm was fading. I got a smile and a polite welcome, but it was about genuine as a plastic pink daffodil. Familiarity with me, may not be breeding contempt, but it was applying to adopt fatigue.

He all but sighed, when he asked me how he could help me now. The "now" was given a heavy emphasis.

'Jackie thinks that she once heard Noah Walker mention that he worked for a company called Strictly L Solutions. I spoke to Booker Campbell who remembers the firm, but not Walker working there. The owner was a nightmare and extremely hawkish in his attitude to the strikers. I was wondering if you remembered him?'

'Hmm, so Noah worked there, did he? That surprises me, because over the duration of the dispute, I had a fair number of dealings with the company, so I'd have expected to have come across him, but I'm afraid, I still don't remember him. Booker's right though about the owner, he was a complete bastard.'

'Don't suppose you remember his name, do you?'

He answered instantly: 'Stuart Midgley.'

'Do we know if he still lives in Southampton?'

Maybe his keenness to get rid of me was igniting Reeves' memory because to my surprise he could once again provide me with information. 'Oh no, he's moved here. Well, when I say here, I mean London. Lives in Putney. The party's London offices will have his address on file. Believe it or not, the toe-rag applied to join the party a few months back. Because of the reputation he gained from the dispute, the membership secretary asked me for my opinion. Seems now that we're in power, Mister Midgley is now comrade Stu. He had a whole number of references and quoted a long list of good solid Trotskyist deeds, but I still said no way. People can change, but I don't believe he truly has. It's pure opportunism. I'll be honest, even if he has experienced a change of heart, it wouldn't be enough to compensate what he was responsible for during that strike. You know about the home invasions?'

I indicated that I did.

'Well, take one guess where that idea came from? Yes indeed, it was Stuart Midgley. The amount of blood he has on his hands, he should be in jail, not the party. Seems other comrades from Southampton agreed with me, and he was turned down.'

I searched the membership request files and found that we did have it, which was why I was travelling deep in South-west London. Vic hadn't been in the greatest of moods when I had rung her back. It had only been half an hour after my last call to her, but something in that small amount of time had managed to piss her off. She had irritably informed me that she was too busy to join me. Clearly not willing to spend much time to placate me, she had simply volunteered Asher to "hold my hand".

After parking my bike, I walked up to the man who I was to be palm in palm with. He was leaning against a muddy green Ford, a community loan car from the pool. It was quite a step away from Vic's set of wheels.

'I see only Vic gets the flash motor,' I said, pointing to it.

He smiled, shrugged and simply replied, 'It suits me.'

Our past hostilities had ceased, and there was now a certain politeness between us, but it would be too much to call it a friendship. It was more of a business partnership. I couldn't actually think of a previous time when it had been just him and me. We had never socialised any further than sharing a coffee and pastry for a morning briefing session. He was usually in his laboratory, peering at test tubes or cutting open cadavers. It was his way of having fun, I guess. I liked to think that I, meanwhile, was chasing down class enemies. Just recently, however, it was pretty much my own tail, I was chasing. This, then, was our first date. As was often the case with such things, there was a touch of nerves.

'Sorry to drag you down here. As I said on the phone, from what I've heard about this Stuart Midgley, he'll respond better if there's two of us, and we puff up the formality a bit.'

I had noticed that Asher was in his jacket and trouser combination, which I'd only occasionally seen him in before. With his party badge and ID, he looked just the right level of officialdom.

'No prob, Pete. Actually, it makes a nice change.'

It was a slow start. You couldn't really say there was a connection between us. Not an electric one, in any case.

'Vic seemed a bit irritable.'

He smiled. 'Don't take it personally. She often gets like that when she's frustrated. She gets a bit twitchy when she knows what she's looking for and has a fair idea on how to find it, but is unable to do so.'

'I've not seen her like that before,' I said.

He gave me a look which I couldn't translate. 'No, I wouldn't have thought you would have. You're different, Pete, she's not like that with you.'

I looked back at him and tried to read his face. It looked fairly friendly and there didn't seem to be any hint of antagonism or sarcasm, so he wasn't trying to be funny. In which case, I desperately hoped that he wasn't suggesting that she had a crush on me; I know I was aging well, but the thought did make my stomach turn in on itself.

'She's too much respect for you to get snappy with you.' He gave a deep chuckle. 'Which says a lot about me and Roij, I suppose.'

'Respect?' I was genuinely surprised. The thought of her respecting me was not something I had really considered. I'd always thought that she considered me, if not a joke, then an amusing anecdote – one that was to be tolerated. But again, I couldn't detect any hostile intentions behind his comment.

He quite evidently had seen my reaction and understood it. Another deep chuckle vibrated up from within his gut, before he explained, 'You've been in the party since the beginning, she respects that. Actually, we all do. You've gone through the frustrating and the hard, the inspiring and the dangerous times. She and us, on the other hand, are "newly joins".'

The use of the unflattering sobriquet for those who had joined within the last five years, stirred an unusual feeling inside me – guilt. It was frowned upon in the party as being elitist and uncomradely, which of course hadn't stopped me from using it – quite the opposite actually. Including on more than one occasion, about the three of them. To my credit, I had ceased doing that now. With the Cribs being regarded with more than a little suspicion, I was becoming less choosy about my companions and so was watching my tongue.

Before I had time to say 'Shucks', Asher was heading off to Stuart Midgley's house. 'I believe it's a few doors this way.'

He wasn't the fastest of men, so I quickly joined him, which was just as well, because it didn't take too long to find it – a large red flag hung outside and revolutionary posters smothered the windows.

'Good grief,' Asher said with a grin.

Short of having a full red army choir and a forty-metre high stone statue of Friedrich Engels outside, it was difficult to see how he could proclaim his new allegiance any more.

'Can he be any more blatant?'

I agreed. 'I haven't seen that much OTT declaration of party affiliation, since I last took a ride in Vic's car.'

He turned and looked at me, and then after a second of silence, roared with laughter. The ice had been broken; the first date was warming up.

'Newly-joins, hey, Pete?'

I smirked. 'He's more like tried-to-joins.'

'Shall we?' He rang the bell.

A voice from inside the house told us that he was coming. Then a minute later, the door opened and a man with a gelled pony-tail answered. He had clear, tanned white skin, and alert eyes, and looked in his early thirties, although I knew for a fact that he was 46. That was a big black mark against him for starters. He was wearing a skin-tight white tee-shirt and tight black shorts, which combined to show that he liked a good workout.

He looked first at Asher and then me. 'Yes? What...' He clocked our party badges, and all of a sudden, his attitude altered, from the curt to the welcoming. 'How can I help you, comrades?'

It was Asher who answered, 'My name is Asher Joseph and this is Pete Kalder. We're from Crib. Are we right in thinking that you are Stuart Midgley?'

'Yes, that's right...'

'Good. We were hoping that you could help us with our enquiries.'

Before he had a chance to say anything more, we touched our ID badges to show our full visual identification. He looked at them and then at us. 'Of course. I'm only happy to help the revolution. How can...'

'You could invite us in,' Asher suggested.

'Of course. Of course,' he spluttered. 'Please come in, comrades.'

His front room was small but tastefully decorated. 'Please take a seat. Would you like a drink?'

We declined both offers and remained standing. Asher busied himself looking at the expensive homecom, leaving me to do the talking. Noticeably, Midgley also remained standing. He seemed apprehensive but not that scared. There was a fixed smarmy smile glued to his face.

'So, comrades, how can I help? I'm a firm believer and supporter of the revolution and will do everything I can to further it.'

'Yes.' I smiled back. 'We saw the flag, didn't we, Ash?'

'We did, Pete. It was a big one.'

'A very big one, Ash. I've rarely seen such a large one.'

He looked at the both of us, trying to work out why we were here, and how he could get the best out of our visit.

'Is this about my application to join the party?' he asked.

That was disappointing. I had expected more from him than that. He knew full well that two Crib members wouldn't be on a membership request. Frankly, I found it rather insulting.

His smile was as realistic as a plastic flamingo in a cocktail. 'Comrade, I'm keen to serve anyway I can.'

His smarm was beginning to irritate me, but I tried to remain professional and friendly. 'That's good to hear. So, Stuart – may I call you Stuart?'

He replied that I could. I had the distinct impression that I could have called him anything I wanted to and he would keep this puppy dog act up. All the names under the sun and he would still have been on his back, with his legs up in the air. 'Thank you, Stuart; am I correct that presently, you're a home worker?'

'Yes. Yes. I design websites. From home mainly. I'm presently working on one for the food co-op down the road. My wife works there. It's a great community scheme. Is this why you're here?'

Was he taking the piss? If it was highly unlikely that Cribs went on membership applications, then we certainly didn't go on house calls on whether the free-range eggs were up to standard at the local co-op!

Behind me, Asher sighed heavily. 'Come on, comrade, enough of this BS. I can see that your homecom is set to multiple news programmes and social media discussion groups. I can also see that they're registered as favourites, so I'm sure you will have seen plenty of coverage concerning the investigation we're currently engaged on. You might not have seen me – I'm somewhat bashful of publicity – but comrade Kalder is positively a star. Aren't you, Pete?'

'I'm far too modest to answer that, Ash.'

Asher folded his arms. 'The thing is, Stuart, that you know full well that we wouldn't come here, to either join you up or to ask about your work for a co-op.'

Using our advantage in numbers, I spoke before he had a chance to reply. 'No,' I said. 'We're more interested in your work with Strictly L Solutions. Or to be more precise, the company called Strictly L Solutions, which you owned.'

Visibly, he tensed. Clearly here was his dirty little secret which he didn't want airing. He looked in turns at the pair of us, visibly growing concerned as to what the purpose of our visit actually was. 'That was a long time ago, comrade. I know I did a lot of regrettable things back then, things which I'm ashamed of. I know that, I admit it. But I've changed. The person I was back then isn't the person I am now. Comrade Payne has said that, "Social relations help mould our social consciousness and help create the people who we are. If those relations are changed, then it follows that it gives us to change ourselves. This is why we must welcome people to our movement who have previously not only not supported us, but who have actively opposed us".'

'Very impressive,' I said. 'That's quite a speech. Not everyone can quote Jackie Payne verbatim.' Or needs to, I said to myself. 'But you didn't continue with the rest of it. She goes on to say that: "those who sincerely swap sides and risk much by doing so, will find a home in the party". Now Ash over there, used to be a cop – in the Met Police. I have no idea what he did back then, but the thing is, Ash joined us not only well before the revolution, but when things were looking grim for us. I'm ashamed to say that it took a me a while to appreciate what Ash had done. I'm sure you know Jackie's quote about how conservative we longstanding comrades can become. That, I'm afraid, is what happened to me, Stu. Asher didn't jump ship when the wind changed, but he did so, when it was an extremely dangerous action to take. You could say, that when he joined, the forecast was the likelihood of the wind changing directions, and blowing right back into his face.'

'Nice analogy, Pete.'

'Thanks, Ash. But then there's you, Stu. You're very different. You applied to join us six months *after* we achieved power. I'm sure you are doing great work now, and such great work that we could barely exist without it, but before we start dishing out the gongs, let's talk about Strictly L Solutions.'

His jaw almost visibly dropped. Quite obviously he didn't have warm and fuzzy memories of his time as Hampshire's uber local business leader, because all of sudden, he wasn't acting so smooth and smarmy. I could feel the worry, the fear and the tension all pushing him down. There was a real concern that this possibly rather important witness was going to be forced into the earth's core.

Finally, he spoke. His voice was deliberate and possibly even deeper than it had been previously. 'It's ancient history. Things have a changed a lot since then. I mean, I've changed. It was a lifetime ago.'

'Eight years ago,' I said.

'Which *is* a lifetime ago, if you're an eight-year-old,' Asher pointed out.

'That's certainly true, comrade.' I grinned, throwing him a glance, wishing I'd said that. Returning my gaze to Midgley, I lost the smile. 'So, eight years ago, you were owner of Strictly L Solutions. It was doing very well and you had a comfortable life, with hot and cold running bourgeois entitlement. You weren't seen as being greatly political back then, although you were a member of the local Conservative Party.' I stopped and looked at him.

He didn't look too pleased to be reminded of his political origins. I patiently waited for what would no doubt be an inspiring and deeply moving account of how he had become radicalised, but I was to be disappointed. All I got was a mumbled repetition of the fact that it was eight years ago. Obviously, two less than ten was an important number for this guy.

'Yes, eight years ago you were a blue-rinse member, but from what I have gathered, you weren't a particularly active one. In the minutes of their meetings, there's no listing of you ever attending. You just paid your subs and occasionally turned up at their socials.'

He shifted from foot to foot, wondering if the fact that he had been a paper member only made our visit any easier. It didn't; in fact, it made me feel even more suspicious of him. I continued, 'Then the Small Firms Strike began. At first your firm wasn't directly involved – you must have thought you'd escaped and could continue profit-making. But then those ungratefuls who worked for you and who took a salary from you, only went and had a union meeting, and god-damn democracy, they went and joined the strike. For a while, you contented yourself with moaning and whining. But then you changed gear...'

I joined Asher looking at him intently. It wasn't for his former membership of the Tory party that I despised him. Well, not totally. No, it was the actions which he was, at least in part, responsible for when moved up those gears, that made my skin crawl, and why in fact, Reeves Wilkinson had been so against him being allowed to join the party. 'You decided to be more proactive. You and several others helped found the Freedom to Work group which proclaimed itself as an organisation combating what it called, "communist militancy".'

I paused again, but this time he didn't say anything. It looked like he felt that telling me that it was eight years ago wasn't now going to be enough. I stared at his face and tried to read his emotions. He was swallowing hard and his breathing rate had increased. He wasn't shaking in terror, but he was most definitely unnerved.

'Stuart,' I said louder than perhaps was normal, so that I could attract his attention. 'I don't need to go into a detailed history of what that charming little group got up to, because let's face it, you'll know better than I would...'

Asher broke away from examining some shelf ornaments, which had caught his eye, and taken him away from the coffee tables, and told me that he at least would like to hear what the Freedom to Work group had done.

'Okay, I will do, Asher,' I said. 'Their actions were shameful, and were designed to bully people by means that you would have expected from a totalitarian state, rather than one which claimed it was a democracy. But I'll give a brief recount of its greatest hits. I'm sure Stuart here, will correct any inaccuracies I may make. I suppose the first I should mention is how the group actively campaigned for court orders to be taken out against the strikers. All those on strike, *and* their families and friends, had their bank accounts frozen. Donations, financial or food, were deemed illegal, all in an attempt to starve them back to work. The most infamous action though, was the policy which the state termed, "Controlling domestic workplace illegality" but was more widely known as "home invasions". This saw the police dragging home workers from their own homes and arresting them.'

He was now shrinking even further into his tasteful floor covering. As well the little shit should do.

'I presume you remember Nicholas Gates and Katarina Jackson?'

He muttered that he did.

'I'm glad, *comrade,* that you do. They were a couple, Asher, who dared to decline the kind offer of being dragged out into the street, in front of their two children. You'll no doubt remember with your marvellous memory, that the coalition government was panicking. An industrial dispute from people previously seen as unreachable, was inspiring millions who were in a similar position. Scared them shitless. Your little group were at the forefront of pushing for such aggressive action.'

He all but whined, 'We wanted assertive action, not aggressive. We just wanted the same controls for home workers as those in larger, more centralised workplaces.' He quickly remembered himself. 'Obviously, I admit that even that was reprehensible. I wouldn't dream of doing that now. I support the revolution.'

I ignored what he had said. 'It was then that the state decided to go in *really* hard. The hope was that the fact that the majority of the strikers were isolated in their homes, meant that they could frighten them back into work, and so smash the strike. Even those actually in a workplace tended to be in ones of less than ten, and so didn't experience the strength from the solidarity of a large workforce.

'You and the Freedom to Work group didn't just support the clampdown, you energetically advocated it. And I'm also reliably informed, in that group, the person who was the most vociferous in demanding that the state take a tough stance was your good self.'

He started to shuffle about on his toes, maybe to see how they moved. His buttocks were going up and down like he had eels in his jockey shorts. I could see red spreading around his neck. It wasn't a great image.

'One particular night in March, armed police broke into every home of every striker. You will remember that, the Freedom to Work group made a statement applauding such *assertive* action. Nicholas Gates and Katarina Jackson were a couple who both worked for a data analysis company. Their door was smashed in and the police stormed upstairs to arrest them. They resisted, and resisted bravely. The police claim they did so by arming themselves with kitchen knives. It was never explained how they managed to get downstairs to their kitchen, leaving their three-year-old twins upstairs on their own, and past coppers on the stairs and manage to grab a knife each. But every one of the police inside their home swore that's what they did.

'Everyone who knew them, said they were peaceful people who abhorred violence. Yet we were told that they ran downstairs, bypassing riot police and grabbed the nearest knife they could find. They then tackled police who had tasers, truncheons and guns. Now it was said that those eight muscled members of the invading police contingent, who had smashed their way into their family home, were terrified that their body armour, pepper spray, tasers and automatic weapons wouldn't save them from two analysts with peeling knives. So, understandably, they shot them dead. Each were shot four times. Once each in the back. Shot dead in their family kitchen. Their children heard their screams and the gun shots from their bedrooms upstairs.' I stopped. Anger had constricted my vocal cords and I couldn't speak.

He didn't have the same problem. He looked up and stared at me. Words vomited out of his mouth: 'They were different times, comrade. I was different. Yes, it was horrible, and I was wrong, but I hadn't expected that. No-one had. It was the Government who gave the order to use maximum violence. Not us. We were just business men and women. We were as horrified as everyone else. It wasn't what we wanted – we didn't want violence and murder. We just wanted the authorities to enforce the law, and, yes, we were wrong. *I was wrong.*'

A flash of hope appeared in his eyes. '*Is that* why you're here? You need to remember, comrades, that Jackie Payne said that the crimes of old will not be punished if the perpetrators are sincere in their regret and have learnt that their future lies with the working class, not against it. If these people have realised that the crimes they committed against the class were wrong, and they are now actively building the revolution, then we will be forgiven. I don't understand why you're here. It's not fair.'

I felt paralysed. Fury was coursing around my veins. I did not know what to say. Did he really just say that it was unfair? The fact that two eleven-year old children are living today without their mum and dad was unfair. That two normal people lost their lives because they dared to withdraw their labour was unfair. What was not unfair was that we were in his lounge, asking him to justify his actions. Out of the corner of my eye, I could see Asher looking at me. This was a Pete Kalder he had not seen before. No smart-arse comments or swaggering irreverence, but serious, real and raw class hatred. I tried to keep it together, and remember the actual reason for our visit. I sensed that Asher was about to step in, whilst I just stood and stared at the man who was squirming in front of me.

But I wanted to finish. I snarled out the words: 'We're not here for that – more's the pity. You should know that I'm one of those party members who feel Jackie was wrong to call for reconciliation. Frankly, I think you should face the strictest revolutionary justice possible. But as I said, that's not why we're here. What we are interested in is that three weeks from the end of the dispute you employed someone called Noah Walker. You were in the middle of a strike, which was making national news, with both sides knowing that the result would have important political ramifications, and yet you decided to recruit – why? It wasn't as if he was taken on as scab labour. On the day you put him on the payroll, he went straight on strike! For the final three weeks he never worked. So why did you employ him, *comrade*?'

He didn't answer. He looked pale and stood motionless. His face screamed pure, undiluted terror.

'Well?' Asher asked. 'Please answer the question.'

Still no words were uttered, and not an inkling of movement showed. Sweat was now clearly showing on his brow and on the top of his lip. I was no expert on recruitment practices, but I was pretty sure that it wasn't generally considered a frightening question to be asked why someone got a job. I would have thought the usual reply might be that he was most qualified or that he was impressive in his interview.

Finally, he decided to speak. 'Erm, oh yeah, that's right. I remember now.' He made a big play of his memory returning, with a big blink. 'I took him on because I could see that the dispute was drawing to a close and thought fresh blood would be good for the firm. If I remember correctly, he showed a real flair in design. I didn't ask him if he was going to work during the strike or take industrial action, because it isn't the type of question I ask in interviews. I don't think that's even legal. It's not a big surprise that he went out, the rest of the company were, so there'd have been no work for him to do, so I'm not sure he had much choice. Little did I know that he was later going to be a regular on the news channels. But then, you can't tell that much from an hour-long interview, can you?'

'You're telling me that you employed him because he was going to revitalise your company?'

'Exactly,' he replied, looking a little less worried. Obviously, he hadn't registered my sarcasm.

'Have you any records from that time? Employment, pay, HR or such like?'

'No. No, I got rid of them all. I didn't see the point of keeping them. I mean, I've moved on.'

That was one name for it. Trying to conceal his disgusting past would be another way of putting it. I asked him again, trying to prod his memory of the possibility of a dormant computer file lying about on some old computer somewhere, or a box file of paper documents. He maintained that he had destroyed them when he had embarked on his trek up the road to the socialist Damascus. It was obvious that he wasn't going to change his mind on the matter. In my humble opinion, Stuart Midgley's memory was functioning perfectly; it was his will that was debatable. The revolution's newest and keenest supporter didn't really have a yearning for his blood-soaked past to be widely advertised, or at least shown to two members of the president's Crib.

He had dried his face and his confidence was returning, his wobble had gone and he was talking clearer than he had been. Going from floor-gazing to looking straight at me with an unctuous tone and an ingratiating smile. The number of times he said comrades increased as he spoke. If he'd been sponsored, then he would have raised a tidy sum for charity.

I exchanged a look with Asher, who indicated that we wouldn't get much further with him. He nodded to the door. Midway through yet another self-mythologizing monologue, I cut Midgley short. 'Well thank you, Stuart, we'll be in touch.' Asher was already leaving the room, by the time I had spun on my heels to leave. Midgley's smug face followed me out.

Fearing that I would either throw up or give him a slap, I stopped at his front door. Asher was waiting outside, but before I joined him, I said my tender goodbyes to the revolution's newest supporter. 'Listen, *comrade*. We'll be looking very closely at what happened back in Southampton. That includes your recruitment processes. Oh, and, comrade, one more thing, if all these flags, banners and posters, are not down within the hour, I will instruct the local militia to take them down themselves.' I leant forward. 'And I will make sure they do so *assertively*. Do I make myself clear?'

Walking with Asher, away from Midgley, I breathed heavily, taking in as much air as possible. Partly, this was to calm myself down, but partly because I wanted some clean summer air to remove the stench of the man's hypocrisy. After a few moments of therapeutic breathing and silent contemplation, we finally spoke and both agreed that we needed to return to Somerset House to follow up what we'd learnt.

'Utter scumbag,' Asher snarled. 'I have to admit that it was great to see how you made him squirm. I did enjoy the double act bit. Is that how you are with Vic?'

'No,' I said, reaching his car. 'She usually just prowls about, looking mean and scary.'

# CHAPTER 33:
# THE DANCE OF THE VILLAGERS

I had finished the mysterious tale of Noah Walker in Southampton, when Odette added an epilogue. 'Pete and Ash sent me the names of three people who also worked for Strictly L, so I checked up on them...'

Quite plainly, all of us baking in the office, thought exactly the same thing, and we all gaped at her. Roijin stopped her futile fanning, and was about to let rip with a rebuke. Asher rested his arms on his stomach. Vic, as usual, adopted her resting attitude, which was quiet aggression. As for me, I just waited for the worst.

With an olive between her fingers, she held her hands up. 'Chill, chill, comrades. I phoned them. *I just phoned them!*' There was a palpable relief in the room. Roijin moved back onto her bottom and Asher smiled reassuringly. Vic and I remained as we were. 'I mean, what sort of person do you think I am?'

She really didn't want to know the answer to that.

After the brief cloud had interrupted the eternal happiness, which is Odette Lacomte, it quickly dispersed, and her usual self was back with us. 'Anyways, I spoke to them and they all confirmed that Walker did indeed join the company. It was late in the strike and they were all very surprised that he threw himself straight into the action. There'd been rumours that the owner, this Midgley guy, was going to recruit a replacement workforce. He'd already advertised for them. The word was, that he was going to be taking on twenty or thirty new workers to act as a scab workforce. But for some reason, they were withdrawn.'

'But instead, he employed Noah Walker, who joined the strike,' Vic said to herself as much as to anyone else.

The olive was quickly consumed before Odette continued with what she was telling us. 'Yeah, Vic, exactly. They all said he was an eager-beaver.

Got involved with everything. I have to say that they were extremely complimentary about just how involved he was. How one of them put it was – "If chairs needed to be put out for a meeting, he'd be the one doing it". They did say something which might interest you...' She paused. We waited. We were indeed interested. 'He was quite publicity shy.'

There weren't gasps of surprise or howls of shock, but there could well have been. Noah Walker declining the limelight was a concept that was difficult to comprehend. Just as you wouldn't expect the Pope to go without praying, you wouldn't expect Walker not to have his face in front of a camera.

I broke the silence. 'Midgley – the owner – was evasive in the extreme, as to why he employed him. He just muttered some nonsense about seeing Walker as fresh blood and that he would bring creativity to the company.'

'To the picket line, it seems.' Victoria seeing just how transparent it all looked. 'Any ideas what might have been the real reason for his sudden appearance on the payroll?'

I didn't have the chance to answer, because Asher had noticed something on his wanderings around Midgley's lounge, and had an interesting nugget of information to offer. 'I might have something which could have a bearing on the answer. Stuart Midgley might not live in a mansion, but he does live in a neighbourhood, which pre-revolution was a very pricey area. I also noticed that he had top-of-the-range homecom – a very expensive piece of kit. And I mean *very* expensive. And his furniture is equally from the upper-end of the market; the very topper most. It's bespoke and from a company of a high price tag – a very high price tag. The question is, where did he get the money for it all?'

The implication was obvious – Midgley had been offered money to take on Walker. It was a possibility. But then I would have thought that in any case, as a CEO, Midgley would have a fair few bob in the bank, so it wouldn't be a complete surprise if he had top-notch stuff.

Vic had read my mind. 'Could we check the state of his finances before the dispute and after?' she asked Roijin and Odette jointly.

Odette looked to Roijin and deferred to the older Bolshietech, who answered, 'We can try but it might well be the tired old problem of the records having been wiped.'

'Try anyway,' said Vic.

Odette looked puzzled. 'So you're suggesting that he was planted into the dispute by MI5, but what good would that do them? How could one latecomer have any effect on the course of it? Especially as he pretty much stayed in the background.'

I explained: 'It wasn't to influence the strike. They knew they couldn't do that, by the time he started working there it was clear what the outcome was going to be. I believe they were sussed enough to know that another upturn in union militancy was coming and it was going to be much bigger than they'd seen before. What they were doing was positioning someone in the movement for it. His involvement in the Small Firms' Strike was simply to provide a believable back-story. That's the theory, anyway.'

'Although it's pretty much just that at the moment,' added Roijin.

She was right, it was a theory, but I was developing a sense of these things and it felt right.

Asher asked if Victoria had found anything at the television studios about Walker's exact movements. One look at her face could have told him the answer.

She breathed out heavily. 'There was one cleaner who was fairly sure that he had seen Noah Walker outside the studios for a period of time, but he wouldn't swear to it in court. I also found someone else who thought they saw someone looking similar to Walker, but again was wobbly.' She looked tired and disappointed. 'I have, though, some more circumstantial data, which might be of use. If you look at this.' She put up a timeline. 'You can see that the red line is the attack on the Shard. Now look at the blue. That is the time when Walker is on camera, the green is when he's not.'

'You can see that he goes off the direct visual five minutes before the attack and for the duration of it. And if I fast forward the footage of the audience, when he was in view, you will see, that he almost makes a point of being in shot.'

She was right. Short of dropping his trousers and farting out the hits of Bing Crosby, he couldn't have been more on show. That is, tellingly, until the duration of the drone attack.

It wasn't enough though, and that was what was cheesing her off. Actually, none of what we were finding was enough. Put it all together and it looked suspicious, but when taken individually, it was just random incidents. All of which could be explained away. But then what did we expect? These were spies, after all; they weren't going to have large foam fingers pointing at themselves.

Roijin was next and reported on what she had picked up in her surveillance of Walker's communications. She hadn't found anything which could be deemed reactionary, illegal or counter-revolutionary. 'They're spending all their time arguing their position – all legal and within both NWC and party rules. It's clear that the Anand/Walker faction are making headway and gaining considerable support with a growing number of rank-and-file activists agreeing with them. There's very real fears amongst the class about the safety of the revolution, and there's no doubt that they're effective faction fighters.'

'Which doesn't make them, or their supporters, counter-revolutionaries!'

'No, Ash, it doesn't. We should be clear that both Anand and Walker are fully aware of our suspicions. They've frequently discussed that we're probably monitoring them which could be why we haven't found out anything of note.'

'What's their reaction to our interest been?' Vic asked.

'Anger at first. Especially from Anand, he's furious about it. He's made several complaints to the NWC Security Committee. He's obviously smarting, or pretending that he is, from what he sees as unjustified and insulting accusations. With Walker, it's been less so. He's more philosophical about the investigation, saying that we're only doing our job.'

'How nice of him.'

I looked at Vic, and chuckled. Life was returning to her. She didn't stay down for too long. 'Pete, I think we should have another little chat with comrade Walker.'

I agreed. 'Let's go.'

'Wait!' Odette swung her legs down off the table and jumped onto her feet in one graceful movement. Simultaneously, she threw two olives into the bin and instructed her laptop visual to come up.

It was of a live news stream. Large groups of people were chanting and marching. I could tell from the badges, placards and digital projections above them, that a significant proportion of them were party members. When the camera zoomed in close, I could see their faces, glowing with anger, distorted by fury. The voice, who I assumed was a reporter, announced that "since the revelation", numbers were growing on the protest and that more people were joining it. It was obvious that they were very angry indeed. What was noticeable, was the speed at which they were marching. It was not the speed normally associated with a demo. This was more like rushing to have a fight.

Odette pointed to the second screen, which had just appeared.

'Shit!'

Roijin succinctly summed up the view of the room. This was another news report from another channel. A woman in a well-cut beige trouser-suit was standing in front of a room full of crates. It was a room which myself, Vic and Roijin had been in very recently – Dave Donaldson's storage unit. She was reporting its discovery. Pointing to the crates, she announced what was in them. We knew this already. It sounded like a terrorists' Christmas list for a psycho Santa. These, she informed the viewers, were intended to be used in an uprising against the NWC.

The report prompted more melodramatic exchanging of looks between us. This time it was quite the appropriate response, because this was dramatic. Beige trouser-suit woman went on to say that there were spontaneous gatherings of URSP members outside AF offices across the country. The largest was on its way to the Shard.

That was the angry march which we were watching. Looking at the crowd, I began to recognise the Shard's surroundings. I also recognised the distinct shapes of weapons, being held or holstered.

Odette started to relay what she was monitoring: 'Both the party and the NWC are calling for calm and for the crowds to dissemble. They're requesting that the appropriate NWC authorities be given time to look into the matter. From what I'm hearing, it's still only a minority who are involved in the protests, but it's being described as being a very angry minority. The AF are advising all their members to stay inside and not to engage with any of the crowds. They are instructing all who support the AF and associated groupings and individuals not to react to any provocation. They have also issued a statement that they were unaware of the collection of weapons and have reasserted their support for the NWC and their agreement to work alongside the URSP. Both the anti-social stewards and the NWC militia are being mobilised. The party, AF and the NWC are all emphasising that it is important to show revolutionary discipline and restraint, and to listen to instructions from the stewards. Basically, everyone is calling for calmness and restraint.'

But looking at what could easily be called a mob in front of us, it was pretty obvious that there were quite a few who weren't listening.

Vic turned to her. 'Any word on who leaked the news?'

'The BBC are saying it was an anonymous source, who gave them the information.'

'Noah Walker?'

'Possibly,' I said. 'But I bet he isn't making public announcements urging people onto the streets to lynch the nearest anarcho. No, if he hasn't already, he'll be all statesmanlike and will be calling for calm and thoughtful reflection, and then at the right moment, he'll drop a heavy hint that that should include the questioning of the reliability of the AF.'

'I agree, Pete. Odette, do we know if Dave Donaldson has specifically been named yet?'

'Not so far, Vic.'

In my view that didn't mean anything. 'He will be, but it will be timed just when the outrage seems to be waning, or at the very least, when it needs a boost. It will be carefully choreographed – not too quickly and not too late. This whole thing feels like we've been led on a merry dance, and it isn't going to stop now.'

Asher looked at me, 'So you reckon, he will be named?'

'Most certainly.'

Vic was getting to her feet as she spoke. 'Then we need to find Donaldson, and find him quickly. If Pete is right, and I think he is, then he'll be in very real danger. At the moment the AF are holding back, but I'm guessing that an attack on one of their most prominent supporters could change all that.'

Looking up at Vic, Roijin muttered, 'And his death would be even more provocative.'

I agreed. 'You could even say it would be a red flag to a bull.'

'Yeah, very amusing,' Vic said, quite clearly not meaning it. 'Pete. We need to get to Donaldson immediately.' She was holstering her gun, when she turned towards Odette. 'Where can we find him right at this moment?'

'He's at the Central Cleaning Department, which is his workplace, and it's...'

'We know. Pete, come on!'

Victoria didn't flick her fingers, or shout "Here boy!", but the tone was there. I jumped up and followed my mistress.

# CHAPTER 34:
# DANCE TO THE MUSIC

---

**W**e had been driving for just over ten minutes, before every news channel exploded with the same 'exclusive' that sibling Dave Donaldson was not simply a badly-dressed firebrand anarchist, but was also a keen collector and connoisseur of hand weapons. The world now knew that the arms store belonged to Dave Donaldson. It was then announced publicly the exact location of his workplace. The response of social media was akin to an explosion at a nuclear reactor. The response from the party to all this, sounded as weak as a ten-year old's first attempt at making a cup of tea. It regretted the arsenal's existence, and called for restraint and political maturity. I couldn't see it having much effect on people's opinions. Twenty buglers in one resonant call, five corporals yelling "Charge!", four hundred cavalry officers beginning to gallop, and at the back, a little drummer boy warns of the danger of riding horses too quickly.

Vic's opinion was rather less ornate: 'Well, that's going to achieve fuck-all!'

As rescue parties went, the pair of us seemed somewhat a little inadequate. My concerns multiplied, when we heard that the BBC had learnt from reliable sources that Dave Donaldson had been planning a massacre in the hope that it would provoke a second revolution. Following this revelation, there were numerous clips of Donaldson in full flow demanding that the NWC could only be a transitional instrument of freedom and would have to be replaced in the very near-future. Several so-called experts, who no doubt had studied anarchism at Cambridge University, were painting lurid accounts of the bloodbaths which were being planned. It was political porn for the middle classes.

We reached Donaldson's workplace and, thankfully, it looked that, at least for the moment, the only crowds in the area were either people commuting to and from Euston Station or those enjoying a summer's early evening beverage. Vic wasn't convinced that it would remain like that for too long. I agreed. But then, surely, he wouldn't be so stupid as to hang around here? I had tried to call him but had been unable to get through.

Cole nodded towards a group of men in tight tee-shirts, standing legs apart by the bus stop opposite, and flashed them an anxious and appraising look. Being now quite literate in post-grad Vic Cole body language studies, I guessed that it wasn't from being overly impressed by their muscles. Something about them bothered her, and it wasn't which gym they attended.

She leant over and opened the Aladdin's Cave which passed for her glove compartment and pulled out first a cap boasting a prominent party badge, then a folded green waterproof. I couldn't see why she needed either. Rain was not forecast, it was too hot for such a cap and we had our virtual ID, so who needed a badge? I didn't say a word – she'd have her reasons.

We walked at a steady speed; quick enough for such an emergency but not so quick as to draw attention. That is until we entered the large foyer, where she burst into a sprint. I did my best to keep up, but no Olympic team would be inviting me for trials just yet. By the time I had managed to catch her up, she had passed the evening receptionists and was standing by the lifts. Her visual ID was still floating in front of them, still being read. Seeing the baffled look on their faces, I couldn't be sure if Vic had been let through, or had just invaded the place. The lift doors opened, and with a definite air of conspiracy. she whispered, 'I've asked them to ring up if anyone comes looking for Donaldson.'

They closed and she barked his floor number. That was the only sound either of us uttered. There was no need for anything else. We both knew why we were here and what needed to be done. Maybe it was nerves or maybe excitement, but she looked like some Edwardian bookie with her cap jauntily at an angle on her head, whilst she kept tapping her palm with the rolled-up waterproof.

As the lift doors opened, we jumped out, braced for furious violently-inclined comrades. But it was immediately obvious that the inhabitants of the hive were buzzing elsewhere in town. The floor was deserted. Computer screens appeared to be the only thing moving. That and the man himself. Donaldson was at the far side, busily consuming a large pizza. He turned around as soon as he heard the doors open and looked quizzically at us. No doubt he was hoping that here was someone he could talk to. But like the expression that an infant has when they're opening a present from Santa, hoping it's the season's new footie kit, but it turns out to be six pairs of brown socks from Grandad, it went from expectation to surprise to disappointment. Melted cheese hung from his mouth. Obviously, he wasn't overly excited to see us. There wasn't much chance of a slice of the pizza, then. That was probably just as well, because despite a growing hunger, I wasn't sure that I wanted anything near my mouth, which his bony fingers had touched. Cuffing the cheese aside, he asked, 'What are you two doing here?'

A shadow of wariness crossed his face. From his eyes, I could tell he was calculating the possible reasons for our dramatic entrance. Judging by the fact that he wasn't clutching the pizza box to his heart, he had discounted that we were peckish. From the way we had jumped out the lift, we might conceivably be auditioning for the next Batman and Robin movie. Neither of us had shouted "Holy anarchist arms hauls!", and I was far too old to be a boy anything, let alone wonder, so it couldn't be that. It was odd though, he looked genuinely discombobulated to see us, which suggested he didn't know that his illegal arms cache had been discovered. Whatever emotions were struggling to appear amongst his facial hair, fear wasn't amongst them. Surely, if he was aware that his little secret was out then he would have assumed we were here to arrest him. But then, if he had known that his workplace was now plastered across the net, he wouldn't actually be here. So obviously he hadn't been watching the news. Nor, it would seem, had any of his friends; otherwise, they would have contacted to tell him of his new-found celebrity. I was intrigued as to how he could have missed all the hullabaloo.

'Well?' he demanded. He was now moving towards us. Unfortunately, any feeling of authority was somewhat diminished by the fact that he was limping. His face may be exuding the desire to be striding towards us, but he certainly wasn't.

He saw me looking and jumped to the conclusion that I was in some way interested in the cause of his discomfort. Though, obviously he couldn't jump anywhere. 'I've always had a weak knee, had it since I was a kid, congenital I think. It gets worse from time to time. It's flared up now.'

Probably from hauling boxes of rifles around. The thing was, I wasn't interested in the microscopic slightest, as to why he was limping; just that it was going to slow us down.

Each time he lolloped nearer, particles of pizza base pinged off his half-open shirt, which displayed a chest resembling a xylophone. His ribs poking through his pale skin.

Vic said nothing but strode up to, and then past him, towards the windows. He looked at her in total confusion. His garlic bread was probably safe, but he was now definitely wondering what brought us here. 'If you want Cathy Smith, she's, er, not in,' he spluttered.

Reaching the window, Vic pulled one of the cream bog-standard office blinds aside and looked down at the streets below.

We probably didn't have that much time, so I got straight to the point. 'You haven't been following the news, then?' Him being a news junkie, I would have assumed that he'd be watching it 24/7 and so by now be fully aware that he was the lead item.

It wasn't the response which he had been expecting. Taken aback for the moment, and probably fearing that the tyrannical party had instituted current affairs spot checks, he mumbled a reply, 'No. I think there's a localised cyber-attack, all television and net channels are down. My phone's down as well.'

I looked at mine and saw that all coverage was blanketed. That explained it; they wanted to catch him unawares. He would be happily here at work, all alone, enjoying the novelty of actually *being* at work, when the mob arrived baying for blood – *his* blood. 'You working by yourself tonight?' I asked. It was stating the bleedin' obvious, but I asked it all the same.

He frowned and stared at the empty desks. 'Cathy's supposed to be in; I was certain that it was her shift. There should be a few others as well, but, er, it appears that it's just me.' He laughed nervously. 'Probably having a social down the Railway Arms and not told me.'

I looked at Vic. Neither of us thought there was a piss-up at the local. She pointed downwards at the street. 'People are starting to congregate.'

He looked at her. 'Who are?'

'Dave,' I said loudly, pulling his attention back to me. 'Listen very carefully and don't waste my time by asking questions, and certainly don't bother denying anything, because we really don't have the time.' He went to open his mouth. 'Don't! Not a word! Not a fucking single word.' I slapped one of the old anti-pandemic virus screens hard. It vibrated, making a noise like a cheap thunder sheet. Startled, he closed his mouth. I wasn't known for machismo. My fingertips stung, but I didn't wince – that would rather spoil the affect. I spoke quickly and firmly. 'Your secret store of weapons is presently the main item across all news channels.' He held his hand up and was about to protest. 'No!' I shouted. I looked across at Vic, who shook her head and pointed towards the street below. 'I told you not to interrupt. Please don't insult our intelligence. We've seen it. We've visited your little toy cupboard. You know, the ones in crates, hidden behind the pile of furniture, including that lovely violin.' His eyes widened. 'We got past your CCT, and the little strips of sticky paper and the security dust on the floor. We've known about it for days. Your problem...'

His jaw dropped. Thankfully, all the food had been digested.

'Quickly, Pete,' Vic shouted. 'There's quite a crowd gathering now and I really don't like the look of those men by the bus stop. They look more paramilitary than passengers.'

I did as commanded: '...*Our* problem, is that the narrative being sold is that you were going to conduct a mass uprising, with massacres on every street corner, so as to destabilise the NWC.' He went to speak. 'It doesn't matter whether that's true or not, what matters is that's the story which is being repeated.' I paused and then looked around dramatically. 'Aren't you wondering why you're alone in this office, the only person at work?'

He didn't answer but just stared at me. We didn't have time to debate the matter. My phone went ping as if to underline the point. The phones were back online. Immediately, I rang Cathy Smith, putting her on 3D visual. She accepted the format and answered. She was wearing a red sarong and was sitting in her garden. 'Pete? Hi.' She leant forward and peered at me. 'Are you in my office? What are you doing there?'

I didn't answer. 'Question is – why aren't you, Cathy? Dave, he's here with us, thought you were due in. Presently the workforce consists of him, me, Vic and a pizza.'

Her tone got defensive. 'I got a text from the management committee not to come in as they had enough people rostered. Aren't they there? Dave, does he know about...I've been trying to...'

I didn't want to have this conversation lasting a second longer than it needed to. 'All personal communications have been down. There's not a soul in except for Dave. Could you ring the others to see if they got the same call and then ring me back? Thanks. Bye.'

I didn't wait for a reply and hung up.

Vic had now unholstered her gun and was staring down at what was happening on street level with obvious concern. 'They will have,' she muttered. Looking back at us, she asked, 'Dave, apart from the lift, is there another way out?'

'Er, yes, there's the fire escape. Why?' His eyes were saucers as he stared at her.

'Are you armed?' she snapped.

'Er, no, er, it's not allowed,' he garbled. 'Is it? Armed workers are anti-social, well, except for certain workers.'

Good God! Dave Donaldson has metamorphosed into a responsible citizen who wouldn't dream of breaking the NWC gun laws! Not so much the pinnacle of ironies; more the Mount Everest.

A phone went. It wasn't mine. It was Vic's. She answered it, and spoke rapidly. Even though it was audio only, and I could only hear one side, I gathered that it was the receptionist downstairs. My guess was that she had been joined by a group of people who were expressing a real desire to come upstairs, and it wasn't because they fancied an apprenticeship in street cleaning. Plainly, she was starting to get worried. She wasn't the only one. Vic told her to not put herself in danger but to delay them if she possibly could.

Before she finished, a second call went off. This one was for me; it was from Cathy. As I had expected, all the office had received the same text. I turned and faced him. 'Then it looks exactly what we thought – Dave, my friend, you've been set up to be murdered. There's a crowd down there who are furious – furious with you in particular. They know about your gun collection and have been given a line of what you planned to do with them. They're stirred up and looking to tackle you about it. And here you are – all on your lonesome.'

Cathy was outraged. 'Comrades wouldn't just go up there and kill him in cold blood, no matter what the provocation. We're not animals.'

Vic sharply left the window, and was making her way to us. 'They wouldn't, but a group of mercenary thugs embedded in the crowd might. And I think they're on the way. Cathy, ring...'

Suddenly the connection with Smith was cut and her image disappeared. I looked at my phone and saw no signal. Vic did the same and hers was down too.

Then, like Lazarus, mine returned and lit up once more, coming back to life. A text message arrived. It simply said **J.** No sender's ID could be seen. A second later an **e** came through. Again, no ID appeared and no return message was allowed. Then came **r**, then a **u**. Letters came through each second. I was hypnotised. Despite the pressing time, I sat waiting for the telecommunications Scrabble to finish. After the **m,** I put them together. Not that I needed to, because by the **s** I knew what these were spelling. Donaldson in mortal danger and I get sent the word **Jerusalem**. A feeling spread like a pair of wings across my back – it was fear.

'Jerusalem,' I muttered, looking up and deep into Vic's eyes. I threw my phone in the nearest paper bin and told them to do the same. Vic didn't need to ask why, and with a throw which a baseball pitcher would have been proud of, launched it into one ten metres away. The noise of it hitting the metal bottom, shook Donaldson out of his stunned coma.

'What? Why?' he mumbled.

There was no time to explain what Jerusalem meant or why I had just had it spelt out to me. I did, though, need him to get rid of his phone as soon as possible. One thing was sure, and that was that the message didn't come with a heart emoji. What I did explain, as quickly as I could, to Dopey Dave, was that we'd been hacked and it wasn't beyond the realms of possibility that we were being tracked. That would explain why they seemed be in control of events and seemed to be able to double guess every move we made. Donaldson, though, didn't make the slightest move. He just gawped at us. Vic grabbed his phone, and showed us once more what a fine throwing arm she had. 'Move!' she yelled.

It had the desired effect – he pointed to a door at the end of the floor, just by Cathy's desk. Reaching it, Vic took an impressive jump, and grabbed hold of the Fire Exit sign and tore it off the wall. She was showing off now. It was some alternative pentathlon. Stuffing it in her pocket, she opened the door and scanned the stairs with her gun.

Despite, crouching down to make herself as small as possible a target, and holding her arms out straight ahead of her, she still managed to move quickly down the stairwell. Not so, Donaldson who followed, shuffling down, continually complaining about his knee. She gave him a look which was deadlier than anything else he might face. She hissed through gritted teeth, 'They're in the lift coming upstairs. When they get there and see we've left, they will guess that we've taken the stairs. I counted four doors on your floor. If we're lucky, then they won't know which one leads to the fire exit and will check each one. Even then, that doesn't give us much time. We're talking a couple of minutes at most. Put up with the pain in your dodgy legs or you risk being in a whole lot more after they've finished with you!'

Personally, I thought he wouldn't be in any pain after they had finished with him, because he'd be dead, but now wasn't the time to discuss analogies.

Nor did he. There was a whimper but not a reply. To be fair, he did increase his speed, but it was hardly rapid. Vic moved forwards with both hands grasping her gun, dramatically swinging around every corner, just in case one of them was coming up to join us. I covered our rear. Since I was bricking it, it was appropriate. Pointing my gun upwards, I edged step by step backwards, trying my best to keep my balance and not to fall. Spread-eagled on top of Dave Donaldson wasn't the heroic way I had envisaged my death would be.

Even with Donaldson trying to go as quickly as he could, we were still moving worryingly slow. With each step, considering he probably weighed less than a paper weight, he made a loud thump. As light as he might be, it sounded to me as loud as a sonic boom. Then came a grimace and a grunt. To my ears, they didn't need to check each of the doors, they'd just hear the cacophony of noise he was making. I urged on every movement he made, willing him to speed up.

For what seemed like an eternity, it was clump, grimace, grunt, clump, grimace, grunt. Then I heard two voices above us. Luckily, we were near the bottom, and temporarily, we were hidden by the turns of the stairs, but it wouldn't be that way for long. Finally, we found ourselves on the ground floor, with two doors and an extinguisher for company. She pointed at the doors and whispered to Donaldson, 'Which one?'

He crossed his eyebrows, musing, 'One exits directly out onto the street and one leads into the reception.'

She glanced upwards, before growling, 'Which one to the street? We need to avoid the crowd at the front. You're the number one hate figure there. I think it would be an idea to give them a miss. So, *which door*?' In reply, he made various noises which were impossible to interpret, before scratching his beard and pointing to the one in front of us.

Without wasting a second, she thrust the fire escape bar down. The warm air hit us as it opened and she ran out and straight into 100kg of muscle. Instantly, she reacted and threw a punch at his throat. A ghastly choking sound spat out of his mouth. He didn't have time to register what had just happened, let alone make a counter-move, because she followed it up with two more punches, this time both to his nose. Losing his balance, he fell back from the triple hits, but she didn't pause for a second, and swinging her right foot in an arch, her foot hit his jaw with force. He crashed to the floor. Then, just to prove that her leg was as accurate as her arm, she kicked his face like I'd seen rugby players do converting tries.

Donaldson was clearly shocked – stammering and stuttering, trying to say something.

'He was one of those at the bus stop,' she explained, slightly out of breath.

I shrugged my shoulders. 'Fare evader.' Then started to move in the direction of her car.

Vic snapped, 'No – they'll be watching it, probably tagged anyway. Come on, let's go this way!'

Then came the moment for the waterproof. She unwrapped it and hung it over her right arm in an attempt to hide her gun. Gangster movies from the 1940s used to hiding their guns in their pockets. Personally, I always thought it made them look aroused. There wasn't much in the way of suggestive sexual power with Vic holding a luminous green waterproof around her arm, with a barrel pointing out, but it was about as ineffective.

Running would draw attention to us, so we walked quickly. I hoped the fact that we'd just left a man, with the look of an off-duty bouncer, unconscious on the road with blood spouting out of his nose, wouldn't be too noticeable either. There was also the problem that our bearded companion had his ugly mug plastered all over the media, so anyone could recognise him as the erstwhile leader of the second revolution. Vic had an idea about that as well. She tossed him the cap and then a pair of sunglasses and told him to wear them. This was desperate. His beard and long scar were pretty identifiable. There were so many straws being grasped that it resembled a milkshake convention. He looked at the party badge and pulled a face. If he complained or made some petty sectarian point, we would march him back to his assassins. But he didn't and just pulled it down onto his head.

I wasn't sure that a cap three sizes too small for him, rammed on his head, would fool any MI5 agents in the area. We moved quickly, weaving in and out of the pedestrians. It was impossible to tell which of them were here to demonstrate, to commute or were just off for a pint, so we were wary of them all. Behind us, I still couldn't see anyone.

A few minutes later and we had made it far as Euston Station with no obvious sign that we were being followed. But still, everyone was taking on the stature of possible killers. That young couple for example, lying on the brown grass, looked to be just enjoying a romantic moment, but one could have a flick knife for all we knew.

'Bus or train?' I asked, feeling relieved that we were in such a transport hub.

'Neither.'

'Tram?'

'No.'

We were several blocks from his office, and Vic was slowing down, but I didn't have another chance to play transport trumps. Vic asked Donaldson if there was a community car-pool anywhere near. I shrewdly surmised that it was a car which she wanted. Still clearly not too sure what was happening, he mumbled that there was one around the corner.

She looked at me. 'We can't risk public transport and we need to get him away from here and to safety, as quickly as possible.' Personally, I just thought that she was averse to travelling with other people.

'I agree, but Vic, if you're thinking of hiring one of them, then we have a problem – there's a charge, and we have just left our phones up in the office.'

A pained expression distorted her face, and she frantically looked around. For what I couldn't say. I doubted very much whether it was feasible that we could waltz into a phone shop and purchase one. We really didn't have the time to go in, choose the style, coverage and chat about what colour. Seeing a young woman standing on the corner, wearing both an anti-social behaviour steward's armband and a party badge, gave me an idea. The steward had just finished talking to woman pushing a double pushchair, when I approached her, sporting my most wonderful smile.

I began to introduce myself but she stopped me mid-flow: 'I know who you are, comrade.' Then looking at both Vic and the not-so-heavily disguised Donaldson, added meaningfully, 'I know all three of you. The local council sent me here to help prevent any trouble, so if there's anything I can do to help, I will.'

Now wasn't the time to question how effective she had been, bearing in mind what we were in the middle of. Instead, I explained that we needed a car, and we needed her phone to pay for it. Whether it was her political commitment, my charm or that she was just bored standing there on the corner, I didn't know, but she didn't protest. She reached into her back-jean pocket and slipped it out. I held out my hand, but Vic was too quick and snatched it. 'Comrade, could we also make a call?'

'Of course, comrade Cole.'

'Thank you. Could you tell me your name?'

'Ingrid.'

'Thanks, Ingrid, do your friends call you by that, or is it shortened, or have you a nickname?'

She looked at Vic with a puzzled expression. She wasn't the only one who was wondering why we were wasting time with social niceties. But she replied that yes, her friends called her Ingrid. Well, I was glad that had been sorted out. We were standing here, with an anarchist who wanted to take arms against us, whilst a group of hired thugs was chasing the three of us. Meanwhile, Vic was making friends.

'And where do you work, Ingrid?'

Good grief, was Vic asking her out on a date? Donaldson looked at me, wondering what this was all about. I couldn't tell him; I had no idea myself.

'I work at the dermatology department at the Paddington Hospital, why?'

Vic didn't answer her, but turned her attention to me. She looked worried. I surmised that it wasn't that she was concerned about coming into contact with someone who might give her a skin complaint.

'We need to warn Roijin that they've breached our security.' She started to type rapidly.

*Hi Roij,*

*Thought you'd want to know I'm outside Dave Donaldson's work – YK the anarchist you've been investigating. (Don't worry I've told nobody about it in Padd Derm.) It's Ingrid BTW, in case you didn't recognise the number – had to get a new phone – old one RIP. I'm here on anti-social control duty. Not looking forward to it if gets nasty. There's an angry mob here. Not sure the party's calls for calm are being that effective. Better go. Be good to meet up.*

*Ingrid.*

She pressed send. 'Roijin will understand. Ingrid, there's a car-pool nearby, isn't there?'

'Yes. Just up there, on the left,' she replied.

'Good. Come on.'

Once more, I took up my position of guarding the rear, looking around for anyone who might be following us. To my relief, I still couldn't see anyone. We tapped Ingrid's phone onto the car hire post and returned it, with appreciative thanks. Having done her duty, Ingrid left. We went to choose the car. I offered some suggestions. I feared that she'd go for a bright yellow Porsche with flashing lights on top, which might be her idea of cool, but would stand out like a Belisha beacon. Thankfully, she chose a nondescript family estate.

She got behind the wheel, whilst Dave and myself got in the back. Donaldson couldn't return to his place. Mine was also out of the question, they knew the address and, in any case, after an hour of his company, either I or Red would kill him ourselves. Twenty minutes into the journey, I guessed where we were heading. Beside me, Donaldson had pulled himself out of his shocked state and was keeping up a constant flow of verbiage. He alternated between outraged demands to know where we were taking him and denials that he had done anything wrong. The conversation was one-sided, as neither Vic nor I could be bothered to engage with him. If Vic was anything like me, she was concerning herself more about what the situation was telling us, than what Davey-boy was wittering on about.

Finally, I had had enough and asked him about his phone he'd left in his arms lock up.

'What phone?' he said.

'The one we found hidden by the boxes of guns.'

'Don't know what you're talking about. You forced me to leave my phone back there in the office.'

I looked at his face. It was the picture of incomprehension. I believed him. He had no idea what I was talking about.

The traffic in Brent Cross wasn't too bad and we made good time. Turning off the A41, we headed towards the Walwyn Estate. Built in the 2030s it had previously been named after some Etonian prat, but post-revolution it had been renamed. It was known to be one of the fiercest red estates in London. The standing joke was that the residents who weren't party members had tried to form a football team, but had only managed a five-a-side. Hardly Wildean wit, but it told you the political affiliation of the estate. Taking a sharp right, we entered it. Residents were having picnics on its artificially green slopes. Knowing this place as I did, I would bet twenty Fists that word was already out of the arrival of an unfamiliar car. Four storeys high, it was made up of small courtyards and green open spaces, linked by raised cycle and walkways. The colour red was everywhere – banners, flags, fists, pennants and lights; contrasting sharply with the pristine clean white of the buildings. It hadn't always been like this. Without funding to maintain it, the place had quickly plummeted from award-winning design to slum. That is, until the residents took control.

Skirting around a game of rounders, we parked. Getting out of the car, I could feel dozens of eyes spying on us from the raised walkways. The community spirit here was better than any CCT could ever hope to be. That was why we had asked for Phan Bien to be put under their care and protection. Even the SAS wouldn't stand a chance of getting in here.

By the time Vic had got out from the driver's seat, we had been joined by a welcoming committee. Four men and three women walked up to us. The first spoke: 'Well, well, we are honoured. A personal appearance by none other than Pete Kalder!'

I hugged him, his firm chest pressing onto mine. 'Adam, great to see you – you old bastard!'

He roared with laughter and turned to his mates. 'See how the bureaucrats treat us rank-and-file? Me – resident of the Walwyn for fifteen years, chair of the estate committee, member of the NWC Defence Corps – and he calls me a bastard!'

They all laughed, even more so when a middle-aged woman added, 'Well, he's got a point, hasn't he?'

I had known Adam Hardy for donkey's years – droves of donkeys. He had worked on building sites all his life and been a member since he was in his early teens. He was approximately the same age as me, perhaps a year or two younger, and was one of our most experienced members. He was also one of the most respected.

'You here for Phan? Hope not – we've kind of got used to having her around and I think she likes it here. I expect it's nice for her to get away from you lightweights, and be with us real people, the real working class!' When he saw Vic, he released me and grinned. 'Good to see you too, comrade. You here to make sure he doesn't get his hands dirty?'

She smiled. 'Oh, there's never a danger of that. No, comrade, I'm afraid we are here to ask another favour...'

With perfect timing, Dave Donaldson's lanky leg poked out from the back seat and he emerged still with Cole's cap perched on his head. Hardy looked at him and clenched his jaw. The merriment instantly stopped. The others stared at him with looks which could not be remotely described as being affectionate. This lot had certainly been watching the news.

I spoke first. 'Obviously, you know Dave. Adam, there's been an attempt on his life.' Before anyone had a chance to voice an opinion on whether that was necessarily a bad thing, I explained, 'This has all been choreographed to create friction between the AF and us. They want to murder Dave and pin it on the party.' I didn't have to clarify who the "they" were, but I knew as disciplined as he might be, this was asking a lot of him and the residents here.

Adam chewed his lip and folded his arms. His biceps tightened, before he replied very carefully, 'These guns of his, that they're reporting, don't exist, then?'

In all the rush we had forgot to tell Donaldson to keep his gob shut, so confronted with a group of people, he couldn't help himself. 'Well, sibling, I can explain...'

'Shut up, Donaldson!' Vic snapped.

'We want him alive and unharmed, Adam... but we might look the other way if you have to give him a slap,' I added with a grin. He laughed again. Donaldson didn't, but then he didn't say anything more either. I conceded that it wasn't all totally fiction. 'It's true in part about the arms store, but it was for defensive purposes, in case the party turned on the AF. We know that wouldn't happen, but there's some in the AF who have genuine fears that we would. We've known about it for a while. Like I said, Adam, this is all designed to set us against each other.'

He thought for a second, before saying, 'Fair enough. Come on. Let's see Phan.' He nodded and gave a thumbs up towards a group of children who had just joined us on bikes. They returned the gesture and rode off.

'The local radar?' I said, seeing them ride up the ramp to the higher-level walkways.

He grinned. 'Like to see anyone hack them.'

We followed him, Vic starting up a conversation immediately. His loud voice echoed around the concrete. I heard him ask her if it was true that she used to be a cop. When she replied that it was, he guffawed and started to talk about the run-ins he'd had in the past with the law. Shaking his head in disbelief, he said that he couldn't believe we'd have coppers in the party.

She smiled. 'Nah, Adam, nor did I.'

I walked slowly with Dave behind them. Surprisingly, he wasn't complaining. In fact, he wasn't saying a word. I took the opportunity to tell him exactly what was going to happen: 'You're going to stay here for a while. They'll look after and protect you. You'll be safe. You're free, to a certain extent, to move around the estate, but you're to contact no-one and to avoid social media. The security services won't know you're here and we want to keep it that way. It's unlikely that even if they do, they would launch an attack. They want you dead, but they want it to look like we did it. That wouldn't be the case if they attacked the estate. Let's face it, we're unlikely to attack one of our own red estates, are we? And there's no way they could infiltrate here, not without attracting attention.'

He looked behind at the people following us. I explained, 'They're NWC Defence Corps too. They also, like Adam, happen to live here. They're solid revolutionaries and loyal – unquestionably loyal. They'll keep you safe. *If* you do as they say.'

He replied in a voice which was barely above a whisper, 'You think they'll try again?'

I looked at him. He had a haunted look about him, which I couldn't really blame him for. Quite obviously the truth of his predicament was dawning on him. 'I don't honestly know, Dave, but it's best not to risk it. I'm sorry. I don't think it'll be too long, their plan only had a limited life-span, they'll have another one. We'll contact the AF and tell them you're safe. Obviously, we won't say where you are, just in case.'

'In case we've been infiltrated?' He sadly shook his head. 'God, Kalder, it must be shit doing your job. You end up suspecting everyone.'

'Yep, pretty much so.'

Adam and Vic had gone into one of the flats. We followed them in and saw Phan Bien with a plate of salad on her lap. She was in her familiar linen trousers. Her black hair was tied up into a ponytail. She put the plate by her side and jumped up. 'Vic! Pete! Is it safe to leave...?' She saw Donaldson and understanding crossed her face. 'Ah, so that's it. Dave, mate, I heard all about it? What were you thinking? You total arsehole! How could you do that!'

'It's not what they said, it was...'

'I don't care!' she snapped. 'You bloody fool. You've friends in the party, for God's sake!'

He didn't answer but just looked sheepish.

She closed her eyes. 'But that's for the NWC to sort out.' She didn't pursue the matter, and softened her tone. 'You look wiped out. Fancy a cuppa?' She reached out a hand and stroked his arm.

'I'd love one. Thanks, Phan.'

She took him into the kitchen, with a fraternal arm around his waist. For the first time in quite a while, he visibly relaxed and smiled. He even tentatively laid a palm on her back. It could well be that the plan to force a wedge between us, but by having these two share a hiding place, might just end up making the opposite happen. Who knew what strange things happened nowadays.

I raised an eyebrow and looked at Adam. 'They say he grows on you.'

'Will he be here long enough to?'

I ran my hand through my hair, and briefly closed my eyes. 'I sincerely hope it won't be for too long. It's a precaution more than anything. I don't think they'll spend too much time and effort in killing either Phan or Donaldson, they're a means to an end, it's not that it's vitally important to eliminate either of them.'

Vic agreed. 'They won't be pinning everything on killing either of those two. Bien and Donaldson are small fry.'

Adam looked at the kitchen with a doubtful look on his face.

'We do appreciate it, Adam.'

He brushed away my thanks. 'It's no hassle whatsoever, comrades. Phan's in here with us and we can put Donaldson in a flat along the way. The Macedos have a spare room.'

I could hear the pair of them chatting away. I could even hear the occasional laugh. I wondered if he had a split personality. Affable and friendly to many; to me – a prat.

I changed the subject because something Adam had said on the way here, had given me an idea. 'Adam, what's your take on Noah Walker?'

He snorted. 'Not a great fan to be honest, Pete. Loves the limelight and will do most things to get him centre stage to be in it. Bit like him really.' He directed his nose towards the kitchen. 'But I guess a revolution takes all sorts. I have to say that I fundamentally disagree with his position on strengthening the state. My view is that it if we do that then we risk the state becoming a type which we don't want – the state might get stronger, but the revolution is fatally weakened.'

'Trust him?'

He looked at me hard; his eyes analysing my question. His reply was careful and measured: 'I've no reason not to. I've never particularly seen eye to eye with him; we often seem to be on the opposite side of an argument. But I gather from the fact that you asked the question, that you've doubts. Seems that the social media gossip has a grain of truth to it, then. But to be fair, I've never seen anything which would suggest that he's a renegade.'

Vic leaned towards him, as if she was going to share a secret. 'What do you know about him? Personally, I mean?'

Shrugging, he replied, 'Not a great deal. Made his name in the Small Firms Strike, from Southampton. Since then, if there's an industrial dispute or campaign, he's been involved in it. You can't criticise his level of commitment. There's long been rumours that he's desperate to get on the Central Committee. The way things are looking, he might just do so. Why? What...'

At that point, Bien and Donaldson returned with a cup of tea each, and Donaldson with a handful of chocolate digestives clasped in his hand. She was giggling at what sounded very much like a retelling of our escape. It was far more comic than I remembered, but it was amusing her. She joined in, telling him of her own journey here. They both stopped when they remembered that we were still in Adam's lounge.

Seeing us, Phan changed the subject. 'I was just saying to Dave that he'll be fine here. I won't lie and say that I wouldn't prefer to be back home. I've got tons of stuff to do, which can't be done here.' She stopped and gave him a meaningful look. 'You'll feel the same, but it shouldn't be for too long and there's plenty to do around the estate. They've organised it well; it's like the independent state of Walwyn here.'

He nodded and swallowed a digestive.

A young voice called out from the door, 'Comrades!' We all turned to see a boy on a bike at the door. 'There's another one. Says she's expected.' He described what she looked like, which prompted Vic to look pleased in the extreme and inform us all that it was our lift home. He then sped off to pass on the message to the estate network.

Whilst we were waiting for our visitor, the atmosphere began to relax as Adam entertained everyone with amusing anecdotes about various times when he and I had worked together. For some inexplicable reason, everyone in the room seemed to find them funny – Vic especially. Quite possibly, because they appeared to be mainly at my expense. But then Adam did have a way of making even the most mundane story sound hysterical. By the time the visitor entered the flat, my sides were hurting from laughter.

Roijin took one look at all the merriment and with a mock sigh said, 'And I thought there was an emergency.'

Her arrival was a sign for us to leave the warm family feel of Adam's home and get back to work. Rather surprisingly, Donaldson hadn't made any complaint and even appeared to be looking forward to it. The mask of antagonism had slipped, and the human face beneath it had started to show. Or perhaps it was simply that he realised that the choice basically boiled down to making the best of this, or getting beaten to death by paid counter-revolutionaries.

Sibling Donaldson also needed to be making as many friends as he could right now, because, even assuming that he survived this, he still had a few questions to answer. The main one being – why did he have a gun collection? Now, many people have hobbies; I have an uncle who makes model airplanes; I knew some folks who collect stamps and others who paint watercolours. These are harmless, ones which no-one would object to. Stealing machine guns and rifles from the NWC and storing them up for a possible future civil war didn't quite fall into that category. It wasn't like a squabble over whether the markings on a model Spitfire were accurate or if the perspective of a Cornish harbour scene was correct.

Roijin took out two phones and slid one each to us. 'Got the text, Vic, or should I say, Ingrid.' She chuckled. 'We've scanned all our phones and software again and you're right, they're riddled with spyware. Odette is in shock that they got in without her knowing – she'll soon learn that today's tech wizard is tomorrow's amateur. For the moment, we're going through the motions of using them, just to keep them guessing for a while. Asher's reclaimed your phones. The crowd's still there, by the way, but he didn't see those blokes you described. Odette's taken mine for a ride. They've been playing with us, so we thought we'd do the same. Oh, and guess what? Moments after you sent the text, the dermatology department at the Paddington Hospital received a call enquiring after an Ingrid who worked there.' Roijin gave Vic a mock salute.

'What's the latest score from the match of the day – the party versus the AF?' I asked, not being part of the mutual appreciation society.

'Both sides are calling for restraint. There's been a few minor confrontations but thankfully nothing serious. Jackie's due to make a press statement in an hour's time; rumour is, that she will be accompanied by a leading AF member.'

'Okay, it would be useful to see that,' I replied, feeling both relieved at the news, but somewhat disappointed that she had left it so long to make a statement. 'What about Noah Walker? He said his two pennies worth, yet?'

'He's made statements on social media echoing the calls for peace, but as of yet, no physical appearance.'

'He will,' I sneered. 'Whether he's the person we're after or not, he's not going to miss this golden opportunity to push his agenda.'

'Something you said a few days ago, Pete, struck a chord with me. When we were looking into Dave Donaldson you said we should analyse what he was doing at key moments. I thought we should do likewise with Walker. Seems, he was very active indeed, working for the East London Defence Zone. What's interesting is that one of the days he was working tirelessly for the cause was the day that the Workers' Hall was attacked. He was at the ELDZ control office at the very time of the attack.' She stopped, and looked at each of us in turn.

A light went on in Vic's head. 'The attack came from the east! The ELDZ is the zone which borders the Central Defence Zone *to the east*. It will have passed through it to reach the Workers' Hall. What was Walker's role there?'

With a voice so heavy with emphasis that it was as if gravity had quadrupled, she replied, 'Aerial protection.'

'Didn't alarm bells go off when he failed to notice four US Air Force bomber drones cross his patch on the way to destroy the NWC? The fact that they had US Air Force plastered all over them would have been a clue that they weren't tourist pleasure drones.'

Roijin looked at me. 'He claimed that he'd been a victim of a simultaneous cyber-attack and his monitoring systems were down. Others said the same thing, so everyone just accepted it, but the thing is, when it was investigated afterwards, whilst they found cyber-interference, there was no clear indication as to where it'd come from. The NWC techies couldn't locate its external point of entry into the system. That was odd, but with everything going on and the revolution fighting for its life, there wasn't the time or the inclination, to look into it further.'

Vic spoke: 'Only the leaders of the NWC parties had advance notice of the evacuation of the NWC delegates. He wasn't on the CC so he wouldn't have known. So as far as he'd have known, they'd have been in full session.'

When asked what was the crucial ingredient for a successful revolution, Jackie Payne had replied – "luck". She had meant it only half-heartedly, but here she was quite right. If the evacuation had been a few hours later than it could have toppled the infant state.

I pushed back my chair, and got up. 'I think it's time we have a serious word with comrade Walker. Do we have any idea where he may be?'

Roijin looked at me and replied with a look which conveyed a full understanding that the answer might be surprising, but was nonetheless true, 'He's at the Shard.'

She had expected a reaction from me and she got one: 'What? Are you kidding?'

'No. Odette's been tracking him.'

'Do we know why he's there?'

'No.'

Vic got to her feet, prompting Roijin to do likewise. 'Whatever the reason, whether he is exactly what he says he is or not, it's not going to be a good one.'

# CHAPTER 35:
# SINEW OF OLD ENGLAND

I f the Shard produced loyalty cards, we'd be entitled to a free gift by now. Something more than just a bog-standard kettle, considering how many times we'd been there in the past few days. Not in my wildest dreams though, would have I ever imagined that we'd be there to meet Noah Walker. And if I had indeed had such dreams, I would have been straight to my therapist, pretty sharpish, wanting the pill-dosage upped.

It was still light when we arrived, but the summer's welcoming darkness was closing in fast. After politely pushing our way through a small but vocal protest outside, we were met by six Shard security guards. Obviously, the AF had beefed up their protection (or whatever the vegan equivalent is). Three held back, whilst the other half formed a wall in front of us. Two of them were our old friends who we'd met on the day of the drone attack. Both were still wearing their orange combat trousers, which I sincerely hoped had been washed since our last adventure. Instantly, they recognised Vic and I – who didn't nowadays? Giving us a broad, if conspiratorial, smile. 'Good evening, comrades. Great to see you. Should have guessed you'd be here for it.'

'It?' I asked.

He looked at me as if I'd asked a remarkably stupid question. 'Jackie Payne's media conference!' He looked at his watch. 'Should be starting pretty soon.'

I exchanged a stunned look with Roijin and Vic. 'That's here?' I stuttered.

His expression was one that you might have, if you were talking to a rather confused child. 'Yes, of course, comrades.'

I looked around the foyer, but couldn't see the normal gaggle of people who I would normally associate with Jackie. Being the head of state and having a bloody great target on her forehead, she was usually accompanied by a group of people carrying guns and/or notepads. Certainly, when she had last visited me at two in the morning, there had been consternation in my road. The arrival of a fleet of five dark-tinted vehicles had made our StreetChat group explode with theories.

'I don't see any of her people,' I said.

'She's upstairs, probably getting ready, and yeah, it's just her. She spoke to them outside for a little while, and then came in. Like, I said, not a single person with her. I suppose her security attachment is waiting outside somewhere. Friendly woman, I like her – down to earth – always very approachable; even chatted to us for quite a time. If anyone can get us through all this crap – she can.'

That made sense. It wouldn't have been a good look for her to march in here with gun-toting bodyguards.

'And the media are already up there,' he added.

I noted that he had called us comrades, which I took to signify some level of rapport between us. That was useful because it was something which we might well have to draw upon. Though, now wasn't the time to mention anything to him, because we needed to be up there as well.

'Do you know if Noah Walker is here?' I asked.

'Yeah, he's upstairs. Before that, he spent a good half an hour stirring them up.' He twitched his head towards the demo outside. 'Quite the opposite to Jackie. There's been no trouble, mind – just hot air, a few chants and posing, as far as I can see. Sorry to say that I don't like him. Seems more interested in fighting us than the ruling class. He went up with that Reyansh Anand fella.'

I hoped he was right about the crowd outside, but it was worrying that at an important press conference, specifically designed to calm the tempers of the two sides, both Anand and Walker were present. They were to calmness what a blowtorch was to frozen peas.

Jackie had told me to take the political lead, so here was another chance to do so. 'Comrades, I shouldn't tell you this and no doubt I will get in trouble for doing so.' I leant in towards him, as if sharing a secret. 'But the people we want to question are them. It's extremely concerning to us that those two are here at the exact same time as the press conference. There are, shall I say–' I didn't tap my nose but I might well have done, I was being so OTT hush, hush– 'questions to be asked about *some of their actions*, and what they might be planning. We need your help.'

That had surprised them. By directly involving the AF, we would not only allay the concerns of the security here, but also the other residents of the building. What we were planning on doing needed to be choreographed well, otherwise who knew how it might end. And if nothing else, the six of us would make for a nice publicity shot in the British Isles Revolutionary Scrapbook, that I could do in my dotage. The three of them and the three of us. Obviously, they'd have to be standing at the back, otherwise you wouldn't see us. We at least partially obscure the sight of those trousers of theirs. I was so close to them now, I could have stuck my tongue into his mouth. (Although, I'd have to stand on tip-toes.) 'We have reason to believe that one or both of them were behind the attack here.'

It wasn't just them who were surprised that I had just boldly implicated two leading party members in terrorism. Roijin and Victoria were gob-smacked. Publicly pointing the finger at Walker and Anand might not be in the counter-revolutionary prevention rulebook, but then, that had yet to be written. I thought by doing so, I had brought the security guards into both the warm embrace of confidentiality and the surprising knowledge that it was actually two high-profile party members that we were interested in. Whatever my colleagues might think, it had the desired effect, and the lead orange camouflage muscle-man shared a look with his mates. I couldn't read what it meant, but after a second, he nodded to his associates, and simply said, 'You two come with me, you three stay here. And you two comrades, you can keep your guns.'

When we arrived at the floor, I grimly smiled to myself. It was the same floor that the drone had raked with gunfire, last Thursday. By my side, I felt Vic involuntarily tense. No doubt, she was remembering that time too. The shattered panes of glass had been boarded up and now sported painted tributes to those who had died. The floor had bullet holes spread across it, making it look like Swiss Emmental cheese. Many of the tall upright columns had chunks ripped off. Bullets had shorn them of their confident machismo.

In front of them was a portable projector. In front of which was a large abstract painting. Walking past, I noticed an image of a severed arm reaching out for a sword and immediately recognised Pablo Picasso's Guernica. I grinned. That really was laying it on thickly. But it was an inspired choice; considering it had been painted as a reaction to the Fascist bombing of Guernica in the Spanish Civil War, the link with the drone attack was if not subtle, then at least appropriate. That said, a battered old

2D projector was hardly cutting-edge decor.

Noticing that I had been distracted, Vic tapped my elbows and flashed me a look. Seems now wasn't the time to be looking at art. I tried to look professional, and surveyed the room, with what I hoped was a cool, menacing eye. Or preferably, two of them. A neat, metal black stage had been erected with rows of green seats in front of it. To the left, was the reserved area for the virtual journalists. Behind them, were dozens of cameras of many types – hand-held, robot and mini-drone. Quite obviously, this was going to have a big audience, and that would make our job harder. How we were going to get to chat with Walker and Anand without causing an almighty fuss was going to be quite a challenge. But then, the bigger worry was what type of fuss were they themselves intending?

I looked around for Walker and saw him immediately. It would have been difficult not to with his dress sense. Bright yellow jeans clashed like titans against an orange un-ironed shirt. On his head was a blue beanie. Looking at him made me seriously wonder whether my suspicions were unfounded. Surely a MI5 agent would want to merge into the background and not draw attention to themselves? Unless, he was planning on going undercover in a Smarties factory, then he'd singularly fail to do that. Next to him was Anand, who was a complete contrast. Whereas Walker looked like a walking acid casualty, he was stiff, starched and wearing a crisply ironed uniform. He was the embodiment of military discipline to such a ridiculous extent that it was clichéd.

There were three people on the stage. Jackie was easy to spot. She was wearing a short white skirt and a matching white blouse, with an elegant white beret finishing off the look. She was standing with her hands on her hips, looking around at the journalists, waving and snatching brief conversations. With each, she was polite, charming and determinedly non-political. Opposite her was Art Parker from the Network 56 News, looking extremely dapper. He was also wearing white, but this time, a linen suit. A pale pink shirt added some colour. I possessed a very similar one, but sadly, I didn't have the tall, slim figure which Parker could boast, nor his chiselled jaw, or his smooth skin. Git. The fact that Parker was here meant that this was to be no simple media junket, but a high-profile interview. Parker would never allow himself to be put in the position of being merely a host. No, he was here for an exclusive interview and a chance to lord it over the other journalists present. The major questions would be from him and then he'd regally toss a few crumbs to the others, who would be sitting, watching up at him on the platform. As for the third, the AF member, they were partially hidden by Jackie's imperial stance.

It was whilst Vic was giving instructions to the security guards that Jackie caught sight of us. She looked at me first, then Vic, then Roijin, then the three guards. Aware that she had several pairs of journalists' eyes – and cameras – focussed on her, she hid her surprise at seeing us. I saw her mouth twitch, but nothing else. She didn't really need to, because that was enough. I could almost see the mental calculations being made in her brain. Whether they had been solved or not, I had no idea, but seconds later, she unclenched her jaw, changing it into a diplomatic smile, as she returned her gaze to the audience. When she sat down, she did so deliberately avoiding my gaze.

It was just then that the AF representative came into view. Now it was my turn to be surprised – it was Fiona Bailey! Our initial concern had centred on what might happen to Jackie, but now a second and stark possibility occurred to me – that Bailey could be the intended target. She had been here in the attack and had only been saved by the quick reactions of Vic Cole. I feared that she might be relying on them once more. Or they could want to take out the pair of them. I looked to Roijin, whose dark eyes managed somehow to acknowledge my thoughts. She blew her cheeks out just to underline her concern.

Bailey herself looked the epitome of tranquillity. She was tying up her long hair into a ponytail. Barefoot, with her long legs sprawled in front of her, orange shorts and tight vest, she looked readier for the beach than be the official spokesperson for the AF. Admiring the sunshine, rather than discussing the way forward, looked to be the most likely thing to be on her mind. With her sleepy eye closest to me, one could have been forgiven into thinking that she was about to nod off.

One of the security guards walked behind the stage and stood with his machine gun slung across his chest. His eyes were focussed like laser beams on Noah Walker and Reyansh Anand. Subtle he wasn't.

Roijin began to get herself into position and moved around the back, settling just a few rows behind Anand, and besides an auto-camera. Plainly, it gave her something to hide behind and use for cover if required. Vic skirted around the outside and then moved inwards. She was diagonally behind Walker. Putting it brutally, both sat in a position where they had a clear view – and aim – of the two men's heads. Simultaneously, they unbuttoned their jackets, not because of the temperature, but to allow easy access to their guns.

I found a chair and sat down. Whilst they were almost directly behind the two men, I was at a shallow angle to them. Our timing had been perfect because the second my bottom touched the chair, Parker started his introduction. As smooth as silk, his voice almost made love to the audience. Welcoming them all, he informed those watching around the world that he was coming live from the Shard, and into their homes. I thought to myself that there would be a fair few million who wouldn't mind him literarily being in their homes. He reminded them of the attack and the casualties from it, sombrely naming the victims.

After the briefest of a respectful pause, he went on to articulately describe the present situation and the latest news of the anti-AF demonstrations. 'Including the one outside where we are right now!' he said to add a bit more spice to the mix. Footage of the previous hour's scuffles around the workers' republic appeared above the stage. Viewers were then treated to film of party members hurling abuse at hastily barricaded windows. From there, we went to a previously recorded segment from within Dave Donaldson's arms store. The camera lovingly roamed around the assortment of weapons.

Whilst this was happening, Art Parker checked with his AI floor manager that everything was going okay. Having had it confirmed that it was, he returned to the live feed of us in the bar, the bar which was now his makeshift studio, or perhaps more accurately, his kingdom. You had to admit that he was bloody good at this. He then introduced Jackie and Fiona.

I took a closer look at who exactly was here. Other than Anand and Walker, I could see only three or four people who weren't working for the news channels. They, I recognised, were AF members. That was interesting. Clearly this was a media event, not a public meeting. The worrying question remained as to why Anand and Walker were here. They were having a little dispute at the moment. I could see Walker trying hard to suppress his anger and visibly turning puce, which it had to be said, clashed terribly with his clothes. Anand was shaking his head and palming his hand in the direction of Walker. Obviously, he was disagreeing with something that Walker was saying. Or he was trying to wave that shirt of Walker's away. They were whispering, but at one point, Art Parker did give them a stern look, indicating displeasure at the disturbance. That shut Walker up – the sight of which alone, made our trip worth it.

It was Jackie who spoke first. She was effusive in thanking the AF for allowing her to be here in the Shard and for Art Parker for agreeing to be the interviewer. That was flannel for starters, Parker would have bitten his mother's hand off to get this gig! Although it was plainly obvious that Parker had only wanted her to say a brief hello, she continued into a tribute to the Anarchist Federation. She spoke eloquently of the importance of the AF in the movement and of the work which the party and the AF had done together, including the unity which had been shown when the forces of reaction had launched violence against us. The 'us' was heavily emphasised. When she eventually finished, Parker gave a dazzling smile, but even though his blue eyes were shining and not a single hair had moved, I was guessing that he would have liked a shorter monologue from our illustrious president.

If he was hoping that Fiona Bailey was going to be more concise, he was equally as disappointed. She too, after briefly thanking him, moved into a lengthy and moving tribute to Jackie and the party. It was all one big love-in. We'd have heart-shaped balloons and pink streamers at this rate.

She finished, and then finally, he got to ask his first question. Like a professional at curling, delivering a stone who takes a run up, bends down and sleekly throws, Parker prefaced it with the discovery of Donaldson's arms dump, referring to the reaction, and then he went for the button, by asking Jackie how she felt about it when she heard the news today. The cameras zoomed in. This was the key question and the reply was going to be important. After a brief smile, Jackie answered, 'If you mean was I surprised? Then no, I wasn't. We've been fully aware of it for some time. And I should say that it's not the only one, there's a few others as well. All of them are under close observation. It would have been impossible for any of them to be moved, without us knowing about it. It's regrettable, and I wish they didn't exist, but we have to honestly, and concretely, face the situation which we find ourselves in.'

'You knew?' Parker was visibly taken aback.

'Yes, Art, I did.'

He turned to his other guest. 'And did you know, Fiona?'

'No, I didn't. It was a shock when I heard what Dave had been doing.'

That as may be, but she didn't look shocked at Jackie's admission. My guess was that they had carefully arranged what they were going to say at this conference. With no disrespect to Parker's journalistic skill, but whatever he had hoped for, the reality would soon dawn on him that he was here to facilitate the Bailey and Payne show.

Jackie's answer was, I presumed, a part of her strategy of diffusing the situation, but there was a major problem with it and Parker was too sharp not to have grasped that. 'But if that is the case, did you inform the NWC security committee? As I understand it, because the weapons have been stolen from the NWC, any information relating to them has to be reported to the NWC, otherwise – and please correct me if I'm wrong – that would put you in the position of being involved in the conspiracy. I think I'm correct in that.'

He knew that he was absolutely correct. Now Jackie had some explaining to do. She smiled, nodded and stroked her left eyebrow, before giving him the answer that he had not expected. 'Of course, Art. As soon as I was made aware of them, they were informed. The committee discussed it and then unanimously agreed that we should not publicise its existence for fear of creating conflict.'

Not a moisturised pore on Parker moved. His chiselled jaw didn't so much as tremble. 'Okay, can I ask why? I think our audience would be most interested in hearing what the reason was for withholding the fact that a substantial and illegal arms dump had been discovered. Especially, as you have long boasted that the NWC is the most transparent and democratic government this country has ever had. And yet you kept this secret.'

'It is, Art. But we've never claimed that we will announce every single action which we are forced to take in this war of survival. And, Art, it *is* a war, the workers' republic is fighting for its life. We're not going to make a fetish of transparency, at the expense of furthering the struggle. The question isn't why we kept it from being publicised, but whether the existence of the storage unit posed a credible threat to the workers' republic? To answer that, I would say that of course it was illegal, counter-revolutionary and wrong for Dave Donaldson to have stolen and stored those guns. Trust me, he'll face the consequences. However, the NWC Security knew of it and were united in the decision not to publicise it. Art, please remember that the committee consists of members of the URSP, AF members, a DL delegate and five from other organisations. It represents the politics of the NWC. And we were *and are* united, in protecting the revolution, and spreading it world-wide. Quite simply, no matter how much our enemies might wish it – there is no fracture.' For a second, she paused, before taking over the interview in all but name. Turning towards Fiona, who had been quietly listening and stroking her hair. ' Wouldn't you agree, Fiona?'

'Yes, well, I spoke to the siblings on the Anarchist Federation Organising Committee, and as far as they are concerned, nothing has changed. Donaldson has taken an individualistic, reactionary and adventurist action. We unequivocally condemn his actions. We stand united with the URSP.'

Jackie then asked her what the feeling on the ground was across the different groups within the AF. Going into detail of the myriad organisations, Fiona reiterated that whatever sincere and deep differences they had with us, they still saw an alliance as important for the progressive cause.

This question-and-answer session between the two women went on for a while. Parker sat there, letting it continue. Finally, as it began to veer dangerously close to becoming an inter-organisational romance, he shuffled a piece of paper on his lap and asked them what they would say to the angry crowds outside the Shard. Fiona answered first and spoke in gentle tones of understanding their anger, whilst reiterating the official AF position of condemnation of Donaldson. Jackie, however, was far more forthright concerning the demonstrations, demanding that they return home and let the NWC deal with it. She insisted that they show discipline and maturity. She finished with a withering comment: 'They're behaving like a petty-bourgeois hybrid of a right-wing mob and a seventeenth century Salem witch-hunt. Seeing us at each other's throats must make for glorious viewing for the counter-revolution. What those erstwhile revolutionaries outside must remember is, who our enemies are, and who are our comrades and allies.'

Parker smiled. 'Comrade President, do we know where Dave Donaldson is at the moment? Is he in custody?'

'He's not *formally* in custody, but is under close observation. For his protection, very few people know the location; even I don't know. But Crib are on the case.'

At the mention, I thought I saw Fiona Bailey move her head slightly in my direction. I was now sure that she had seen me.

Parker's follow-up question was the richest of velvet. 'You mention the Crib. Is there any link between the arms haul and the death of Mike Stewart? I ask, because of course, Dave Donaldson, was a housemate of Stewart's.'

'As I was,' Bailey pointed out.

'Of course,' he purred. 'But with the question is it more pertinent to ask of Donaldson?'

Without pausing for breath, Jackie Payne replied with a bland denial, saying that she wasn't aware of any, but that Crib were keeping all their options open.

When she had finished, with a gentleness of stroking a butterfly, he turned in my direction, and asked, 'As we appear to have Pete Kalder here, the political support for the Crib charged with investigating Mike Stewart's murder, perhaps I could ask him – is there a link?'

There's that phrase about that all eyes being on someone, well, it was true right there and then. Fiona turned around, amusement spread across her face. Yes, that sealed it, she'd seen me arrive and she was now looking forward to seeing me squirm. That wasn't quite the reaction I received from either Noah Walker or Reyansh Anand: the former looked surprised and then a little confused; the latter went from surprise to anger. It was safe to say that he wasn't pleased to see me. Anand glared at me, looking very much like he was ready to punch me.

I leant forward and engaged my brain. I quickly needed to work out what the best thing was to say. Knowing this was live, I didn't have much time to think, but an idea did come to me. 'Yes, hello Art. I won't take up much of people's time – I'm here to listen, not to make a statement. But you ask if we think there is a connection between the death of Mike Stewart and the arms theft? Then, yes, we think there is, but not necessarily in the way you mean. First off, we might want to think about who notified the BBC of its existence – and for what purpose? As I understand it, it was an anonymous source.'

I saw some nodding heads. 'Then we might ask why was the location of Donaldson's workplace so quickly publicised – so *provocatively* publicised? As the comrade president has already said, he's presently being kept in a secret location under our protection. We've taken this action because amongst the crowd outside his workplace – his publicly identified workplace – there were armed mercenaries. It was quite obvious to us that they were there for one reason and that was to murder him.' I paused. I could feel the tension in the room. A murmur rippled around the floor. This had them hooked. The folks at home were bound to be equally as focussed. Nothing like the news of a gang of armed vigilantes to draw attention away from the pasta supper. I had a chance here to both defuse the situation, and to further our investigation. I took it. 'We believe that the intention was to make it look like Dave Donaldson had been murdered at the hands of a rabid URSP mob. And who would have benefited most from such a thing? Certainly not the URSP, not the AF, not the NWC. Although, we're keeping an open mind, and he remains a person of interest, we think the link isn't him per se, but the strategy to divide the URSP and the AF.'

I wondered if I was talking for too long. Art Parker had asked a simple question and I was turning my reply into a doctorate thesis. Looking at him though, I couldn't see any sign of impatience. Jackie, too, seemed happy to let me speak. Seems like it was presently my show. 'It's a desperate tactic, but they'll try anything. The fact is, the vast majority of URSP members aren't on the streets, baying for blood, but are at home or at work. Nor are the AF. They've not taken to the streets to challenge the protestors. They've not been provoked, but have remained inside. Both sides understand their responsibility to the class and have heeded the calls from the network of workers' councils, and remained calm.'

I stopped. Partly to draw breath, but also because the hovering of a camera drone so close to my face had brought home to me what exactly was going on here. I was reeling off theories and pontificating, whilst Roijin and Vic concentrated on what Anand and Walker were doing; making sure that it was nothing more violent than the odd snarl. I was expounding theories, whilst someone in the room might be planning the death of the president of the workers' republic and/or a prominent AF figure.

Parker seemed not to mind in the slightest. Maybe, it was because he liked the cut of my suit, but he didn't return to Fiona or Jackie, but instead, directed his next question to me. 'You seem, Pete, to be trying to underplay these crates full of guns. I find that very interesting.'

I glanced at Jackie. With just the slightest nod, she indicated that I should continue. 'The thing is, Art,' I replied. 'Who'd use those guns of Donaldson's? Sure, there's a few ultra-leftist adventurers out there, who hold romantic notions of once more charging the barricades, but they're only a handful. They're no more of a threat to the state than a group of traffic wardens.' A couple of the journalists chuckled. Obviously, they didn't have relatives in the service. 'We believe that Dave Donaldson is merely a useful idiot. He's been used, just like the cowardly and deceitful murder of Mike Stewart, like the public slurs against our Crib and the savage drone attack here.' I stopped to hold out my hand in the direction of the shot-up windows. The camera whirred as they focussed on the damage. 'All to provoke a civil war. Our enemies have taken note of the old trade union slogan of unity is strength. They've come together to coordinate their action, whilst attempting to sew disunity on our side. And that's all I want to say, Art, so I will say no more. Nor,' I added, 'will I take any questions. I defer to sisters Payne and Bailey.'

I breathed out heavily. For a second, I didn't dare look at Roijin or Vic for fear of what kind of look I would get as a reply. I was pleased though, to see Jackie smile. The look in her eyes seemed to me to say that I had done well. Like a primary school boy being congratulated on his work on fractions, I felt a warm glow inside.

There wasn't time for Jackie to write a certificate or give me a star, before Parker thanked me, and then swung around to Fiona. 'So, Fiona Bailey – Dave Donaldson – "a useful idiot" – what would you say to that?'

As the three on the stage continued the discussion, I looked at the other two of my own triumvirate. I could only see them in profile because they were focussed on Anand and Walker, so I couldn't tell what they had thought of what I had said. It didn't appear to be a pressing priority for them. The two men being watched, seemed to have calmed down a bit. Whether that was because my contribution had soothed their troubled brows or not, I didn't know, but they seemed strangely relaxed. Both sat, arms crossed and listened.

After ten minutes, Parker turned to face the journalists and announced, in that friendly, warm, yet authoritative voice he always had marinating, that there would be a short period of time for questions. Hands shot up from across the media. Anand and Walker remained still. This, surely, was the time for one or both of them to act. Even if they were here for the most innocent of motives, they would surely take this chance to make a statement in front of the large TV audience. Headlines would loom large across the networks, if they confronted Bailey and Cole here. Now was the moment to attack what they saw as the conservatism of the NWC and the failure to deal with the threat it faced. But they said nothing. They didn't move. Nor did they do so, until Parker wound up the press conference. With fake humbleness, he thanked everyone and ended it.

Both Anand and Walker got to their feet and stretched. Behind them, Cole and Kemal also stood, only a lot quicker. Their hands weren't outstretched, but both had their right hand resting across their stomach. It wasn't from indigestion; both were ready to pull out their guns if need be.

Walker slowly moved towards Jackie. I tensed. I could see that Vic had started to move in close behind him. She was ready to spring if need be. Roijin hadn't moved because Anand hadn't. He was standing rigid, arms across his chest, staring at Walker's back. Roijin herself was shuffling about, pretending to be deeply interested in one of the cameras.

A journalist tried to get between Vic and Walker to ask a question, but she swept him aside with a few words. From my limited ability at mouth reading, I could see that a fair percentage of them were profanities. Walker was now directly in front of Jackie, talking, for the moment at least, all seemed to be quiet and civil.

A looming face suddenly appeared, obscuring my view. 'Well, who's the star then!' Fiona Bailey grinned.

'Uh, huh?' I wasn't listening, as she talked about how the conference had gone. I was far too concerned at what Walker's next move might be. He was now very close to Jackie. Very close indeed. He wouldn't need a gun – a knife would suffice. Vic was tensing. She was calculating the risk potential as to whether waiting for him to act or not, was the safest strategy. He was close enough to hug Jackie. Or stab her. If she waited, it might be too late. The three security guards had also moved closer. One of them was now a metre or so behind her. He had moved to an angle, so as to get a clear view of Walker.

Walker himself seemed totally unaware of the fact that he was the centre of attention. He looked in deep conversation with Jackie. It looked serious and grave, but not angry. That was what it *looked* like, anyway.

Just then, I felt someone other than Bailey, looking at me. I glanced over to see Reyansh Anand staring at me with a quizzical expression. Judging from how he shot further looks at Vic and the AF guards, he had seen what was happening. He obviously wasn't happy, but what exactly was the cause of his annoyance was difficult to guess. He turned to see what was behind him, and came bang, slap, face-to-face with Roijin. She smiled an officious smile and whispered something. Whatever it was, it made him move and he turned back to Walker. In reply, she quickly and firmly grabbed his right arm, pulling him back. Before he could do or say anything, she whispered something in his ear. He looked deep into her eyes, which I shrewdly guessed wasn't from passion – not the romantic kind in any rate. And froze.

Bailey also seemed oblivious to not only my concern, but what was being played out in the room. 'A good speech, have to say, Pete, I've never heard you speak so well.'

'You too,' I mumbled, looking round her.

Eventually seeing that I wasn't focussed on her, she turned around to see what was of more interest to me.

'Oh sorry. Are you waiting to talk to Jackie?' She laughed. 'I'm sure she will be with you in a minute. Anything to get away from Noah.'

'Yeah, good.' I dared to move my attention back to her – just for a second. 'Sorry, Fiona. Do you think this will have any effect?'

'What, this little shindig? Yeah, I think so. To be honest, Pete. I'm not sure that it was a serious attempt to cause a civil war, more of the latest in a line of destabilising actions. The forces opposing the revolution are more astute than they are given credit for.'

Walker moved his hand. I saw Vic reach inside her jacket. My hands were now a puddle of sweat. I had been training hard with the militia and could now boast a fair aim, but I was worried that I'd have difficulty holding onto the thing. My heart was beating so loud that it appeared to be drowning out the constant stream of words coming out of Fiona's mouth.

I caught just a small fraction of them… 'The question is, Pete, did you get any clear look at the guys who were after Donaldson?'

'Huh? Er, no. Vic gave one of them a slap, but we kept away from them.'

She giggled, which seemed completely incongruous to what might soon happen here. 'Well, I think you're doing a great job. We've been very impressed. Maybe you've been underestimated.'

Then Walker moved. He flung his arm up and stormed away from Jackie. Reyansh yanked his arm from Roijin's, and followed him to the lifts. Seeing where they were headed, one of the guards got in a lift first. Reyansh and Walker followed him. The other, looking as if he was casually surveying the floor to see if he could get his face on TV, joined them.

'Yeah, look sorry, Fiona. I got to go.'

'Well. I'll try not to take it too personally. Seems you have more pressing concerns.' She laughed. 'Obviously I have to wait my turn.'

I didn't reply and joined Roijin and Vic. The third orange combat dude was there too. We were all in the lift, with Anand and Walker in the middle, and us surrounding them. A case of piggies in the middle, perhaps.

The door closed, but it didn't move.

Vic spoke. 'Comrades Noah and Reyansh, with the power invested in Crib, we need to formally question you both, concerning threats to the workers' republic. But first we need to search you. Do you consent to that?'

Before Reyansh had a chance to argue, which from the thunderous look he had on his face, was what exactly he was going to, Noah raised his arms as if to surrender. It gave us a full glimpse of the multi-coloured ensemble that he was wearing. We should arrest him for that, alone.

'Of course, comrades. You know I support your work, totally.'

Vic moved forward and patted him down. He stood with a pleasant smile on his face. Looking for all the world that he had no cares whatsoever. Reyansh Anand didn't move. He just glared. Walker spoke to him in what I swear was an amused voice, 'Now then, Rey, help the good Cribbers.'

With a grunt, he followed his leader. Roijin searched him, whilst I, and our trio of burly anarcho-chums, watched and braced for any repercussions.

'Clean,' said Vic.

'Clean, here too,' added Roijin.

'I should hope so,' grinned Walker. 'I had a shower this morning and I know Rey has a cold one every morning.'

No-one replied. I could feel the faint movement of the lift.

Unable to contain his anger anymore, Anand snarled, 'What the...'

Vic cut him short. 'All in good time, comrade. All in good time. We are all serving the revolution, after all.'

The doors opened, but not at the ground floor. She pointed towards the open space and said, 'We will be interviewing you. You will not be under arrest, but under NWC anti-terrorism law, we have the right to ask any question we choose and take whatever forensic evidence we require. If we feel the need to arrest you, you will be read your rights and taken to a station. You will then be given the right to legal representation.'

'But...'

'Comrade Anand—' she held up a hand to stop him. 'Please come with us. We understand it is awkward and uncomfortable and don't want to create a scene. We would like this to be as civil as possible. There's no need for this to be unpleasant. We're all comrades here, and want to protect the state. But please understand, this needs to be done, and we will take *whatever action is necessary.*'

# CHAPTER 36:
# THE CARD PLAYERS

Asher met us with two more guards. After adjusting his kippah, he nodded to one side. 'We've the use of a couple of rooms, they're just the right size, usually used for meditation.' He chuckled. 'Quite appropriate, really.'

Anand gave him a fierce stare. He didn't think the comment was big or clever. Rage shone behind his eyes. He looked ready to explode. His partner had obviously noticed, and tried to soothe his temper, 'Rey, they're just doing their job. Just let them ask their questions. It won't take long and then we can go.'

He didn't reply, but instead started to take deep breaths, closed his eyes and opened up his hands, palms upwards. Obviously, surprised as I was, Asher stared at him and then at me. Anand was bloody mediating. I mean, he could at least wait to get in the room before he started to chant Umm! I felt my lips begin to move, I was just about to ask him if he needed a scented candle, a warm towel and some bland music, when I felt Vic gently squeeze my arm. I looked at her and she shook her head. Seems Vic could read my mind now and guessed that I wasn't going to say anything helpful. Making an incredibly rare double discovery, I suddenly found both some discipline and maturity, and kept my comments to myself. It was probably just as well, because after a few moments of inhaling and exhaling, and without the need for any chanting, he started to relax a fraction. A small fraction that is, with a very big denominator. Let's just say that he had been very, very pissed off, but now he was just pissed off. Catching the touchy-feely vibe off Vic, Walker gently put his hand on the small of his back.

It appeared to do the trick because Anand didn't put up any opposition when we led him into one of the rooms. Which was pretty lucky as those hands of his could probably kill. Certainly, his looks could. Noah was far more placid and almost happily went into the other room. The doors closed, with Noah and Anand safely ensconced in each, with an AF guard keeping them company.

'That wasn't as difficult as I feared it might be,' I said.

Vic gave me a serious look. 'Probably won over by your speech back in the meeting.' A hint of a grin appeared. 'Sorry,' she muttered, remembering why the hell we were here. Returning to her usual intensive mode, she did what she was seemingly designed to do: she took control. 'I suggest that Pete and I formally interview them. We take one of them, whilst you Roij – and Ash – chat to the other. Roij, get down every personal detail you can think of – nothing is too trivial. I want to know where they were born, the schools they went to, who they lost their virginity to – everything! National and local computer files may have been shredded, but there may be some hard copies, or even people who remember either of them. If that's not possible, that might indicate something – as Pete found out at the museum. Not being known is telling in itself. Contact the workers' councils in the relevant areas, they can coordinate the searches. Get them to go everywhere, like veins through a body. We have a network in our society, use it.'

'Okay, Vic. Understood.'

'Ash – do the complete forensic works on them. Cover every nook and cranny of their bodies.'

I flinched. I did like my florid descriptions, but there were limits, and that really did conjure up images, which I'd rather not have.

'Process them. Buzz everything to the forensic team who are at the TV studios at the moment. Also buzz them to Dr Lopez and tell her to drop everything she is doing and get back to Mike Stewart's house. Use Jackie's name as leverage if you have to.'

'No prob. I'll try some BTWs as well.'

Both Vic and Roijin grinned; I had no idea what he meant. Seeing my puzzlement, Vic explained, 'Something Ash is great at is small talk when taking swabs. Must be the link with medical procedures and care, but in the past, suspects have surprisingly often let slip useful titbits of info, when he's doing it. We call them his "By the Way" moments.'

I politely smiled. My, they were a wacky crew.

'Anyway, Pete. We'll start with Anand. He's quite plainly wound-up, or at least pretending to be, so let's see what we can find out. I think it would be best if you took the lead. If one of them is our man then he'll be trained in interrogation techniques, predictable questions from an ex-copper will be easy meat for him. With you, they'll not know what to expect. And if either or both of them are simply good solid comrades, then they're less likely to object to being questioned by you than they will be by me.'

It was possibly the first time that I had ever been thought as being unlikely to be antagonistic. Strangely, I was looking forward to this.

'Why not?' I replied. Pointing to the door, I said, 'Shall we?'

We went through one, whilst Roijin, Asher and his BTWs, went through the other. I was extremely pleased to see that this meditation room wasn't as bad as I feared. Sure, there were mats and cushions, but thankfully there were three chairs and a table. The room was windowless, and the walls were all in plain cream, and the floor stripped pine. Two large pots of houseplants stood at the back. I wondered how they could survive without sunlight. Maybe Ash could find out with one of his BTWs.

Sitting at the table was Anand, who was doing his usual impression of a toy soldier. His spine was rigid and his buttons shone. My first thought was that we needed to loosen him up a bit, and a large anarchist cradling a machine gun behind him wasn't going to do that. This man wasn't easily intimidated. He was angry, but not in the slightest bit scared. If we gave out medals, then comrade Anand would have his entire chest covered in them. I looked at the guard and nodded in the direction of the door. He understood immediately and left us without a word. I'd never known armed anarchists be so amenable. Maybe I did have a commanding air about me? More likely though, he was glad to be out of here. Playing at being a prison officer wasn't the type of thing he had ever envisaged himself being involved in. I could sympathise with that.

We sat down and I crossed my legs. I did so, simply to give myself time to think of the approach I should take. Coercing him was out of the question; whether he was a revolutionary soldier or a spy, or both, he wasn't going to crack under a few words of abuse, some fabulous word-play and the threat that we could take him somewhere, where there were no pot plants. On the other hand, pretending to be his friend wasn't going to work either. I decided to try to be simply straightforward, be who I was, and accept, at least for the moment, he was who he claimed to be.

I began by reminding him of his rights under the Workers' Republic's Constitution and explained that it was our duty to follow whatever leads we might have. I thought using "duty" might be apt here. That was why I was here. 'But if you don't mind, comrade, could I ask what brings you here?' I asked. I was friendly and polite, trying to sound more intrigued, than antagonistic.

'We wanted to hear what Jackie had to say,' he replied coldly. As reasons went, it was as limp as a two-month-old lettuce.

I sighed heavily; I really did not want to spend hours in this soft-furnished cupboard, trying to get the most basic of honest answers out of him. 'Please, comrade, don't disrespect us. We're not fools. As I explained, we're here on official counter-insurgency business. If you're as committed to the revolution as you say, then you'll want to assist us in every way you can. If all you wanted to know was what Jackie was going to say, then you could have watched it on your phone.'

For a moment, he did not reply, but just looked at me. It had to be said that he had quite a scary look. I started to regret dismissing the guard. Vic was queen of kung-fu and stuff, but she'd have no chance against him. He wasn't trying to frighten me (I hoped). More likely, he was weighing up what he was going to say. For a few seconds he continued to stare at me. I calculated the time it would take me to reach the door and shout for help if he lunged at me. Finally, he made his decision. No lunge, just an honest answer. 'We were going to use it as a platform to demand that the NWC take firmer measures against the insurgency.'

'But you didn't.'

'No, once we were in there, I felt that it would be too much like attacking the NWC and in particular Jackie, rather than defending it, and that isn't what I'm about. I want the NWC strengthened, not weakened.'

'Is that why you and Noah were arguing?'

'Yeah. Noah thought I was being too squeamish, too liberal.'

'He was keen to make the intervention?'

'Yes. Very much so.' He smiled.

'So why didn't he?'

'That's down to you, comrade. He said your speech made it difficult to say anything because you'd polarised the positions. If we spoke, it would sound like we were supporting the rebels, so it was best to choose another time.'

I didn't say anything and let silence hang in the air for a few seconds, purely for theatrical affect. After hopefully a suitable impression of absorbing the thoughts of the walls, I spoke. 'Of course, you and Walker were also here at the time of the drone attack – came from Britain Today studios for the Do We Need to Take a Step Back debate, weren't you?'

'Yes?' he said warily.

'Can you confirm, comrade, that neither you or Noah Walker, left the TV Studios until you did so to come here?'

He looked directly at me again, and I could see that his annoyance at being asked these questions. It wasn't love, then, they were straining at the cords of self-control. His answer was in a tightly regulated tone, 'As I've told you before, I was in there the whole time.'

'And you didn't see Noah Walker leave at any time?'

Carefully pronouncing every syllable and every vowel, he repeated that he hadn't seen Noah for the entire time, but then, he hadn't seen him leave either.

Remaining the diplomatic, respectful and polite comrade-in-arms, I apologised for having to ask these questions. 'Comrade, you of all people will understand why I have to. We face an existential threat – one you have brought to the attention of the class on many occasions – and have been right to do so. Believe me, that Crib value your support and it pains us to do this. But we must be seen as impartial. The revolution is bigger than individual egos – as again, you have said many times. Please understand that we take no joy in having to ask these questions of someone like yourself.'

He shrugged it away; he was now beginning to relax a little. The Kalder charm couldn't be resisted for too long. 'Yes – I understand, comrade. Everyone knows how high the stakes are. We have to be very careful how we progress. Difficult decisions will have to be made, decisions which may upset our allies. No-one is ignorant of the danger of a rift between the AF and the party – certainly not Noah and me. We've no wish to see that. All we want is the NWC to give itself the necessary tools to do the job of defending itself. We have to be realistic. We've all seen what the forces of reaction are planning in the shadows, and I include in that, Dave Donaldson, who *amongst others* has been stockpiling weapons for *our* destruction.' His facial expression grew more serious. 'I'll be frank, comrades, I find it amazing that you knew – *that the president knew* – about them. I mean, there's freedom and liberty, and then there's the freedom and liberty of our enemies to overthrow us. I thought we were Marxists, not bleeding-heart liberals.'

He had a point. He and his mate next door had been making similar ones ad-nauseam over the past few days, but now wasn't the time for a debate. This Q & A was one that I was conducting. 'You didn't know anything about the weaponry, then?'

'If I had, I would have raided it and arrested him!' he snarled.

'Okay, thank you, Anand.' I made a fractional move, as if to leave, but then, as if a thought had just occurred to me: 'Actually, one last thing. If I said Jerusalem to you – what would be the first thing which came into your head?'

He looked wide-eyed at me, as if I was mad. He shrugged. 'Er, the place where Christians believe that Jesus was crucified?'

'Nothing else?'

A touch of irritation accompanied his bemusement. 'Well if you give me a minute, I'll try and come up with a few more answers, but you asked for the first thing which I thought of. Is this an IQ test?'

I faked a laugh. 'Nothing so reactionary, just asking.' Then looked at Vic to see if she had anything to add. She shook her head. We both got up.

'That's it?' he said, surprised that after all the melodrama, it was going to be as short as that.

'Yes, comrade. Our colleagues will be in to take forensic samples and some personal details. Are you okay with that?'

He looked at me. I could almost see the mental discussion as to whether he would agree. Finally, he just replied, 'Sure. Of course.'

We left him and stood outside, and waited for Roijin and Asher. Neither of us spoke, because the fact was, that there was little to say at this point. We both knew what needed to be done, but whether we could actually do it, was the question. As we had been finding out all too painfully, we had smashed the superstructure of one state, but it wasn't instantaneously possible to build a new one.

The other door opened and Roijin and Asher emerged.

'All yours!' Asher grinned.

'Any problems?' Vic asked.

'Nah. He's being one big pussy cat.'

'Good. Time to tickle his tummy. You ready, Pete?'

'Coming, comrade.'

It was true, Walker did resemble one big, snoozing, dayglo cat. As we entered, he barely stirred, but sat lying back in his chair, legs sprawled in front of him and his hands supporting his neck. The room was identical to the one we had just left. Good for karma, I guessed. I dismissed the guard, as I had done in the other room. She too seemed pleased to go.

Walker smirked. 'Hello again.'

If he was concerned that we were about to uncover his secret and expose him to the unforgiving glare of the proletariat, then he wasn't showing it.

He was laid back in the extreme, almost literally.

I reminded him of his rights, then spoke gently. 'Noah – comrade – do you mind if we ask you a few questions? We just need to get a few things straight.'

'Of course, of course!' He spoke as if I was asking his permission to sit down, not questioning his loyalty. We had already taken our seats, so he can't have been confused.

'Thank you, comrade, that is kind. We do appreciate how this must seem, but we've a job to do. Before we begin, can you tell me why you were at the press conference?'

He breathed out heavily. 'Well it's not a secret, we were going to use it to argue that the party was not taking the threats seriously enough.' He could have left it there, but Noah being Noah, had to continue into a long political discourse. I let him speak because let's face it, we were here to listen. Not that there was anything new, he went from the well-worn to the petty. 'I mean, for fuck's sake, there was even that memo about not capitalising the word Party, so as not to appear that we were setting ourselves as being the only one. By having lower-case, it shows that we're one of many. I mean – really! Can we be any more pathetic?'

I didn't reply. He didn't really want me to. He didn't give a toss what I thought. I thanked him and then, despite fearing that I would be at the receiving end of another speech, asked him why he hadn't in fact spoken at the media conference.

To my blessed relief, his reply was short and to the point: 'In the circumstances, I would have sounded anti-NWC, which could easily have been misinterpreted.'

On TV, I'd seen the fictional detectives suddenly change the topic as a way of wrong-footing suspects. Being that programmes were basically my training videos, I tried one out. 'Did you know about Dave Donaldson's armaments dump?'

If I had expected a give-way tick or huge faux-pas, I was disappointed. His reply was the epitome of conversational casualness: 'Not at all. Not until everyone else did.'

'You've never been there then?' I asked. I knew full well that he was hardly going to say, "Oh yes, I drop off missile launchers every Sunday", but I wanted to see his reaction. TV dicks did things like that. But once more I was disappointed. He simply looked surprised that I had even asked him such a question, and replied that, no, he hadn't.

'Okay, thanks.' I paused. ' Actually, Noah, just to get our files in order, and something which I should have asked right at the beginning – how long have you been in the party?'

He thought for a second. 'Must be almost nine years now. I joined during the Small Firms Strike, it was whilst I was back in Southampton. I was, what you might call, a left-wing Labour type, before then.'

'Were you a member of the Labour Party?'

He laughed. 'You really are trying to find out my secrets, aren't you?' He knew full well what secrets, exactly, we were trying to find out. 'Nah, more of a fellow traveller.'

It was pointless to camouflage anything. If ever there was a case of *he knows, I know*, then it was now. The obvious thing was just to go straight in. 'I'm a bit intrigued about your experience during the strike, I mean, you joined Strictly L Solutions during its height, when the entire company's workforce was on strike, and then you went straight out yourself. Not the usual thing, you have to admit.'

He threw his head back, and laughed again. 'What can I say? I convinced him that I was the man for the job and then screwed him over when I got it. I told him that I was a solid Tory and that I despised unions, and he could count on me to help the firm through the dispute. He believed me. I got the job – I went on strike.'

I was, I had to admit, rather surprised at his candour. 'Good at deception, are you?' I asked.

'Only with Tory scumbag bosses.' He gave me a toothy grin. He was enjoying this a great deal and quite obviously wasn't bothered in the micro-slightest by any of my questions.

However, my patience didn't snap; I had decided to be straight-forward, but pleasant, no matter how much it was being stretched. I changed direction again. 'Previously, you told us that at the time of the drone attack here you and comrade Anand were at a televised debate at the Britain Today studios.'

'That's correct.'

'Previously, you said that you were in there for the whole time, yet we have a witness who saw you leave before then – a cleaner.'

The only response I did get was that he leant forward and rested his elbows on the table. His grin remained. 'I'm afraid, they're mistaken. The debate was far too important to leave early. We're facing a crucial moment in the revolution and it's important, it is my duty, to...'

I cut him short. 'Yes, you've previously said.' I had heard the speech many times. 'Have you any ideas who may have been behind the drone attack?'

This time there was a snarl rather than a smile. 'Some low-life murdering fascist, who needs strung up, but as to their identity, I have no idea. I wish I did, comrade, I really do.'

'I think a lot of people would agree with you, Noah. We know that you've been unwavering in your commitment to the party ever since you joined the party. I will be honest with you, comrade, that I don't agree with your position which you're taking right now, but I understand where you're coming from. Right from the start, you've been one of the staunchest advocates of revolutionary action. You were heavily involved in the civil war, I understand.'

He pulled a face. I think it was his attempt at humility, 'I did my bit, like every other comrade. I should tell you that no-one worked harder than me during that stressful time. As you're obviously checking up on me, ask around, comrades will tell you.'

'Just filling in some gaps,' I replied blandly, before continuing the question. 'You were in the East London Defence Zone during it, weren't you?'

A smile tickled the corner of his mouth, betraying the fact that he knew what I was going to ask. 'I was comrade, yes.'

'I've been told that there were some technical difficulties on the day of the attack on the Workers' Hall?'

'I guess that you're referring to the cyber-attack which nullified our defence systems, and allowed the attack drones to reach their target. Yes, it was very well-organised. To be honest, comrade, we were lucky that Jackie had had the foresight to evacuate the building, which meant that the fatalities were kept to the minimum. Those we did lose will be sorely missed. They were solid proletarians who gave their lives to the revolution.'

I furrowed my brow. 'It's worrying they never found the route of the hack. I mean, I'd worry that they could repeat the trick. You didn't have any idea how they managed it? You being an IT expert, and all.'

Once more, a sign of amusement appeared in the crease of his mouth. 'In a very different field, comrade. It would be like saying a brain surgeon knows all about feet.'

I nodded but did not pursue the matter. I drummed the tables with my fingers, and moved my weight, to suggest that I was about to get up. 'Before

I go, can I ask – if I said Jerusalem to you, what would that mean to you?'

'Artichokes – Jerusalem artichokes – lovely in a smoky haddock bake. Why, are you asking for recipes?'

Funny man. I ignored his goading, and asked him again. 'Nothing else, apart from the cookery reference – nothing suspicious?'

'No, I haven't.' He leant forward towards me. His body language was not menacing, but rather one of fascination. 'Why?'

I deflected his question and after a more few bland platitudes, ended the interview and left him alone.

Outside, I asked Vic what she had thought of both our guests. After a long preamble, she basically indicated that they'd given us nothing. 'The answer lies in their past, we need to research that further.'

I agreed. 'That can be done at home.' Then, without waiting for any opposition, I said a brief goodbye. 'Anything else I need to know, ping it over to me.' I needed space and I needed thinking time.

It was midnight when I arrived home. I dragged myself into the kitchen and found some scraps of food. At least there was a three-quarters of a bottle of red wine on the side. Closing my eyes, I requested some Miles Davis and crashed back into my armchair. Victoria had already compiled an extended list of things for all of us to do, from information which Roijin and Asher had obtained from our two likely-lads. Before I made a start, I rang my sister. Despite murder and terrorism taking up much of my thoughts, our confrontation was troubling me. Any chance of reopening diplomatic relationships was shot down, when she declined the call.

Our troubled relationship couldn't be allowed to get in the way, so I pushed her back into the mental compartment labelled "sister issues" and focussed on what I had to do. I instructed the living room screen to appear and display our files on Noah Walker. Dates and places of his life – his birth, school, workplaces, party branches, union membership, homes – and so on, and so on. Say what you like about her, Roijin was thorough. She and Odette had trawled the electronic archives from a variety of sources and built a network around everything which Walker had told her at the Shard.

'Let's start with what we know, hey sweetheart,' I said to Red, who had sniffed my Merlot, decided that the grape wasn't to his liking, and had settled onto my lap. 'Work from the present and go backwards.' I was good at this sort of thing, I spread out what we knew in front of me, and instructed the homecom AI to interrogate it, flashing-up possible links.

Tonight was going to be long and drawn out. As well as staring directly ahead of me at the random biographical facts, it was going to be a lot of leaving messages for people who were sensibly asleep, and hoping that they would get back to me in the morning.

What to wear for these messages was the next question. The 3D visual, I decided, was going to be the best, but then, me sitting here in a sweat-soaked shirt, with a cat and a glass of wine, probably wasn't the best image to convey. So, I shooed the cat away and put on a fresh, more formal – and clean – shirt. Even though it was still ridiculously warm, I thought a jacket might add a little gravitas, so got a dog-toothed half-lined three button, no vents number. The look was slightly spoilt when I sat back down and Red immediately jumped back on me. Now for some calls.

# CHAPTER 37:
# RAIN, STEAM AND SPEED

As I had feared, it had been a long and pretty fruitless night. Anything less than seven hours of sleep usually meant that Comrade Peter Kalder was not fully operative. Right now, I felt barely switched on. I had accumulated less than three. And rather than enjoying a luxurious lie in, I was back at the office.

Opposite me sat Odette, sprightly and full of annoying energy. She was operating the surveillance drones, which we had acquired from the NEC Defence Corps. They were shadowing Walker and Reyansh, but from the running commentary, exaggerated movements and all-but frantic munching of a variety of fruit, she could easily have been playing a late 2020s war game. Not that from what I could see, there was anything to get too excited about. They were in bed, but she wasn't indulging in guilty porn, as both men were fast asleep. Lucky gits.

Just behind her, sat a more subdued Vic Cole. She certainly looked in need of some shut-eye. She wasn't having the fun that Odette was having, but was arranging in-person visits to all key offices and workplace, to follow up what little I'd achieved during the night. Asher was helping her. As for Roijin, she was the epitome of concentration, whilst she examined the computer software of the East London Defence Zone.

Surrounding us were virtual boards, which Yelena was continually updating, like hyper-active train departure boards. Although, not quite so exciting. Roijin had added graphics and colour-coding to spice them up. She had explained that "on-going avenues of investigation" were in black; dead-ends were green; and awaiting information were red. Not surprisingly, the green and red vastly outnumbered the black. Anything highlighted in yellow was of special interest. There was very little of that colour.

As the morning grew older, information came in and went up. The reports of Anand's military training were one of the first up. Then former

Southampton Labour party members confirmed that Walker had attended a few meetings of theirs but had never joined. "Thought we were too reformist for him", one woman had said. Then the doctor's surgery near where Reyansh's parents lived, phoned to confirm that they had his medical records on file and he had been a 3.4kg healthy lad. And so, it went on. As each piece of the puzzle appeared, Yelena sorting it. The only picture appearing was that they were two normal, and very committed, people. There wasn't a secret in a closet, or even a closet, just yet.

From Odette came continual crunching and munching, accompanied occasionally with a slight shuffle and a muttered comment. She announced big news at 11.30am: Anand had left his house, shut his front door and got into his car. If that wasn't excitement enough, the euphoria increased when Odette informed us that he was heading towards the administrative offices of the party's soldiers' faction. Walker, meanwhile, remained at home.

The rest of us were chivvying people up to prioritise our requests above anything else. None of the people we were contacting, were just sitting there, counting paper clips, waiting for a chance to help. Most had good reasons not to drop everything to rifle through dusty paper records and laptop memory hard-drives. We couldn't force anyone to do anything. We had official standing and, legally, all organisations and citizens of the republic should aid and help the work of Cribs, but in reality, we were reliant on goodwill and cooperation. Thankfully, we received it. No-one could fail to notice the tension in the country and most people were keen to do what they could. We waded through the steam of data flowing in. A medical centre in Eastleigh rang me at 12.15pm to let me know that they had found the records of Noah Walker who had been born weighing 3.6kg, basically healthy, but with a urinary tract infection. That had been treated and had been cleared up.

I was beginning to OD on caffeine. Sitting here steering a desk, could be nullifying at the best of times, but with so little sleep I was beginning to drop off, so to compensate, I was drinking cup after cup of coffee. It was keeping me alert, but I could feel a headache strolling up to keep the fatigue company.

Lunchtime was announced by my stomach making odd noises beneath the tailoring. Coffee just wasn't enough to stop it. A lush salad would have been nice, but I made do with a pile of cheese and crackers. I looked around and perhaps from a shared hunger, all the team looked up and caught each other's eyes. We took it in turns to announce that whilst we had found a couple of interesting avenues to explore, we had nothing concrete. In other words, we'd found sod all. The cheddar was about the best discovery. Basically, everything checked out with Walker and Anand – they were who they said they were. In an attempt to dilute the office coffee, I was now sipping from a glass of ice-cold water, with a slice of lemon on top. My little luxury.

A call came in from the secretary at Walker's old primary school. Her local council had visited her at home and in response, she'd delved into the labyrinth of the archives in the school's basement. By doing so, she could confirm that Noah David Walker had been a pupil there. I thanked her, trying not to dribble cheese down my front.

I needed to stretch my legs, so I went outside by the embankment and tried my sister again, but despite it being obvious that she was at work, she refused to take it. Vic had marched out ten minutes earlier, loudly proclaiming the need for a break. She was a little further along the wall, watching the river buses passing by on the Thames. I shuffled along and stood next to her. She turned to face me, flicking her cigarette onto the floor. Not quite in keeping with our strictures on looking after the world around us, but as her face looked like thunder, I wasn't going to say anything. Having one woman being pissed off with me was enough for me at any particular time.

'Anything of note?' she asked, sounding like she didn't expect there to be.

Despite a barrel full of coffee, I was growing in befuddlement from the lack of sleep. I wasn't sure who or what she exactly meant. Did she mean the complex, tangled relationship between my sister and me, or did she mean the investigation? Or was it something else – like the renaissance masterpieces which had disappeared two months earlier? Too exhausted to decide which it was, I kept my reply neutral. 'Not really.'

For a moment, she didn't say anything to my momentous reply, but just wearily shook her head, and sighed. She was a tired bunny too. Turning back to face the river, she spoke to herself as much as to me, 'We just have to keep on keeping on.'

Neither of us said a word.

Our quiet contemplation was loudly interrupted by Roijin shouting at us. We turned around to see her striding towards us and grinning triumphantly. 'Got something you might be interested in!' she yelled.

If she had wanted to attract our attention, she had succeeded.

'What?' Vic asked, managing to sound simultaneously fatigued and eager for something which we could use – something to get her away from the office.

Joining us, Roijin was like a burst of pressurised air into two deflated balloons. Holding her phone in triumph. A small 2D projection, approximately ten centimetres square appeared. We both looked. I hoped Vic had some idea what we were looking at because it looked like just a stream of consciousness algebra to me.

Looking bemused, Vic asked, 'Okay, Roij, could you explain what this means?'

Roijin looked as if she was going to cheer. Words streamed out: 'The camouflage for the hack, the one which crashed the system, and let the drones through our defence air-space, you know, for the attack on the Royal Albert Hall? Well, it was sophisticated in the extreme. That's why the NWC techies had such difficulties in tracking it down. But I've managed to.' She paused, perhaps waiting for a firework display, or at least a standing ovation.

'You've found out who crashed the defence system?' Vic asked, having neither Catherine Wheels nor rockets, and we were already standing.

Not feeling perturbed at the lack of appreciation, Roijin continued. 'These here,' she said, highlighting some numbers and dashes, 'indicate the point of attack. As I said, it is cleverly disguised, but look at the *34/09* there – that tells us that it was internally initiated.'

That prodded Vic awake. Indeed, she almost jumped down her throat. '"Internally initiated"? Does that mean you can prove that the virus came from Walker's terminal?'

Roijin didn't need to speak because the look on her face gave the answer. 'No, Vic, sorry. But what that does tell us is that the cyber-attack came from within the defence zone's internal network. Which, I found out, had forty people online at the time.'

I nodded in encouragement. It was important but not conclusive. It was certainly more than either Vic or I had managed to find, but then, any legal defence rep could simply point out that even if Roijin was right, it was entirely possible that one of the other thirty-nine could have been the culprit.

Seeing our lack of partying celebration, Roijin's grin widened. All of a sudden, I had the impression that Roijin here was playing with us, having some fun as she built up to a climax. 'And see these six symbols – *56?^\*3?* Well, that code shows that it was routed via the monitoring office, which was responsible for – amongst other things – aerial surveillance against drone attacks. The code was linked to what we call a time-bomb. In other words, a time for it to begin. From that I can see that the virus was installed at 9.15am and set to be triggered at 2pm that day.'

'Two in the afternoon? When was the time of the attack?' Vic asked.

'The drones passed through their zone's air-space at 2.33.'

'So, thirty-three minutes after the cyber-attack starts, the drone attack does.'

'Precisely. And Vic, Pete, there were ten people who were online at the time of its installation and can be linked by that coding.'

'Which means that there's a ten per cent chance that it was him?'

Roijin nodded. From her expression I could see that she had not quite finished. 'But only one person was present at the time of installation, the cyber-attack and the drone attack itself, and that was...'

'Noah Walker?'

'Exactly, Victoria!'

Suddenly, as if by magic, I didn't feel tired anymore. Energy was running through me. From the look of Victoria, the same was happening to her. 'We have the bastard!' she shouted. A few passers-by looked at her but she didn't care. ' Well done, Roij! Time to pay comrade Walker a visit, I think. Do we know where he is this minute?'

'Still at home.'

'Come on then, Pete. Grab your jacket, and let's go! We'll take my car. It's quicker than your moped.'

'Scooter. It's a scooter.'

'Whatever. Come on.' She marched off, before turning and shouting, 'That really is great work, Roij! Come on, Pete!'

'Woof, woof,' I muttered to myself. 'Good doggie is following his master.'

It hadn't taken us too long for us to make the journey from Somerset House to Noah Walker's house in Brent Cross. His was your common-or-garden 1930s detached house with a bay window and paved-over front, where his car sat. Odette had patched us into the surveillance drone sensors. According to the heat outline, he was presently in his front room.

The curtains were drawn shut, so whatever he was doing, we couldn't see. Vic rang the bell and waited. Nobody came. Standing there, I looked down at my phone and the imaging. Far from coming to the door, Walker had gone upstairs. Obviously, comrade Walker wanted to be alone today.

It was Sunday, so maybe he had the newspapers to read, or he was off to church. Or there was a roast to cook, with accompanying veg. Whatever the reason, he was upstairs in the front bedroom when Vic rang again. This prompted no movement whatsoever. He just stayed there. Vic bent down and shouted through the letter box. Not what you call high-tech. It certainly wasn't effective, because he remained in his bedroom.

We discussed what we should do next. He was inside; we were outside. What action should – or indeed could – we take, wasn't an easy question to answer. We had enough to closely question him, but we could hardly do that through the letter box. Should we smash down the door? Did what we have justify that? The trouble was, we didn't have much in the way of alternatives. Our decision was to return to Vic's car and wait.

So, we sat there, aircon on, and monitoring screens up. Several were showing our virtual boards back at Somerset House and their steady inflow of information. Another was from the drone following Anand, who was seemingly having lunch with a woman on a park bench. Roijin had identified her as being his older sister. The conversation we were picking up on was of great importance and interest, focusing as it did, on the sister's unhappiness at how Anand wasn't visiting his mum enough. It seemed that I wasn't the only one who had fraught issues with family members.

Then suddenly, my thoughts on families were rudely interrupted, with Vic slapping her knees. 'Shit! What an idiot!' She phoned Roijin and spoke rapidly, allowing for little in the way of replies. 'Roij, me again. Look, I've just realised that we haven't done something, which we bloody well should have! Who's the first people we usually talk to when we're trying to find out about someone?' She paused before almost shouting, 'Yes! Bloody right! Family members! Looking at Anand and his sister reminded me – talk to their family! The time for subtlety has long gone. Could you prioritise that? Cheers.'

Commands delivered, she looked at me and shook her head. I pulled what I hoped was an understanding face and returned to staring at the screen showing the movements of Noah Walker. He had now moved from the main to the spare bedroom. He though, had left his phone in his bedroom. We had turned it on and could see the ceiling, which had a hairline crack along the edge. Neither of us were over-pleased to be sitting here. Vic especially was cursing the drone, which she said was a museum-piece, only having thermal imaging. She had a point: this had been standard technology when I had been still at school. But here we were, like we were trapped in a time-machine, watching a fuzzy glow of red and orange silhouette move around his house. When confronted by Victoria's howls of complaint, Roijin had explained that it was the only type which we could presently get our hands on because of our previous rulers' scorched earth policy with regard to the country's IT infrastructure.

I had no idea what people passing thought about the pair of us. The car itself looked too upmarket and conspicuous to be a getaway for a burglary. More for drug dealers, I'd guess. Or they thought we were having an illicit affair and this was our bolt-hole. Certainly, one elderly woman using a walking frame stopped to have a good nosey at us. Her pet pooch sealed the interest by pissing up against the left front wheel. Nice.

We could have been there for the rest of our lives, if an excited Roijin hadn't rang us. 'Vic, Pete, you're watching crap! I've just been looking at the programming coding and it's not what it seems. Basically, there's a simulation being inserted into our system by the house's AI. What you're seeing is fiction.'

For the second time in half an hour, Vic swore and slapped her knees. She'd have arthritis, if she carried on doing that. Out of her glove compartment, she took what looked like a three-dimensional trapezium and all but leapt out of the car, announcing that we now had every right to break in.

Before I had a chance to make a reply, she had pressed her gadget against the front door's keypad and pressed a red light. A small bang went off and the door shuddered, and she gently pushed the door. It swung open. Quite a magic trick. I wondered if she could pull a rabbit out of a hat too. Instead, she pulled out her gun. I did likewise. Nowadays, I was pretty good at doing this. I could usually manage it without it catching – too often – on my jacket lining.

Once in, the first place we looked was the front room. It was one you'd expect to find in your common-or-garden London activist's home. It was neat and tidy, with inexpensive, but decent flat-pack pine furniture, and a floor-to-ceiling bookshelf, with all the titles you'd expect from a leading revolutionary. Finding the room lacking a Noah Walker, we tried the kitchen. In there was neat, inexpensive but well-made furniture, but no Noah Walker.

It was the same story when we searched the upstairs, the two bedrooms and the bathroom. All were neat and tasteful, but empty.

'See anything out of place?' Vic asked, whilst she holstered her gun.

I looked around. 'What – aside from the fact that Noah Walker isn't at home? No, it all looks, well, it looks, er, normal.'

Her voice was urgent and very angry. She had been made a fool of and Vic did not like that one little bit. She reeled out instructions: 'Roijin, you there? Good. Issue a warrant for his arrest. This time it's going to be more than a cosy little chat. That little bastard has a few questions which need to be answered. I'm going to talk to the neighbours and see if they have any idea where he might be.' She shot me a look. Her face was red and her eyes pretty much were too. 'Pete, you stay here, look around, see if you can find anything.'

Unsure what that might be, I wandered around, looking at the books. Nothing was out of place and a good number of them were in my collection. I picked a few out, flicking the crisp pages. All were neat and mint. After finding myself getting immersed in a classic on race and class, I remembered why I was here and pulled myself away and headed back upstairs.

Opening up his wardrobe, I saw a dazzling array of truly hideous jackets and trousers. He obviously didn't do subtlety, or indeed wear anything that didn't cause blindness. The same applied to his drawers. Painfully coloured shirts and socks lay neatly folded. Lying on top of the chest of drawers was his fabled phone.

Walking into the other bedroom, I pulled out more drawers. Déjà vu hit me with a soggy mallet. Another house, another search. Finding nothing but naff taste, I moved to another unit, looking indistinguishable from the rest. However, this one did not contain more of his atrocious socks, but a filing cabinet. It wasn't locked, so I pulled open a tray and looked inside. Kneeling down, I flicked through the metal dividers, I was impressed at his system. It was easy to follow and extensive.

A shout from Vic, broke my concentration. 'Pete?'

I grabbed a bundle of the files and headed downstairs. She was standing by the door, with what looked like a torn sack at her feet. I didn't have a chance to ask her if she'd been playing Santa, because she had spotted the files in my hands. 'Found something, Pete?'

I nodded towards the lounge. 'I think so. Let me show you.'

She followed me, leaving the sack at the door. I sat on the sofa and laid them out on the Ottoman footstool. She sat by me and looked at them.

'These are his examination certificates, all in chronological order.' She took a few seconds to look at each. 'This is the hard copy of an email inviting him to a job interview. Behind it is the print-out of the email confirming that he got the job. Then there's payslips from that company. Here are rent receipts. Upstairs, there's loads more of this type of stuff. From what I can see, every job, every place where he lived, every doctor he ever visited is evidenced. All are crisp, intact, neat and perfectly filed.'

She took some examples off me and looked closely at them. 'Twenty years old and in perfect condition. What a careful and neat man he is.' She looked at me, with knowing eyes.

'Yes, he is. I'm quite an ordered person myself; I've documents from years back. Thing is, mine get creased after a month or two. The same goes for those books.' I nodded towards them. 'There's nothing unusual in the fact that a comrade has books, nor that they are looked after. People who have physical books often feel almost love for them. I'm the same. But my books are also used; they're not for show, they're to be referenced. That usage cannot but mean that there will be signs that they have been opened and studied. But his look straight off the press. There's a stiffness when they are opened.'

She nodded, and spoke as much to herself as to me. 'What careful man he is – keeping documents from every stage of his life. Which does means that what we have here is a wealth of information, which we have been searching for, everything we have been mobilising workers' councils for, is here nicely filed. That's convenient.' Sarcasm dripped from the final word. She paused. 'We can use it to check up on his life-story.' She paused again.

She was, of course, correct, and I knew exactly what was coming next.

'Okay, so we can get the office to chase all this up. I've already called, and Roij and Ash are on their way. They need to do a full forensic sweep.' The poor bastards always had to do the legwork.

'One thing, I've already found, is this.' She held up a small bottle of hair dye. On closer inspection, I could see that it was empty. 'Also, in the sack is a three-quarters full tube of glue, the type theatres use to stick false facial hair. The neighbours saw a dark green hydrogen Peugeot, reg starting with REH, pick him up about half an hour before we arrived. They say he was wearing a black bomber jacket, blue denim jeans and a dark blue, possibly black, baseball cap. That's obviously to hide his hair. Seems today, he wants to be invisible. He's doing a runner, Pete. I've called all transport hubs to be on the alert. I've put out a call across party and NWC media that he is someone we wish to help us in our enquiries, but it isn't going to be easy. He'll have an escape route all planned out for him. I'm hoping that the timeframe means that he's still in the country, but that still leaves a large area to search.'

'Excellent – any ideas what else we can do?' I asked, hoping that she did, because as far as I could see, we had just allowed a mass killer to get clean away. One who had the blood of Mike Stewart and those at the Shard on his hands. He was safe and sound, whilst we admired his show home. All it had taken was a hacked drone and some fake whiskers. It had been that simple. *We were that simple.*

Vic looked thoughtful. 'This is a long shot, but then the way I see it, we don't have too many options, so it's the best I can think of, but we could talk to Reyansh Anand. He's been working closely with him for the past year. Now, whilst we can't completely rule Anand out, I think the fact that he is still here, means that he probably isn't directly involved, so would be willing to help us. Walker might have inadvertently told him something, which could help us. I would have thought that no matter how good a spy-cop you are, you can't be in a role every minute of the day. Anand is an intelligent man, he might remember something which is of use to us. We don't have that long, if Walker hasn't already left the country, then he will be doing so very soon.'

She was right, it was a long shot, but then they often made the best goals. The trouble was that for every one which went hurtling in, twenty went flying into the stands. I, though, couldn't think of anything better. We had to somehow make up for lost time.

A wry smile crossed her face. 'Reyansh Anand has just been detained by members of the NWC Corps. As time is of the essence, I've arranged for him to be brought directly here. Luckily for us, he was pretty local, his sister lives in Edgware, which is only twenty minutes away. My guess is that he will be here soon. Let's get ready, Pete. This has to be done well. We need to be at the top of our game, and we need a lot of luck.'

By the time all our house guests had arrived, we were ready and hoping for luck. Not that we looked particularly efficient. I was actually in Walker's kitchen making drinks for everyone. Roijin was at the kitchen table, surrounded by papers and virtual screens, as she went through Walker's personal archive. She and Asher had arrived half an hour after Anand had. Asher himself was upstairs looking for things like concealed compartments and basically anything which looked remotely spyware.

Anand had been the first of our invited guests to walk through the front door, closely followed by a four strong NWC Defence Corps escort, and a string of expletives. Despite the assurance from his guards that they had been polite and discreet, he was fuming at what he called his abduction. Looking at the four of them, I did feel some sympathy. I wasn't sure how such a muscular quartet of armed women could possibly be anywhere near discreet.

Victoria had been assertive with him, which was no surprise, but she had also been calming and even soothing. Which *was* a surprise. Patiently explaining what we had found and why we needed him – *really* needed him. Whilst he hadn't fallen in love with her, the four-letter words had decreased in frequency. He still didn't believe that Walker could be a mole and still thought we were on the bequest of Jackie Payne to clamp down on any internal dissent, but at least he wasn't now tearing up the atmosphere.

I poured the tea out, whilst following the strict instructions on the amount of milk, sweetener and sugar which should be in each. Putting the cups on a plain red tray, I took the NWC guards theirs first. Whether this was from hospitality to sisters from a fellow NWC organisation, or simply that they were bloody intimidating, I couldn't say. Vic had expelled them from the lounge, saying that she wanted a more relaxed atmosphere. One was stationed on a stool by the door, whilst another was at the bottom of the stairs. The remaining two were sunning themselves on the front doorstep. I exchanged some polite small talk, gave them their beverages and then headed upstairs. Asher was on his knees, closely studying a socket in the main bedroom. I put his drink on a bedside cabinet. 'Ash, your tea. Sorry, there's no biscuits. Found anything?' I asked.

He shook his head, got to his feet and stretched. 'Nah, nothing so far, it's all clinically and forensically neat, tidy and normal. I'll keep at it, though. How's Anand? I can't hear him anymore – is he being more amenable?'

'I wouldn't go that far, but he's dropped the hostility level somewhat. Vic is having a cosy chat with him.'

Asher had obviously caught the note of amusement in my voice, because he grinned. 'It may be difficult to believe, but Vic can be very encouraging when she wants to. She can equally play good or bad cop. She's a highly effective interviewer. I've seen her be the wild lion and at other times, a pussy cat. She can play any role. '

I didn't disagree, although the thought of Victoria Cole being a tame feline was something even my vivid imagination couldn't comprehend. Instead, I just muttered something inane, and headed downstairs to finish my tea-round.

After boiling the kettle again for the second sitting, I let it settle in the teapot. In the meantime, I poured myself out a coffee, took a few sips, before pouring out a tea each for Roijin, Vic and Anand. I was just leaving, when Roijin let out huge scream. I almost dropped the cups on the floor, and it was only due to some previously unknown juggling skills, that I didn't. The guard in the hall was more proactive, and came running in, gun drawn. It was certain that her arrival wasn't from fear of hot drink spillage. However, the huge triumphant smile on Roijin's face, and her clenched fist punching the air, was the give-away that the guard's sprint and my circus tricks had been wasted. There was nothing to worry about. All was well. Seeing what she had caused, Roijin apologised profusely and reassured us that all was well. 'Very well, in fact,' she beamed. The guard had barely left the kitchen to return to her stool, before Roijin was waving pieces of paper in front of her, and pointing at an image in front of the both of us.

'This is Noah's birth certificate, and host of medical files, blood group and his old National Insurance number. There're masses of other personal stuff. They match with his primary school records. The thing is though, that the Noah Walker they relate to, died in a road traffic accident when he was thirteen years old.'

'Are you sure?'

'Totally. Look, here's the photograph of the boy–' she pointed to the virtual image in front of us, which looked like a news blog from the period, headlined, "Dangerous Game, Claims Another Victim". 'It's from a local paper's report on the accident. I think they published it as a warning, he and his mates were playing chicken – who could run out of cars at the last minute. He misjudged it, tripped on his flared trousers and fell. He was on a life-support for three weeks, before the plug was eventually pulled. The article gives some background info, which I cross-matched. It all fits. The poor lad was born on that date, was born at the same hospital, same blood type, had the same jabs at the same time, went to the same nursery and the same school, etc, etc. Basically, Pete, this is Noah Walker!'

The picture of the boy in the report, who even allowing for the passing of years, didn't look remotely like the Noah Walker who we knew. His eyes were smaller, ears bigger and his nose was longer.

'He took a dead child's identity?' I asked, aware of what she was suggesting, but wanted to make doubly sure.

'And look at his bio-tech ID, it...'

I held up my hand, indicating that I was confused. 'I thought all the BIFs had been wiped – by our side? Before, even, the dual power of parliament and the NWC. It was seen as an important moment, the techies organising and hitting back. The BIFs were a symbol of cyber-authoritarianism and the action was a blow against it.'

The who hacked and wiped what, and when, was a rather twisted and complicated thread in the history of class struggle. True, it didn't have the romance of street battles and mass pickets, but it was nonetheless an important part of it. There was also a great deal of irony to which side was attacking particular areas of cyber-space and who was defending it, and how that could dramatically change, depending on the state of the struggle. Rather like two armies fighting over no-man's land in the 1914-1918 World War, it could change pretty quickly. The bio-tech Identity files, or BIFs as they were known, had been hated by our side, and yet here we were, grieving at their loss.

'You're right. But like most such actions, there are scraps of them left. His is one such.'

That was lucky. 'Is that common? I mean how much is left?'

She shrugged. 'I'd say approx. 9%.'

Very lucky, then.

'And it proves that 'our' Noah Walker is a fake one?'

'Yes and no.'

'How can it be both? It either confirms your suspicion or it doesn't! And that looks exactly the same photo that was in the newspaper clipping.'

'It is.'

My little brain was lost. Did this mean that we hadn't made any progress? Just a newspaper clipping and a guess. How did this fit with the other Noah Walker being killed in a car crash?

She enlightened me. 'Obviously, that's why his BIF is still there, or bits of it. It's just like all these paper files, it's to 'prove' who he is. It's cleverly done, there are scraps of the real Noah – the dead Noah in there. Look closely at the photo: it's smudged and fuzzy. I think it's been doctored, it's the real and legit picture. It even has the address of the photographer who took it. He's long-since died, but he existed, and so did his shop. But it's nowhere as clear as the one in the newspaper report. Unless we spent long hours of research, we couldn't prove that it isn't our Walker. Even the outline of the face has been smudged so as to confuse, or at least off-put face-recog. The later pictures are much clearer and are obviously of our

Walker. It stops at a time when it is said that he was nineteen. There's nothing suspicious in that, because of the cyber-struggle.'

'Why?' I was still finding this a touch confusing.

'To make it look genuine, Pete. See it like a scrap piece of paper. To have a full intact BIF right up and until our cyber-action, would have looked too suspicious. Whoever was responsible for that part of his cover-story knew what they were doing. I don't think this was ever intended to stop any investigation completely, just to slow it down. My bet is that they thought that if the party was going to the trouble of fact-checking his Bio-Tech ID then his cover had already been blown. But I didn't need to do that.' She grinned. 'I simply analysed the photograph and found it has been changed using a completely different program from any mass-data wipe. And I could even date when it had been done. And guess what? The date is four weeks before he applied for a job at Strictly L Solutions! Without boring you with techie-speak, this is a fake ID and I can prove it. Classic spy-cop procedure. He's not even from Southampton. Actually, it was the first thing I did – I used a voice-scan on some of his broadcastings. It came back as 94% certain that he was born and spent at least until his early teens in mid-Dorset.

'Brilliant!' My grin matched hers. 'Could you relay it all over to my phone? Vic and Anand need to see this.'

'Of course.'

'Great! Vic is going to enjoy this, even more than my tea.'

One of the NWC guards in the hall opened the lounge door. On entering the room, I found Reyansh Anand sitting on one of the armchairs, leaning forward, resting his elbows on his bare knees. Vic was opposite him, and was also leaning forward, her hands clasped together. It almost looked romantic. Almost. Although they were both talking quietly, I could still sense an atmosphere in here. His voice was no longer expletive-heavy, but I could hear him repeating what he had been saying since he had arrived, that he did not believe that Noah was a traitor and we had shown him nothing that could be taken as proof. 'From what you've said, what you've got basically boils down to several guesses and pseudo-facts.'

I put the tray down and passed the drinks around, and waited for the right moment. Anand nodded a thank you as he took his drink, took a sip. He spoke: 'I can't see that having neat filing is in any way suspicious.' He raised an eyebrow, which I presumed, indicated disbelief, rather than disapproval of my tea-making abilities.

'I admit, what we have isn't conclusive, comrade,' Vic replied, oozing empathy, 'but you can help us to either find further proof, or conversely, prove his innocence.' Her entire attention was on him, barely acknowledging my existence; despite hovering by her shoulder, with her cup. She merely pointed to the floor. I did as I was bid, and put it down. 'Secret agents rarely leave too much in the way of evidence behind – they're trained not to. There won't be a signed confession...'

And there was my cue to speak. The tea boy could now deliver his lines. My big break! 'Maybe not, Vic, but there might be a data-file, which acts as one...'

Having grabbed their attention, I put my phone on project and then palmed the screens into an order. 'Okay, let' start with these from the early years of Noah Walker...' I went on, making sure that I did so in stages and all the while looking directly at Anand.

Five minutes later, and he had his head in his hands. If muscles could talk then his quads and biceps were narrating a story of anger. They'd have to shout, mind, because out of his mouth, outrage was bellowing out. Swearing had made a comeback – big time. Not this time at us, though. 'Treacherous fucking bastard' was one of the less-heated names he was using. Was this rage at a traitor, I wondered, or a betrayal of a friendship? Or was the outrage designed to persuade us that he had known nothing of Walker's activities? He looked at me intently. 'I had no idea, comrade. No idea, whatsoever. You do believe that, don't you?' When neither of us answered, concern crossed his face. 'Am I a suspect? Comrades, do you really think that I'm involved in all this? That I'm his, his...' He grappled for the right description. 'Fellow spy, his accomplice?' Before adding bitterly, 'No, I'm just his dumb patsy!'

This time, Vic did answer, still using the calmness which she was giving an airing. 'No, I don't actually think that you are. I'll be honest, and I'm sure that this will come as no surprise to you, for a period of time, you have been someone we've had concerns about. You will remain a person of interest, but in all honesty, at this moment, no, I don't believe that you've been duplicitous in any shape or form. But as I said, we'll keep checking.'

He gritted his teeth and clenched his hands together, but again the anger did not appear to be directed at us, but at his former ally. 'The fucking treacherous bastard. What has he done? How many has that piece of ruling class scum had killed, or actually killed himself? I've been such a fool. It never crossed my mind. I thought you were just against what he, what we, were arguing. Christ, I've been a mug! How could I have been so stupid!'

I sat by him, and said in a low voice, 'We've all been. That's why he has these documents, it's called his "legend" – his fake life story. He's been in deep cover with the party for years which makes it hard for any of us to believe. I mean, we've put out an NWC nation-wide call, but do you really think that every single person who hears it will believe it, or will some just think, as you did, that this is the dominant faction of the party merely clamping down on dissent?'

That thought seemed to stir him some life back into him and he looked up, unclamping his hands. 'Well that's something I can do, to start making up for what I've done – you could put me on one of the call-outs. Me and him have always been seen as bloody Tweedle Dee and bloody Tweedle Dum, so if I am involved, then people are less likely to be suspicious.'

'I think it's a very good idea,' I replied. 'But before we get to that, can you think of anything he might have let slip or mentioned that you thought was out of place?'

He blew out his cheeks. 'Vic's been asking me the same thing, but nothing springs to mind. I mean, I've known him for almost three years. We've had a lot of conversations in that time. What exactly do you mean? What might he have said?'

'Did he mention anyone that you didn't know?' Vic asked.

He looked at her, as if she was stupid. 'He mentioned quite a few people I've never met.'

'Anyone he seemed a bit secretive about?'

Again, he flashed her a look, which was far from being flattering. My guess was that he wasn't over-whelmed with our razor-sharp questioning. He didn't answer, but shook his head. He was being somewhat unfair, as it was pretty hard to think what incisive questions we could actually ask.

'Think, Reyansh, please think – it could be vital!'

Was it my imagination, or was Vic sounding distinctly desperate? She'd be pleading at this rate.

'Sorry, I'd love to be able to help, but what constitutes being secretive?'

He had a point.

'Was there anyone only he met, or contacted by himself?'

'Well, we weren't joined at the hip. There'd be quite a few that we didn't see together. I don't think he ever met my mum for starters. But no, sorry, I can't think of anyone who he deliberately kept me away from. No, I am sorry, comrade, but I really can't think of anyone.'

Vic thought about his answer. I wasn't sure there was too much to think about. 'Okay, can you think of anything, anything at all, which might be of help?' This new approach could best be described as desperate.

He started to tap under his chin, before shaking his head.

The sole benefit of my intervention was to make hers seem less naff.

She took over the chief integrator role.

'Have any thoughts of where he might have run to?'

He looked at her. 'How on earth would I know that? It could be anywhere!'

'True.' She jutted her chin towards one of the screens. 'Did he ever talk much about Southampton?'

'Sometimes. He'd talk about the Small Firms Strike and how it changed him. Little did I know, just how much it had – to a spy cop. All just a pack of lies. That's probably why he was so reluctant to have anything to do with the place. Never wanted to visit there – would avoid it like the plague. He'd travel halfway around the world to stand on a picket line, anywhere except Southampton. Bloody obvious to see why, now.'

'Anything stand out when he was talking about the place?'

She was met with thoughtful silence. With one eye on the clock, she urged him again to think. If Walker was doing a runner, then time was of the essence. The desperation monitor was swinging into the red.

He went back to tapping. All of a sudden, he tilted his head. It was obvious that something had just occurred to him. 'Well, I once overheard him on a telephone mentioning something about a boat. It seemed he was being told about one, which I thought was odd. I mean, why would he want a boat? Alright, he was called Noah, but I never had him down as a boat kind of guy!'

I smiled at his joke. It was a good one, I wish I'd thought of it.

'I asked him about it, asked him whether he was buying a boat, but he brushed it off, saying that I'd misheard. I knew I hadn't, but I let it go. After a few days though, he got another call, and I was sure I heard a marina mentioned. I asked him whether it was about his boat again. I did it half in jest, but he got quite angry and told me to stop eavesdropping and imagining conversations. I let it go, basically cos I didn't care, but he wasn't happy. I just put it down to stress.' A thought struck him. 'Actually, this was about the time, you started to investigate that anarchist's death – Mike Stewart.'

Vic and I exchanged a look.

His back straightened. 'Yeah, I don't know if it means anything, but he was very odd about that. He was always transparent with what he was doing.' He laughed ruefully. 'Or pretended to be. Hiding in plain sight, I guess. But with this, he all but snarled at me to keep my nose out of his business. He got really pissed-off.'

She asked, 'Do you remember anything which may point to where it was berthed?'

'I got the impression he knew the place.' He stopped and closed his eyes, trying to remember the call. He spoke slowly: 'He...said something...what was it?' He clicked his fingers twice. He wasn't going to launch into The Addams Family theme song – he'd thought of something. 'He said, "avoid that place". Yeah, that's right, he said, "I thought you wanted me to avoid that place".' Anand looked at us. 'The place must have been Southampton!'

In seconds, Vic was on the phone to Odette. 'We think Noah Walker is trying to get to Southampton. Yeah, well, we're not certain, but what we know points to that. Get all the Southampton Workers' Councils – actually – get all the workers' organisations you can think of, to look out for a dark green hydrogen Peugeot, registration starting with the letters REH, heading towards the south-east coast.'

Anand mumbled to himself, 'Pointing?'

'Sorry?

'Pointing, that reminds me.' His finger-snapping increased. He'd be recording a single at this rate. 'I'm sure I heard Noah say the name of the boat, he asked whoever had called, what it was called and then repeated the name. Now what was it? It was something about pointing. That's right, the boat was called arrow something, arrow, no arrows, that's it. Arrow of something. Arrows of – of love, romance?'

'Arrows of desire,' I said. 'Was it Arrows of Desire?'

He slapped his side. (Proving that he was adept at using various parts of his anatomy for percussive accompaniment.) 'That's it! How the hell did you know that, comrade?'

'It's from a famous hymn, "Bring me my bow of burning gold/Bring me my arrows of desire".' I turned to face Victoria. 'It's from Jerusalem.'

# CHAPTER 38: THE GREEN WAVE

T he journey to Southampton had taken a lot less time than the arrangement for the transport to make it. I had pointed out the salient fact – or perhaps it should be the sailing fact – that this boat – if it existed – could be found in a marina anywhere in the country. It didn't have to be at Southampton. Walker could have been told to avoid a multitude of places – maybe he had ex-wives dotted around the country. My doubts were compounded by the fact that the snippet of conversation, which Anand had overheard, sounded to me like it wasn't actually his personal boat; it sounded more like one that his masters were offering him. It was his getaway ride, or getaway sail, if you will. But if someone was offering me a new bike, would they park it by my old primary school or the primary school I pretended to have gone to? A glazed look of disbelief had met my comments. (Or incomprehension at my strangled metaphor.) Obviously, my thinking sounded better in my head than in hers. That hadn't stopped me from also suggesting that even if she was correct in that the boat was moored near his fictional home, it could just as easily be Portsmouth. That was only twenty miles up the road from where he claimed he was from. In all honesty, she had only been half-listening because Vic was busy galvanising the Hampshire class into action.

There was another detail – there were twelve marinas in the Southampton area. None of this had even made her pause for thought – she had decided. Nothing was going to stop her. And it appeared that we *had* to go by helicopter. All this talk of super-spies seemed to be affecting her. She had demanded a chopper. Locating one and seeking permission for its use had led to drawn out arguments with party and NWC officials. Vic had spent much time regretting the lack of *Protocol #5,* because if she had it, we'd not have had this trouble.

The delay had been of some benefit though, because by the time we were hovering over the marina, we had received concrete confirmation that he had been spotted driving through Eastleigh, on the outskirts of the city. Odette's communications had been effective. Quickly, she had organised a mobile-division of cars, bikes, motorbikes, hover-boards, joggers and pedestrians, from here to the Solent, all travelling in never-ending circles on the lookout for him.

Over the news channels, Reyansh Anand was appealing for comrades to help locate Walker. He had strenuously reassured viewers that this was not an attempt to stifle debate and oppress opposition, but was one of defending the revolution. He had made it highly personal, talking about how both the revolution and he himself had been betrayed. I found it ironic that it was probably the best I had ever heard him speak.

We had been airborne for only a couple of minutes, when we were gifted yet another piece of luck – the boat itself had been found in the Sarah Fiona Davies Marina. The news that both boat and renegade were in Southampton had provoked an incredibly painful smug look on Vic's face, something which I had to endure all the way. Thankfully it had been a short journey.

The chopper had dropped us off a life buoy's throw away from the boat. The Arrow of Desire turned out to be like so many people I know: scruffy and nondescript on the outside, but a treasure-trove inside. Externally, the boat looked run-down and in dire need of a lick of paint. With the shutters down, it simply looked like a 12-metre motorboat that a Hedge Fund manager might have once bought on a whim, after a bottle of champers and three lines of coke. Then had promptly forgotten about it. Two clues gave it away that all was not what it seemed. The first was the fact that it had three engines instead of the usual one. The second, was the high-tech security it boasted. Not that it prevented us from gaining entry.

Inside was very different. The look of commonplace was purely for camouflage because the interior was rammed with surveillance and communications equipment of the highest order. There wasn't much in the way of comfort, but there was a wealth of stuff that an up-to-date spy would find useful, including an array of weaponry.

We'd had ten minutes to nose about before we heard him tapping his pass code to get into the security pad. We had relocked the door and reset all his security devices, so he wouldn't know that we were here, waiting to toast his arrival.

Vic and I were sitting by a small round Formica table in the cabin, opposite the outside door, or hatch, or whatever the entrances and exit holes on a boat were called. She looked cool and calm, her attention focussed on the door. I tried to adopt the same, but excitement was turning my body into a summer fun-fair – we had finally caught the murdering bastard.

He came down the small five-step ladder. His head was down and he was typing a message into his phone, so for a moment he didn't see us. Gone were his garish clothes. Across his shoulder was a small brown leather bag. His hair was dyed black. The only hint of colour was a pair of pastel striped espadrilles. He looked like your average middle-class guy off for a spin in his floating toy. Strangely, it also made him look younger.

Although both Vic and I hadn't moved a millimetre, something must have stirred in the air or caught his eye. His head jerked up. In a split-second, his eyes went from registering surprise to steely purpose. His hand went for the bag.

Vic though, was quicker. She lifted her gun and pointed it at his head. 'Don't! I really wouldn't do that if I was you!' she snarled. A second later, the door to the downstairs berth flew open and Asher's two arms shot out, grasping a gun, pointing at what looked to me, like Walker's groin. Walker's eyes darted from one to the other. Before he had time to decide on what action to take, the last of our merry gang shoved her pistol into the top of his skull. Behind him, standing in the doorway, Roijin hissed, 'Drop it, Walker!'

'Or should we call you Christian James?' I said, holding a passport we had found in his packed case downstairs. His mug was in the photo section and it was under the name of Mr Christian James. I was holding a gun in the other hand because everyone else was, and I didn't want to be left out. But it was the passport which was most dangerous. 'Or is that another identity you stole off a dead child?'

He didn't say a word and simply put his hands up.

'Come off the stairs and stand on the deck,' Vic commanded. 'Keep your hands up and don't make any sudden movements, or we'll have the pleasure of restraining you – by shooting you.'

Without saying a word, he did as she had instructed.

Roijin followed him down and relieved him of his bag, sliding the strap up over his arm, and tossed it to Asher. With impressive agility, she managed to do so without her gun arm wavering even a fraction. With equal dexterity, he caught it one handed, again, with his gun arm remaining on target. I was impressed, and for a split-second idly pondered whether we could form a cricket team. These two would be great in the slips.

That could wait. This was another thing which Vic had got right: it had been her idea for all four of us to come here. Vic had haggled for two helicopters, instead of just the one, but with us all in here, it felt right. The team together, arresting this piece of scumbag. Poor Odette was staffing the office, but she could at least enjoy our tales of adventure when we returned.

The scumbag in question – Walker (I couldn't get my head around calling him James) – was surreptitiously looking around, weighing up his options. I decided to point out the obvious, that there were three guns aimed directly at him, plus mine, which was dangling vaguely in his general direction, so he didn't have many to choose from. 'By the way, even if you did somehow manage to get past us, there are up to a dozen NWC Defence comrades outside, so I wouldn't do anything stupid, if I was you.'

He didn't say a word, but nor did he do anything else. It was only after Roijin had patted him down, and told him that he could put his hands down, did he move. But only his hands.

Vic read him his rights: 'The citizen, we understand to be Christian James, also known by the alias, Noah Walker, I must advise you of your rights. My name is Victoria Cole, I am an investigator with Crib. Under the workers' republic constitution, I must advise you that you have the right not to say anything, but anything you do say may be given in evidence against you.' His eyes did not even flicker. She continued, 'So do we call you Christian? We know it's not Noah, but is Christian your real name, or do we call you something else?'

Still, he didn't speak. I stared at his face and saw a countenance of impassivity. It was like one of those plastic masks you buy at high-street joke shops. Not that anyone was laughing. I guessed that my compadres felt the same as I did – happiness at catching him, but aware that we still had work to do.

'Okay, at least for the time being, we will call you Christian – Christian, you're going to be taken to a Community Social Responsibility Hub, where you'll be detained for questioning. We have enough to keep you for 48 hours. We're pretty sure that in that time we will be able to get enough to keep you longer, when you go before a judge. You may choose a defence representative or we can appoint one. You should be aware that we are confident that we will be able to link you with the murder of five citizens. In which case, it is clear that it is in your best interests to tell us what you know.'

He just looked at her.

Her manner changed. She lowered the formality, and adopted a friendlier, almost advisory manner. 'Christian, you must know that you don't stand a chance. You'll stand trial on five counts of murder. We'll also charge you with organising reactionary violence with the intention of undermining the revolution and of passing on information to hostile powers. You risk spending the rest of your life – or should I say *lives,* real and fictional – in jail. It would have been less, but ironically, you're the one who is responsible for toughening up the sentences.' She smiled, as if sharing a joke over a pint.

He didn't join in. Not a muscle of his moved.

Vic nodded at Roijin, who with only the slightest nod in return, took both of his arms and pulled them behind his back. He didn't struggle in the slightest, but let his arms go limp as she put handcuffs on him.

Vic spoke again: 'Talk to us, James. You're obviously a highly intelligent person, so you'll appreciate that you're finished. We've been on this boat for less than a quarter of an hour and we have already found evidence that there's arrangements for you to flee to a hostile nation. Numbers stored on the ship's com are of foreign spy agencies. When we have more time, we'll get more. Your cover is blown and as an agent, you're useless. But, Christian, we can make life easier for you when you're serving time. Maybe get you a reduced sentence for your cooperation. There could even be a possibility of a prisoner-swap with your employers, but that will only happen if you give us some information.'

She didn't even get a "No Comment".

Every question she asked, received the same response. He stood almost to attention, staring at the window behind my shoulder. After several minutes of this charade, she paused.

I took my turn. 'So what about "Jerusalem"? Is it a real organisation? Is it a cover name for the coordination of foreign agencies or is it just a game? I mean, there's the visit to my home, seemingly for the sole purpose of turning over a page of the atlas; the text messages to me, and even the name of this boat is a phrase from it. I have to say, that it all sounds childish to me. Why advertise it? Is it all some sort of joke? If it is, at least let us in on it.'

If I was expecting my cheeky-boy good looks and male-model on a catwalk sense of style to get him to speak, then I was disappointed, because he just stared straight ahead.

Vic sighed. 'Okay, have it your way, James, Walker, or whoever you are. Roijin, get the comrades outside to take him away. We'll talk to him later.'

He had been driven to the nearest Community Social Responsibility Hub. CSRHs had been created to act as centres where the community organised the policing of itself. Sometimes, like the one where we had taken Christian James, they were based in the surviving police stations, and converted to their new role. There had been an attempt to make it look like a community project rather than agent of oppression with soft furnishings and pretty pictures. Much of the locked off rooms had been opened up. Our heavily armed arrival had been rather incongruous, as we had marched through a meeting discussing how improved rubbish collection would be beneficial for the area.

We had deposited our particular pile of trash in one of the underground cells, which still existed for the detention of anti-social elements who needed more than a stern talking-to and a reminder of their revolutionary duty. For the next four hours, he had moved between the cell and one of the interrogation rooms, where the four of us had taken it in turns to question him. All of us had met with total failure. He just looked at us with a hint of faint amusement.

For the moment, he was back in his cell, sitting alone, eating a salad and drinking a glass of water. We were in a side room, reviewing what we had learnt since his arrest. From the scumbag himself, nothing. He had kept speaking to an extreme minimum, only doing so to request a drink or to say yes to food, or request a visit to the toilet. For everything else, not a word. He hadn't even responded to our offer of legal representation. But then, as Roijin had pointed out, that was something in itself, because most people would have done.

If nothing else, this all proved just how much Noah Walker was an act, Noah Walker was someone who couldn't keep his trap shut. He'd speak for hours on any subject, and always put himself in the middle of it. Revolutionary movements, Marxist theory or pigeon racing – Walker could make epic-long speeches. Here, he was almost non-verbal.

'Why is he not even denying our accusations?' I asked. My frustration obvious to everyone.

Vic replied, though I got the impression that Asher or Roijin could have equally done so. 'He wants to keep all communications to a minimum. The first thing you want to do when you're interviewing a suspect is to establish a relationship, so later, your hope is to use it as a pathway of dialogue.

He's preventing that. Him not talking, makes a relationship very difficult to form. It's also a very good way to move the balance of power. We feel frustrated and powerless, waiting for him to have some kind of relationship with us. He has the power. Then we start to get angry and lose control of the situation.'

Well, it was working with me at least. 'Is it that he doesn't fear us?'

'Possibly that too, Pete. If he's in this for ideological reasons, then he'll believe that the foundations of our state are wobbling and that we've a year or two at most. After that, he'll be released as a hero! The death penalty, torture and inhuman imprisonment are illegal, so, he's no worries on that score.'

'It could also be that he fears what his side might do if he does talk,' Roijin added.

From her expression, I could tell that Vic considered that a reasonable thing to infer, but not necessarily the main reason. 'Could be. I'd say though, that it's more likely that he sincerely believes in what he's doing. He'll not give up anyone, or anything, about his work. We need to build up a case against him ourselves and in doing so, hope that we get a little luck and be able to uncover the network he works in.'

'You believe there's a network?' I asked.

'Absolutely. It might go under the moniker of Jerusalem, or it may not, but there'll be one.' She stopped and looked around the room as if she was hoping for answers to pop out the walls. 'So, what have we in the way of evidence against him?'

Asher spoke first. 'I'm waiting for the results of some tests to come through. The whole boat has fingerprints and fibres from just four people – and those people are in this room – us. From top to bottom, it's been sprayed with anti-forensic chemicals. It's totally clean.'

A pained expression crossed Vic's face. I hoped it wasn't the tea I'd made her. The milk had looked a bit ropey, it had to be said. 'Okay, thanks, Ash. Roij?'

'I had a look at his com equipment. All CIA tech, even has their logo on. Their security protocols weren't too difficult to get past, my guess is that they didn't expect the boat to be found, and even if it was, we'd be unable to link it to anyone. Anyway, whatever the reason, I was able to confirm that there's been contact between him and various foreign powers. None of the conversations were recorded, but I can, for certain, link him with at least two other intelligence agencies – the French and Germans.'

I was confused. 'But I thought we had established that he had never been to this boat before? Anand told us that in the phone conversation he'd overheard, Walker had to be told the name of the boat twice, implying that he didn't know of it. That call was made only a week ago. Do we think that with everything going on, he'd have time to check it out first? See if the drinks shelf is adequately stocked? I mean, we don't have anyone who saw him here previously, do we?'

Vic shook her head. 'No-one's seen him there before, and in fact, everyone at the marina that we spoke to, had never heard of him. The suitcase we found on the boat looked very much like something you would pack for someone else, someone else who's about to make a break for it. Certainly, there's nothing in the way of DNA we can get from it and the clothes look brand new. We can try to chase where they may have been purchased, but that'll take time.'

No-one had answered my question, but then Roijin finally did. 'It's been accessed externally, Pete, through a series of passwords and voice recognition. That *was* recorded and yes, it's the voice of the man we've locked up here. It was a signal. Once he did that, they knew that he was getting out. From what I can see, we arrived just in time. The message also remotely set up all the boat's systems so it was ready for launch – all ready to go.'

'Have we confirmed that Christian James is actually his name?' Vic asked.

Asher sighed. 'We've a passport, driver's and boat licence, and a set of credit cards. They look legit, but then so did all those documents under the name of Noah Walker. Personally, I'm minded to be suspicious of them, bearing in mind, they're here, but he never was. Plus, Christian, Noah?' He pulled a face as if he'd just tasted a sour lemon. I knew what he was getting at – the Biblical link was just too quaint.

Vic rubbed her forehead. 'We probably have enough to make a reasonable case to extend his detention. I mean, we've evidence of collaboration with hostile nations, but the stumbling block is the evidence of linking him with murder. By my way of thinking it's pretty circumstantial. We need to get a whole lot more if we're going to charge him with multiple murders and terrorist atrocities. Pete, anything to add? What's the public reaction to his arrest been like?'

'Pretty positive so far. The combination of public statements by Jackie and Anand have been effective in quelling any disquiet.'

Asher added in a complimentary tone, 'And from yourself, Pete. I thought you were measured and professional. ' He grinned. 'And you looked fabulous. The coastal sky behind you went well with your suit.'

'Thanks, mate. I was just hoping that the seagulls didn't shit on me!'

The comment relieved the tension a little. Obviously, birds crapping on me was a source of light entertainment. Not wanting to dwell too much on what that might mean, I continued, 'But seriously, also, credit where credit is due, Fiona Bailey's played a blinder. Her statements have been important, both congratulating us and praising our work. I think that she and other leading AF members being so positive has gone a long way in preventing any demonstrations or more violent acts against the party. It's not beyond the realms of possibility, that the AF could have used it as a stick to beat us with – metaphorically and literally. It could so easily have turned sour, when you consider that for the past few days there's been demonstrations against them, calling for the arrest of Dave Donaldson. They could have taken revenge, once the news came out that Walker is in custody. But of course, all this doesn't help our investigation. Fact is, no-one has come forward with anything which we might use.'

With a voice sounding equally resigned and committed, Vic said, 'Come on, Pete. Let's have another go at him. I think it's our turn. I know you think I like the sound of my own voice, so, with me doing all the talking, whilst he just sits there, staring at me, will provide me with endless joy.'

'And for me,' I added.

Our prisoner was being held in a standard prison cell set up, or at least that was what I had been told by Vic on our arrival here. Each cell had a concrete ceiling and floor, with three concrete walls. The one closest, and the door within it, were made from reinforced glass, which had the strength of concrete. At a flick of a switch the glass wall could be made transparent, translucent or opaque, depending on the jailor's wish.

Out of politeness, Vic informed Christian that we were going to turn it to transparent and then would enter the cell. He was actually on his feet, stretching and looking intently at the glass wall. She told him to sit and lay his hands on the arms of the chair, and his heels against the front legs. Without opposition, he did.

On entering the room, I could see that his plastic tray, along with the plastic plate, cutlery and cup were sitting neatly on the floor. A green light indicated that his wrists and ankles were in position. If they moved more than a few millimetres, restraining bands would instantly wrap around them. For further safety, he was being watched by two armed guards. Not that it particularly looked like we needed protecting because at present he was as about threatening as a new-born lamb.

'Christian, we want to know if you're okay. Was the food adequate?'

He looked at her and simply replied, 'Yes. Thank you.'

'We would like to ask you some more questions. May we?'

This time, she didn't receive a reply.

I had noticed that on the few times he did speak, not a facial muscle appeared to move. It was like those early face-lifts, back in the 2020s, when actors and actresses would appear on chat shows to plug their latest movie, with only their mouth moving. The plastic surgery paralysing everything else. Vic was right, this was evidence in itself – you'd have to be trained to be this impressively impassive. It was to antagonise his captors. It reminded me of those times when you are having a disagreement with your partner: you're ranting and raving, and generally getting very hot under the collar, whilst they calmly just look at you – claiming to have no idea what the problem is.

Vic though, wasn't getting frustrated – she just continued with the interview. 'We can now confirm that you have been in contact with two foreign intelligence agencies. We can also prove that you had planned to escape, using another identity than the one which you are known as. Could you at least give us your first name?'

He did not say a word.

And on it went. It didn't matter whether it was me or Victoria asking the questions. Just as it hadn't when Ash and Roijin had questioned him, we didn't receive a single reply. Indeed, we didn't even get a twitch of a muscle.

We had been in there for about ten minutes, although it seemed like ten days, when Asher appeared, loudly tapping on the glass, beckoning Vic out. I watched them. He leant towards her and spoke into her ear, whilst showing her an image projection. He had switched on the security visual shield so all we could see was a foggy sheet, roughly the size of an A4 paper. Every so often, Asher would look up at the prisoner. The interest wasn't reciprocated, at least not obviously. Although it was clearly something pertaining to him, Christian/Noah didn't once change the direction of his eyes, which since we had first entered the cell, had been looking directly to my right-hand side.

After five minutes, Vic returned. I resumed my pose of the ever-vigilant guardian of the revolution. Christian/Noah continued his impersonation of a statue. A childhood memory came into my mind, when people would spray themselves gold or silver and remain still for hours on end. Covent Garden would always be full of them, all standing in the hope of some small change coming their way. He was as annoying as they had been.

Vic took her phone out, and projected an image in front of us.

'This, Christian, is your bag, which you were carrying when we arrested you. Inside, we found a Maly X15, which as you no doubt know is a Czech pistol. We also found a spare round of ammo. Then there was some sunblock and an almost finished packet of tissues. Aside from the fact that it is good to see His Majesty's secret agents protecting themselves against skin cancer, it's the tissues which interests us.'

With her palm against the image of the bag, she dragged out pictures of the gun, ammunition, sun-block and tissues. Whether he liked it or not, he was looking at them. She smiled. I knew that smile – it was her smile of triumph. Whether he knew it or not, he had lost. Big time. She flicked the packet. 'These tissues are standard issue. They come in a wrapped pack of eight. You've obviously used them, because your fingerprints are on the outside wrapping. The makers of them boast that they are highly absorbent. There was one left, hanging out of the packet.' She flicked up another image. This time it was of a mobile phone. 'Let me show you this – it's the phone which was used to direct the drone attack on the Shard. It is a YP3 made by Estmorr. Model number LX389111723. It was wiped clean – we could find no prints or anything on it. So forensically not very useful. Except...' She moved forward and grinned. 'When we looked at the ultra-absorbent tissue in your man-bag, it matched the type used to clean down the phone. Okay, that doesn't directly implicate you, because there're probably tens of thousands of these packs produced. But the thing is, when we tested the one tissue left, on the top edges, the exposed part, we could find elements from an Estmorr phone on it. We can narrow it down to the model type YP3, then even further down to model number LX389111723. Oh, and each phone has an individual unique number. We can prove that the phone used to murder four people in the Shard was in contact with this tissue. I presume that you used the tissues to clean it with anti-forensic spray, and threw them away, but you hadn't realised that the one which you hadn't used, also had been in contact with it.' She paused.

He did not move, but had I imagined it, or did he move weight on his feet and his eyes flicker? She, though, was not finished.

'But let's look at the outside of this very stylish bag. So stylish that I think Pete would probably use it.' I wouldn't have, but I figured that wasn't the key thing here, so didn't correct her. 'It's a nice leather case, very nice. Also, it happens to be rather absorbent as well. We tested it and found traces of a Vengeov violin, which a few years ago, was a pretty popular make of violin. We also found traces of a resin used on the maintenance of the wood of violins. Again, pretty popular. But then we found more! You could say that there was a veritable treasure chest of finds. We found a microscopic trace of china. What has that to do with a violin you might ask? Well, it comes from the china used to make figurines, figurines such as ornaments of musicians. This we can trace to a particular chipped ornament of, you guessed it, a violinist. All these traces can be proved to have been in contact with your bag at the same time, so if we could find a place where there is a Vengeov violin which has been cleaned using a particular resin, which just so happens to be next to our tiny ornament, then we could locate *exactly* where this bag had been placed. And you know, Christian, we can! In the storage unit belonging to Dave Donaldson, there was just such a combination. You'll remember, that was the place where the phone was found. Where *you* left it to incriminate Donaldson. The problem for you is that you must have put your bag down, and when you did, you rested it against the violin and the figurine. If you were in a talking mood, you might now ask us what the margin of error for this forensic evidence may be? Well, you needn't ask, because, I can tell you – zero percent. Yep, comrade, there's no margin of error. We can prove that your bag was there; which means that you were. Which means, that we have you.'

She got to her feet. 'Citizen, you will face murder charges, which will amount to a long time in a revolutionary republic jail. Oh, don't worry about speaking now, it really isn't worth it.'

For the first time, his head moved to look at the evidence. He knew she was right. We could prove he was a murderer.

# CHAPTER 39:
# WAITING FOR THE VERDICT

E njoying a leisurely Monday morning, without any specific demands on my mental energies, had been a hugely pleasant experience. I'd got up, made myself two Espressos, shaved and then gone to the swimming pool. Not exactly humming a happy tune, but at least thinking of one. There, I managed to complete fifty lengths almost effortlessly – front crawl, breast and back stroke. After the shower, and a further coffee, this time – being post-swim – a latte, I scootered here to Jackie Payne's London office.

I had arrived at 11am. Predictably, Jackie had been in a meeting, which turned out to be with a motley group of teenage comrades. Seeing me, she had quickly, but politely, ushered them out. With arms outstretched, friendly but with determination, she had shepherded them past me. There had been brief introductions (so as not to appear impolite). I was from Crib and they were from the HRG – the History Recognition Group. After the last of them had left, no doubt honoured to be in the presence of the president, she explained to me that they had been here to, amongst other things, attempt to solve the naming situation in the country. Despite the subject of statues and street names being a hot issue for several decades, it had taken centre stage since the revolution. What the HRG was attempting to do was to settle it once and for all. As Jackie pointed out, Hyde Park had been renamed at least three times in the last twelve months. Sometimes, like having three rival popes there had been competing names for the same place. Their recommendation for Hyde Park was that it should be known as Toussaint Louverture Park.

She sighed wearily. 'I really do hope this will be the end of the matter. I mean, I understand that the task of reappraising the past and honouring the struggles of the brave people who ultimately led us here is an important one. Of course, I do. Like every other decent citizen, I also understand that honouring past imperialists and ruling class warriors should end. But right now, we're in a life and death struggle and there's far more important matters to deal with than the names of cul-de-sacs. Still, we need to sort it out.' Her final comment was as dry as a Kent field in a summer drought. 'At the very least we should be able to remember what they're bloody-well called.'

Once the HRG were downstairs and there was no-one was within earshot, we took a seat each. Our body language eloquently spoke of our differing emotions. I sat there, my spine snugly fitting the back of the chair, legs crossed, feeling somewhat content with life. Some might even say, smug. And why not? In less than a week we had uncovered a counter-revolutionary spy who was a traitor and a multiple murderer. True, there were many things we still didn't know, for starters – what his name actually was. He, like Hyde Park, had many. The media had solved the onomastic conundrum by simply sticking with Noah Walker. Official party releases had referred to him as the "comrade formerly known as Noah Walker". With Vic's discovery that Christian James was probably also fake, we at Crib had reverted back to calling him Noah Walker. We all agreed that the link of the first names of Christian and Noah just had to be false. In truth, I did so with a twinge of guilt because it seemed disrespectful to the dead child, but then we could hardly keep calling him 'the spy', 'the person known as Noah Walker' or 'treacherous git'.

Jackie offered, and I accepted, a coffee. 'You look happy.' She smiled, pouring it out. 'And so you should be. Good work, Pete. I hope to pop into your office some time to pass on my congratulations and gratitude. I must say that it comes as a shock that Noah's a spy. I know that after all this time, I shouldn't be surprised by anything, but still.'

I took a sip. It was a pretty weak coffee. Obviously, the president's office was not involved in black market purchasing and just went for the legit, cheap stuff. Principled, honest and sound – just a crap taste. Forcing the tang down, I decided to speak before my tongue dissolved. 'We believe that he was given a fake identity and with the connivance of its owner, was parachuted into a company called Strictly L Solutions during the Small Firms Dispute. We don't think the owner knew exactly who or what he was getting, but he'd guessed that he was connected to the police in some way. Walker used the strike to add to his political CV when he joined the party. And there he remained – fooling us all.'

I could see her shaking her head with regret. I tried to lighten the tone. 'Simple rule of thumb, Jacks – distrust anyone who believes that they've been perfection from conception. Any comrade who comes over as if they learnt their phonics from the Communist Manifesto is, if not dodgy, then a total prat, who should be avoided.'

She laughed, showing her teeth and making her eyes sparkle. 'I'll bear that in mind. So where are we at?'

Attempting to keep a cool nonchalant tone, I went through everything we had on him. That included Roijin managing to prove that at the precise moment when the drone's controls had been over-ridden, this phone had been outside the TV studios.

'Fantastic,' muttered Jackie. But then paused and face-palmed. 'Wait a sec, just so I'm clear, because there seems so many mobiles – we're *not* talking here about the phone which was actually used to operate the drone, and which you found in Donaldson's storage unit?'

'That's right, Jacks. *That* phone's been completely wiped; we haven't been able to get anything from it. Then there's his personal phone, which he used every day. Even before his arrest, we'd accessed it and were monitoring his communications. But this is another one.'

'So, what was this third phone used for?' She looked at me, confused.

'Our guess is that it was for his work with the security agencies. Like a drug dealer might have one for personal, and one for dealing...'

'Except you're saying that Walker had three?'

'Right. The third one was solely used for controlling the drone and was placed in the arms lock-up, purely to incriminate Donaldson.'

'But it's the "business" phone – his "drug dealer phone" – which you can locate outside the TV studios?'

'Yes.'

'Christ! How many did he have? Couldn't he have just keep changing the comcards?'

'No,' I replied. 'We could still have recognised the broadcast echo.' My reply sounded impressive and sounded like I knew what I was talking about, but the truth was, that I had got that snippet of info off Roijin. Fingers crossed that Jackie wouldn't ask me to elaborate.

'Could someone else have had the phone – this "drug dealer phone" of his – the one used to contact his lords and masters?'

'Possibly, but that would mean one of two things: That Walker had handed it to that person, or they stole it off him. We can locate it in

Walker's home during the night, then it moves into the studio when the debate begins. At precisely the time the studio cameras lose sight of Walker, it moves outside. If it was someone taking it off him then they also returned it directly after the attack had finished, because we can also trace it to the Shard at the very time he was there – at the time when he met us.'

'Wasn't Reyansh Anand there as well? Could it be him?'

'It's possible. But that would suggest that it was the pair of them in it together, and we think that's unlikely.

'We think at the time of the TV debate he left his legit "everyday" phone inside, so as to give the impression that he was present for its duration. He knew full well that we had hacked that one.'

She thought for a second, processing what I had just told her. I could almost see her wince at the implications. However, she quickly accepted my explanation and with a professional voice asked, 'Okay, so what does Walker say about all this?'

'Nothing.'

'Nothing? Nothing, as in not much, or as in a denial or as in completely non-verbal?'

I tried not to look sheepish, because I had been coming over as being pretty damn impressive – if I said so, myself – but the truth was that whilst Asher and Roijin had been building a case, Vic and I had been getting absolutely nowhere with questioning him. Drawing a huge blank – getting a multi-dimensional sod-all.

She looked surprised. 'Not even a denial?'

'No denial, no admission – nothing.' Again, I tried to sound knowledgeable. 'It's a technique used to shift the sense of control from the jailor to the prisoner. The prisoner is the one who is controlling the flow of conversation, and so not allowing any chance of developing a rapport between questioner and the questioned.' This time, it was Vic's knowledge.

'Do you think we can get him to talk? Offer him some incentive to confess and even pass on information? I presume we think that he's not a lone wolf, but is a part of a wider conspiracy?'

'No doubt, there's a conspiracy. The international ruling class are getting desperate. The revolution has lasted far longer than they predicted, and we remain a potent threat. They'll be trying every way they can to isolate and preferably topple us. They'd wear a pink bunny outfit and chew a carrot, if they thought it would further their cause, and hinder ours.'

For a moment she looked confused by my comment, before mentally filing it away with the explanation that this was Pete Kalder talking, so that's the type of thing he said.

I continued: 'Jacks, if only that it was just him! The revolution would be very lucky if it was. But Cribs across the countries are unearthing all kinds of plots. No doubt, there're many which we don't know. But he won't talk. I've met people of all different shades of political allegiance, and I think I can tell a true believer when I see one. In my opinion, we won't be able to get anything from him. He believes what he was doing was right. That's why he lived a lie for all those years. There isn't an incentive we could offer him that would induce him to betray that. I'm sure a prison sentence won't bother him because he believes it will be short, because he believes the revolution won't last. He can sit this out for a couple of years, max, until the revolution is overthrown – then he gets liberated and is hailed as a hero.'

She nodded and stroked her eyebrow. I was pleased that she agreed, because this for a change, was coming from me. I didn't want her to think I was here just for my looks.

'And you believe there's an organisation called Jerusalem?'

I shrugged. 'We really didn't know. What's for sure is that they're organising themselves better, there's more international cooperation. Even if it's not by that particular name, there's something like it. I mean, wouldn't we?' That all sounded logical, but here's when it got surreal. 'What's truly odd though, is the nonsense which went with it. I mean, calling the boat after a line in the hymn, Jerusalem. Texting me with the name! Not to mention, going to the bother of visiting my house to leave a clue. All seems rather strange behaviour for a top-secret organisation, don't you think? Simply naming themselves after such an iconic hymn sounds to me like someone likes playing games.'

'Was it Walker then, who broke into your home?'

'Don't know. We can't locate him being there. But then, he might have just left his personal phone at home. He did, after all, have at least two others.' I smirked.

A faint smile approached her lips, but she didn't let it grow. 'Okay, so that's the drone attack. What of Mike Stewart – what about him? I was speaking to his mother earlier.' Her eyelids briefly closed at the memory. 'She's kindly asked me to speak at his funeral tomorrow, which I've accepted – and she asked if Walker was going to be charged with her son's murder. I couldn't say anything, and to be brutally honest, Pete, I would really like to be able to. She's concerned that his death has been over-shadowed by the Shard atrocity. To be honest, I think she may have a point. Can we link him with his murder?'

I blew my cheeks out, because this was where it was going to get even messier. 'Not really, no; Anand claims that he was having a meeting with him at that time. He's been pretty vague on the details on what they were exactly discussing, but it is related to their side's demand for a more authoritarian state approach...'

'I think they wouldn't use quite such terms. Proactive or assertive are words which feature heavily in their media when dealing with reactionary threats.'

I scoffed, 'Considering what we now know about Walker, you have a banner for irony, right there!'

'Indeed.'

'Earlier this morning, Roijin and Odette looked at their tech-com for the time, and it does give the codes and broadcasts from the address they claim to have been at the time.'

She looked at me suspiciously. 'Claim?'

'There's a Com-Shielding Device – a CSD – connected to the house-com. It's something which both Roijin and Odette have seen before but it's above even their impressive tech capabilities, and they can't access it. What they do know is that amongst its many possible uses, it can act like a camouflaging piece of kit. Which suggests that something is being hidden, but we can't access it.'

She blinked slowly. 'Okay, so have you, or Odette or Roijin, any idea what exactly it might be hiding?'

'Honestly, we don't know, but the very fact that it is on Anand's home communications set-up is highly suspect in itself. It may be perfectly innocent but then why have it and where did he get it from? It's not the sort of thing you can buy online.'

'You know, Pete, things were so much easier for previous generations – leaflets and fly-posting was all they had to deal with. Now I find myself in the middle of a bloody computer programmer's wet dream. Are they even called computer programmers nowadays?' She thought for a second. I hoped she wasn't waiting for an answer from me. Not getting one, she continued, 'So if Walker claims to be at Anand's, and wasn't, he could use one of his three phones and route it through this shield to make it look like he was there, when in reality he could have been anywhere – like providing a utility bill to support a fake address?'

Inwardly, I smiled at the fact that Jackie was as old-school as I was. Luckily, I was ancient enough to remember envelopes and utility bills, so I got the comparison. 'Yes.'

She rubbed her eyes. 'Which could mean that Noah Walker was not at Anand's?

'Yes – it could.'

Her hands were still over her eyes, as she might do to hide them from a glare. 'Which would then pose the question as to why Reyansh said they were.'

'Yes.'

'Christ, this just gets worse.' Something occurred to her. She tilted. 'But wait, you said Odette and Roijin only checked this morning, why wasn't this done earlier?'

'We had a witness who said she saw him there. Her name is Mia Lewes – do you know her?'

'Vaguely. Active in the car construction trade unions – party member – been one for a few years.' I could almost hear a reluctance to ask the next question for fear of what the answer might be. 'Why – do you think she's also involved?'

'She also happens to live with Reyansh's Anand. She's his partner.'

Jackie winced. 'Jesus, how bad is this going to get?'

'Don't jump to any conclusions; we're not accusing her of anything, we haven't found anything dodgy about her, but then to be honest, we haven't looked that closely. We've called her into the office so we can have a chat. Previously, she was interviewed by the local council's reps; she told them that Walker was with her and Anand for the specific hours concerned. We're having her in to see if there is anything else she can say, or might want to add, or change. Or where she bought the CSD.'

'Okay. So where does this all leave Reyansh? I have to say, since the arrest, he's been brilliant – really been pushing himself forward for interviews and briefings. He has been strident in his condemnation of Walker, which has been especially poignant because of their close-working relationship. Do you think he's involved?'

I had actually heard some of Anand's interviews myself, whilst I'd been swimming because they'd been playing over the sports centre's system. I agreed with Jackie, they had been articulate and powerful, but what they said about his loyalties wasn't clear. He may be sincere, but then that's also the sort of thing he'd do even if he was involved in the conspiracy, perhaps *especially* if he was. He knows we have suspicions and would want to cover his retreat. I left that all unsaid, and simply replied, 'We still consider him a person of interest. He's not under arrest but we have him under surveillance. We'll be talking to him again.'

She nodded. She had heard my unspoken thoughts. 'I think Anand has a lot to prove.' She glanced up at the clock. 'Not least, right now. He is talking to the Soldier's Council, about his involvement and actions over the past few days.' Again, she stopped for moment, before letting out a long sigh. 'So, the thinking remains that the purpose of all this carnage was simply to further friction between the AF and us?'

I told her that it was.

She sighed. 'Christ Almighty...'

'That still seems to be the most logical reason. Jacks, you're the best placed to know how effective it has been, I only watch the news, you make it. How do you see the situation?'

'Tense, Pete, very tense. Oh, both sides are saying the right things. We've comrades queuing up to condemn Walker and to big up you Cribbers. You're the stars of the moment – once more the whole revolution loves you. Even Marie Williams has given an interview where she congratulated the work of Crib, and indeed, you in particular, in the most effusive terms!'

'Following party orders, was she? Was it that or the gulag?' My smile and light tone hopefully indicated that the comment was from a place of self-effacement rather than bitterness.

'Not at all.' She held her hands up. Jackie had taken it for bitterness. 'Totally sincere.'

'Well, I'm truly flattered. Not sure what her sudden conversion means, but anyway.'

Jackie seemed to be in a very relaxed mood. 'Oh, there's more, Pete. On the same programme, Reeves Wilkinson said the revolution owed you a huge debt of gratitude. Although I think that was partly due to the fact that he was being closely questioned on his association with Walker; him formerly being the Southampton organiser. For much of the interview he was on the defensive, denying that he knew anything, and that he never had the slightest suspicion of Noah Walker. Which, I guess, is pretty much true of all of us. He sounded guilt-ridden, poor man. He really shouldn't be, but I guess many of us are feeling guilty – I know I am and that's fair enough. I have to admit that I am finding it all very difficult to take in. I mean, his name isn't even Noah Walker!'

There wasn't much I could say. The thing with this strategy of embedding agents to undermine us was that even if they were discovered, the destabilising effect continued. The more of them we found, the more suspicion was aroused, the more it undermined us. 'And the AF?' I asked.

Her shoulders ever-so tensed beneath the white dress. This was a subject where it was difficult to feel relaxed about. She carefully chose every word. 'It's been patchy. There's some in the Anarchist Federation who are using the whole debacle to argue that we're not to be trusted and that the very nature of our organisation facilitates the Noah Walkers of this world. There's no way around the fact that this doesn't make us look good at all. I don't blame them for doing so, because, well, that's politics. If Anand and Mia Lewes are also found to be involved in Stewart's murder, then, well, that'll only exacerbate the situation.'

I knew only too well that politics rarely had time for sentiment, but this did smack of opportunism. 'Surely, the fact that it was a Crib full of party members who uncovered him has some kudos?'

'To a certain extent, yes, but there's even some who are saying that you have just made a scapegoat of him so as to cover the real conspiracy.'

'Which is?' I asked.

She shrugged her shoulders and changed the subject. 'I saw Dave Donaldson on the news, with Fiona Bailey. Both were flattering about you and Vic. He was quite emotional, actually. Good Lord, Donaldson, praising a Crib. I would never have imagined that. Obviously, you've released him.'

I nodded.

'Is that wise? You think he's safe?'

'We think so, we're all agreed that they – they being Jerusalem or whoever – would be hard pushed to frame him now, so we let him go.'

'Hmm. If that's what you think.'

'I don't think it'll be Crib who decides his future – what's going to happen to him, concerning the storing of illegal weapons?'

'That's under discussion.'

'Surely, he's not going to be let off?' I was shocked. I wasn't totally naive and knew that in days like these, there was a certain amount of horse-trading, which had to be done to keep our allies happy, but keeping quiet about an arms dump intended to be used against us was equine commerce to Seventh Cavalry levels.

She merely repeated, 'It's under discussion.'

I knew that was the end of the matter. I wasn't happy, but there was nothing that I could do.

I gazed out the windows at the pure blue skies. How good it would be to be up there. 'How's Phan Bien doing?' I asked, thinking of Donaldson's fellow hideaway, who was now also tasting freedom.

'Shaky. Phan may give off happy vibes, but I think deep down she's a rather sensitive soul. She'll have found this all rather hard to take. My guess is that she's having a hot bath and a glass or two of wine. Maybe having a good cry. And I don't blame her. I think some time off would do her good. If that's possible.'

Neither of us spoke for a moment. I can't say what was going through her mind, but I was just thinking how I was looking forward to something similar. I would take a couple of days' leave once the loose ends had been sewn up. A train trip up to the Yorkshire Dales would be an idea. I could get away from all this stress and just go for long hikes and try out some real ales. Not that I was a real ale type, or indeed a hiker, but a change would do me good. I could totally understand where Phan Bien was coming from. The line of work I had found myself in seemed to have as much stress in one day as most jobs have in a month. And it wasn't getting easier, quite the opposite.

Jackie must have sensed what I was thinking, because she leant forward and gently touched my hand. I looked at her face and saw a dear friend. One who looked back with the same affection and perhaps something which looked like pride. 'You've done a great job, Pete. The revolution appreciates it – *I appreciate it!*' She smiled, tapped my knuckles, before getting to her feet. 'Please pass that on to everyone. I'll be addressing NWC tonight and making a public appreciation of your work. Thanks so much.'

I joined her standing. This time I was given a warm embrace. It was one of gratitude, coupled with more than a touch of weary regret, and a polite way of telling me to get on my bike. So, I did, or at least on my scooter. I did, in any case, need to be off, because I had this meeting with Mia Lewes.

I hadn't left her office before she was contacting people for a 3D conference. As they came online, she turned and yelled after me, 'Keep me posted!'

The journey to Somerset House was uneventful. My stomach even managed to digest Jackie's coffee. My arrival at the office hadn't been met by a fanfare, but there had been a display of grins and smiles. The hum of chatter stopped as I entered the room. The team looked up and said hi. Even Odette, who was stretched out, legs on her table, talking on her phone, and eating her obligatory piece of fruit, interrupted her flow of words to breathlessly welcome me. Roijin was leaning back on her chair, hands behind her head, looking for all the world like the cat had got several long-haul tankers' worth of cream. She gave me a thumbs up.

I asked Asher, 'What's up?' – he had said the loudest and longest hello, adding several ees to my first name, as he had.

'Just finished talking to Mia Lewes,' he replied.

I looked at my watch. It said ten past one; her appointment had been for half past. 'She's been in already?' I said, putting my helmet on my desk, trying to hide my unhappiness at the fact that she'd come early, but my colleagues and comrades hadn't thought it important to wait for me and had interviewed her. That was a bit of a slap to my ego, it had to be said.

However, not wanting to appear juvenile, I adopted a lofty tone: 'And?'

I had expected Vic to speak. She usually did. But it was Roijin who shot forward in her chair, so quickly in fact, I thought she was going to rugby tackle me. With a wide smirk and looking as if she was someone who had managed to have her cake and eat it. But then what was the point of having cake, if you didn't? Words cascaded out of her mouth. 'She denied even knowing what a CSD was, let alone having one. She reckoned it must be Walker who planted it. Vic asked her why he would do that; she couldn't answer that. She confirmed that she'd been with Walker in a meeting.' Roijin laughed and shook her head in disbelief. 'Good grief, did the girl talk about that. Ranted about how unhappy she is with the direction of the party – unapologetically critical of how soft the party is. "Drowning in liberalism" was how she described us. She confirmed *again,* what both Anand and Walker claimed, that they were planning a campaign to position Walker for a bid to go on the Central Committee.' Roijin stopped.

I could sense a big *but* coming; however, I did not want to spoil her fun, so I asked it – 'and?'.

She took the prompt. 'She now says, that after thinking about it, she might have – in her words "underestimated the time" when she left. Previously, she thought it was nine when she left, but *now* thinks that she wasn't with them for as long as she thought she was. She now thinks that she left the house at just gone eight.'

This was indeed news; the new timing was now almost an hour earlier. I could see why Roijin had been looking pleased with herself. 'That's quite a difference. It's not like a minute or two out, is it? Why wasn't she more concise when the stewards spoke to her?' I asked.

'She said that she was flustered.'

'Flustered? She was flustered – like some Jane Austen character waiting for the arrival of a neighbouring hunk in riding breeches?'

'That's the word she used. I *know* – it's weak.'

'To put it, *weakly,*' I muttered. 'You believe her?'

'Maybe, maybe not. Certainly, she didn't seem like the flustering type.'

'But she maintains it was simply a mistake and not a cover-up?'

'That's what she says.'

Roijin clearly felt that Lewes had now been dealt with and was merely just a detail. She was keen to return to Walker, who, after all, was the person we were most interested in. 'Anyway, with her amended statement – amended for whatever reason – it means that we only have Anand's word that Walker was there. We can't even check their online work because of the CSD. Certainly, the time she now says she left, means that if he had left soon after her, he would have been able to get to Stewart's house before Bailey and Williams. That's getting very close to Noah Walker having no alibi for the time of Stewart's death.'

'So, Anand is an important witness here. Have you had a chance to talk to him about his partner learning to tell the time in the past few days?' I looked directly at Vic.

This time she answered, her tone was measured. 'Not yet, but I agree with you, Pete, it's important that we do. It's true that we may have let Mike Stewart slip from our attention. Odette is contacting all transport unions to see if anyone saw Anand or Walker, or both, on public transport between Anand's house and Stewart's.'

On hearing her name mentioned, Odette gave a large wave and smiled. Vic replied with a thin smile and continued: 'She's also contacted all the road safety stewards, to see if any of the roads' traffic control cameras are in operation. If we can get a sighting of him en route, then that could confirm him as also being Stewart's killer.' She ran her hands through her hair. 'Of course, if their original statement is true, and they both really did stay until gone half nine, then that would mean that Noah Walker couldn't have killed Mike Stewart. In which case, his killer is still out there.'

I folded my arms. 'It could be that Reyansh Anand was not only an ally in the faction, but in destabilising the revolution as well.'

Asher agreed. 'Simply put, he provided an alibi because he's a spy too.'

Vic nodded, seeing the possibility, but although she herself had actually raised it, I sense that she had doubts. 'Could be, but it seems strange to me that they'd have two, possibly three, important assets in such close proximity – wouldn't they want to spread them out? You know, have them in different parts of the country or something? Having them based in the same area of London, working almost side by side, sounds like putting all your eggs in one basket. And surely, by having one providing the alibi for the other, draws attention to the other. If one is caught, then the other one goes down as well, and drags Lewes with him. To me, that seems a very inefficient and unproductive way of working.'

Asher nodded, seeing the logic, if not totally buying into it.

Personally, I thought it quite plausible that Anand and Walker might team up. The pair of them had been very effective in tandem. Let's face it, unity was strength. Their interventions had, whether we liked it or not, helped frame the national political narrative.

'So, what do we do, Vic?' Asher asked. 'Have another go with Walker?'

Her mouth turned downwards. 'We'll keep trying, but quite honestly, I really don't think Walker is going to say anything more than he has. He's too professional. He won't crack.'

For some reason, I put my hand up like a Year 3 kid might in maths. 'Sorry to get off the point, but do we actually know Noah Walker's real name yet?'

Odette answered in a voice bouncing like a tennis ball: 'Not really, I've linked seven possible names with him so far but nothing definite. Sorreee.'

'Then, we'll stick to Noah Walker,' I mumbled.

Vic stroked her chin. 'Keep going, Odette. We'll find it. As for Anand, well, it won't harm anyone to have another conversation with him. Now his partner has...' she made bunny ears with her fingers... '"underestimated the time" he might have too. Perhaps time-keeping is an issue in that household. It's worth asking in any case.' She looked around the room. 'Anyone have an idea where we might find him?'

Heads shook. Mine didn't, because I actually did know where he could be found. I told her and suggested that we ring him. This was an interview, which I could be involved in.

Vic agreed.

I noted that they'd also decided to allocate duties without waiting for me. We went next door. The room was in the middle of being renovated and being made fit for purpose as extra office space. New IT equipment had been installed and the walls had enjoyed a fresh lick of paint. The large external window was now bullet-proof. Up already was our new logo. The design was the C and B were in capital letters, with the C encasing a much smaller r and i in lowercase, and all in bold red.

'Like it?' I asked, pointing my nose in its direction.

She pouted. 'Yeah it looks okay. Reminds me of a fish or maybe a rocket.'

I snorted, 'Well I could only do so much with the name we're saddled with.'

She grinned. 'Let's give Anand a ring. Mind if I take the lead?' I had no problem with that whatsoever and sat beside her. It was 3D visual and was positioned so as to locate us directly in front of the logo. Something, I was sure, would become iconic.

The call was answered by a pencil-straight, upright, muscular soldier, wearing a red arm-band and closely cropped hair. She barked her answer: 'The NWC National Headquarters of the Soldiers' Committee. This is Comrade Michaela Groves. How can I help you, comrade?'

It hadn't really been necessary for her to answer the call as she might in a parade ground, but old habits die hard, I guess. She had called herself comrade and abiding by the NWC directive, didn't appear to be wearing any sign of rank, but she spoke as if she was a sergeant-major.

Vic introduced us in a much softer tone and requested an interview with Reyansh Anand. The reply came straight back like a bullet: 'That won't be possible, I'm afraid, comrade, because unfortunately he is in a session with the Soldiers' Disciplinary Committee.' It had been said with all the comradely politeness one could have asked for, but still, this was one comrade whom I'd not want to cross.

Vic though, wasn't as easily overawed as I was. With a fixed smile and voice sounding as if she had tasted something distinctly off – maybe Jackie Payne's coffee – she replied, 'That, comrade, is incorrect. You can, *and will*, seek an adjournment, whilst we talk to comrade Anand. As I clearly explained in the beginning, we are Crib – the Counter-Revolutionary Intelligence Bureau. By NWC Directive *Number 45436, Civilian Protection* you will be aware that we hold jurisdiction over civilian issues – in particular, those we deem to be a threat to the safety and maintenance of the revolution. The military have none whatsoever. As Reyansh Anand is being questioned over purely military issues, we take precedence. His working comrade-in-arms, known as Noah Walker, has been unveiled as a reactionary renegade. It is quite possible that Anand has been in league with him. Therefore, we have the right – the duty – to question him.'

For no more than a split second, Vic paused, before resuming in a voice, which, if possible, sounded even more sour. 'Which means, *comrade Grove*, that you cannot deny our right revolutionary duty to question him.'

You could almost see our soldier comrade biting her tongue. But discipline won out and Groves replied through clenched teeth, 'I'll put you through, comrade.'

Two more soldier cadre tried to put up similar resistance, but both had been met with an equally fierce response. Both quickly realised that it was futile to argue.

Finally, the man himself appeared in front of us, looking sharp in his pressed uniform, but not in his expression. Although not a hair looked out of place, it was obvious that he had been grilled closely by his fellow military revolutionaries. He met us with a resigned smile.

Vic returned it, and instantly her tone changed. Whereas before, she had been strident and commanding, now she sounded as she might when meeting a friend, one who was having a bad day. 'Hi Reyansh, thank you for waiting. I know that you're keen to get home, so we won't keep you long. We just want to confirm a few things.'

His voice was heavy with fatigue. 'Yeah, sure. Fire away.'

'Thanks, comrade. I understand that the Soldiers' Committee are considering charging you with bringing disrepute and dispute to the revolutionary forces of the state?'

He didn't say anything but gave a small nod of his head.

'Okay; of course, that's not a matter for us. We also understand that the party's disciplinary committee is considering whether you have or have not broken any of its rules considering appropriate behaviour of a comrade. Again, Reyansh, that's not directly our concern.' She made what I guessed had been intended to be a sympathetic expression, but it looked more like she was suffering from a touch of wind. 'Now, there are a number of outcomes here, Reyansh – ranging from complete exoneration, to expulsion from both the army and the party, to ultimately imprisonment. We do have some say in what choices are made and can testify on your behalf. Put bluntly, comrade – you help us, we can help you.'

He nodded, but still didn't say anything.

'Right. You maintain your innocence.'

'Yes. Absolutely. I'm no traitor. I'm loyal to the international workers' revolution.' Those words could have so easily sounded like a defiant roar, but in reality, they sounded defeated.

Vic flashed me a look. We had decided that we were going to just ask him questions and hear his answers. They'd be no challenges or debates. We'd simply just listen. 'Okay, understood. That's good to hear. And you never had any hint that Noah Walker was?'

'Never.'

'Not even in retrospect perhaps? Something which you now look back on and think that it was not as it first seemed?'

'No, sorry. I'm not going to lie. I never saw anything that made me have doubts about him – then or now. He always seemed to be a committed and passionate socialist. That's the truth. Which might make me naive, but it doesn't make me corrupt. You can believe me or not, but it's the truth.'

'Okay, so really there's only one more thing. Walker told the anti-social behaviour stewards that he was in a meeting with you and your partner Mia on Tuesday morning. He said that the three of you had a meeting. Mia confirmed with them that you both were there but has now changed her statement. She was mistaken in the time which she originally gave for her leaving. She now *remembers* that she left the pair of you much earlier.'

An expression crossed his face, but I couldn't say what it signified. It might have been either embarrassment or concern, or something else entirely. 'Yes, that's right. What with everything going on, she got her times wrong.'

Vic didn't react, her face was deadpan. I tried to do likewise and not convey my opinion that his reason was down there with the dog ate my homework as an excuse. Indeed, the canine excuse might have the edge for believability. She smiled. 'And of course, you got it mixed up as well.' She left her smile hanging.

'Yes, er, we both got confused.'

That dog really was being well-fed. Vic though, did not challenge it. 'We totally understand, we do really. Now you have had time to think, what time do you remember her leaving?'

He made a show of thinking. Rodin would be along any minute to make a statue out of his pose. That told me that he and Mia would had talked about this. After some painful acting of a man wracking his brain, he replied, 'Not long after eight, I guess.' Then with all the subtlety of a mime artist, his expression changed to one of surprise. 'I thought she was going to talk to you?'

Vic kept her face deadpan. 'We'd like *you* to talk to us. What time did you and Walker leave your house?'

'I've told you. I'll tell you again – just after half past nine.'

'Now, you're sure? No chance of a mistake here as well?'

'Yes, I'm sure, it was 09.30 hours. There is no mistake.'

'Are you certain? This is important.'

'I'm certain, comrade.'

It was now that she gave her facial muscles some exercise, by pulling an expression, which could be best described as one of concern. 'The thing is, Reyansh, we can't find anyone who saw either of you until just after eleven. Which, you'll understand, is a problem for us; well, it's a problem for you as well, when you think about it.'

He shrugged, 'I can only repeat that we spent the morning discussing the possibilities of getting Noah elected to the CC. We left together 9.30*ish*, it may have been a few minutes either way, I can't remember exactly. From there, I went for a walk to think about what we'd decided. Then I took a bus here, I mean, to here. Surely, whilst we were at home, we were on the house computer, searching party files, we even contacted a few people – can't you trace our digital movements?'

'We have, and to a certain extent, it does confirm your story, but it can be faked. Which reminds me, comrade, why do you have you a CSD?'

He looked, I had to say, from where I was sitting, to be genuinely puzzled at the question. 'Er, I don't know what a CSD is. Isn't it, diseases like gonorrhoea?'

I stifled a laugh. Vic answered totally seriously, 'That's an STD, comrade. A CSD is a Com- Shielding Device, which is a very special bit of kit which protects all communications systems.' Once more, Vic was proving the more grown up of the two of us. She didn't miss a heartbeat. 'Could you please tell us how come you have one?'

For the first time he seemed wrong-footed, 'I don't know, Mia deals with all the tech stuff. Why, what exactly does it do?'

Vic chose to ignore his question. Whatever he said, we were accepting. 'Right, so you have no idea what it is and have never had it installed?'

'No, like I said, it's...'

'It's Mia who deals with the tech side. Okay, we got that. So, comrade Anand, have you anything else to add?'

'No, sorry, comrade, that's it, I'm afraid. I realise that it isn't much, but I can't make things up, even if it might benefit me. If...'

She had evidently heard enough. A brief smile of thanks appeared, before she said, 'Well thanks. Good luck. We will be contacting you again to clarify a few more things.'

Then, she cut the link, and turned to look at me. 'Think he's telling the truth?'

'About the time? About Mia providing an alibi or the CSD?'

'Any and all.'

'I honestly don't know. I do think it's odd that both him and Mia managed to accidently give the incorrect time of her leaving. I might believe that if it was ten minutes, but an hour? And if we were talking years ago, then possibly, but a matter of days? That's hard to accept.'

'Agreed. Which could suggest that the three of them are involved in a conspiracy.'

'Or that there's so much bad feeling between what is perceived to be the establishment wing of the party, which we're associated with, and them, they feel the need to lie to us.'

'Indeed. Which is actually more depressing than the thought that they're spies!'

# CHAPTER 40: THE LAST SLEEP OF ARTHUR IN AVALON

The office hummed with life. Like a pre-climate change, healthy eco-system, the menagerie of ours simultaneously existed individually, with our own tasks, our own cycle of life, but were also interdependent, working together and feeding off each other. The world we had created was, it seems, a robust and productive one. That made it sound colourful, dazzling and interesting, but in reality, it was grey, wearisome, routine work. But we persevered, trying to find the final piece of evidence so we could close the Noah Walker case. Whatever our foibles and failings, we collectively have a strong sense of justice. What we had on Walker was enough to send him down for long time and we had smashed his operations. But we wanted to convict him for Mike's death as well. Mike Stewart was owed that.

Our youngest, most sparkling and lively species in the Crib habitat was the winged Odette. She was once more following up people who had been in the vicinity of Mike Stewart's home at the time of his death. Most had already been interviewed but she was giving it one more go, just in case she might be able to jog something new out of busy memories. In the main, she, as we all were, was focussing on Noah Walker, but our minds were almost equally as open to the thought that comrade Anand might also be involved.

Odette's older tech-sister, Roijin, was multi-tasking. She was keeping an eye on the man himself and his movements. He and his partner, Mia Lewes, were taking advantage of the milder and more liveable temperatures to taking a lengthy urban walk to reflect on what the future might hold for him after the revelation that his best-bud was a spy and many in the country thought that he might be too. There were a couple in the office who also thought that.

In between snooping on the couple, Roijin had also been checking his comcalls and Red Cloud usage. Which did appear to confirm the times when Walker and Anand claimed that they were home. According to the log, the last call made from that location was by Walker at 9.25am, to a comrade in Bolton. The comrade had not been available to take it, but the call had been made. The echo from both their devices confirmed this. But as Roijin had pointed out, with the Com-Shielding Device fitted, that didn't necessarily mean anything. The CSD could easily duplicate that. As for Mia, Roijin was trying to confirm that she had arrived at work at the time which she said she had. If all that wasn't enough for Roijin, she was also working her way through Mia's communications.

Asher was studiously scanning the forensic analysis from Stewart's home and from the deceased's body itself. From what I could see, they ranged from impenetrable scientific jargon to lurid photographs. Neither seemed to bother him.

After helping herself to a glass of water, with ice and a slice of lemon, Vic settled down to also re-read reports which she had previously read before. These were the eye-witness statements for the morning of his death. From where I was sitting, I could see the edged blur of her virtual screen. Her eyes were locked onto them, silently moving from left to right as, once again, she tried to recreate the day's timeline. No doubt once more, looking closely for the MHG – our 'Mystery Hoodie Guy' – where he might have come from and gone to, and whether he had any connection to Mike Stewart's murder.

Copying Vic, I grabbed a cold drink, and sat down. I had been intending to help her out with the statements, but all my energy appeared to have been drained from me. After a brief look, I found myself getting distracted and instead asked Yelena to collate the speeches of the past few days, which related to our enquiries. If nothing else, I was getting used to calling an AI by a name. I'd be having chats with her soon. Jackie had said that the answer would be political so maybe the answer could be found there. Truth be told, right this minute, I couldn't think of many other places to look. Yelena obviously didn't particularly have a crystal-clear idea either, because she had asked me a series of questions, which I didn't really have answers for.

Making do with what I had said, and graciously accepting my apologies for such non-specific search parameters, she had flagged up a selection for me to watch and listen to. There were the early announcements from the investigation. Others were by Jackie and Marie Williams on the tragedy of Stewart's passing. Dave Donaldson appeared numerous times. There were numerous clips of Fiona Bailey. Scores of recordings were on the growing tension between the AF and us, which had been intensified by the Shard attack. A whole number of people – Donaldson, Anand, Walker and Sophia Brownswood – were heard and seen, stoking it all up, risking – maybe even encouraging – a permanent split.

In front of me was a collage of ever-changing allies and alliances – some personal, some political, some both. As the situation changed so did the alliances. I relaxed back into my chair, and requested from Yelena a precis of what was currently trending in the media concerning our investigation. A motley ensemble of material appeared. Predictably, the majority centred on the unmasking of Noah Walker. The initial standing ovations across the media for our work had started to decrease, with the praise visibly declining, and instead questions were being asked about how he had managed to get away with it for so long. Was the party riddled with enemy agents and indeed, what effect would this have on class' trust in it? Everyone had an opinion, but no-one had an answer.

Dave Donaldson, for one, should be happy for the never-ending circle of talking-heads pontificating on the subject. It meant that the news of his little armaments collection had become a minor item. I did see a small piece on the vote taken at the NWC which indicated that he would be facing possible charges, but it was a sign of how dominant the Walker news was, that the fact that he and the cabal of extreme anarchists hoped for a second civil war was deemed as almost trivial.

Looking at it all, I started to feel disconnected from what was the pressing issue here – to finish off this case. I needed to get back to facts. The answer may well be political, but politics was based on empirical evidence. I swiped the news items down and drew up the witness statements from the day of Mike Stewart's murder. Unfortunately, very quickly it became obvious that nothing leapt out. Reading statements from neighbours who had seen Marie stop a few doors down from the house to make a phone call really did not seem to be that telling. We still seemed hazy on so much of the details of the day. Our guidance to the stewards as to what to ask and how to record it, had been vague. There was no consistency and many of them were incomplete. Whether that was from inexperience or from an initial doubt that there was anything actually to find out, I couldn't say; however, what I could state without fear of contradiction, was that there were too many gaps. But something had started to pulling on my brain, and it was beginning to pull harder.

As anyone who has been lost in a fog will tell you, there is no point in wishing for better vision, you just have to use whatever ill-defined shapes you can see and use them as a guide. In actual fact, I'd never been in a fog, but I figured the principle was a good one. I decided that I'd risk ridicule, and leant over and spoke to Vic, about what I was thinking. She looked doubtful, but listened nonetheless. After I had finished, she didn't reply for a moment or two and gazed ahead into space. I couldn't tell whether she thought what I had said was brilliant or ridiculous. Even when she rose to her feet, I wasn't sure. She coughed and then addressed the others: 'We're popping out. Pete's got something he wants to follow up on, which may be worth looking at. We shouldn't be too long.'

Feeling all eyes on me, suddenly, I felt rather shy, which was very unlike me. 'It's probably nothing,' I said sheepishly, with my palms upwards.

On the way out, Vic surprised me by sharing some thoughts of her own. Thoughts which went a long way to explaining why she hadn't laughed me out of the office.

Our journey there had consisted of us discussing what we were both now thinking; could we think of anything which might support it? When we arrived, Vic got out and using whatever her gadget was called, let me into the house. We were back at Mike Stewart's home. Vic was going to explore a few leads herself, whilst I had another look around. I walked through straight into the kitchen. This was where he had been poisoned. I looked down onto the floor. There wasn't anything there now, it had been thoroughly cleaned. For some superstitious reason, I was careful not to stand on the spot where he had lain. My feet were about thirty centimetres from where his head had been.

Without sounding hippy-dippy and all mystical, I had felt that it was important that I was back inside the house. The answer lay here. No-one was home, we knew where Donaldson and Bailey were, which meant that I could nose around. It had already been searched at least twice. But I was sure that the house held the answer. Yes, I was indeed sounding hippy-dippy. I'd be wearing kaftans soon. I walked up the stairs to the bedroom, and headed first to Stewart's. It still reminded me of a provincial budget B&B. I looked around and saw utility but nothing more. His real life was in the other room. I went in and gazed at the stunning models of future cities. This was the world he wanted to create. A world which was beautiful in its appearance and its functionality. The ergonomic was essential to the aesthetic. They were incredible in their imagination. It had been on the news that the NWC had voted to start a phased introduction of his City Nature Synthesis. Which would be a fitting memorial for a man of such forward thinking. He was visionary in every way. I walked around them and admired the skill of their construction and the vision of his ideals.

I was still drifting around in the mental fog, seeing shapes. I left and went into Donaldson's and then Bailey's bedroom. Nothing was new here. I hadn't expected there to be. It was highly unlikely that anything had been missed. I had wanted to come here just to order things in my head. After Vic returned to the house, we would go to the person who I was now sure was someone we needed to detain. Roijin was tracking them, whilst we were here.

I returned to the kitchen and stood leaning against the table, once again looking out the window into the garden. The lengthy period of heat had had an effect on it, even though it was predominately drought-hardy plants. I could see that much of the green had turned shades of brown. I knew the feeling. What had I achieved by drifting around the house? I just hoped Vic was having more luck than I was. It was then that I heard something, then something blue caught my eye. I felt sharp pain at the back of my head, then my neck. Then darkness.

I can't have been unconscious for too long, because I could feel my arms being pulled behind my back and my wrists being tied by what felt like a plastic tag. The ridged metal of the radiator pressed against my back as the tag was tightened around the inflow pipe. Pain stabbed my temple, worsening as my vision began to return. I could see green trainers moving around me. Through my blurry vision, I thought they had now left the ground and were suspended in mid-air. Above them were sweatpants, no socks. Despite the pain feeling like a metal wrench was being shoved down the back of my neck, I looked up. Dampness clung on the back of my neck, which I guessed was blood from the wound inflicted by the blow. My vision started to clear and my brain became reactivated. I could see someone sitting on the kitchen table. Someone was emerging from the fog. The outline was still fuzzy and colours were blurred. Blue was smudged all around the outline – the material of a blue hoodie. It was the Mystery Hoodie Guy, right there, in front of me, on the kitchen table. My focus moved to her hands and the two guns, which lay by her right – mine and what looked like a vastly more impressive one; one which no doubt was standard issue for MI5 agents. Next to that was a mound of red. I swallowed hard and forced out some words: 'How come...?'

A giggle didn't let me finish. 'That I'm here, yet Red Roijin is tracking me at the Shard? You lot really are quite dumb, aren't you?' She shook her head, which somehow hurt mine. 'And you seriously think you can run the world – Jesus! It really is quite simple, all I need to do is put my phone in the bag of a sibling and hey presto, I'm somewhere else.'

Fiona Bailey came into view. Her long hair had disappeared, it was now closely cropped and black. I realised that the red lump was a wig, formerly what I had taken to be her hair. She was smiling and swinging her legs as a child might on a chair which was too big for them. For some reason, she reminded me of Odette. Although Odette hadn't, as of yet, brained me with the butt of a pistol. She saw me looking at the wig.

'Top of the range this. Stays on whatever activity you're doing.' She grinned. 'Even dearest Janine, my ever-so loving partner for the past year, not only has no idea of my proper job, but isn't even aware that it's a wig – and believe me, we get up to some activities which test its adhesive qualities.'

I ignored her attempt at levity, the pain in my skull wasn't conducive for banter. 'You're the Mystery Hoodie Guy.'

She clapped her hands, looking genuinely pleased. She scratched her closely shaved head. 'That's me, the MHG. Good little outfit this – the material expands, so you can wear padded clothes underneath, so it makes it look like a much larger person. Like what they used to have back in the day, fat-suits I think they called them. You must know them, it's your era. Excellent for disguise.'

I winced, as I tried to get as comfortable as I could, sitting on the floor, with my hands wrenched behind my back and my head throbbing like a bass of a repetitive dance beat. 'So, you travelled back from Hammersmith, then changed clothes when you got here. Why?'

She was genuinely disappointed in me. 'Come on, Pete. Who were you lot looking for? You spent hours searching for Mystery Hoodie Guy, instead of someone who was right under your nose.'

'Didn't...er...Mike,' I was still finding it hard to speak. 'Didn't he think it odd that you were in a blow-up running kit?'

'I just told him I was jog-sweating, you know, to get fitter. Mike, bless him, was far too nice a bloke to–' she changed her voice to impersonate his– '*invade my personal space by asking personal details.* Questioning what I was wearing and why I was wearing them, would have sounded far too identity-critical.'

'Where did you change? I mean, I guess that you must have put them on between the bus depot and here. We know you weren't wearing them on the bus.'

'The corner of the street, behind the newsagent's bins.'

My brain might still be fractured, but something didn't make sense to me. I couldn't see what she meant. 'But Asher Joseph did a full forensic sweep on you and found no fibres which would match the hoodie or sweatpants.'

'Oh, these aren't the type you find at your common or garden sports shop. They're especially designed to be forensically clean – not a single trace is left. Which is operationally useful, but frankly it's also one hell of a pain! They cost a bloody fortune; I wasn't allowed to simply dump them, I had to hide the clothes there and sneak back and pick them up when I could. I tell you, Pete, I'm doing my best to bring you lot down, but the number-crunchers are obsessed about their finances. You see, we have to watch our budgets too. They are, after all, funded from the public purse.' She laughed. 'Like you, I'm a state employee.'

'What state would that be?'

She let out a victorious laugh. 'Pete, I'm an internationalist. We're so alike, you and me. I work for many states.'

If my brain could concentrate, I would return to that later. I wanted to keep her talking for as long as possible. Vic would be returning soon. ' So... you...er then came in, injected Stewart, then left, changed back into your travelling clothes, so you could arrive in time at the front door to meet Marie Williams. You came in and "found" him dead. That way, she gave you an alibi.'

'That's about right. When I first arrived, he was conveniently sitting in the kitchen, but then he often was at that time of day, day-dreaming about his cities of the future.'

I couldn't keep my admiration out of my voice. 'Risky, it must have taken split-second timing and a lot of luck!'

'I've always had that. And if something is worth doing then you have to be prepared to take a gamble or two.'

'Slick.'

'Thank you.' She was flattered. But a thought flashed across her eyes and a frown appeared on her face. 'I'm still not quite sure how you knew it was me.'

A metallic sharp pain pushed my head back against the radiator. It had been how Jackie had behaved with me when we had last met. How she had laid her hands on mine. 'The injection must have been made horizontally, which would suggest that his hands were flat on the table. To force it in, would have involved abrasions and bruises. But it was done with the person resting their hand on top of his, in an affectionate manner. A stranger doing that, would be surprising and would have meant that the natural reaction would have been for Stewart to look down – and see the syringe and pull their hand away in time. But when someone close to you does it, like you were to him, you keep your eyes on the face. He literally didn't see anything strange, he was simply talking to you and in a moment of tenderness you rested your hand on his. He would only have felt a prick and it would have been too late.'

She nodded, appreciating the logic. 'Good thinking, comrade. Exactly, as it happened. I came in with tears in my eyes that Janine had dumped me,' she scoffed, 'as if she would. She knew she'd struck gold. Anyway, I came in and sat in front of him, crying, I laid my hands on his – and that was that.' She tilted her head. 'And it was the injection which gave you the clue?' She seemed genuinely interested in how I'd guessed it was her.

Again, Jackie came into my mind. The answer she had said, was political. 'Yes, that, and your speeches,' I replied. 'It was noticeable that at certain times you were highly effective, able to influence and motivate people to a level I've rarely seen, but then at others, you seemed barely articulate. In the beginning, when there was anger directed at the party, you superficially spoke in favour of the alliance, making it appear that you were arguing for exactly the opposite of what the world ruling class would want – a strong and stable alliance. That threw attention away from you. But as you did so, you were hesitant, weak and half-hearted. What exactly you said, and how you said it, wouldn't convince a dickie-bird.'

She positively glowed with pride. 'I'm glad you noticed that. The idea was that Noah Walker would be pushing hard against the continuation of the alliance, whilst I weakly pushed the other way, for it to be kept. That way, it appeared that I was opposing what he was arguing, but actually in being so ineffectual, it was all but a pull force. If I say so myself, I was rather good at that. But when you caught Noah, I needed to maintain my cover, became stronger in support of the coalition.' She sighed. 'I enjoyed my role. It was fun, but hearing what you lot were doing in your office I pretty much guessed that it was coming to an end.'

'So why the rush to kill Mike Stewart? Surely, you being the one who not only killed him, but claimed to have found him, put you at risk of being the prime suspect?'

A knowing smile crossed her face; she spoke with satisfaction. 'Needs must. I always knew that it was a possibility that I'd have to use my position to cancel AF members, and quite probably it would be Mike. Which was a shame, he was a nice lad, actually. I liked him. But when you get your orders, you have to follow them. Not that Mike was the first. I lost that particular virginity, years ago.'

I let the comment pass. When we had this woman in custody, we could find out who else she had helped butcher. For now, I wanted to keep to the subject of Mike Stewart. 'Was it that you feared that his City Nature Synthesis scheme would cement the alliance between the party and the AF? Or was he just a high-profile figure who needed to be got rid of and one whose death could be used to stir discontent?'

Her smile broadened and swung her legs. 'All the above.'

'And you deliberately made his death look like a tragic accident, in the hope we wouldn't take it seriously. So, you could use it as an example of how the NWC, and in particular, Crib, have little regard for anyone except the party comrades. Surely a sign of how the party was betraying the revolution. Is that why you demanded that it be us who investigated it?'

'Correct again. Your reputation needed to take a few dents. I thought asking for you personally would be fun, what with your track record of going off at all angles.' She threw her head back and guffawed.

I ignored the ridicule. 'Which is why you made a big thing about how we didn't care about his death. The fact that Mike was a popular and respected sibling, and highly regarded across the political spectrum, would make it even more controversial.'

'Correct again, and it worked well for a while.'

'And the whispered threats and hand-written notes, which you told us that he had received?'

'All crap. I thought it would be fun to add an element of Victorian melodrama, a touch of Arthur Conan Doyle, to it all. Make it even more unbelievable. More proof of you lot not taking a witness seriously. Anyways, it amused me, and there's no harm in enjoying your work, is there?' She laughed.

Seems the death of a 'nice bloke' was a bit of fun. I changed the subject. 'And the Shard attack was to divert attention?'

She didn't answer for a second, but instead nimbly jumped off the table. She glanced at her watch and pouted.

'Waiting for someone?' I asked. I knew I was.

'My lift. He's just messaged. Stuck in traffic apparently, but should be here in fifteen minutes. Yes indeed, you've won this round, comrade Kalder – I'm finished in this role – Fiona Bailey will have to move on. Oh, and you won't catch me as easily as you did Walker. I'm too valuable an asset just to be packed off on a small boat.'

'And you *are* Fiona Bailey?' I asked, remembering that our background check on her had found nothing which looked fake.'

She walked over to the sink, talking behind her as she did. 'Oh yes, I am she. I'm what you looked into – superficially – at least. All the dates are correct. All my family are my family. Mum is retired and Dad works on the buses. They know nothing about my real job. But what you didn't find out was that whilst I was at sixth form, I started to pass information about the militant eco-warriors who were there on to Special Branch. After some initial scepticism on their part, they soon found that I was good at doing that – bloody good in fact. And to cut a long story short, my career began to take off.'

She poured herself another glass of water. With her back turned, I took the opportunity to feel behind mine with my fingertips, around the tag and the pipe I was attached to. At various points I gave it a tug. She turned and a smile flickered on the corner of her mouth.

I stopped my wriggling and to divert her attention, I asked her again about the Shard.

'Ah yes, the Shard, now that was thrilling. Oh, and by the way–' she pointed with her eyes towards the two guns on the table. 'If you do manage to get yourself loose, go for mine, it's self-aiming, far more dependable.' She chuckled. 'Especially, as you'll have to tear your hands off to free yourself, which will make holding it rather problematic.

'But anyway, the Shard – God, I did enjoy that. We were always going to do a spectacular to light a fire under things. Once you found out that Stewart had been murdered it was also a great way to throw you off the scent. How can I be the killer when I'm being shot at? An ideal way to confuse things. We knew you were on the way there, so we took our chance. Noah is quite multi-skilled at weaponry and easily controlled the drone. We had hoped to take out Phan Bien as well, but we didn't manage that.' She almost muttered the final sentence to herself, 'Never mind, there'll be another time.'

I ignored her. 'You were there for the attack, but never in actual danger, the arc of the fire was away from you.'

'That was always the plan. Took some trust in his skill but hey, it added some excitement, didn't it! Of course, your Victoria Cole intervened to make it even better. Ah yes,' an odd expression crossed her face. 'Good for Vicky Cole. Dragging the pair of us under the sofa was wonderfully dramatic. And being face to face made for the perfect witness that it couldn't possibly have been me controlling the drone, and so by implication wasn't me who killed Mike. We figured on you being too slow-witted to think that there could be more than one of us.' She stopped and took a sip, then the mask of good humour slipped for a second. 'You couldn't even comprehend that there were two of us.' A sneer appeared. 'Pete, my friend, you should wish that it was the case that there are *only* two of us involved. You've no idea how riddled your revolution is with our agents.' She blinked, and the plastic bonhomie returned. 'Sometimes, I think it would be easier for the agents just to go on strike, you'd get nothing done!' She laughed. It wasn't a pleasant or sincere one.

A watched clock never seems to move; the same could be said of waiting to be rescued. Time seemed to have stopped. I asked more questions which right this very moment I didn't give a toss about. 'I'm guessing that once Noah Walker was incriminated, you tried to link him with Stewart's murder by placing the CSD at Reyansh's home. He could take the fall for both and let you off the hook. I assume Anand is not one of yours?'

'That's about right. Noah was toast, so hanging Stewart on him would at least slow you down. And no, dear Anand isn't one of ours. Although him and his partner were brilliant at looking like they were.' She chuckled. 'Noah couldn't believe his luck when Mia Lewes suggested that she give them a fake alibi for the time of Mike's death. They were both convinced that you were going to fit Anand up for it.' She lifted her glass and made a toast: 'To paranoia!'

'And it was to foster this paranoia that you broke into my house and messed with the atlas – I guess it was you?'

She nodded, grinning.

'Wasn't it a bit, well, childish?'

Again, her humour slipped and a snarl prepared to appear. She was straining to say something cutting or even do some actual cutting, but something held her back. She forced a smile and between her teeth, replied, 'Like I said, I like to have fun. Anyways, with you looking behind your back, you wouldn't be looking ahead.'

'And the cumbersome attempt to frighten my sister?'

A look of regret appeared. 'Ahh, now that wasn't my idea. You're right, it was designed to intimidate you and further spread worry, but that initiative came from Washington. I thought it was a waste of resources, but they were keen, so we did as we were told.'

'You've mentioned "we" and Washington, is that Jerusalem? Or is Jerusalem just part of the game?'

She finished her glass and turned to pour herself another one. I was certain that it wasn't that she was thirsty, but more that she enjoyed me desperately attempting to find a way to free myself. I didn't have much choice, so I did the predictable and did just that. The plastic cut into my wrists, and rust from the pipe caught under my fingernails, but by the time she turned back to face me, I hadn't achieved very much.

'Jerusalem? Yes, that exists, the organisation I mean, and you're right that it's an umbrella organisation for various security agencies. It's based in Washington, obviously the CIA have a big say, and the little hearts like to have their office near their homes, but there's a fair few countries now pitching in, and not just all those who consider themselves our allies. The initiative didn't come from me, that comes from much higher up. But I suggested the name.'

I swear she looked proud.

'I thought you having such intellectual pretensions would appreciate the allusion to William Blake.' Her head went back and she gave what I would guess was actually a genuine laugh. 'When I first suggested it they were puzzled what it had to do with Israel or the Middle East. I had to explain who Blake was and what the hymn represents. I told them it's like all those great paintings of stately homes and grand countrysides, praising a mythical past. Finally, some of the suits got it, or at least couldn't see that it would do any harm, so the name stuck! Jerusalem it is, quite cool I think.'

If my arms weren't now aching from their unusual position, I would have challenged the "intellectual pretensions" remark, but instead I asked, 'Why tell us about it, though?'

She shrugged. 'Why not? The CIA knew the KGB existed in the cold war of the 1950s, it didn't help them? Quite probably, the opposite. I mean, every nation's security service has known of their opposite numbers, but knowledge isn't always power. Not since the internet, anyway!' A smile briefly appeared, before something far more determined replaced it. Carefully, she placed the glass in the sink and looked at me as if I was stupid. She moved to her right and with a theatrical flourish, spread out her arms, catching the door slightly, pushing it so it was half-closed. 'The knowledge of each other's existence only helped to spread...'

I finished her sentence, 'Paranoia.'

'Absolutely, Pete. You now have a bogey figure to give you all nightmares. But the question the great proletariat will be asking itself, is whether Jerusalem actually does exist or is it simply a creation of the ruling faction of the NWC, designed to usher in a more authoritarian regime? Doubts and arguments about the threat the revolution faces will cause fractures.'

'Or make us stronger!' I replied.

'Possibly, Pete, possibly. We shall have to see how the game turns out, won't we?'

At that precise moment, the door crashed open. It viciously swung towards Bailey.

Vic ran into the room. Her arms out-stretched; gun out-stretched. I didn't have time to warn her before Bailey had grabbed the door's edge with both hands and with all her weight, shoved it back hard. Vic was in mid-turn, having seen or sensed, where the danger lay, but she was too slow. The door hit her arms with force, and she went sprawling onto the floor with the impact. Like a cat, Bailey pounced on her, grasping the gun. In one movement, she held Vic's wrists, while lifting her knee up high, burying it deep into Vic's stomach. I saw Vic gasp for breath.

I was now shouting, tugging and yanking at my restraints. Surely, I could get this poxy pipe loose.

Elegantly, Bailey jumped back onto her feet. She was like a floor gymnast. But this wasn't to cartwheel, this was to stamp on Vic's wrists. Vic screamed. Bailey's weight forcing her to release the gun. Bailey didn't even attempt to pick it up, but kicked it away. What happened next wasn't a manic attack by some psychopath, but a quick and expert series of blows to Vic's neck and head.

I screamed. I tugged. I yanked. I swore.

Seconds later, Bailey had stopped and Vic lay still.

'Vic,' I whispered. 'Vic.'

Grabbing her by the top of her shirt, Bailey pulled her over to the other end of the radiator. Pulling out a plastic tag she pulled her life-less arms behind her, and bound her.

'Vic...'

She was slumped over, I couldn't see any sign of breathing.

Bailey wiped a small bead of sweat away from her brow and walked leisurely to the sink.

'Vic, Vic...'

After consuming a glass of water, Bailey filled it up again and walked back over to Victoria, knelt and threw it full up her nose. Vic spluttered with the sensation of drowning and groggily tried to see where she was. Blood was coming from her lips and her nose.

'Vic?'

Bailey turned and faced me, pulling a face; she sighed. 'Oh for fuck's sake, don't be such a drama-queen, Kalder. She's fine. A bit sore, but she's fine. What do you take me for – a barbarian?'

I didn't answer, but instead watched Bailey move towards the table and pick up her gun. Presumably, she was of the view that carrying firearms, didn't make you a barbarian.

'I try not to kill with my bare hands. It's too messy and too much effort.'

'Injections are easy and clean, I suppose?'

My sarcasm didn't seem to faze her, one bit. Instead, she boasted of her skills. Holding her gun loosely in her right hand and vaguely pointing it halfway between me and the floor, she nodded towards Vic, who was now making slight whimpering sounds. 'Didn't I tell you that I was listening in to everything you were doing? I knew she was checking the Neighbourhood Centre and has now found out that I never visited the place on the way here that morning. I'd operated the printer and computer remotely. You should have really checked that in the first place. Pete, if you're going to play detectives, then you should get better at it. I'm sure Vicky here has also had a word with the lovely young neighbour, Janice Bromptom, who told her where exactly she had met me. And Ms Cole has worked out that if I had been walking from the Neighbourhood Centre to here, I wouldn't have been where Janice saw me. Actually, we met soon after I had changed out of the "Mystery Hoodie Guy" guise. Like a superhero really! She didn't see me changing my clothes, but the location was a problem. Luckily, I could rely on your incompetence, so I didn't have to liquidate her. You were too busy looking for the Mystery Hoodie Guy – I do like that name by the way.' She paused, and looked at her watch. 'Good. My lift is here.' She spoke into it: 'Termination almost completed. Exit in two.'

She turned to face me, pointing the gun in turns at the pair of us. 'I have to say that your cobbled-together team have done rather well. Noah Walker is a good man. He was a highly effective agent who did much good for the cause of freedom. You've stopped that. You've also somehow managed to stop my work too, for the moment at least. I was hoping to be doing it for a few more years, yet. But alas, that's now impossible. I'm forced to congratulate you, I really must. You've made a few cock-ups, but you got there in the end. We had a good chance to drive a wedge between the AF and your party. The powers-that-be were very excited at the project. We shall continue to do that, but we'll have to try other methods. How did you put it? That we would wear pink bunny outfits if we thought it would be effective.' She laughed. 'That might have to be the case, but this particular campaign has ended. You've won this battle, but the war continues. And now, I must say goodbye!'

I looked down the barrel of her gun. At that moment my life did not flash before me. Strangely, I did not think of my wife or my daughter. I did not remember the good times we had shared and the love we had. I did not even go back in time to that road in Italy, where a car crash had ended their lives. Instead, I looked at Vic and thought that if I was going to die, then it might as well be with her. I just wished that this radiator wasn't separating us. It would be good to go holding hands.

A tear ran down my cheek.

She aimed at my head. 'Bang!'

Nothingness didn't appear. Instead, Bailey was doubled up in front of us, laughing. The sound had come from her mouth, not the barrel of her gun. 'Oh, for Christ sake, Kalder. Pull yourself together. I'm not going to kill you!' She slipped the gun into her trouser pocket. 'That would make martyrs out of the pair of you. This case has put Crib in the ascendency – you're all-conquering heroes at the moment; the last thing we need is for Crib to get even more glory. Your death would strengthen the revolution, not weaken it. No, killing you two won't serve any purpose, but your survival might. No, I'm off – leaving you to try and explain to the likes of Dave Donaldson and chums, how you let a senior Jerusalem agent escape without a shot being fired. You can explain why this senior agent explained to you her mission, and then left you both alive, not even gagged. That will be fun to watch. The conspiracy nuts will have a field day!' She let out a howl of laughter, before turning and marching towards the door; but just as she was leaving, she stopped and swung around. 'Aren't the last lines of Jerusalem about not allowing a sword to sleep in my hand? Well, mine is well-awake! You must realise, Pete – no way am I going to stop, "till we have built Jerusalem in England's green and pleasant land".' She grinned.

'Anyway, I've an event to organise. Until we meet again, comrade!'

Printed in Great Britain
by Amazon

24999146R00271